For my dad…who taught me the value of integrity above winning.

And

For athletes everywhere who act honorably even when the stakes are the highest.

Patrick Sinclair

Chalk Wars: Pommel Clock and the Incredulous Cost of Integrity

AUSTIN MACAULEY PUBLISHERS®
LONDON * CAMBRIDGE * NEW YORK * SHARJAH

Copyright © Patrick Sinclair 2025

All rights reserved. No part of this publication may be reproduced, distributed, or transmitted in any form or by any means, including photocopying, recording, or other electronic or mechanical methods, without the prior written permission of the publisher, except in the case of brief quotations embodied in critical reviews and certain other non-commercial uses permitted by copyright law. For permission requests, write to the publisher.

Any person who commits any unauthorized act in relation to this publication may be liable to criminal prosecution and civil claims for damages.

This is a work of fiction. Names, characters, businesses, places, events, locales, and incidents are either the products of the author's imagination or used in a fictitious manner. Any resemblance to actual persons, living or dead, or actual events is purely coincidental.

Ordering Information
Quantity sales: Special discounts are available on quantity purchases by corporations, associations, and others. For details, contact the publisher at the address below.

Publisher's Cataloging-in-Publication data
Sinclair, Patrick
Chalk Wars: Pommel Clock and the Incredulous Cost of Integrity

ISBN 9798891550469 (Paperback)
ISBN 9798891550476 (Hardback)
ISBN 9798891550483 (ePub e-book)

Library of Congress Control Number: 2024921781

www.austinmacauley.com/us

First Published 2025
Austin Macauley Publishers LLC
40 Wall Street, 33rd Floor, Suite 3302
New York, NY 10005
USA

mail-usa@austinmacauley.com
+1 (646) 5125767

Table of Contents

Chapter 1: The Fall	1
Chapter 2: Ferry Ride	4
Chapter 3: Campus Tour	18
Chapter 4: Tryouts	26
Chapter 5: Meet Schedule	36
Chapter 6: Kickoff Party and Opening Ceremonies	38
Chapter 7: Uniform Day	49
Chapter 8: Underwear Predicament	60
Chapter 9: Aspen Gets Bullied	74
Chapter 10: Starting Lineups	84
Chapter 11: Dr. Hewitt's Secret Meeting	91
Chapter 12: Pre-Meet Festivities	92
Chapter 13: First Meet—Day 1	106
Chapter 14: First Meet—Day 2	120
Chapter 15: Gisele's Failure	138
Chapter 16: Meet v. Homework	139
Chapter 17: Challenge Project	148
Chapter 18: Bribing Gymnasts	157
Chapter 19: Hacking Dr. Hewitt's Messages	164
Chapter 20: Dr. Hewitt's Mistake	181
Chapter 21: Decrypting Scoresheets	183
Chapter 22: Parents Ball	198
Chapter 23: Hendricks the Gambler	217

Chapter 24: Ice Cream Sundae Surprise	228
Chapter 25: SYPHUS	236
Chapter 26: Ugu's Clever Tactic	238
Chapter 27: Hendricks Confronts Bibb	249
Chapter 28: Gen. Gibson Hack	252
Chapter 29: Ugu's Birthday	261
Chapter 30: Bank 'Heist'	273
Chapter 31: All-Star Week	286
Chapter 32: Ugu's Bad Behavior	300
Chapter 33: Retrieval Mission	308
Chapter 34: Birthday Planning	323
Chapter 35: The Glass Box	336
Chapter 36: Cheating at Seven Bridges	343
Chapter 37: Entrance Exams	356
Chapter 38: Ugu's Research Meeting	364
Chapter 39: Entrance Exams Restolen	379
Chapter 40: Meet Failure	394
Chapter 41: The Planning Stage	403
Chapter 42: Awards	412
Chapter 43: Lord Sirroc's Gala	427
Chapter 44: Team Championships	445
Chapter 45: Individual Championships	462
Chapter 46: Revelations	484
Chapter 47; Whitfield's Birthday Bash	496
Chapter 48: Yuri's Deception	512

Chapter 49: End-of-Year Celebration 524

Chapter 50: The Captain 540

Chapter 1
The Fall

The sign hanging outside the Mitchell's modest three-bedroom starter house on a busy cul-de-sac set just north of downtown read 'World Championships Watch Party—GO MORTON'.

Shouting over the crowd, Livvy pointed at the screen. "I think I just saw him!"

Understanding his wife's excitement, Aldrich tried calming her. "Honey, you did not just see Hendricks. There are over 150 thousand people at that arena. You didn't spot him."

"Fine, maybe I didn't. It's just so cool that he went, though."

"Yeah, well, Morton invited us and obviously we couldn't go, so Hendricks went instead."

"Yeah, but Morton doesn't know that. Hendricks didn't even take the tickets Morton sent us. Said he was going to pick up a ticket out there."

The Mitchell's neighbor, Kole, chimed in, "yeah, good luck with that—tickets for World Championships are crazy expensive."

"If you can even find one," Wells was speaking from experience.

Livvy was undeterred. "Oh, Hendricks will find one. No doubts there."

"Honey, could you go check on Aspen? I think he's waking up from his nap."

"Sure, dear. Hey, Whitfield, go sit with Daddy. He'll let you help fill out the Fantasy StickHit Bracket. Only a few minutes left until the meet starts."

Whitfield was so excited to stay up late to watch his heroes compete. "Yay! Dad, I want Morton on every event. Every duel matchup."

Aldrich was so proud of his son. He couldn't help but smile from ear to ear sharing this experience with his pride and joy. "Every one? That's a lot, champ. Are you sure?"

"Yes. Morton's the best."

Wells agreed, "kid's got a point, Aldrich. Morton is still the champ."

Livvy came out of the bedroom with baby Aspen and found her spot on the wraparound sofa in time to catch the end of the pre-meet analysis. The biggest meet of the season was about to begin, and not a moment too soon, as the network announcers were running out of superlatives to describe 5-time World Champion Morton Cheesestock.

For the past six years, Livvy and Aldrich happily hosted their friends for an all-weekend watch party to view the two-day World Championships event. The guest list grew each year, and with the addition of baby Aspen, well over 40 attendees were present at this year's gathering.

Sitting next to Whitfield, Bradley asked, "hey, Whitfield, you think Morton is going to land his triple double tonight?"

Whitfield thought for a brief moment and responded emphatically, "no!"

Knowing how much Whitfield idolized Morton, Bradley's sister, Kristy expressed her surprise. "No? What do you mean, no?"

"He's not going to land his triple double, because he's going to do a quadruple-double. No. He's doing a quadruple-triple. Going to stick it and then come back and do an amazing front-triple layout punch to another triple pike and stick that too." Whitfield acted out his imagined tumbling sequence on the floor in front of everyone.

The gathered crown all laughed, and Bradley gave Whitfield a fist bump. "Yeah, buddy, that's what I'm talking about. This kid knows his stuff."

Whitfield loved all the attention, but as soon as the meet started, he was locked in. At just three years old, he already knew everyone's routines, on all eight events. He spotted deductions that even the judges sometimes missed, and computed difficulty and execution scores in his head with ease. During intermissions, Whitfield would get up and entertain guests with handstand walks, pommel circles, and a whole array of other gymnastics skills, but as soon as the meet resumed, his focus returned in full force to the video screens.

For two days, Livvy and Aldrich had a blast hosting their friends and watching the biggest meet of the year. All eyes were focused squarely on Morton, his every movement, every twist, every routine. The whole house seemed to shake from all the cheering after every successful routine. As the final session neared, Morton was firmly in the lead and only needed to score a 17.34 on his final event to avoid losing a major decision and win an unprecedented sixth World Championship title.

Whitfield couldn't hide his enthusiasm. "I told you; he's going to win. Morton never falls on Pommel Clock. He has such a big lead; he'd have to fall three times to get a score that low. This is so great! Morton is the best!"

With big eyes, Whitfield watched as Morton stepped up to begin his final routine. That's when life for the Mitchell family changed forever.

Morton's first fall brought a chorus of gasps and shrieks from the crowd gathered at Livvy and Aldrich's house, not to mention among the hundreds of millions of fans watching across the world. After Morton's second fall, the Mitchell house grew deathly quiet, as utter and complete shock set in. All eyes began to focus on Livvy and Aldrich. A third fall would be devastating, and everyone gathered in that house knew it.

Morton's third fall was absolutely horrifying. It wasn't that Morton suffered an injury. He didn't. It wasn't that Morton had just cost himself a shot at a sixth World Championship title—he did—instead, it was all about what was about to happen to Livvy and Aldrich.

Desperate and fearful, Livvy and Aldrich stared hopelessly into each other's eyes. The only sounds were made by Whitfield, who was crying as he awaited the final score, even though he already knew it wouldn't be enough.

One by one, the guests hurriedly gathered their belongings and made their way out of the house. Livvy and Aldrich were temporarily paralyzed with shock. They were stunned, and it wasn't until Whitfield came running over to put his arms around his dad that the two parents awoke from their trance.

"Aldrich, we have to get out of here. I'll get our things." Livvy was visibly shaking.

"There's no time. We have to leave now. I'll take Whitfield. You grab Aspen."

With tears streaming down her face, Livvy desperately asked, "where can we go?"

"I don't know. As far away as possible."

Livvy and Aldrich quickly threw a few things into a single bag, took their children, and got into the car and started driving. After a few minutes, Whitfield dried his eyes with his sleeve and finally asked the question. "Mommy. Daddy. What's going on? Why are we leaving?"

Livvy was terrified. She looked over at her husband, both of them holding back tears.

"Mommy, I'm scared. What's going on?"

Chapter 2
Ferry Ride

Ten years later.

"C'mon, Whitfield. We don't want to miss it."

"Relax, Aspen. We still have plenty of time before the ferry leaves."

"No, we don't. C'mon."

"All right. All right. Hey, which one is it?"

Aspen and Whitfield were sprinting down the docks, trying to avoid other people as best as they could, while holding two heavy bags each.

Breathing heavily, Aspen reminded Whitfield, "Hendricks said it would be all the way down at the end of the pier. Besides, he said we would know it when we see it."

"I don't know how that's possible. We've never even been to the school. How are we supposed to know what the ferry taking us there looks like?"

Hendricks, fit, toned, and experienced, was trailing behind the two anxious boys. His gait was smooth, swift, and despite the boys' eagerness, Hendricks only trailed by a few steps. "You'll know. Trust me."

Whitfield, Aspen, and Hendricks hurriedly continued through the throngs of new arrivals and soon-to-be departing passengers. As they raced toward the end of the pier, Whitfield looked up and suddenly stopped short.

"Uhm, Hendricks. Is that our ferry?"

Hendricks smiled. "What do you think?"

Whitfield was awestruck as he gazed upon the ferry boat. "I think that's the biggest, nicest, most spectacular ferry I've ever seen."

"Well, yes, that may be true, for now. Remember, you haven't left our humble estate in ten years. The world has a lot of spectacular sights never before seen by those curious, blue eyes of yours."

Suddenly, the gravity of his current situation hit Whitfield. "You're right. Hendricks, I don't know if I'm ready for this."

"You are ready. More ready than you know."

"But..."

Hendricks stopped walking. So did Whitfield. "But, nothing. You and Aspen are special boys. I've raised you since you were three years old; and Aspen since he was a baby. I've taught you everything you need to know to be successful. You are smart, clever, resourceful, and a young man with the highest integrity."

Whitfield was still unsure of himself. He had never been on his own before. "Thank you for saying that, but I'm still not sure I'm ready. I've already missed the first two years of school. Everyone else in my year is so far ahead of me. And I don't know how I'm going to even make the team this year. They have so many really good gymnasts, and national titles and..."

Hendricks knelt down beside Whitfield and flashed a stern look across his face. "Whitfield. Relax. Do you trust me?"

"What?"

"Answer the question. Do you trust me?" The words came out even more sternly than Hendricks had intended.

"Yes. Of course, I do."

"Then trust me now when I say that you are ready. Aspen. He is ready, too. I have taught you both exceptionally well. You are both about to experience adventures beyond your wildest dreams and your lives will change. You can be sure of that."

Aspen, who had run ahead to check out the ferry up close, returned to encourage Whitfield and Hendricks to hurry and board the vessel.

Hendricks gave Whitfield one final nod, and stood up. "OK, Aspen. OK. We are coming, but first, can I have a word with both of you?"

Aspen reluctantly stood still to take in one more piece of advice from his beloved guardian. "Sure. What is it?"

"Now, I am going to take the ride out to Seven Bridges with you, but once we are there, you're on your own. You need to be strong. Remember your training. Always be watchful. Practice hard. Study harder. Know now, and forever remember, I am proud of you. Your parents would be proud of you too. Not just because you are their boys, but because of the men you are becoming."

Whitfield starting tearing up. "Thank you, Hendricks. We'll keep trying to make you proud of us."

Aspen was less emotional than his older brother, but still appreciated Hendricks' words. "Yeah, thanks, Hendricks. I'm going to miss you."

"Me too, Aspen. Me too."

With that, Whitfield and Aspen each hugged Hendricks, and then proceeded to board the biggest, nicest, most spectacular ferry either of them had ever seen.

****

Seven Bridges Academy is a highly selective co-ed boarding school set on 283 acres of the world's most beautiful landscape. The primary campus of 158 acres is pentagon-shaped, surrounded on each side by five large mansions, each sitting on five acres of land, where all 1,050 SBA students reside, 42 students per mansion. Set beyond each row of mansions is a unique environment.

The waterfront side includes a spectacular white sand beach and crystal-clear waters, where students can swim, surf, kayak, and access (across the canal) any of Seven Bridges' large fleet of mid- and large-size boats, from 25-foot speedboats to giant mega-yachts. The waterfall side contains magnificent gorges, streams, cascading waterfalls, a rain forest, and nestled slightly further back, a wondrous safari, home to many exotic birds and other wildlife.

Beyond majestic views, the mountain side offers year-round opportunities for skiing, snowboarding, snow-tubing, and a plethora of other snow-filled activities, all within a 12-minute ski lift ride, which means students could swim and sunbathe all afternoon on the waterfront side and within thirty minutes find themselves swooshing down a magnificent ski slope or cozying up fireside in the luxurious ski lodge on the mountaintop.

Abutting the mountains, the garden side is home to the most beautiful flowers and plants in the known universe, with glorious tree-lined paths and intricately carved gazebos welcoming students for bouts of quiet contemplation or private conversation.

Rounding out the pentagon, is the only true student-made environment, a rotating, multilevel labyrinth where students can exercise both their minds and bodies as they face down obstacles, swing across bridges, and lose themselves inside the enormous adventure maze.

Due to Seven Bridges' unique geographic positioning, all traffic into and out of campus is restricted to three options: ferry (docking on the waterfront side, with awaiting kayaks to traverse the canal toward campus), train (an underground subway system with a single local station located directly underneath Arlington Gymnastics Center), and flying drone taxis, limos, and buses (to be parked in designated rooftop holding areas sitting atop each of four hotel buildings adorning the four open corners of the Pentagon).

Admission to Seven Bridges Academy is among the highest and most prestigious achievements a young person could attain. The application process is rigorous, with intense focus on academics, integrity, character, athleticism, and potential for life-long success. Students are hand-picked from across the country, with strict limits on enrollment numbers. Each year, 150 new students, exactly 75 boys and 75 girls, enroll at Seven Bridges to begin their seven-year journey toward graduation.

The academic calendar is set to include six 7-week class terms during the year, with one week off in between terms and five weeks off after the school year. Students take four courses during each of five terms and secure an internship for the remaining term. Classes are held in the mornings, Monday through Thursday, two classes per day, with afternoons reserved for physical activity and homework. Gymnastics practices are held every weekday evening, and while the 25 team members are in practice, all other students have specifically identified roles to play in supporting their assigned gymnast.

With the start of each new year, hope springs anew for scores of students trying to earn a coveted spot on the gymnastics team for the upcoming season. Hundreds of students opt to come to school early, a full two weeks before classes start, to either try out for the team or to support friends in their own quest for a roster spot.

Whitfield and Aspen are in the former group, gymnastics team hopefuls eager to earn a spot on the team, but knowing that the odds are stacked against them. Whitfield, a 13-year-old incoming third-year transfer student, had no prior competition experience, as he had always been home-schooled, but did train gymnastics with Hendricks.

Likewise, Aspen had been home-schooled and trained with Hendricks, but he was only 10-years old and had received a special exemption waiver directly from the school headmaster, Sir Arlington, to enroll as the youngest first-year student ever at Seven Bridges Academy. The odds of either brother, especially Aspen, securing a spot on the team this year were nearly incomprehensible.

****

The ferry ride got off to an uneasy start for Whitfield and Aspen. Shortly after boarding together, Hendricks encouraged the boys to stay out on the outdoor level and start mingling with the other students, while he went downstairs with the rest of the parents and guardians to catch up with some old friends. Whitfield and Aspen were both relatively shy, particularly when first introduced to a new environment. They stood next to each other, staring out at the passing scenery for a while, only pretending not to notice how happy all the other students appeared to be while catching up with each other, many for the first time since leaving after the previous school year's end-of-year celebration.

Looking around, Whitfield noticed that there was an open table toward the middle of the eating area, and asked Aspen if he wanted to sit down.

"Sure. I'm getting a bit hungry though."

"No problem, Aspen. Go grab that table over there and I'll get us some food."

"OK."

Whitfield walked over to the concession counter while Aspen grabbed a seat. On his way, Whitfield noticed a few things. First, nearly everyone on the boat truly seemed happy and glad to see each other. Second, the wait staff and concession workers were among the friendliest people he had ever encountered in his life. Third, and later on Whitfield would kick himself for not noticing this first, he saw the most beautiful girl, with the perfect smile, perfect hair, perfect...well, everything as far as Whitfield was concerned. She was standing with a large group of friends, all laughing and smiling, and it seemed that everyone on the boat knew who she was and genuinely liked her.

Whitfield was entranced. He couldn't move. His legs just wouldn't work, and as other students simply walked around him to retrieve their own concessions from the counter, Whitfield stayed, locked in the same position, for what felt like days, until finally, Keegan, an older boy with dark hair and a bright smile, came up behind Whitfield and put his arm around the shy, lovestruck newcomer.

"Hey, brother, like what you see?"

Whitfield remained stoic for a second longer and then was stunned out of his trance. "Uhh...what? I wasn't staring."

Keegan laughed. "Hey, relax. Don't sweat it. I feel you. She's a hottie."

Whitfield pretended not to know what Keegan was talking about. "Who?"

"Oh, please. Are you going to tell me you weren't just staring at that fine girl over there? I mean, I just had to step over your tongue. You're drooling, man."

"I am not." Feeling slightly embarrassed, Whitfield finally admitted, "I mean, well, maybe I noticed her. Who is she? She's incredible."

"That, my friend, is Ugu. She's great! Want to meet her?"

Whitfield nearly lost his composure. "What? You know her?"

"Oh yeah, that's my girl." And then, without further warning, Keegan yelled out across the way, "hey, Ugu, my man here wants to meet you."

Whitfield turned bright red and quickly turned away from Ugu's direction. "Stop it! What are you doing?"

"What, you don't want to meet her?" Keegan was loving just messing around with the new guy.

"Not like this. Stop it."

"OK." Keegan proceeded to yell out in Ugu's direction yet again. "Never mind, Ugu. He's shy. Says maybe later. He does think you're hot though."

Whitfield was mortified.

"See. Now isn't that better?"

Whitfield's face was even redder now. "How is that any better? Do you know how embarrassing that was?"

Keegan pretended not to notice. "Embarrassing? For who?"

"For me."

"Ah, cuz, you're thinking about this the wrong way. If anyone should be embarrassed, it should be me, but don't worry, I'm not, or maybe Ugu, but she's not embarrassed either. Trust me. But what she is now is curious. She hasn't seen you before, right?" Whitfield shook his head. "So now she's wondering who you are. I guarantee you she's over there with her friends right now asking everyone about you."

Whitfield hadn't thought about it that way. "Really?"

"Absolutely. Does anyone over there know you?"

Again, Whitfield shook his head. "No. I'm a transfer student. I don't know anyone here. Well, except for my brother." Whitfield pointed toward Aspen.

"OK, perfect. None of her friends know you, which means she's going to have to do some research on her own. She could send one of her friends over, but not Ugu. She likes to do things herself. I bet her friends all come over to me after I leave you, though."

Whitfield was still confused. "Why you?"

"To ask me about you, stupid. But also, because they can't keep their hands off me. They all want me." Keegan's confidence was off the charts.

Whitfield wasn't convinced. "Is that so?"

"Of course. But, don't worry about me. I'm used to it by now. It's kind of a curse being this good-looking and all."

Whitfield smiled and stifled a chuckle. "Ahh. I see."

"Well, look, great meeting you. I'm going to bounce over there. Don't worry about Ugu. She'll come find you."

Whitfield wasn't quite sure what to make of this crazy, impromptu interaction, but thought he should be polite, nonetheless. "Thanks."

"Hey, brother, what's your name?"

"Whitfield. What's yours?"

"Keegan. I'll see you around."

With that, Keegan left and Whitfield gathered his and Aspen's food and went over to meet his brother at the table. Whitfield was still trying to process what had just happened, and even thought he had caught sight of Ugu looking in his direction, he quickly averted his eyes, turning instead to look down at his feet, which is perhaps why he didn't notice Jonathan approaching from his right side. Jonathan, a cantankerous, mean-spirited second-year student, intentionally crossed paths with Whitfield, bumping into him, knocking all the food Whitfield was carrying onto the floor. Whitfield's first reaction was to apologize for walking into Jonathan by accident, but quickly realized the incident was not merely an accident.

As Whitfield stood, somewhat befuddled, Jonathan took a step closer, such that he was uncomfortably close to Whitfield's face. Neither said a word. Whitfield felt some anger stirring up in the pit of his stomach, but remained in control of his actions. Jonathan continued staring right into Whitfield's eyes from only a few inches away, let out a low grumble, and continued on his way, kicking one of the fallen wrapped sandwiches away, stepping on a fruit cup, and intentionally bumping into Whitfield's shoulder as he passed by.

Whitfield had the sudden urge to punch Jonathan in his smug face, but instead, calmed his emotions and bent down to pick up any of the food and drink he could salvage. As Whitfield knelt down, he noticed that Jonathan had met up with three of his friends, who were all laughing at Whitfield and congratulating Jonathan for his recent altercation. Jonathan, however, looked dissatisfied, with a hint of anger still boiling over in him. Whitfield remained calm, although as he turned to look in Ugu's direction, he felt a wave of embarrassment all over again.

Fortunately, Whitfield thought, Ugu was no longer standing amidst her crowd of friends. Whitfield looked all around and couldn't find her, and feeling some relief that maybe she hadn't seen what just happened, he sat down at the table with Aspen, who was clearly quite hungry.

"Hey, what took so long? I'm starving."

"Sorry, Aspen. You didn't see?"

"No, what? I was looking out at the water. What happened?"

Whitfield thought better of burdening Aspen with what just happened. He didn't want Aspen thinking there might be any trouble before even arriving at school. "Oh, nothing. Don't worry about it. Here's a salad and some snacks for you." Whitfield handed what remaining food he was holding to Aspen.

"Great! Thank you." Aspen starting eating right away. "Hey, I thought you were hungry too. Where's your food?"

"Oh, it's...uhh..."

Just then, Whitfield felt the soft touch of a hand on his shoulder and the sweetest voice he had ever heard.

"Excuse me, but the nice gentleman at the concession stand thought you might like to try one of his homemade sandwiches. It's really good. I actually have one myself and if you don't mind, could I sit here with you two?"

Whitfield was stunned. Ugu was even more beautiful up close. For a moment, he had forgotten how to speak. Fortunately for Whitfield, Aspen was there, and he didn't seem so tongue-tied.

"Sure. Please come sit with us."

"Oh, great. Thank you. I'm Ugu. I don't think we've met before. What's your name?"

"Hi. I'm Aspen. He's my brother, Whitfield."

"Well, very nice to meet you, Aspen. And you too, Whitfield."

Whitfield was still, inexplicably, unable to speak. Ugu sat down next to Whitfield and placed a sandwich in front Whitfield and one in front of herself.

"So, Aspen, are you starting at Seven Bridges this year? You look so young."

"Yes. I'm starting my first year. I'm only ten and had to get special permission from Sir Arlington to start school this year."

"Wow. That is really cool. I don't think we've ever had a 10-year-old at Seven Bridges." Ugu was clearly impressed. Aspen liked how she seemed genuinely interested in him. "Where did you go to school before?"

"Yeah, Sir Arlington said I was the youngest student ever. We were both home-schooled, so all this is all really new to us."

"Really? Well, I would be happy to show you guys around...if you want. I'm sure you are going to love it at SBA. We are so happy to have you here." Ugu smiled at both Aspen and Whitfield. Whitfield was still silent.

"Yes, I'm really excited to go to Seven Bridges."

Ugu turned toward Whitfield to try to coax him into saying something. Anything. "And Whitfield, what year are you?"

Whitfield turned red, and seemed to still lack the ability to speak.

Ugu smiled and let out a slight giggle. "Oh, I'm sorry, I didn't bring you a drink. Please, share some of mine. You have to try it. It's a peanut butter and banana smoothie. Please, have some."

Whitfield smiled awkwardly and reached for the cup as Ugu handed it to him. As he reached out for the cup, his fingers inadvertently brushed up against Ugu's fingers, and when they did, he lifted his eyes to hers, and felt a surge of tingling energy shoot up his spine, forcing the corners of his mouth to curl upward. They both smiled, and after another moment, Whitfield was finally able to speak.

"Thank you."

Ok, so it wasn't exactly romantic poetry escaping his lips, but it was a start.

Whitfield took a sip of the smoothie, placed it back on the table directly between himself and Ugu and slowly started to speak.

"I'm sorry, I didn't mean to be rude before."

Ugu was still smiling. "Oh, not at all. I thought you were very nice."

Surprised by just how kind she was treating him, Whitfield relaxed, just a bit. "I'm Whitfield."

"Yes, your brother told me." Ugu let out another giggle, which let Whitfield know she wasn't being mean or sarcastic.

"Right. Yes, have you met my brother, Aspen?"

Aspen slapped his hand up to his forehead and let out a groan. Ugu, however, remained enchanting. "Yeesss...he introduced himself."

"Right. I'm sorry, I'm just a little off right now." Whitfield was starting to collect his thoughts now, and realizing just how awkward he was being.

Aspen kicked his brother's shin under the table and in a low grumble, said, "hey, bro, get it together."

"No, Aspen, your brother is doing fine."

"Thank you. Umm...yes, I'm starting at Seven Bridges this year."

"Good. What year?"

"Third-year."

Ugu's eyes grew wider. "Oh, wow. Me too. I mean, I'm a third-year too. I've already been here for two years though."

"Yes, I umm...kind of noticed you standing over there with a lot of other students."

"Oh, yeah, we were just catching up. After the end-of-year celebration, everyone takes off for a few weeks to either go home, go on vacation, or whatever. Even though it's only for a few weeks, it's really the longest any of us are apart from each other, so the ferry ride back to campus is a good time to catch up."

Aspen asked, "did you go home, or take a vacation?"

"I spent some time at home, but only for one week. I stayed here, I mean, at Seven Bridges, for a couple weeks after everyone left at the end of the year."

"Why?"

"Just working on a few projects. Helping Sir Arlington with some things." For the first time, Whitfield thought he saw some uneasiness in Ugu's response. Almost as though she didn't really want to talk about what she was working on over the break. Whitfield quickly put it out of his head, though, when Ugu changed the subject. "Anyway, Whitfield, are you trying out for the gymnastics team?"

Stunned at how Ugu could possibly know that, Whitfield responded, "why would you ask that?"

"Well, because classes do not start for another two weeks and since you do not seem to know any of the gymnasts already on the team, I figured you must be trying out. And, Aspen, I assume you are here to help your brother?"

Whitfield was satisfied with Ugu's response. Aspen, however, was quick to share his own intention to try out for the team.

"Actually, we are both trying out for the team."

"Really?" Ugu appeared surprised and took a moment to collect herself, before continuing enthusiastically. "Well, that is awesome! Ohh, I hope you both make the team. My best friend is a gymnast. It would be so cool if you two can make the team too."

Whitfield appreciated her support. "Thanks for the enthusiasm, but it's not so easy to make the team. Odds are we're not going to make it, and even if one of us does, the other probably will not."

"Oh, don't think that way. Have you competed before?"

Aspen quickly responded, "nope."

"Oh, that's right, you said you were home-schooled. Well, no matter. You can still make the team."

"Are you trying out too?" Aspen was hoping she was, so that he might know someone else, besides his brother, at tryouts.

"Oh, no. I'm afraid not. I'm not good enough to make this team."

Whitfield wanted to compliment her with the same confidence as she had just shown them, but couldn't find the right words. Instead, he just focused on her words about them. "So, what makes you think we're good enough?"

"Just a hunch. You seem to have good judgment."

That comment caught Whitfield off guard. He looked directly into Ugu's eyes, and said, "a hunch? How do you know whether or not we have good judgment?"

Ugu met Whitfield's eyes. "Well, put it this way. When most new students board the ferry, they rush over to the snack bar, grab some ice cream, climb up to the top level, or act in some crazy way. When the two of you boarded the ferry, you stayed together, scoped out your surroundings, took note of what others were doing, and waited until you had enough information to make a move."

Still locking eyes, Whitfield retorted, "maybe we're just shy."

"I thought about that, and perhaps you are, but so are many of the other new students. Then I saw Aspen grab a table while you went to the concession stand."

Aspen was now quick to join the discussion. "We just wanted to make sure we had a place to sit with our food."

"Right. Thoughtful. Might be a small thing, but still, more thoughtful than most of the others around here. But the clincher, was how Whitfield responded when Jonathan ran into him."

Whitfield finally broke eye contact and looked away, feeling embarrassed all over again. "Oh, you saw that?"

"Saw what? What happened?"

"It was nothing, Aspen. Actually, it was worse than nothing. I did nothing. I just stood there. Oh, I'm so embarrassed." Whitfield hung his head.

Ugu reached over and lifted Whitfield's chin with her hand. "Not at all. You handled that situation like a true gentleman. If you were going to be embarrassed, it should have been when you were standing with Keegan. He's such a show-off, but I love him."

Even though they had just met, Whitfield's heart sank a notch, hearing those words. "Oh. So, is he like, your boyfriend or something?"

Ugu laughed out loud. "Oh, no, nothing like that. He's like a big brother. That's it. But back to you, no, the way you handled yourself, controlling your emotions, standing firm, not giving any ground, but at the same time, not antagonizing or provoking the situation. That took courage."

"Whitfield, someone ran into you? Who was it?" Aspen started looking over the crowd, hoping to find the coward who ran into his brother.

Ugu encouraged Aspen to let it go. "He's one of our less-well-mannered students. Jonathan. He's always looking for trouble. I've seen him pull that stunt before and it typically doesn't end well for whoever he targets. But, not this time."

As Ugu was talking, a thought entered Whitfield's mind. "Wait a second. How do you know all this? Were you watching us this whole time? From the time we boarded the ferry?"

Now, it was Ugu who was caught off guard. Still, she maintained her composure, and smiled. "Umm…well. Perhaps. Maybe."

Whitfield was intrigued. "Why?"

"Why were you staring at me when you were over by the concession counter?" Ugu was trying to change the subject.

"Uhh…Because…"

"Because?"

Whitfield stopped trying to come up with an explanation, not wanting to say that he thought she was the most beautiful girl he had ever seen. Instead, he just smiled, and Ugu returned his smile with one of her own. They sat quietly for a while, interrupted only by the occasional returning student stopping to say 'hi' to Ugu and give her a welcome back to school hug. Ugu was always super sweet and nice to everyone she met. This time, Whitfield was the one who broke the silence.

"You seem really popular. Do you know everyone here?"

"Maybe not everyone, but I do like to meet people. I also serve on some school committees, so I get to meet people that way too."

Aspen was happy to meet a new friend. "I'm glad we got to meet you."

"Aww…that's so sweet of you. I'm really glad to have met you too."

Just then, the edge of campus started to come into view. Whitfield and Aspen took notice of the beautiful scenery—snow-capped mountains in the distance, glorious waterfalls, amazing gardens; but, above anything else, they noticed the incredibly large and palatial mansions lining the perimeter of campus. Just on the waterfront, Whitfield noticed five majestically large houses with unbelievable pools and grounds.

"Whoa!"

"Wow! Whitfield, look at those houses."

"Those aren't houses, Aspen. Those are enormous mansions."

"I wonder who lives there."

Ugu responded, "we do, silly."

Whitfield couldn't believe it. "Get out. No, really, who lives there?"

"I'm serious. Which one do you want to live in?"

Whitfield was completely confused. "Wait, are you serious? You mean we get to live in one of those houses?"

"Of course. All students live in mansions here."

Aspen let out a big gasp. "Whoa. That's crazy! Which one do we get to live in?"

"Well, that depends. Each house contains one member of the gymnastics team and 41 other students, and a house supervisor—usually a teacher at the school. In addition to taking classes, each student works on his or her gymnast's staff."

Whitfield was starting to realize just how little he knew about the school. "Do students just get assigned to gymnasts?"

"No, not exactly. Each gymnast gets to select which students they want in the house. But the system leaves out a lot of students and not everyone gets picked, and most of us do not know the incoming first-years or transfers. So, every student makes a list of their top five houses they want to live in, top five gymnasts they want to work with, and top five staff jobs they would like to have, such as security, stylist, PR rep, or any number of other positions. There are 25 total houses—25 gymnasts on the team. Some students will simply write down a particular house they want—for example, some want to live near the water, others by the ski area, others by the waterfalls. You getting all this?"

"Not really, but go on."

"I know. It seems really complicated now, but you'll get it in no time. Anyway, while some students pick the house, others pick a particular staff job or the particular gymnast they want to live with. These other paths could be a little tricky though, because if your gymnast is older than you, when they graduate, you'll be looking for a new house or need to break in with a new gymnast. That's what I'm having to do now. I was with Gabe for the past two years—see, in that house right there." Ugu pointed to a gorgeous house on the waterfront. "But he graduated last year."

Whitfield's eyes grew big. "Ohh...so where are you going to live now?" Whitfield hoped his question didn't come off as sounding too hopeful that they might end up in the same house together.

"My best friend, Flaherty, is on the team. I'm going to live with her. She lives in that house right there, right on the waterfront side." Ugu pointed toward another beautiful mansion.

"Oh, too bad. I think my brother wants to live with you."

Whitfield's face turned bright red. "Aspen! No. I mean, well, yeah. Uhh...what I mean is..."

Ugu put her hand on Whitfield's arm. "That's OK. We'll see where you guys end up. If you do make the team, you would have your own house. If not, you can put Flaherty's house at the top of your list. I'll put in a good word for you." Ugu winked, and Whitfield's heart melted.

At that moment, for the first time in his life, Whitfield thought twice about whether he wanted to continue being a gymnast. The thought of living in the same house as Ugu was almost more than he could bear at the moment. As the ferry started to pull up to the dock, Ugu wished Whitfield and Aspen good luck and offered some assistance in getting acclimated to campus.

"Hey, I have to meet with Sir Arlington after our welcome meeting and then I have a few other things lined up, but if you guys aren't doing anything later tonight, I'd be happy to give you a campus tour."

Aspen jumped at the opportunity. "Really? That would be great!"

Ugu smiled and looked at Whitfield. "Yeah?"

"I'm not sure if we have anything else planned. Do you know if the school has us doing anything tonight?"

"Typically, the school does offer a cursory tour. They'll show you some of the classrooms and dining options, but I can give you a better tour. And I can introduce you to Flaherty."

Whitfield didn't need any more convincing. "OK. That sounds great! Let's meet up tonight."

"Great!"

Ugu walked away and Whitfield and Aspen stood up from the table, looked at each other and smiled. They both shared the same thought: *This is going to be a great year!*

Chapter 3
Campus Tour

The ferry arrived at campus at noon on Sunday. All passengers debarked and after saying their goodbyes to parents and guardians, the students headed toward Arlington Gymnastics Center, while parents and guardians were whisked off to the Alumni Center for cocktails and entertainment. Whitfield caught sight of Hendricks speaking with an elderly man, whom he quickly identified as the school's headmaster. Sir Arlington's picture could be seen in multiple locations around campus, nowhere more prominently, however, than near the main entrance to the largest facility on campus, Arlington Gymnastics Center, which as per tradition at Seven Bridges Academy adorns the name of the school's current headmaster. As Whitfield and Aspen followed the throngs of students into the enormous gymnastics center, taking in all of the scenery, Hendricks and Sir Arlington exchanged a friendly greeting.

"Good to see you again, Arlington."

"Likewise. Thank you for doing this, Hendricks."

"You really left me no other choice."

"They will be safe here. What do they know about why they are here?"

"Only what they need to know."

"And are they prepared…you know, physically?"

"Arlington, I've prepared them myself. They'll be fine."

"And Aspen? I'm sticking my neck on the line here admitting a student so young. Not everyone on the Board approves of this decision."

"I give you my word. Aspen is the most talented gymnast I've ever seen at his age. And his intuition, acumen, and academic skills are world-class. He'll fit in just fine. You just make sure they are both protected at all times."

"I swear it. You have my word."

****

Whitfield and Aspen were both overwhelmed by how many students came to campus early for tryouts. The number of students from the ferry nearly tripled once all three modes of transportation arrived on campus in unison. Whitfield noticed hordes of students appearing from both below the gymnastics center (those arriving by train) and from above (those arriving via flying vehicles). In total, almost 500 students, nearly half of the total student body had arrived on campus early for the two-week tryout period. Once inside Arlington Gymnastics Center, Whitfield and Aspen heard Ugu calling out for them to come over to meet Flaherty. The four students sat together for the opening welcome meeting.

In total, one hundred fifty-six students were trying out for the gymnastics team this year. Only 25 students would ultimately make the roster. Nineteen students were returning from last year's championship team, which had boasted six individual national champions, one of which was Gabe, the 3x National Gymnast of the Year and first pick in the draft following his fourth-year, and now competing professionally for the Long Neck Crocodiles. SBA lost four gymnasts to graduation and two to injury. The 19 returning members were not guaranteed a spot on this year's team, but in reality, about 14-15 spots were all but certain, and the other 4-5 gymnasts were all really good too, and would likely keep their spots on the team.

At last year's ending ceremony, the graduating gymnasts each selected their replacement—which does not constitute an official roster change, as it is more just a cursory gesture and tradition than anything else, but there were four students who were loosely 'promised' spots on this year's team. So, counting the 19 returning gymnasts and four anointed replacements, there were really only two open roster spots available over which the remaining one hundred thirty-three gymnasts would compete.

The welcome meeting lasted about 30 minutes. Afterwards, returning students were able to go back to their houses and settle in prior to the first tryout session at 19:00. New students and transfers without housing were welcome to stay in the gymnastics center for the duration of the tryout period, or find another student to temporarily bunk with for the next ten days.

Flaherty gladly welcomed Whitfield and Aspen to stay in her mansion; however, Whitfield and Aspen opted to stay in the gym. The twenty-two other first-years and four transfer students all opted to find mansions to live in for the duration of the tryout period.

After looking around Arlington Gymnastics Center and storing their bags under their gym cots, Whitfield and Aspen only had about four hours remaining until their first tryout session. Flaherty dropped off hers and Ugu's bags at her locker and caught up with Whitfield and Aspen. They chatted with each other for about 20 minutes while waiting for Ugu, who was meeting with Sir Arlington. Once her meeting ended, Ugu met up with the others and the four new friends decided to explore campus, with Ugu and Flaherty leading the way. The campus seemed huge to Whitfield and Aspen, but Ugu was able to make sense of it all. She was a terrific campus tour guide.

"OK, so as you may have seen from the ferry, the campus is shaped as a giant pentagon. Surrounding each side are five houses, or mansions. The houses are technically considered non-academic areas, but the school still owns them anyway. Inside the main campus area, we have the Inner Bowl, where we're now standing and then the eight academic areas: International Affairs; Engineering; Law; Advanced Medicine; Business; Computer Science; Applied Mathematics and Quantitative Economics; and Gymnastics, each with their own library, eating areas, and other cool features specific to their discipline. Most gymnasts just major in gymnastics, right Flaherty?"

"Right. Some say they are easier classes and the teachers all love the gymnasts, so they get easy As."

"Figures. But Flaherty is the odd duck though. She majors in Engineering."

"It's so cool. I have to show you guys the labs sometime. They're amazing!" Flaherty was always excited to talk about the engineering labs at SBA.

Ugu continued, "each academic area has color-coded turf and a different event practice gym marking its entrance. See over there, the Parallel Planks practice gym marks the entrance to the Computer Science campus. You'll notice the lampposts, signs, and other little things all have Parallel Planks on them and share the same color as the turf."

Aspen was really impressed with the campus. "That's cool. Is that where we practice? I mean, if we make the team. We have to go around to different gyms for each event?"

Flaherty understood his confusion. "No, not if you make the team. We practice inside Arlington Center. These practice gyms are for the rest of the student body."

"Yeah, the gymnasts have their own practice area, but don't worry, these practice gyms are all really nice. They do get super busy in the afternoons though. Students take the House Point Challenge kind of seriously around here." Ugu was about to continue, when Aspen interrupted.

"House what challenge? What is that?"

Flaherty fielded Aspen's question. "The House Point Challenge. We all have these trackers that we keep on our legs. You'll get them at tryouts tonight. The rest of the first-years will pick up their trackers at the Kickoff Party. They're really cool and can be used to get into certain building around campus and operate the Outer Loop slide system, which Ugu will talk about in a minute, but they also keep track of our exercise."

Now, Whitfield was impressed. "Really?"

"Yeah, it's pretty cool tech. So, whenever a student does a push-up or pommel circle or rope climb or whatever, they earn points for their house. At the end of the year, whichever house has earned the most points, wins."

"That sounds really cool."

"It is, Aspen. But any exercise you do inside Arlington Center for practice or at meets does not count. Isn't that right, Flaherty? I think it's just one of the rules."

"Correct. I know. Doesn't really seem fair, especially since that's the time many other students are out on campus working out, but whatever."

"Yes, Flaherty is working on getting that rule changed, but I don't think her proposal is getting a lot of support."

"Typical."

Ugu knew this was a hot button issue for Flaherty, so swiftly changed topics. "Anyway, Craig Library, the Uniform Galleria, Administration Building, Seven Bridges Bank, Post Office, Flaxen Hall, the Police House, Cheesestock Hospital, Alumni Center, and some other buildings are all located near the entrance area over that way."

Flaherty was quick to add, "the middle of campus is the most fun. Obviously, Arlington Center is right in the middle, but surrounding it, we have trampolines embedded in the walkways, pommel horses, inclined monkey bars, rope climbs…you name it, we probably have it around here. And if we don't, just submit a suggestion, and if enough students want it, we'll likely get it."

"That's right. Flaherty's actually responsible for a few of the upgrades around here, isn't that right?"

Flaherty just smiled and nodded.

"I'm sure you've also noticed the slides and large tubes surrounding campus." The group of four looked skyward to the complex array of slides and tubes hovering above even the tallest buildings on campus.

"This is how most of us get back and forth from campus to our houses or to classes across campus. You see, each of the academic campuses is connected via the Inner Loop. You can walk from one campus building to another on the third floor of each building without ever stepping on the grounds. The buildings are connected via walkways, or bridges."

Flaherty chimed in, "hence, where Seven Bridges Academy gets its name."

"Right. You can also zip-line down from the Inner Loop to the middle of campus. Sometimes it's easier to use the zip-line, especially if you have class directly across campus."

Flaherty added, "each main campus building has two slides, or inclined runways, leading to the Outer Loop. The Outer Loop connects to the four hotels and Arlington Center, and has four long slides, or ramps, to each of the houses surrounding campus."

Whitfield and Aspen looked out toward the Outer Loop in awe. Ugu followed up with, "so, you can take a slide after class back home and arrive on either the east or west side, or upper level or ground level of your house. The entire Outer Loop spans over two miles, so it makes for a nice run too. It's also a great place to watch meets or concerts."

Whitfield was confused. "Wait, how can people watch meets when they're not inside the arena?"

"The roof of the Center is lined with video boards that show everything going on inside. Sometimes it's difficult to see every event, especially when seated far away or on different levels inside the Center, so some people just prefer to watch from up there."

"Ugu's right. Also, tickets for non-students are really expensive, and we're always sold-out, so this gives others an opportunity to still see us compete."

"Yeah, the Outer Loop gets packed during meets. It also has scrolling LCD screens that update scores throughout meets. They'll also post scores from meets around the world, along with other relevant news items."

"Yup. You'll see them scrolling constantly throughout the day. That's usually how we find out how other meets are going. The boards will replay highlights during the week."

Whitfield's head was spinning. This was all a lot to take in. "So, could we get up to the Outer Loop from down here?"

"Sure." Flaherty glanced over at Ugu. "Should we take them up there?"

Ugu nodded. "Yes. I think we should."

Flaherty immediately perked up, like she was about to start a competition. "OK. So, there are lots of different ways get up to the Inner Loop, and then from there it's pretty easy to get to the Outer Loop. Every academic campus has their own way of accessing the Inner Loop from outside. Of course, you can always just enter a building and head up to the third floor to access the Inner Loop, but that's the boring way. These other ways are much more fun. My personal favorites are the rope climb over on the AMQE campus, the tramps over on the Gymnastics campus, and the wall pegs on the Engineering campus. That one may be the toughest. But also, so satisfying when you reach the top."

Ugu could sense the boys were having a tough time following, but that didn't stop her from adding on. "There are also the reverse treadmills, rising stumps, spider wall, and salmon ladder. We could also use the hand bikes over here by the zip-lines. I never really got the hang of those, but there are some kids here that can really fly up the line on those."

Always the competitor, Flaherty asked the only question on her mind. "You want to have a race?"

"Yes!" Aspen replied without even considering how he was going to find the start or finish lines.

Whitfield was a little more thoughtful. "Uhh, sure, but we don't really know where we're going."

Ugu tried to calm Whitfield's apprehension. "No worries. Look, you see that statue over there? Run over there and just past it, you'll see the rope climb. Climb the rope up to the third floor and then go left once you are in the Inner Loop. Look for the first Outer Loop sign, turn right and run up the ramp. The ramp is kind of long, so you may be out of breath by the time you reach to top, especially for your first time. Once you get up there, turn left again and we'll meet at the SBA IV Hotel extension. Got it?"

"I think so."

"Good. Aspen, you're going to go that way. Run toward the Pommel statue and just past it, you'll see the pommel lift. All you have to do is start doing circles on the pommel horse and the platform will rise. Keep going. You may have to do about 60 circles to reach the third floor. Do you think you can do that many?"

"No problem."

"Good. Once you get to the Inner Loop, turn right. Look for the first sign for the Outer Loop, turn left and run up the ramp. Again, you may be tired by the time you reach the top. Once you get there, turn right and run until you reach the SBA IV Hotel extension."

"Sounds fun!"

"Oh, it is. Ugu will take the Escalating Tramps and will likely get to the top first, but she'll have a longer run on the Outer Loop to the meeting point. I'll head over to the Vault-Pegs area. Like I said, it's probably the toughest, but it's also my favorite, and I think I may still be able to beat you to the meeting spot. Does everyone know where they're going?"

Whitfield and Aspen both responded, "yes."

Ugu counted them down. "OK. Ready. Go!"

All four took off in different directions. Despite not being on the team, Ugu was clearly the fastest runner. She made it to the Escalating Tramps in less than 40 seconds and was already halfway up the tramps before Aspen had reached the pommel lift. Aspen found the lift with relative ease. He ran straight toward the statue at first and then hesitated while deciding on which direction to pass the statue. He went right, but later realized that the left side would have been a little faster. He spotted the pommel lift about 100 feet ahead of him to the left of the building's main central entrance.

Aspen hopped on the platform, and the entire circular stand lifted about two inches off the ground. Aspen stretched his fingers and immediately started doing circles on the pommel horse. With each circle, the entire platform lifted higher off the ground. It wasn't long before Aspen had reached the third floor.

Whitfield was having a slightly more difficult time, as he got lost once he reached and passed the Handstand Obstacle statue. Even though the AMQE building holding the ropes was directly in front of him, Whitfield decided to run toward his left for a few seconds and then after not seeing the ropes, he did a complete 180 and ran to the right of the statue.

Again, he could not find the ropes. It wasn't until he came back to the statue and bent forward to catch his breath that he saw what had been in front of him the entire time—a very large academic building with four ropes hanging down from just above the third floor's Inner Loop entrance. Whitfield ran toward the ropes and grabbed hold of one of them and started climbing. Whitfield was an excellent rope climber and reached the Inner Loop in a matter of seconds.

Flaherty had climbed the Peg Wall outside the Engineering building too many times to count. She knew she could climb that wall faster than anyone in the school, but even now, when it was just a race for fun, she couldn't bring herself to slow down and enjoy the climb. No, Flaherty had an inner need to keep improving—to be better than she was the day before. No one else at the school even came close to beating her time at the Peg Wall, but she still challenged herself to do better. As she raced up the wall, Flaherty nearly forgot that she was in a fun race against three other competitors. It was just her and the wall, until she remembered why she was there in the first place. After reaching the top, she quickly sprinted through the Inner Loop, up the ramp to the Outer Loop, and made a quick left to join the others.

Ugu was the first to arrive at the SBA IV Hotel extension, getting there just a few seconds before Whitfield. Even though he had lost some time finding the ropes, Whitfield was still surprised that he hadn't finished first. Ugu had to run over a mile around the Outer Loop just to get there, and from what he could see, Ugu didn't have a bead of sweat on her. She wasn't even breathing heavy. *How could she have gotten here so fast, ran so far, without even a hint of exhaustion?*

Whitfield, on the other hand, was doubled over, his pulse racing, and breathing heavily. Ugu patted Whitfield on the shoulder and told him he did a nice job. Ugu's hand on Whitfield's shoulder sent shivers down his spine. He never felt that sensation before; well, once before, on the ferry, but this time was different. He didn't exactly know why, but he liked it.

Whitfield started to say something, but just as he did, he noticed Flaherty running around the bend to join them. Aspen was coming from the other end just a few seconds behind. All four completed the race. They treated themselves to a leisurely stroll around the Outer Loop, admiring the houses and pristine scenery on their left and a more elevated view of campus on the right. The four friends shared lots of laughs and smiles during their stroll together, but it was getting close to 19:00, which meant Flaherty, Whitfield, and Aspen would need to make it back to Arlington Gymnastics Center for tryouts.

Fortunately, they could just take a slide from the Outer Loop directly into the upper level of the Center and head down the stairs to find their stored gear and change clothes before practice. Whitfield and Aspen could not believe their luck in becoming fast friends with Ugu and Flaherty, nor did they completely understand why these two amazing girls had chosen to spend their entire afternoon with them, but one thing was for certain—if Whitfield and Aspen were going to continue being friends with Ugu and Flaherty, they were going to have to get in better shape.

Chapter 4
Tryouts

Arlington Gymnastics Center was by far the largest standalone structure on Seven Bridges Academy's entire campus. Holding seats for an impressive 150,000 spectators, space for hundreds of video boards, and a huge multilevel competition floor, Arlington Center easily ranked as one of the grandest arenas in the entire country. To accommodate all eight competition events simultaneously, the main competition area spanned eight levels, each level home to a different event, holding a minimum of four sets of competition-ready equipment, plus additional practice equipment, to accommodate the eight teams competing at a typical meet.

Each level held about 18,500 seats in a horseshoe shape while the remaining wall supported 100 twenty-person floating luxury suites, which allowed fans to take control of the suite and move to different floors as desired without ever leaving the comfort of their seat.

Whitfield and Aspen stood in awe of the impressive facility when Flaherty reminded them that they needed to get changed for tryouts. As they descended the stadium stairs, Whitfield started to have a sinking feeling in his gut.

"What if I don't make it? I'm not sure I could compete at this level."

Aspen was his brother's biggest fan and was quick to lift his spirits. "Don't worry, bro...if you completely wipe out, you can always live with Flaherty and Ugu."

"Thanks. But, I'm serious. I never competed at this level before. I just don't know."

"Look, Whitfield, you are the best gymnast in this gym. No, seriously. Look at those banners from past champions. Gabe. He won the pommel title last year. Your routine is already better than his. Oslo. He won the Vault-Pegs title. You already have him beat. Cassidy on Parallel Planks. McKayla on Tri-Bars. You are better than all of them. Don't be so uptight. You got this."

"Thanks, Aspen. I'm really glad you're here."

"Me too…now, if we could just fix your handstand lines." Aspen loved teasing his brother about the arch in his handstands.

"Oh, really, you're going to talk about my handstand. What about your vault run? You look like a baby bird learning to walk and fly for the first time."

"I do not. Well, you…"

The two brothers continued laughing and teasing each other down to their cots to pick up their gear.

Whitfield and Aspen arrived at the practice gym early. Only a handful of other hopefuls were already there, but no one had actually started warming up yet, when Whitfield and Aspen decided to step out onto the floor to stretch. Tryouts were not being held on any of the main competition floors, but rather in the basement-level practice area. All the equipment was laid out nicely, but without the enormity of space and 150,000 empty seats. Whitfield was immediately comforted by this more intimate setting, and Aspen felt the same way. Despite displaying more confidence than his older brother, Aspen, too, was nervous and somewhat insecure about his abilities at this new level.

Despite Whitfield and Aspen stretching out on the floor, none of the other team hopefuls had dared step onto the floor. It wasn't until Flaherty showed up a few minutes later and walked out onto the floor that others slowly joined in. Flaherty was one of the more popular gymnasts returning from last year's squad, and projected to be one of, if not the, best on the team. Everyone liked her. She tried introducing Whitfield and Aspen to some returning team members and other hopefuls, but after a few moments, Flaherty got pulled into several other conversations as everyone awaited the coaches' arrival.

At exactly 19:00, all 18 coaches arrived and formed a semi-circle on one side of the main practice floor. Accompanying the coaches, but standing rigidly behind them were about a dozen student assistants, all seventh-years. The coaches certainly commanded respect in the room, as all chatter abruptly stopped and everyone remained laser-focused on whichever coach was about to speak. The lead assistant, Coach Daza, second in charge, was the first to speak.

"Over these next ten days, you will have 28 three-hour sessions—three per day, following tonight's lone session. Every member of the coaching staff will be evaluating your performance throughout the tryout period. Every circle. Every handstand. Every push-up. Every rope climb. You will be pushed to the point of exhaustion. And beyond."

Whitfield and Aspen looked at each other, with both anxiety and fortitude in their eyes.

Coach Daza continued, "you will be evaluated on the basis of your pure gymnastics abilities, your character, your strength, your flexibility, your ability to recovery, adapt, and improve. We will be conducting interviews with each of you; multiple times over the tryout period. Remember why you are here. Each member of our team not only represents our school, but fights for every resource we have at our disposal. Our clothes. Our food. Our houses. Our technology. All that we have is provided for out on this equipment. This week, it is our job to make sure we select the best of the best to fight for us.

"After that, our job shifts toward training those 25 members to squeeze out every ounce of talent, ability, drive, and determination so that the rest of us can enjoy the fruits of their labor. Being a gymnast at this school is neither a privilege nor a right. It is an honor, and those selected have a duty to uphold, to all of us. Just as those who ultimately do not make the team will have the honor, and duty, to work with and for one of the team members. It takes every single person at this school to make it function properly. Whether you are a gymnast or personal assistant—you add value to this school and are counted upon to do your duty. Let's have a great tryout period. Go get 'em!"

Whitfield was pumped, and a little frightened. "Wow! That was intense."

Flaherty could sense his apprehension. "Yeah. Daza's actually a really nice guy. I don't think he enjoys cutting anyone from the squad, so I think he thinks if he comes off as a bit intense now that some of the students who might not really want to be on the team bad enough will just voluntarily remove themselves, so he doesn't have to do it later."

Coach Cassidy was the next to speak in front of the gathered hopefuls. "OK, so I'm Coach Cassidy and this is Coach Vespi. We are the Parallel Planks coaches, and we are going to lead you though an opening workout. Those of you who successfully make it through can then head over to your first event or workout station. For anyone new, or if you possibly forgot, you can find your individual tryout schedule on your tracker on your upper thigh. Any first-years or transfers who do not yet have a tracker, go see Coach Larissa after the warmup. She will get you squared away. We made sure to allow time for each of you to showcase for the coaches on your preferred event prior to the first scheduled cuts, which are tomorrow night. OK, let's get started."

The opening workouts were tough. Two people quit within the first fifteen minutes. *Quitting on the first day?* That seemed bizarre to Whitfield, who had waited so long just to be here. There was no way he was going to quit, no matter how hard they pushed him. Whitfield had spent years developing his body to the muscular frame that it is today. He wasn't going to let a few rope climbs, pull-ups, and L-holds knock him off his path. He glanced over at Aspen, and knew Aspen was thinking the same thing. Aspen was undoubtedly the strongest gymnast, pound-for-pound, in the gym. The only problem was that he only weighed about 70 pounds.

After a quick hydration break, Whitfield and Aspen hurried over to Coach Larissa to get their trackers and then Whitfield went over to VH-Bars (Vertical-Horizontal) while Aspen rushed over to Pommel Clock. The VH-Bars were undoubtedly Whitfield's least favorite event, even though he could perform a few high-level skills. His form was not as clean as it could be, and he still struggled with the transition from vertical bar back up to horizontal. Whitfield was scheduled to go up second, so he quickly strapped on his grips and hit the practice bars.

The tryout schedule was very regimented. For the first few sessions, each gymnast had a scheduled five-minute evaluation period on the apparatus with the event's two coaches. Gymnasts could warm up on the practice set immediately before their 5-minute evaluation block, but otherwise they were asked to complete an intense circuit of exercises, workouts, and flexibility training in between evaluations. As more hopefuls were cut, the remaining gymnasts saw multiple 5-minute evaluation periods with coaches on each event. With this being Whitfield's first evaluation period, he wanted to make sure he was ready.

After a somewhat sluggish start to his practice set, Whitfield started to complete some front giant and back giant work on the horizontal bars, a few flagpole stands on the verticals, and even made a smooth transition from horizontal to vertical. He did not have time to practice any release moves before his time was up and needed to show the coaches what he could do. To his surprise, the coaches simply asked Whitfield to complete a very basic routine, without any transitions, pirouettes, or release moves.

The coaches evaluated Whitfield's hand placements, lines, shapes, and body positioning. The coaches asked if Whitfield was comfortable doing a series of skills, but did not actually test whether Whitfield could complete those skills. The coaches offered some feedback to Whitfield, including some advice on removing a slight arch in his back while in handstand and before he knew it, his five minutes were up and Whitfield's time on VH-Bars was over for Tryout Session 1. He really had no idea how he did, but considering the limited time spent doing higher-level skills, Whitfield thought his evaluation could not have been that strong. Aspen, on the other hand, was enjoying an epic start to his tryout period.

After cranking out over a hundred dips, squats, and handstand shoulder taps, Aspen's evaluation period on Pommel Clock was up next. He approached the practice area with high confidence and began his usual warmup routine. Even after completing thousands of circles while training at home with Hendricks, Aspen could still never just hit his routine cold. He needed a few touches before hitting his rhythm.

After just a couple attempts though, Aspen successfully traveled down one horse, transitioned to the next horse, traveled back down and made the tricky pirouette transition using the leather stand filling the wide gap between the second and third horses. Aspen traveled up and down the next few horses before finally stalling out on the ramp leading from 6 o'clock back up to 12 o'clock on the clock. Not a bad first effort for his practice set. When the buzzer sounded for his evaluation period to begin, Aspen was already at the first pommel waiting to start.

Similar to Whitfield's experience on VH-Bars, the Pommel coaches kept things very simple for Aspen. They simply asked Aspen to complete two circles. Then they asked for two flairs. Then they asked if Aspen could travel down one pommel horse. Aspen completed each of these tasks expertly. Just when Aspen started growing a little frustrated with not being able to show the coaches what he could actually do on Pommel, the coaches allowed Aspen to start a routine.

Without glancing up from his notes, Coach Mayflower calmly instructed Aspen. "Now, Aspen, complete as much of the clock as you can. We'll time you, count how many circles, and keep track of skills. We'll be looking for deductions, but will not compute a score for you yet."

Yes! I finally get to show them something.

Aspen closed his eyes, took a deep breath, and was off. Aspen completed his first pass in three circles, two of which in flair position. He easily pivoted to the second horse, maintaining his flairs, legs spread at 135 degrees, toes pointed, and hips well above the horse. Aspen then completed his signature move—he went up to handstand with his legs straddled, pirouetted across the wide gap to the third horse and traveled down the horse in handstand while completing two 360 degree turns. Both Pommel Clock coaches stood there in awe. Aspen then came back down to flairs as he traveled up and down horses four, five, and six.

By this point in Aspen's routine, the entire gym had stopped to watch this incredible exhibition. Aspen proceeded to complete a triple wide-armed front-support circle series across the ramp, making it all the way across to the 12 o'clock horse. Aspen continued to work through horses 11, 10, and 9 while mixing in double-leg circles, half-turns, and reverse full turns. No other gymnast had ever made it this far during the first day of tryouts, and no other first-year had ever made it this far in any practice or competition. Was it possible? Could Aspen complete the entire clock and dismount? A feat that had only been completed by the most skilled gymnasts in the world.

As Aspen approached Horse 8, he was starting to get winded, but still made it back up to handstand and wowed the, now cheering, crowd with another helicopter spin travel and pivot to Horse 7. Aspen came back down to flairs and was about to make the transition to Horse 6 and his ultimate half-travel on the ramp to dismount, when his left hand slipped off the horse and he fell with a thud to the mats below.

In sum, Aspen's epic routine had taken 93 seconds, while completing 45 circles, four handstand helicopter spins, eight half-turns, two full turns, ten flawless horse transitions, and one incredible ramp travel. The crowd cheered for over 30 seconds. Whitfield ran over to Aspen to hug him and check if he was OK. Aspen's eyes were watery, and Whitfield knew it wasn't happy tears, nor was it because he was injured.

"You're upset, aren't you?"

Aspen was trying, unsuccessfully, to hold back his tears. "Yes. I should have made it. I was so close."

"Aspen, listen to everyone. They're clapping and cheering your name. You did great!"

Aspen stood up and the crowd roared again. Aspen let out a small smile, and turned directly to the coaches.

"Can I go again? I know I can make it this time." The coaches simply smiled and shook their heads.

Flaherty came running over to give Aspen a big hug. The other returning gymnasts all came over to congratulate Aspen. Hugs and high fives lasted for another few minutes, and then the video board came to life, announcing that Aspen had set a new tryout record for Most Impressive Pommel Clock routine. At last, Aspen could no longer hold back his smile.

****

Tryout Session 1 concluded without any more drama; however, four more hopefuls quit. The selection process was down to 150 potential gymnasts. Cuts would be made after the second session each day from now until the final day, until only 30 prospective gymnasts remained. Each day grew more difficult, as athletes became more exhausted. With each passing cut list, the remaining athletes were asked to take more turns, execute higher-level skills, and complete longer routines.

Each session became a blur to Whitfield and Aspen. They would wake up, go to the morning session, eat lunch, go to the afternoon session, eat dinner, go to the evening session, shower, and crash hard on their cots. For several days, they hadn't even gone outside the Center. It wasn't until Ugu showed up on Day 5 that Whitfield and Aspen left Arlington Center to have lunch with Ugu and Flaherty at Plank 'N Steins Outdoor Cafe on the Computer Science campus. Flaherty had been going home to sleep in her house every night, but for the boys, it was nice to be outside for a change.

Whitfield was happy to finally see Ugu again. "Hey, Ugu, where have you been? I haven't seen you in so long."

Ugu was just as happy to see Whitfield. "Well, that's what happens when you lock yourself in the gym for five days. I've been getting ready for the Kickoff Party, getting Flaherty's house in order, and, of course, prepping for the start of the school year."

Flaherty put her arm around Ugu. "Yes, Ugu kind of goes crazy this time of year. She reads all of her assigned books cover to cover BEFORE the term even starts. I guess that's why she's the smartest student at school."

"Wow! Impressive."

"Well, thank you for the compliment, Whitfield. Not sure if it's true, but it's nice to be thought of that way. Anyway, Aspen, I heard about your school record. That's so amazing! That's all everyone is talking about out here…you know, in our small world outside of the gym."

Ugu gave Aspen a hug.

The four friends happily ate, laughed, and talked during lunch. They were all having fun together until Flaherty noticed the time.

"Hey, guys, this has been great, but we have to get back to the gym."

Tryouts were down to 100 athletes, and 20 more were to be cut after this afternoon's session. Until now, Whitfield and Aspen still felt cautiously optimistic that they would make it through the day's cuts, but looking around, there were a lot of really good gymnasts left, and not many remained that they felt confident in them being superior gymnasts.

Day 7 marked a significant shift in Aspen's comfort level at tryouts. With only 80 athletes left, Aspen's chances of being the youngest ever member of the team were growing; however, those growing odds also made him the target of some unwanted teasing and bullying at the hands of Jonathan, who relished in his role as one of the anointed four from last year's end-of-year celebration. Jonathan was certainly a terrific gymnast. He had all the skills required to make an All-Star appearance this year. Many of the coaches, however, questioned Jonathan's character and motivation.

Jonathan took pleasure in teasing Aspen. "Hey, Aspen, I hear you couldn't even reach the pegs after your vault. I guess that's why we don't put shrimps on the team."

A few of Jonathan's friends chuckled and pushed Aspen as they walked past him.

Jonathan continued his assault. "Hey, Aspen, I saw your handstand routine earlier. Maybe when you stop being a baby you can finally reach the top."

This had been going on for a couple sessions now, but it was getting more and more frequent as the two adversaries came into contact more often, with fewer athletes around.

Aspen didn't say anything to Whitfield about Jonathan's bullying, but Whitfield could tell something was bothering him that night. Whitfield thought he had even heard Aspen crying in his cot next to him, but when he asked what was the matter, Aspen said nothing and just continued to cry himself to sleep.

On Day 8, Jonathan's bullying went too far. While Aspen was getting set to complete his Tri-Bars routine during that evening's session, Jonathan loosened one of the bars. Aspen started his routine wonderfully, with a kip handstand, giant, pirouette, and then threw himself over the middle bar in a front pike, but when he went to land in support, the outside bar shifted and Aspen came crashing down, bruising his left shoulder, and spraining his wrist. Aspen started to cry, less from the pain, and more from the embarrassment of falling while being evaluated.

Whitfield saw Aspen's fall, and made a move to help his brother off the ground, but out of the corner of his eye, he spotted Jonathan chuckling with his friends, while displaying a guilty, mischievous grin. Whitfield wanted to charge over there and punch Jonathan right in his nose, but instead tended to his brother and made sure the seventh-year assistants took care of Aspen.

After practice, while Aspen was getting some treatment, Whitfield walked out of the gym with Flaherty. They were going to meet up with Ugu for a quick snack. Whitfield almost passed on the invitation as he was still fuming about what Jonathan did to Aspen, but it had been a few days since he last saw Ugu at lunch, and thought just seeing her again might lift his spirits. As Ugu, Flaherty, and

Whitfield sat down for some late-evening yogurt, Jonathan and his friends came walking by.

"Hey, new kid, I hope your baby brother doesn't cry too much tonight." Jonathan and his cronies chuckled.

Whitfield stood up and walked toward Jonathan. "What did you say?"

"Hey, back off, new kid."

"What did you do to those bars?" Whitfield and Jonathan were standing nose-to-nose. Ugu stood closely behind Whitfield.

"Hey, relax. What, your brother can't take a joke?"

"Did you loosen the spinlock before Aspen's turn?"

"So, what if I did?"

Whitfield pulled his right fist back and just before he lunged forward to pop Jonathan, Ugu held him back.

"Whitfield, he's not worth it. Look at me. He is not worth it. Aspen is going to be fine. Jonathan, go home. Stop bullying Aspen. Stop bullying, period. Grow up."

Jonathan left, snickering.

"Whitfield, c'mon, let's finish our yogurt. You just focus on tryouts. Let me deal with Jonathan."

"You?"

"Yeah, me. What, you don't think I can handle myself? And protect my friends."

"It's not that. I'm sure you can."

They exchanged a look. Whitfield finished his yogurt, almost forgetting that Flaherty was still there, watching the two of them intently.

Flaherty thought she noticed a spark between Whitfield and Ugu. "Uhh, what is going on here?"

"Umm…nothing. I should probably get back and check on Aspen." Whitfield was still upset with Jonathan's antics, but decided that Ugu was right. Jonathan wasn't worth it.

"Hey, Whitfield, two days left. Go be a champion!"

"Thanks."

With that, Whitfield left to return to the gym. Ugu and Flaherty turned to walk back home, with Flaherty asking Ugu, "so, what was up with that look you gave Whitfield?"

Ugu looked away. "I have no idea what you're talking about."

The two girls smiled at each other, and Flaherty thought it was best not to pry any further. The final two days of tryouts were the most intense all week. Each of the remaining athletes had multiple evaluation periods on each event, multiple interviews, and barely a minute to rest. After the final tryout session, only 30 gymnasts remained. 25 would make the team. Whitfield and Aspen were still standing. Tryouts were over. They wouldn't find out if they made the team until tomorrow. As for tonight, they slept.

Chapter 5
Meet Schedule

"Ahh, Dr. Hewitt. Thank you for stopping by. I presume you are here to deliver this year's meet schedule."

"Yes, Sir Arlington, I am. Here you go."

Dr. Hewitt handed Sir Arlington a binder containing this year's upcoming meet schedule. Sir Arlington studied its contents meticulously. After several minutes, he looked up from the binder with disdain.

"What is the meaning of this?"

"Sir?"

"This schedule. It's garbage." Sir Arlington closed the binder and tossed it across his desk back in Dr. Hewitt's direction.

"With all due respect, Sir, what do you mean? General Gibson assured me this schedule adheres to all of the proper guidelines and regulations."

"No. No. No, it is not that. I mean, where is the competition? We do not have any of our top competitors on this schedule."

"Ahh, I see. Well, again, with all due respect, should that not make it easier to win and even easier to amass greater resources for the school? I should think you would be happy."

"Is that all you care about, Dr. Hewitt? Winning. Resources. Our gymnasts are competitors, first and foremost. We want to pit ourselves against the very best in competition and see who comes out ahead."

"Sir, I am not sure everyone on the team, or in this administration, or my colleagues serving of the faculty, would agree with you. We do have a culture of winning at this school, and for many students, winning is all they know. Take that away, and they may rebel."

"Is that so? I refuse to believe that."

"Well, sir, I believe it is you who once said that losing builds character. Our younger students simply have not tasted defeat. Now, I believe that is a good thing.

Winning can build character too. Why would you want to take that away from our students?"

"I simply want a fair schedule. Fair competition."

"And I assure you, Sir Arlington, Gen. Gibson has done his very best to ensure this schedule is fair."

Sir Arlington looked dubious. "Doubtful."

Chapter 6
Kickoff Party and Opening Ceremonies

For the first time since they arrived on campus, Whitfield and Aspen were able to sleep in and not worry about getting changed into practice gear and going through intense warmup routines. Even though they both needed the extra sleep and felt good laying in their cots for a few extra minutes in the morning, they both missed the intensity, the movement, and the sweat. It wasn't long before Whitfield and Aspen both decided to get up a get a few reps in before packing up their belongings. They weren't going to be sleeping in the gym any more—tonight they would be moving into their new home for the school year, maybe even their own mansions.

It was arrival day for all first-years and all returning students that weren't already on campus for tryouts. It was still morning, but campus was bustling. Students, along with their parents or guardians, flooded campus from all directions, which was somewhat surprising since Seven Bridges Academy only allowed for three ways to arrive on campus: ferry, train, and flying vehicle. Campus tours were scheduled throughout the morning.

Whitfield and Aspen decided to skip the tours, since they already had seen much of campus during their personal tour with Ugu and Flaherty, and decided to meet up with the girls for lunch at Half-In Full-Out Restaurant on the Applied Mathematics and Quantitative Economics (AMQE) campus before joining the rest of the students across campus for the Kickoff Party at 13:00 in Flaxen Hall.

By the time Whitfield and Aspen walked into the restaurant, Ugu and Flaherty were already seated, sipping on milkshakes, talking, and giggling. They certainly seemed to be in a good mood, and both got up and hugged the boys when they approached their table.

Ugu was the first to speak, "congratulations on making it all the way through tryouts!"

"I was just telling Ugu about Whitfield's last turn around the Pommel Clock and his sick dismount to ring the bell. I think Gabe was the last one to complete the Clock at tryouts and that was a few years ago, right?"

Ugu seemed to recall everything that Gabe did on campus. "Yeah, he did it going into his fifth-year, a year before we got here."

Aspen was feeling a little jealous. "I could have made it all the way around too. They just wouldn't let me keep going after the first day."

"Oh, I know, sweetie. You still have the record. We all saw the video. It's been playing all over campus all week."

Flaherty added, "Aspen, I told you that the coaches already saw how awesome you are at Pommel. I wouldn't be surprised if you made the starting lineup this year. They just wanted to see how good you are on the other events. Ugu, Aspen's Handstand Obstacle routine and Tri-Bars were amazing! He can already do a double-full switchback to upper arms."

"Wow! That's incredible, Aspen! You are so awesome!"

The attention and recognition of Aspen's skills made him feel better right away. Ugu caught Whitfield's eye as he mouthed the words "Thank You." Ugu returned the gesture with a quick wink and smile.

Changing the subject back to today's events, Whitfield inquired, "so, what should we expect from this meeting today? Three hours in an event hall seems kind of strange, and long, for a Kickoff Party."

"Oh no. Sir Arlington makes the meeting super fun. You'll see." Ugu was already excited for the Kickoff Party.

"When do we find out who made the team?"

"Well, Aspen, this is the first time we are all back on campus together in over a month, since last year's end-of-year celebration, so Sir Arlington will catch us all up on what's been going on. He'll introduce any new teachers and welcome the first-years and transfer students. That will just take a few minutes. Then, he'll probably give an update on each academic area. As he does that, the teachers get up and demonstrate any new toys, gadgets, or other cool things they've been working on since last term. They really are trying to recruit students to their classes…so it's pretty wild. After that, Sir Arlington will likely run down a list of new resources we earned over the past year."

Flaherty chimed in with a basic rundown of resources earned by the school. "We had a really good season, so we got lots of new stuff. All new uniforms. Four new mega-yachts parked in the harbor. All new drone buses and taxis. New holographic engineering lab equipment. An all-new heavy-gravity training wing in the gymnastics center. Tons of jewelry, diamonds, rubies, and gold. Watches. Spices. Food. We got a bunch of stuff for the school."

"We also got a brand-new library and all new equipment for Advanced Medicine, right?"

"That's right. I almost forgot."

"See. There's a long list. Sir Arlington will tell us what we can use and any changes that need to be made."

Finally, Flaherty added, "he'll also announce the new gymnastics team roster."

Aspen was excited. "Yes!"

"Anyone who made the team will join him on stage. He'll say something about each member and then reveal the schedule."

"Flaherty is right. This is a big moment, as our resources all come from the schedule. Different meets have different payouts."

Whitfield was confused. "What do you mean?"

"It's a little complicated, but it works this way. Each meet has a theme. Let's take our first home meet, the Precious Gems meet, as an example."

"Wait. Ugu, how do you know that's going to be our first meet?"

"Oh, I already saw the schedule."

Aspen was curious. "How?"

"Don't ask. Ugu's involved in everything at this school. You'll learn that soon enough. Anyway, we competed at that meet last year too. We came in first. I won all 7 of my head-to-heads on Vault-Pegs and I think about 21 out of 26 overall, or something like that." It was hard for anyone to rattle off those kinds of stats about themselves without it sounding like bragging, but somehow, when Flaherty said it, it just came out as sounding sweet and sincere.

"Yes, you were awesome that meet. Anyway, teams from all over will bid to gain entrance to the meet. So many precious gems are on the line, and not just diamonds, rubies, emeralds, and sapphire; but, also tanzanite, black opal, red beryl, musgravite, alexandrite, jadeite, taaffeite, benitoite, poudretteite, grandidierite, and I'm sure I'm missing a few others. The WGF sets a minimum bid for each meet, but most teams bid more to try to secure their spot. Only eight teams are selected to participate."

Whitfield was impressed. "How do you know all of this? I haven't even heard of half of those gems."

"Oh, I interned at the WGF last year. I handled a lot of the incoming bids and sat in on some of the selection meetings."

Whitfield rolled his eyes. "Sorry, I should have known."

Aspen asked, "I'm sorry, but what is the WGF?"

"The World Gymnastics Federation. They control just about all resource allocation in the world. Really powerful organization."

"Ugu's right. See, I told you she's involved in everything."

"Thanks. Once teams are selected, that's when all the side deals happen."

"What side deals?"

Ugu was happy Aspen asked the question. "Teams will start calling each other to set up additional wagers, such as an extra 10,000 carats for whichever team finishes higher head-to-head. Stuff like that. I wasn't really involved much on those deals, so I'm not really sure how they work, but I know they exist. The WGF keeps 10% of the entire pot. Teams are supposed to report all side deals, but we know, I mean, the WGF strongly suspects, that teams under-report these deals.

"Anyway, the WGF collects their 10% and establishes the payout rates. For example, the first-place team may take home 60% of the remaining pot, second place 30%, third place 10%. It's usually something like that. Oh, and the winning team also gets favorable pricing if they want to purchase more goods on the open market for up to one year after the meet. I think the favorable pricing ends at the end of the calendar year. Though, I may be mistaken."

"What do you mean, favorable pricing?" Whitfield seemed really interested in learning more.

"It means that the winning team, let's say it's us, we can then buy diamonds, for example, at a steep discount for the rest of the year. Instead of paying the market rate, let's say $1,000, we would only pay $350, or something like that. There may be some limits to how much we can buy, but I know some of the pro teams will use their favorable pricing to buy a lot of extra goods."

Now Flaherty seemed interested. "Why?"

"Depends. But I think some teams will buy goods at a discount and then sell them back to the original owner at full price."

Always thoughtful, Aspen didn't like what he was hearing. "That doesn't seem right."

"I know. But that's just the way things work sometimes. Not everyone is as thoughtful of others, like you are."

Flaherty noticed the time. "Well, we better get going if we are going to make it to the Kickoff Party on time."

Aspen still had questions about the resource allocation arrangement, but at the moment, cared more about finding out if he made the team. "Wait, when do the team members get announced?"

They all got up to leave and started walking toward Flaxen Hall. As they walked across campus, Ugu addressed Aspen's question.

"Oh, that's right. Well, right after the teachers' demonstration, students are given some time to enroll in classes using their electronic trackers. Sir Arlington will then announce the team members. After the team members are introduced, and Sir Arlington discusses the schedule, the meeting will shift focus to the gymnasts and housing assignments. The gymnasts spend a few minutes deciding upon their own houses. Out of courtesy, returning gymnasts are usually allowed to stay in their previous house, but changes can be made. While the gymnasts decide on their houses, all the other students fill out their preferences, according to gymnast, house, and job assignment."

"Job assignment?" This was all very new to Whitfield.

Flaherty jumped in to answer Whitfield. "Yes, every member of the gymnast's staff has an assignment. Security. Practice Judge. Nutritionist. Trainer. Stylist. Tutor. Lots of different roles to play. Some students prefer a specific role, others prefer a gymnast or particular house. Since you are new, and most people here do not know you, if you do make the team, your staff applications may be on the lighter side. I'd recommend you spend some time networking during that part of the meeting."

Now Aspen seemed concerned. "Networking? Application? I'm sorry, you lost me."

Ugu was quick to calm Aspen. "Don't worry, Aspen. I can introduce you to some good students."

With that, Whitfield, Aspen, Ugu, and Flaherty arrived at Flaxen Hall and entered the gigantic event center. What a spectacular sight! All 1,050 students found their seats in the high-tech auditorium and eagerly awaited Sir Arlington's arrival. The teachers and staff all sat together in the front two rows. Everyone stood and cheered upon Sir Arlington taking the stage.

The meeting went very much according to Ugu's outline, with Sir Arlington welcoming everyone back, paying particular attention to the 150 first-years and five transfer students. He also introduced two new teachers, both in the Advanced Medicine department. Sir Arlington discussed some of the campus improvements and read through the Honor Code. Whitfield keyed in on the statement: "Any violation of the Honor Code or breach of the Acts of Character will result in your immediate arrest and incarceration. We have three detention chambers, each one more vile than the last. Please do not find yourself on the wrong side of those walls."

Whitfield looked over at Ugu with concern. "Wow! They really take cheating and discipline seriously around here."

"That's right. We have a strict code of conduct. Just make sure you always do your own work. Be nice to others. Help out when you can, and you'll be fine. You don't want to get in trouble here. The penalties are really harsh."

"I can tell. Have you ever been arrested?"

Flaherty chuckled. "Please. Ugu? She's an angel. She would never step out of line."

"I would...well, maybe. No, I haven't been arrested. Nor do I want to be, thank you very much."

Despite Sir Arlington's stark warning for violators, the mood in the room was generally upbeat and happy. The time had come for teachers to display their new classroom gadgets, attempting to sway students to take their classes. The first one up, Dr. Slippenfall, a Law professor, opened with a holographic reenactment of the school's founding 123 years ago, with amazing detail and fourth dimension technology.

Next, an Advanced Medicine teacher, Dr. Wooks, brought out a human cadaver and a live patient and actually performed a live transplant right there in Flaxen Hall, taking ligaments out of the cadaver's ankle and attaching them inside the patient's knee. Within 20 minutes, the patient was able to walk up and down stairs. It was amazing!

Not to be outdone, Dr. Spylock, an International Affairs teacher, laid out 12 items on the table in front of the room. She had successfully pick-pocketed all twelve items from teachers during the previous 30 minutes, and temporarily hijacked control of the video board and displayed her official bank records. With a few keystrokes, the balance in her bank account grew by $5,000. She proceeded to stand up, return each of the pick-pocketed items to their rightful owners, along with $1,000 each to the five Applied Mathematics teachers sitting in the second row.

She thanked them, and instructed each of them to check their accounts, and lo and behold, each one had had $1,000 withdrawn from their account in the last five minutes, only to be made whole again by the thieving professor.

Continuing with the professor presentations, Dr. Randle, an Engineering professor, took out three sheets of paper from his briefcase, and folded them into paper airplanes. He then gave the following instructions to the audience.

"I am going the throw each of these planes into the crowd. Whoever grabs hold of a plane, I want you to write your name on the inside flap of the plane. Fold it over again, and throw it in a different direction, still in the crowd though. I want the second person to write your name on the inside flap, fold it over, and send the plane on one more test flight. I want the third plane holder to do the same thing; write your name on the inside flap and then pass the plane back up to the front of the room."

After announcing his instructions, Dr. Randle launched his paper airplanes into the crowd. The students had fun with this exercise, even if they had no idea why they were doing it. In the end, none of the planes had come close to landing near Whitfield, Ugu, Flaherty, or Aspen, but they still laughed throughout the exercise, watching as other students tried to catch and throw the planes.

In the end, something amazing happened. Dr. Randle took the first plane, and read the three names written on the inside flap and proceeded to also list every student who had touched the plane during the exercise. He called them the flight crew. He did the same thing with the second plane. He verified the names on the inside flap and the flight crew names.

Whitfield was stunned. "Wow. That's pretty amazing. He has some memory, being able to see and recall everyone who touched that particular plane."

Ugu was equally impressed. "Yeah, I wish I could do that."

Flaherty, however, was an engineering major and had taken Dr. Randle's class before. She knew Dr. Randle wasn't just recalling the names from memory. "Umm…just wait. I don't think it's from memory at all. Just watch."

With the third plane, Dr. Randle was just about to read off the names on the inside flap, when he stopped.

"It seems we have some deception afoot."

The crowd of students didn't really know how to respond. Was this a joke or was he serious?

The Engineering professor continued, "is Graciela here?"

Surprised to hear her name being called, Graciela answered, "yes, sir. I'm right here."

"Can you please come down here, dear?"

"Sure."

As Graciela made her way down to the front of the room, the crowd started whispering with puzzled looks and glances all around.

"My dear, I see that your name is written here on the inside flap, but you didn't write it did you?"

Graciela was shocked. "No. I didn't even touch the planes. Why is my name written there?"

"Why, indeed. That is the question. That's right, dear. It seems that you have an admirer."

Jonathan shouted from his seat. "I'll bet it was Reid. He's still in love with her."

The crowd chuckled a bit. Reid got all red, before firing back, "stuff it, Jonathan."

"Thank you, gentlemen. That's enough, Reid. Jonathan, thank you for contributing to this little mystery of ours. It seems that the mystery forger is none other than…yourself. Perhaps it is you that is in love with our lovely Graciela."

The whole crowd burst into laughter.

Ugu raised her hand. "Excuse me. Dr. Randle, how did you know it was Jonathan who wrote Graciela's name?"

"Ahh…the answer is right here. But, to truly understand, you'll need to take my class."

Ugu was not happy with the professor's little tease. She turned to her best friend. "Flaherty, how did he do that?"

"He weaves a special GPS and fingerscan tracking device in the paper. He's a little paranoid and thinks someone might steal some of his notes, so he invented this cool tech. He told us about it in class. It's really pretty cool."

Several other professors continued to wow students with various tricks and treats. By the end of the demonstrations, only 90 minutes remained in the Kickoff Party and the gymnastics team rosters were yet to be unveiled.

****

The time had come. Sir Arlington took the stage again and with great fanfare and cheers, he started reading down the list of this year's Gymnastics Team members.

"First, the returning team members: Fenway; Ippy; Kayleigh; Keegan; Flaherty; Wilson; Vail; Reid; Sydney; Diego; Bailey; Brooks; McKenzie; Morocco; Ryne; Swindell; Kylie; Bella; and Chloe. All 19 returning gymnasts have been selected to return."

Sir Arlington paused to allow the crowd of students to cheer and for the selected gymnasts to make their way to the front.

"We do still have two current students who were members from last year's team, but neither are ready to compete as they are still recovering from injury. We hope to see you back soon. Now, on to the remaining six spots. Seraphina. Dakota. Whitfield."

Whitfield burst into tears. He had actually made the team. A huge wave of relief poured over him, as Aspen and Ugu both leaned over to hug him before he joined Flaherty and the rest of his new teammates on stage.

"Three more to go. Please. Please." Aspen clenched his fists, hoping to hear his name called.

Ugu was right there, pulling for Aspen's name to be called. "C'mon. Just say Aspen. Say Aspen."

"Hutchison. Pryce."

"Oh no. Just one more to go. Please."

At this point, Jonathan stood up and obnoxiously bragged for all around him to hear, "ahh, yes…saving the best for last" and started walking up to the front of the room.

Sir Arlington initially paused, just for effect, but grew increasingly annoyed at this show of egotism.

"Excuse me, but please have a seat, young Jonathan. You were not selected."

Jonathan stopped in his tracks and stood in disbelief, as Sir Arlington proceeded to read out the final name.

"Rounding out this year's roster is the youngest ever member of a gymnastics team at this fine institution. Aspen."

An enormous roar from the crowd shook the walls. Everyone stood, cheering. Some for Aspen. Some for the 24 other gymnasts. Aspen was smiling from ear to ear. Both he and his brother had made the team. He couldn't be happier. Aspen rushed to the stage and was immediately met by his brother, greeting him with open arms.

****

With the entire gymnastics team together on stage, the next item on the agenda was to determine housing. Without really knowing anything about the different houses, Whitfield and Aspen were happy to just take whichever houses were left after everyone else made their selections. Fortunately, Sir Arlington intervened, and strongly 'suggested' that Aspen be placed in House 19, on the garden side, and Whitfield in House 6, on the waterfall side, closest to the waterfront. Given the respect everyone had for Sir Arlington, no one dared argue, even though it left some on the team less than thrilled with their new housing assignments.

Once the gymnasts' housing assignments were completed and posted to the video boards, the application and matching process began. Students would input their housing preferences on their personal trackers, while mingling with others in the room, trying to coordinate living arrangements. Flaherty was busy taking Aspen around to meet students and trying to build out his staff. Whitfield went straight to find Ugu. It was pretty clear to Flaherty, that Ugu was already starting to develop strong feelings for Whitfield, but it was less clear to Whitfield himself, how he felt about Ugu and, just as important, how Ugu felt about him.

When it came to telling who might have a crush on him, Whitfield was hopeless. He didn't have a clue. When Whitfield approached Ugu and asked her to come close because he had to ask her something, Ugu immediately thought he was going to ask her to join his house, and she started to panic.

Ugu and Flaherty had already discussed this possibility the previous night, and after much consideration, Ugu had decided that she wouldn't move into Whitfield's house because she didn't want to ruin their budding friendship, but now that Whitfield was standing right in front of her, she didn't know if she could turn him down. With her mind racing, Ugu stared into Whitfield's deep blue eyes.

"Ugu, I want to ask you something, and it's OK if you say no, but I was wondering…"

It's happening…it's really happening. What do I do? Eeeek.

"Would you consider living in Aspen's house?"

Huh? What? What just happened?

"Look, I need someone to look out for him, and you are really the only one I trust around here. I love Aspen and I know with you there; he would be safe. I know it's asking a lot and you already told Flaherty…"

"Of course. Yes! I'd love to look after Aspen."

"Really, you will? That's great!" Whitfield was truly relieved that Ugu would be there to look after his younger brother.

Whitfield gave Ugu a big hug. Just as he started to move away, he noticed that Ugu hadn't yet let go. After a quick moment, and prolonged eye contact, where Whitfield noticed a little speck of green in Ugu's beautiful brown eyes, Ugu stepped back and told Whitfield that she'll go tell Flaherty the news. Whitfield hesitated. He wanted to know if that extra split second where Ugu was still hugging him meant anything. But the moment passed. Ugu disappeared into the crowd. Whitfield was happy that he made the team.

He was happy Aspen made the team. He was happy Ugu would be in Aspen's house looking after him. Well, mostly happy. He knew he would be happier with Ugu in his own house, but he needed to think of his brother first. After some contemplation, Whitfield decided that he did the right thing, and proceeded to mingle with the other students, who all seemed eager to congratulate him on making the team.

Chapter 7
Uniform Day

Whitfield's first night in his new house was a whirlwind. After his conversation with Ugu at the Kickoff Party, he was bombarded with students applying to join his staff, and by extension, his house. Whitfield felt as though he spoke with over a hundred students at the meeting, and well over fifty more showed up at his house later that evening. He wondered if Aspen was going through the same thing, but then thought better of it. *Of course not. Aspen has Ugu taking care of everything. He probably already has his staff all selected and is enjoying some free time in the pool.*

Whitfield had to select 41 students to join his staff. Ugu had told him what positions to look for. Specifically, she had offered him the following advice:

"First, you need to cover your gymnastics training. I suggest 8 trainers (one for each event); an athletic trainer; strength and conditioning coach; nutritionist; psychologist; equipment manager; and two judges. For your academics, I suggest four tutors (one for each subject). For your personal appearance, image, and safety, I suggest bringing in a stylist; photographer; digital media specialist; interview coach; publicist; endorsement rep; agent; four field security agents; a chief of security, and two covert operatives, or spies. I'd also recommend bringing on board a chef; business manager; paralegal; financial planner; personal assistant; chief technology officer; and of course, a chief-of-staff to manage everyone."

Ugu had stressed that the chief-of-staff should be brought in first. Regrettably, Whitfield failed to heed this most important piece of advice.

Whitfield had a bunch of questions, such as: why do I need so much security on campus? Do I really need all those extra trainers? A stylist, really? What's wrong with the way I look already? And, two spies? Really?

Ugu had assured Whitfield that all of these positions were warranted. Even though all students at the school must pass the Acts of Character test prior to admission, jealously still exists and some students will go to great lengths to make the team. Also, occasionally the school hosts students from other schools. It's always nice to have some extra protection, just in case. But mostly, security was for off-campus travel engagements, including meets.

Ugu continued by convincing Whitfield that it's always important to look his best, speak intelligibly, and have all his affairs in order at all times. He is now on the big stage, and people are always watching.

Whitfield thought these job assignments might be too huge a burden for the other students, but then rationalized it by acknowledging each student was only taking care of one gymnast at a time. By the time Whitfield had finalized his staff of 41, it was late and he was exhausted. Whitfield never even made it up to his room that night. In fact, he never even made it inside the house, except once, to use the bathroom. He slept on a hammock outside, near the fire pit, alone…with 41 strangers occupying ten-bedroom suites and Dr. Hewitt, the cryptography professor assigned to his house, who was supposed to help with staffing but was nowhere to be found, occupying the basement loft area.

The professional butler and two maids assigned to the house would begin work tomorrow. Whitfield didn't even notice when Ugu stopped by to check on him. She was out for her nightly run, which had been delayed due to the day's hectic schedule. He was already asleep when she arrived. Ugu simply found a nearby blanket and covered Whitfield. She whispered good night, and continued with her run.

****

The next morning, Whitfield and Aspen had decided to meet up for breakfast at Pike's on the Advanced Medicine campus near Aspen's house. Ugu and Flaherty joined them. With all the commotion from yesterday's move-in circus, neither Whitfield nor Aspen realized until that morning that last night was the first time they hadn't slept under the same roof for as long as they could remember. Still, Whitfield decided he would let Aspen know he was thinking about him. Flaherty and Whitfield were the first to arrive.

"Hey, Flaherty! How was move-in yesterday?"

"Hi Whitfield. A little hectic, you know, without Ugu, but I managed just fine." Flaherty flashed Whitfield a quick smile to let him know she was only teasing.

"Oh, yeah. Sorry about that."

"That's fine. I completely understand. Ugu is the best. Aspen is in good hands."

Just then, Ugu and Aspen walked in and sat down.

"Hey, bro. Missed you last night. How was move-in?"

"It was great! You have to come over and see my house. It has everything. Whitfield, it's huge. We have three pools, huge kitchens, a game room—with skeeball and a ping-pong table, two movie theaters—with popcorn machines and seats that go all the way back. We have a huge backyard, with tramps, zip-lines, and an obstacle course. Whitfield, you have to see it." Clearly, Aspen was excited.

"That's great, bro. Did you pick out your staff yet?"

"Oh, yeah. Ugu did that."

"Yes. I was able to fill all 41 spots. We had most of it done at the meeting. I just had to make a few calls afterwards to track some people down, but yes, we are all set. Whitfield, did you see Jackson, Jordana, and Amber? I sent them to your house after the meeting. They are all really good."

"Uhh, I think so. Honestly, it was all a blur."

Ugu looked skeptical. "Who did you pick for your chief-of-staff?"

"Umm…I forgot."

"What do you mean you forgot?"

"Well, everyone just started showing up and telling me why they would be a good fit and how I should bring them on board. It was all a bit too much."

"Didn't you hire a chief-of-staff first, like I told you?"

Whitfield looked defeated. "Sorry."

"Oh, Whitfield."

Whitfield felt a little embarrassed, but mostly, just tired.

"Look, I can help you. I'll come over tonight and we can go through your staff list. I know most of the students, so I can tell you which students are hard workers and should be given more responsibility and which ones to avoid. I can even help broker some trades if you want."

"No, you don't have to go out of your way for me. I can figure it out. Wait, did you say trades?"

"Whitfield, really, it's no trouble at all. It would be my pleasure."

Flaherty sensed that Ugu wanted to help, and maybe even spend some quality time together with Whitfield. "Let her help, Whitfield. I told you; she's the best."

"Thank you, Flaherty. Yes, you can trade staff members. Especially early on in the school year. Some gymnasts may have brought in too many field security agents or realize too late that they need a hair stylist, or they don't have a nutritionist on staff. I'll be able to find a new home for anyone you don't want on your staff, and bring in harder-working students."

Aspen was intrigued by all of this. "How can you do all that?"

"Ugu is top of our class in International Affairs. She's crazy smart, an expert negotiator, has great people skills, and is super-cute. Look at her, she's adorable. Who wouldn't just fall in love her? Whitfield, isn't she cute?"

Whitfield felt completely embarrassed for being put on the spot, and for maybe staring a bit too long at Ugu's brown eyes, long blonde hair, and comforting smile. "Umm…sure. I mean, of course. She's…err…cute. I guess."

"Oh, come on. Don't be embarrassed. She's a hottie. But she'll also kick your butt if you step out of line."

Now, it was Ugu's turn to feel slightly embarrassed from all the attention, especially from Whitfield staring at her. "Thank you. So, what do you say, Whitfield? Can I help?"

Flaherty kept pushing. "Whitfield, just say yes. You know you're not going to win an argument with her. She's too good."

"Well, when you put it that way. OK. You can come over tonight. We'll discuss my staffing issues."

Flaherty looked pleased. "Great! It's settled."

Ugu just smiled and noticed Flaherty's huge grin as she looked directly at her. Ever since she found out about how Ugu felt about Whitfield, Flaherty had been trying to get the two of them together.

****

After breakfast, the four friends took a quick stroll around the Inner Bowl on campus while waiting for the Uniform Galleria to open. Today was Uniform Day, and even though the galleria was usually open 24-hours a day during the school year, it had been closed since yesterday afternoon to get ready for today's extravaganza. All students are required to wear officially approved school attire while on campus, starting on the first day of classes and running through the end-of-year celebration.

All uniforms must display the school crest. Students are required to wear classroom uniforms during classes, except when physical strain requires more athletic apparel. Classes run from Monday through Thursday. Classroom uniforms for girls include silk tops and black slacks; and for boys, includes button-down shirts, vests, and gray slacks. Uniform tops are color-coordinated by year: Year 1 (green); Year 2 (red); Year 3 (purple); Year 4 (blue); Year 5 (white); Year 6 (gray); and Year 7 (peach).

Students may change into casual/athletic wear after classes (and on Fridays and weekends); however, they must maintain color coordination and display the school crest at all times. Students may opt for a third change of clothes for evening activities (same color and crest rules apply). Students also may select pajamas from the Uniform Galleria. Gymnasts are required to wear workout gear for practice.

The Uniform Galleria is an enormous structure located near the front entrance of campus, between the Administration Building and Cheesestock Hospital. On the ground floor (basement level) is the laundry service and dry cleaners. Students can pick up and drop off clothes for cleaning. While this service is available at all hours, most students fall into a routine of dropping off clothes once a week, either on weekends or on their way to class, but vary quite a bit on pick up.

The dropped off clothes are almost always available for pick up within 72 hours, save for the need for additional sewing, stitching, or other tailoring; however, students have the option to pick up different clothes entirely. Students could shop for clothes themselves, or use one of the galleria's many talented personal stylists to pick out clothes for them and have them ready for pickup at a moment's notice. The galleria does not offer standard delivery or remote pickup service.

The Uniform Galleria's first floor holds the school store, filled with school merchandise, clothes for visitors and family members, stationery, and other novelties and school swag. This floor gets packed during Parents and Alumni Week, home meet weekends, alumni events, and a variety of other concert and entertainment events hosted on campus.

The second floor contains a huge selection of classroom uniforms. This floor is divided into seven large sections, color-coded by class year. Students can find silk tops, button-down shirts, vests, slacks, trousers, bras, underwear, socks, and other pertinent classroom uniform attire. Personal stylists and tailors are always available to assist students with finding the right look and fit.

Casual wear and formal wear are located on the third floor. The selection on this floor includes a vast array of shorts, tees, jeans, polo shirts, hoodies, pullovers, sweaters, bathing suits, ski gear, socks, sneakers, and other miscellaneous items on the casual side; and tuxedos, suits, evening gowns, blazers, shoes, and other intricate items on the formal wear side.

The fourth floor holds all accessories, including: hats, watches, more shoes, jewelry, belts, fragrances, makeup, handkerchiefs, handbags, etc. The fifth floor is reserved for gymnasts (and their equipment managers) and includes workout gear, leotards, sports bras, grips, and certain portable exercise equipment.

Whitfield, Aspen, Ugu, and Flaherty arrived at the entrance of the Uniform Galleria about ten minutes before the doors opened, and were already joined by about 300 other students eager to see the new styles for this year and snatch up the coolest looks. While most of the other students jostled with each other trying to get nearer the front doors, Ugu remained perfectly calm and advised her small group to hold back and follow her lead. Whitfield was wondering how she could possibly control this situation too. He wasn't disappointed.

"So, Ugu, what's your plan for once we get in there? Assuming we don't get trampled out here first."

"Don't worry about it. It's really quite simple. Everyone out here is going to rush right up to the second floor and grab as many uniforms as they can, and fight over a few of the newer styles…especially the girls. Isn't that right, Flaherty?"

"That's right. The girls here do not like wearing the same exact uniform as anyone else."

Aspen didn't quite understand. "Aren't they all the same anyway?"

Ugu saw Flaherty's eyes light up, but before her friend could lecture Aspen on the finer points of girls' clothing choices, Ugu calmly explained, "you'd think so, but no. Well, for the boys, that's pretty much true. The shirts will have different collars, some shirts will have stripes, others have a different pattern. But most of it is covered by your vest anyway. And those have less variation. You all wear pretty much the same style pants. Shoes can vary, and so can your belt, handkerchief, and watch. That's why I'd recommend you two both go straight to the fourth floor and pick out your accessories first."

Flaherty calmed down and added, "the stylists know your basic uniform, so they can help you pick out anything, if you are unsure."

"Right. Now, for girls, it's much different. Flaherty and I are going straight downstairs."

Whitfield remembered noticing the layout of the galleria on the front doors. "Wait, isn't that the laundry room?"

"Exactly," Flaherty was impressed with Whitfield's attention to detail.

"Since classes haven't started yet, they are really not that busy down there. They might still be taking care of workout clothes from tryouts and students could drop off their personal clothes from when they arrived on campus, but most do not think to do that ahead of time."

"Unfortunately, Ugu's right. Students mostly just throw their personal clothes in with their school uniforms at the end of the first week."

"OK, so they're not busy right now. But, why go down there?"

Ugu smiled. "Ahh, two reasons. First, what most students around here do not realize is that the laundry staff keeps at least one article of each piece of inventory in a holding area. They do it for inventory tracking purposes, but Flaherty and I use it for our own personal shopping spree."

"That's right. The colors they hold downstairs don't always line up with our year. This year we're purple." Flaherty pointed to herself, Ugu, and Whitfield. "Aspen, you're green. But it doesn't matter. Any style in one color, can easily be ordered in any other, if they don't already have it out on the floor or in the off-campus storage warehouse."

"So, while others are upstairs looking only at their own color section and fighting over a tiny sampling of what's really available, we'll be downstairs combing through the entire catalog." Ugu gave Flaherty a celebratory fist bump.

"Clever. But you said there was a second reason?"

"Oh, right. Upstairs, after you select your clothes, you go find a tailor and they help take measurements, to see if anything changed over the past year. Plus, the first-years haven't been measured before, so it takes a little longer to build out their sizing profile. This all takes a bit of time. Flaherty and I already came over here last week, after tryouts one evening, to get resized. Our profiles have already been updated in the system. I also may have hacked into the system last year to override the checkout system."

Whitfield was surprised to hear that Ugu may have broken a school rule. "Wait. I thought you never did anything wrong. I thought you were an angel." Whitfield gave a sly smile to indicate he was not offended by Ugu's behavior.

"Wipe that smile off your face. I did it for a class assignment. We were supposed to hack into a school system. I got an A." Ugu held her head up high.

"Oh, really?" Whitfield couldn't help but continue smiling.

Ugu returned Whitfield's smile with one of her own. "But thanks for calling me an angel."

Flaherty was happy to see Ugu and Whitfield getting along so well. "Aww, that's sweet. Yeah, Ugu's hack works really well. See, we just point to the clothes and accessories we want and click. Poof. Done."

"Usually, it's the tailors or stylists that have to scan the items into the student's account. But after my 'tweak', Flaherty and I can do it ourselves. It also has one more added benefit. I actually programmed this feature in myself afterwards."

"Yeah, for extra credit."

"Shut up. The system now records every student who has taken and worn that particular uniform and when. So, if you are about to check out, for example, a button-down Milano silk blouse with gold buttons, the system can alert you if someone one else has already worn that same shirt."

"So, what difference does that make?" Aspen still clearly had not learned how girls think about clothes.

Flaherty quickly retorted, "oh Aspen. Trust me. It's a big deal for girls."

Whitfield whispered to Aspen, "I know, Aspen. I don't get it either."

Flaherty and Ugu just rolled the eyes, looked at each other, and at the same time, said, "boys."

It was 10:00 and the Uniform Galleria was about to open. The throngs of students all rushed in and, as Ugu predicted, they all headed for the second floor. Ugu and Flaherty casually walked downstairs, while Whitfield and Aspen, heeding Ugu's advice, went to the fourth floor. They couldn't believe their eyes. Everything on the floor seemed to sparkle. Diamonds, rubies, sapphires, and black opal appeared everywhere. Watches. Sunglasses. Belts. Shoes. Everything seemed lined with gems or the most expensive materials known to exist. Whitfield and Aspen just froze.

"Aspen, don't touch anything. I think there must be a mistake. We don't belong here. This stuff is way too nice."

Noticing their hesitation, Alyssa, a personal stylist, approached the boys. "Hi. How can I help you?"

Whitfield didn't know what was going on. For the first time since they arrived on campus, he and Aspen were left alone to figure things out for themselves. Whitfield panicked. "Uhh...sorry, I think we are on the wrong floor."

"Are you sure? What are your names?"

Whitfield didn't know if he should answer. Aspen was less reluctant. "I'm Aspen. This is Whitfield."

"Oh my! I thought that was you. You're the one I've been watching on the video board. That Pommel Clock routine at tryouts was amazing. And, Whitfield, I saw your triple layout full onto the second level in your Floor Exercise. It's really an honor to meet you both." Alyssa extended her hand to formally greet each of them.

Shaking Alyssa's hand, Whitfield felt a little more at ease. "Thank you. It's an honor to be here."

"Well, look around. Take your time. Let me know if you have any questions."

"Thank you."

Whitfield and Aspen walked around, but didn't dare touch anything. They stayed away from the most expensive stuff, and tried to keep mostly to themselves. A few other students eventually made their way up to the fourth floor, and Alyssa's attention was diverted away from the boys.

Meanwhile, Flaherty and Ugu were enjoying themselves in the basement, shopping for clothes, when Ugu decided to check on Whitfield and Aspen. She pulled up the video monitor from the fourth floor and after a quick scan, spotted the boys standing in the corner, alone.

"What are they doing? Flaherty, come look at this."

"Umm...I don't know. Maybe they have gas and don't want anyone else to hear, or smell, them."

Ugu nearly choked on her drink.

"Flaherty! That's awful. I'm going to check on them. They seem lost."

"No, you stay. I'll go. Keep on shopping. Remember, we have three meets coming up this term and at least two other formals. I need you to pick out something stunning for me."

"You got it. Just make sure they are OK."

Flaherty left. Ugu couldn't help staring at the screen. *What are they doing in the corner?*

Flaherty arrived on the fourth floor, just as the boys were nearing the exit to leave. "What's wrong?"

Whitfield was relieved to see a friendly face, but still felt awkward being surrounded by such opulence. "Uhh...nothing. We are just going to wait outside. Come on, Aspen."

"Wait. Did you pick up anything? You are going to need clothes and accessories for class."

Whitfield felt embarrassed and didn't want anyone to overhear his concern, so he whispered in Flaherty's ear. "Yeah...look, we just can't afford to be in here. This stuff is way too nice."

Flaherty didn't quite understand. "What do you mean?"

"Look, it's a little embarrassing, but we can't afford this stuff. We don't have any money."

Flaherty laughed, but quickly composed herself. "Aww...now, I understand. Look, all this stuff is free. The school owns it and gives it to us. We don't have to pay for any of it."

Aspen perked up right away. "Wow! Really?"

"Uhh…that can't be right."

"Uh-huh. Do you really think I could afford all this?" Flaherty was holding several items that she picked up on her way to meet the boys. "I don't come from a wealthy family. My parents are school counselors. In fact, most of the students here come from working families. None of us could afford this stuff…well, most of us anyway." Whitfield followed Flaherty's eyes motioning toward Jonathan standing a few feet away. "The school makes a lot of money off the gymnastics team, and as long as we keep winning, we keep getting all this stuff."

Overhearing their conversation, Jonathan rudely interjected, "yeah, that's right, punks. We win and we live like kings. So, don't screw it up!" Jonathan was still clearly upset at not making the team, and directed his anger squarely on Whitfield and Aspen.

The gravity of Jonathan's words finally hit Whitfield. *Was he right? Did the fate of the school's resources really lie with his team's performance at meets?*

Flaherty could see Whitfield was a bit rattled. "Don't listen to him. He's still just bitter that Aspen took his spot on the team."

"Is it true, though? Does the school afford all this stuff because of our performance? If we lose, does all this go away?"

"Well, sort of. But, don't stress about it. We have a really good team. Our coaches prepare us well. You'll see. Hey, anyway, you guys are amazing! There's no way we'll lose now." Flaherty picked up a nearby hat and placed in on Aspen's head.

"Yeah, as long as we don't screw up."

"You'll do great! Let's forget all about that now. Let's get you guys dressed."

Flaherty called over to Alyssa, who came right over and the two hugged. "Alyssa, these are two of my best friends. Whitfield and Aspen."

"Yes, we met earlier."

"Great! Aspen is a first-year and Whitfield is a third-year. They are both gymnasts so they need to look good ALL the time. Work your magic."

"My pleasure. So, do you see anything you like?"

Aspen was the first to speak up. He liked everything. Following Flaherty's pep talk, Whitfield and Aspen felt more relaxed and walked around the entire floor with Alyssa, picking out a whole host of accessories. Whitfield was still reticent to pick out fancy items, but Aspen felt right at home.

****

After they finished picking out accessories, Flaherty, Whitfield, and Aspen headed upstairs to the gymnasts-only floor. Here, Whitfield and Aspen felt most comfortable. Aspen ran over to pick out new grips and look at the shorts. Flaherty stayed with Whitfield a moment longer.

"Is all the stuff on this floor free too?"

"Yes. Everything in the whole building. Well, the whole campus, really."

"Get out! Really? Food. Books. Everything…is free?"

Whitfield couldn't believe it.

"Yes. Really!"

"Whoa!"

"You really didn't know? Huh. Who did you think was paying for those meals we had together?"

"Umm. Honestly, I guess I didn't really think about it at first. And then I thought maybe you and Ugu were spotting us. I felt really bad about it, so I wrote Ugu a letter thanking her for taking us to all those meals, and…well, some other stuff is in there too."

Flaherty's face lit up. She completely skipped over the fact that Whitfield wrote a letter thanking Ugu but not her. In her mind, just the fact that Whitfield wrote Ugu a letter was huge. "You wrote her a letter? Really? Can I see it?"

"No way."

"What does it say? Oh, come on…you have to tell me."

"Nope. Can't do it."

"Do you like her?"

"Uhh…I don't know…maybe. I mean, she's so beautiful. And smart. And funny. And she always knows the right thing to say. And her smile. I mean, she's so…"

Flaherty cupped her hands over her mouth. "Oh my gosh. You really do like her, don't you?"

Whitfield blushed. He knew there was no sense in hiding his feelings from Flaherty. "Yeah, I guess I do. But you can't say anything. Please don't say anything to her. Not about the letter. Not about any of this."

"OK. Fine. I promise."

Flaherty didn't have to say anything. Ugu was watching the whole conversation from the basement. She heard everything.

Chapter 8
Underwear Predicament

The weekend just before the start of Term 1 classes was always a time for students to relax and chill with friends, both old and new. Aside from getting acclimated to their new houses and finalizing staffing assignments, the only real responsibility for students was completing their course schedules. At the end of each term, all returning students selected their course schedules for the upcoming term, while first-year students and transfers selected courses during the application process.

But after the teacher demonstrations during the Kickoff Party and talking with their friends, students sometimes desired to change their schedule. Students have until 22:00 Sunday night before the term begins to change their schedule. Other than these, mostly, minor changes to their course schedules, and, of course, gymnastics team commitments, students were free to enjoy their final weekend before classes began.

Seven Bridges Academy always hosts a few events on campus during opening weekend, including a kickoff concert with some hot new artist or celebrity in the making. This year's headliner was Lucie Greene. She just broke onto the music scene last year, and already had three songs in the top ten on the charts, including "What I Wouldn't Do" and "Chalk on My Body." Whitfield didn't notice that he was still humming the hook to *Chalk on My Body* when he stepped into the practice gym and saw Aspen.

"Hey, Whitfield. What are you listening to?"

"What? Oh nothing. I guess that song is still stuck in my head from last night."

"What happened last night? Oh, right…Ugu came over, didn't she?"

Flaherty arrived just in time. "Yeah, she did! So, what happened? I mean, I know what happened, because Ugu tells me everything. But I want to hear it from you. What happened?"

"Nothing. She just came over and we worked on putting my staff together."

Aspen was not impressed. "That's it? Pretty boring. I tested out every slide into my house. I went up to the Outer Loop and tested all of them. I like 19-WL the best. It drops you off on the west side, lower level, right next to the pool."

"Yeah, that slide is awesome."

"How do you know, Flaherty?"

"I went over to Aspen's last night. A few of us from the team went over there. It was a fun time. We would have invited you, but...ahem...you were busy. Hehe."

"What's that supposed to mean?"

"Oh nothing. By the way, Ugu said she accidentally left her scrunchie at your place last night."

"No, she didn't. She had the scrunchie in her hair when she showed up and we sat down on the back patio. The wind blew a few strands out, covering part of her face and she crinkled her nose a bit. When she went to tuck her hair behind her right ear, the clasp on her watch got a little stuck and she let out the cutest little sound. Anyway, I helped to free her hand, and she took off the scrunchie, put it in her bag, and just wore her hair down the rest of the night."

At this point, several members of the team were listening to Whitfield's story.

Flaherty had a huge smile. "Oh, that's right. Silly me. She did find the scrunchie in her bag. My mistake. Hehe."

"What? I don't get it."

Flaherty was going to have to spell it out for Whitfield. "Crinkled nose. Cutest little sound. Hair behind her right ear. Mm...Hmmm." Whitfield still didn't get why Flaherty was smiling so much. Flaherty simply walked away.

"What?"

"Nothing, Whitfield. See you out on the floor."

Flaherty didn't have to say anything. Several of the guys on the team said it loud and clear.

Morocco just came out with it. "Dude. You're in love."

Brooks concurred, "yup. No doubt."

Whitfield shook his head. "That's crazy. I am not."

"OK, if you say so." Morocco turned away from Whitfield to head out onto the practice floor with Brooks, and Whitfield overheard them talking. "He's in love."

"Yup. No doubt."

****

Whitfield and Aspen both enjoyed getting back in the gym and the intensity of practice, but were really disappointed that not everyone on the team seemed to be working as hard as they could. Sure, other's lack of effort would all but assure that Whitfield and Aspen would crack the starting lineup, but the meet results depended on everyone contributing, not just the two of them.

As practice ended, Aspen caught up with Whitfield.

"Hey Whitfield, you have a good practice?"

With 25 gymnasts and 18 coaches, it was difficult to know what every other gymnast was doing at all times.

"Yes. I think I did good. How about you?"

"It was awesome. I got a new skill."

"Really? What?"

"I was able to make a front pike half on the Parallel Planks."

"Wow, Aspen. That's great! Was it across the gap, or on a single plank?"

"Across the gap! It was going down from the third to fourth plank, but I think I'll be able to do it on the first transition soon. That's only a slight rise in height."

"That's great, bro. Good job."

Aspen noticed that Whitfield didn't quite seem himself. "Anything bothering you, Whitfield?"

"Yeah, as a matter of fact. Wilson. Did you notice that he doesn't complete any of his circuit work between turns? The same with Reid and Diego. They just seem to goof off more than they work."

"Not really. I just focused on my own stuff. I did see those three joking around by the VH-Bars though. It was my turn, and they were just sitting on the bars talking."

"Right. It's so frustrating."

"Nothing we can do about it. Just keep working. That's all we can do, right?"

"I suppose you're right, Aspen. Let's grab Flaherty. We're meeting with Ugu to go over your class schedule."

Whitfield, Aspen, and Flaherty arrived at the International Affairs library just in time to find Ugu seated at a large table with stacks of folders and over a dozen charts laid out across the surface. She had been drawing up several course schedule options for Aspen. Ugu had already finalized her own course schedule before the final term ended last year. Truthfully, she had already mapped out her schedule for her entire academic career, all six terms for each of her seven years at Seven Bridges.

Students take 20 courses per year: four courses in each of five terms plus a term-long internship every year. Additionally, students take a year-long staffing class, based on each individual student's staffing position (i.e., all security agents take a class together; all publicists take a class together, and so on). This year, Ugu would be taking the following courses in Term 1:

Complex Variables
Underground Economics
World Intelligence Agencies
Cyber Espionage
Staffing Class: *Chief-of-Staff*

Whitfield glanced over all the charts on the table.
"Thank you for putting all this together for Aspen."
"Oh, it was nothing. I just saw what classes Aspen was eligible to take from his admission exams."
Flaherty was quick to add, "which you hacked into…"
"Oh, come on. That was super easy. Anyone could hack into those."
"Well, just because it's easy, doesn't mean you should."
"No, that's OK, Flaherty. I don't mind."
"Thank you, Aspen. And, by the way, nice job on your exams! Highest scores I've ever seen…for a first-year."
"Thanks. Hendricks taught us really well."
"I can see that. First, I need to ask—a lot of gymnasts simply major in gymnastics. They take classes in judging, announcing, building routines, meet operations, and stuff like that. They still take some other classes across campus, but usually take two gymnastics courses per term and a minimum number of other courses. Does that sound good to you?"
"Actually, no. I want to take a bunch of other classes. I'm probably going to learn all that other stuff anyway just being on the team. I want to learn other stuff too."
Flaherty opened her eyes in shock. She was super impressed by Aspen's academic ambitions. "I really like this kid."
"Good. That's what I was hoping you'd say. Well, I see you already put together a nice schedule. But, might I make a few suggestions?"
"Yes, please."

"Great. With your scores, you do not need to take Mathematics I or II. I know they suggest that all first-years take it, and that's probably why you have it on your schedule, but you are way too smart to sit through those courses. I'd recommend either *Geometric Topography* or *Linear Optimization*."

"What about *Multidimensional Calculus?*"

"Perfect. Whitfield is taking that course this term too. You two can study together."

Of course, Ugu had already memorized Whitfield's schedule, after having just gone through it with him the night before. Whitfield was taking:

Intermediate Cryptography
Algorithmic Optimization
Lying, Cheating, Stealing, and Deception
Multidimensional Calculus
Staffing Class: *Gymnast*

Sadly, Ugu would not have any of the same classes with Whitfield this term, but if everything went according to plan, they would have two classes together in Term 2.

Ugu continued to work with Aspen on his schedule. "Now, I see you have *Countries of the World* on your schedule. That would be an easy A. I took it as a first-year and was bored out of my mind. I think you would get a lot more out of the *International Studies* sequence—*Politics*; *Culture*; *History*; and *Economics*. I know, it's four courses instead of one, but well worth it. You'll still learn about all the countries, but these courses are so much better."

"OK, I trust you."

"Great. I'll sign you up for *International Politics* first. I got an A in that class. I'd be happy to review the course material with you."

"Thanks."

"OK, now, for your other two courses, I think you should be fine taking *Crystal Ball Technology I* this term."

"Is it true that you can use the crystal ball to see into the future?"

"Not exactly. You will, however, learn how to see across great distances."

"Wow. How?"

Flaherty had taken *CBT I* and *II* already and was a self-proclaimed expert in the area. "I'm sure you know that we have surveillance cameras set up all around campus, right?"

"Yes."

"Well, it's not just here on campus. Cameras and other devices are set up virtually everywhere. Stores. Parks. Buildings. Everywhere. The *Crystal Ball Tech* classes teach you how to access those cameras."

Whitfield wasn't quite sold yet. "Whoa. Really?"

Ugu corroborated Flaherty's description. "Yes. All students here are required to take at least two terms of *CBT*. That way, everyone knows how to access the cameras in their own house and certain eateries and classroom buildings on campus. Beyond that, though, you need to take more *CBT* classes to learn how to access more. With *CBT III*, you can access cameras in other gymnasts' houses and even unlock doors around campus. *CBT IV* teaches you how to access certain library cameras, remote access computers, and even spy on some off-campus buildings."

Aspen was super excited. "Ooh…that seems so cool."

Whitfield was starting to come around too. "Yeah, it really does. But can't you do all that already, Ugu?"

"No, not exactly. I can hack into some school systems, but hacking into a place, like, say the WGF, is top level. I don't have clearance, and don't know how to do that…yet."

"I definitely want to take those courses."

"I don't blame you, Aspen. I'm going to take it with you."

"Really?"

"Yes. Flaherty is going to take *CBT III* with you this term. All the *CBT* classes levels are held together. Whitfield and I are taking *CBT* next term. You'll have your internship in Term II, Aspen, and I think it would be better if you already had *CBT* first."

"Yeah, I decided to take it this term with you, Aspen. Usually, Ugu and I take that course together, but I didn't want you taking the course alone, so I decided to switch."

"Aww, Flaherty. You don't have to do that for me."

"Oh, it's my pleasure. Besides, without Ugu in there, maybe I'll have a chance to score the highest grade."

"I don't know, Flaherty. My brother's really smart."

Aspen nodded. "I really am."

Flaherty threw her arms up in the air. "Oh great. Second again."

They all chuckled.

Ugu was on a roll now. "Three down. One to go. I noticed you had *Underground Economics* on your application list."

"Yes, that course sounds so cool. All about how terrorists, drug dealers, and other bad guys get away with smuggling money and stuff—and how to catch them. I want to be able to stop all the bad people from doing bad things."

Ugu remembered having already read that exact line from one of Aspen's application essays. "Hmm…me too. You know, I think I'm going to take that course with you."

Aspen's eyes grew large. "Really? You will?"

"Yup."

"Aww…you two really are the best. Ugu, now I know why my brother likes you so much."

Whitfield, who had been taking a sip of water, immediately spit it out. "Aspen! Uhh…he doesn't know what he's talking about. Err…uhh…so, glad we got Aspen's schedule all squared away. Who's hungry?"

Ugu was keenly aware that Whitfield was growing uncomfortable, and decided not to embarrass him anymore. "That's OK, Aspen. I like your brother too. And I like you."

Ugu tapped her finger on the tip of Aspen's nose. For a quick second, Whitfield's eyes widened, but when Ugu said she liked Aspen too, he understood that Ugu was just being nice. Still, Whitfield was left wondering whether Ugu really did like him, or if he was alone in feeling that way about her.

****

The first week of classes surpassed Whitfield and Aspen's wildest dreams. They absolutely loved their classes. Aspen had *International Politics* and *Underground Economics* on Monday and Wednesday, and *Crystal Ball Technology I* and *Multidimensional Calculus* on Tuesday and Thursday. Each class lasted two hours, but seemed to fly by. He had a one-hour staffing class all four days, but since that class was with all 25 gymnasts on the team, it seemed more like a friendly social gathering than actual classwork.

Whitfield's favorite class so far was *Intermediate Cryptography* on Monday and Wednesday with Dr. Hewitt, his house supervisor. Ever since his inconspicuous absence at the Kickoff Party and Whitfield's subsequent staffing debacle, Dr. Hewitt had made himself widely available around the house and had really taken a shine to Whitfield. In just one week, Whitfield already learned a lot about encryption. Dr. Hewitt is a great teacher.

Whitfield really enjoyed his other classes too, even though he had a feeling his *Lying, Cheating, Stealing, and Deception* class might be challenging for him. Whitfield was never really that good at lying, and was even worse at detecting when someone else was being untruthful. He had a lot of work ahead of him if he was going to score well in that class.

Flaherty and Ugu loved their classes too, which is not a surprise, since they are both excellent students. Flaherty loves her *Holographic Technology* class and is already excited about working on a class project and Ugu is enjoying her *Underground Economics* class with Aspen. She is starting to appreciate just how smart Aspen really is.

The only negative all week was that Aspen had to endure some more teasing at the hands of Jonathan in his *International Politics* class. Being the youngest, and smallest, student at Seven Bridges Academy made Aspen an easy target for bullies. Aspen was very friendly and super smart, but wasn't particularly good at standing up for himself. He had always had his older brother around to stick up for him, but now, in his *International Politics* class, he was alone. Or at least it seemed that way.

Unfortunately for Aspen, the bullying did not end there. Although he hadn't been a direct target, Aspen's *Multidimensional Calculus* teacher, Dr. Crawfish, seemed to get annoyed at the slightest disturbance in class. He ridiculed students for getting answers wrong, chastised anyone who was late, and even yelled at another teacher when she got in his way leaving class on Thursday. He made a student take gum out of her mouth, hand it to him, and he proceeded to put it in the student's own hair because she was chewing too loudly in class. Whitfield and Aspen did not like the teacher, but really liked the course material. They knew it would be wise to avoid getting in Dr. Crawfish's way.

Fortunately, everyone survived week one, and had a fun and enjoyable weekend. Just as Whitfield and Aspen started to get into a routine, the second week of classes took a turn for the worse.

On Monday morning, Jonathan came into class in a bad mood. He shoved past a few students on his way to his seat and even knocked over someone's breakfast as he sat down. Aspen got out of his seat to help Elin retrieve her breakfast, and Jonathan yelled at Aspen.

"Hey Aspen, maybe while you're down there, you can scrub my shoes too. That's all you're good for anyway." Aspen tried to ignore Jonathan. He picked up the rest of Elin's breakfast and sat back down. "Good boy. Maybe you can come by my house later and clean my dishes."

Colin, another student in class, tried coming to Aspen's defense. "Why don't you just leave him alone?"

"Shut up, loser."

Colin mumbled under his breath, "you're the loser."

This set Jonathan off. He aggressively stood up and approached Colin. "What did you say? Let's go, right now."

The *International Politics* professor, Dr. Speights, took control of the class. "All right, that's enough. Now, students, today…"

Dr. Speights started her lecture, but Aspen was only partially paying attention. His eyes started tearing up. He was so mad, but didn't know what he could do about it. Jonathan kept glaring over at Colin.

Jonathan was fuming in his seat, muttering to himself. "Nobody calls me a loser. He's going to pay."

Colin and Aspen weren't exactly friends. They were in two classes together, and Colin served as a tutor on Aspen's staff, even though Aspen was definitely the smarter of the two. Aspen found Colin to be a little annoying, but other than that, didn't really have anything against the kid.

Jonathan spent the next day planning his revenge on Colin. He knew Colin and Aspen had *Multidimensional Calculus* together and he was also well-aware of Dr. Crawfish's reputation for doling out harsh punishments to students who stepped out of line. That's when the idea hit him. Before their next class, Jonathan waited outside the *Multidimensional Calculus* room for Colin to arrive. Colin was walking to class with Whitfield and Aspen.

Upon seeing the three of them together, Jonathan thought '*this is perfect*'.

Whitfield, who was seeing Jonathan for the first time since Aspen told him what had happened in class earlier in the week, had a few words for the troublemaker. "Hey, Jonathan! That's my brother you were talking to the other day. I heard what you said. You owe him an apology."

"You're absolutely right. That's why I'm here. I've been looking everywhere for you. I just wanted to apologize for the other day. Aspen, I'm really sorry for what I said to you. I was having a bad day, and I took it out on you. Please accept my apology."

Aspen appeared dumbfounded. He was not expecting an apology, especially coming from Jonathan. "Uhh, sure, OK."

Jonathan continued, "Whitfield, I want to apologize to you too. I never should have spoken to your brother that way. I'm sorry."

Whitfield wasn't buying Jonathan's obviously fake attempt at sincerity, but decided not to make matters any worse. "Sure, OK."

Jonathan had one more apology to make. "Colin, I really want to apologize to you too. Look, I was angry and it wasn't your fault, and…"

Just then, the buzzer sounded, signaling the start of class.

Whitfield put his arm around Aspen. "Hey, bro, we have to get to class. C'mon Colin."

Jonathan implored, "please, just give us another minute. This is important."

Colin was actually feeling quite happy that Jonathan was apologizing directly to him. In his mind, this was a sincere attempt at a reconciliation. "It's OK. You go ahead."

Whitfield and Aspen gave each other a quizzical look, but then went into class.

Jonathan put his arm around Colin. "Look, Colin, I've always liked you. I know we've had some differences, and I'm not the easiest guy to get along with, but I respect you."

"Really?"

"Yes. Of course. Here, I want you to have my watch. It's the only one of its kind. The Uniform Galleria only brings in one per year and I was fortunate enough to get it this year."

In truth, Jonathan stole it from another student's bag at the Uniform Galleria when he was looking the other way.

"Wow! I can't take your watch. You love that watch."

"I do. But I value our friendship more." Jonathan was really laying it on thick now. Jonathan handed the watch to Colin, hugged him, and watched as Colin entered class.

Colin was late for class, which meant a severe scolding from Dr. Crawfish. Colin took it in stride. For the first time in his life, he actually didn't mind getting yelled at. He made a new friend. Colin pulled up a seat next to Whitfield and Aspen and told them what had just happened. Whitfield and Aspen looked at each other, confused and befuddled.

Whitfield leaned over to Aspen and whispered, "what's his angle? Why is Jonathan doing this?"

"I don't know. Maybe he wanted Colin to be late for class and get yelled at. I know I wouldn't want that."

"I guess. But, why give him his watch?"

Dr. Crawfish stopped lecturing, and looked directly in Whitfield's direction, clearly annoyed by all the chatter. "Ahem…if I may continue."

Whitfield and Aspen promptly stopped talking.

A few minutes went by with Colin still admiring his new watch, when the door burst open. It was Jonathan. He was in tears. His uniform was all disheveled, with his underwear hanging out of the back.

"Excuse me. Jonathan, you do not belong in here. Explain yourself." Dr. Crawfish was quite displeased with the interruption.

Jonathan appeared to be crying, but right away, Whitfield could tell they were fake tears. "I'm sorry, Dr. Crawfish, but one of your students just beat me up and stole my watch."

The class let out a collective gasp. Whitfield, Aspen, and Colin looked at each other in disbelief.

Jonathan continued, speaking through his fake whimpers. "I came over to apologize for saying something rude to Colin the other day, and he punched me in the gut, spun me around and gave me a wedgie. And then he stole my watch."

Dr. Crawfish was outraged. "Colin. Is this true?"

Like most students, Colin was afraid of Dr. Crawfish, but still tried to defend himself. "No, sir, not at all."

"Well, do you have this young man's watch, or not?"

"Well, yes, sir, but I didn't take it."

Dr. Crawfish was appalled. "Come down here at once and return that watch to its rightful owner."

Now, Colin started to tear up. "But Dr. Crawfish…"

"Quiet! Jonathan, I want you to go to the nurse. You will be excused from your class." Jonathan stumbled out of the room, and Whitfield swore he saw Jonathan smile as he was exiting. "As for you, Colin. You like giving wedgies, do you?"

Colin, with real tears starting to flow, could barely answer. "No sir."

"QUIET! Come down here this instant. I want you to sit up there on that stool facing the class." Dr. Crawfish reached into his desk and pulled out a pair of old underwear. "You will wear this pair of underwear on your head for the remainder of the class period."

Whitfield couldn't believe the punishment about to be doled out by his professor. He yelled out from his seat, "excuse me, sir. But Colin didn't do what Jonathan said."

Dr. Crawfish flashed an angry look in Whitfield's direction. "Were you there? Did you see their interaction?"

"Well, the first part of it, but then we came to class."

"That's right. As well you should. As this poor excuse up here should have done as well." Colin was in full tears now, embarrassed, ashamed, and really mad at Jonathan.

Whitfield was still incredulous. "But, that's not fair. Colin didn't do anything wrong."

"I am warning you." Dr. Crawfish's face was turning dark red. "You are out of line. This is my classroom, and I will run it as I see fit."

"Does he really have to wear underwear on his head, sir?"

"Yes. Maybe this will teach him…and all of you…not to abuse others by stretching their underwear up out of their pants and over their…well, I don't even want to think about it. That poor boy." Dr. Crawfish shook his head at the mere thought of a wedgie.

"But, sir…"

"SILENCE!"

Colin's face was beet red. Well, at least the part of his face still visible past the teacher's mighty large underwear sitting atop Colin's head. Despite the intensity of the room, some of the students were chuckling and pointing fingers at the mortified Colin. Whitfield had to do something. He couldn't let this spectacle continue. He wasn't sure if he would consider Colin a friend as of yet, but it didn't matter. What was being done was wrong. Whitfield had to do something.

It didn't take long before the idea struck him. Aspen noticed Whitfield starting to squirm in his seat. "What are you doing?"

"You'll see."

After about a minute, Whitfield returned upright. He managed to successfully take off his own underwear and proceeded to place them atop his head, and continued taking notes. Aspen let out a short, but audible, chuckle, alerting others around him to turn around.

At first, Dr. Crawfish did not notice what Whitfield had done. "What is the meaning of this disturbance?"

From his seat, Whitfield calmly said, "for Colin."

Students started laughing and pointing at Whitfield. Dr. Crawfish was not happy. Aspen was the next to squirm out of his own underwear, and place them atop his head. From his seat, Aspen calmly said, "for Colin."

Callahan, Ander, and Antonella all followed suit. They each took off their underwear and placed them atop their heads, and in doing so, each firmly stated, "for Colin."

Pretty soon, the entire class took off their underwear and placed it atop their heads. "For Colin!"

Colin was quite touched by this gesture. His tears dried up and now he was smiling and laughing. He looked out and saw the whole class, with underwear on their heads.

Dr. Crawfish was even more outraged. His students were defiant.

The dust settled, and the students all sat there at attention, waiting for the teacher to continue. A student in the front row even handed Colin a piece of paper and a pencil so that he may turn around and continue taking notes.

From across the courtyard, a once proud of himself Jonathan, looked on in agonizing disbelief. His plan for sweet revenge had backfired.

When the bell rang, all the students got up and patted Colin on his back and gave him high fives and fist bumps, on their way out of the classroom. Dr. Crawfish started to storm out, but paused right as Whitfield approached.

Dr. Crawfish looked as though he wanted to bite Whitfield's head off. He let out a low grumble. Whitfield stood his ground. That's when Dr. Crawfish broke the silence. "Well-played, son. Well-played."

Whitfield nodded. Dr. Crawfish left in a huff. Colin walked out of the room with Whitfield and Aspen.

"Thank you, Whitfield. I can't believe you did that for me." Colin was extremely grateful for Whitfield's quick thinking and empathy.

"Hey. It wasn't right what Jonathan did and you shouldn't have been blamed for it. Dr. Crawfish was wrong for punishing you that way."

"I know. Just, thanks, anyway. You're a good friend."

After class, Whitfield and Aspen were going to study in the Applied Mathematics library together, but first Whitfield had to drop off an assignment for his *Lying, Cheating, Stealing, and Deception* class on the International Affairs campus.

"I'll be back in 15 minutes, Aspen. You can get started on the problem set."

Whitfield ran across the Inner Bowl, using the embedded tramps to speed himself up at times. Other students kept waving at him. He was starting to feel more comfortable around campus, and it really seemed as though people were starting to know him. Maybe it was because he was gymnast. Maybe they all were friends with Ugu and they always see her with him. Maybe it was just because he was a nice guy and they were starting to get to know the real him.

Whitfield dropped off his assignment and started to head back, when who does he see standing right in front of him?

"Ugu. Hey, I wasn't expecting to see you until after practice." Whitfield had decided to join Ugu on her nightly runs.

"I can see that."

"Huh?"

Ugu tried to stifle a chuckle, but couldn't help herself. "Oh nothing. Hehe. I was just heading to the IA library to study. What are you doing?"

"Same here. I'm studying with Aspen over at the Applied Mathematics library. I just had to drop off an assignment here." Whitfield was still confused why Ugu kept chuckling.

"Oh. Well, I guess I'll see you tonight after practice?"

"Yes. Looking forward to it."

Why does she keep laughing?

"Umm...Whitfield?"

"Yes."

"Why do you have underwear on your head?"

Whitfield had forgotten to take his underwear off his head. Now he knew why so many students were waving and pointing at him as he walked across campus. Whitfield reached his hand up and pulled his underwear off his head. Completely embarrassed, Whitfield could only utter, "umm..."

Ugu was finally able to compose herself. "That's OK. You don't have to tell me. I'm sure it will be on the evening news."

Whitfield's face was red with embarrassment. Of all days, why did he have to wear his "I Heart Monkeys" underwear today!

Chapter 9
Aspen Gets Bullied

Whitfield was still shaking his head from embarrassment as he walked across the Inner Bowl back toward the AMQE campus to meet Aspen at the library. When he got there, Whitfield heard a commotion coming from the corner study area where he and Aspen had been working all week. As Whitfield approached, he saw a small crowd of students surrounding the table, where Jonathan was yelling at Aspen. "You are such a baby. How did you ever make the team over me?"

Aspen replied quietly, "leave me alone."

"Aww, what's the matter? The little shrimp can't handle himself without his brother around to protect him. Well, go get him. I'll knock out both of you. I'm not afraid of anyone."

"You wanted to see me?" Whitfield entered the library, walked past several tables, and calmly approached Jonathan, standing mere inches away from him. "You're going to knock me out?"

Jonathan stumbled over his words. "Uhh...well."

Whitfield desperately wanted to punch Jonathan, but kept his composure. "You see, Jonathan, everyone here knows you're just a pathetic bully, and can't back up any of your tough talk." Whitfield inched even closed to Jonathan, so they were practically nose-to-nose. "But, after what you did to Colin, now everyone around here is going to know what a gutless coward and rotten person you are."

Jonathan was fuming mad. "You jerk!"

Jonathan raised both hands and shoved his palms into Whitfield's chest, hoping to push him down. Instead, Jonathan was the one who took two steps backward. Whitfield, solid as a rock, remained in the same spot. Unshaken. Whitfield folded his arms across his chest and asked, "do you really want to do this? Do you want me to embarrass you in front of all these people?"

Jonathan was visibly shaken. "You're such a jerk. I hate you. Your brother too. Why don't you just leave this school."

At this point, Mr. Redallot, the head librarian, and two guards, came over to break up the escalating fracas.

"This ends now." Mr. Redallot was emphatic. "Jonathan. Whitfield. Aspen. Follow me."

One guard took hold of Jonathan's arm and guided him out of the main study area, down a flight of steps, into a somewhat smaller study area. The other guard followed, while escorting Whitfield and Aspen, who was still clearly upset by the whole situation. Sir Arlington, whose office was just beyond the smaller study area, entered through a separate door moments after the three students arrived.

Sir Arlington looked displeased, but otherwise had a calming presence about him. "I have already seen the recordings from the library incident…and from Dr. Crawfish's classroom earlier today. Both inside, and outside, the classroom," Sir Arlington added this last piece while glaring directly at Jonathan. "I have also seen the recordings from tryouts last week when young Jonathan shoved young Aspen, pushed him into a trash receptacle, heckled Aspen, and callously conspired with his comrades to continue inflicting harm on both Aspen and Whitfield."

Whitfield turned to Aspen. "You didn't tell me he pushed you into the garbage."

Aspen looked down to the floor. "Yeah, it was embarrassing. I just wanted to forget about it." Whitfield glared at Jonathan, who was looking the other way.

Sir Arlington continued, "now, I am not interested in recounting any of the events that have already transpired. I am, however, interested in hearing from young Jonathan, since he appears to be the instigator in each of these incidents. Young Jonathan, why are you targeting these two students?"

Jonathan was emotional and red-faced while yelling, at no one in particular. "They shouldn't even be at the school. Sir, you know it's true. They come out of nowhere, and now, all of the sudden, shrimpy little Aspen is on the team, and I'm not. It's not fair. That spot was mine."

Aspen was offended. "I earned that spot on the team."

Whitfield picked up on a different part of Jonathan's ramblings. "Wait, what do you mean, we shouldn't be at this school?"

"Oh, come on. You know you only got in because of your parents. My mom is on the Board of Directors. She saw your files. I know you only got in because…"

Aspen interrupted Jonathan in mid-sentence. "Our parents are dead. They died just after I was born."

Jonathan smirked. "Lucky for them."

Aspen lunged after Jonathan, but Whitfield was able to hold him back.

It was clear to Sir Arlington that strict punishments needed to be doled out. "I see. Young Jonathan, I am sentencing you to Level 2 Detention for your repeated violations of the Acts of Character. You will not need to carry out the Level 1 incarceration since you have not previously been arrested and did not, apparently, have enough time to reflect upon and learn from your errant ways. I will not seek further punishment for your behavior during tryouts, as those violations were left unreported."

Sir Arlington glanced over at both Whitfield and Aspen, as though to say he was disappointed that they did not report these incidents at the time. "I will, however, add each incident to your official record, and have my staff review all recordings from your time here at Seven Bridges and document every violation. Further sentencing may be warranted. Guard, please arrest young Jonathan and escort him to the Level 2 Detention area."

The guard left with Jonathan in tow.

Sir Arlington turned his full attention to Whitfield and Aspen. "As for you two…first, do you have any questions?"

Whitfield spoke first. "Yes sir, was Jonathan right? Do we not belong here? Are we only here because of our parents?"

"Three questions. Here are three answers: No. No. No."

Aspen did not immediately see the humor. "Uhh…that's it?"

"Of course not. I was just trying to lighten the mood. Look, did you take the admission tests?"

Whitfield and Aspen both answered, "yes."

"Did you pass these tests?"

Again, both boys replied, "yes."

"That is quite an understatement, for both of you. First place on all incoming exams for your class year, if I recall correctly. Young Whitfield, you even scored higher than young Ugu, if memory serves me well." With a wink, Sir Arlington added, "just don't mention that to her."

Whitfield smiled.

"Did you pass the Acts of Character?"

"Yes."

"Did you complete every requirement asked of every other student here?"

"I think so."

"So, you belong here."

Whitfield still wasn't convinced. "But, what about our parents?"

Sir Arlington thought deeply. "Ahh, well, that is a bit more complicated. All I can say is Hendricks raised you, Whitfield, from the time you were 3; and Aspen, he raised you since the day you were born. I should know. I was there."

Aspen had no idea. "You knew our parents?"

"Yes. Wonderful people. I will share their story with you when the time is right, but for now, just know that Hendricks is the one responsible for raising you, and preparing you so well to be here. You are two of our shining stars and we are thrilled to have you here."

Aspen accepted the compliment. "Thank you."

Whitfield too. "Yes, thank you."

"But that does not mean you are immune from punishment. Aspen, I am adding a note to your record that you failed to report known violations of the Acts of Character. You will avoid punishment…this time. But see to it that this does not happen again."

Aspen was not happy with having a note added to his permanent record, but mostly was disappointed in himself for not reporting Jonathan. "Yes, sir."

"And as for you Whitfield. I commend you for your restraint. I think I would have knocked Jonathan's block off if I were in your shoes. Keep setting a fine example. You are being watched, and will be rewarded."

With that, Whitfield and Aspen were excused. Whitfield, however, had one more question. "Sir, would it be possible to stay in here to complete our problem set? I just think that if we head back out there, we might get bombarded with questions from other students."

"Certainly. Here, use my study chambers. I think you will find the space suitable."

Whitfield and Aspen stayed for another hour, completing their problem set, before heading over to practice.

****

With one week remaining until the first meet, the intensity in practice was palpable. Team members were not just working out the kinks in their routines, many were aiming for perfection, or as least as close to perfect as possible. Coaches were trying to keep the gymnasts loose, but their relaxed vibe felt out of place with the voracity with which many of the gymnasts practiced. The coaches' main job was to select a starting lineup for their upcoming home meet.

Not an easy task with a team full of such hard-working and talented gymnasts. Well, that is most gymnasts on the team exhibited this insatiable desire to improve and with it, crack the starting lineup. There were still several gymnasts that didn't seem to put forth much effort.

During a brief water break, Whitfield caught up with Aspen. "Can you believe Wilson and Diego? They haven't taken a single turn on Pommel Clock since practice started?"

"I know. They just keep getting in my way. I couldn't even take my last turn."

Whitfield couldn't believe it. "You missed your turn?"

"Yeah, they wouldn't move."

Whitfield decided he had had enough. He approached the Pommel Clock area. "Hey, Wilson, what's up? My brother was trying to take his turn and you wouldn't get out of the way?"

"Oh, hey, my bad. Go ahead, Aspen." Wilson climbed down from the horse and let Aspen use up the rest of his own time on Pommel Clock.

"Thank you."

"Hey, no problem." Wilson appeared sincere.

"Thanks, Wilson. You didn't have to give up your own time."

"Nah, Whitfield, that's OK. I'm good."

Whitfield was about to walk away, but curiosity nagged at him. "Hey, Wilson, why aren't you practicing? We have a meet next weekend. Don't you want to get better?"

Wilson, along with Diego and Reid, who had now joined the other two in resting, all chuckled. Diego uttered, "Wilson doesn't need to practice, man."

Wilson followed up with, "that's right. We gonna win anyway." Wilson slapped hands with the other two.

Whitfield didn't understand. "What do you mean? We have some tough competition this weekend."

"Look, man, don't you get it? We always win." Wilson's confidence appeared to be masking something else.

"Yeah, only if we practice hard and hit our routines in the meet, right?"

"No, man, you really don't get it. It doesn't matter how we do at the meet. We're going to win anyway."

"How is that?"

Wilson stood up and spoke directly to Whitfield. "Look, I don't know how it works, it just does. We had a meet last year where every one of us fell on Parallel Planks and we still won. At the same meet, Morocco didn't make it past the third pommel on any of his routines all weekend and Keegan couldn't even catch the pegs after his vault. Even on his second chance. Even Flaherty fell so many times on VH-Bars. All of that happened, and we still won. What can I say, we're the chosen ones."

Whitfield didn't believe in Wilson's conclusion. "Well, I'd still like to get better. And so does Aspen. So, I'd appreciate it if we can still get our work in."

"Be my guest. You got it. We won't get in your way. Just don't try too hard. Enjoy being a gymnast at SBA. We got it made."

Whitfield went back to his circuit work by Escalating Tramps. He was satisfied that Wilson and his group wouldn't get in Aspen's way anymore, but something still stuck with him. What did Wilson mean when he said, "we always win" and it didn't matter if we practice or not? Something just didn't seem right.

That can't be right. We don't always win. Do we?

****

Whitfield kept mulling over this question through the rest of practice and during his nightly run with Ugu, where he was uncharacteristically quiet. The phrase "we always win" stuck with him like an itch all the way home that evening.

His restless sleep left Whitfield slightly more tired than usual Saturday morning. That still didn't stop him from getting in his morning workout. But something else did manage to cut into his morning workout routine. The doorbell. Whitfield remembered that his house butler, Torrington, doesn't work on weekends, and even though there were over 40 other students living there, he was already up and ready to go, so he answered the door.

"Uhh, hello?"

No one was at the door. Whitfield looked all around, but didn't see anyone standing outside.

But what was there, was a dozen or so giant baskets of…cookies? As Whitfield rummaged through the baskets, he found cookies (of all shapes and varieties); cakes; pies; muffins; bagels; candy; fruit, and all sorts of baked goods. He kept digging, and saw smoothies; juices; scones; other assorted pastries and chocolates…lots of chocolate.

As Whitfield tried to make sense of this mystery delivery, he dug deep down into one of the baskets and finally spotted a card. "Happy Birthday Keegan!" OK, now it made sense. It must be Keegan's birthday and whoever sent this enormous pallet of sweets, maybe his mom, just got the wrong house number.

Ahh. Simple mistake. But this is a lot of stuff for one person. I guess Keegan likes his sweets.

Whitfield couldn't possibly take every basket over to Keegan's house himself; at least, not all in one trip. Instead of calling Keegan to tell him to pick up his delivery, or wake up his own fellow housemates to lug everything over to Keegan's mansion this early in the morning, Whitfield decided to head on over to his teammate's house personally and be one of the first to wish Keegan a happy birthday. He grabbed a box of cookies to show Keegan that a delivery did in fact arrive from his mom.

Keegan lived over on the garden side, almost directly across campus from Whitfield. Still wanting to get some exercise in, Whitfield decided to run up the slide ramp to the Outer Loop, take the stairs down to the Inner Loop, zip-line down to the Inner Bowl, hop on a few tramps across to the Law campus and race up the Rising Stumps back to the Inner Loop, head back up the stairs to the Outer Loop, run a quarter mile, and take Slide 16-EL down to Keegan's house. When he got to the slide entrance to Keegan's mansion, it was locked, as expected.

Whitfield scanned his tracker and spoke into the receiver, "here to wish Keegan a happy birthday." He waited a few seconds before Keegan's security team gave him the green light. As Whitfield waited, he noticed that Keegan's neighbors, on the left, also had what appeared to be the same dozen or so large baskets of goodies sitting outside their front door. It was still pretty far away, but Whitfield was almost sure it was the same baskets.

Slide 16-EL took Whitfield down to the east wing of Keegan's mansion, at the ground level. He spotted Keegan almost immediately, walking toward him. Keegan's security team almost assuredly had relayed Whitfield's message.

"Whitfield! So good to see you. What brings you here this morning?"

"Hey, buddy. Happy birthday!"

"Thanks. Yeah, 17 years old. Where did the time go?"

"Hey, I think maybe your mom sent your birthday gift to the wrong house. I have about a dozen large baskets filled with a whole bunch of cookies and pies and stuff. See, just like this." Whitfield held out the box of cookies he took with him. They were pretty much all crumpled now, after his adventurous jaunt through campus. "Uh. Sorry."

"Oh, don't sweat it. They're yours, actually."

"What do you mean? The card inside said 'Happy Birthday Keegan!'"

"I know. I wrote it."

"Huh? That doesn't make any sense."

Keegan sat down with Whitfield on a bench overlooking the garden in front of the house. "Sure it does. Whenever someone on the team has a birthday, the whole house gets together and either sends out gifts to the other houses or does something nice for the school. Last year, Morocco sent out personalized leather-bound journals to everyone. Brooks found out everyone's favorite food and had his chefs prepare custom meals for every student, faculty member, and school staff—that was a nice touch.

"Sydney's a really talented artist, so she drew portraits of every student on campus and had her staff frame them, jazz them up a bit, and deliver them. Reid, yeah, I know he's kind of a toolbag, but he had everyone on his staff come out and do gardening work, fix up any loose fence posts, clean pools, scrub windows, and a whole lot of other yard work. His staff was amazing, and he didn't shirk at all. He was the last one standing, still working away well past 02:00."

"Wow, that's incredible. Does everyone do these amazing things on their birthday?"

"Either on their birthday or the closest non-meet weekend. But, no, not everyone. Ryne simply hosted a party at his house. He said his gift to the other students was the invitation. What a tool."

Whitfield chuckled. "No way. Did you go?"

"Yeah, I went. The party sucked. I peed in his pool. Then left."

Whitfield laughed, but then caught himself. "That's mean."

"Ahh, he deserved it."

"What about Flaherty?" Whitfield was curious about what Ugu did for her birthday, but he felt self-conscious asking about Ugu, since everyone on the team already thinks he likes her, so he decided to ask about Flaherty instead.

"Nah, I don't think she peed in his pool. She did knock him on his butt though."

"Really?"

"Oh yeah. She popped him right in his nose, then kicked him upside his head. Everyone knows you do not mess with Flaherty."

"Why? I mean what happened?"

"I just told you. Oh, you mean why did she do it? Well, you know that Ugu had a bit of a crush on Gabe last year, right?"

"Yeah, I heard." Whitfield did not like hearing about Ugu's past crush.

"Don't sweat it. Nothing ever happened. Gabe is a great guy. All the girls here had a crush on him. He was like a God here. Anyway, we're all dressed up at this party and Ryne was messing around and nearly knocked Gabe off the balcony over the pool. Ugu lunged after Gabe to stop him from falling, but in the process got in Ryne's way and he knocked her off balance. She fell over the balcony edge and dropped two stories into the pool. Gabe rushed down to check on Ugu, but Flaherty saw what happened, and just hauled off whooped Ryne's ass."

"Did Flaherty get in trouble?"

"No, Ryne never reported the incident. He claims it was an accident, you know, knocking Ugu off the balcony, but too many people saw him acting all crazy. He wore sunglasses for the next week in class, but you could still see his black eye in the meet photos from the following week. I actually have a photo from that meet hanging up in my room just for that very reason."

Whitfield and Keegan shared a laugh.

"Hey, why don't you come inside? I'll have Adrian make us some breakfast. He's already cooking for the staff. What's one more?"

"OK, sounds good. I can stay for a little while."

Whitfield and Keegan went inside and laughed and told stories. Whitfield met much of Keegan's staff and had a great time as they all took turns telling embarrassing Keegan stories. Even Whitfield was able to share a funny story from practice earlier in the week. Throughout the morning and well into the afternoon, the whole house was alive with laughter and good times.

The doorbell kept ringing. Every 5-10 minutes, another girl, usually a sixth- or seventh-year, would show up at the door, Keegan would walk over, open the door and the girl would say, "happy birthday, Keegan," place a flowered necklace over his head, and give him a kiss. Some girls stayed and hung out in the mansion or out by the pool; others just stopped by for their greeting and kiss, and left.

Whitfield was shocked by the whole scene. He couldn't believe Keegan was kissing all these girls. He couldn't believe all these girls had even wanted to kiss Keegan. *Why would any girl want to kiss him after he's already kissed dozens of others that same day?*

"Is this how all birthdays are celebrated here?"

Brooks, who was eating some snacks in the kitchen, answered, "no. Keegan's special. The girls around here love him."

Reid followed. "Yeah, now that Gabe is gone, right."

Several students within earshot laughed. Just then the doorbell rang again.

Keegan yelled out from the bathroom, where he was washing his face. "Hey, guys, my lips are starting to get tired. Could someone else answer the door?"

Even though it wasn't his house, Whitfield was feeling right at home. So much so, that he offered to get the door. "I'll get it."

"Thanks, Whitfield. You can even pretend you're me if you want."

More laughter. Whitfield opened the door and couldn't believe his eyes.

"Hey, Ugu. What are you doing here?"

Chapter 10
Starting Lineups

"I'm here to wish Keegan a happy birthday. And, I have something for him."

Whitfield looked down and mumbled under his breath. "Yeah, I bet I know what it is too."

"Are you OK?"

"Uhh...I'm actually not feeling too good. I'm going to head home now." Whitfield walked past Ugu and started heading home.

"Wait. Do you want me to walk with you?"

Whitfield just kept walking. Keegan finally came over to the door to see what was taking Whitfield so long.

"Oh, hey, Ugu. Nice to see you. Did you see where Whitfield went?"

"Happy birthday, Keegan." Ugu handed Keegan a gift. "Whitfield said he wasn't feeling well and took off."

Keegan took notice of the situation. "Oh no. I bet I know what's up. Hey, just wait here. Go inside, help yourself. Hey, Whitfield, wait up."

Whitfield was running toward campus, but Keegan was faster. He kept calling after Whitfield, and before long, caught up with him. "Hey, buddy, what's up?"

Whitfield already had a tear running down his face. "Nothing. I just have to go."

"Oh, man, you have it all wrong. Ugu didn't stop by to give me a kiss. She always drops off a gift for anyone's birthday—and not just for gymnasts, but everyone. That's just what she does—she's Ugu."

Whitfield wiped his tear away. "You mean, you weren't going to kiss her?"

"No way, man. She's like a sister to me. Gabe and I were boys on the team for five years. When Ugu got here, Gabe kind of took her under his wing. Yeah, she had a little crush on him, but that's only because he's Gabe. We took her everywhere. Introduced her to everyone on campus. We saw how really smart she was and wanted to help her any way we could. She's going to go far and we wanted to help her get there."

"Really? So, you're not interested in her?"

"Dude. I know she's cool and hot and all, but no. I could never. She's way too smart for me. You know, I need a girl with a little dumb in her. Makes me look smarter."

Whitfield laughed a little. "All right. Thanks."

"So, you really like her, huh?"

Whitfield put his head down. "I don't know. Maybe."

"Well. Can I give you some advice then?"

"Sure."

"Don't wait, man. Tell her how you feel. I told you I wouldn't ask her out, but there are 500 other dudes on campus, and she is the number one hottie on everyone's radar. Give me the word, and I'll clear a path for you, but I can only hold everyone off for so long."

"Thanks, Keegan. Really. But I just don't know yet. I can't really think about all that right now. We have a meet coming up and I need to focus on that."

"Well, let me know. I don't mind throwing some kids around. I got your back, homes."

"Thanks man."

"You're all right, Whitfield."

"You too, Keegan."

Whitfield and Keegan shared a bro hug. Whitfield turned and started running toward campus again. He stopped after a few yards and half-turned back around. "Hey Keegan. Happy birthday!"

"Thanks. And lay off those doughnuts. They're for the staff. We have a meet coming up."

"You got it."

Keegan walked back to his house. Ugu was already walking out.

"Is Whitfield OK?"

"That depends."

"On what?"

"Ugu, would you ever consider going out with me?"

"Eww. Not even in your dreams."

Keegan smiled. "Yup. He'll be fine."

****

Thursday. The final day before meet weekend. Practice had just ended and the coaches were deliberating one final time before announcing the starting lineups.

It was called meet weekend for a reason. Meets ran for two whole days, three if you count the opening festivities. The Friday before a meet, all eight teams arrive and the host school typically hosts a banquet and concert. The athletes get all dressed up in formal attire and parade around the red carpet. Photographers, journalists, reporters, and all sorts of media types show up in droves. With so much media attention, the work put in by the gymnasts' personal stylists and interview coaches are on full display.

The competition runs as follows: each team puts up four athletes per event, eight events in total, for a combined 32 routines per session for each team. Athletes may compete in more than one event. Each of the four team athletes on a particular event are assigned to a different bracket.

In total, there are four brackets per session, each consisting of 8 athletes, one from each team. Athletes may switch brackets for each event. Competition arenas hold at minimum four sets of each apparatus, one for each bracket, plus practice sets.

Points are awarded via head-to-head competition. Athletes compete head-to-head against each other member of their event bracket during the meet weekend, across seven sessions. Each athlete may compete up to seven times per event during the 2-day competition. Athletes earn team points by scoring higher than their opponent in head-to-head competition, or duels. Team points from head-to-head duels range from 0-5 points, based on margin of victory.

Day 1 of the competition is typically held on Saturday (this can change during All-Star Week and playoffs) and lasts about ten hours. The first four sessions take place on Day 1; the remaining three sessions on Day 2. Competition on Day 2 lasts about eight hours.

The coaches finished their deliberations and were ready to announce the starting lineups for the first meet of the year. Team members anxiously gathered on the competition floor awaiting the lineups.

Coach Daza stepped out of the coach's room to address the team. "In a moment, the video boards will display the starting lineups. For those of you whose name appears, congratulations. For those not listed, stay ready. We will be making substitutions as needed throughout the weekend."

The video boards came to life, one at a time, displaying the starting lineups:

Tri-Bars
1. Morocco
1. Flaherty
2. Whitfield
3. Aspen

Escalating Tramps
1. Sydney
2. Flaherty
3. Seraphina
4. Whitfield

Vault-Pegs
1. Flaherty
2. Fenway
3. Whitfield
4. Bella

Handstand Obstacle
1. Whitfield
2. Keegan
3. Wilson
4. Flaherty

Pommel Clock
1. Whitfield
2. Aspen
3. Flaherty
4. Kayleigh

VH-Bars
1. Flaherty
2. Diego
3. Whitfield
4. Ippy

Parallel Planks
1. Flaherty
2. Whitfield
3. Chloe
4. Ryne

Floor Exercise
1. Flaherty
2. Keegan
3. Whitfield
4. Swindell

Aspen could not believe his eyes. He had cracked the lineup. Not just once, but in two events. Aspen, the youngest athlete to ever be selected to join the school team, would now be the youngest ever to compete in a school meet. Likewise, Whitfield was ecstatic with being named an All-Arounder. Just a few weeks ago, he questioned whether he even belonged on the team. Now, his team was counting on both him and Flaherty to compete in all eight events. Which, of course, meant they would each be asked to complete 56 routines over two days. Not an easy task, even for the most skilled, and most fit, gymnasts in the world.

Whitfield carried his elation with him when he met up with Ugu for their nightly run. The past week had been awkward between the two of them, as Whitfield remained quiet and seemed to have something on his mind. Ugu, to her credit, remained positive throughout, and let Whitfield have his space. Ugu knew something was bothering Whitfield but he wasn't quite ready to talk about it.

Ugu thought maybe he was just feeling the pressure of the upcoming meet, but she was really good at reading people, and strongly suspected there was something else too. Pressing him on the issue might drive him further away, and Ugu was quickly realizing that she wanted, and needed, Whitfield in her life. She had grown to depend on Whitfield for his advice, perspective, and comfort.

Also, for his charm, wit, humor, and the way he looked at her and smiled and laughed at just about anything funny she ever said or did. But, most of all, she just loved the way Whitfield made her feel about herself, about school, about everything. Ugu wasn't quite yet ready to admit she was in love with Whitfield, even if she knew how much she cared for him.

Despite the awkwardness of the past week, tonight was different. Whitfield couldn't wait to tell Ugu about this weekend's lineup. Whitfield ran over toward Ugu at their normal meeting place inside the Outer Loop.

"Ugu, guess what?"

Ugu saw how excited Whitfield was, and knew that could only mean one thing. "You made the lineup?"

"Yes!"

Ugu was so excited for Whitfield. "That's great! I'm so proud of you." Ugu moved in to give Whitfield a hug, but he put his hands on her hips to stop her.

"But, wait, there's more."

"Aspen made the lineup too?"

"He did! It's so incredible."

"Aaaaahhhh! I'm so excited for you both."

Ugu pushed past Whitfield's temporary restraint and wrapped her arms around his neck and squeezed so tight. Whitfield returned the hug, but couldn't hold back his enthusiasm, and took a step back. Ugu still had her hands clasped around the back of Whitfield's neck, and as he spoke, Whitfield reached up and slid her arms down so he could grab hold of her hands. "But, wait, there's more."

"Did Flaherty make All-Around?"

"Yes. Wow, you're really good. How do you know all this?"

Ugu pulled her hands away and covered her mouth. She was so excited for her best friend. "Wow! That's great! She's worked so hard. I can't wait to congratulate her."

"Yeah, she really is awesome. Probably the best on the team."

"Is there anything else?"

"Well, yes, as a matter of fact, there is."

Whitfield stepped closer, and grabbed Ugu's hands in his own. He looked deep into her eyes. "I made the All-Around too."

Ugu screamed. She started to shake. Of all the news Whitfield just shared, this was the most unexpected. Ugu didn't know what to do, or say. After taking a couple steps backward, she rushed toward Whitfield and jumped into his arms and wrapped her arms and legs around him in a tight embrace. Whitfield was really caught off guard and almost toppled backward, but his elite balance kicked in and he remained on his feet. He twirled around with Ugu in his arms and her face buried in his neck.

Ugu jumped down and before she knew what she was doing, grabbed Whitfield's shirt with both hands, pulled him close, and gave Whitfield a big kiss.

Whitfield was stunned, but did manage to return the kiss. Clearly, not his best effort, but still.

It only lasted for a second or two before Ugu pulled herself away.

"Oops. I'm so sorry. I didn't mean to…"

"No, really, it's OK."

"No, I know you're not ready. I'm not ready. This was…"

"No, it's OK."

Ugu was all flustered. "Stop saying it's OK. We haven't ever talked about this. I mean I don't know how you feel. I mean, I think you like me, but I'm not sure. And then you hardly talk to me all week. And I know there's a meet coming up, so I gave you space. And then you don't know how I feel. I don't even know how I feel. I mean, do I like you? Well, yes, but like, like you? I don't know. Maybe. Do I think you like me? Maybe. I mean, I think you like me, but I don't know. This whole thing is just really confusing."

Ugu continued rambling, and Whitfield just smiled. Even when she was confused and totally out of control, Whitfield still thought Ugu was beautiful. Whitfield grabbed Ugu's hands.

"Ugu. It's OK. Trust me. Let's just start our run."

Ugu looked straight into Whitfield's blue eyes, and all her stress just melted away. "OK." They started their run together. They ran for longer than they had ever run together before.

They completed four laps around the Outer Loop. They both had a lot of energy to burn off. Whitfield was about to drop, and even Ugu had a deep sweat working. They decided to call it a night and Whitfield walked Ugu to the slides leading to Aspen's mansion, where Ugu lived.

"Well, good night."

Not knowing where to look or exactly what to do, Ugu hesitated. "Yeah, good night."

Ugu swiped her tracker and the green light above Slide 19-EU flashed. Whitfield was about to walk away, but paused momentarily. Ugu was about to head down the slide, but she paused as well.

"Look, let's not make this complicated. You have a big meet coming up. Concentrate on that. I'll be cheering like crazy for you and I'll still be here after the meet."

Whitfield, again realizing the gravity of what's at stake this weekend, temporarily froze. "I just hope I don't let everyone down. Or worse, let you down."

Ugu took a step toward Whitfield. "You won't let me down. Believe in yourself. Your teammates and coaches believe in you. Your school believes in you. I believe in you. I'll be here for you no matter what happens at the meet."

"Really?"

"Well, maybe not if you fall ten times and your shorts fall down and you trip over your feet and everyone stares at your 'I Heart Monkeys' underwear and…"

Whitfield smiled. "Haha. Very funny. You know, not everyone can pull off that look, with underwear on their head. I thought I was looking rather fine."

Ugu laughed. "You are so dumb."

"Yeah."

Ugu stopped laughing, but kept her smile. "Yeah. Go get some rest. Big weekend coming up."

"Right."

Whitfield started to jog toward his own house slide. Ugu called out to him. "Whitfield."

Whitfield stopped in his tracks and turned around. "Yeah?"

Ugu didn't say anything else. She didn't have to. Whitfield just smiled at her, turned back around, and ran home. Ugu held her hands to her heart, took a deep breath, and slid home.

Chapter 11
Dr. Hewitt's Secret Meeting

High atop the mountainside, in a dark, remote corner of the ski lodge, Dr. Hewitt was meeting with Gisele, a known gang member and hired hand.

"Here's the list. Take the envelopes and make sure they get into the proper hands."

"No problem. We know how to handle our business."

"I'm counting on it."

"Are we free to roam around the grounds?"

"Just stick to the plan. But, yeah, the school doesn't know I'm using you for this, so you shouldn't set off any alarms."

"That's good. We'll hit the banquet. Maybe the hotel too. Anyone we miss, we'll get before the meet starts."

"NO! They all have to be distributed by Friday night. No exceptions. We can't risk day of the meet changes. Some of the gymnasts have been told to fake injuries. They'll need enough time to alert their coaches to make the lineup changes."

"Whatever you say. Anything else?"

"Check the list. I believe you're giving two food poisoning, delivering news of a death in the family, and don't forget the phony job interview. We'll save the bogus grade misconduct for another meet."

"I know. I know. We already discussed all that."

"I'm just making sure you get it all. We can't afford any mistakes. The founders are keeping an eye on us this year. We're really ramping up our activity."

"As long as we get paid, I don't care how many gymnasts we bribe or poison. Your boss can take down the entire system for all I care."

Dr. Hewitt smiled. "Careful what you wish for. It just may come true." He handed Gisele the remaining envelopes and the two parted ways. Once he was alone again, Dr. Hewitt placed a call.

"It's done. Seven Bridges will win this weekend. You can bet on it!"

Chapter 12
Pre-Meet Festivities

Friday. With classes done for the week, all eyes focused on the upcoming home meet, the first meet of the season. Seven other teams would be descending upon campus today, with all visiting athletes, coaches, and personnel staying at the SBA I Hotel on the Northeast corner of campus. Seven Bridges students were busy all week preparing campus for their arrival, along with making sure their own assigned gymnasts were ready for the opening meet weekend.

By noon, four teams had already arrived, with the other three due to arrive shortly. Each of the four outdoor amphitheaters were alive with sound and lighting checks for tonight's concerts. Fans were in for a real treat as four top musicians and bands were scheduled to perform, each with their own outstanding opening acts scheduled as well. The Outer Loop was already jam-packed with fans waiting to rock out to Chalk Bucket; Mynt Chico Chip; Diamond Eyes; and Lucie Greene, who was making her second appearance on campus in less than a month. All four campus hotels were sold out, with hundreds of thousands of fans scheduled to arrive on campus over the three-day spectacle.

Each of the eight event practice facilities around campus would welcome fans for watch parties. Every gymnast assigned designated staff members to host additional watch parties for friends and family at their homes. Even the on-campus eateries would be packed to the gills with fans trying to catch a glimpse of the meet. As for Ugu, as usual, she took on multiple roles during meet weekend. Her top priority was making sure Aspen was completely prepared for the meet and had everything he needed for Friday night's gymnast banquet and for the remainder of the competition weekend.

Ugu had also volunteered to host the Alumni Ball, not so coincidentally taking place at roughly the same time as the gymnast banquet on Friday night. Luckily for Ugu, she could wear the same formal attire for both events. As more luck would have it, even though the events took place in different buildings, one in the Alumni

Center and the other in Flaxen Hall, the buildings were located in close proximity to each other near the main campus entrance.

Ugu did not technically have to make an appearance at the gymnast banquet, but each gymnast was allowed to bring a guest, or date, and Aspen asked if she would accompany him, as he was a bit nervous about wearing a tuxedo for the first time and didn't know what to expect. Ugu gladly accepted Aspen's invitation as it would give her a chance to personally make sure Aspen was OK, and had the added bonus of seeing Whitfield in his own tuxedo. She also wanted Whitfield to see her in her stunning new dress, picked out specifically for tonight's events.

Whitfield and Aspen's meet weekend started even before the first visiting team arrived. At 08:00, Whitfield, Aspen, Flaherty, and about a dozen other team members and three coaches visited the local children's hospital to visit with patients and their families. This visit had become a team tradition a few years back after one of the gymnasts' younger sister got sick and nearly died.

Now, before every home opener, members of the team visit the Ginger Holliday Children's Hospital to try to lift the children's spirits. Aspen was particularly motivated to go as he was the youngest on the team, and closest in age to many of the patients.

In total, twenty team members, seventeen of the twenty-five rostered gymnasts and three coaches, all rode together to the hospital on the team's official drone bus, but only sixteen rode back together after the team's official two-hour visit had ended. Whitfield, Aspen, and Flaherty stayed an extra hour, as each had connected with a different family and asked if they could prolong the visit. Coach Mayflower agreed to stay with them and escort them back. The other coaches said they would send a drone taxi back for them when they were ready. It was about 11:30 when the trio decided to head back to campus.

Aspen's staff was getting anxious when he did not immediately return with the bus. This delay was going to cause some scheduling issues, as time was running short and there was still a lot to do. Being the youngest ever member of the team and making the starting lineup was a very big deal.

Combine that with the Pommel Clock video from the first day of tryouts now going viral, Aspen was quickly becoming the school's newest celebrity. Aspen's staff had been fielding media inquiries and endorsement proposals ever since the lineups were announced to the public late Thursday night. The first call came in at 22:37 last night, and the inquiries hadn't let up all through the night. It seems that everyone wanted to talk with Aspen.

Aspen's first interview, scheduled for noon, had to be pushed back 20 minutes. Fortunately, it was a phone interview, and Aspen could talk as his stylist was still working on Aspen's hair and clothes. Aspen's interview coach was going over some last-minute tips, while his publicist and endorsement manager were both trying to keep Aspen updated with new requests and offers.

Aspen's nutritionist was trying to get him to eat a quick protein bar to keep up his energy. Amidst all the chaos, Aspen managed to keep his cool and show his gratitude and appreciation for everyone in the room. This was something that Ugu had stressed to Aspen all week, and he rose to the occasion, like a seasoned pro.

Meanwhile, Whitfield was dealing with his own packed schedule of media requests and endorsement offers. Many of the returning gymnasts already had endorsement deals and shared their experiences, both good and bad, with Whitfield. He immediately recognized some of the brands, but had to be educated on others. This was all a lot to take in, especially right now, with competition starting in less than 24 hours.

In the brand advertisers' defense, final rosters were not publicly released until just a few days ago, and most companies did not want to take a huge gamble on someone who they had never heard of before or who wouldn't even see action in a meet. So, it made sense for companies to wait until the starting lineups were announced before making their offers. Still, for Whitfield and Aspen, the timing of these offers just added to the pressure they were already feeling.

By the time 17:00 rolled around, Whitfield and Aspen had already completed a combined 23 interviews and met with seven endorsement reps. Neither had signed any contracts, as they needed to give their own legal advisors time to review the deals. Aspen also had the added security of having Ugu review any deals and offer her own advice. It was now time for Whitfield and Aspen to get dressed and head over to the red carpet for pictures and more interviews. As advised by their coaches, they each ate a quick meal at home before heading over to Flaxen Hall, where most of the cameras had already set up.

For the only time all year, luxury drone limos were able to pick up gymnasts and their security detail on the roof of their mansions and circle around to the campus entrance. Aside from the landing zones atop each of the four hotels, campus was strictly a no-fly zone, so the drones had to be careful not to breach the campus perimeter as they hovered over the crowd. The coaches were the first to arrive, followed by the non-starters, and then the single-event specialists. This meant that Whitfield, Aspen, Flaherty, and Keegan would be the final four gymnasts to arrive. Aspen arrived first.

The roar from the crowd was deafening. The entire area surrounding Flaxen Hall, the Outer Loop, and even the nearby rooftops, was overflowing with screaming fans waiting to catch a glimpse of the youngest star in school history. With cameras flashing and holographic images of fans taking enhanced selfies whizzing by, Aspen, handsomely outfitted in a crisp black tuxedo bearing the school crest on his left lapel and custom green-tinted cufflinks, designating his class year, stepped out of his ride and calmly walked toward the pop-up media stage, smiling, waving, and shaking hands with his fans.

Aspen paused to pose for the occasional photo op, always with his security team firmly in place, but offering him some space to be seen. Aspen hadn't even completed a routine in competition yet, and had already reached heartthrob celebrity status—at ten years old.

Aspen was just about to stop and talk with the reporter from *Gymnastics Tonight* when Keegan arrived in his luxury drone. Another roar from the crowd. This one a little more high-pitched as screaming girls with a huge fantasy crush on the sixth-year gymnast made their voices heard. Keegan loved all the attention, soaking up every minute of it.

A rabid fan managed to temporarily break through Keegan's security team and get close enough to touch Keegan's hand before she was pulled away. Keegan took it all in stride. He even stopped to kneel down by a young girl and handed her a signed trading card from his rookie season and hugged her. He then stood up and asked her parents if they had tickets to the meet.

Her dad said, "no, we just came to watch from the loop." Keegan reached into his pocket and handed the little girl's parents four weekend passes to his mansion's personal watch party. The little girl and her brother opened their eyes wide and gasped. The mom reached out, hugged Keegan, and planted a kiss right on his lips. Even the dad was overcome with emotion. Keegan thought he saw a tear in the dad's eye before he gave a fist bump to the little girl's brother and continued on through the crowd toward the media staging area.

Two more drones were hovering nearby. Whitfield and Flaherty, the only two gymnasts yet to arrive and the team's only All-Arounders, were viewing the scene from above, while chatting with each other through their earpieces.

"Flaherty, is it always like this? I've never seen anything this wild."

"Yup. Every meet."

"You mean, just the home meets, right?"

"No, we'll get a lot of attention on the road too, being defending champs and all. Maybe not to this extent, but, yeah, it's a lot."

"I'm not sure I can handle all this."

"Oh, sure you can. You were nervous at the start of tryouts too. Remember? And that turned out just fine."

"Well, yeah, but that was different. I didn't have some reporter asking me about setting records or random moms asking me to date their daughters."

"Haha…don't worry. I'll tell them that you're already taken…and deeply in love."

"What! No, don't do that."

Flaherty laughed. "So, you want to date their daughters? OK. I'll let them know. They'll be very happy, but I think I know someone who might be a little upset and not want to have a second first kiss with you."

"Oh, she told you about that, huh?"

"Of course, she did. I told you; she tells me everything."

"Hey, what do you mean, second first kiss?"

"Oh yeah. She said that first one doesn't count. Too rushed."

Whitfield agreed, "yeah, it kind of was."

"Anyway, she has a whole plan for her first real kiss. Very romantic."

"Wow. Well, let me ask you. Does her plan include me?"

"I don't know."

"Yes, you do. You two talk about everything."

"OK. You got me. Of course, I know. I'm just not going to tell you."

"Oh, come on. I thought we were friends."

"We are. I'm just not sharing this one with you. Besides, you have more pressing things to think about."

"I know. The meet."

"Well, yeah, but I was thinking about something even scarier. Loads more pressure."

Whitfield was getting worried. "More pressure than this? What's that?"

"Oh, she didn't tell you? Ugu's dad is coming to the meet. She told him about you. He wants to meet you."

Stunned silence. "Whitfield? Are you there?"

"Uhh…WHAT?"

"Yup. He'll probably be at the Alumni Ball tonight. Might mosey on over to the banquet to check you out. No pressure."

"Uhh, Flaherty. That's not funny. I think I'm going to be sick."

"No time for that now, you're about to land. Smile for the cameras." Flaherty signed off with a devilish chuckle.

"Flaherty!"

Whitfield's luxury drone limo landed and he stepped out. Whitfield could hear the screams from inside his ride, but nothing could have prepared him for the intense volume and roar of the crowd that came rushing in as soon as his door lifted. Still a little weary from his conversation with Flaherty, Whitfield shook it off quickly and managed to smile for the crowd. He was more rigid than Aspen and Keegan. Didn't stop quite as often to interact with the crowd.

Despite being well-spoken and highly intelligent, Whitfield didn't possess the same people skills as his younger brother or certain other members of the team. He wasn't rude or offensive; he just didn't really know how to act in these situations and wasn't comfortable without an exact road map detailing his every movement. Fortunately, Jordana, Whitfield's personal assistant, mapped out a detailed agenda for him. Whitfield stuck to his schedule, with little improvisation.

If there was an exact opposite to Whitfield's social naivete, it was Flaherty. Flaherty's arrival generated the loudest cheers of the past hour. She was clearly the face of the team, the most skilled gymnast, and the heir apparent to Gabe's legacy as SBA's top performer. The crowd loved Flaherty. She was charming, beautiful, smart, friendly, the defending champion on Vault-Pegs and the preseason favorite for the Cheesestock Trophy, given to the Most Outstanding Gymnast of the Year and named after the greatest gymnast to ever compete, and an honored school alumnus, Morton Cheesestock.

Flaherty was the epitome of elegance in her formal attire, moving gracefully over the red carpet, almost gliding. She stopped several times for pictures and to speak with fans.

Flaherty had the unbelievable ability to remember faces and names of everyone she came across and stunned a pair of fans when she called out to them by name. She remembered they had come to last year's home opener and had stood in just about the same spot as a year ago. She asked how they have been and took a photo with them. Flaherty was the star of stars this evening, and everyone knew it.

The banquet took place inside the Grand State Room on the third level of Flaxen Hall. All 200 rostered gymnasts from the meet's participating teams were invited to attend the banquet. Each gymnast was allowed one guest plus one security agent. Other members of gymnasts' security detail would be asked to patrol the areas either outside the building, or inside the vast atrium. Security was tight. Other invited guests included coaches and other pertinent team personnel (up to 8 per team), meet organizers, WGF officials, and trade representatives from the most lucrative major precious gem producers in the world.

As the gymnasts arrived, they were allowed to select from a variety of jewels and gems to adorn their necks, wrists, fingers, and ears. Most of the Seven Bridges students were already adequately outfitted with jewels, by virtue of winning the Precious Gems meet each of the past six years; however, many of the visiting gymnasts took great enjoyment in wearing expensive jewelry for the evening.

Aspen, Whitfield, and Flaherty waited by the top of the stairs, outside the Grand State Room, for Ugu, who said she would arrive at exactly 19:30 to escort Aspen into the banquet. Right on time, Whitfield was the first to spot Ugu as she ascended the stairs. *An angel.* Whitfield was stunned. This was the first time he had seen Ugu in formal wear, outside of her classroom uniform, and wow. He was speechless. Ugu was the most beautiful girl he had ever seen. Ugu reached the top of the stairs and Whitfield was still mesmerized by her beauty.

"Hi Flaherty. You look stunning. Aspen, you are so handsome. And Whitfield. My you clean up nicely."

"Thank you. Ugu. You are absolutely beautiful." Flaherty and Ugu exchanged kisses on their cheeks.

"You look very nice, Ugu. Thank you for coming to this. I'm a bit nervous." Aspen was still adjusting his tie.

After a moment, Flaherty nudged Whitfield. "Whitfield, aren't you going to say anything to Ugu?"

Whitfield remained frozen.

Aspen, being goofy, stood behind Whitfield and while moving Whitfield's arms, mimicked Whitfield's voice. "Hey, Ugu. You look really beautiful. Don't mind me. I'm not very smooth. My brother is much better at talking to girls than I am. He's much cuter too. You should go into the banquet with him."

Flaherty laughed. Ugu smiled. Whitfield…remained frozen.

"Well, thank you for those kind words, err, Whitfield. I'm going to escort your brother into the banquet now. I hope to see you inside."

Whitfield said…nothing. He was still frozen.

"I'll meet up with you two inside." Flaherty turned to Whitfield. "Will you get your act together?" Flaherty then proceeded to punch Whitfield in the gut. That seemed to have woken Whitfield from his trance.

"Hey."

"Oh, you can speak? What was that?"

"I…I…I don't know. I just saw her and froze. She's just so…so…"

Flaherty softened her tone and smiled. "I know. Let's just go inside."

Despite having an extra ticket each, at the request of their coaches, Whitfield and Flaherty decided not to bring a date to the banquet. Instead, each were allowed to have two security agents inside the Grand State Room. As such, Flaherty and Whitfield decided to enter the banquet together.

The banquet itself was enjoyable. Whitfield, Aspen, Flaherty, and Ugu all mingled with the other gymnasts and coaches. Ugu knew a lot of gymnasts from the other teams, having accompanied Gabe at several of these events over the past two years.

Whitfield met many of the other schools' coaches and athletes on his own, by the dessert table, while Aspen and Flaherty made their way around the dance floor and even sat at several tables, talking with whoever was there. With Aspen smiling and having a good time, Ugu decided to duck out of the banquet and head over to the Alumni Center, but said she would return in about an hour.

While the banquet was mostly just a meet-and-greet type of event, there were some scheduled speakers. The band stopped playing and Coach Brockport, Seven Bridges' head coach, got up to speak. Without the band playing, the guests were able to make out the faint sounds of the outdoor concerts, which were in full swing. Coach Brockport welcomed everyone to campus and introduced General Gibson, a representative from the WGF.

Gen. Gibson gave a brief talk about the meet and all that was at stake. Thanks to Ugu, Whitfield and Aspen already knew the importance of the meet in determining the allocation of precious gems across the participating schools, but they were both surprised to learn just how many gems were up for grabs this weekend. The winning school would have complete control over several diamond mines; ruby and emerald processing factories; and large stakes in the worldwide supply of red beryl, musgravite, alexandrite, jadeite, and a few other precious gems. The global precious gem market was valued at about $300 billion. About a third of that value was officially at stake in this meet.

Gen. Gibson wrapped up his talk and the band started to play again. Aspen was having a great time meeting people and even Whitfield managed to loosen up a bit. Whitfield was busy chatting with a visiting gymnast, when he noticed Gen. Gibson speaking with Dr. Hewitt. The two seemed to be friendly with each other, but the conversation was tense. Gen. Gibson was clearly in charge and seemed to be asking Dr. Hewitt a bunch of questions.

Whitfield was too far away to hear any of the conversation or to read lips, not that he knew how to do that anyway. The conversation ended, and Gen. Gibson rejoined the party. Dr. Hewitt walked the other way, toward the exit beyond where Whitfield was standing.

"Whitfield. How are you? Enjoying the banquet?"

"Dr. Hewitt. Yes, sir. I'm having a good time."

"Bravo. Let me know if I can do anything for you. I have to run along now, and I will likely not be arriving back at the house until quite late—possibly not until morning. But, if you need anything, don't hesitate to contact me."

"Sure. Is everything OK? I saw you chatting with Gen. Gibson."

Whitfield thought he saw a slight twitch in Dr. Hewitt's face. Ever since taking his *Lying, Cheating, Stealing, and Deception* class, Whitfield had been trying to pick up on these subtleties in conversation, but until now hadn't found any success.

"Oh, that. Gen. Gibson and I are old chaps from our school days. We were just reminiscing about the old days. Nothing to concern yourself with."

"OK. See you at the meet tomorrow?"

"I may not make it there tomorrow, but I'll be watching. Cheerio." Dr. Hewitt hustled along without stopping again before reaching the exit.

Whitfield only had a moment's time to reflect on his conversation with Dr. Hewitt, and to contemplate the reasons why he had to leave the banquet so early and why he wouldn't attend tomorrow's competition, when he became mesmerized, once again. There she was. Ugu was standing across the Grand State Room, smiling so beautifully, perfect in every way…well, every way except one. She was standing there with her arm entangled in an older gentleman's arm on her right, and carrying on a conversation with him and another woman standing on her left. Whitfield didn't know what to think. *What is going on?*

Whitfield tried not to stare, but couldn't help it. Keegan came over and playfully punched Whitfield in the ribs.

"Hey buddy, enjoying the party?"

"Look." Whitfield motioned across the floor in Ugu's direction.

"Yeah. So?"

"Who's that she's with?"

"Dude. That's her father. She must have brought him over from the Alumni Ball. That woman standing next to her on the other side is Vanessa Klein."

"THE Vanessa Klein?"

"Yeah. World Champion. 3x Pro League MOG. Second greatest All-Arounder in school history. Well, until Gabe broke most of her records. Yeah, that Vanessa Klein."

"Wow. Ugu really does know everyone."

"Yeah, Ugu's got connections. But I wouldn't worry about Vanessa."

"Why's that?"

"Because I think Ugu's just spotted you and she's coming over here with her dad. C'mon, I'll introduce you."

"Wait. WHAT?" Before he could say anything else, Keegan put his arm around Whitfield's shoulder and proceeded to walk toward Ugu and her father.

"Mr. Gugurutruv. Nice to see you again, sir. Ugu, you didn't tell me your father was coming to the banquet."

"Keegan."

"Dad was over at the Alumni Ball and wanted to come over to check out Vanessa's speech."

"Oh, how nice. She is one of our most honored alumni. We are so proud to have her here."

"Can it, Keegan." Ugu's dad was a stern man. No nonsense.

"All right, sir."

There was a long awkward pause before anyone spoke again. Ugu's dad was staring right at Whitfield. Whitfield was scared.

Keegan sensed that he should leave. "Well, I am going to…go anywhere else. Good luck, buddy." Keegan patted Whitfield on the back and quickly left.

"Daddy, this is Whitfield. The boy I told you about."

Whitfield, as nervous as he's ever been, but remembering every word of Flaherty's last-minute advice before she left his side, tried to make a good first impression. "Sir, it's a pleasure to meet you. I'm Whitfield and I've been seeing your daughter."

Ugu's eyes widened. Her dad's face remained stoic.

"No, not seeing each other, sir. That's not what I meant. I mean we kissed. Well, it wasn't really a kiss. I mean it didn't count. Well, she doesn't think it counts. She wants a more romantic kiss…"

Ugu's eyes got even wider. Her dad's face remained unchanged.

"Wait. NO. That's not what I meant either. I mean, we're friends. Well, maybe more than friends. I don't know. I mean, I like her. I think she likes me. I don't know. She did see my underwear."

Ugu covered her eyes with her hands. Ugu's dad raised an eyebrow, but otherwise, remained stoic.

Whitfield continued fumbling for the right words. "Haha…did I just say underwear. It's not what you think. The underwear was on my head."

He did not find the right words. Ugu was stunned.

"Not that I always wear underwear on my head, sir. No, I was helping out a friend. There was an incident with a wedgie, and…"

Ugu had enough. "Excuse us, Daddy." She grabbed Whitfield's hand and pulled him over to the side. "What is wrong with you?"

Whitfield was in complete shock over what he just said to her dad. "I don't know. I didn't know what to say."

"So, you decided to lead with 'I wear underwear on my head'?"

"Yeah. That probably wasn't good, was it?"

"Uhh…no. Not your best effort."

"OK. Give me a moment." Whitfield took a deep breath. "Give me another chance."

"Oh boy!"

"Hey, did I mention that you look beautiful tonight? But, if I may…I think I like your hair better behind your left shoulder, like you had it when you were walking up the stairs. You have the cutest little freckle below your ear, by your neck." Whitfield brushed her hair behind her left shoulder. Ugu stood there trembling. "What's wrong?"

Ugu simply stood there. Smiling. "Nothing. Absolutely nothing."

It was amazing. Whitfield knew every little detail of Ugu's face. He had a way of turning any of Ugu's insecurities or imperfections into a flawless masterpiece. Always seeing the butterfly in her caterpillar frame. Seeing herself through Whitfield's eyes was a magical source of warmth, comfort, and dizzying magnificence.

Whitfield smiled, and Ugu forgot all about his ramblings to her father. Whitfield walked back over to Ugu's dad. "Sir, I was wondering if we can start over?"

With the hint of a smile, Ugu's dad accepted. "All right."

"Thank you. Sir, it's a pleasure to meet you. I am Whitfield. I'm a third-year student and member of the gymnastics team."

"Whitfield. Nice to meet you. How do you know my daughter?"

"Well, sir. We are in the same class year, but we do not share any classes together. She is, however, the chief-of-staff in my brother's house."

"Oh? Your brother is a gymnast too?"

"Yes. Aspen. He is here somewhere. Anyway, Ugu, Flaherty, Aspen, and I have become close friends during this first month at school. Ugu has really helped with Aspen and I transitioning to Seven Bridges."

"Yes. Daddy, Whitfield is a transfer student."

"Hmm. I see. Where were you before?"

"Home-schooled, sir."

"By your parents?"

"Uhh, Daddy. Whitfield's parents died when he was young."

"Oh. Sorry to hear that. What are your plans for while you are here at Seven Bridges?"

"Well, sir. With all due respect, I'm not really sure." Ugu's dad appeared less than happy with this response, but Whitfield clarified his answer. "What I mean is there is so much to do here. I came here thinking that I wanted to study Applied Mathematics and Quantitative Economics, and maybe even Computer Science and Technology. I'm really interested in cryptanalysis. After doing some more homework, though, I think I may give International Affairs a look. I like the idea of being able to address problems on a more global scale."

"Daddy, Whitfield actually had the highest scores on his entrance exams since the school started keeping records."

"Hmm. Even higher than yours, dear?"

"And yours, Daddy."

Whitfield turned toward Ugu. "Oh, you know about that?"

Ugu waved her hand. "Oh, please. That was just a simple hack."

Whitfield smiled. "Sometimes I forget how smart you are."

"Don't worry. I'll keep reminding you."

Ugu and Whitfield shared a smile. "I'm sure you will."

"Well, Whitfield, I was wondering if you'd care to join me across the way over at the Alumni Ball. I think the event will likely wrap up soon over here, so you will not miss much."

Whitfield was nervous. "I thought you wanted to hear Vanessa's talk."

"Oh, heaven's no. I've heard her speech a thousand times already. Even helped her write most of it. Come on."

Whitfield looked over at Ugu, for guidance. Ugu gave a quick wink.

"Sir, I'd love to accompany you back over to the Alumni Center. I'll give you a moment with your daughter while I let my brother know where I'm going."

Aspen was out on the dance floor. He had already taken off his jacket and seemed to be having a great time.

"Don't bother. Ugu can let your brother know."

Now Whitfield was really nervous. "Oh, she's not coming with us?"

"No, it will just be us guys. She'll come by a little later, won't you, dear?"

Ugu nodded. "Of course."

"OK. Sure. Well, sir, would it be OK if I have a moment with your daughter before leaving?"

Mr. Gugurutruv, who had ever so briefly appeared to relax a bit, regained his stern demeanor. "Sure. I'll give you two a minute." Ugu's dad stepped back and left Whitfield and Ugu some space to say goodbye.

"Any words of advice?"

"Just be yourself."

"Ha. You saw how that worked earlier."

"You recovered fine. Just be yourself, and he'll love you, just like I…do."

Whitfield's jaw nearly fell to the ground. He was stunned. He froze again. This time it wasn't Flaherty's right cross to his gut that jarred him back to life, but Mr. Gugurutruv's hand on the back of his neck that gave Whitfield a jolt.

"Ready to go?"

"Uhh, sure."

Ugu still couldn't believe what she had just let slip out. She just stood there, unable to move.

Whitfield left Flaxen Hall with Ugu's dad, both talking along the way. To his credit, Whitfield managed to keep up his end of the conversation. The pair entered the Alumni Center and Ugu's dad introduced Whitfield to all the most powerful and influential alumni in the room. The alumni event did not end until just after midnight. Whitfield and Mr. Gugurutruv walked back to SBA IV together and said goodbye.

"You're a good kid, Whitfield. My daughter likes you. As long as she likes you, I'll like you. Got it?"

"Yes, sir. And thank you. For everything. Tonight was enjoyable. I appreciate your showing me around."

"You bet. Get some rest. Big day tomorrow."

"Good night, sir."

Whitfield and his security detail, who had followed him at a distance throughout the evening, walked through the Outer Loop together, back to their house. While walking past the mountain side, Whitfield spotted a shadowy figure, carrying a large suitcase, get inside the ski lift suite. He was by himself. It vaguely looked like Dr. Hewitt, but Whitfield wasn't sure. *Why would anyone be heading up the mountain at this time? Strange.* But Whitfield didn't have time to think about it.

He used Slide 06-WU to head straight toward his bedroom. He got changed into his pajamas and crawled right into bed and fell asleep, completely missing the flashing message on his tracker. It was from Aspen.

22:47: *Hey, bro, come over here. It's important!*

Chapter 13
First Meet—Day 1

Saturday. All gymnasts were scheduled to arrive at Arlington Gymnastics Center by 08:00 on Day 1. Despite the late night, Whitfield arrived early, ready to go. He still hadn't checked his messages from the night before when Aspen rushed over to him.

"Hey, bro, thanks for calling me back."

"What do you mean?"

"I called you like ten times last night."

"Oh, really? I'm sorry. I was out late with Ugu's dad. What's up?"

"Yeah? How'd that go?"

"Fine. I can tell you about it later. What's so important?"

"Right. So, yesterday, I was sitting down talking with some of the gymnasts from Triplepike Academy. They have a boy named Aspen on their team too. I was sitting in his seat."

"OK. What's so important about all this?"

"Just listen. So, I'm sitting there listening to a funny story about monkeys, which made me think of you, you know, I heart monkeys…"

"Aspen."

"Yes, anyway this cute girl sits down next to me. She asks if I'm Aspen. I say yes. She hands me an envelope and tells me to put it in my jacket. We talk for a few minutes and then I got up to get some more water and she disappeared."

"What do you mean disappeared?"

"She left. Didn't say anything. Just left. I looked around and couldn't find her for a few minutes. Then, I spotted her talking to someone else standing by the dessert table, where you were earlier. I was going to go over there, but I saw her hand someone else the same envelope as she handed me."

"OK. So where are you going with this?"

"Whitfield. I followed her for the rest of the night. I saw her hand out five envelopes plus the one she gave me."

"Did she say who she was?"

"I didn't ask for her name. She just said she was here for the meet."

"OK. Probably someone's date."

"I thought the same thing. But then, after the banquet, on my way back home, I saw her again. She was outside getting onto the ski lift drone suite. Whitfield, it was dark out already."

Whitfield immediately perked up. "Did you say the ski lift drone?"

"Yes."

Now, Whitfield was concerned. "Aspen, was she alone?"

"Yes. I mean I think she was. I didn't see anyone else, but it was dark outside."

Whitfield thought deeply before asking this next question. "Aspen, what was in the envelope?"

Aspen opened his gym bag to show Whitfield. "$20,000!"

Whitfield jumped back. He closed the bag quickly and looked around to make sure no one else saw what was inside Aspen's bag. "No. No. No. This is bad."

"There was also a note."

"What did the note say?"

Aspen handed Whitfield the note. Whitfield cupped his hands around the note to shield it from any nosy spectators. The note simply listed four lines.

Session 2	**PP**	**Br3**
Session 3	**VH**	**Br2**
Session 5	**VH**	**Br2**
Session 6	**PP**	**Br4**

Whitfield studied the note. "Seems to be someone's schedule for the weekend. Maybe it's a substitute?"

"Maybe. But, what's with the money?"

"I don't know, but it's probably not good. I think it would be better if you did not have that money in your bag during the meet. Here, put it in my bag." Aspen discreetly took the envelope with the wad of cash out of his bag and shoved it into Whitfield's gym bag. "No, wait, I can't have it in my bag either. Shoot. OK, you only have two events, so you can keep the bag close to you most of the time. Keep it in your bag."

Aspen took the contents out of Whitfield's bag and shoved it back into his own bag, and zipped it closed.

"OK, we don't have time to deal with this now. We have to get out on the floor. We'll deal with this later."

"Sounds good to me."

****

The competition was about to start. The meet's four-bracket system meant that the four Seven Bridges competitors would be dispersed evenly across the four sets of equipment on each of the eight main competition floors. Event coaches stay on their event floor throughout the competition, while Coach Brockport and Coach Daza float around all eight floors, depending on which athletes were competing at a particular time.

The meet coordinator has the challenging task of scheduling all 896 head-to-head duels, making sure that no single athlete is scheduled to compete on two separate events at the same exact time. As such, scheduling typically begins with slotting the 16 All-Arounders, two from each school, first. The coordinator will then work backward, filling in those gymnasts competing in 7 events, then 6 events, all the way down to single-event specialists.

Head-to-head duels are scheduled in half-hour increments, with each athlete given 15 minutes for warmup and competition. Each session includes four head-to-head duels per event bracket, resulting in All-Arounders having to compete on two separate events during the same half-hour block.

After team introductions and a general warmup period, Whitfield's schedule for Session 01 was as follows:

Session	Time	Event	Bracket	A	B
01	09:30-10:00	VP	3	Whitfield	Timmy
		HO	1	Rondo	Whitfield
01	10:00-10:30	TB	3	Whitfield	Jacelyn
		PC	1	Sofia	Whitfield
01	10:30-11:00	PP	2	Whitfield	Faye
		VH	3	George	Whitfield
01	11:00-11:30	FE	2	Whitfield	Roger
		ET	4	Willamina	Whitfield

All gymnasts would have a thirty-minute rest period during Intermission 1, followed by Session 2, starting promptly at 12:00. Whitfield's first event at his first-ever school meet was Vault-Pegs, one of his favorite events, but also one of the most challenging. Gymnasts start by running 20-25 yards down a long runway, hurdle onto a springboard and using their hands, spring over a vault table. While in the air, the gymnast reaches upward to grab hold of two vertical pegs, hanging freely from a pair of cables affixed to a titanium frame. The peg height may be adjusted from 6-8 feet above the table height, depending on gymnast preference.

Gymnasts complete a series of swing, strength, and hold elements on the first set of pegs before releasing forward onto a second set of pegs, hanging at the same height as the first set. Gymnasts complete further swing, strength, and hold elements, before releasing forward onto a third set of pegs. Gymnasts complete a final set of swing, strength, and hold elements before dismounting onto raised mats.

A floor-level trampoline spans from just beyond the vault table to the raised mats under the third set of pegs. If a gymnast fails to grab hold of the pegs following the first vault attempt, they may use one jump on the trampoline to propel themselves upwards to grab hold of the pegs (0.5-point deduction). If the gymnast cannot grab hold of the pegs after one jump, they may perform a second vault attempt (1.0-point deduction). Once on the pegs, if a gymnast falls, they may use one jump on the trampoline to regain their hold on the pegs (1.0-point deduction per fall).

Whitfield started his first 15-minute block with a few warmup runs on the vault runway. He tested out both the springboard and tramp, even though he had hoped to not use the trampoline at all during his actual routine. During his warmup period, however, Whitfield made use of the tramp to hop up to the hanging pegs.

Whitfield completed a few swings and released to the second set of pegs, where he completed a few more swings. Whitfield dropped to the tramp and sprung up to the third set of pegs, where he completed a few more practice swings, and added in some strength and hold elements. With his remaining warmup time, Whitfield went back over to the runway, and executed a few vaults up to the pegs.

Satisfied that he was ready, Whitfield returned to the vault runway strip and waited for the judges to salute, signaling the start of his official routine. The crowd was awesome, cheering wildly. The video boards around the arena were shining brightly, including the one almost directly in front of him, showing a massive closeup of his face. His nose was over four feet tall. He wished they hadn't shown the pimple that was forming on the right side of his chin; but at least his hair looked good. He'd have to thank his stylist later.

Whitfield closed his eyes and tried to clear his head. He needed to block out all the distractions and just focus on his routine. No more thinking about Dr. Hewitt and the mystery girl taking a trip up the mountain last night. No more thinking about the $20,000 in Aspen's bag. No more thinking about Wilson's "we always win" comment. No more thinking about Ugu.

Ahh Ugu. She's just so perfect. I wish I could see her smile right now. No, snap out of it. Focus. But, her hair. No. Focus. Vault. Pegs. Focus.

Whitfield gave himself a pep talk under his breath. "Nothing can stop me. I'm Whitfield. Nothing can stop me."

Whitfield took a deep breath and opened his eyes just in time to see the judges salute. Whitfield saluted and stepped onto the runway. His gymnastics career had just begun. Whitfield started his run. Nothing was going to stop him...nothing except perhaps the giant beach ball that had escaped from the crowd and had rolled directly onto the runway five feet in front of the springboard.

Whitfield had quickly decided that he would hurdle the ball and keep going, but McKenzie, one of Whitfield's teammates, decided he would reach over to try to poke the ball out of Whitfield's way, but he slipped, and now was lying face down on the runway strip. Now Whitfield had to navigate around the ball, which was still on the runway and his teammate who was scrambling to get up. All of this was too much. Whitfield's valiant attempt to avoid disaster had resulted in his kicking the beach ball right into the first judge's head, knocking off his glasses, stepping on McKenzie's butt, and totally missing the springboard as he dove headfirst over the vault table, missing it completely, and crashing into the protective mats lining the edges on the trampoline.

The mats toppled over and landed on top of Whitfield, covering him almost entirely, with just his ankles and feet showing. Not exactly the start Whitfield, or his teammates were hoping for.

After some careful deliberation, the panel of four judges determined that Whitfield could repeat his first attempt, without deduction, as he never touched the springboard or table, and the obstruction was not directly caused by the competitor himself. Whitfield's coach asked if time could be extended. The judges conferred, and agreed; however, the schedule for remaining events would not be altered, so

Whitfield would still need to complete his next scheduled event within the designated 30-minute duel time.

Whitfield cleaned himself off and tried to refocus. Luckily, he was not injured. He had a scratch on his left arm, but he didn't even notice it. Whitfield stepped back up to the vault runway.

Focus. I am Whitfield. Nothing can stop me.

The judges saluted. Whitfield saluted. This time there were no unexpected obstacles in his way. Whitfield flew down the runway, hurdled onto the springboard, hit the table, and with a superbly executed front handspring half, Whitfield caught the first set of pegs blindly, facing the vault table. Whitfield used his momentum to carry him into a handstand position, lowered into a straight planche, held for three seconds, back up to handstand, held for three, front giant, hold, swing down, release, half twist onto the second set of pegs.

Whitfield continued to perform swing, strength, and hold elements on the second, and then, third set of pegs. He performed a relatively safe half-in half-out dismount, and stuck his landing. The crowd, who moments ago had been laughing at Whitfield's incredible misfortune, was now cheering wildly. What a performance! The judges awarded Whitfield a score of 25.85 (out of a possible 30.00—a few years ago, the WGF set the start value for all routines at 30.00). Whitfield's score ranked ninth best in school history on that event.

Whitfield saluted, let out a giant yell, and joined his teammates and coaches for some high fives and hugs. His elation from successfully completing his first routine would be short lived though as he was already late for his next event, Handstand Obstacle. Whitfield would have to wait until later to see if he won the VP duel.

Fortunately, Whitfield did not need much warmup time for his next event. Handstand Obstacle included a series of 13 elements, all to be completed on the gymnasts' hands, without any other body part touching the floor, for the duration of the routine.

The elements include: S-curve forward; S-curve backward; left side walk; right side walk; full pirouette (4 hand placements); twist (quarter, half, or full); lowering into a straddle position and back up; lower to L-sit and back up; walking up three stairs; walking down three stairs; hopping back and forth over a rod (2-5 inches off the ground based on gymnast preference); 20 shoulder taps (10 with each hand); and inclined step-ladder on parallettes. Most gymnasts need about 4 to 4 1/2 minutes to complete the course, and fall an average of five times. The school record for completing the course with no falls was 1:42. Whitfield's personal best in practice was 2:01, with one fall.

Due to the 'beach ball' delay, Whitfield arrived late and only had 8 minutes left on his warmup and compete clock. Whitfield got right to work. He did some simple handstand exercises, hopping around and really working on taking the arch out of his back. He walked around a bit and practiced some pirouettes, but never touched the course until it was time to perform. Most gymnasts like to get a feel for the course during warmups, but Whitfield felt comfortable enough to begin. He only had 2:30 on the clock when his routine began. He was going to have to run through the course smoothly, if he was going to complete his routine on time. The penalty for an 'incomplete routine' was a 3.0-point deduction and a disciplinary infraction warning. Three warnings, and you were ejected from the competition.

Whitfield ran through the first part of the course cleanly, but stumbled on his half twist. He messed up his hand placement and fell coming out of the twist. Worse still, he only got credit for a quarter twist, as his hand touched slightly before the halfway line. Whitfield recovered nicely, completing the rest of the course with only one more fall. In total, Whitfield completed the course in 2:19, with two falls. Not bad. Score: 20.80.

Whitfield arrived at his third event, Tri-Bars, with 12 minutes still on the clock. Plenty of time to warm up and compete. He was back on schedule and doing well. Flaherty, for her part, was flawless. She was executing every one of her routines superbly, without a single fall, and nary a stumble. Not only was Flaherty the best gymnast in the arena, she was also the most fit, barely breaking a sweat through the first several events.

Aspen's Day 1 performance was one for the record books. Competing in only two events, Aspen's Session 01 schedule looked a lot less daunting than his brother's:

Session	Time	Event	Bracket	A	B
01	09:30-10:00				
01	10:00-10:30				
		TB	4	Flaky	Aspen
01	10:30-11:00				
01	11:00-11:30	PC	2	Aspen	Olivia

Aspen's first event was Tri-Bars, a set of three parallel bars, made of a hard, but pliable, wood-like substance, with each bar set slightly more than shoulder-width apart and supported seven feet above the ground. Gymnasts complete a customized series of swing, hold, twist, and release elements, before dismounting onto mats stacked around the edges of the apparatus. Even though Aspen was competing against Flaky head-to-head, he found himself trying to catch a glimpse of Whitfield's routine over on the Bracket 3 quadrant of the competition floor during the A set. Aspen gave a fist pump after Whitfield stuck his dismount and then returned his focus to the task at hand.

Aspen had started his warmup set the same as always, with a few swings, glide kips, and handstand work. He sprinkled in some easy release moves to get the right feel and then more difficult releases, as he moved from the right set of bars to the left, flying over the center bar. Aspen had been working on an upgrade to a release combo that he saw Morocco perform in practice. Aspen only hit the combo twice before in practice, but his coaches agreed that if Aspen felt comfortable adding it into his routine during the meet, he had their permission to do so. And as of now, Aspen was feeling good. He knew he would go for it in the first routine of his career.

Unlike Whitfield, Aspen's opening performance was free from distraction; that is, aside from the hordes of screaming fans shaking the arena. Aspen mounted the bars and quickly moved into handstand position. Aspen was so light and strong that he was able to pop up from the bars with each swing handstand and release move. Aspen's routine was going smoothly when the moment of truth came. It was decision time. Go for it or play it safe? Aspen went for it. He swung down and popped up high, releasing into a backward double pike, full twist over the center bar, landing in support.

Without hesitation, Aspen swung up to handstand, pirouetted over the center bar, and completed the same skill again, only this time tucked (instead of piked) and stopped on a dime in a perfect handstand position. This combination had never been attempted in competition before and Aspen nailed it on his first try. He added two more release moves and a relatively simple dismount to complete his routine. The crowd went absolutely bonkers! Aspen screamed out in joy and almost forgot to salute the judges, one of which happened to be Professor Marino, Aspen's own house supervisor, before joining his teammates in celebration. Score: 19.27.

Aspen's teammates were outraged. "What! That's not fair." Boos started raining down on the judges. Coach Javier started yelling in the judges' direction and, through his earpiece, urged Coach Brockport to come down to speak to the judges. But even after Coach Brockport had his say, the score remained unchanged. Aspen had lost his first duel matchup. His teammates turned their attention to trying to cheer Aspen up, as tears welled up in his eyes.

Seraphina put her arm around Aspen. "Your routine was awesome, Aspen."

McKenzie agreed, "yeah, those judges are terrible. You should have scored way higher."

Aspen was still sniffling, holding back even more tears. "Thanks. I've got to go get ready for Pommel." Aspen kicked his bag and quickly moved away, walking toward the gymnast elevators to make his way up to the Pommel Clock floor.

Coach Brockport caught up to Aspen and rode the elevator with him. "Aspen. I saw the video. Your routine was good. I had it at a 26.0, maybe even 26.2. You had all the elements. Sometimes these things happen in competition. You can't let one score affect another performance."

Aspen knew his coach was right. Hendricks had drilled that into him a thousand times before. "I know, Coach. I just thought…"

"I know. Let me worry about the scores. You're still my guy. You just go out there and do what we all know you can do on Pommel. I'm going to stay with you for your routine."

"Thanks, but you don't have to. I'm OK. Really." Aspen seemed to regain his composure.

"Are you kidding? I want to be here." The elevator doors opened, and several fans spotted Aspen walking off the elevator started screaming. "You hear that? They are all here supporting you. No matter what happens from here on out, just know that these people love you. Your teammates—they love you, too. You are going to accomplish great things here. This is just Day 1. Every champion has to start somewhere. This is your beginning."

Aspen felt a whole lot better. He really did feel loved. His coach was right. Every champion has to start somewhere, and Aspen was determined to be a champion.

Aspen still had about 20 minutes left before his scheduled warmup. He used that time to visualize his routine, take a few breaths, and calm himself. Aspen reached down to grab his wrist guards out of his bag and…

"Where'd it go? Where's my bag?"

Coach Brockport was standing right beside Aspen. "I don't know. Did you leave it downstairs?"

Aspen was frantic. "I must have."

"Don't worry. I'll get it."

"NO! I'll get it." Aspen remembered it wasn't just his wrist guards inside the bag. He couldn't risk anyone finding what he was storing inside his gym bag. Aspen ran back to the elevators. When he arrived back to where he competed on the Tri-Bars floor, his bag was gone.

"No. No. No. No." He saw some of his teammates cheering on Flaherty over on Bracket 2.

Aspen ran over to them. "Chloe, have you seen my bag?"

"Hi Aspen. Nice routine before. Tough judge though, right?"

"My bag. Have you seen it?"

"No. Why, what's up? Do you need to borrow my grips or something?"

"No. It's just really important that I find my bag."

"OK, don't stress out about it."

"I'm sorry. Really. I don't mean to be rude. I just need to find it, that's all."

Keegan ran up beside Aspen and grabbed him in a big bear hug, lifting Aspen off the ground. "Hey, Aspen! What's up?"

"Have you seen my bag?"

"Yeah, you left if over on Bracket 4. I picked it up and brought it over here. I was going to head up to Pommel in a minute to give it back to you. A bunch of us want to see your routine, especially after you crushed it on Tri-Bars."

Aspen was so relieved. "Oh, thank you. Thank you."

"Hey, no problem, buddy."

Keegan handed Aspen his bag. Aspen thanked him again, grasped the bag tightly in his arms, and ran back toward the elevators. While running, Aspen checked to make sure the envelope was still in there. It was. *Phew.* So were his wrist guards. His warmup clock was about to begin.

After the viral video and the story *Gymnastics Today* ran on Aspen's Pommel Clock prowess and the upcoming article *Pommel Quarterly* teased on the air this morning, Aspen's Pommel Clock routine was the most anticipated event of the entire weekend. With a hundred school meets taking place across the country this weekend, this one gymnast on this one event was the must-see event for fans across the globe. And Aspen did not disappoint.

52 circles. Six handstand helicopter spins. Eight half-turns. Four full turns. Eleven flawless horse transitions. One spectacular ramp travel. And a never-before-seen half-travel backward piked half dismount. 108 seconds to immortality. Score 29.12. Highest Pommel Clock score in history. Not just school history. Aspen's 29.12 was the highest Pommel Clock score ever recorded at any level, anywhere!

****

Session 01 ended with Seven Bridges Academy on top of the team standings:

Seven Bridges Academy	55
Triplepike Academy	50
Pancake Batter Prep	47
Fallburn	39
Muppet Grove	30
Matwood	27
Plank Spring Prep	19
Scapula Research Inst.	7

Seven Bridges won 24 out of their 32 duels, with Flaherty (8-0) and Whitfield (7-1) leading the way. Flaherty earned 19 team points with her stellar performance. Whitfield added 17, with his only loss coming on Tri-Bars, and Aspen chipped in five big points with his huge victory on Pommel Clock. Sydney also added five team points with her huge win on Escalating Tramps. Even though she fell twice, her opponent crashed five times and did not even reach the top before time had expired.

The team met in the locker room during the first intermission. Whitfield was exhausted, but let his coaches know he still had a lot more in the tank. Flaherty was as fresh as ever, and the rest of the team all seemed energized and ready to go. To his credit, Coach Brockport did not make any mention of the scoreboard or call anyone out for sub-par performances.

"We had a nice first session. Get some rest. You have about 25 minutes before we go out there and do it all over again…hopefully, without any beach balls this time." Coach Brockport flashed a smile in Whitfield's direction.

By now, everyone on the team, except for Flaherty, had seen a replay of Whitfield's blooper reel. They all laughed.

"What was that? What happened?"

Keegan stood up and mimicked Whitfield's fall. "Oh, don't worry about it, Flaherty. You'll be seeing it over and over again all week. Whitfield thought he was surfing on the beach. Hey, McKenzie, how's your butt?"

The team all laughed again. Flaherty looked at Whitfield for answers.

"Uhh…I can't explain it. You'll just have to see it for yourself."

Flaherty let it go and just closed her eyes to relax. Whitfield did the same thing. Aspen farted.

It was loud.

"Excuse me." The team all laughed again. Several others made similar sounds. Not all the sounds came from their mouths.

The coaches met in their office as the athletes rested.

With five minutes to go, the coaches announced that no changes would be made for Session 2, but that Vail, Reid, Diego, and Kylie should prepare for Session 3. Soon after, the team members all got loose and walked back out onto the competition floor. The cheerleaders and dance squads were still performing for the sold-out crowd when Whitfield and Flaherty arrived at their first event.

Whitfield continued with his self-motivating pep talks. *OK. Focus. I am Whitfield. Nothing can stop me.*

Session 2 was under way. Seven Bridges increased their lead on the competition by putting up another 57 team points. Aspen repeated his full Pommel Clock routine, scoring a 29.00, showing everyone that his Session 1 routine was no fluke. Flaherty continued her brilliance and Whitfield remained steady, as usual. Both All-Arounders swept their duels, earning a combined 40 points for the team. The only hiccup came on Tri-Bars, as both Whitfield and Aspen continued to earn low scores, despite solid routines.

As Sessions 3 and 4 rolled on, Whitfield was starting to lose some of his sharpness. He continued earning team points, but his scores slipped some. That's what happens after completing 32 routines over ten hours. Even Flaherty showed some signs of fatigue, as she posted her lowest scores of the day on six out of eight events during the final session of Day 1.

Aspen continued his strong overall performance, despite registering his first fall on Pommel Clock, during Session 3. He still earned his team 5 points as his opponent did not have a good showing. All in all, Seven Bridges Academy ended Day 1 with a commanding 19-point lead on the competition.

Aspen nearly had to drag Whitfield up to the Outer Loop after the team meeting following Session 4. Lack of sleep from the night before was really starting to catch up with Whitfield. The Outer Loop was still jam-packed at 20:00. For many, the festivities were just getting started. More concerts. More tailgating. More of everything, as the parties would likely continue deep into the night and continue on into the morning. Highlights from the meet continued to play on the video boards outside Arlington Gymnastics Center and around the Outer Loop, and Whitfield caught a glimpse of his beach ball incident.

"Aww, man. That video is going to be played forever, isn't it? I can't believe I hit that judge with the ball."

"Probably. Hey, next time, maybe you can direct that kick to Professor Marino. What was his deal today? He kept giving me low scores."

"I know. Me too."

"Yeah. I crushed my first routine and I only got a 19.27."

"Really? I saw your score and I figured you just fell…a couple times."

"Nope. I nailed it. He just doesn't like us, I guess."

"Nah. It's probably something else. Don't worry about it, Aspen. You still did great. We'll get 'em tomorrow."

Whitfield had really wanted to see Ugu tonight, but decided it would be better to get some rest. "Aspen, can you just tell Ugu that I'll catch up with her tomorrow?"

"Sure. I know she'll understand. She's good like that."

"Thanks."

"What should I do about the money?"

"Oh, right. Keep it tucked away in your room somewhere. Do not bring it to the meet tomorrow. We'll tell Sir Arlington about it on Monday."

"Are you sure you want to wait that long?"

"Aspen, I'm sorry. I'm just too tired right now."

"I understand. Get some sleep, Whitfield. I'll see you tomorrow."

"Thanks. Good night, Aspen."

"Good night. And hey, you did great today."

"Thanks, bro. You were awesome."

They hugged each other and Whitfield went down Slide 06-WU and went straight to bed, without even eating dinner. Aspen wasn't as exhausted, having competed in just two events all day. Sure, it was eight routines, but Aspen had unlimited energy. He couldn't wait to be an All-Arounder someday. But, for now, Aspen knew the smart thing to do was return home, eat dinner, and get some rest. He started to walk around the crowded Outer Loop toward his mansion when he saw Ugu coming from the other direction. She was carrying a picnic basket.

"Hey, Ugu."

"Aspen! Hi!" Ugu was very happy to see Aspen and gave him a big hug. "You were outstanding today. I am so proud of you."

"Thanks."

"Where's Whitfield? I thought we were all eating together."

"Oh, he was exhausted, and just wanted to get some sleep. I just dropped him off."

Ugu was a little disappointed, but didn't show it. She had really wanted to give Whitfield a hug following his amazing performance. "Oh, I understand. He did have a long day."

"I can still eat though."

"Great! Let's head home."

Ugu and Aspen started to head home when Aspen spotted the strange girl from last night standing in the distance in the Outer Loop. "Oh hey, that's the girl I was talking to last night. Hi!"

Off in the distance, the strange girl from last night could be seen pointing at Aspen and talking to another boy. "That's him."

Ugu looked up and saw the girl.

"Aspen. We need to get out of here. Now!"

Chapter 14
First Meet—Day 2

Aspen and Ugu were almost out of breath from running in the Outer Loop, away from the mystery girl and her friend. The loop was crowded, so they used Ugu's tracker to unlock a nearby stairway down to the Inner Loop. Ugu and Aspen raced around the Inner Loop, pausing only for a second when they heard the door they had just come through open again.

"Shoot. She must have forged a tracker."

"What? Why are we running?"

"Aspen, do you know who that is?"

"She never told me her name, but I met her at the banquet last night."

"She was there? Oh no, this isn't good. Why would she be there?"

"She gave me this envelope." Aspen took out the envelope and Ugu immediately recognized it as a bribe.

"You took it?"

"I didn't know what it was. She told me to just put it in my pocket. I didn't realize what it was until I got home. I called Whitfield, but he was out with your dad. Who is she?"

"I'll tell you later. First, we need to get to Sir Arlington." Ugu and Aspen ran through the Inner Loop as fast as they could toward the AMQE campus. The main building was locked and Ugu's tracker didn't work to unlock it. "Maybe we can use your tracker. You're taking a math class this term, right? It might open for you."

Aspen fumbled for his tracker.

"Hurry up. They are almost here." Aspen finally reached his tracker and it worked. The door opened. Ugu and Aspen each grabbed hold of the zip-lines designated for the library and were on their way. They each heard some banging at the door behind them. Luckily, the forged tracker did not unlock the academic buildings. "Let's hope Sir Arlington is still here. He has to know what's going on."

Ugu and Aspen arrived at the AMQE library and headed straight downstairs to Sir Arlington's office and knocked three times. Almost immediately, the door opened. Aspen and Ugu stepped inside and the door closed swiftly. Sir Arlington calmly walked out of his study chambers to greet them. "Ugu. Aspen. To what do I owe this most unexpected visit?"

"Sir. Isadora's Gang is here."

Sir Arlington looked deeply concerned. "Are you sure?"

"Yes. I just saw Gisele in the Outer Loop. She made contact with Aspen yesterday, and spotted him again tonight. She was just chasing after us."

"I see. Come inside. Tell me everything." Sir Arlington gave a quick look down the hallway before shutting the door. Aspen proceeded to tell Sir Arlington and Ugu everything about his interaction with the mystery girl from last night. "And you say there were other envelopes just like this one?"

"Yes. Five others, I think. Maybe six."

Ugu did not wait for Sir Arlington to ask the question. "Do you know who else she gave the envelopes to?"

"Not really."

Sir Arlington attempted to bring calm to the situation. "Not to worry. I will be able to comb through the surveillance records."

"Sir, I didn't realize there were cameras in Flaxen Hall?"

"Ahh, young Ugu. That's because you've only taken *CBT II* and are not yet all-knowing. Might I suggest another few terms of *CBT* courses?"

Ugu recognized that Sir Arlington was right and smiled. "Yes, sir."

"Am I in trouble?"

"Oh, not at all, my dear Aspen."

"Well, what's going on?"

"Ugu? You can feel free to share."

Ugu appreciated Sir Arlington's trust. "Sure. Isadora's Gang is really big into gambling."

Aspen remembered hearing about the gang in his *Underground Economics* class. "But I thought gambling was legal."

"It is. But, they do more than just gamble. They try to affect the outcome by bribing athletes. That's probably what was going on here with your envelope. Gisele probably thought you were the Aspen from Triplepike Academy. You said you were sitting in his seat when Gisele approached you, right?"

"Right."

"You see this note? I'll bet Aspen, I mean, the other Aspen, was scheduled to compete in the events listed here at these exact times."

Sir Arlington checked the master meet schedule. "Would you look at that. It appears that is indeed correct."

"I knew it. The other Aspen was supposed to take a fall on these events. When he didn't, the gang got suspicious. That's when Gisele told her boss that she may have given the money to the wrong person. When she spotted you, she was going to ask, or worse, take, the money back to correct her error from last night. Look here, two of the sessions where the other Aspen is supposed to fall are scheduled for tomorrow."

"Wow! You are really smart. How do you know all this?"

"Thank you. During my internship with the WGF last year, we worked on breaking up Isadora's Gang. We, I mean WGF Law Enforcement, arrested Isadora, Laurel, Gimlet, and a few of her other goons. I actually found a key piece of evidence to help bring them in."

"I thought you only worked on schedules and meet bids?"

"I'm versatile."

Sir Arlington agreed, "yes, she is. Clever student. I am troubled by something though."

Aspen and Ugu both asked at the same time, "what's that, sir?"

"Well, we know Gisele wouldn't be acting alone."

"She wasn't. Aspen and I saw someone with her in the Outer Loop."

Sir Arlington pulled up footage from the banquet. "You are correct. No, she wasn't acting alone. She had a partner. Was this the young lad you saw in the Outer Loop earlier?" Sir Arlington pointed to an image of a boy passing out similar-looking envelopes at the banquet.

"Yes, that's him."

"And Aspen? You said you saw her taking a ski lift drone suite up the mountain last night?"

"Yes, sir. After the party."

With a few more keystrokes, Sir Arlington was able to find the footage of Gisele ascending the mountain. Five minutes later, footage appeared of her partner ascending the same mountain. Sir Arlington quickly scanned footage from the previous and next 30 minutes and found no other movement up or down the mountain.

"I do not think they were acting alone. They are working for someone. I'll place a call into Chipwood Prison. I want to talk with Isadora myself. See if she's involved. As for you two—Aspen, you need to get some rest. Another big day tomorrow. Ugu, call your security team. Have them meet Aspen upstairs in the Inner Loop. They can escort him home through the Outer Loop slides. It's busy up there, but I do not think he'll be in any danger."

"Yes, sir."

Just then, Sir Arlington had another thought. "Ugu."

"Yes sir?"

"Tell them to bring a change of clothes for you."

"Sir?"

"Better still…Aspen, who is your chief of security?"

"Francesca."

"Ugu, have Francesca swing by the galleria. Tell her to pick up a rush order for you. I'm sending it over now. Tell Francesca to simply drop it off in my mail slot. And after that, please pull these books from the library and bring them to me?" Sir Arlington handed Ugu a slip of paper with three book titles.

Ugu took the slip of paper and scanned the titles. She was confused, but did not question her orders. "Yes, sir." Ugu went into the hallway to call Francesca and put Sir Arlington's plan, whatever it was, into motion. Sir Arlington stayed with Aspen for another minute.

"Sir, I'm a little scared."

"My, yes, Aspen, I'm sure you are. I understand how you feel. A lot has happened today. I saw your Pommel Clock routine. A new record, I believe. Impressive!"

"Thank you, sir. But I know what you're doing. You're just trying to change the subject."

"Yes. I am."

"Is this the part where you tell me to go home, go to sleep, and not to worry about any of this?"

"Well, how about two of those three?"

"Which two?"

"I am going to tell you to go home. I am going to tell you to not worry about any of this. Trust me, you are unlikely to ever see Gisele again. I have flagged both her and her partner. They will not step foot onto campus again. OK?"

"Good. That's comforting. But, wait, does that mean you're not going to tell me to go to sleep?"

"Heavens no! You're young and have the energy of a thousand suns. I have a project for you. Two, actually."

Aspen was not expecting this. He immediately perked up. "Really? What are they?"

"I noticed on your entrance application that you have a fond interest in solving puzzles and 'stopping bad people from doing bad things', if I recall correctly."

"Yes, sir." Aspen was impressed that Sir Arlington actually read through his application himself, and had actually remembered what was written.

"Well, I happen to think there might be some bad people out there planning to do some very bad things. I need you to help me with something." Before Sir Arlington could continue, Ugu arrived back in his chambers carrying three books, as requested. "Ahh. Perfect timing. Aspen, this is a book on Bank Scanning and Safety Protocols. The bills in your envelope were minted over seven years ago, but were crisp, which means they did not change hands often. I want to know which banks held these particular bills and when they were withdrawn."

Ugu felt the need to interject, "sir. The banks have scanners that keep track of all that. Each serial number is scanned with every transaction. You can just ask for the bank records, or I can hack…"

"Yes, yes, my dear Ugu, I know all that. But I would like to obtain this information without alerting the banks. Aspen, I'm not asking you to recreate the bank's scanning software, but with the information held in this book and your impressive computer coding skills and knack for solving problems, I think you may be able to discern from where these bills originated, and where they may have been stored. That would give us a nice head start in our investigation."

Aspen was unsure of exactly how he would solve this particular puzzle, but didn't want to disappoint Sir Arlington. "OK. I think I may be able to do that."

"Good."

"You said there was a second project?"

"Ahh, yes. I have a mystery novel here by one of my favorite authors, Miyagi White. Have you heard of him?"

Aspen's eyes lit up. "Yes! He writes a series of brain teasers and crypto-puzzles for kids. I always like solving them."

"Wonderful. Then this should be enjoyable for you. In White's novels, he always introduces a new puzzle for the reader to figure out on their own. It's usually the key the main protagonist uses to help solve the mystery. It's become one of my favorite pastimes on a quiet Sunday evening—attempting to solve the puzzle before the end of the novel. But, this latest novel has me befuddled. I've been working on it for weeks now, and can't seem to crack it. I was hoping a smart guy like you might offer some assistance?"

Aspen felt incredible that Sir Arlington would come to him for help. "Wow. Sure. I'd love to help. This sounds great."

"Smashing! Here, take the novel and perhaps this other, rather heavy, book may offer some insights as well."

Aspen immediately recognized the other book. "Hey, I think my brother has that book. He's taking *Intermediate Cryptography* this term."

"Yes, our very own Dr. Hewitt authored this textbook on cryptanalysis. I thought it might offer some insights into the puzzle you are about to solve. Happy hunting!"

"Thanks!" Aspen picked up his bag and carried the three books with him as he got up to leave Sir Arlington's chambers. He was smiling, when a curious thought came to mind. "Sir. What does this novel have to do with the money or Isadora's Gang?"

Sir Arlington smiled. "Oh, just a hunch." Aspen knew Sir Arlington wasn't telling him something, but he was excited to get started, nonetheless. "Now, head upstairs to the Inner Loop. Your security team should be there waiting for you."

Ugu confirmed, "yes, they are."

As Aspen walked past Ugu, he just kept staring at the covers of the three books in his arms. "And Aspen." Sir Arlington waited for Aspen to turn around and make eye contact. "You have my permission to use any means necessary to solve this puzzle. Any means necessary."

Aspen wasn't sure why Sir Arlington had emphasized that last part, but didn't question it. "OK. Thanks."

Ugu stepped forward to open the door for Aspen. "Aspen, try not to stay up past 24:00. It's really important that you do well tomorrow. We're counting on you." Ugu gave Aspen a kiss on the cheek and said good night. It took Ugu's reminder to snap Aspen's mind back into the here and now.

"Right. I'll make sure to get some sleep. Thanks again." Aspen rushed out of the room and climbed upstairs to the Inner Loop where his security team was waiting.

Back in Sir Arlington's office, Ugu awaited further instructions. "Sir, what would you like me to do?"

Sir Arlington stepped behind his desk, unlocked his mail deposit and retrieved the package awaiting him. "Here. Change into these clothes. I'm sending you up the mountaintop to the lodge…right after you break into young Jonathan's room."

"Sir?"

****

Sunday. Whitfield woke up early and, although a bit sore from yesterday, felt refreshed...and hungry. He went into the kitchen and snacked on some of the few remaining leftover goodies from Keegan's birthday delivery, while he waited for his chef to finish making breakfast. Twenty minutes later, Whitfield was well-fed and ready to go. Before leaving to go to the gymnastics center, he remembered to check his messages. Oh boy, he had 72 messages. *Oh, come on. This is ridiculous.*

Most of the messages were of the simple 'congratulations' variety. He decided he would get back to them later. He did, however, read all four messages from Ugu.

19:40: *Congratulations! You did awesome. I am so proud of you. I am coming over now, with dinner.*

"Aww...that's sweet. Oh no, she brought dinner, and I missed it. I am such a dunderhead."

19:42: Image: Beach Ball *Hehehe...I couldn't resist.*

"Very funny."

01:27: *Hey sweetie. I just saw the news report that Tommy Chen is pulling out of the competition. Hurt back. Bad break. I know you wanted to go H2H with him. Maybe next time.*

"Oh no. That stinks. I really wanted to beat him today. I wonder what happened."

02:40: *Good Luck today! I'll be thinking of you. Remember—keep your security team with you ALL day.*

"Aww...thanks for reminding me. Doesn't she ever sleep?"

With his security detail accompanying him, Whitfield walked to Arlington Gymnastics Center. Even though he was the first gymnast to arrive, he immediately started stretching and loosening up. He felt good, and didn't want to tighten up today, like he did toward the end of Day 1. Other gymnasts started to filter into the gymnastics center. Today, it was Aspen's turn to arrive looking a little more tired than he should. "Hey, bro, what's up?"

Aspen let out a big yawn before responding. "Hi Whitfield. I'm tired. I stayed up until 02:00."

"What? Why? You didn't go to any of the parties, did you? Coach warned us about that."

"No, nothing like that. I was reading."

"Reading? For class?"

"No. Sir Arlington gave me some reading to do."

"Sir Arlington? When?"

"Last night."

"Why were you with Sir Arlington last night?"

"Because we were being chased."

"Who's we?"

"Ugu and I."

"Ugu? Who was chasing you?"

"Isadora's Gang."

"WHAT?"

"Whitfield, look, it's too early for all these questions. I need to warm up."

Whitfield looked completed befuddled, and concerned. "What is going on here?"

"I'll tell you all about it later."

"Are you in trouble? Where's Ugu?"

"I'm not in trouble. I don't know where Ugu is. She didn't come home last night."

"WHAT?"

"Whitfield. Don't worry about it. I'm sure she's safe."

"How can you be sure?"

Just as Whitfield was about to lose his mind worrying about Ugu, he felt a friendly tap on his shoulder. "Because I'm right behind you."

Whitfield turned around and a rush of relief washed over him. "Ugu!" Whitfield gave Ugu a big hug. "Are you OK?"

"Yes. I figured you might be a little concerned about me, so I wanted to stop by and show you that I am, in fact, OK."

"Phew, I am so relieved. What happened last night?"

"It's a long story, and I will tell you all about it tonight…at dinner?"

Whitfield was just so relieved to see Ugu. "You got it. I am never going to bed early again."

"See all the stuff you miss when you break a date with me?" Ugu shoved a friendly elbow in Whitfield's side.

"What? Wait. That was a date? I'm so sorry. I…"

"No, of course not. I'm just teasing you. Look, go out there and be great today. I'm going to be watching from my dad's suite. I think you made a good impression on him."

"Really? So, all of that clumsiness worked?"

"No. I'm just kidding. He doesn't like you at all." Ugu was really starting to enjoy teasing Whitfield.

"Really?"

Ugu simply shrugged. "Hmm…not sure."

"Where were you last night? You messaged me really late."

"Oh, I was out all night on a secret mission to save Seven Bridges Academy. You know, breaking into houses, climbing mountains, all that stuff."

"No, really."

Ugu flashed her most innocent smile. "You think I'm lying to you?"

"I don't know. I can't tell when you're lying."

"Hmm. You need to pay more attention in class. Look for the clues." Ugu gave Whitfield a quick kiss on the cheek and started toward her seat.

"Does your dad really not like me?"

Ugu didn't bother turning around. "Look for the clues."

Whitfield stared at her as she continued walking away. Aspen noticed Whitfield's eyes. "Uhh, bro. I do not think the clues she's talking about are on her butt."

"Huh? What? No, I wasn't staring at her butt."

Keegan overheard the word 'butt' and couldn't help himself. He put his arm around Whitfield. "Whose butt are we staring at?"

Whitfield shook his head. "No one's."

"Too bad. Because I was just staring at that those two girls over there." Keegan looked over toward the southwest corner of the gym and made eye contact with two members of the Muppet Grove dance team. "Whitfield, you interested?"

Whitfield followed Keegan's eyes and gave a quick glance in their direction before turning away. "No thanks."

"Aspen? How about you?"

"Keegan. I'm 10."

"That's OK. You can still come over and make a new friend."

"That's OK. I'm going to head over to the floor and warm up."

"OK. Suit yourself. I'll just have to make two new friends." Keegan went over to talk with the dancers. Whitfield and Aspen went onto the floor to stretch.

****

Session 5 started with Whitfield on Escalating Tramps and Flaherty on Pommel Clock. Aspen's first routine wasn't until the third duel period, and then he would go back-to-back with Tri-Bars and Pommel Clock.

The crowd arrived a little later than the day before, undoubtedly a little worn down from two nights of excessive partying, but was already at full throat by the time Flaherty became just the fourth gymnast at this meet to make it all the way around the Pommel Clock, joining her two teammates, Aspen and Whitfield, and Tommy Chen, who had accomplished the feat in Session 4 the day before.

Flaherty's routine wasn't as flashy as Aspen's, but she still earned a 25.76, and five team points for her effort. Whitfield also earned five team points with his effort on Escalating Tramps, successfully ascending to the top of the giant spiral, hitting all 28 tramps just once each, without a single fall, and managed to complete all seven distinct element groups with ease. Whitfield's 27.90 placed him near the top of the weekend's ET leaderboard.

Despite some early sluggishness during warmups, Aspen nailed his Tri-Bars routine and came close to making it all the way around the Pommel Clock again in Session 5. During the day's first intermission, Coach Brockport approached Aspen and asked if he would be able to take Ryne's spot on Parallel Planks in Session 6. Ryne had been struggling on the apparatus throughout the first five sessions, and Coach thought a change was in order.

"What do you say, Aspen? Think you're up for it?"

Aspen returned an enthusiastic, "absolutely!"

The motivation underlying this particular substitution was driven partially by Ryne's performance and partially by Aspen's rising celebrity status. Ryne's performance was poor, there was no denying that. He needed to be removed from the lineup, but Hutchison had performed marginally better than Aspen on Parallel Planks in practice. He was the next best option to replace Ryne. Instead, Coach Brockport decided to give the media what they wanted, and what they all wanted was very clear. They wanted more Aspen.

The meet coordinator was easily able to slot Aspen into Ryne's spot on the schedule. Despite already scheduled for two other events in Session 6, Aspen had an open spot in his schedule where Ryne had been scheduled to compete. Now, that spot was Aspen's. Aspen was slotted into Bracket 4, Competitor B, which meant he would compete second in his duel. His competitor was none other than Aspen from Triplepike Academy. Triplepike's Aspen had a great Day 1, but SBA's Aspen was unsure whether Isadora's Gang had finally caught up with him.

Aspen's question was answered in short order, as his counterpart posted a personal best 24.77, without any falls, on Parallel Planks. In order for SBA's Aspen to win the duel, Whitfield's brother was going to have to nail his routine and include his front pike half earlier in his routine than he would have preferred. It was going to be challenging, but Aspen was confident he could do it.

Parallel Planks consists of five raised planks, each four-and-a-half inches wide, spaced three-and-a-half feet apart from each other, each standing between 5-7 feet above the ground. Gymnasts must perform a series of acrobatic skills, traveling up and down each plank, and leap, jump, or hop from one plank to the next, without falling. Each fall counts as a 1.0-point deduction. In order, from the first plank to the last, the official heights are 6-feet, 7-feet, 6-feet, 5-feet, and 7-feet, meaning gymnasts must navigate one-foot drops and one foot rises for the first three plank transitions and a two-foot rise on their transition to the final plank. Gymnasts then dismount onto mats.

Aspen saluted the judges and mounted the first plank by hitting the springboard, placing his hands on the plank and moving right into a series of three flairs and two handstand helicopter spins while traveling up and down the plank before his feet ever touched. The crowd went crazy! Feeding off the crowd's energy, Aspen stuck a front pike half transition to Plank 2 and continued to deliver oohs and aahs to the packed crowd with every twist, leap, and layout. Aspen stumbled briefly on his final transition, but stuck his triple double dismount. Score 26.82.

As Aspen was awaiting his score, he walked over to his competition and congratulated him on his routine.

"Hey, Aspen. You had a great routine."

"Thanks. You too. That was a sick dismount."

"Thanks. I'm surprised I stuck it. Hey, didn't I see you at the banquet?"

"Yeah. I think you were sitting in my seat."

"Oh. Sorry about that."

"Don't be. I was happy to get up anyway."

"You're having a really good meet."

"Thanks. I didn't even think I was going to compete this much."

"Why?"

"Oh, no reason." Triplepike's Aspen realized that he probably shouldn't say what he was thinking. "I was just expecting to sit, that's all."

Aspen picked up on his counterpart's hesitation. "Oh, you don't usually compete?"

"Oh, no, I do. It's not that. It's just…look, I'm not supposed to say anything, but I was told to expect something at the banquet and if I got it that would probably mean I would not compete…or maybe even something else."

Aspen decided to just go for it. "What, like fall on purpose?"

Triplepike's Aspen looked surprised. "How did you know? Did you get a secret message too?"

Aspen needed to think quickly. "Uhh…yeah, mine was a call though. Strange voice. Didn't know who it was from. I wish I received a digital message. Then I would be able to see who it came from."

"No, that didn't work. I tried to trace it, but it was encrypted."

"Do you still have it?"

"No. The message said to delete it right away. I was scared so I did. I was supposed to get an envelope at the banquet, but it never came. Hey, if you got a call, how come you didn't fall today?"

"Oh, same thing. No one showed up at the banquet."

"That's funny. I guess they didn't need us after all. Probably some gambling thing. I'm just glad that's over. I hate when I have to fall on purpose."

"Has that happened to you before?"

"Yeah. Twice last year. I didn't feel good about it, but it was nice having the money." Just then, Aspen's score was announced. The cheering crowd made it hard to hear. "Hey, congratulations on the win. You deserved it."

"Thanks. You're a really good gymnast. Hope to see you again."

"Me too."

With that, the two Aspens shook hands and Whitfield's brother left to join his team members in the locker room for the fifth, and final, intermission of the weekend. Seven Bridges Academy was well ahead in the standings, and Coach Brockport took the opportunity to put in all of his remaining substitutes. Dakota and Pryce were thrilled. As first-years, neither thought they would see any action this meet. The whole team seemed really happy for them. Even Keegan, who was being replaced on Handstand Obstacle, cheered wildly for the substitutes.

"Go get 'em, Dakota. I'm your biggest fan."

Bailey was right there with Keegan, cheering on the substitutes. "Yeah, Dakota, you got this. You too, Pryce."

With a renewed energy going into the final session, SBA's team charged out of the locker room. Coach Daza stopped Flaherty, Whitfield, and Aspen for a quick word.

"How are you guys feeling?"

They all responded, "fine, coach."

"Great. Now even though we've all but sewn up first place, we still need the three of you to perform well. A lot of side action is still riding on you two finishing 1-2 in the All-Around." Whitfield looked concerned. "Either order is fine. Whitfield, don't worry. Second place is still good."

"Phew. You got me worried, coach." Whitfield was trailing Flaherty by over 22 points.

Coach Daza continued, "Flaherty, we do have some bets on your floor routine. Just do what you do. The world will be watching. Aspen, some heavy action came in last night, and throughout the day today, on your Pommel Clock. Now, I know you missed on both your attempts today, but we need you to pull it together here for your final routine."

"No problem, coach. I can do it. I'll be focused." Aspen was always confident on Pommel Clock.

"Good. That's why we're pulling you from Tri-Bars for this session."

Aspen looked hurt. "But, coach, I can handle it. It's Professor Marino. He just doesn't like me." Aspen was still performing well on Tri-Bars, but like yesterday, continued receiving low scores from Judge Marino.

"I know you can handle it. You've had a wonderful weekend on Tri-Bars. You're still our starter. And, I'm really considering telling Coach Brockport to start you on Tri-Bars and Planks next meet. But, for now, we just really need you to focus on Pommel."

Aspen was disappointed, but accepted the lineup change. "I understand. Can I still do Planks this session?"

"I'd really like to see what Hutchison can do on Planks. But, you're still my guy."

Again, Aspen was disappointed. He hung his head low. "OK. I understand."

Whitfield was standing quietly nearby, but felt the urge to stand up for his brother. "Coach, Aspen worked really hard for this. Does he really have to sit out both events?"

Flaherty didn't want Whitfield drawing the ire of Coach Daza, or especially Coach Brockport, so quickly stepped in. "Whitfield, Coach Brockport knows what he's doing."

Coach Daza stood by the decision, "trust me. This is what's best for everyone." Whitfield relented, "yes sir."

Whitfield, Aspen, and Flaherty walked out to their respective events. Whitfield and Flaherty were scheduled to compete right away. Aspen still had another hour before the world would be watching his final Pommel Clock routine of opening weekend.

Session 7 was always the most highly anticipated session of any meet. It was often the time when team titles were decided, All-Around and event champions were crowned, and all final bets were settled. Even though the team title and most event champions were already decided heading into this final session, there was still a lot of excitement left for the fans. The two most anticipated routines of the final session were Aspen's Pommel Clock and Flaherty's Floor Exercise, which the meet coordinator intentionally scheduled last, to bring in the highest expected audience, worldwide. With Aspen's Pommel Clock routine scheduled in the penultimate duel time slot, ratings peaked 30 minutes earlier than expected, bringing in additional millions in broadcasting revenues.

While the official pot for the Precious Gems meet started the weekend just shy of $99.6 billion in precious gems and related mining rights, after all reported side bets were included, the total pot had grown to $114.2 billion before new bets were cut off at the start of Session 7. It was estimated that an additional $24 billion in unreported side bets and roughly $37 billion in underground gambling was to change hands over the course of the weekend. Of that amount, $4.2 billion, at a minimum, was about to change hands in the next 100 seconds or so, depending upon whether Aspen could successfully complete his Pommel Clock routine, for the fifth time this weekend.

Aspen stepped up to the first pommel. Closed his eyes. Visualized his routine. Let out some gas. Opened his eyes. Saluted. And was off. 105 seconds later, Seven Bridges Academy was at least $4.2 billion richer. Aspen set another new record. Score: 29.25.

Only one time slot remained. Flaherty was about to perform her floor routine. Despite her personal declaration of Vault-Pegs being her favorite event, Flaherty's floor routine was utterly magnificent, as if she was sent by heaven and angels had choreographed her every movement. Such grace. Such beauty. Her lines. Her toes always perfectly pointed. Despite being one of the most powerful gymnasts at the meet, her movements all appeared effortless. A goddess, in a leotard.

Floor Exercise spans two levels. The bottom level consists of a 50ft x 50ft spring floor, with four embedded trampolines, one located in each of the four quadrants. The second level, located 14 feet above the bottom level, contains a 50ft x 50ft spring floor with four large triangles cut out. The resulting structure includes an eight-foot-wide perimeter border and two five-foot wide diagonal strips. Gymnasts perform a choreographed sequence of acrobatic and non-acrobatic elements, using the embedded tramps to alternate levels.

Ever since Flaherty's Floor Exercise at last year's Individual Championships, she has been a media darling. As such, Seven Bridges Academy was able to increase their broadcasting rates above last year, even with Gabe turning pro and no longer competing on the school team. Flaherty is a bona fide superstar. And, now, with the addition of Aspen and Whitfield, SBA would surely continue to bring in high viewership for all their meets.

Flaherty wowed the crowd one final time with one high-flying tumbling pass after another. Triple-doubles. Triple-triples. Triple turns with one leg held high in split position. Straddle jumps with double turns. Double salto backward straight with triple twist. Double layout with full twist in second salto. Double full-in double full-out. Quadruple back. Flaherty's routine had it all.

Score: 28.95. Another five team points. After all was said and done, Seven Bridges Academy concluded the meet with another team title.

Final standings:

Seven Bridges Academy	337
Triplepike Academy	296
Fallburn	277
Pancake Batter Prep	251
Muppet Grove	198
Plank Spring Prep	121
Matwood	119
Scapula Research Inst.	52

Flaherty (52-4) won the All-Around title. Whitfield (48-8) finished second. Aspen (11-3), despite only completing 14 routines, contributed the third most points to the team total (28). Flaherty won event titles on Floor Exercise; Vault-Pegs; VH-Bars; and Parallel Planks. Whitfield won the Handstand Obstacle title and Aspen won the Pommel Clock title.

After the meet, many of the gymnasts and coaches gathered on the first level of the main competition floor. Whitfield was busy shaking hands and receiving congratulations, when he spotted Tommy Chen.

"Hey, Tommy. I'm Whitfield, nice to meet you."

The two competitors shook hands.

"Hey, Whitfield. Congrats on a nice meet."

"Thanks. Yeah, sorry you had to pull out of the meet. I was looking forward to our duel today."

"Yeah. Me too. Sorry about that. My knee was acting up."

"I thought it your back?"

Tommy realized he had made a mistake. "Oh, that's right. Umm…first it was my back last night. But then my knee started hurting more today."

Whitfield saw it. No eye contact. Looking down. Facial tic. Unusual rise in tone. Excessive fidgeting. Whitfield spotted the clues. Tommy was lying.

"Well, hey, I just wanted to say hi. Thanks for coming anyway. Hope your back, and knee, feel better soon."

"Yeah, thanks. Hope to see you again soon."

Whitfield started to walk away, but stopped short, when Tommy opened his bag to put his grips away. There, inside Tommy's bag, tucked away, was the same envelope Aspen received at the banquet and carried around in his own bag all day yesterday. What did it all mean? *It has to mean something, right?*

Whitfield went back to the locker room to change, shower, and get dressed. The first meet was over. Whitfield was exhausted, but there was no way he was going to skip out on another dinner with Ugu. *Oh, man. What if her dad is staying for dinner? It doesn't matter. I just want to see her.*

"Hey, bro. We did it. We won!" Aspen came over and gave his brother a huge hug.

"That's right. So proud of you, little bro."

Wilson walked by Whitfield's locker. "See, buddy. I told you we always win." Whitfield didn't think anything of it, and just enjoyed the moment. They won. That's all that mattered.

After they all showered and changed, the team had to meet with the media. Since everyone contributed, everyone had at least one reporter asking them questions, but the largest stable of reporters found their way to Flaherty, Whitfield, and Aspen. For the next hour, the trio answered questions about their performance, goals for the season, training regimens, and a host of other questions. A reporter even asked Whitfield if he was currently dating anyone.

Flaherty was quick to seize the moment, and jumped in to answer. "Yes. We have been dating each other for over a month now. I just can't pry myself away from those baby blue eyes of his." Flaherty playfully wrapped her arms around Whitfield's neck. Ugu wasn't the only one who enjoyed teasing Whitfield. The reporters all seemed to get a laugh, and no one took Flaherty's comments seriously.

Whitfield took the playfulness in stride. "Thanks, Flaherty."

"No problem…Honey Bear."

Whitfield was startled. He quietly spoke in Flaherty's ear. "Honey Bear? How did you…she really does tell you everything."

"Relax. I was looking over your shoulder as you checked your messages. If she calls you Honey Bear, what's your pet name for her?"

Whitfield shot a quick glance toward the reporters, before turning back toward Flaherty. "We are not doing this here."

Flaherty unwrapped her arms from Whitfield's neck. "Suit yourself. I'll find out later." The media circus abated, and the team members were free to go. Whitfield, Aspen, and Flaherty all met up with Ugu, whose dad left shortly after the meet. The four friends all hugged.

"My dad said he was sorry he couldn't stay for dinner. He'll be back for Parents and Alumni Week, though."

"Does he really not like me?"

Ugu laughed. "Well, you did tell him you kissed his daughter and wear underwear on your head."

"Well, not at the same time. Now, that would be grounds to dislike me."

They all laughed and continued to walk out of Arlington Gymnastics Center to find a place on campus to eat. "Now, can you guys finally tell me what happened last night?"

"Yes. At dinner."

Flaherty didn't know what happened last night either. "What's he talking about? What happened?"

"We'll tell you both at dinner."

"Oh, Aspen, I spoke with Tommy Chen after the meet. Guess what? He had the same envelope as you got from that girl at the banquet."

Ugu stopped in her tracks. "What?"

Whitfield repeated himself.

Ugu mumbled under her breath. "He wasn't on the video feed from the banquet. He wasn't removed from the lineup until late last night. She must have gotten to him *after* they discovered they tried to bribe to wrong Aspen." No one could make out what Ugu was muttering.

Then, she spoke up. "Uhh, guys, I have to go check on something."

Flaherty wanted Ugu to stay. "What? Now?"

"Can it wait until after dinner?" Aspen also wanted Ugu to stay.

"No. Sorry, it's just something I have to look into."

"Do you want me to come with you?"

"Thank you, Flaherty, but no. It's OK. I'll be fine."

"Ugu?" Whitfield really wanted Ugu to stay.

"I am so sorry. I really want to celebrate with you. I don't know how long this will take, but I'll meet up with you guys later. Aspen, you can fill them in on last night."

Whitfield grabbed hold of Ugu's hand. "You sure you're OK?"

"Yes, sweetie, I'm fine. Go enjoy dinner. I'll meet up with you later."

Ugu left, sprinting across campus.

"I hope she's OK."

"She'll be fine." Flaherty knew Ugu better than anyone. They arrived at Nolan's Surf Bar & Bucket on the Business campus and sat down to eat. "So, Aspen, tell us about last night."

Chapter 15
Gisele's Failure

In a dark corner of her one-room apartment, the phone rang. Gisele was dreading this moment.

She lifted the phone to her ear, but didn't say anything. The caller spoke first. "You failed us."

Through her tears, Gisele's words were barely audible. "But it all worked out anyway."

"Wrong. We counted on you to do a job and you failed."

"I didn't know there would be two with the same name. They switched seats."

"We do not tolerate excuses."

"I fixed it later."

"You are now on their 'No Admit' list. You are no longer of any value to us."

"I can still get by their security. I can hide my face."

"We do not take chances."

"Wait. The next meet. It's not on campus. It's at P'socto. I can still do my job."

"Arlington will share the security footage with other schools. You will not be allowed on their campus either."

"I can do my job off-campus."

"The Seven Bridges students have already identified you."

"They will not see me again. I promise."

The caller hesitated. "If you fail us again."

"I won't. You have my word."

Chapter 16
Meet v. Homework

Seven Bridges Academy students were still in good spirits following the huge meet victory over the weekend. Teachers on the Gymnastics campus collectively decided to cancel their classes on Monday, to allow students an extra day to recover, and, perhaps, to afford themselves the same comfort. As for the rest of campus, it was back to business as usual. Students arrived at their morning classes with breakfast waiting for them at their seats, as usual. Whitfield had a few extra 'Congratulations!' and 'Awesome job' notes waiting for him at his station in *Intermediate Cryptography*. Even Dr. Hewitt made a big deal about Whitfield's debut performance. Flaherty's entire class brought in flowers, diamonds, and assorted gems for her. She accepted the gifts with humility and grace, as only Flaherty could.

Aspen was asked to stand up in front of his *International Politics* class and recap his experiences at the meet. Since most students in class didn't really know Aspen beforehand, this brief public speaking engagement served as much of an introduction as anything else. When Aspen concluded, the whole class stood and cheered, showering Aspen with praise. Aspen returned to his seat, happy and smiling.

The attention directed toward Flaherty, Whitfield, and Aspen in class paled in comparison to the innumerable requests bestowed upon the trio's staffs. Their publicists were fielding requests for interviews and appearances; agents and endorsement managers dealt with pitches and sponsorship opportunities; photographers were being hounded for magazine covers and shots of all varieties; even their chefs and trainers were being pestered to share recipes and workout programs. The world wanted to know more about these three standout gymnasts. What did they eat? How do they prepare for a meet? Would Flaherty be my son's date for his prom?

To their credit, Whitfield, Aspen, Flaherty, and all of their teammates, each seemed to handle the increased attention in stride. As per team protocol, each gymnast made themselves available, at their locker, to reporters for 15 minutes before practice, and 25 minutes after practice. Reporters were not allowed inside the locker room, but through enhanced holographic technology, athletes would be made to appear as though they were sitting right next to reporters.

Thursdays were considered a hands-off media day, and since the team had off from practice on Saturdays, athletes were not required to speak to the media; however, many gymnasts would satisfy media requests from their homes on Saturday mornings. Whitfield, Aspen, Flaherty, and even Keegan, who was drawing some increased attention, especially from teenage girls, each set up enhanced media rooms, with their coaches' permission, in their homes to handle the excessive media requests.

The gymnasts found it easier to have a home studio to handle requests from around the globe. This way, they could still appear live, albeit through a hologram, on morning talk shows on the other side of the world, without leaving their homes. Per Coach Daza's request, these media sessions were limited to one hour per day during the week, and 3 hours on Saturday. No in-home media requests were to be granted on Sundays.

With classes, practice, loads of studying and homework, media requests, and additional workout reps for the House Point Challenge, Whitfield still found time to meet Ugu every day for their nightly run. This was the highlight of both of their days. It was a time to just be themselves and relax.

No pressure to perform in front of teachers or coaches. They could just lose themselves in each other's company. And, ever since Whitfield learned about Isadora's Gang and Ugu's secret mission to tap into the ski lodge's mainframe, plant floor trackers, and break into Jonathan's room to set up additional surveillance cameras overlooking the mountainside and immediate surrounding areas, Whitfield was more than happy to have this daily check in, in-person, with Ugu.

As for Ugu, she was just as busy with class projects and all of her volunteer assignments. In fact, after their run, when Whitfield usually went home to sleep, Ugu would stay up and complete more schoolwork for another hour or two before turning in for the night. Whitfield had grown accustomed to waking up in the morning to see what time Ugu sent him her "Good night, Honey Bear" message.

After tonight's run, they came to a stop at the slides leading to Ugu's house. "Hey, you're getting faster. I almost broke a sweat tonight."

"Very funny. I could beat you if I really tried."

Ugu had to cover her mouth to prevent herself from spitting out her water. "Ha! You really think so?"

"Sure, give me a minute to catch my breath and I'll beat you."

"OK. Loser carries the other's clothes to the galleria's laundry drop off for a month."

"Uhh, on second thought. Maybe not. But it's not fair. You're like this superstar runner. It's like trying to keep up with a jaguar."

"And you're a superstar gymnast. Or did you forget? Let me remind you..." Ugu thought for second, trying to recall the exact words as laid out in the latest magazine article about SBA's new star gymnast. "... 'Whitfield, Seven Bridge's newest star gymnast, wows the crowd with his boyish charm, deep blue eyes, and incredible strength and tumbling ability. A sure-fire rockstar.' Does that sound about right?" Ugu's words were dripping with sarcasm.

"Oh, come on, it didn't mention anything about my eyes."

"OK. Maybe I threw that one in. But the rest was all in there."

"OK, but you know I didn't write that."

"I know. It's just..." For the first time, Whitfield sensed some insecurity from Ugu.

"Hey, look, you know I don't care about any of that stuff. I just want to do my best out on the floor, and in the classroom, and be with you. I lo..." Whitfield stopped short of saying the words.

Ugu gasped, and smiled, "you said it."

"I did not."

"You were about to say it."

"Nuh-uh."

"Liar. You know you were about to say it."

"Uhh..."

Ug started laughing. "Ha. *Elementary Seduction* strikes again. Tip #8: Act vulnerable and he'll tell you the most comforting thing on his mind."

Whitfield was confused. "Wait, you were playing me?"

"Yup. Now we're even."

"I'm confused."

"That's right. Because I am smarter than you."

"Well, that's not what the entrance exams say."

"Shut up. I am smarter and you know it."

"Hmm."

"I am. Anyway, I was about to say something at the banquet, but I didn't say it. Well, not really. But now, you said it."

"I did not."

Ugu started to walk away. "Uh-huh."

"Wait, where are you going?"

"Taking my victory lap."

"Oh, no you don't." Whitfield started to run in the same direction. He passed Ugu. "Now we'll see who's faster. And your shoe is untied."

"Ooh, you little…" Ugu bent down and tied her shoe. For good measure, she untied and retied her other shoe. Then, Ugu started to run. For real, this time. Whitfield ran as fast as he could, for as long as he could. The Outer Loop spanned 2.54 miles, and they had already run three laps tonight, but Whitfield was determined. He had been training hard, running with Ugu every night. Now was his time to show Ugu who was really faster, even if he did get a head start. He dug in and sprinted as fast as he could.

Ugu passed Whitfield before they reached the three-quarter mile marker. By the halfway point, Whitfield could no longer see Ugu in front of him, around the curve. By the time she reached the two-mile marker, Ugu knew she had at least a 90-second lead on Whitfield. She decided to have a little fun with him. Ugu sprinted the final quarter mile, reached her slides and went down Slide 19-EU.

Ugu ran into her bedroom suite and quickly changed clothes. She removed her sports bra and leggings and threw on a loose-fitting hoodie and shorts. She grabbed some underwear from her dresser drawer, an apple from the kitchen, wrote a quick note, took her clothes with her and scaled the ramp back up to the Outer Loop in record time. Whitfield was still about 30 seconds away. Ugu ran in Whitfield's direction and dropped the clothes she was carrying, spreading them a few feet apart, ran back to the slide entrance, and hid.

Whitfield, breathing heavy, and about to collapse, was almost at the finish line, when he spotted Ugu's shirt laying on the ground. *What? Why is Ugu's top here?* A few feet ahead, Whitfield noticed Ugu's leggings. *Why did she take her clothes off?* A few feet later, Whitfield saw a pair of underwear. *Is she naked up there?* A few feet later, Whitfield spotted a note. *I hope she's OK.*

Whitfield picked up the note and read it. "Decided to go swimming." Whitfield was stunned.

Ugu was going to go swimming in her pool…naked?

Whitfield stopped to think. *What is she thinking? I guess it's OK. It is nighttime. No one will see her. Wait, does she want me to join her? Probably, right? Why else would she have changed out of her clothes up here and left me this note. She wants me to go swimming with her. And she wants me to be naked too. Oh boy, this is crazy. But, why not? I'm doing it.*

Whitfield peeled off his shirt and shorts. He looked in both directions, and, satisfied that no one else was around at this time of night, took off his underwear. Whitfield picked up Ugu's clothes and his own and went over to Slide 19-EL. Instead of reaching for his tracker, Whitfield just relied on the hand reader to unlock the door. Aspen had Whitfield coded into the system so that he can come over any time, so he knew the door would open. What he didn't know was that standing on the other side of the door was a fully dressed Ugu, holding a camera.

Whitfield quickly positioned the pile of clothes he was holding in front of his private area.

"I thought you'd want to get a start on bringing my clothes to the laundry."

Whitfield's face turned beet red. "Uhh…"

"Oh, I see you decided to take your clothes over there too. Good thinking."

"Uhh…"

"Here, have an apple." Ugu tossed the apple in her hands to Whitfield, who, without thinking dropped the clothes in his hands to reach up and catch the apple, leaving himself fully exposed. As the slide door closed, Ugu called out, "you know you love me!"

Whitfield just stood there…completely naked…holding an apple. "Uhh…"

****

On Saturday, the gymnastics team got together, first over Keegan's house, then at Seraphina's house, to watch the PGL (Professional Gymnastics League) meets. Several Seven Bridges alums were scheduled to compete, including Gabe, who after his first two meets, was one of the favorites for Rookie of the Year. Seraphina was happy to host the evening watch party, as she was having some difficulty with her staff, especially Jonathan, and welcomed the distraction. The gathering wasn't exclusive to gymnasts. Chloe brought two friends from her staff, Keegan brought two girls, neither from his own staff, and Aspen walked in with Flaherty, Ugu and Colin. Whitfield showed up late with Liam and Sarah, two trainers from his staff.

Everyone was laughing and enjoying themselves, except for Jonathan, who was clearly annoyed, and still upset about not making the team.

"What's HE doing in my house?" Jonathan was clearly signaling for Aspen to leave.

Keegan stood up for his teammate, and friend. "We invited him. He belongs with us."

"And this isn't YOUR house. It's mine. And I want him here." Seraphina had enough of Jonathan's attitude, which had made life in her mansion miserable for weeks. Aspen smiled. He liked Seraphina…as a friend.

"Oh please, YOUR house. For now."

"What's that supposed to mean?"

"Everyone knows you're the weak link on the team. Couldn't even score more than two measly points. Pathetic."

Seraphina grew quiet. Her feelings were clearly hurt.

Once again, Keegan spoke up to defend his friends. "Hey, why don't you watch your mouth? Seraphina is a bigger part of this team than you'll ever be."

Flaherty tried to prevent things from escalating. "Guys. Let's just stop all this and enjoy the meet. Here, Seraphina, I have some room next to me."

"Can it, princess." Jonathan didn't care whom he offended or ridiculed.

Whitfield sensed that Ugu was about to say something, and even though she, and Flaherty, were perfectly capable of handling themselves, Whitfield stood up first. "Jonathan, it seems to me that you really want to be on the team. And, you think you deserve to be on the team, right?"

Jonathan scoffed. "Everyone knows I'm the best gymnast here. Better than all of you, that's for sure."

A few others returned derogatory remarks and jeered. "No. No. Look, Jonathan is very good. We've all seen him during tryouts. I, for one, was very impressed with his form and technique, especially on VH-Bars."

"Yeah, what would you know about form, you loser."

More hissing and jeering.

"No, that's OK. He's entitled to his opinion. I want to help you make the team." Looks of surprise filled the room.

Even Jonathan appeared taken aback by Whitfield's comment. "Yeah, right."

"No, seriously. Look, your temper and bad attitude aren't going to help you make the team. Being a gymnast at Seven Bridges is about more than just your skill out on the floor. You need a strong work ethic. Empathy. Humility. A helping hand. Look, we have enough votes in this room right now to block your selection. But, if you want, I can help to change that."

Sydney spoke out against Whitfield's budding plan. "What are you doing? He's a jerk. We don't want him."

"I know. But he is a really good gymnast, and I think, underneath it all, a good person. Here is what I propose. I'll work out with you once a week. At one of the practice gyms. Others are welcome to join us. But, once a week, for the next six months, you agree to attend the staff mental health class."

"Yeah right. That's not happening."

"No wait. There's more. One of us on the team will go with you each week. That way, you'll have one-on-one time with everyone on this year's team. I'll volunteer to go first. What do you say?"

Flaherty supported Whitfield's suggestion. "Wow. I like that idea." Chloe and Seraphina also supported Whitfield's idea.

Keegan was still on the fence. "I'm not crazy about spending an hour with Jonathan, but whatever is best for the team. I'm in."

Whitfield reached out his hand. "Jonathan?"

Jonathan looked out at everyone gathered around, all looking at him. "You losers are all pathetic. I don't need any of your help. I'm the best gymnast here. You'll see." Jonathan stormed upstairs to his room and slammed the door.

Ugu grabbed Whitfield's arm and pulled him close to her. "Whitfield. That was a really good idea. He's just not ready yet. You did the right thing."

"Yeah, homes, give him time. He'll come around." Keegan patted Whitfield on his shoulder.

"Thanks for trying, Whitfield." Seraphina was starting to like Whitfield.

"Hey, what are we all looking down for. Our boy, Gabe is about to go on Vault-Pegs. Let's Go, Gabe!" They all shifted focus back to the meet coverage on the video screens and with another solid routine by Gabe, the cheering and good vibes returned. The rest of the night was fun.

****

Another week went by, and so far, Whitfield and Aspen's first term at Seven Bridges was going well. Better than that actually. They loved their classes. They loved the team. And Whitfield loved...well, let's just say the Mitchell boys both found a lot of new friends. The term was not without its challenges though. Jonathan was still being a pain. Isadora's Gang had shown up out of the blue at the last meet. Who knows if they would be at the next one? What was Dr. Hewitt's connection with the gang? Why did Seven Bridges always win? And now, five weeks into the term, a new challenge.

On Thursday morning, Sir Arlington interrupted the students' lunches with an announcement on the holoscreens:

"Greetings. It is time for our time-honored school tradition awaiting all new students at our school—The Grand Curriculum Development Challenge. Every first-year and transfer student shall submit a project. You may work with a partner. Project submissions must include at least one substantially new curricular resource, with practical applications, ready to be implemented by next year, for an existing course at Seven Bridges, or a fully developed and researched new course proposal. Project submissions will be evaluated based on creativity, practicality, and student support. For further details, see the school's e-message board."

Whitfield just happened to be sitting next to two first-years, both majoring in gymnastics, at the assigned rotating four-person lunch round-tables, when the announcement came through. Both students seemed very excited about the project.

Rodolfo spoke first. "Wow. This is awesome. We can work together."

Quan replied, "I know. What do you want to do?"

"Maybe we can submit our design for automated Tri-Bars judging at meets."

"Yeah. We could have students from Engineering and Computer Science work on it."

"And Applied Mathematics."

"Right. We are definitely going to win."

Whitfield was intrigued by Rodolfo and Quan's idea for automated judging, but he really perked up when he heard them talk about winning. "Win? What do you mean win?"

Just then, Sir Arlington reappeared on the holoscreens.

"Apologies for the second interruption. Two more things. First, don't think I forgot about the prizes. Students with winning submissions receive an all-expenses paid trip for two to the destination of their choice and have the option to teach their designed curriculum to Seven Bridges students next year. Second, the deadline for submissions is this Monday at 08:00. Enjoy your weekend!"

Quan pointed to the screen. "See. That's what I mean."

Whitfield felt energized. A free trip to anywhere in the world...with Ugu. The option to teach at Seven Bridges. He was in. But how in the world could he complete the project by Monday morning? He had another meet this weekend.

After lunch, Aspen and Whitfield both scrambled to find each other. Aspen was just as excited as Whitfield. "We have to do this."

"I know, Aspen. I want to do it too, but how? We only have until Monday. It's already Thursday."

"Let's ask Flaherty how she did it." On their way to find Flaherty, they ran across Morocco, Bella, and Kayleigh.

"Hi Whitfield. Hi Aspen. What's up?"

Aspen liked Bella. She had always been nice to him. "Hey Bella, have you seen Flaherty?"

Kayleigh pointed behind her. "Yeah, I think I saw her heading over to Advanced Medicine. She's working on a class project."

"That's OK." Whitfield didn't want to be rude. "What we really wanted to know is how did you guys get your challenge project done on time?"

Morocco and Bella both chuckled. Morocco finally admitted, "aww, man. I totally messed that one up. I told Dr. Futenmouth that I did it but then someone must have stolen it while I was sleeping. He didn't believe me and I got arrested. Level 2 Detention."

Bella continued laughing. "Yeah, that was bad. I didn't hand mine in on time either, but didn't come up with some crazy story either. I still got arrested. Level 1 Detention."

"But then I found out the following year that Keegan just asked for an extension. He got it. No questions asked. I think Dr. Futenmouth wasn't happy about it, but still…no detention? Man, Keegan's a lucky guy. I had to spend a week in the Glass Box."

Kayleigh was the only one of the three that had actually competed the project on time. "I actually handed mine in on time, but I asked Coach Brockport if I could be excused from the meet. It was my first year, and I wasn't going to compete much anyway. He wasn't happy, but let me sit out the meet. I still traveled with the team anyway. I think he would have preferred I stayed home."

Whitfield didn't seem too enthused with these choices. "So, those are our options? Either don't do it and get detention. Do it and miss the meet and get coach upset with us. Or ask for an extension."

"Yeah, that's about it. Well, you could try to complete the project at the meet, but you're an All-Arounder. When would you have time? And, Aspen, coach said you're probably going to start on three events. You wouldn't have time either." Morocco shook his head, indicating that he was out of other ideas.

"He's right, Whitfield. It seems impossible to complete the project on time and still compete in the meet."

Whitfield sensed his dreams of going on vacation with Ugu were quickly being dashed away, but he wasn't willing to give up just yet. "Hmm…impossible? I wonder."

Chapter 17
Challenge Project

As Whitfield and Aspen packed for their first away meet of the season, their minds were consumed with the Curriculum Development Challenge. Teaching at Seven Bridges Academy was a great honor. Several seventh-year students were already teaching their own classes, and every year at least one or two students receive offers to join the faculty full-time after graduation. A job at Seven Bridges Academy, coupled with the potential to spend a week with Ugu at an island resort, or anywhere else in the world, was all the motivation Whitfield needed to think hard about completing his project on time.

"Hey Whitfield, do you think they would let each of us bring someone on vacation if we win?"

"I don't see why not."

"Good. I think I might ask Seraphina to go with us."

"Ooh. You like Seraphina?"

"She's cool. And she's always been nice to me."

"She is cool. But, before we can think about any of that, we have to come up with a plan. How are we going to get this project done, Aspen?"

"I don't know. What did Ugu do?"

"Well, you know your *International Politics* class?"

"Yeah?"

"Well, she designed it."

"Get out."

"No, really. And not just that. Ugu designed the entire four-course sequence: *Politics*, *Culture*, *History*, and *Economics*. Before she came up with the curriculum, students just had a class on *Countries of the World* and some generic *International Studies* course."

"Wow. That's amazing! No wonder she said she could help me with the course."

"Yeah, she's incredible."

"Sure is. But, wait. I thought she said she got an A in the course. How could she get an A if she never took it? She only designed it."

"Because she did take it. All of them actually. Usually, students who come up with course proposals take a few more years to develop materials and then are asked to teach the course in their sixth and seventh years, but Ugu already had all the materials developed and ready to go by the end of her first year. Sir Arlington didn't think students would respond well to having a second-year teaching them, and Ugu agreed. Instead, Ugu decided to take each of the four classes, as a student, and give the faculty members teaching the class feedback after each class, all while still coming up with the course materials herself."

Aspen had never been more impressed. "Whitfield, I don't think we can design four courses."

"No, of course not, but we don't have to. I have an idea."

****

Whitfield, Aspen, and Flaherty boarded the team's drone bus at 07:00 on Friday morning for the long three-hour flight to P'socto Academy. All week long, Ugu had been planning on heading to P'socto with the team. Flaherty even got special permission from Coach Brockport for Ugu to ride with the them, but at the last minute, Ugu decided to stay on campus. She had really wanted to go to support her friends, and to keep an eye out for Gisele and her partner, but she had just stumbled upon something interesting.

Ever since being unable to track down Tommy Chen before his bus left after the opening meet, Ugu had been reviewing video footage from all pre-meet festivities from the previous year, including all Friday night banquets the team attended last season. To get all of the footage, Ugu had to pull some strings, using Sir Arlington's credentials, and occasionally pull a harmless computer hack. Ugu had Sir Arlington's full support in her investigation.

Of last season's twelve regular season meets, Ugu was able to retrieve, and review, footage from nine pre-meet banquets. She was still working on gaining access to the surveillance tapes from the other three meets and all the playoff and championship tapes. Ugu had spotted Gisele at three different banquets, passing out a total of 13 envelopes. With some careful attention to detail, Ugu spotted four other suspicious characters distributing similar-looking envelopes.

Ugu immediately identified one of the characters as a member of Isadora's Gang who had since been convicted of bribery, among other petty crimes, and incarcerated. The other two characters, one boy and one girl, were both close in age to Gisele with similar athletic builds.

Ugu was starting to build her case. *It seems that whoever this mystery villain is has a particular type when recruiting henchmen to do his dirty work.*

In total, Ugu spotted 38 different envelope transactions across the nine meets. Some of the camera footage was a bit murky, and didn't cover all areas of the room, so she was confident she didn't catch every such transaction. Ugu then pulled the recordings from the respective meets. Without seeing the enclosed notes, it was difficult to know exactly in which sessions and on which events the targeted athletes were supposed to fall, so Ugu watched every routine carefully. Every second. In painstaking detail.

Ugu even pulled multiple camera angles from those routines where more than one view was available, to see if she could get a view of their eyes during the routine. After two plus years of taking classes in deception, cheating, seduction, and espionage, Ugu was well-trained in looking for clues, and Rule #3 was to look into a person's eyes.

After countless hours combing through video footage, Ugu couldn't conclude a whole lot. The evidence showed that every gymnast receiving an envelope either fell at least once during competition or was replaced in the lineup at some point. Neither of these consistencies amounted to much, as gymnasts fall quite often, especially when competing seven times on each event during a single competition.

Ugu computed the odds of randomly selecting 38 gymnasts who each ultimately fell at least once or were substituted for during the meet and the probability of such an occurrence was really low, but not low enough for Ugu to make a hard case. Perhaps if she could see what was written on the notes inside the envelope, she could make a better case. Ugu was able to spot facial tic and eye movement disruptions for six gymnasts just prior to their falls, but with only six cases, she didn't feel that she had enough evidence…yet. She had to keep searching for more evidence. *I have to be missing something. What is it?*

****

Whitfield and Aspen sat together on the drone bus working on their plan for the Curriculum Development Challenge project.

"Whitfield, are you sure this is going to work?"

"I think so. Coach Daza agreed to let the *Holographic Engineering* class come. They are traveling on a different drone bus."

"Yeah, but how do we know if they'll be allowed on the floor?"

"I already called the meet coordinator and said it's for a school project. He was happy to allow it. Just mentioned that if any of our students get in the way, he'd have them all pulled."

"Better make sure you tell them that."

"I will."

"What about the gymnasts from the other teams?"

"I reached out to the other coaches. Only one agreed so far, as long as it was for educational purposes. I explained our idea and she loved it. Said she would like a copy of it when we're done. May even suggest it to the faculty at her own school."

"Cool. Hey, maybe we could travel all over and…"

"Aspen. Stay focused."

"Right."

"P'socto's coach had a request of her own. She said if we agreed, she could probably get the other coaches to agree to our request."

"Great! What was her request?"

"Simple. I think you'll like it. You'll see when we get there."

"OK."

"We should probably talk to all the other coaches tonight at the banquet, you know, just in case they are hesitant. I hope we can convince them on our own, and not have to rely on P'socto's coach."

"Yeah. Too bad Ugu isn't here. She can get anyone to do anything."

Whitfield recalled the apple incident. "I know. Don't remind me."

"What's that supposed to mean?" Aspen still didn't know what had happened on the Outer Loop between his brother and Ugu.

"Nothing. I'll tell you later. Is there anyone else who can…" Whitfield didn't even need to finish his sentence.

In unison, both Whitfield and Aspen said, "Flaherty!" Whitfield and Aspen both got up and stood next to Flaherty, who was busy reading for class.

"Hey, Flaherty, sorry to bother you."

"Oh, hi Whitfield. Aspen. No bother at all. Come, sit. What's up?"

"We have something to ask you?" Aspen wasn't shy around Flaherty. She treated him like he was her own little brother.

"Sure, what is it?"

Whitfield and Aspen shared their plan with Flaherty, and she enthusiastically agreed to help. Like Ugu, Flaherty had incredible people skills. She, too, was well-trained in seduction and persuasion, and was just naturally likable. And with the task in front of her, it didn't hurt that she was also the best gymnast at the meet.

****

When the drone bus landed at the hotel, the team members quickly found their way to their rooms, dropped off their bags, and headed downstairs for the team lunch. Whitfield and Aspen asked Coach Daza if they may be excused, and explained where they were going. Coach Daza agreed to let them go, with their security detail close behind, of course.

Flaherty asked, "where are you two going?"

"P'socto's coach asked if we would stop by the senior center to sit with her dad for a little while. It's just a block over that way. Apparently, he never misses a meet on his holovision and wanted to meet Aspen and I. You're welcome to join us. I'm sure he'd love to meet you too."

"Aww, of course. I'd love to go. Let me just ask coach. Wait here."

Flaherty asked Coach Daza if she could go, and with the same caveat of bringing her security detail with her, he agreed. Whitfield, Aspen, and Flaherty, with 12 members of their security teams, walked up the block and met Yonca, the P'socto head coach, outside the senior center.

Yonca was thrilled to see them. "Whitfield. Aspen. So nice to meet you. Thank you so much for doing this. Aahhh…Flaherty! So nice to see you again." Flaherty and Yonca hugged. Flaherty had attended several elite camps when she was young, and Yonca had been one of her instructors.

Aspen turned to Whitfield. "Wow. Just like Ugu. Flaherty knows everyone."

Flaherty was happy to see Yonca. "So nice to see you, again. How are you?"

"Good. Real good. Well, except for my dad. He's not doing so hot. But I think seeing you three will lift his spirits." They all followed Yonca up the stairs, into the senior center. Yonca's dad was sitting in the main sitting room, watching highlights from last weekend's meets, along with previews of this weekend's matchups. "Dad, there are some people here to see you."

Yonca's dad, Felix, was old and frail, but loved seeing his daughter every time she came to visit. "Hi sugar. So nice to see you. Who came to see me?" Felix turned around and instantly recognized SBA's three most popular gymnasts. "Oh my. Is this really happening? Are you actually here?"

Whitfield held out his hand. "Yes, sir. It's a pleasure to meet you. I've heard so many wonderful things about you."

"Sir. Nice to meet you. I'm Aspen."

"Felix. I am so happy to finally meet you. You have such a wonderful daughter. I see where she gets her sparkling eyes." Flaherty was so skilled at making people feel good about themselves.

Felix blushed. "Aren't you the sweetest?"

Flaherty continued her charming ways. "I hear you are a big fan. A former gymnast, too, I presume." Flaherty grabbed hold of his upper arm, and squeezed it gently.

"Class of '52. All-Arounder, until my shoulder gave out. Never missed a meet though."

"Seems like you could still go a few rounds on the pommel." Flaherty was still holding Felix's arm, but lightly touched his chest and stomach area too.

"Oh, that's sweet of you to say. I could probably still do a few tricks, but not like what you can do. Aspen, your Pommel Clock routine is outstanding. Whitfield, how did you stick that landing on Parallel Planks?"

"Thank you, sir."

"It wasn't easy, sir. Just got lucky, I guess."

"Oh, I'm sure that's not it. Lots of practice, I bet. Yeah, you guys are the present and the future. I just enjoy watching every routine."

"Well, with such wisdom, I'm sure you have a lot of knowledge to share." Flaherty knew exactly what buttons to press to get Felix to smile.

"That's what I keep telling my daughter."

Flaherty sat down right next to the old man. "Let me ask you, did you happen to catch our meet last weekend?"

"Watched the whole thing on Sunday night and all Monday. Sorry, I had to watch my daughter's team live."

"Of course."

"Anyway. Saw every one of your routines. All of yours too." Felix pointed a crooked finger at both Whitfield and Aspen.

"Great. I am having a little trouble on my Tri-Bars dismount. Do you think you could help? Any advice would be very much appreciated."

Felix had a proud, albeit defiant, look come over him. He looked directly at his daughter. "See, I told you. I knew something wasn't right with her dismount." He looked back at Flaherty, "she didn't believe me."

"Yonca, you should listen to your dad. He's very wise."

"Thank you. You're letting go too early. You need to hold on a smidge longer and lift your hips higher before you rotate. Then really bring that shoulder around hard to complete that second twist."

In truth, Flaherty's dismount on Tri-Bars was nearly flawless. She had stuck every landing and felt good about each one. She just had a way of making the old man feel important, and needed. Flaherty was a master at getting people to feel good about themselves, and in turn, about her.

Whitfield, Aspen, and Flaherty stayed with Felix for another hour. More elderly ladies and gentlemen filled the seats in the grand meeting room. Lots of laughs were shared. The trio had injected a youthful spirit into the room that lasted well after the three had left. All through the weekend actually, as Whitfield, Aspen, and Flaherty had won over the small group of seniors. Felix still supported his daughter, but now, he was happy to root for Seven Bridges Academy as well.

Yonca walked the three gymnasts out, and thanked them all for being so gracious with their time. She hugged each of them and promised Whitfield and Aspen that she would speak with the other coaches on their behalf concerning their school project. As Whitfield, Aspen, and Flaherty walked back to the hotel, they all felt good about themselves.

"That was fun. Thank you for letting me tag along."

"Are you kidding? Thank you. Flaherty, you were great in there."

Aspen agreed, "that was fun. And, Whitfield, she said she would get the other coaches to help with our project. I'm so excited."

****

The three friends arrived back at the hotel in enough time to change into their formal attire and get ready for the red carpet and upcoming banquet. With a travel allotment of six staff members each, excluding security, each gymnast still had plenty of assistance in getting ready for the media frenzy that was about to begin. Unlike their home meet, where they each arrived in personal luxury drones, the Seven Bridges gymnasts arrived at this red-carpet scene together. One by one, they stopped for photos and to briefly speak with reporters, before being ushered into a grand staging area, awaiting entrance into the banquet hall.

There was no sign of Gisele at the banquet, but Whitfield and Aspen kept a watchful eye. They also warned their security team to stay alert. Everyone enjoyed themselves at the banquet, and although the event was relatively drama-free, Whitfield did spot a guest handing a gymnast an envelope that he was sure looked exactly like the one Aspen had received two weeks earlier. He immediately sent Ugu a message to let her know. He only spotted that one transaction, although admittedly, wasn't paying as much attention as he could have, as he got caught up in the festivities and having a good time.

Even Flaherty seemed to get caught up in the fun as she was dancing with a boy for a good part of the evening. That night, before going to bed, Whitfield sent Ugu a message to let her know he was thinking about her. Ugu returned the sentiment and asked how the event had been. Whitfield told her about their trip to the senior center and the banquet, and told her he missed her.

23:11: *I miss you too, Honey Bear. Good luck tomorrow.*

23:11: *Thanks*

23:12: *By the way, did the other coaches agree to your project request?*

23:12: *Yes. Flaherty helped. They all agreed.*

23:13: *Great. She is hard to say no to.*

23:13: *Agreed.*

23:13: *Just like me.*

23:13: *Oh really?*

23:14: *You know you can't say no to me. You love me too much.*

23:14: *Me? What about you?*

Whitfield thought about saying 'I love you', but thought he should say it for the first time in person instead. Ugu also wanted to say 'I love you', but didn't, for the same reason. She had really wanted Whitfield to say those words. She was hoping to see them before going to bed. She missed him so much. They both waited for the other to say it. Neither did. They both fell asleep without even saying good night.

****

The Agricultural Commodities meet was another Seven Bridges victory. For their efforts over the two-day meet weekend, the school earned enough corn, oats, soybeans, wheat, rice grains, cattle, hogs, milk, and lumber to last for the next ten years. Once again, Flaherty led the way, with Whitfield finishing second in the All-Around. Aspen continued to impress, going a combined 17-4, notching another perfect meet record on Pommel Clock. He continued to hit each of his Tri-Bars routines, but still earned scores much lower than expected.

Whitfield and Aspen were busy working on their project on the drone bus ride home. After stopping for a team meal, it was 22:00 before the bus arrived back on campus, which meant Whitfield and Aspen had only ten hours left to submit their project. They decided to head straight to the AMQE library to complete their work. They thought they would need every bit of the ten hours left to finish, but if they completed it in time, they were confident they could actually win the prize.

"Aspen, we have to hurry. I don't think we are going to have enough time left."

"We can do it. Just stay focused. Maybe we can call Ugu for some extra help with the finishing touches."

"No. We should probably finish this all on our own." Just then, Whitfield received a message from Ugu.

"Wow, bro. She must have known we were talking about her."

"She's probably just sending a good night message. Let me get back to her quickly and we can finish this up."

Whitfield checked Ugu's message:

00:43: *Whitfield. I found something. I need to see you. Can you come over now?*

Chapter 18
Bribing Gymnasts

"Aspen, pack up. We have to go."

"But we're not done yet."

"It's Ugu. She needs us."

"Is she OK?"

"I don't know. She said she found something and needs to see me now."

"OK. Where is she?"

"At home, I guess. Why?"

"Well, it's just that Ugu never works at home. If she found something, that means she's probably working somewhere else."

"Good thinking. I'll ask where she is." It turns out Ugu had been working in Sir Arlington's study chambers, inside the AMQE library, just one floor beneath where Whitfield and Aspen were working. The two boys headed downstairs and knocked on the door three times. The door opened swiftly. Ugu was working at a desk just inside the chambers.

"Wow. That was fast!"

"We were right upstairs working on our curriculum challenge project."

"Are you OK?"

"Yes, I'm fine. But, here, check this out. After you sent me that message about the envelope transfer, I decided to pull up the live feed from the surveillance cameras inside the banquet hall. I spotted four other transfers."

"Really? Sorry, I only spotted that one."

"I know. You were having a good time. I saw you talking with a lot of the other coaches."

"Yeah, that was for our project."

"And Aspen, I saw you spending some time with Seraphina. Anything going on there?"

"We're just friends. She's nice."

Ugu and Whitfield looked at each other and smiled. "OK. Well, anyway, I spotted one envelope going to a fifth-year boy from Pancake Batter Prep. I connected with Flaherty and asked if she could work some of her magic to get a good look at the note inside the envelope."

"Was that the boy she was dancing with?"

"You got it, Aspen. As expected, Flaherty delivered. She just flashed her smile, laughed at some of his corny jokes, and while he was busy falling in love with her, she was able to get a look inside the envelope. $15,000 and a note that looked just like the one Aspen received, listing three specific events and sessions."

Whitfield raised his eyebrows. "Good work, Flaherty. Not surprised, though. The way she looked that night, I don't know anyone that could have turned her down." Whitfield did not mean for his comment to come out the way it did.

Ugu stared at Whitfield. "Oh, really?"

"Well, I mean…I'm sure someone would be able to say no. Umm…I definitely would have said no."

Ugu rolled her eyes. "Mmm-hmmm."

"No, really." Whitfield was digging a hole for himself.

Aspen decided to help his brother. "Whitfield. Just stop talking."

"Thank you, Aspen. Anyway, I looked at the three events on the meet tapes and guess what?"

"What?"

"He fell on every single event listed on the note."

Aspen didn't think that was too unusual though. "Did he fall any other times?"

"Well, yes, two other times during the weekend, but these three events were his worst scores of the entire competition. He performed 22 routines in competition and fell five times, three of which were on the events listed on that note tied to the money."

Whitfield was perplexed. "So, what does all this mean?"

Sir Arlington, who had entered the room just a moment earlier, offered a broad synopsis. "It means that someone is bribing athletes to take falls during meets."

Whitfield continued pondering the situation, "do we know who is handing out the bribes?"

"No. Sir Arlington was able to contact Isadora at Chipwood and he's convinced she is not the one pulling the strings, even though whoever is behind this bribery scheme is using her goons at the ground level."

"Is there any connection among the gymnasts?"

"Good thought, Whitfield. Other than competing at the same meet, no. At least, I haven't been able to connect them at all. They come from all different schools."

Aspen asked, "anyone from Seven Bridges?"

"No. I didn't see anyone from Seven Bridges receiving a bribe. Well, except for Aspen, of course, but we know that was a mistake. It doesn't mean that Seven Bridges is clean though."

Whitfield shuddered to think what might happen if one of his teammates received a bribe attempt. "Yeah, whoever was handing out bribes might have contacted our gymnasts outside the banquet hall somewhere."

"Exactly. Look, we have some evidence identifying the gymnasts who received bribes and those handing out the bribes, but that's about it. I can spot some distorted eye movements before the gymnasts took a fall, but without knowing for sure which events were compromised, it's difficult to run a full analysis." Ugu desperately wanted to solve this case, but was growing frustrated with the limited evidence at hand.

Whitfield thought back to this weekend's meet. "What about the boy from Pancake Batter Prep? You knew when he was compromised, right?"

"Oh yeah. It was easy to tell with him. His arms went limp right before he was about to fall."

This gave Whitfield an idea. "Wait right here. I'll be right back." Whitfield ran upstairs to retrieve his project. While Whitfield was gone, Aspen offered a suggestion.

"Have you compared their falls in the meets in question to falls in other meets? Maybe you can see some differences there?"

"Good idea. But I'm not sure which falls were compromised, even in the meets where we knew they were bribed, and which ones were real. If only I knew the connection. Aarggh...this is so frustrating."

As usual, Sir Arlington tried reinforcing calm. "Young Ugu, my dear. Let's not lose our patience. You will see the bigger picture soon enough. I have faith in you."

"You haven't found any connection?"

Ugu threw her arms down by her side. "None. I've looked at every routine. Every angle. I pulled their profiles. Even pulled school records, well, those I could access without getting into too much trouble. Nothing. No connection."

Aspen thought for a minute. "Who were they competing against?"

"What?"

"Did you look at who they were competing against? You know, head-to-head? Maybe there's a connection there?"

Ugu and Sir Arlington looked at each other. Sir Arlington smiled. "Very good, young Aspen. Perhaps that could be the missing connection." Ugu went to work. First, she pulled up the master schedule from the most recent meet, since she knew in which events a particular gymnast fell on purpose. In each of the three events, the duel opponent was from Seven Bridges. "Let's not get ahead of ourselves. Could be a coincidence. Keep checking."

Ugu pulled up meet records from the past year, involving all the gymnasts in question. In every case, a bribed gymnast either had a fall or pulled out of the duel matchup when competing against a Seven Bridges gymnast.

Sir Arlington took great pride in his youngest student. "Young Aspen. I believe you have found our connection." Aspen and Ugu both smiled.

Whitfield re-entered the room as Ugu was pulling up footage and Aspen caught him up to speed. "That's great, Aspen. Now, we see the connection."

"Well, this is good. But I still don't know if it's enough to go to the WGF with. Their standards for evidence are pretty high."

"Well, Ugu, perhaps this can help." Whitfield held up a data drive.

"What do you have there, young Whitfield?"

Whitfield was about to answer, but Aspen cut him off. "Sir, it's our project for the Curriculum Development Challenge. Well, it's not finished yet. Sorry, but I don't think we'll have time to finish it by the 08:00 deadline. We didn't want to ask for an extension and thought we could get it done in time."

Whitfield assured Aspen that the deadline was secondary, at the moment. "That's OK, Aspen. This is more important."

"Yeah, but what about the prize? You wanted to take Ugu on vacation and..."

"Aspen! Shut up, please."

Ugu just sat there and smiled.

Sir Arlington offered some comfort. "Well, perhaps we can see what can be done about any late submissions. Just share with us how you think this can help."

Whitfield continued to share the idea behind their almost completed project with the group. "We brought some engineers with us to the meet to scan the athletes as they competed. We wanted to model the force of their movements across multidimensional space. We measured pressure exerted on each apparatus in pounds per square inch and torque for each rotational element. We figured the applications for this data would hit across multiple disciplines. Applied mathematics; physiology; engineering; and even biology and mechanics."

Aspen jumped in. "Yeah. The gymnastics classes could use it for training and conditioning too."

"Right. We're still mapping out the use cases, but the technology and data is all there."

Ugu had never dreamed of such a project. "That is brilliant!"

Even Sir Arlington was quite impressed. "How did you come up with this idea?"

This time, Whitfield deferred to Aspen. "Flaherty told us she had been working with safe, radiation-free multidimensional scanners for mapping underwater surfaces and we asked if the technology would work with human movements. She said sure. They were already working with fish and other sea creatures that move way faster than humans."

Whitfield continued, "we contacted Dr. Rothsfeld, the *Holographic Engineering* professor, Thursday afternoon, and he was ecstatic about the idea. Even offered to send his entire class to the meet. We got the OK from Coach Brockport and the meet coordinator. All the other head coaches agreed to let us scan their athletes during competition too."

Sir Arlington was speechless. "Well done. Both of you."

Ugu was floored. She was so impressed with their idea. Like a bolt of lightning, Ugu came to realize that she could use their project in her own research. "Hey, do you have the scans with you?"

"Sure do. Here you go." Whitfield handed Ugu the data drive, confident that she was now on the same page as him regarding how his and Aspen's project could be used to detect intentional falls.

"What are you planning to do with that device?"

"Sir, I can use these scans to identify the muscle movements for every gymnast during their competition. With these scans, I can identify every intentional fall."

"I do not follow."

As Ugu uploaded the scanned images, Whitfield explained, "it's really quite simple, sir. When a gymnast is performing, they always fire and relax their muscles in the same order and time of their routine. Think of drinking a cup of water. You contract muscles to hold the cup in your hand, fire the muscles in your forearm and bicep to raise the cup to your mouth, and continue to grip the cup as your drink."

Aspen continued, "but, if you want the cup to spill, you'll loosen your grip on the cup, allowing the cup to fall. You signal your muscles to change their routine prior to the cup falling."

Whitfield concluded, "if the spill was an accident, you wouldn't change your muscle patterns prior to the accident. Just like stepping on a wet spot or gripping the cup too high or too low. The accident would happen without changing your muscle pattern beforehand."

Sir Arlington finally seemed to be catching on. "So, by identifying changes in muscle patterns prior to the fall, you can identify which gymnasts fell on purpose, and which fell accidentally."

"Exactly."

"Well, boys, I must say, your project is certainly inspiring. I will have a word with the committee about your late submission issue."

Aspen was happy. "Thank you, sir, but we are really close to wrapping it up. I think we may be able to hit the deadline. Maybe. If we stay up all night."

"Very well. Young Ugu, let me know what you find."

"Yes, sir."

"Well done. All of you. I will retire now. As should each of you. Tomorrow is another day. Good night, all."

Ugu and Whitfield said in unison, "good night, sir."

Aspen had one more thing to share with Sir Arlington. "Oh, excuse me. Sir?"

"Yes, young Aspen."

"I have some news to share with you about my other project. You remember? From the novel. I think I figured it out."

"Wonderful. Oh, I am so delighted. Come see me tomorrow after class. I would love hear all about it." Sir Arlington let out a brief yawn.

"Sure. Thanks. Good night."

Whitfield, Aspen, and Ugu had decided to pick up their investigation again tomorrow. They had found the connection among the bribed gymnasts, but the question remained as to why someone was bribing gymnasts to take a fall against Seven Bridges. Was it just gamblers, or was it something else? Something bigger? These questions lingered as Whitfield, Aspen and Ugu walked out of the study chambers together.

"Whitfield! We still have a chance to win."

"That's right. You two should definitely finish up your project and submit it. Do you need any help?"

"Thanks, Ugu. We'd love to have your input, but we're going to just put the finishing touches on our submission first. If we are selected to continue developing it, we'd love to bring you on board."

"It would be my pleasure." Ugu opted for a quick change of topic before leaving the library for the night. "So, what's this I hear about you wanting to take me on vacation?"

"Oh well…Aspen must have misunderstood. I said I wonder if Ugu would be upset if I took Flaherty to a tropical island somewhere. You know, she was looking good this weekend."

Ugu smacked Whitfield on his arm.

"Just kidding. I haven't decided who I would take if we win."

"Really? Well, that's OK. I'm not sure I would go with you anyway."

"You know you can't say no to me."

"Maybe. I don't know. I mean, why do I need to go to an island resort with you. I've already seen you naked."

Aspen's jaw dropped. "WHAT? She's seen you naked?"

"Uhh…"

"Don't worry, Aspen. It's not what you think. We were in the Outer Loop."

Aspen started to laugh. "Ha. Why were you naked in the Outer Loop?"

"Yeah, Whitfield, why were you naked?" Ugu pulled out an apple from her bag and bit into it.

"Uhh…I was…it was…uhh."

"You're right, Aspen. Your brother is smooth when talking with girls. Good night, boys."

Ugu walked back to Aspen's mansion alone. Whitfield and Aspen went back to their desk in the library. They were determined to get their project submitted by 08:00. Even with Sir Arlington promising to smooth things over with the committee, Whitfield and Aspen wanted to show they could still meet the deadline on their own. Monday classes might be tough and both would be super tired at practice, but if all went well, they would submit their project on time and feel proud of a job well done.

Chapter 19
Hacking Dr. Hewitt's Messages

After classes on Monday, Aspen and Whitfield both went to the Applied Mathematics and Quantitative Economics library to meet with Sir Arlington. The boys were tired from pulling an all-nighter, but at least they completed their Curriculum Development Challenge project and submitted it on time, and had managed to stay awake during their two class periods. Whitfield had thought maybe he could use this time before practice, usually dedicated to studying and recreation activities, for a quick nap, but Aspen was eager to share with Sir Arlington his progress on the puzzle and Whitfield figured this would be a good time to see if Ugu needed any assistance with her investigation.

"Ahh, young Aspen. Right on time. I am most eager to hear of your progress. And young Whitfield, I presume you are not here to see me, but rather to cure young Ugu of any loneliness?" Sir Arlington flashed a kind smile.

"Well, I guess, sir. I do want to see if Ugu needs any assistance, but I also want to speak with you about something Aspen found. It can wait until Aspen tells you about the puzzle though."

"Hmm…most interesting. We will call you in when the moment is right. For now, you are welcome to make your inquiry with young Ugu. However, I believe she has already found a capable assistant. Perhaps two are better than one though."

Whitfield was surprised when he entered Sir Arlington's study chambers. "Flaherty? What are you…" It appeared that Ugu and Flaherty had arrived a few minutes earlier, and the two were already giggling when Whitfield walked in, and his entrance only brought about more laughs.

Flaherty finished Whitfield's question. "…doing here? Why, I could ask you the same thing."

"I just came to see if Ugu needed any help, you know, with her investigation."

"Same here," Flaherty continued giggling.

"Look, I can use help from both of you. Whitfield, thanks for coming. I've been able to access footage from the remaining meets and all the post-season meets from last season. Flaherty is going to help me go through the banquet footage. Perhaps you can review the meet footage?"

"Sure." Whitfield, Flaherty, and Ugu immersed themselves in work. Meanwhile, Aspen and Sir Arlington met inside Sir Arlington's office.

"Young Aspen. What do you have for me?"

"Well, sir, first, I wanted to tell you I am still working on tracking the money. I found out that the bills were minted seven years ago at Rutherford Mint in Parkette Falls and shipped straight to WGF Bank. They were stored in the vault there until three years ago when they were sent to Seven Bridges Bank on campus. The dates seem to line up with our meet season, so perhaps it was part of a settlement after a meet?"

"Yes, that would make sense."

"Good. The bills were then shipped to an external bank, Greater Bison Trust, about a week later. Perhaps for an additional resource purchase at a discounted rate?"

"Hmm…not likely. Did you follow up on that purchase?"

"I tried, sir. But nothing came back. I'll continue searching though."

"Please do."

"Sure. I didn't find any further bank-to-bank transactions involving these bills. The bills were withdrawn from Greater Bison three days before our first banquet this season, when I received them. It was a private bank account number, and without accessing the bank mainframe directly, I haven't been able to trace the account owner."

"Well done, young Aspen. I am proud of you. You have delivered much information in a short period of time. Kudos. Now, tell me, young Aspen, did you enjoy the novel I handed you?"

"Yes, very much. I want to read more."

"Well, I believe you will find many more available titles right here inside these walls. You are most welcome to read any title you wish."

"Thank you, sir."

"Tell me, what do you believe is the key to this particular novel's mysterious puzzle? How did the killer know where to find his targets? Ms. Collier never spoke directly with him. How did he know?"

"Well, she did sort of speak directly to him."

Sir Arlington raised an eyebrow. "When? I must have missed it in my reading."

"Through the upcoming wedding announcements. Remember, throughout the book, Ms. Collier's job was to post upcoming weddings at the Event Hall. Every Thursday, she would post five wedding announcements, but the Event Hall only had four grand halls big enough to host wedding receptions."

"Very good eye, young Aspen. Wonderful attention to detail. But I am still confused. I do not recall any of the names in the wedding announcements matching the names of the victims. Nor were there any other identifying features of when or where the murder eventually took place written in the announcements."

"Right. That's where it got a little tricky. So, I had to do a little research."

"Ahh, so the textbook came in handy then?"

Aspen hesitated. "Not exactly. I…I…"

"Young Aspen, it's OK. What do you want to say?"

"Well, remember when you said I could use any means necessary?"

"Yes. Oh, did you ask Dr. Hewitt for his assistance?"

"Oh, no, nothing like that. It's just that when I finished reading the novel, I figured that the wedding announcements were important, possibly even encrypted messages, but I still didn't know exactly how to break the code. I went back, determined to read the book again cover to cover, when I came across the acknowledgments page."

"Yes?"

"I noticed that Dr. Hewitt was thanked for his contributions to the book."

"Clever child. I noticed that too. That is why I handed his textbook to you."

"Yes, but the textbook you handed me was published four years ago and the novel was written just last year."

"So, you think Dr. Hewitt has developed a new encryption method?"

"I know he did."

"Oh? How can you know that?"

"Because I hacked into his account." Aspen couldn't believe how quickly, and nonchalantly, he uttered those words. He was scared that Sir Arlington would get mad and arrest him for hacking into a teacher's account.

Sir Arlington paused, with a look of total surprise, before speaking. "That's…brilliant, young Aspen! Why didn't I think of that?"

"So, you're not mad?"

"Of course not. I mean, you shouldn't go about hacking into your teachers' private accounts just for fun, but this was a quest for knowledge. Well done."

Aspen was quite relieved. "Thank you, sir."

"So, what did you find?"

"Quite a lot, actually. Maybe a bit too much. It's why Whitfield came with me today."

"Oh? Shall we call him in now?"

"In a minute. First, let me tell you about the book's encryption. I first came across messages with Dr. Hewitt's publisher. He is working on another textbook, so I asked Whitfield to help me, and we read through all of his notes and new book chapters and still didn't find this particular encryption process, so I kept digging. I went back over a year and I finally found it."

"Found what?"

"Dr. Hewitt's communication records with the author, Miyagi White. See, Mr. White asked Dr. Hewitt for help with the coded messaging. It was Dr. Hewitt's idea to put the messages in a public setting, so the bad guys could avoid taking the risk of meeting each other in person or having their conversations recorded. That's where the idea for the wedding announcements came from. Then, Dr. Hewitt created some sample encoded announcements and sent over the decrypted messages. It seems that Mr. White himself still couldn't figure out the decryption process, and asked for a detailed explanation."

"Ahh, so you read the decryption process right from Dr. Hewitt's own hand. Well done!"

"No, not exactly. Dr. Hewitt refused to give away his code. He insisted that Miyagi send over any character names that he wanted to use and other scene details of where and when he wanted the crime to be committed. Dr. Hewitt then replied with his own encrypted messaging for the announcement."

"So, Miyagi White doesn't even know how the encryption in his own book works?"

"Doesn't have a clue. He's not happy about it either, judging by the messages. He said he doesn't want to work with Dr. Hewitt again."

"So, if Dr. Hewitt never sent over the code, then you don't know it either, I presume."

"Well, that's not exactly true either."

"What do you mean?"

"I cracked it."

"Excuse me."

"I figured it out. I know how he does it."

Sir Arlington beamed with pride. "Such a brilliant young man. How does he do it?"

"Well, I got both the encrypted and decrypted messages from Dr. Hewitt's accounts. From there I went to work. I figured it wasn't going to be a simple mono-alphabetic substitution cipher, so I played around with a few poly-alphabetic and permutation ciphers. A few public and private-key cryptography elements, and before long, I got it."

"That's amazing! Young Aspen, I am impressed."

Aspen smiled from ear to ear. He felt proud of himself. "Thank you, sir."

"Do you think you can show me how the code used in the book works?"

"Sure. Do you have some paper?" Aspen spent the next 25 minutes demonstrating the encryption code used in Miyagi White's mystery novel to Sir Arlington. In the end, the headmaster was astonished.

"Young Aspen, that may have been the most utterly enjoyable teaching lesson I have ever received. Simply brilliant!"

"Thank you, sir."

"Now, I believe you have another purpose in stopping by. One that includes your brother?"

"Yes, sir." Aspen went to the door and asked if Whitfield could come in. Whitfield thought it would be best for Flaherty and Ugu to join them as well. Flaherty, because what they had to tell Sir Arlington affected the gymnastics team, and Ugu, because, well, she just may be the smartest student at Seven Bridges, and would likely find out eventually.

"Now that we have a nice gathering, what would you like to share?"

"Well, sir, when I was going through Dr. Hewitt's messages, I stumbled across these." Aspen handed out copies of several pages to Sir Arlington, Ugu, and Flaherty. Whitfield already had his own.

Flaherty recognized the formatting immediately. "Scoresheets?"

Whitfield confirmed, "yes, from our first meet."

Sir Arlington knew exactly what these were. "Yes, Dr. Hewitt is our school's treasurer and record-keeper. He receives these sheets directly from the WGF to update our school's records. They also serve as confirmation when receiving our winning allocation and for related purchases."

Aspen wasn't done yet. "Yes, well sir, we believe the scores have been tainted."

Now, Sir Arlington looked quizzical. "Explain."

"Well, sir, if you look…"

Flaherty quickly cut off Aspen, interjecting her disbelief. "Hey, I didn't score a 19.62 on Vault-Pegs in the first meet." Flaherty continued flipping through a few pages. "Wait, all my scores are off. And Whitfield's too. Look, they even misspelled Chloe's last name. One T, not two."

"That's what my brother is trying to say, sir. Our scores on these scoresheets do not reflect what we actually scored in the meet. Most of my scores are lower on these sheets. Aspen's scores are mostly lower too. We checked the others, and some are up but most are down, and none are correct."

Flaherty continued examining the sheets. "The scores for the other teams appear accurate, though."

"They are. We checked."

Aspen was relieved, and oddly satisfied, that Sir Arlington, along with the rest of the group, appeared to be taking this issue seriously.

"Curious. What are you suggesting, young Aspen?"

Whitfield answered first. "We think someone is trying to lower our scores on purpose."

"And we think we know who."

Sir Arlington peered out above his glasses. "Who?"

"Professor Marino."

"Oh, that's nonsense. Professor Marino has been a trusted member of this faculty for 20 years."

Aspen didn't appreciate how quickly Sir Arlington dismissed his claim. "Sir, he always gives us low scores on Tri-Bars. He's not fair."

Whitfield concurred, "that's right. And, if you look at the judge's signatures at the top of the page, Professor Marino's is the final one. He was the last to sign off on the sheets before they were submitted."

"I do not believe Professor Marino would engage in such behavior; however, I will investigate this matter immediately." Sir Arlington called Professor Marino, who was still on campus, and asked him to come to his office immediately. For good measure, Sir Arlington also called Dr. Hewitt into his office. Both professors arrived within 20 minutes.

"Gentlemen. It appears that we have an inquiry from these students regarding a matter of improper score keeping. I have stumbled upon these scoresheets from our first meet. Professor Marino, is this your signature?" Sir Arlington showed the scoresheets to Professor Marino.

"Yes, sir, it is."

Dr. Hewitt appeared concerned. "Where did you happen to come across these sheets, sir, if I may ask?"

Aspen looked guilty and was hoping Sir Arlington would cover for him. "On my direction, one of these students hacked into your account in search of a vital piece of information. In doing so, this student happened to stumble upon these sheets, which appear to have incorrect scores inputted into them. Can either of you explain?"

Professor Marino took a closer look at the scoresheets. "Let me see that. I have never inputted an incorrect score. This is outrageous."

Aspen blurted out under his breath, "yeah right." Professor Marino heard, and glared over at Aspen. Whitfield urged Aspen to stay quiet.

Dr. Hewitt finally cleared the air. "Ahh, I think I know what is going on here. First, whichever one of you hacked into my account…nice job. That wasn't an easy firewall to break through. Kudos. Anyway, I know what the issue is. You pulled the first set of sheets that came through. There is always an issue with the first transmission. For as long as I can remember. A glitch of some kind. If you bothered to continue checking my messages, you would notice a second set of scoresheets coming through five minutes after the first. Happens all the time. Here, let me show you. If I may?"

Sir Arlington allowed Dr. Hewitt to take control of the large screen in his office. Dr. Hewitt pulled up his messages, which, unsurprisingly, looked very familiar to Aspen. Dr. Hewitt highlighted all messages coming in from Gen. Gibson at the WGF. He was right. Following every meet, a message reading 'Official Meet Scoresheets' came in on Tuesday at 19:00, followed by another message reading 'Correction: Official Meet Scoresheets' timestamped exactly five minutes later. Dr. Hewitt opened the 'Corrected' scoresheets and let everyone in the room inspect them.

Sir Arlington watched as his students reviewed the evidence. "Well, students? Are those the correct scores?"

Whitfield felt deflated, and embarrassed. "Yes, sir."

Flaherty felt the same way. "Yes, sir."

"Wait…" Aspen desperately wanted Professor Marino to be guilty of something, anything, but even he had to relent. "…yes, sir."

"And just to satisfy any lingering concerns, let me show you one more thing." Dr. Hewitt logged into his school treasurer and record-keeper account, and pulled up the tab where official scores were archived. "Look. I just want to show everyone here that the scores recorded in the official archives are indeed the scores you each earned in the meet." Every score was correctly recorded.

"Gentlemen. Thank you for coming on such short notice. Please accept my deepest apologies for this inquiry. Your integrity, once again, has been proven admirable."

Professor Marino and Dr. Hewitt turned to leave Sir Arlington's office, but before they exited, Whitfield stood and cleared his throat. "Sirs. I just want to apologize for all of this. Flaherty and Ugu had nothing to do with any of this. Aspen and I found the account. We just thought…well…we're really sorry."

Professor Marino was gracious. "Apology accepted." He bowed, and walked out.

Dr. Hewitt was equally gracious. "No apologies needed. You found something out of place, and immediately pursued it. Even if it meant challenging a figure of some authority around here. You are to be commended. Keep up the great work!" With a wink and a head nod, Dr. Hewitt left as well.

Whitfield turned his attention to Sir Arlington. "Sir, I'm really sorry about this."

Aspen offered his sincere apologies too. "Yeah, me too. I should have opened the other messages first."

"Boys. Do not be too hard on yourselves. I happen to agree with Dr. Hewitt. Yes, young Aspen, you could have exercised more diligence, but perhaps it was I who was too impetuous with requesting such a meeting. You have all been performing at a high level. Please, take the rest of the afternoon off. Enjoy yourselves."

"Thank you, sir. But we have practice coming up in a few minutes."

"Ooh, Aspen…you're right. We have to go." Flaherty rushed to gather her things.

"Well, after practice, take tonight and tomorrow afternoon off. Young Ugu, I am locking my door. You four are under strict orders to have fun. Failure to do so will result in your arrest." Sir Arlington flashed a warm smile.

All four responded affirmatively. "Yes sir!" Whitfield, Aspen, Ugu, and Flaherty all got up, threw away their copies of the 'glitch' scoresheets, left Sir Arlington's office, and exited the library.

Flaherty put her arm around Aspen. "Don't worry, Aspen. I would have had the same questions about the scoresheets."

"Thanks, Flaherty. I still don't think it makes sense."

Whitfield felt the same as his brother. "Me too. Something isn't right about all this."

The three gymnasts headed straight for Arlington Gymnastics Center. Ugu, who had been sitting quietly during the meeting in Sir Arlington's office, but listening intently, also wasn't quite satisfied with letting go of Aspen's scoresheet inquiry. "Hey, let's catch up after practice. I'm going to head over to the IA library to see if I can make any further sense of all this."

Whitfield was happy to hear that Ugu was also uneasy about these altered scoresheets. "You got it. We'll see you soon."

****

Aspen did not have a good practice. He just couldn't find his rhythm on Pommel Clock or Escalating Tramps, and fell a lot on VH-Bars and Parallel Planks. Something was bothering him.

Sure, he was still tired from not getting any sleep the night before, but there was something else. He wasn't entirely satisfied with Dr. Hewitt's quick, and almost too smooth, response to the whole scoresheet issue. During a quick break, Whitfield caught up with Aspen.

"You OK, bro?"

"I just don't have it today."

"Me neither. Really tired. We both need to get some rest."

"Do you think Ugu will find anything?"

"Well, if anyone can, it's her."

With their minds elsewhere, Whitfield and Aspen decided to play it smart during the rest of practice. They opted to focus more on strength training and flexibility, rather than risk getting hurt while attempting difficult skills on an apparatus. After practice, they waited for Flaherty, who was having a great practice, as usual, and they all met up with Ugu at the International Affairs library.

Aspen was most anxious to learn about Ugu's progress. "Hey, Ugu. Find anything?"

"Hi guys. Nothing much. But I'm stuck trying to hack into Dr. Hewitt's account."

Flaherty wasn't used to hearing Ugu struggling with what appeared to be a simple hack. "Why are you trying to access his account anyway?"

"Because I threw away the scoresheets Aspen printed out, and I wanted to check something. Did any of you keep your sheets?"

No one did.

Whitfield thought he might lighten the mood by picking on Ugu just a little. "Wait. Did you say you couldn't hack into Dr. Hewitt's account? You? The smartest student at Seven Bridges Academy!"

"Ha ha." Ugu wasn't really in the mood for jokes.

"Aspen. Show her how it's done."

Aspen sat down and went to work. Before long, he…still couldn't get in. "No. This isn't right. Why can't I get in? This is strange. It's not letting me in."

"Let me see." Ugu reviewed Aspen's work. "Yeah, that's just how I tried to get in. Why isn't it working? This is how you got in the other day, right?"

"Yeah. You don't think he updated his security, do you?"

Flaherty thought this might be a possibility. "Well, you did just tell him you hacked into his account. I'd probably want to strengthen my security too."

Whitfield thought something wasn't quite right. "Yeah, but this fast?"

Flaherty agreed, "that does seem a little strange."

"You think he's trying to hide something?"

"I don't know, Whitfield. It is suspicious."

"Ugu's right. It is suspicious. How can we get a look at those scoresheets again?" Flaherty asked the question that no one seemed to have a good answer to. That is, until Ugu came up with a clever idea.

"Aspen, where did you look at the scoresheets?"

"What do you mean?"

"I mean, exactly where were you when the scoresheets were out in the open?"

"Just in the library and Sir Arlington's office. But I only had the sheets on my computer screen in the library. I printed out copies and just shoved them into my bag. Why?"

"Well, it looks like it's Sir Arlington's office then."

Whitfield recalled Sir Arlington's orders that they were to stay away from work and 'just have fun'. "Ugu, Sir Arlington said he was locking his door. We can't break in there. He'll have us arrested."

With just a quick second or two of eye contact, Flaherty was the first to catch onto Ugu's plan. It seemed as though the two best friends had an entire conversation with each other without speaking. "We're not going to break into his office. Ugu, you know what this means?"

"Yup. We'll have to get changed."

Whitfield and Aspen were totally confused.

"Boys. I think you two can finally go home and get some sleep. Ugu and I have some work to do."

"Uhh…what does that mean?" Whitfield loved that Ugu and Flaherty were best friends, but sometimes felt left out of their private connection.

"Oh, it's nothing, really. We just have to access the surveillance cameras in Sir Arlington's office."

Flaherty added, "and you need to have *CBT V* clearance for that."

Whitfield acknowledged the huge hole in their plan. "But you don't have *CBT V* clearance."

Ugu and Flaherty smiled at each other. "Right. But Spencer does."

"Who's Spencer?"

"He's a fifth-year. Kind of a loner. But, he also kind of has a crush on Ugu."

"Nuh-uh…he likes you more."

"No way."

"Yeah, he does."

Whitfield needed to put an end to this silly back and forth. "Whoa. What are you talking about?"

Flaherty could see Whitfield and Aspen were totally clueless. "It's simple. Spencer has access to the cameras we need inside Sir Arlington's office."

"OK. But he can't just give you access, and he's not just going to hack into Sir Arlington's office on his own."

Ugu offered a sly smile. "Well…not intentionally. Look, he likes both of us. We'll just flirt with him a little, distract him enough to get what we need, and leave. Piece of cake."

Aspen was on board with the plan. "That sounds like a great idea."

"No, it doesn't. I don't think you should manipulate Spencer like that."

"Oh really. You're concerned about Spencer?"

"Yes."

"And it has nothing to do with Ugu flirting with an older boy?"

"Well…"

Ugu got up, grabbed Whitfield's hand, and walked a few steps away so the others couldn't hear. "Whitfield? What's wrong?"

"Look, I just don't feel comfortable with you flirting with another boy for personal gain."

"Whitfield, sweetie, we need to get those scoresheets back. This plan will work. But I'll only go ahead with this if you're on board. Would you like to flirt with Spencer?"

"No. Of course not. He's too tall for me." Whitfield forced out a smile.

Ugu returned a smile of her own. "I promise nothing will happen with Spencer."

"How can you be sure?"

"Because I think I've already fallen for someone else."

Whitfield tried playing it cool. "Oh really? Who's that?"

Ugu squeezed Whitfield's hands and pulled him in closer. Her body pressed against his. She leaned in, and with her lips lightly brushing his ear, whispered softly, "Felipe." Ugu took a step back and continued teasing Whitfield. "He's a new transfer student. Fourth-year. Super hot. Surprised you haven't met him yet."

Flaherty and Aspen started laughing. Whitfield fell for Ugu's tricks again. He thought he might call her out this time. "You're lying."

"Really? How can you tell?"

"Clues."

"What clues? You couldn't see my eyes. I spoke in a whisper. No clues."

"Your heart."

"Excuse me?"

Whitfield took a step forward, gently pressing his body against Ugu's and looked deep into her eyes. "I felt your heart beating super fast. When you were pressed against me. I bet Felipe doesn't affect your heart that way."

Ugu wanted to come back with a witty retort, some comment to show that she still held the upper hand, but she couldn't. She was melting away standing this close to Whitfield. She wanted to kiss him. Their first real kiss. Her heart starting beating even faster. If he wasn't going to kiss her, she would make the first move. Right here. Right now. It didn't matter that Aspen and Flaherty were right there. Ugu prepped herself. She leaned in. She was ready.

Whitfield continued staring deep into her eyes. Flaherty was on the edge of her seat, desperately hoping for Ugu and Whitfield to finally kiss. Ugu softened her lips. Whitfield…yawned. He yawned! Whitfield turned his head, partially covered his mouth, and let out a huge yawn.

Ugu slipped out of her temporary trance. "What was that?"

"Oh no…I am so sorry. We were going to kiss, weren't we? No. No. Here, I'm ready. Oh no…" Whitfield yawned again. He was so tired. "I am so tired. Sorry. I meant to say, I am so sorry."

Any girl in the world would have felt embarrassed, frustrated, and even a little mad at the boy they had a crush on ruining the perfect moment by yawning. Every girl, that is, except for Ugu. "That's OK. I understand." Ugu stepped away. The mood was gone. "Flaherty, come on, let's get ready."

Ugu turned to leave, but Whitfield pulled her closer. "Ugu. Look, I want to kiss you. I really do. If you don't believe me, here." Whitfield brought Ugu's palm to his muscular chest and held it there. "Feel that? My heart races every time I'm with you. Every time I think of you. I want our first kiss to be special, but…"

Ugu stood there, listening to Whitfield's words, feeling Whitfield's heart, and falling even deeper in love. "It's OK. I understand. Really, I do. I'll wait for you. Go home. Get some sleep. I'll send you a message when I get home tonight."

Ugu and Flaherty went upstairs toward the Outer Loop to go home and get ready.

Aspen wasn't sure exactly what just happened, but saw a strange look on Whitfield's face. "You OK, bro?"

Whitfield snapped out of his own trance. "I think so. Just tired. Can I crash at your place tonight?"

"Sure."

"Thanks. Let's just take the long way. I have a feeling I do not want to see what Ugu is going to be wearing tonight."

****

Flaherty checked the student directory and surprisingly, saw that Spencer was currently doing circles on a pommel in the Inner Bowl. He was by himself, working on adding points for the House Point Challenge. Flaherty and Ugu decided against putting on party dresses, and opted instead for leggings and sports bras. They headed straight for the Inner Bowl.

Flaherty and Ugu lightly jogged around the Inner Bowl, which was brightly illuminated by moonlight, lampposts, and the brightly-lit scrolling news feed affixed to the Outer Loop. They spotted Spencer, struggling to complete circles over on one of the practice pommels, and jogged over in his direction.

"Hey, Spencer. How are you?"

Spencer fell off the apparatus. He was excited that Flaherty even recognized him. "Oh…hi Flaherty."

The girls stopped running and stood next to Spencer. "Hey Spencer, what are you doing?"

"Hi Ugu. Umm…I was just trying to add some points for the House Point Challenge."

"Wow. That's really decent of you. I wish more people in our house were as dedicated as you."

"Yeah, me too. I can't believe how selfish many of the students in my house are."

"It's nothing, really. I'm not really that good. I keep falling off. I was trying to get to 100, but I don't think I'll make it tonight."

Flaherty was impressed with Spencer's goal for the night. "What are you up to?"

Spencer lowered his head, and muttered, "twelve."

Flaherty wasn't expecting such a low number, given how sweaty Spencer was already. Ugu expressed some empathy. "Oh, well, that's not bad. You just got here, right?"

"I've been here for about 25 minutes."

Ugu was struggling to remain positive, but it was in her nature to be uplifting. "Oh, well…that's still good. I couldn't even do twelve if you gave me an hour." That was a lie. "Maybe Flaherty could give you some pointers."

"Really?"

"Of course, I'd be happy to." Flaherty and Ugu continued to offer Spencer some guidance and tips on completing circles on the pommel, making certain to touch Spencer as often as they could. Flaherty even pretended to lose her balance several times so that she and Spencer bumped into each other more often. Spencer loved the attention, and was having a good time. The girls, although their motives were not pure, were having a good time as well. Spencer was fun to hang out with.

After a while, Ugu and Flaherty made eye contact with each other and decided to further their plan. "Spencer, this has been really fun, but it's getting late. I think we should be getting home now."

"Home? No. Ugu, you promised you were going to help me with my project."

"Oh shoot. I forgot. OK. I'll go to the Advanced Medicine library with you. Not sure how much help I'll be, but maybe…" Ugu dropped the act. She turned to Spencer. "Wait, I can't do this."

"Do what?"

"Spencer. You're a really nice guy, and we had a lot of fun with you tonight, but our meeting wasn't just a coincidence."

Flaherty decided to come clean too. "Yeah, we kind of sought you out. We need *CBT V* access to look inside Sir Arlington's office for something, and we were going to try to trick you into helping us, but, darn it, you are just too nice. We can't do that to you."

"We are so sorry. We did have fun with you, though. Really." Ugu and Flaherty started to walk away.

"Wait. What is it that you need from Sir Arlington's office?"

"Well, it's not exactly in his office."

"Flaherty's right. We were in there earlier today, and long story short, we were reviewing a document with him…"

"Only, we threw the pages away before leaving the office, and now, we kind of need them back."

"I thought you said what you needed wasn't in Sir Arlington's office. Why don't you just go back in there and get the documents out of the trash?"

"We can't. Well, not until later in the week. Anyway, we were hoping we could pull the surveillance videos from our earlier meeting to recover the document." Ugu implored Spencer to help them.

"Sure. I can help with that."

Ugu was not expecting it to be this easy. "Really? I thought you couldn't share *CBT V* secrets with third-year students?"

"Well, sure. We're not supposed to share with anyone who doesn't have clearance. So, you can just tell me what you're looking for, and I can pull it for you."

Flaherty knew that wouldn't work. "Spencer. That's not going to work. We can't have you see the document."

"Why not?"

Ugu sensed Spencer's concern and didn't want to lose their only chance at pulling this off. "It's confidential. But I promise you it's something that we are fully entitled to see. We were the ones who brought the document into Sir Arlington's office in the first place."

Spencer was not convinced. "If you had the document, why didn't you just make extra copies?"

"We did. We just threw those out as well." Flaherty wasn't sure if the truth was going to work, but was committed to following Ugu's lead.

"Something just doesn't seem right with all this."

"I know. If it was me, I'd be really skeptical as well." Ugu grabbed Spencer's hand. "I'm just asking you. Please. Help us retrieve this document. We promise it's for a good cause."

Spencer was reluctant, but agreed. Flaherty, Ugu, and Spencer went into the Advanced Medicine library, and Spencer used his credentials to pull up the surveillance footage from Sir Arlington's office and then stepped aside while Flaherty and Ugu reviewed the tapes.

Ugu pointed to the corner of the screen. "Here it is. Shoot I can only see the top half of the page over Aspen's shoulder."

"That's not enough. We need the whole thing."

Overhearing their frustration, Spencer spoke over his shoulder. "Are there any video screens or mirrors in the office?"

"Yes. Lots of video screens. Why?"

"See if you can use the reflection from the screens to piece together the rest of the document."

"That's a great idea! Ugu?"

"Yes. I think we can. Look, right there. On Sir Arlington's desk. I can see the bottom half of the document. Now, if we just move the video forward a bit...no, he doesn't ever flip through the pages."

"But I did! Change the angle. Look at the reflection peering over my shoulder."

"Flaherty, you're a genius." Ugu and Flaherty took all the screenshots they needed from the surveillance footage.

"Spencer. We can't thank you enough for this. You really helped us a lot." Ugu gave Spencer a hug.

"Spencer. You're the best." Flaherty gave Spencer a kiss on the cheek.

Ugu and Flaherty left the library and ran back to Ugu's house. Spencer just stood in place and spoke softly to himself. "I just broke every rule of *CBT*. I gave access to unauthorized students. Let them manipulate me. Let them take screenshots of the footage..." Random students studying nearby, gave Spencer two thumbs up after seeing Ugu and Flaherty hug and kiss Spencer. "...totally worth it!"

****

Ugu and Flaherty arrived at Aspen's house at 01:27. They found Aspen and Whitfield asleep on the couches in the sitting room. Flaherty put a blanket over Aspen. Ugu did the same for Whitfield.

"You should have kissed him earlier."

"I know."

"Why didn't you."

"I don't know."

"You know whenever it happens, it's going to be perfect. Even if it's all messed up."

"I know…because it's going to be with him."

"Oh, you are so in love."

Ugu just stood there, staring at Whitfield. "Yeah, I am."

"He's a lucky guy."

"Hey, did I ever tell you about the time I saw him naked?"

Chapter 20
Dr. Hewitt's Mistake

Sitting at his desk in his basement loft inside Whitfield's mansion, Dr. Hewitt seemed fidgety. He needed to make the call, but was hesitant. When all went well, he loved chatting with General Gibson. Even considered him a friend. But he hated delivering bad news. Especially to his friend. And even more so, when it involved something that he, himself, could have prevented. But he could no longer delay making the dreaded phone call. Gen Gibson had to be made aware of the situation. Reluctantly, Dr. Hewitt placed the call.

"Sir, we may have a problem."

"I'm listening."

"Sir Arlington has seen the files. He may be on to us."

"How could you let this happen? You assured me he would never suspect you."

"It wasn't him. Not directly, at least. He had help."

"Who?"

"Two students. They hacked into my message center."

"Students! You let students hack you?"

"They caught me off guard. But, don't worry, I've upgraded my security. They will not be able to hack in again."

"What do they know?"

"Nothing, I think. They simply thought they were given lower scores than they earned at the meet. I handled it. Sir Arlington seemed satisfied."

"Gymnasts, huh? Always concerned about their own scores. Blinds them to the point they fail to see the big picture. Still, I am displeased. Our whole operation is dependent upon these transactions. We cannot afford any more screw ups. Is that clear?"

"Yes, sir."

"Is there anything else?"

"Sir, yes, I'm afraid there is."

"What is it?"

"The students. The ones who hacked into my messages."

"What about them?"

"It was Whitfield and Aspen, sir."

"The Mitchell boys?"

"Yes, sir."

"Livvy and Aldrich's boys hacked into your messages and may now be in possession of data that could destroy us all?"

"I am sorry sir."

"This is worse than I thought. If they figure out what they saw, they may alert Hendricks. We have to get to him, and them, first. I'll alert the founders. You are hereby on alert. Do not fail us again."

Chapter 21
Decrypting Scoresheets

The end of Term 1 was fast approaching and SBA students were busy with class projects and studying for exams and placement tests for next term's classes. Students not only had to pass the current term's classes, but before Term 1 was over, also decide which classes they wanted to take next term and pass the qualifying exams before enrolling. The school's method of testing into certain classes mirrored the pure meritocracy found in greater society. All positions, including those of teachers, government officials, law enforcement, judges, coaches, and beyond required annual appointment, or re-appointment, testing. It did not matter for how long someone held a position or how powerful the role was, all individuals holding a job must comply with the annual testing requirement. Even Sir Arlington, who had been headmaster at Seven Bridges Academy for 27 years, and Lord Sirroc, who has served as President of the WGF for the past 12 years, were each required to pass annual assessments. By requiring students to take qualifying exams before enrolling in classes, Sir Arlington felt he was preparing students for the real world.

Students had until Friday at 17:00 to complete all exams, but since Whitfield, Aspen, and Flaherty were leaving Friday morning for the pre-meet festivities for their third meet of the season, they were working extra diligently to complete all testing and submit all projects by Thursday night. Aspen, along with all other first-years, was excused from course placement testing as they would be on their internships in Term 2.

Instead, Aspen had to choose an internship and pass any related qualifying exams. Aspen really wanted to intern at Seven Bridges Bank on campus, but those spots were typically reserved for third-years and up. He thought that perhaps Sir Arlington could help secure a spot for him.

Ugu, who once again had wanted to travel with the team but couldn't due to her on-campus obligations preparing for the upcoming Parents and Alumni Week, felt less pressure to submit her work as early as her friends; however, with the level of perfection Ugu demanded of herself, she was every bit as busy as the other three. Furthermore, Ugu was still hard at work tracking down other bribe attempts and identifying additional intentional falls at meets.

So far, Aspen's idea of looking at the head-to-head duel opponent was right on point for regular season meets, as in every case, the bribed gymnasts went head-to-head against a Seven Bridges competitor; however, this connection broke down in the playoffs, as bribed gymnasts appeared to take intentional falls when competing against other schools as well. Ugu was not yet able to see the bigger picture or detect a pattern involving the post-season bribes.

As for Aspen, in addition to completing his coursework, prepping for his potentially upcoming bank internship placement testing, and working hard at gymnastics practice, he was still consumed with the mystery of the money transfers and the riddle of the 'glitch' scoresheets he found in Dr. Hewitt's account.

Working late at the AMQE library on Thursday night, Whitfield had finally submitted his last project. "Aaannndddd…done! That's it, I submitted my last project. No more testing. How are you doing, bro?" Aspen was hard at work, not paying attention to Whitfield. "Hey, Aspen. Hello? You, OK?"

"Oh, yeah. I'm fine."

"You still working on your *Underground Economics* project?"

"No, I submitted it already."

"Well, then, *International Politics*?"

"Nope. All done."

"Cool. Well, then what are you doing? We already submitted our final problem set for *Multidimensional Calculus*. You aced your *CBT I* final. And, you don't know if you can take the bank internship exam yet, so what are you working on?"

"Just give me one more minute."

"Aspen."

"Please."

"Sure." Whitfield allowed himself to relax for a minute. He sent Ugu a quick message to see how she was doing. She responded promptly with a sweet, but curt, message. Whitfield knew she was still working hard and that he shouldn't bother her.

"I did it. I got it…I think."

"Got what?"

Aspen packed up his belongings. "Come on, let's go see Ugu. We'll grab Flaherty on the way."

"Aspen, it's after midnight. They are both still very busy. Can't this wait?"

"No. We're leaving tomorrow, and if I don't tell them now, it'll have to wait until Monday."

"And, so? Can it wait?"

Aspen thought for a moment. "No, it has to be now. We have to at least tell Ugu. We can tell Flaherty tomorrow morning on the bus."

Whitfield saw that Aspen wasn't going to let this go. "OK. Let's go see Ugu." Whitfield and Aspen ran across campus to the International Affairs library, stopping quickly to pick up a protein shake. Aspen was able to use his tracker for late-night entry into the IA library, and they both found Ugu working in her usual study spot. Whitfield placed the shake in front of her on the table and she showed her appreciation, despite there being a shake bar just 20 feet from where she was sitting in the library.

"Thank you so much. This is so thoughtful of you. Are you two done for the term?"

"Yup. Everything is submitted. Feels good."

"Oh, I'm so jealous. I still have two projects to submit. Are you done too, Aspen?"

"Yup. At least you took all your placement tests, right?"

"Yes. I got them out of the way on Monday, when they first opened up. I knew the rest of the week was going to be super busy, so I wanted to get those out of the way first."

"Do you know when we hear back on our placement assessments?"

"Classes for which you are eligible to take based on your scores will be updated on Monday. You'll then have until Friday to set your final course schedule. Whitfield, you're not worried about any of the assessments you took, are you?"

"Nah. I was just curious."

"What about you, Aspen? Worried about any of your finals?"

"No, not really. I think I did well on all of them."

"Great! So, are you two just heading home now?"

"Actually, I know you are really busy, but Aspen came across something and wanted to share it with you. I told him you were busy, but he said it couldn't wait until Monday and since we're leaving in the morning…"

"Sure. No problem. What is it?" Ugu closed the book in front of her to give Aspen her full, undivided attention.

"Thanks. So, I've been going through the scoresheets."

"The 'glitch' ones?"

"Right. Well, I think I found something."

"Really? That's great. What is it?"

"Well, remember how it's just the Seven Bridges scores that were inputted incorrectly?"

"Yes."

"Well, I don't think it was a glitch. I think it was done intentionally. I think it's an encrypted message."

Whitfield and Ugu both opened their eyes wide. "Get out. Really?"

"How?"

"Well, check this out." Aspen proceeded to show Whitfield and Ugu a page with just the first five Seven Bridges gymnasts names, leaving off their ranking and scores.

Sydney Truxler
Kayleigh Bourner
Keegan Carpeligian
Chloe Chatterlov
Flaherty Sumner

"Do you notice anything?"

Ugu caught something right away. "Yes. Chloe's name is misspelled. Flaherty already pointed that out in Sir Arlington's office."

"Right. Anything else?"

Whitfield studied the names closely. "No. Not really."

"They all have the same number of characters."

"Uhh…bro, sorry to burst your bubble, but no they don't."

"Aspen, Whitfield's right. Sydney Truxler has 13 letters and Kayleigh Bourner has 15 letters."

"Right! Which makes it the perfect disguise."

Whitfield looked at Ugu to see if she was following Aspen's train of thought. She just shrugged. "Aspen, you're not making any sense."

Aspen was growing frustrated, but realized that he was still seeing the names through a decrypted lens. He needed to take a step back. "Look. Let me explain."

"Please."

"You need to convert every letter to its corresponding number. A=1; B=2; C=3. Get it?"

Whitfield understood the mechanics of the code, but still didn't see it.

"OK. I guess. But..."

Aspen was growing impatient. "Here. I'll do it for you." Aspen took the first name on the list, Sydney Truxler, and with zero hesitation, wrote down a series of numbers: 19254145252018212412518, and triumphantly slapped the table. "Now do you see it?"

Whitfield thought Aspen might be losing it. "No. Aspen, maybe you just need some more sleep. You've been working really hard."

"No, Whitfield, let him explain. Go ahead, Aspen, we just need a little more time to catch up. Could you help us get there?"

"Sure. Look, S is the 19th letter of the alphabet, so we write down 19. Y is the 25th letter, so we write down 25. We keep going all the way to the last R in Truxler, which is the 18th letter. See it now?"

Ugu's eyes lit up. "Yeah, now I do. It's all right there. Good work. But what is it? This just seems like a random set of numbers."

"Right, but how many numbers?"

Whitfield and Ugu both counted. As usual, Ugu was faster. "Twenty-three."

"Exactly!"

"OK, but I'm still not getting it. What's the significance of 23 numbers?"

"Well, I have a theory. But, before I tell you, you should know that every Seven Bridges name on the scoresheets translates to 23 numbers, exactly. Well, after a few names are misspelled, that is. But by adding the extra T in Chloe's last name and the extra L in Wilson's first name, like the fake scoresheets did, all translations come to 23 numbers."

Whitfield's interest was piqued. "That's incredible. Does it work that way for the other gymnasts, not from Seven Bridges?"

"Nope. I mean some names do, but they are all over the place. Some have 20, or 25, or 26. Really, it's all over the place. But for Seven Bridges, all the gymnasts' names, as recorded on these sheets, fit. Look, they even cut off the last names of five other Seven Bridges gymnasts just to get them to fit into the 23-digit transcription."

Ugu glanced over at Whitfield. "That can't just be a coincidence. So, what do we know that has exactly 23 numbers in it?"

"School IDs? No. Licenses? No."

"Medical records?"

Aspen was enjoying seeing his brother and Ugu struggling to figure it out. "Close. But no. Do you guys have it yet?"

Just like that, a spark hit both Ugu and Whitfield at the same time. "Bank accounts!"

"Exactly!"

Whitfield couldn't believe it. "You think these are bank account numbers?"

"Yes."

Ugu remained cautious. "Did you confirm that?"

"No, not yet. Remember, Sir Arlington doesn't want us hacking into our bank's mainframe."

"Right, he doesn't want to tip them off to anything suspicious, you know, just in case someone in there is guilty of something."

"Ugu, do we know anyone working inside the bank?"

"Well, the fifth-years are just wrapping up their internship term. I can ask Spencer for help."

Whitfield rolled his eyes. "Oh, him again."

"Whitfield, relax. I told you nothing happened. He's actually a really nice guy. In fact, I think Flaherty had dinner with him a couple nights ago."

"Really? I didn't know about that. I'm just not comfortable…"

Aspen didn't want to blow this opportunity. "Whitfield."

"OK, I guess it's all right. You can ask Spencer if he can help identify if these are indeed bank account numbers. That might give us clue as to what some of the other numbers on the scoresheets mean."

"Great. I'll ask Spencer tomorrow. Great work, Aspen! You are a genius!"

Aspen felt really good about himself. "Thanks."

Whitfield sighed, with the slightest hint of jealousy. "Oh, don't give him a big head."

"Oh, Whitfield. I think you're a genius too. Just…not as smart as your brother…or me."

"Yeah, well…" Whitfield caught a glimpse of Ugu's sweet smile. "…you're probably right."

"As usual."

Whitfield just smiled, said good night, and as the boys left to go home, Ugu continued to work deep into the night.

****

The next morning, Whitfield, Aspen, and Flaherty met at Pike's for a quick breakfast before getting onto the team bus. On their way to their third meet of the year, the Energy meet, Aspen and Whitfield informed Flaherty of their conversation with Ugu from the night before.

"Wow, Aspen! That's awesome. I can't believe you figured that all out."

"Thanks. It was nothing, really. So, do you think Spencer could help see if these are really bank account numbers?"

"I'm sure he would if he could, but his internship ended yesterday. I don't think he'll have access to the bank's mainframe anymore. Sorry."

"That stinks. Well, Aspen, if you get the internship at the bank, you'll be able check yourself."

Flaherty was curious. "What internship?"

"Aspen is applying for the bank internship for Term 2."

"I know they usually don't take students before third-year, but I was hoping Sir Arlington could pull a few strings for me."

Flaherty felt bad being the bearer of bad news. "Sorry, but I don't think that's going to work either. Dr. Hewitt is in charge of the bank internship, and Spencer said he doesn't even want third-years anymore. Said Dr. Hewitt's really trying to shut down student access to some of the banking records."

"Oh no. I was really hoping I could intern there. Plus, I need to check on these account numbers."

"Sorry, bro."

"Hey, Aspen, look, there's a bunch of good internships available for first-years. You can work at the hospital; the Holographic Design and Engineering Lab is always looking for interns. You can go into Campus Planning, Architecture, and Design; Flying Vehicle Design; or maybe Curriculum Development."

Whitfield tried offering yet another option. "Or maybe Security and Surveillance."

Flaherty shook her head. "No, those are only open to students who have already passed *CBT III*."

"Oh, sorry."

"No problem. Look, there are about five or six internship opportunities available where you wouldn't even have to take a qualifications exam. If you really wanted to get into a different internship, you can stop by the Administration Building early on Monday and maybe they'll let you take the qualifications exam late."

Aspen was disappointed. "Thanks. I'll think about it and maybe see Sir Arlington on Monday. I really thought he'd be able to take care of this for me."

After another 20 minutes or so, Ugu contacted Whitfield. She basically confirmed everything Flaherty had just told them about Spencer's internship coming to an end and no longer having access to the bank's mainframe and Dr. Hewitt's insistence that bank internships be reserved for upperclassmen.

"Yeah, that's just what Flaherty said. She said Spencer wasn't sure if it was Sir Arlington or Dr. Hewitt that wanted to restrict younger students' access to bank records."

"Interesting."

"Yeah, but either way, it's a real bummer for Aspen. He said he still wants to talk with Sir Arlington Monday morning. Even if he can't get into the bank internship, maybe Sir Arlington will have another idea."

"Hey, do me a favor. Tell Aspen to hold off on talking to Sir Arlington. I overheard a conversation between Sir Arlington and Lord Sirroc today…"

"Who?"

"Lord Sirroc, the President of the WGF."

"Oh, right."

"Yes, well they were talking a lot about gambling, bribes, and I even heard Sir Arlington mention Isadora's Gang."

"Maybe he was just informing Lord Sirroc of what's been going on."

"No, I think it was more than that. It was tough to hear, but I think I heard that Lord Sirroc failed his re-appointment exam."

Whitfield was not expecting to hear that bombshell of a news item. "Whoa. That's major!"

"I know. They also said something about if they don't find the funds soon, he may not be allowed to retake the exam. Lord Sirroc mentioned needing Sir Arlington's help to keep Gen. Gibson from taking over his position and Sir Arlington told him they should go to Isadora for help. What do make of all of that?"

"Hmm…it doesn't sound good. Do you think Sir Arlington might be the one bribing gymnasts to take falls?"

"I can't believe that, but I guess it would make some sense. All the bribes are, in a way, helping Seven Bridges win. Sir Arlington is our headmaster and certainly gains from our success."

"He wouldn't do that though, would he?"

"I really hope not, but until we know for sure, let's pull back on how much we share with him. Whitfield, we'll need to pursue this ourselves. With Flaherty and Aspen too, of course."

"Agreed. Are you going to find somewhere else to review the surveillance footage?"

"I thought about that, but Sir Arlington's office is really the only place where I have full access, and he might get suspicious if I stop coming around. Besides, it will give me an opportunity to keep an ear to the ground. I've been there so much lately that I think he forgets I'm even there. Some of the things I've heard him say on the phone or in one-on-one meetings. Wow."

"Really? Like what?"

"Nothing really relevant for what we're doing. I can fill you in later on some of the juicy stuff."

"Fair enough. What should I tell Aspen to do about his internship?"

"Well, I do have an idea. Tell him to meet me in the IA library at 06:00 Monday morning. It's a longshot but I think it just might work."

"Are you going to tell me what it is?"

Ugu loved playing coy with Whitfield. "Nope. It's probably best that you two just focus on the meet this weekend. Aspen doesn't need to do any additional prep work. Just tell him don't be late."

"OK. You're lucky I trust you."

"It's not luck. You love me."

"Oh, so you wouldn't consider yourself lucky if I were in love with you?"

"Excellent point. So, do you consider yourself lucky?"

"Yeah, I guess I do."

"Why?"

"Well, I have a loving family with Hendricks and Aspen. I am at this amazing school and part of the gymnastics team. And I have the second smartest student in my class hopelessly in love with me. Yeah, I'd say I'm a lucky guy."

"Second smartest? Oh, that right. I guess you do love yourself."

"Ouch! That's not what I meant."

"Good luck in the meet! Goodbye, Honey Bear!"

****

The Energy meet resulted in another Seven Bridges win and a clean sweep of the individual event titles. Once again, Flaherty led the way with a 46-4 record and contributed 97 team points. Coach Brockport allowed Flaherty to rest most of Session 6 as her ankle was bothering her a little. Whitfield went the whole way, compiling a 50-6 record and contributing 96 team points. Aspen continued performing well, competing on Pommel Clock, Tri-Bars, Parallel Planks, and made his season debut on VH-Bars.

Ugu watched both the banquet and meet live, and continued to document instances of bribery and intentional falls. Flaherty didn't work any of her magic at the pre-meet festivities this time, but Ugu was still able to spot eight envelope transfers, six at the banquet and two others at the hotel, where Ugu was able to tap into the live hallway camera feed.

She didn't have access to any of the envelopes' embedded notes, so wasn't sure exactly which routines were meant to be corrupted, but sure enough, just about every time a bribed gymnast from another school went head-to-head against a Seven Bridges gymnast, the result was the same—a significant fall, or multiple falls, resulting in a major duel victory for Seven Bridges. Ugu monitored the publicly available gambling action, and, as usual, saw some heavy money coming in on Seven Bridges to win, but curiously, also identified particularly high spikes in wagering activity when bribed gymnasts were set to compete.

Ugu knew she was onto something. *Clearly, someone knows who is about to take a fall, and betting big on Seven Bridges. But who?* Without access to the mainframes of the primary sportsbooks taking bets, Ugu could not identify specific accounts or the perpetrators of any individual transactions.

In the end, roughly $440 billion of the world's $7 trillion energy market shifted hands over the weekend. Seven Bridges Academy earned the lion's share of the winnings, and now had complete control over three of the world's largest uranium mines and the largest methanol reactor in the world. Seven Bridges also controlled massive amounts of crude oil reserves and petroleum naphtha, and had won the rights to purchase more energy reserves from state-owned providers at bargain prices. In addition to owning the largest endowment of precious gems and agricultural commodities in the country, Seven Bridges Academy continued to serve as a global leader in the energy market.

When the team arrived back home Sunday night, campus was buzzing. Students were lining the Inner Bowl, cheering and congratulating the team on the weekend's successful meet. Whitfield reminded Aspen that he should go straight home to get some rest since he was meeting with Ugu in the morning.

Even though part of him had wanted to stay up and enjoy his growing celebrity status, even if just for a little bit, Aspen knew his brother was right. Aspen went straight home, showered, set his alarm, and crashed in his bed. Whitfield and Flaherty avoided the crowds and ducked into the Advanced Medicine library to grab a quick snack before calling it a night.

Whitfield was still getting accustomed to all the fanfare. "Phew, that was close. It's crazy to think all those students, our classmates, are cheering for us."

"I know. I don't think I'll ever get used to it. But we can't let it get inside our heads. One slip-up and our whole world could change."

"Yeah, I guess."

"Something bothering you?"

"It's just…I can't get what Wilson said out of my head."

"When? This weekend?"

"No. Back during tryouts. He said 'we always win'. Like it didn't even matter if we practiced hard or performed well at the meet. Like we would win anyway. And now, with all these bribes and gymnasts taking falls when they compete against us. I don't know, it just doesn't feel right."

"I know what you mean. All weekend, I was looking forward to my duel with Mikaela. She's the defending champ on Planks and I wanted to see if I could beat her, fair and square. Only, she pulled out at the last minute. Said it was her shoulder, but I saw her go on Handstand Obstacle like 20 minutes later."

"Why would her shoulder keep her out of the Parallel Planks anyway?"

"Right? It wasn't even a good fake excuse."

"Well, should we say something?"

"To who?"

"I don't know. We can't say anything to Sir Arlington. I don't even want to talk to Professor Marino. He still has it in for Aspen and me. What about Dr. Hewitt? He seems to care a lot about us and always enjoys talking about our meets."

"I don't know. I know he's your house supervisor and all, but those messages from the WGF went straight to him. We don't know if he's involved in all this, and if he is, in what capacity. Besides, don't you think it's a little suspicious how quickly he updated his security after he found out Aspen hacked into it?"

"You're right. I guess we should just keep this all to ourselves. For now."

"Let's do a little more digging. We have Parents and Alumni Week coming up. No classes. We should have some time to sit back and really think about what's going on here."

"I guess."

Flaherty saw an opportunity to change the subject. "By the way, is Hendricks coming this week?"

Whitfield was grateful for the change in topic and excited to talk about Hendricks. "Yes. I can't wait to see him. This is the longest Aspen and I have ever been away from him. You're going to love him."

"I'm sure I will. I can't wait to meet him. Did you tell him about you and Ugu?"

"What? What's there to tell?"

"Uhh, only that you're in love with her."

"I am not...I mean, sorry, just a kneejerk reaction."

"Did you forget who you're talking to?"

"Yeah, I guess I did for a moment."

"Well, I'm sure he'll find out tomorrow night when we're all sitting together, with Ugu and her dad, at the Parents Ball."

"Oh, that's right. I totally forgot."

"You did pick out your suit, right?"

"Uhh..."

"Oh, Whitfield. Come on. Let's go to the Uniform Galleria. We can sneak into the basement level. I'll pick out something good for you."

"Thanks, you're a lifesaver. Oh, and can we..."

"Yes, I'll get Aspen a suit too."

"You're the best. What am I going to talk to Ugu's dad about? I mean, I didn't really make such a good first impression the last time I saw him."

Flaherty laughed thinking about that moment from the first pre-meet banquet. "I know. That was so funny. Ugu told me about it."

"Thanks. You can stop laughing now."

"Don't worry about it. I'm sure you'll come up with something to say. Besides, you have something else to worry about."

"Again? What? Nothing could be scarier that talking with Ugu's dad."

"Oh really? Well, then, what are you getting Ugu for her birthday?"

Whitfield stopped cold. Flaherty's question took him completely by surprise. "What?"

"Ugu's birthday. It's in two weeks. You didn't forget, did you?"

"Oops."

"Oh, Whitfield."

****

At 06:00 on Monday morning, Aspen met Ugu at the IA library. At first, Aspen thought they would leave the house and walk over together, but Ugu left a note saying that she was heading over to Flaxen Hall at 05:00 for some prep work for tonight's Parents Ball and would meet Aspen at the library.

"Don't you ever sleep?" Aspen was still wiping crust away from his eyes when he spotted Ugu in the library, whereas Ugu looked refreshed and ready to start the day.

"Sometimes."

"I don't know when. Well, what are we doing here?"

"I have an idea for your internship."

"OK. What is it?"

"How would you like to intern at the WGF?"

"Really?" That seemed to jolt Aspen awake. "That's not on the list of first-year internship opportunities."

"I know. It's usually only for second-years and up and you need to take a qualifying exam."

"But I already missed the deadline. Wasn't it last week?"

"Not for the WGF. They're different. They only take the most highly qualified, exceptional students. They typically do not take first-years because they need to see a record of course achievement first and the application process usually takes about a year to complete."

"So, how does that help me? My internship period starts a week from today."

"Well, I may have pulled a few strings. I spoke to the internship director, and she said it helps that you already took *Multidimensional Calculus*. That shows that you're really smart; I mean, you're the only first-year on record having ever taken that course. Your success at meets, thus far, and all your interviews, show that you can perform under pressure and are well-spoken."

"So that got me in?"

"Not quite. As a former intern, I wrote a glowing letter of recommendation for you."

"Aww...thank you, Ugu. So, that's what got me in?"

"Not quite."

Aspen was confused. "Well, what else is there? Do I have to take the qualifying exams?"

"No, they agreed to waive all other requirements if I was able to convince Gabe to do some charity work for them. I called him last night and set the whole thing up."

"Wait, so none of that other stuff mattered? They just wanted Gabe?"

"No. I'm sure the other stuff mattered too. Maybe."

"Thanks. Well, what am I supposed to do there anyway?"

Ugu shifted a little in her seat. She didn't quite know how to tell Aspen what he would be doing during his internship. "Well, as a first-year, there's not much they were willing to give you to do, so I…"

"Ugu?"

"I signed you up for…"

"Ugu?"

Ugu couldn't delay telling Aspen any longer. "You're going to be a chicken."

"What?"

"I kind of agreed that you would dress up as the World Gymnastics Federation bird mascot for any in-week promotional events and some Pro and Minor League meets, whenever they do not conflict with your school and meet schedule."

Aspen didn't believe Ugu. He figured she must be joking. "Oh, come on. I took *Multidimensional Calculus* and *International Politics*. Why would I want to dress up as a chicken?"

"Umm…yeah, that's not all."

Aspen thought this must be where Ugu drops the joke and tells him what he would really be doing at the WGF. "What else is there?"

"In the mornings, you have to dress in the bird suit and entertain kids at the WGF Family Entertainment Zone by letting them dunk you in water and…"

"And?"

"…shoot you with rubber arrows as you fly overhead in a pressurized air flow duct."

Aspen realized this wasn't a joke. "WHAT! No way. That's going to be so embarrassing. I can't do that."

"Hey, no one will know it's you. You'll be in costume the whole time."

Aspen was not happy, and was quite excitable. "Ugu, why are you doing this to me?"

"I need you to be inside WGF headquarters."

"Why? So I can be embarrassed in front of the whole world?"

"No."

"Then why?"

"Because we are going to get to the bottom of all this bribery and bank account corruption."

"How? You want me to lay some eggs on the bad guys?"

"No. I want you to hack into Gen. Gibson's account to find out what's really going on."

Aspen paused for minute and calmed down. "So, I'm going to be kind of like an undercover agent?"

"Exactly. Memphis Reigns 2.0."

"Cool."

"In a chicken suit."

"Less cool."

"Are you in?"

Aspen thought deeply for another minute. "OK. You bet! What do I need to do?"

Ugu was ecstatic. "Just fill this out and submit it before 07:00, and I believe that's it. You'll officially be the new WGF mascot for Term 2."

"And are you sure no one will know it's me in that suit?"

"Just you, me…and a few people at the WGF."

"Good. Let's keep it that way."

Chapter 22
Parents Ball

Parents and Alumni Week (PAW) was one of the highlights of the entire school year at Seven Bridges Academy. For seven days, campus was transformed into a festival of games, events, entertainment, and joyous exploits. As always, the week kicked off with the Parents Ball, where parents and their children came together to laugh, reminisce, and dance the night away. It's also when the winners of the Grand Curriculum Design Challenge would be announced.

As for the rest of the week, Ugu, PAW's lead organizer, scheduled a catalog of events for all comers to enjoy. Tuesday included mansion walk-through tours; cooking lessons with student chefs; hair, makeup, and personal image consulting with student stylists; a variety of water games; and harbor cruises and boat rides, with open-air floating dance floors. On Wednesday, former members of the gymnastics team were celebrated, along with former members of the cheerleading and dance squads.

Alumni and parents were scheduled to square off in a mock gymnastics meet, with special events where parents could throw a pie in their student's face and alums could dunk their favorite teachers in a giant water tank. Ugu had even designed what she called the Ultimate Ice Cream Sundae Surprise, a special rotating conveyor belt with seven levels, where current students and teachers, wearing special sticky suits, sat inside large ice cream bowls, as conveyor belts moved them along the course, and parents and alums, standing at a distance, fired foam objects at them, sprayed them with water, doused them with whipped cream, drizzled chocolate syrup on top of them, and threw softball-sized soft cherries at them, ultimately knocking participants backward into tubs of colored sprinkles.

Any student or teacher who reached the end of the top level without being knocked off with a cherry, found themselves either falling sideways into a vat of green slime or perched atop a giant waffle cone, only to be slowly tilted down to a slick strawberry jam slide ending up in a tub of chocolate chips. Ugu really outdid herself with that one.

The remainder of Wednesday's scheduled activities included a waterfall photo shoot; three-minute student research presentations; and the Alumni Achievement Awards Banquet. Thursday's schedule included a scavenger hunt; ski trip; fashion show; student talent show; and the Fantasy Student Draft, where alums and parents competed against each other in a fantasy league by drafting current students and earning points based on their students' classroom performance, physical activity, service work, and internship evaluations. Student bios are distributed beforehand, and prizes are awarded at the end-of-year celebration, resulting in many parents and alums taking the draft seriously, despite its fun intention.

For Friday, Ugu scheduled a family festival to take place in the flower gardens, followed by a day of service, where parents and alums are to be divided into small groups to complete various community service and engagement projects. The day concludes with the Precious Gems and Agricultural Commodities Auction and a special trivia night. Over the weekend, parents and alums are welcome to watch any, or all, of the 15 professional gymnastics meets that will be displayed on monitors throughout campus, and make special use of the on-campus sportsbook for all wagering activity.

In addition, the final weekend includes a music festival, starring twelve of the greatest living bands in history; a celebration of the 10th anniversary of Seven Bridges Academy's first national championship team; a wine and spirits tasting; a curriculum development workshop; and the annual students v. alumni v. parents physical challenge competition. When adding in all the various academic discipline alumni gatherings and class reunions, Ugu led a student team in organizing, staging, and scheduling well over 100 events for the one week.

As always, the kickoff to Parents and Alumni Week was Monday evening's Parents Ball. Since students completed Term 1 and did not have classes all week, and therefore had no need for classroom uniforms, the Uniform Galleria converted its second floor to a parents and alumni-only open closet for all their clothing needs for the week. Formal wear, boating attire, party dresses, casual wear, anything and everything that parents and alumni would need for the week was made available, free of charge. Sweetening the pot even more, parents were provided a $10,000 credit for any clothes they wanted to take home with them after the week was over; alumni were given a $5,000 credit.

For those select few, like Ugu's dad, who was both parent of a current Seven Bridges student and alumnus, a full $15,000 credit was awarded; however, many decided that $10,000 was plenty, and graciously gifted the remaining $5,000 back to the galleria, or to fellow parents or alums. Any other clothes that were worn, but not taken home, were simply dropped off at the laundry by the end of the week.

As many of the parents descended upon the second floor of the Uniform Galleria to get properly outfitted for tonight's ball, Ugu, satisfied that the committee she left in charge of running the event could function in her absence for at least an hour, decided to get ready for the ball at Flaherty's house, while Whitfield made his way over to Aspen's house to get ready.

"Hey Aspen, you excited to see Hendricks tonight?"

"Yeah, definitely. I miss him a lot."

"I know. Me too. What do you think he's been doing since we left?"

"Probably the same stuff as when we were there: work out, read, work out, beat up on some sparring partners, read some more, and maybe travel a little. You know how he was always disappearing for a weekend every now and then."

"Yeah, I know. I always pictured him as a spy, going on secret missions."

Aspen mumbled under his breath. "Yeah, but I bet he wasn't wearing a chicken suit."

"What was that?"

"Nothing."

"Do you think he's been watching our meets?"

"Probably not. You know he never liked watching meets."

"I know. He would always work with us, train us on every shape, movement, hand placement, even told us exactly when to inhale and exhale during a routine, but never seemed to want to watch any meets."

"Yeah, we would have to sneak downstairs to catch some of the meets when he was busy with something else."

"Well, it doesn't matter if he's watched any of our meets. I'm still excited to see him."

"Me too."

Meanwhile, over at Flaherty's house, the girls were busy getting ready on their own. "Hey Flaherty, are you excited to see your folks tonight?"

"I guess. I mean, I didn't get to see them much over break. With national team camps, elite training, and working at the lab, I was hardly home. They continued to travel for work, so they weren't home much either. When we were together, it would start off nice, but eventually we'd argue about something. You know the story. Dad thinks I'm not cut out for gymnastics and should focus on something else. Mom doesn't think I'm cut out for, well, much of anything. Nothing is ever good enough for her."

"Oh, come on. They are both wonderful people. They love you so much."

"I suppose. I think they still wish I was more like you."

"Nonsense. I wish I was more like you."

"That's nice of you to say. I guess we are both pretty OK."

The girls took a break from trying on jewelry to look at themselves in the mirror, standing next to each other. "We are better than OK. We are awesome. And you, wow, look at you in that dress! Flaherty, do me a favor and don't stand anywhere near me tonight. You are too beautiful."

"Yeah right. Do you see yourself? You are gorgeous."

"Our parents are very lucky to have daughters like us."

"Agreed. So, you think your dad will freak out when you tell him about you and Whitfield?"

"What? What's there to tell?"

"Ugu. Come on."

"Daddy will be fine. He likes Whitfield."

"Really?"

"Yes. After a slow start, he warmed up to him. Daddy said Whitfield was really sweet and respectful, and well-spoken when he took him back to the alumni function. Dad said a lot of his friends were impressed with Whitfield, and now that Whitfield is such a celebrity gymnast, I'm sure Dad loves him even more."

"Well, good. I hope your dad does like Whitfield. You two are great together. I can't wait to start planning the wedding."

"Thanks…wait, what? Wedding? Whoa, slow down, princess. Let's not get carried away. Too soon for that."

"I know. Just teasing…but, you know you've already thought about it."

Ugu blushed. "We haven't even kissed yet."

"Yeah…and?"

"And…I haven't even met Hendricks yet."

"Yeah…and?"

"And…so, what if I've already thought about it. It doesn't mean anything."

"Uh-huh."

"Shut up."

"My lips are sealed."

"Besides, maybe he's not even a good kisser. I mean, he did yawn when I tried to kiss him."

"Ugu. He had just stayed up all night...but sorry, not saying another word."

"And so what if he has like the perfect body. Maybe he doesn't even know how to tie a tie correctly or the proper way to button up a jacket?"

Flaherty knew her friend was just grasping at straws now. "Proper way to button a jacket?"

"I don't know...look, he's not perfect. OK, fine, maybe his eyes are the perfect shade of blue. And he has the perfect smile. And he always knows the right thing to say, except when talking with my dad, but even that, he was so cute, stumbling over his words like that."

"Ugu."

"He told Daddy that we were seeing each other, which means he wanted to go out with me, even back then. Wait, where was I?"

Flaherty rolled her eyes. "You were telling me about how Whitfield is not perfect."

"Right. He's not. Like did you see when he bit into that crepe at breakfast and some of it ran down his chin, and then he grabbed my napkin by mistake and it had whipped cream on it and he smeared it all over his cheek? That wasn't perfect, was it? I mean, we did all laugh. It was the funniest thing that happened that day. I mean, I was sitting in *Cyber Espionage* class later that day, just thinking back to that moment and let out a laugh in class, right when the teacher was talking about this case where four people were arrested over hacking into a bank's mainframe and stealing millions of dollars. Everyone just stared at me and thought I was crazy for laughing. See? Now, that wasn't perfect, was it?"

Flaherty didn't say anything. She just kept staring at Ugu.

"Shut up, Flaherty. He's not perfect."

"OK, whatever you say. I am with you all the way. Let's get going." With one final look in the mirror, Ugu and Flaherty left to head over to Flaxen Hall.

Back at Aspen's house, Whitfield was still struggling with his tie. "Aspen, did you see Ugu's dress before she left?"

"No, why?"

"Just curious. I wanted to know if I should get her a corsage for her wrist or one for up by her shoulder."

"Uhh...neither. Dude, this isn't a date."

"Huh?"

"Whitfield, it's a Parents Ball. If anything, her dad is going to be her date."

"Oh, right. I knew that."

"Are you OK?"

"Yeah, I guess I'm just a little nervous, that's all. I mean, the last time I saw Ugu really dressed up, I froze. And then, I started saying all kinds of weird stuff to her dad. I just don't want a repeat of that night."

"Just relax. You really hit is off with her dad at that alumni thing, right?"

"I guess so. I mean, he was nice to me and everything."

"Just be yourself. Ugu really likes you, so I'm sure her dad will like you too."

"But what if I say something dumb again?"

Aspen tried to calm his brother's nerves. "You won't. You'll be smooth. You'll be cool. Just don't say anything about kissing his daughter this time."

"Right. That was bad. I'll do better tonight."

"How do I look?"

"You're fine. How about me?"

"Good."

"OK, let's go."

****

Whitfield and Aspen walked over to Flaxen Hall together with most of the other members of Aspen's house, with Ugu being an obvious exception. As they neared the magnificent event hall, they recognized some of their other classmates.

"Hey, there's Seraphina and Dakota. I'm going to say hi."

"Sure."

Keegan came up from behind, and put his arm around Whitfield. "Hey, cuz, looking good."

"Hey, Keegan. Right back at you."

"Yeah, I know. But, thanks for noticing. Hey, do you know Danielle and Alison?" Keegan introduced the two girls he was with to Whitfield.

"Uhh...no. Nice to meet you."

"Hi Whitfield. You're cute."

"Hey Whitfield. She's right, you are cute."

"Danielle and Alison go to Matwood. They're both on the cheerleading squad."

Danielle held onto Whitfield's arm for a brief time. "Hey, where's your date for the evening, Whitfield?"

"Date? Uhh, I don't have one."

"Aww...that's so sad."

Alison reached over and grabbed Whitfield's other arm. "Yeah. Hey, maybe you can join us. Can he, Keegan?"

Whitfield was astounded. "Keegan, you brought dates to the Parents Ball?"

Danielle unwrapped her arms from Whitfield's. "Parents Ball? Keegan, what's he talking about? You said this was your school's prom."

Keegan stumbled a bit over his words. "It is…let's not get carried away. I'm sure Whitfield has someone he's meeting inside. Can I speak with you for a minute? Excuse us for a second."

Keegan pulled Whitfield over the side.

"Keegan, what are you doing?"

"Look, my parents aren't coming to this thing. They never do. So, I figured what's the harm in bringing two lovely ladies to the ball with me. Everyone else gets to bring two people."

"Yeah, those two people are called parents."

"Well, maybe if I'm bad, they'll send me to my room later."

Whitfield smiled, "you are such a dog."

"Oowww!"

"Get out of here."

Keegan returned to his dates for the evening. "Ladies. Whitfield has graciously decided to allow you both to accompany me inside. He has a special lady friend awaiting him inside."

The girls were very nice to Whitfield. "It was nice meeting you."

"Maybe we'll see you inside. I'll save a dance for you."

Whitfield slowed down to get some distance between himself and Keegan and his dates. "Oh, thank you, but that's OK…" The girls and Keegan were already several paces ahead.

Keegan yelled back. "Oh Whitfield, try to keep your clothes on tonight." Keegan reached into his pocket, pulled out an apple, and tossed it to Whitfield.

Whitfield caught the apple and came to a complete stop. *He knows? How many people did Ugu tell?*

As was customary for big events, Flaxen Hall was spectacularly decorated, and Ugu had even staged two red-carpet and interview stations, one for students and the other for parents, for each to express their last second emotions and heartfelt sentiments to each other minutes before reuniting for the first time in weeks in the Grand Presidential Hall. The interviews and red-carpet photos were elegantly displayed on monitors lining the exterior of the giant hall.

Aspen didn't wait for Whitfield. He was too busy chatting with Seraphina and Dakota to notice that Whitfield had fallen back in the crowd. Aspen posed for his red-carpet shots and said a few words into the camera, directed at Hendricks, before entering Flaxen Hall. Whitfield looked around outside and spotted Ugu and Flaherty walking up the steps. Once again, Whitfield was mesmerized by Ugu's beauty; however, this time, he quickly snapped out of it and walked across the divide to catch up with the two beauties.

Flaherty spotted Whitfield first. "Oh look, there's Whitfield."

Ugu quickly turned around, hoping to spot Whitfield. "Where? You see him?"

"Relax. He's walking this way. And, for some reason, he's holding an apple. Are you two playing some kind of game?" Ugu blushed.

"Hey, Flaherty. You look amazing! Great dress!" Whitfield gave Flaherty a hug and kiss on the cheek.

"Oh, what a gentleman. Might I say that you are looking rather fine yourself."

"Thank you. And who is this angel beside you?"

"Oh her? Just some stray I found on the streets."

"Nonsense. She must have been sent from heaven. Perfect in every way." Whitfield tried to push the apple he was holding into his pocket. Only half of it fit.

"Did he just say perfect?"

"Shut up, Flaherty. Well, thank you for the kind words, sir. You certainly are a smooth talker."

Whitfield grabbed Ugu's hands in his own and looked deep into her eyes. "It must be your beauty that fills my heart with such poetic verse."

Flaherty did a double-take and coughed. "Oh gag."

Ugu looked quizzical, and somewhat annoyed. "Yeah, that one went a bit too far. You've been talking with Keegan, haven't you?"

Whitfield knew he had been caught. "How could you tell?"

"I've heard him use that same line on Graciela, Kayleigh…"

Flaherty added, "Amanda, Georgia…"

"Oh, who was that girl from Pancake Batter Prep?"

"Leah."

"Right. Leah."

Whitfield pulled away a bit. "So, I guess not so smooth then, huh?"

"Look, you don't need to get tips from Keegan of all people on how to talk to me. Just be yourself."

Whitfield appeared saddened and looked down, shuffling his feet. "I guess. But I saw you in that dress and I just really want you to like me, and, I don't know…"

Ugu was flattered. "Whitfield, you don't need to talk smooth for me. I love y…oh, wait a minute." Ugu finally caught on. "Are you acting vulnerable on purpose just to get me to say…"

Whitfield let out a sly smile. "To say what exactly? What was it? Tip #8: Act vulnerable and she'll tell you the most comforting thing on top of her mind."

Ugu and Flaherty both gasped, "oh, that was so mean."

Whitfield was rather proud of himself. "No, I think you mean to say it was clever."

Flaherty had to agree. "OK. That was pretty good."

"Shut up, Flaherty. You're supposed to be on my side."

"I'm on both of your sides. This whole thing is getting silly. You are both so obviously in love with each other. Look, I'll prove it." Flaherty scanned the nearby crowd, and found a teammate. "Morocco, come over here."

"Oh, hey, Flaherty. Looking good. Mmm…save me a dance tonight?"

"Yeah, maybe."

"Nice. What's up, Whitfield?" Morocco punched Whitfield in the arm. "Ugu, you are looking hot!"

"Hey, Morocco, how come you just asked me to dance tonight but not Ugu?"

Without hesitation, Morocco shot a quick glance to Whitfield. "Dang, 'cause I wouldn't do that to my man right here."

"What do you mean?"

"Well, that's his girl, right? I mean, she's all he ever talks about."

Flaherty asked Morocco the next question while staring straight at Whitfield. "So, would you say he likes Ugu?"

"Likes? Shhh please. My man is devoted. He's hopeless. So, in love with her."

Whitfield's face reddened. "Thanks, Morocco. That wasn't embarrassing at all."

"You got it, brother." Morocco turned to Flaherty. "I'll see you inside, pretty lady." Then, he turned toward the Flaxen Hall entrance, and shouted to no one in particular, "make way, Morocco is coming."

Ugu stood on top of the steps leading into Flaxen Hall with a big grin on her face, as though she had just won an argument. Flaherty, however, decided to rein in her best friend's victory. "Hey, I don't know what you're gloating about. You are just as much in love with him. Did I not just see you writing 'Ugu and Whitfield in Love Together Forever' all over your notebook?" Now it was Whitfield's turn to smile. "And didn't you decide to wear that uncomfortable lace bra just hoping that he would notice?"

Ugu opened her eyes wide and gasped. Whitfield felt a little uncomfortable. He had been looking at Ugu's dress, but now he diverted his eyes away. "OK, maybe I shouldn't have shared that last one. But, come on. You two are perfect for each other. If you're not going to kiss, at least hold hands or something."

Whitfield and Ugu looked into each other's eyes. At the same time, they felt for each other's hand, and finally, Whitfield held Ugu's right hand in his left, and just like that, they seemingly were announcing to the world that they were indeed a couple. They posed together for pictures on the red carpet, but did give separate statements into the camera; Ugu for her dad and Whitfield for Hendricks.

The newly minted couple walked into the Grand Presidential Hall together and Whitfield was amazed. Inside, the hall was transformed into a majestic winter wonderland, with shimmering ice crystals floating from the ceiling, starlit drapery, shades of arctic blue, sapphire, and cobalt, mixed with pure white, and low-hanging, ankle high, swirling fog, which gave the impression of walking on clouds.

A light gray and white layer of cushiony grass turf covered the floor, adding to the feel of walking on air. Tables were adorned with ice sculptures, with floating fruit trays meandering their way around each statue on a lazy river of melted ice.

Whitfield was awestruck as he looked around the room. "You did this?"

Ugu appreciated Whitfield's look of amazement. "Well, the team and I put it together. Actually, they did most of the 'putting together'. I just designed it."

"You really are incredible." Whitfield kissed Ugu on the cheek.

"Thank you. Do you see Hendricks yet?"

Whitfield scanned the crowd. "Not yet. I'm sure he's here somewhere. How about your dad?"

"No. Not yet. Perhaps they are over at the table. I put us together. I hope you don't mind."

"Don't be silly. Let's make our way over there. Where are we sitting?"

"Over there, next to the emcee stand. I want to be close, in case they need any help with the awards later."

"That's right. We find out who won the Grand Curriculum Development Challenge tonight, right?"

"Yup. I think you have a good chance."

"Thanks, but I'm not even thinking about that now. I'm just happy here with you." Whitfield squeezed Ugu's hand and the couple started walking toward their table, when Whitfield stopped short.

"What is that decoration by our table?"

"Oh, that," Ugu chuckled. "It's a winter apple tree. I thought it would be a nice touch."

Whitfield shot Ugu a sideways glance. "Apple tree? Really? Apple?"

"Oh, keep your pants on. It's just a decoration."

They reached the table at almost the same time as Hendricks arrived. Ugu's dad was not there yet.

"Hendricks! I'm so happy you came."

Hendricks grabbed Whitfield in a giant bear hug. "Whitfield, my boy. So glad to see you. Let me look at you. How are you?"

"Doing great, Hendricks. Really."

Hendricks looked behind Whitfield. "And where is Aspen?"

"He's around here somewhere." Whitfield looked out toward the crowd. "There he is. Talking with those two girls."

Hendricks grinned. "Ah, yes. I should have known. And who is this lovely young lady?"

"Hendricks, I'd like you to meet Ugu. She's my…well, her and I…umm…" Whitfield turned toward Ugu. "You want to help me out?"

"Hello, sir. I am Ugu. I'm in the same year as Whitfield at BBA. We've become very good friends over the past couple months. He's really a wonderful person."

Hendricks noticed the two of them had been holding hands when they entered, and even now, Ugu wrapped her one arm around Whitfield's arm. "Ahh. Brilliant. I am so happy for you both."

Whitfield whispered to Ugu, "smooth."

Ugu whispered back, "smoother than you were with my dad."

"Speaking of your dad, isn't that him over there?"

Ugu's face lit up. "Yes. Excuse me for just a moment. I'm going to go grab my dad. I'll be right back." Ugu glided across the floor to greet her dad. Whitfield motioned for Aspen to come over.

Aspen jumped into Hendricks' waiting arms. He wanted to tell Hendricks all about his first term at Seven Bridges, but asked if he could go back and wait with Seraphina and Dakota until their parents showed up. Hendricks agreed.

Ugu reached up to give her dad a kiss on the cheek. "Daddy!"

"Sweetheart. So good to see you. You really outdid yourself with all of this." Mr. Gugurutruv put his arm around his daughter.

"Thank you. You like it?"

"It's beautiful, dear. A winter wonderland! How did you come up with this?"

"Well, I wanted to do something different. We are going to have a lot of warm weather outdoorsy activities planned for tomorrow, so I thought about what might be a nice juxtaposition for tonight. I traded in the swimming, sun, and surf for ice crystals and floating on clouds. Instead of waterslides, we have ice slides. Instead of apple bobbing, we have a winter apple tree…although, now that I'm looking at it, I'm not sure I like how it's so close to some of the ice crystals. It's hiding some of the fringe."

"It's perfect, dear." Ugu and her dad hugged. She brought her dad over to meet Hendricks and to see Whitfield again.

Whitfield held out his hand to greet Ugu's dad. "Sir, so happy to see you again. This is my guardian, Hendricks."

When Hendricks turned around to meet Ugu's dad, it was as though he had seen a ghost. Whitfield had rarely ever seen that look in Hendricks' eyes, but on those few occasions when he had, it was always bad news for the other guy. Whitfield was hoping Hendricks would control himself in this situation.

Mr. Gugurutruv spoke first. "Hendricks? Is that really you? How long has it been?"

"Yuri. About ten years." Hendricks remained calm on the outside, but Whitfield knew, deep down inside, Hendricks was fuming. He didn't know why, though.

"You two know each other?"

"We went to school here together, isn't that right, Hendricks? Not the same year, of course, but yes, we shared some good times. Didn't we, chum?"

"Yes, we did."

Ugu wasn't as tuned into the subtleties of Hendricks' behavior, so she was oblivious to the tension. "I don't believe this. You didn't tell me you knew Whitfield's…" Ugu caught herself, stopping short of saying parents. "…I mean, Hendricks."

"Oh, I didn't know Hendricks was his guardian. This is splendid. So, sweetheart, are you and Whitfield still…ahem, seeing each other." For the first time since locking eyes with Hendricks, Ugu's dad broke eye contact to look at his daughter.

"Yes, Daddy."

Hendricks overcame his initial shock, and returned to his normal self. "Well, I think that's wonderful. You have quite the daughter there."

"Thank you. Your son...oh, I mean Whitfield, is quite exceptional, as well."

Whitfield hoped to avoid any further confrontation. "Well, did you both know that Ugu organized all the events for this week, including designing the hall for tonight's Parents Ball. Isn't it spectacular?"

Hendricks offered another cursory look around the room. "You designed this, dear?"

"Yes."

"Very impressive. Truly magnificent."

"Yes, my daughter was just sharing with me her inspiration for the winter wonderland concept. What was it dear, apples, slides, and swimming?" Whitfield's eyes almost popped out of his head. *Apples! Slides! Swimming!* Ugu's dad continued, each word making Whitfield even more nervous. "Although she's not happy with apples hiding such delicate figures, I think it's just fine. Why shouldn't there be some icy surprise hidden behind an apple tree?"

Whitfield was unable to control himself. "Ugu! I can't believe you told your dad you saw me naked!"

For the second time in as many meetings between Whitfield and her dad, Ugu was mortified. "Whitfield, I never told him about that."

Mr. Gugurutruv looked puzzled, and just a tad angry. "Excuse me! What's that? My daughter saw you naked?" Mr. Gugurutruv's voice rose to a level not quite yelling or shouting, but loud enough such that those nearby stopped their own conversations to listen.

Whitfield quietly asked Ugu, "you didn't tell him?"

"No."

"Then how does he know about the apple and the slide and my icy surprise?"

"I told him about the ice slides and the apple tree. And I don't know anything about your icy surprise."

Whitfield wondered how he was going to recover from this one. He started laughing uncomfortably as he turned toward Ugu's dad. "Ha Ha Ha. This is all just a misunderstanding."

Mr. Gugurutruv did not appear to be in a joking mood. "Did you expose yourself to my daughter?"

"Not exactly. Well, technically, yes, but it's not what you think."

"Why were you naked in front of my daughter?"

"Because I thought we were going swimming, sir."

"So, you decided you would go swimming with my daughter while you were naked?"

"Well, sir, I actually thought she was naked too."

Ugu covered her face with her hands. "Oh boy. You are not good at this."

"Was my daughter naked?"

"No, sir, she was not. She was fully clothed. She did take a naked picture of me though. Me naked, not her."

Ugu couldn't take it anymore. "You need to stop talking. No one was naked, dad. No one went swimming. It was just a simple prank that may have led to one of us…OK, him, taking off his clothes. I did not see anything. Nothing in the private area. No icy surprise. Just a harmless prank."

Whitfield couldn't help himself. "Well, harmless for you. I had to run to the Uniform Galleria in my underwear."

Ugu turned to face Whitfield. "Shut up."

"Yes, dear."

Hendricks offered some assistance. "Well, now that we have that cleared up, how about we check out some of the food around here. I'm starving." Hendricks placed his arm around Whitfield's shoulder, and calmly walked with Whitfield away from their table.

****

For the next two hours, Whitfield tried his best to avoid putting his foot in his mouth, especially around Ugu's dad. He spent more time than he usually would out on the dance floor, partially because Ugu kept asking him to dance and partially to avoid awkward conversation with her dad. Aspen stayed out on the dance floor almost the entire time, along with Flaherty, Keegan, and several other members of the gymnastics team.

Many other students and parents danced the night away, while others, among them Hendricks and Yuri Gugurutruv, remained mostly on the fringes, observing and talking among themselves; although Yuri did manage to come out onto the dance floor for a pair of slow songs to dance with his daughter. It wasn't clear to Whitfield, but he thought he saw Hendricks and Ugu's dad engaged in a heated discussion at the table when no one else was around, but quickly dispelled those thoughts when he saw both men smile when he and Ugu arrived back at the table.

Dr. Hewitt was the emcee for the evening, and despite some minor interruptions early in the evening, the night ran smoothly. By 21:30, it was time to announce the winners of this year's Grand Curriculum Design Challenge. Dr. Hewitt asked Sir Arlington to come up to say a few words about the Challenge and its rich history. Many of the programs and courses currently being offered at Seven Bridges Academy originated out of this competition. Twelve current faculty members were past winners of the contest. By the end of Sir Arlington's prepared remarks, the entire crowd was on the edge of their seats.

Dr. Hewitt introduced the three finalists and gave a brief overview of their submissions. "The three finalists are:

"Whitfield and Aspen for their N-Dimensional Scanning Technology for Muscle Tension and Release, with Applications for Applied Mathematics; Physiology; Engineering; Biology and Mechanics; and Gymnastics.

"Rodolfo and Quan for their Algorithmic Optimization Approach to Judging and Scoring Tri-Bars Performance with Applications for Computer Science; Deep Machine Learning; and Gymnastics.

"Mariska for her new course proposal on Stock Trading Anomalies and Gymnastics Performance: A Critical Analysis of 50 Years of Trading Activity with Applications for Business; Psychology; and Gymnastics."

The crowd cheered after each of the finalists was announced.

"Let me remind you that the winning submission will be cultivated and added to the Seven Bridges curriculum. Winners receive a generous budget to fully design and roll out the class lesson or full course program next year, or as early as reasonably conceivable, at Seven Bridges. Additionally, winners will receive an all-expenses paid trip for two to a destination of their choosing, anywhere in the world."

The crowd was buzzing with anticipation.

"And the winners of this year's Grand Curriculum Design Challenge are: Whitfield and Aspen. And I recently received word that the WGF will adopt their technology for use in all upcoming meets this season."

The crowd stood and cheered. The roar was deafening. Whitfield and Aspen were in complete shock. They embraced each other by their table before going up to receive their award.

"Whitfield, we won!"

"I know. That's incredible."

Ugu hugged both Whitfield and Aspen. "I am so proud of you two."

Hendricks hugged both boys. Mr. Gugurutruv, who also stood and clapped, shook their hands. "Well done, Aspen. Well done, Whitfield. That is quite an honor. My daughter won this award two years ago."

"Yes, I know, sir. She really inspired me to submit this project."

"Come on, Whitfield. Let's get up there." Whitfield and Aspen went up to the stage to accept their award. They were asked to say a few words.

Aspen took the microphone first. "Thank you everyone who voted for us. This is awesome. I don't know what to say. I'm so happy. Thank you."

Everyone clapped.

Aspen handed the microphone to Whitfield, who remained quiet for a moment to collect his thoughts before speaking. "I want to thank you all too. This being the Parents Ball and all, it wouldn't be right to accept this award without thanking the man who means the world to Aspen and I. It's really because of him that we're standing up here. Thank you, Hendricks, for everything."

Hendricks smiled, and the crowd gave a nice round of applause.

"And I want to say one more thing. This night wouldn't have been possible without the hard work of one of the former winners of this award, someone who inspires me to achieve more and more every day, and the person who designed this entire winter wonderland in here tonight and every event that's planned for the entire week. I know all the students here already know her, but I wanted to introduce her to all the parents as well. No matter what class year your student is, or what classes they are taking, Ugu has had a positive impact on your son or daughter.

"Just ask them. I'm sure they'll share some story of how Ugu has inspired them during their time here. And this isn't me standing up here feeling vulnerable or insecure. I just wanted to make sure her dad, who is sitting with her right over there, knows how truly special his daughter is, and how we ALL love her. This award is for you."

Ugu was in tears. Flaherty was in tears. Even Ugu's dad had tears welling up in his eyes. The audience, many with tears in their eyes, gave a huge ovation to this year's Grand Curriculum Design Challenge winners as they walked off the stage. Ugu could not wait until Whitfield got back to the table. She ran into his arms, told him she loves him, and gave him a big kiss, in front of the entire room. Above the applause, several of Whitfield's teammates could be heard.

Keegan yelled out, "that's my boy. Way to go!"

Through her tears, Chloe screamed, "you two are the best!"

Ippy shouted, "that's how gymnasts do it!"

Morocco bellowed, "rock on, Whitfield!" Then he added, "Flaherty, that's you and me next, babe!"

Fenway countered with, "keep dreaming, Morocco."

The mood quickly shifted to one of cheerful frivolity and joy. The music started to play again, and the crowd rushed to the dance floor. Whitfield and Ugu hadn't moved from their embrace.

Ugu held onto Whitfield so tightly. "So, does this mean you really do love me?"

"I don't know. Do you see any clues?"

"Hmm…increased heart rate, deep eye contact, and I think that's an apple sticking out of your pocket."

"Let me make this simple for you." Whitfield looked deep into Ugu's eyes. "Ugu. I love you!" They kissed again.

Ugu's dad came over and, after affording the couple some extra time, partially to wipe away another of his own tears, politely interrupted. "Whitfield. Son. Thank you for what you said up there. I know we haven't exactly gotten off on the right foot…"

"Mostly because I keep sticking mine in my mouth."

"True. But I can tell you love my daughter, and she loves you. That's enough for me."

"Thank you, sir. And yes, we are in love. And, even though I haven't asked her to go yet, if I do decide to share my prize and ask her to accompany me on a vacation, would she have your blessing to go?"

"On one condition."

"Name It."

"Make sure you keep your bathing suit on if you decide to go swimming." Ugu's dad smiled, and flashed a wink in Whitfield's direction.

Whitfield laughed. "You got it, sir."

Mr. Gugurutruv walked away and Hendricks, who was just congratulating Aspen, joined the happy couple. "Thank you for your kind words. That was really nice of you. Ugu, I've never seen him like this. You've really made an impression on him."

"Thank you, Hendricks."

"Whitfield, can I have a word in private? Sorry, my dear, this will only take a minute. It was lovely meeting you."

"Sure. You two go ahead. I want to congratulate Aspen again."

Whitfield and Hendricks left the crowd and found a secluded corner of the Grand Presidential Hall. "Hey, Hendricks, what's up?"

"Whitfield, I have to go."

"OK, sure. I'll still see you tomorrow morning, right? You're coming over to the house."

"No, I'm afraid not. Something's come up that I have to take care of."

"Oh. Will you be back this week?"

"Too difficult to tell right now. I'll try my best. Tell your brother I said goodbye. I love you both very much."

Whitfield was beyond confused. "I love you too."

Whitfield and Hendricks hugged, and Hendricks walked away, exiting the hall. Whitfield was confused with Hendricks' decision to abruptly leave. With his eyes, Whitfield followed Hendricks as he made his way toward the exit, stopping first to place his hand on Sir Arlington's shoulder, presumably to say his goodbyes, and then just like that, he was gone.

****

A few minutes after exiting the Grand Presidential Hall, Hendricks was joined by Sir Arlington in the private walkway. "Hendricks, my friend, what is it? You said we needed to talk."

"That's right. We have a problem! And I think you know what it is."

"Ahh…you must be referring to Mr. Gugurutruv."

"How can you allow Whitfield and get so caught up in a relationship with his daughter?"

"Young Ugu is a fine student. A wonderful person. They are in love."

"You know what kind of man he is. What makes you think he hasn't instructed his daughter to manipulate Whitfield?"

"I assure you; their love is pure."

"You'll forgive me if I have my doubts. But, even if that is true, it will not stop SYPHUS from using her against him. Their relationship places her in danger. They will stop at nothing to get to him."

"Remember, my dear friend, it was your idea to enroll Livvy and Aldrich's two boys here. It was your idea to use them as bait to draw out SYPHUS."

"And you swore to protect them!"

"I believe I am upholding my commitment. Hendricks, let's not lose sight of the bigger picture. Your quarrel is not with me. We are on the same side in this fight."

"And Marino? Which side is he on?"

"Professor Marino remains loyal to our cause. As you know, he has never approved of using the boys as bait, and continues to try to undermine their celebrity, in his own way."

Hendricks was not convinced. "Yeah, a lot of good that's doing. The latest polls have them both making the All-Star roster."

"True. They are truly exceptional gymnasts. I believe we have you to thank for that."

"Perhaps blame is the better word."

"We will keep them protected. If your plan is to work, they will need to receive even greater media attention. If that means All-Star appearances, interviews, elite camps, or anything else, so be it. We have allowed them to conduct interviews with foreign outlets from their homes, so as to limit travel. We will continue to protect them at meets, both on campus and off. We are doing our best."

"Let's hope your best is good enough. I will not lose them."

"We all share your love for these boys. And for Livvy and Aldrich…and Morton. We'll get them back. All of them."

"I hope so." Hendricks took a step toward the door.

"Are you leaving?"

"You know I can't be seen with them now. Yuri has his spies everywhere. I'll stay close. You know how to reach me."

"Hendricks, remember, this is a school. I will not have this institution turned into a battlefield."

"Too late. It already is."

Chapter 23
Hendricks the Gambler

Whitfield did not let Hendricks' sudden departure dampen his spirits. He and Ugu were in love and that's all that really mattered to him at the moment. Aspen was sad to see Hendricks leave, but he had made a lot of friends at school, and was genuinely happy. On Tuesday morning, parents visited their children's homes. The walk-through tours at each mansion were all organized differently. For example, Bella had organized a huge backyard breakfast and had parents leave in small groups to tour the house with their children. Swindell set up a scavenger hunt throughout his mansion, promising prizes for parents who filled out the related scorecard. The prizes ranged from decorative towels to personalized t-shirts, but since he ended up handing out prizes to everyone who stopped by, completing the scavenger hunt was really just a fun added bonus. He also handed out passes to his house's floating dance floor party for later that afternoon.

Keegan had one of the more memorable mansion visits, as he gathered all parents in the backyard and directed each of his staff members to go inside and find a bathroom. With all 33 bathrooms attended to, Keegan counted down from 10, and a few second later, 3…2…1…FLUSH! All 33 toilets flushed at the same time, triggering a massive swirling motion in the giant backyard swimming pool. Then, the pool water started to drain as a full breakfast bar, with on-site chef, rose from the depths of the water. The crowd all laughed and cheered. Keegan felt like a hero.

Aspen's mansion walk-through was well-organized, thanks to Ugu. She had assigned every staff member a particular role in welcoming guests, and with seven floors, 23 in-resident bedrooms plus four more for overnight guests (not including the house supervisor's basement loft area, which was off-limits to the tour), two movie theaters, a game room, a full-sized workout room, one outdoor and three indoor kitchens, numerous sitting areas, and an entire outdoor paradise, including three large swimming pools, it was easy for guests to get lost without knowledgeable guides leading the way.

Whitfield's mansion was just as large as Aspen's, with just as many rooms, but instead of three swimming pools, his backyard was replete with trampolines, zip-lines, and rope bridges. Whitfield had planned a special walk-through for Hendricks, but since learning of his sudden departure, Whitfield opted instead to switch roles with his staff, as best as he could for the morning. He prepared breakfast, laid out clothes, welcomed parents and other guests, gave about 20 full tours, and in all other ways tried his best to make his staff feel like royalty while their parents were visiting.

Whitfield's staff members all appreciated Whitfield's sentiment and even chipped in when they saw he could use some extra help. For Whitfield, staying busy helped to take his mind off Hendricks' absence.

After the mansion tours, all parents and students made their way down to the waterfront for various water games, boat rides, and relaxing walks along the beach. The five gymnasts who lived on the waterfront side all agreed to open their houses for a variety of activities: cooking lessons with student chefs; stylist lessons with student stylists; private guitar jam sessions with several of the musicians scheduled to play on stage during the week; and various obstacle courses connecting the five backyards. For those still wanting to enjoy the weather, but less inclined toward physical activity, Ugu scheduled eight luxury drone suites to hover high above the water and take occasional laps around the campus perimeter and nearby areas so parents could take in the different environments surrounding campus, all while seated comfortably.

With the afternoon in full swing, parents and students started making their way toward the large mega-yachts floating in the harbor. Alumni also started showing up on campus, so the waterfront area got a bit crowded. Many students rode across the water with their parents in kayaks, canoes, and rafts; other guests opted for drone taxis or small boat service across the harbor.

Guests boarded one of five large mega-yachts, where they would be spending the rest of their day and night out at sea, enjoying games, entertainment, food, and dancing. Each mega-yacht was equipped with five floating dance floors. Each dance floor could comfortably hold 120 guests plus service staff, including DJs and waiters. Each dance floor would rise high above the boat. By the time the sun set, all 25 dance floors, full of happy guests, were scattered across the brilliant sky, splashed with majestic pink, purple, and orange streaks.

Dozens of drone taxis escorted guests, two to four at a time, back and forth, from dance floor to large boat, or from one dance party to another. Ugu had her own dedicated drone taxi shuttling her across all dance floors and boats. As the lead organizer for all PAW events, Ugu needed to make sure she was on top on any mishaps or unexpected needs. Whitfield decided to keep Aspen company on his dance floor. Without Hendricks, Aspen and Whitfield were two of only about a dozen students whose parents or guardians were not in attendance.

"Hey bro, how are you holding up?"

"Hi Whitfield. I'm fine. This is pretty fun, isn't it?"

"Yeah, these flying dance floors are incredible. The view is amazing."

"I know. You can almost see the whole campus from up here. I even thought I saw Hendricks standing on the Outer Loop earlier. Crazy, right?"

"That's so funny. I thought I saw him over by the waterfalls earlier this morning, when I was taking out some trash."

"I guess we just really miss him, huh?"

Whitfield put his arm around Aspen. "Yeah. I wonder why he had to leave so early."

Just then, a familiar face interrupted their conversation, walking up from behind Whitfield.

"Ahh, here you are. The most recent winners of the prestigious Grand Curriculum Development Challenge. How are you two fine gentlemen this evening?"

Aspen spoke first. "Oh, hi Ugu's dad. I'm good. How are you?"

"Splendid, Aspen. And how about you, Whitfield?"

"Hi sir. Yes, I'm doing OK. We were just admiring the job your daughter did with organizing all this."

"Yes. She certainly outdid herself yet again. Two for two so far. Can't wait to see what tomorrow brings."

"Me too. I believe we have some reunion stuff for the gymnastics team tomorrow."

"And the parents and alumni mock meet. Ugu said she has a cool Ice Cream Sundae Surprise event planned. I can't wait." Aspen was really excited for all of the extra fun events Ugu planned for the week.

"Yes. She told me the same thing. Aspen, if you are interested in getting an early start, I believe I saw the chefs working on a special ice cream dessert for tonight. I'm sure if you took a taxi down to the boat, they would let you have a taste."

Aspen's eyes lit up. "Really? OK. Whitfield, are you coming?"

Mr. Gugurutruv spoke on Whitfield's behalf, "Whitfield will be down there in a few minutes. I want a word with him first." Aspen looked over at Whitfield before moving.

"It's OK, Aspen. I'll catch up with you in a few minutes. You can ask Colin if he'll ride down with you."

"OK." Aspen left. He found Colin, and the two rode down to the boat together. Whitfield was nervous that Mr. Gugurutruv might say something about not wanting him to see his daughter anymore, so quickly decided to steer the conversation elsewhere.

"So, sir, I didn't know that you knew Hendricks. Were you two friends in school?"

"That's actually what I wanted to talk with you about. Hendricks and I were very good friends in school. Of course, he was a few years older than I, but we were in the same house, along with your parents."

Whitfield was shocked. "Wait! You knew my parents?"

"Yes, very well."

"How come you didn't say anything to me before?"

"I didn't want to bring up any painful memories for you. Besides, I wanted our relationship to stand on its own two feet, and I never told my daughter any of this, or what I am about to tell you. I'd appreciate the same courtesy from you."

Whitfield felt uneasy about this unusual request. "Are you asking me to keep something from Ugu?"

"I know. It's not fair of a dad to tell his daughter's boyfriend to keep secrets, but I think we can make an exception in this case." It was the first time Whitfield had ever really thought of himself as Ugu's boyfriend. The word brought a smile to his face. Mr. Gugurutruv must have noticed. "Good. I see we are in agreement. As I was saying, yes, the five of us were very good friends. Inseparable."

"Five?"

"Oh, yes, your parents, Hendricks, me, and, of course, a little later on, Morton."

"Morton?"

"Yes, Morton Cheesestock. The gymnast whose house we all lived in together."

"Whoa! No way. You all lived with Morton Cheesestock? The greatest gymnast to ever live. World Champion on every event. Morton Cheesestock. You lived with that Morton Cheesestock?"

"Yes. Yes, that one. Of course, he wasn't World Champion at that time. He was quite a bit younger than the four of us, but we still shared a house with him. For two years. Those were some really good times. I'm surprised Hendricks never mentioned that to you."

Whitfield wondered why Hendricks had kept this from him for all these years. "Yeah, me too. Hendricks doesn't really talk about his past at all."

"Doesn't surprise me. I don't think Hendricks ever forgave himself for what happened with your parents."

Again, Whitfield looked shocked. "What are you talking about?"

"I'm not sure Hendricks would want me telling you this."

"It's OK. I want to know what happened to my parents."

"OK, son. I understand. This isn't going to be easy for you to hear. Just like it's not easy for me to say. Your parents were great people. Everyone loved them. I loved them. After we all graduated, and Morton started winning more professional meets and winning championships, a lot more fame and fortune came along with it. Your parents were always with Morton, but never asked for anything. Not a dime. But Morton took care of them anyway. Like he did for all his friends.

"Only, Hendricks was greedy. He always wanted more. And to Morton's credit, he always gave Hendricks anything he asked for, but it was never enough. Hendricks convinced your parents to name him as trustee on their estate, around the same time as they named him your guardian should they ever meet an untimely death. I don't know, I guess he was just taking advantage of your parents' trusting nature."

This all came as news to Whitfield. He never thought of Hendricks as greedy or even capable of taking advantage of anyone.

"Anyway, like I said, nothing was ever enough for Hendricks. He started gambling on gymnastics meets, from your parents' accounts, so his identity would stay hidden. He was betting big on Morton to win. Well, one day, Morton didn't win. Hendricks lost millions. When people finally tracked down your parents to collect their money, Hendricks was there.

"Your parents denied knowing anything about it. And how could they. They were innocent. Hendricks left the room with you and your brother and let those savages kill your parents. Your parents are dead because of Hendricks."

Whitfield listened in stunned silence. His eyes welled up. He started crying. Why hadn't he ever heard this before?

"I know, son. This is hard. Unfortunately, that's not all." Whitfield looked up at Mr. Gugurutruv, but couldn't say anything. "We think Hendricks may be gambling again. We've been noticing some abnormal activity in the sportsbooks and…"

Whitfield's eyes lit up. "And what?"

"Well, don't repeat this to anyone, but we think he's paying off gymnasts to take falls in meets."

Whitfield looked at Mr. Gugurutruv in shock, with a million thoughts running through his head. *Could Hendricks really be the one that is bribing gymnasts to take falls? All the bribes are helping Seven Bridges win. All the big bets are coming in on Seven Bridges' side. Hendricks trained two of the best gymnasts on the team. If what Mr. Gugurutruv said it true, Hendricks has a long history of gambling.* Whitfield shook his head, not wanting to believe any of it, but then recalled something. *Hendricks refused to watch meets. Instead, he would disappear for entire weekends. What if he was out paying off other gymnasts? He's not here right now. What if he's out bribing gymnasts before the next meet?*

Mr. Gugurutruv recognized that Whitfield was really struggling trying to process everything he just heard. "Whitfield, my boy, I am sorry for being the bearer of bad news. I really am. I know how much you must care for Hendricks. Look, how about you go find my daughter. I'm sure she can take some time off from her responsibilities and relax for a little while. I'm sure she would love to see you. You know, I've never seen her so in love before."

Whitfield still didn't know what to make of all this. "Sure. I guess. Umm, thank you, sir." Whitfield reached out his hand. Mr. Gugurutruv brought Whitfield in for a hug. Whitfield hopped into a drone taxi in search for Ugu, but really, just to spend some time by himself. He rode around for an hour, before heading back to Aspen's boat.

"Hey, bro, where have you been?"

"Oh, just…nowhere. Just wondering around. Look, I'm going to call it a night. If you see Ugu, tell her I went home." Whitfield couldn't bear the thought of sharing this news with Aspen. Not yet. He needed to sort things out on his own first; and maybe even approach Hendricks directly. Regardless of what he had just heard, Whitfield still felt he owed Hendricks an opportunity to defend himself against these allegations.

"You OK?"

"Yeah, I'll be fine. Just tired. I'll see you tomorrow."

"OK. Good night." Aspen looked at Whitfield with concern, but trusted his brother when he said he was just tired.

Whitfield walked down the stairs and left the mega-yacht. Flaherty spotted Whitfield as he was leaving. She called out to him from her mega-yacht, but he must not have heard her because he didn't stop walking. Flaherty followed Whitfield with her eyes and noticed that he stopped at a quiet, dark spot facing the water. He was all by himself, and Flaherty suspected something wasn't right. Flaherty left her own party to go talk to Whitfield.

"Hey, there you are. We have a bunch of the team alums back on our boat. I was looking for you. Wanted to introduce you. Gabe, Patel, Lyla, they're all there."

Whitfield didn't bother turning around. "No thanks. I just want to be alone right now."

Flaherty came closer. "Hey, are you OK?"

"I'm fine."

Flaherty sensed that something was not fine. "Whitfield. It's me. You can talk to me." Flaherty stepped in front of Whitfield and saw that he had been crying. "Whitfield, what's wrong?"

Whitfield wiped away some tears. "Nothing."

"Whitfield."

"Nothing. I'm fine. Just go away."

"OK. Sure. I'll go." Flaherty took a few steps back toward the boat, and then stopped abruptly and turned around. "No, on second thought, I think I'm going to stay, and you are going to tell me what's bothering you. And don't say nothing, because I will kick your ass."

"Flaherty, I'm not in the mood."

"That's close enough." Flaherty punched Whitfield square in the nose. She then kicked Whitfield in the back of his left knee and he toppled over like sack of potatoes. As Whitfield was lying flat on his back, struggling to catch his breath, Flaherty reached her hand out to help Whitfield up. "Now, we are going to try this again. I am going to ask you what's wrong and you are going to tell me what's bothering you because that's what family does."

Whitfield struggled to find his footing after being helped up. "Family? But, we're not family."

Flaherty didn't care for Whitfield's response and proceeded to kick Whitfield in the ribs, which he partially blocked, but he couldn't lift his hand up quick enough to block Flaherty's straight jab to his right eye. Whitfield fell for the second time, and for the second time, Flaherty extended a hand to help him up.

"What was that for?"

"Because we are family. Ugu is like my sister. Which means you're practically my brother. And even without Ugu, you and I have been through a lot together. You're my best friend on the team. Seven Bridges' 1-2 punch, remember?"

Whitfield held his hand over his right eye. "Yeah, well, let's leave the punching out of this."

"Well, stop saying stupid things."

"That's kind of my thing, or haven't you noticed."

"I have noticed. You say the right things more often than you give yourself credit for. Now, prove me right, and say the right thing. What's wrong?"

Whitfield finally let his guard down, not that it was doing much good with Flaherty anyway. "I just had a long talk with Ugu's dad."

"Oh no. He didn't ask you to stop seeing Ugu did he?"

"No."

"Good, because I didn't want to have to kick his ass too. I mean, I would if I had to."

"I'm sure you would. No. It's nothing like that. It's about Hendricks."

"Hendricks? What about him?" Whitfield proceeded to tell Flaherty all about his conversation with Mr. Gugurutruv. Flaherty shook her head in disbelief. "That's awful. I'm so sorry. I can't believe Hendricks would do any of that. He seems so sweet."

"I know. That's what I can't figure out. None of this makes any sense. Hendricks is the least greedy person I know. He never asks for anything. He's always been good to Aspen and I. He loves us. How could he do that to my parents?"

"Maybe he didn't. Maybe Ugu's dad got some facts mixed up. I mean, he said he hadn't seen Hendricks in ten years, right? So, maybe the truth got mixed up somewhere."

"I suppose. But why wouldn't Hendricks tell me about Morton Cheesestock. I mean, Aspen and I loved him. We had posters of him all over our room. We'd always watch old videos of his routines, you know, before he got old and started falling all the time."

"I don't know. Maybe Hendricks and Morton had a falling out. Maybe it was like Ugu's dad said and Hendricks didn't want to bring up his past. I don't know, but I think you owe it to Hendricks to talk with him before jumping to any conclusions."

"Yeah, I know I do."

"Does Aspen know yet?"

"No, I didn't tell him. He went downstairs for ice cream just before Ugu's dad told me everything."

"Maybe you should talk to Hendricks first. No sense in upsetting Aspen if you don't really know what happened."

"Yeah, you're probably right. Hey, thanks."

"For what?"

"For kicking my butt."

Flaherty smiled. "Anytime." Flaherty and Whitfield just stood there staring out at the water without talking for a few minutes. "Hey, you feeling better?"

"I guess so. Still don't know what to make of all this."

"Well, there's nothing for you to figure out right now. You'll just have to speak to Hendricks to get some answers. But for now, there are about 40 former gymnasts on that mega-yacht right there waiting to meet you."

"Ahh…I don't know."

"Don't make me knock you out again. You're coming."

"OK. OK. You know, you don't have to punch me every time you want to make a point."

"Yeah, I know, but none of the others will let me beat them up."

"What's their secret?"

"That's just the price you pay if you want to date my Ugu."

"Really? Now, I'm not so sure."

Flaherty raised a fist. "Don't even think about it. You don't want to know the price you'll pay for breaking her heart."

Whitfield let Flaherty know he was just joking. "I got you. We're good."

"I thought so. Now, let's get back to the party."

"How am I going to explain this black eye?"

"I'll tell them I thought you were trying to grab my butt."

"I don't know. Morocco might think that's a fair trade."

"Yeah? Watch what I do to him if he ever does try. He'll be wishing for just a black eye." The two friends laughed and joked with each other as they walked back to the boat together. Flaherty introduced Whitfield to the team alums. Aspen was already there. He had met everyone and seemed to already be best friends with Gabe.

"Hey, Whitfield, I told Gabe about you and Ugu."

"Thanks bro."

Gabe stood up and extended his hand. "Hey, Whitfield. Great to meet you. I've been watching your meets. You've got some real talent."

"Oh, hey, thanks. That means a lot coming from you. You've really been doing great for the Crocodiles."

"Thanks. I wouldn't say great, but I appreciate the compliment."

"You been working on anything new?"

"I have. I…"

Aspen interrupted, having already discussed this topic with Gabe earlier. "Gabe said he's been watching my Pommel Clock routine and he wants to know how I do the helicopter spin out of the reverse circle."

Gabe smiled at Aspen. "That's right, little man. I just can't seem to get that one."

Aspen put his hand on Gabe's shoulder. "Stop by the gym tomorrow. I'll show you." Those close to the conversation all laughed. Aspen felt on top of the world.

"So, Whitfield. I heard about you and Ugu. Congratulations, man. She really is a great girl."

"Thanks, Gabe. She still thinks the world of you."

"Aww, that's sweet. I always knew she was going places. I really hope you two are happy together." Gabe truly seemed genuine in his well-wishes for Whitfield and Ugu.

Whitfield, Aspen, Flaherty, Gabe and the rest of the alumni gang all continued talking, laughing, and telling stories through the late hours of the night. By the time Ugu showed up, Whitfield had long since fell asleep. Aspen was asleep too. Flaherty, as one of the two current team members still awake, was getting tired too. Only Keegan seemed to have the energy to match the alums.

"Ugu! Come join the party!"

"Hi everyone. So nice to see you all again." Everyone said hi and those who could, got up and gave Ugu a hug. "Oh, my goodness. Gabe! I didn't think you were coming in until tomorrow."

"Yeah. Got to leave practice a little early. Wanted to surprise everyone." Ugu and Gabe hugged, and Ugu sat down next to him.

The group continued telling stories, as Gabe spoke softly to Ugu, "I met Whitfield. Seems like a great guy."

"Yeah, he really is."

"So, are you two happy?"

"We really are."

"Does he know yet?"

"Know what?"

"About your dad."

Ugu averted her eyes. "No. I haven't told him yet."

"Don't you think you should?"

"Yes. It's just…complicated. You know that."

"I know. But if you are serious about him, he needs to know."

Ugu looked at Whitfield, who was curled up in the corner, fast asleep. "I know. And I do love him. I just don't know what this will do to him."

"Ugu. He needs to know."

"You're right. I'll tell him before the week is up."

"That's my girl."

Chapter 24
Ice Cream Sundae Surprise

As the sun rose on Wednesday of PAW, Whitfield and Aspen found themselves nicely tucked into their beds, with notes adorning their bedside nightstands:

Breakfast at Flaherty's—07:00—Don't Be Late

The entire current gymnastics team and all returning team alums were to gather at Flaherty's house for their annual breakfast before the official on-campus gymnastics alumni reunion. Breakfast was already in full swing when Aspen and Whitfield arrived, minutes apart from each other.

"Hey. Whitfield is in the house!"

"Hey, Morocco."

Keegan was the next to greet them. "What's up brother? You guys have a good night sleep?" The alums present in the kitchen all laughed.

"Yeah, I guess. Sorry, I fell asleep last night. I don't even remember how I got home."

"Me neither." Aspen didn't recall much of how he arrived home either.

One of the recent alums, Melinda, placed full breakfast plates in front of the boys. "Yeah, a full day in the sun, followed by dancing up on those floating floors will knock you out."

Gabe looked refreshed. "Don't worry, guys. In full alumni tradition, we carried you guys all the way home and put you in your beds before hitting the sack ourselves."

Aspen was confused. "Wait. You carried us home?"

Randy, another alum, spoke from experience. "That's right, dude. Every year, same thing. You young guys start out strong, but in the end, can't hang with the big dogs."

"Speak for yourself. My boy Gabe and I rocked it last night." Keegan threw up both arms and waited for high fives that didn't come.

Skye was the first to throw cold water on Keegan's hype. "Oh really, Keegan? Is that why after we brought Wilson and Kayleigh home and got back to the boat, you were face down next to the dessert cart?"

Morocco jumped into the mix. "Yeah, I heard your pants were hanging off the flagpole and someone wrote 'Big Butt Man' all over your underwear."

Melinda confessed. "Yeah, that was me."

"What? You took my pants off and wrote on my underwear?"

Melinda corrected any misperceptions. "No, your pants were already off."

Harper acknowledged her role in last night's shenanigans. "Yeah, I took those off after you fell asleep."

"So, Harper, you took my pants off and Melinda couldn't help herself and fondled my butt? I'll take that as a win."

"There was no fondling."

"Yeah, that's what you say now."

The whole mood at breakfast was happy, with everyone joking around. Whitfield made his way over to Gabe.

"Hey, Gabe, you didn't by any chance bring Ugu home last night, did you?"

"Nah, man. Don't sweat it. Ugu and Flaherty were awake enough to walk back here last night. Ugu crashed with Flaherty."

"Oh good. Wait, so is she here?"

"She left about an hour ago. Went home to shower and change. I imagine she's getting everything ready for today's events."

"Yeah, she's always working hard."

"Hey, Whitfield, I just want to let you know something. Ugu's a good kid. You can trust her."

Whitfield didn't know exactly where this was coming from. "Thanks, but I already know that."

"Well, you may hear some things." Whitfield looked concerned. "No, not really about her. But others. I don't want to say too much. She's going to talk with you. I just want you to know that you can trust her."

Whitfield remained somewhat confused, wondering what Gabe was not telling him, but expressed gratitude for the advice. "Thanks, Gabe. I appreciate that. Really, I do."

****

After breakfast, current and former gymnasts all stopped by the waterfalls for their annual photo session, before heading over to Arlington Gymnastics Center for the reunion event. As usual, Ugu planned a magnificent day. At previous team reunions, outside media was given full access to athletes and several major news outlets televised coverage from inside the gymnastics center. This year, however, Ugu banned media coverage during the entire official reunion event, allowing team members, alumni, and parents to simply enjoy themselves, without the pressures of giving interviews or posing for pictures.

For the athletes, it was a welcome change, and for the parents and other alums, it was a great opportunity to share stories, laugh, and have fun with their children and former classmates. The cheer and dance squad reunion also took place in the gymnastics center, so despite not hosting a full meet, several thousand guests still gathered and celebrated together.

The alumni and parents mock meet took place outside the gymnastics center, in the Inner Bowl. Current gymnastics team members served as judges as participants competed in ten events, including zip-line relay races; crab walks; (assisted) handstand obstacle courses; trampoline golf, where parents and alums jumped on trampolines that had small golf balls spread out on them to see who could get the most balls to jump off the tramps and into designated rings surrounding the apparatus; and various other fun activities. The pinnacle of the mock meet was Ugu's amazing Ice Cream Sundae Surprise.

Parents got a real kick out of dowsing their children with chocolate sauce and whipped cream and hurling red cherry-colored balls at them, trying to knock them backward into vats of awaiting colored sprinkles. Alumni seemed to enjoy the new featured event just as much, as several former classmates took pleasure in teaming up to turn their friends into giant ice cream sundaes. Current and former gymnasts attracted the largest crowds, with their ultimate demise, whether sprinkles, green slime, or strawberry jam, universally cheered by adoring participants.

Aspen enjoyed firing foam objects at his friends and getting them all messy, but was a little reluctant to sit in the ice cream bowl himself. Once he did though, he loved every second of it, even when his brother took the final shot and knocked Aspen down from the seventh level into a vat of sprinkles. Flaherty only made it to the fifth level before Bella knocked her backward. Whitfield was knocked off his perch on the second level, but because enough people complained that it wasn't fair that he was only up there for such a short while, he was encouraged to go a second time.

This time, everyone made sure they got their shots in, particularly Aspen, who was more than happy to pour loads of chocolate sauce on his brother's head. Flaherty made sure she got her shots in too. Ugu, though, couldn't bring herself to throw, pour, or fling anything at Whitfield. As Whitfield reached the seventh level, the crowd all started to cheer for Ugu to whack Whitfield with the cherry. She didn't want to, but the crowd kept cheering.

"Ugu! Ugu! Ugu!"

Just before Whitfield was about the topple over into the green slime, Ugu fired and hit Whitfield square in the forehead with a cherry. Whitfield was knocked over and the crowd roared with approval.

When it was Ugu's turn, the current students were all pretty nice and didn't fill her bowl as much as they had for others. The alumni were not as reserved, as several young alums fired away. By the time Ugu had reached the top level, her bowl was filled about half as much as Whitfield's was at the same point. The crowd was every bit as boisterous though, as they all cheered for Whitfield to knock her off with the final blow.

"Whitfield! Whitfield! Whitfield!"

Though her face was partially covered in chocolate sauce and whipped cream, Whitfield could still see her eyes. Her beautiful brown eyes. The crowd's cheers grew louder. Whitfield picked up the ball and...threw it ten feet over Ugu's head. Ugu had reached the end and sat perched atop the giant waffle cone, and was slowly lowered down to the strawberry jam slide, where Whitfield stood at the bottom waiting for her.

"Sorry, I just couldn't hit you with the ball."

"Wimp!"

"Hey, I was being sweet."

"Oh please, you tried to hit me. You just missed, that's all."

"Oh, really? Is that what you think?"

"That's right."

"You saw I hit Morocco when he went. And my brother. Knocked them both backward."

"Mmm-hmm. You missed me by ten feet."

"Oh, come on, you know I could hit you any time."

Just then, a voice came from behind, startling Whitfield. "I certainly hope you have no intentions of ever hitting my daughter."

"Oh, sir. Uhh...no, never. I was talking about the game. I..." *How does he keep doing that?*

"Daddy! You came."

"Of course, dear. Everyone seems to be having a grand time. Congratulations, dear. You are truly something." Ugu's dad gave her a kiss on her head, and then took a handkerchief out of his shirt pocket to clean himself off.

"Sir, are you taking a turn on the Ice Cream Sundae ride?"

"Why? Would you like to hit me as well?"

"No. Not at all. It's just…fun. That's all."

"Relax, Whitfield. I know you love my daughter. And wouldn't want to see any harm come to her…or to me, for the matter."

"Of course not, sir."

"Good. Well, with regret, I must decline. I must get back to the hotel to get ready for tonight's awards banquet."

"Awards banquet?"

"Yes, tonight Seven Bridges Academy is hosting the Alumni Achievement Awards. Surely, you must have heard?"

"Oh. Of course. My mistake. Are you up for any awards this year?"

"Oh, heaven's no. I received my award several years ago. No, I am on the committee though, and we have some outstanding recipients this year. I need to go make sure I'm well prepared."

"OK, Daddy. Thank you for coming. I'll see you tonight."

"Good. And, darling, bring your boyfriend." Mr. Gugurutruv motioned in Whitfield's direction with a slight head nod. Ugu's dad gave Whitfield a wink and walked away. Whitfield, still covered in whipped cream, chocolate sauce, and colored sprinkled, stood next to Ugu, who was covered mostly in strawberry jam.

"So, your dad wants you to bring your boyfriend? Hmm…who could that be? Does he go to school here? Do I know him?"

"It's you, stupid."

"Stupid? Is that any way to talk to your boyfriend?"

"Oh, shut up and kiss me."

Dripping with chocolate sauce, whipped cream, sprinkles, jam, and assorted other ice cream toppings, Whitfield and Ugu kissed.

****

The Seven Bridges Alumni Achievement Awards banquet recognized those alumni who have made significant achievements in their post-Seven Bridges career. Ugu planned a wonderful evening, full of speeches, award presentations, holographic re-enactments, guest speakers from the WGF, and plenty of food and dining. The evening started with a showcase of current fifth- and sixth-year Seven Bridges students presenting their own research in short three-minute pitches. The presentations helped to remind everyone in the room that grand ideas start here. For the presenting students, it was an opportunity to introduce themselves to some of the most powerful alums in the world, in the hopes of perhaps securing future employment opportunities.

In some respects, tonight's banquet also served as Ugu and Whitfield's first date as a couple. Sure, they had been out together many times before, and had even attended formal affairs at the same time, but tonight was the first time they were actually going to an event of this magnitude, together. As Whitfield was getting ready for the event, he was nervous and kept thinking he was going to mess up and say something dumb again. Only, this time, he didn't. He was a perfect gentleman throughout the evening.

Through her role in organizing this year's event and from previous event interactions, Ugu already knew many of the most powerful and influential alumni in the room. She introduced Whitfield as her boyfriend to everyone she knew.

Several alums remembered Whitfield from the previous alumni function where Mr. Gugurutruv had introduced him, but now that Whitfield's celebrity status as a star gymnast had skyrocketed over the past several weeks, the handshakes and greetings were much more enthusiastic this time around.

There was no denying it; Whitfield and Ugu made the perfect couple, and were clearly the main attraction of the evening. The awards came and went, speeches delivered and forgotten, but the undeniable love and affection Whitfield and Ugu shared for each other resonated throughout the room.

While many current students opted to sit out this banquet in favor of an outdoor movie double feature showing on the four campus amphitheaters, Flaherty, along with several other gymnasts, decided to support Ugu by attending. She also decided to bring Aspen as her date.

Flaherty had contemplated bringing Spencer, but he was busy preparing for his research presentation and she didn't want him to read anything into her asking him to accompany her. She also didn't want to subject herself to Keegan's or Morocco's constant advances, so decided that Aspen would be the perfect date for the evening. Besides, she really enjoyed spending time with him. Aspen was quickly becoming like a little brother to her.

Toward the end of the evening, Whitfield, Aspen, Ugu, and Flaherty gathered around the dessert table. "Ugu. Again, can I just tell you how amazing you look? This banquet is spectacular."

"Aww, thank you, Flaherty. You look stunning, as always. And might I say, your date is the most handsome man in the place."

Aspen blushed. "Thank you. See, Whitfield, even Ugu thinks I am more handsome than you. And she's the smartest student in the whole school."

Whitfield passed on the opportunity to argue with his little brother. "Well, this time, I happen to agree with her. You do look handsome, bro."

"Yes, I do." Aspen adjusted his bow tie.

Flaherty had an idea. "Hey, some of the guys on the team just asked if we wanted to stop by the amphitheaters and catch the last movie. I figured we can go home first and change into more comfortable clothes, and then relax at the movie. What do you think?"

"Umm…thanks, but I'm going to stay with Ugu. I'm sure she wants to make sure the evening wraps up OK."

"Actually, you know what, Flaherty. That sounds perfect. I've been working like crazy all week. I need some time to just relax…and maybe snuggle up next to the second most handsome guy in the place."

Ugu's dad appeared out of nowhere, and joined the conversation. "Second most handsome? Who's more handsome than me?"

How does he keep doing that?

"Hi Daddy."

"Hello, sir."

"Flaherty, angel. You look gorgeous."

"Good evening, sir." Whitfield didn't know if he should extend his hand. After some quiet contemplation, he decided the moment had passed and was going to put his arm around Ugu, but then thought he saw her dad glare at him. Eventually, he decided to just keep his hands in his pockets.

"Me. I'm the most handsome."

"Well, Aspen, you'll get no argument from me. You look quite dashing."

"Thank you, sir."

"Ugu, sweetheart, now that the banquet is almost over, several of the alums and I are heading over to the Alumni Center for a nightcap. I thought maybe you and Whitfield could join us."

"Well, Daddy, actually Whitfield and I were going to join these guys and catch the movie out at the amphitheaters. But, if you really want us there, we'll go."

For a brief moment, Mr. Gugurutruv's face offered a hint of disappointment, but he quickly regained his composure. "Nonsense. You two go and have a great time. This will just be a bunch of old guys and gals talking about the good ol' days. You kids go have some fun. Make your own memories."

Whitfield did not want to disappoint Ugu's dad. "Sir, thank you. But, if you really want, we would be happy to join you."

"Don't give it another thought. You take care of my daughter. There will be plenty of time for you to join me later."

"Thank you, sir."

Whitfield, Aspen, Ugu, and Flaherty all went back to Aspen's house to get changed. Flaherty simply borrowed some of Ugu's clothes and Whitfield always kept some of his clothes over at Aspen's mansion for just such an occasion. They all got changed into more comfortable clothing, still color-coordinated by class year and adorned with the school crest, of course, and met up with their friends at the amphitheater. They all laughed, joked, and just enjoyed being kids for a night. Ugu fell asleep in Whitfield's arms. He wrapped his arms tightly around her, and thought this is what heaven must be like.

Chapter 25
SYPHUS

Over in the Alumni Center, on the top floor, in a dark, secluded meeting room in the northwest turret, Yuri Gugurutruv, Dr. Hewitt, Gen. Gibson, and several others convened. Yuri glared out the window, where moments ago, he saw his daughter laughing and enjoying time with her friends.

"Thank you all for coming. Everything is proceeding as planned. However, we do have a potential threat on our hands."

The group started to murmur.

Gen. Gibson took his cue to speak. "You mean besides the boy and your daughter discovering those envelopes and finding our transaction paper trail? Both of which may have been prevented if not for the utter incompetence displayed by Dr. Hewitt."

Dr. Hewitt bowed his head. "I am ashamed of my ignorance. I will not fail again."

Hon. Cornelia was unaware of Dr. Hewitt's failure. "Please explain."

"Yes, Dr. Hewitt brought in those incompetent kids from Isadora's Gang to bribe gymnasts. They were discovered. He then allowed a child to hack into his account, leaving our trail out in the open."

Yuri turned to face the group, and silence prevailed. "Please, if I may. The envelopes are not the problem. And the children, as you say, have not even begun to understand the significance of the altered scoresheets. Although, it would be wise to not allow any more hacks into our system." Yuri glared in Dr. Hewitt's direction.

"Already taken care of, Grand Founder."

"Good. The real problem is Hendricks. He's back." More murmuring from the group swept through the room. This time, even louder, and more fearful. "I have already begun to turn the boy against his guardian, and with a little help from my daughter, I believe he will be ours."

Col. Drachlich added an inquiry, "and his brother? He is just as talented."

"Yes, we will turn him as well. In due time."

Sterling expressed concern, "how should we proceed regarding Hendricks?"

Lt. Smedvik offered a suggestion. "Should we bring in some muscle?"

"No. I am not interested in starting another war. Not at this time. That is what put us in this precarious position in the first place."

Lane was the only seated member that appeared on equal footing with Yuri. "The Grand Founder is right. We need to exercise caution."

Gerola spoke from the far corner of the room. "How are our reserves?"

Gen. Gibson addressed this concern. "We are almost at our prior levels. Our target schools are all contributing nicely."

Col. Drachlich asked for additional confirmation. "Any programs resign yet?"

"We have had twelve schools submit paperwork, effectively canceling their gymnastics teams. We fully expect another 35 or 40 by the end of the season."

"That is still short of our goal."

"Yes, over 760 programs will likely make it through the season. Unless…"

Yuri raised his hand to signal Gen. Gibson to stop going any further. "No, we are not yet ready to move so aggressively. The old man is still in power."

Gen. Gibson conceded, but followed with additional information from inside the WGF. "He has already failed his first re-appointment exam. I made sure of that. He has friends. So, he will likely be granted a probationary period to pass the exam."

Gerola adamantly followed. "Then we should make sure he does not pass."

Sterling presented another potential obstacle to their plan. "Even if he does fail again, there is no guarantee Gen. Gibson will become the next president."

Once again, Yuri silenced the group with a wave of his hand. "We have made arrangements."

"That is good enough for me."

Yuri continued, "I wish for our reserves to grow. Dr. Hewitt, continue making the necessary arrangements. Be certain to use competent soldiers this time. Gen. Gibson, we need more favorable scheduling. Make it happen."

"Yes, Grand Founder," Dr. Hewitt bowed his head.

"Yes, Grand Founder," Gen. Gibson bowed his head.

"I will pay Morton a visit. It is time that he lives up to his legendary status."

Sterling and Col. Drachlich each nodded. "Agreed."

Yuri concluded the meeting. "We are…"

All those in attendance, replied, "…SYPHUS."

Chapter 26
Ugu's Clever Tactic

As the week continued, the buzz around campus was that this was by far the best PAW in Seven Bridges' history. The Thursday morning scavenger hunt and afternoon ski session brought parents, students, and alums together for a fun day of outdoor activities and good times. By evening, with some physical exhaustion setting in, parents were particularly pleased to sit back and relax as students took the spotlight with the annual fashion show and student talent show. After a brief interlude, students were back in the spotlight as the subjects of the annual Student Fantasy Draft. This year's draft was capped at 42 teams, with each team selecting 25 current students to fill their roster. Points would be earned based on draftees' grades (weighted by course difficulty); contributions to the House Point Challenge; service points collected during days of service periods and extracurricular activities; and scores provided on their internship evaluations.

The Student Fantasy Draft first appeared at Seven Bridges Academy seven years ago, and has quickly become a cherished tradition, bringing together alumni and current students in a rather unique way. Alumni become vested in their students' academic performance, with many providing additional tutoring services, as well as opening doors for their students during internship terms. Parents and alums review student bios and even interview potential draftees during the evening's draft proceedings.

Prizes are awarded to the winning teams at the end-of-year celebration; however, the biggest prize for many of the past winners has been bragging rights over their fellow Seven Bridges brethren. For the students, a healthy competition emerges as they all want to be part of the winning team. An additional unexpected, but pleasant, benefit of the Student Fantasy Draft is the further development of student relationships that span across houses, as many of the team 'owners' would treat their team to meals, pay for group vacations, and even give priority internship access to members of their fantasy team.

The Student Fantasy Draft was one of the few exceptions at SBA where being a member of the gymnastics team was not a huge benefit. In fact, most gymnasts were often selected near the bottom of the draft, since so many members opted for easy classes and rarely collected points for the House Point Challenge, due to their in-practice and meet weekend physical activities being excluded from House Point Challenge totals.

Despite this reputation, Whitfield, Aspen, and Flaherty were all academically ambitious and capable students, making them three of the most sought-after gymnasts in the Fantasy Draft; however, being new to the school this year meant that many parents and alums were not yet fully aware of Whitfield and Aspen's significant aptitude outside the gym.

As expected, Ugu was the top draft pick, followed by Flaherty at number two. Throughout the rest of the first few rounds, many teams simply selected their own sons or daughters for their fantasy rosters, before making more strategic selections. Kayleigh was the second gymnast selected, 17th overall.

No other gymnasts were selected in the first or second rounds. Whitfield was selected in the third round, pick number 107, and Aspen was picked up in the fourth round, with the 142nd selection. Despite the four friends all being drafted by different teams, their friendship was everlasting. For one thing, they each got to make new friends and meet other parents and alums; but, also, they were each aware that many of the team 'owners' would stay up all night discussing trades and rearranging their rosters throughout the weekend, so while tonight they were on separate fantasy teams, tomorrow could be a whole different story.

****

On Friday morning, Whitfield and Flaherty decided to head over to Aspen's house to discuss their Term 2 schedules, before going over to the flower gardens with Ugu to help oversee the morning family festival.

"Hey Whitfield, were you able to get into all of your classes for Term 2?"

"Hi Flaherty. I think so. I'm taking *World Intelligence Agencies*."

Ugu perked up. "That's a good class. You'll like it. I took it last year, and helped to redesign the curriculum."

Aspen wasn't surprised. "Of course, you did."

Ugu just smiled, and handed Aspen another pastry. "Thanks. I'm also taking *Computer Hacking*, *Counterintelligence Strategy*, and *Crystal Ball Technology*."

"Tough course load. But I think Ugu's in two of those classes, right?"

"Yup. I'm taking *Counterintel* and *CBT*."

Flaherty tried to stir the pot. "Hmm. Two classes together. Uh-oh."

"What is that supposed to mean?"

"Oh nothing. I guess we'll just see who's smarter. You know, Whitfield, I think you may have the advantage. Ugu's not going to be able to concentrate with you sitting next to her."

Ugu did not appreciate the presumption that she would allow herself to be distracted during class. "Yes, I will. I can focus on other things you know."

"Right."

"Oh. Shut up."

Flaherty giggled. "Anyway, Whitfield, you're not the only one taking a class with our lovely Ugu. I'm taking *Advanced Seduction Methods* with her."

"Really. What's that course about?"

"Oh, just going to learn more ways to get others to do what we want them to, right Ugu?"

Aspen rolled his eyes. "Umm…don't you two already get everything you want?"

Ugu and Flaherty both chuckled. "Not everything, Aspen."

"Really, Ugu? I bet you can get my brother to do anything for you."

Whitfield did not agree. "That's not true."

Flaherty was intrigued by Aspen's comment. "Hmm. I'm not so sure. Aspen, that is an excellent idea, though."

Whitfield didn't like where this was going. "What idea?"

"I want to see if Ugu can get Whitfield to do anything she wants."

Whitfield really didn't like where this was going. "Like what?"

"Not sure yet. We'll have to come up with something."

Ugu decided to play along. "It will have to be something good."

"Oh yeah. Definitely."

"Oh, I don't like the sound of this. Aspen, save me."

"Sorry, bro. Here, have a cookie."

"Don't worry, Whitfield. Ugu and I won't torture you…too much." Flaherty and Ugu shared another laugh, before Flaherty remembered something else entirely. "Aspen, I hear you are interning at the WGF."

Aspen opened his eyes wide, wondering what else Ugu may have said to Flaherty. "How did you hear that?"

Right away, Ugu recognized that Aspen was nervous, and wanted to calm him. "I told her. I mentioned that you would just be helping out in the office." Ugu made eye contact with Aspen and flashed a quick wink.

"Oh. Right."

"So, are you excited?"

"I guess so. It'll be weird flying back and forth every day. I wish I could go with someone, but no other first-years can intern there."

Flaherty thought she would offer him some company. "Aspen, if you want, I can ride in the mornings with you, and then catch a ride back in time for class."

Aspen remembered that he is supposed to get changed into his bird suit and land in a fake nest every morning to surprise the visiting children, and did not want Flaherty, or anyone else for that matter, to see him in his bird costume. "Oh, no. That's OK. I'll be fine."

"OK. Just let me know if you change your mind."

Whitfield changed the subject back to Term 2. "Flaherty, what other courses are you taking?"

"Oh, I am slammed this term. I have *Holographic Engineering II*, which is going to be so cool. I also have *Nanotechnology I* and *Neurobiology II*."

"Wow. That sounds like a really tough schedule."

"Tough? Yes. But, also a lot of fun. I really like all my teachers and can't wait for the projects. Should be a blast."

"That's cool." Whitfield noticed the time. "Do we need to head over to the flower gardens yet?"

Ugu checked the clock. "Yes. We should get over there now. And, thank you all again for helping. This really means a lot."

Aspen spoke for the group. "No problem. Happy to help."

The four friends went over to the flower gardens for the family festival. Later in the day, they all pitched in to help tear down the equipment and stands and restore the gardens to their quiet, peaceful nature. Ugu also communicated with her team overseeing day of service projects across campus, and with the exception of a few overzealous parents, everything went smoothly.

Whitfield was pleased to see Dr. Hewitt helping out at the family festival as well. "Hi Dr. Hewitt. What brings you out here today?"

"Whitfield. How nice to see you. I always enjoy helping out when I can. PAW is such a wonderful time for everyone in the Seven Bridges community. Don't you agree?"

"Yes. Very much so."

"So, have you given much thought into how you are going to use your budget from the Grand Curriculum Design Challenge winnings?"

"Yes. Well, a little. We have some ideas on how to apply the data for several math classes, and the engineering applications are pretty straightforward."

"Yes, you and your brother certainly hit on a winner with this idea."

Whitfield appreciated the compliment and was eager to share more about his project. "We were even able to apply it in detecting irregular patterns in gymnasts' routines."

Dr. Hewitt stopped picking up leftover trash and focused all his attention on Whitfield. "What do you mean?"

"Well, gymnasts always follow the same sequence of muscle movements with every routine. We can identify when a gymnast makes a mistake causing a fall. You know, determine whether it was intentional, or simply an accident."

Dr. Hewitt found this latest application quite intriguing. "Intentional? What do you mean? Are you saying some gymnasts make mistakes on purpose?"

Whitfield feared he may have said too much, and attempted to backtrack from his earlier comment. "No. Of course not. I didn't mean intentional. Of course, all falls are on accident. I meant to say that some gymnasts fall because their hands get sweaty or the apparatus gets slippery, while others fall because they forget their routine. Sometimes gymnasts just get tired or aren't as precise as they normally are. Lots of different reasons for falls. I think our tech can detect some of those causes."

Whitfield wasn't quite sure how to read Dr. Hewitt's reaction, but on the surface, the house supervisor seemed satisfied. "Ahh, OK. That's more like it. Well, you have certainly put a lot of thought and ingenuity into this project. I'm proud of you. Keep up the great work. I think I'm going to take a break now and go clean myself up. Good chatting with you."

"Same here."

Dr. Hewitt hurried off across campus to his basement loft in Whitfield's mansion. Whitfield wondered if he shouldn't have told Dr. Hewitt about those alternate uses for his technology. *It's not like I told him about all the bribes we found or that we've already used the technology to identify intentional falls. Everything will be OK.*

The evening brought yet another formal attire event, as Ugu staged the Agricultural Commodities and Precious Gems auctions to run side by side in adjoining rooms in one of the tertiary wings of Flaxen Hall. Many of Seven Bridges Academy's wealthier supporters attended the evening's auctions to help raise additional money for the school. The night ended with a low-key, fun-filled trivia contest.

Whitfield and Aspen were both undeniably knowledgeable about gymnastics trivia, but when it came to Seven Bridges' history and larger societal issues, they both leaned heavily on Ugu and Flaherty for answers. Their strategy worked, as their four-member team took home the top prize. Well, they didn't exactly take the prize home. They used the money to help pay for parents and alums' late-night snacks at Plank 'N Steins. All the parents and alums in attendance were appreciative of this generous, and thoughtful, act of kindness and selflessness.

****

The final weekend of PAW was the perfect culmination of an amazing week. With an all-day music festival filling campus with upbeat energy, a wine and spirits tasting for parents and older alums, a tribute to the 10th anniversary of Seven Bridges' first national championship team, a curriculum design project open to anyone with an idea to share, and the final students v. alumni v. parents competition, the weekend truly had something for everyone. In the midst of all the fun and games, however, Ugu had yet another clever idea.

Of course, all of the available video monitors on campus would be airing the live Professional Gymnastics League (PGL) meets taking place on Saturday and Sunday. Ugu contracted with the WGF to allow on-campus wagering for the pro meets throughout the weekend. Typically, the on-campus sportsbook only accepted bets for school meets. This upgrade allowed parents and alums who were avid gamblers to continue enjoying the weekend on campus and place their bets without ever having to leave their seats.

While certainly appreciated by most, Ugu had another motive entirely for making this change. Still unable to hack into the remote sportsbooks to identify individual account holders, Ugu was, however, able to access the on-campus sportsbook mainframe, which allowed her to link bank account information with gambling IDs and other personal identification data. With her newly-constructed customized algorithm, anyone placing a bet on campus using their personal account would automatically trigger a data feed, whereby Ugu could identify all prior bets placed using the same account number.

It may be a longshot, Ugu thought, but if the person, or persons, placing large bets ahead of bribed gymnasts taking a fall was a Seven Bridges parent or alum, just maybe she could identify the mysterious gamblers this weekend.

Upon reviewing the data on Sunday evening, Ugu's clever tactic had paid off. She needed to tell Whitfield and the others right away. Whitfield, Aspen, and Flaherty were enjoying the final acts of the music festival when they received Ugu's urgent message. They immediately gathered their belongings and rushed off to the IA library to meet up with Ugu. Flaherty was the first to speak, since Whitfield and Aspen were still trying to catch their breath.

"What's up? We got here as fast as we could."

Ugu explained all about how she got the WGF to allow gambling on pro meets on campus over the weekend and how she intended to use the data.

"Wow! Impressive. Quite clever."

"Thank you, Whitfield."

"So, what did you find?"

"With just this weekend's on-campus betting, I was able to successfully match 217 Seven Bridges parents and alums with their personal gambling histories. After screening for size of bets and active gambling activity during our three meets this season, I was able to narrow the results down to just twelve accounts. Of these remaining accounts, four jumped out at me right away. First, Sir Arlington actively wagered on all three of our meets this year, but never specifically on those duels involving a bribed gymnast. He did have one quite large bet on Aspen, though, in the first meet. I have that one flagged for further investigation."

Flaherty raised an eyebrow. "Wow. He must have won big betting on you, Aspen."

"I wonder if that was one of the times I made it all the way around the Pommel Clock."

"It was."

"Cool."

"Second. Dr. Hewitt has the longest history of placing wagers. He's very active, and not just for Seven Bridges meets. He places bets across the board. Other schools. Minor League meets. Pro meets. Everything. And for big money too."

Again, Flaherty was suspicious. "Wow. That's strange."

Whitfield joined her in thinking something was amiss here. "Yeah. How does he afford to gamble so much?"

"Well, here's the thing. He almost never loses."

Aspen tried pushing back on the obvious thought running through each of their heads. "He does really like gymnastics. Maybe he's just good at knowing which gymnasts are better."

Ugu was not convinced. "No one is that good. But, here's an even stranger part. He doesn't have his gambling account tied to his personal bank. He uses a different bank account number. I wasn't able to trace it yet. Whitfield, he's your house supervisor. Do you know if he has distant relatives or a business or something?"

"Not that I know of. We don't really talk about his family."

"That's OK. I'll keep digging."

"Did Dr. Hewitt bet on me to win too?"

"Yes, Aspen, but only once. He actually placed really large bets on the duels that we're looking into. He must know something about the bribes. Maybe even be part of it."

Flaherty turned toward Aspen. "You need to keep working on that fake scoresheet. See if you can find anything else useful in it."

"I will. I'm also going to look into Gen. Gibson's private messages."

Whitfield did not approve. "Aspen. That could be dangerous. I don't think you should do that. What if you get caught?"

Aspen looked at Ugu. "Should we tell them?"

"Only if you want to."

Aspen proceeded to tell Flaherty and Whitfield the plan to have Aspen dress as the WGF mascot to get inside WGF headquarters, and hack into Gen. Gibson's account. Flaherty and Whitfield totally lost control, laughing hysterically. After a good ten minutes of laughing and joking about Aspen wearing a chicken suit, the group composed themselves.

"Oh, is that why you don't want me to ride with you to WGF in the mornings?"

"Yeah. I don't want you to see me in my bird suit."

"I understand. But, Aspen, you know you can trust me. None of us will tell anyone about this. And I promise I will not make fun of you."

"Thank you."

"Yeah, sorry, bro, I can't make that same promise. This is too funny."

"Whitfield, sweetie, shut up and don't make fun of your brother for this. He is sticking his neck on the line for all of us. I think he is very brave."

"You mean he's sticking his chicken neck on the line?"

Aspen was getting upset. "Ugu. Tell him to stop."

"Whitfield."

"Sorry. I'm done. Don't get your feathers all ruffled." Flaherty chuckled and Whitfield laughed at his own joke. "Sorry. I'm done."

Ugu felt like a parent to two toddlers. "Good. This is our best lead so far."

Flaherty brought the conversation back to the gambling accounts Ugu had found. "You mentioned there were four accounts that stood out? So, far you only mentioned two."

"Oh right. One of the other accounts belongs to my dad."

Flaherty knew Ugu's dad liked to gamble, but still feigned surprise. "Really?"

"Yes, I knew my dad wagered for fun occasionally, and that's probably all this was, but his activity did meet all my screens. I also found it strange that his account wasn't linked to our home account, but to another, foreign account. I didn't look into it yet. I may just ask him about it later. He already left this morning, but I'm sure I'll talk with him soon." Ugu shrugged off her dad's gambling activity as though it didn't matter to their current investigation.

Whitfield wasn't so quick to dismiss it though. "Hmm…that's interesting. You don't think he has anything to do with all this, do you?"

"Daddy? No. Of course not." The tone in Ugu's voice was a little higher than she had intended. Both Flaherty and Whitfield picked up on it, but decided to not pursue it any further.

"So, what was the fourth account that caught your eye?"

"Oh, well, I kind of wanted to talk to Whitfield about this one in private."

"Me? Why?"

"It's kind of personal, for you, that is."

Whitfield looked at Flaherty. "It's OK. Whatever you have to say, you can say it in front of Flaherty. She's kind of like a sister to me anyway."

Flaherty smiled.

"OK. The name on the fourth account that stood out was Hendricks."

Flaherty nearly choked. "What?"

Whitfield couldn't believe it. "WHAT?"

Aspen's eyes grew wide. "Hendricks is here?"

"No, of course not, Aspen. He left earlier this week. How could it be Hendricks?"

"OK, so I hope you're not mad at me, but I did some digging."

"No, of course I'm not mad at you. What did you find?"

"This is really weird. Hendricks' name is listed as the primary trade executor on the account, but he is not the primary beneficiary." Whitfield and Flaherty exchanged glances.

Aspen was confused. "What does that mean?"

Ugu tried explaining. "It means that the person listed as the trade executor can place all the bets, but the winnings actually go to someone else."

Flaherty asked the question Whitfield wasn't able to bring himself to ask. "OK. Do we know who is the primary beneficiary?"

"Yes."

Whitfield lowered his voice to a whisper. "Who?"

After an uncomfortably long pause, Ugu rocked Whitfield's world. "The primary beneficiaries listed on the account are your parents, Livvy and Aldrich."

****

Whitfield stood up and started pacing. "That's impossible. They're dead. There must be a mistake."

"I know. It doesn't seem possible, but here it is." Ugu showed the other three the account records she pulled from the in-house sportsbook mainframe. The data showed that Hendricks made several large bets on Saturday afternoon.

Flaherty spoke softly. "Whitfield, do you think it is at all possible that Hendricks placed those bets? You know, after what you heard the other day?"

Ugu didn't know what Flaherty was talking about. "What did you hear?"

"Uhh…nothing. No, wait, sorry. There is something I'm not supposed to tell you, but I will anyway. Just not right now. First, is there any way for someone to place a bet from a remote location?"

"What, for any meet?"

"No. For this weekend's meets. For the on-campus gambling data you pulled from the system."

"No, I only collected data for the bets that were placed on site."

"OK. Can you access the sportsbook cameras to see if Hendricks made an appearance?"

Flaherty was confident she could. "Sure, I can do that. The sportsbook only requires *CBT III* clearance. Which I now have."

"Great! Can you please check the camera feeds?"

"Do you really think you'll find him placing a bet here?" Flaherty wasn't sure what Whitfield was thinking.

"No, I don't. But I just want to be sure. Ugu, I hope you are as good as we all think you are."

"Ooh…that sounds like a challenge is coming. What do you need?"

"I need you to find out who placed those bets that came in under Hendricks' account. If my hunch is correct, someone is trading on my parents' account, and setting up Hendricks by using his name. I need to know who it is." Flaherty now understood exactly what Whitfield was thinking.

"That's going to be really tough, but I guess I can identify through which terminal the trades came in and with Flaherty's *CBT III* access, I can run facial recognition and…"

"You got it. Whatever you need."

"Thanks, Flaherty. OK, let's get started."

"No, not yet. We need to get home first."

Ugu wanted to start on this latest project right away. "You and Aspen are going home?"

"No, we all need to head back to Aspen's mansion together."

Flaherty looked at Ugu, and then back at Whitfield. "Now? Why?"

"Well, tomorrow's a big day for Aspen."

"Come on, Whitfield. I'm not going to practice walking like a chicken in front of everyone."

"No. It's your first day interning at WGF. You're going to hack into Gen. Gibson's account tomorrow. And Ugu is going to teach you how to do it."

Chapter 27
Hendricks Confronts Bibb

Perched high atop Arlington Gymnastics Center, blending in among the ultra-high-def video boards, Hendricks scanned campus and the outlying areas in search of his target. He knew Yuri well, and was convinced that his nemesis was planning to turn his wards against him, or worse, corrupt them into joining SYPHUS. Hendricks was convinced Yuri was using Ugu to get close to Whitfield, and even though it cut him to the bone to leave Whitfield and Aspen by faking his early departure from campus, he knew there was only one way to stop SYPHUS. His way.

Hendricks was always up for a fight. Despite his age, he was in top physical shape and could outmaneuver anyone on the battlefield, but this was different. Unlike past encounters with SYPHUS, when Yuri's henchmen would attack you out in the open, hoping to impose their dominance through numbers, Yuri's henchman now hid in the shadows. Hendricks suspected Yuri was planning something big, and with the constant alerts he received all weekend concerning the balance in his custodial bank account, he knew Yuri was going in for the kill.

Hendricks peered out over campus. *Where are you, you little bug? Show yourself. Just give me a sign, a signal, anything. Where are you hiding?*

Hendricks knew many of Yuri's henchmen from past encounters, and had seen several SYPHUS members convening earlier in the day, and now gathering somewhere inside the Alumni Center, but suspected not all members would be invited to their 'little clubhouse' sessions, as he liked to call them. One member, in particular, was not accounted for, and Hendricks was determined to not let him get away.

And that's when it happened. Under the cloak of darkness, Bibb Tossino was spotted walking through the Law campus toward the waterfalls—he must have thought it was the perfect spot to escape undetected, through the rain forest and out past the safari. He would have been right if anyone else had been out hunting that night. But, not tonight. Not with Hendricks hot on his tail. Hendricks deftly descended the outside of Arlington Gymnastics Center, and expertly traversed the Inner Bowl with speed, prowess, and stealth. Before Bibb had reached the exterior of the rain forest, Hendricks had caught up with him and pinned him against the wet buttressed trunk of a massive kapok tree.

"I thought I smelled a rat."

"Hendricks. How did you find me?"

"That's not important. Why were you making those bets today under my name?"

Bibb was struggling to break free from Hendricks' grasp. "I had to."

"Why? Who told you to do it?"

"General Gibson. He said if I didn't, he'd hurt my family."

"Stop lying. I know you're part of SYPHUS. I know all about you."

Bibb stopped attempting to break free. "It's true. I am part of SYPHUS. But I don't want to see anyone get hurt. Not this time. We're different than you remember."

"Where are Livvy and Aldrich? Are they still alive?"

Bibb flashed an evil, knowing smile. "You have no idea what you are getting into here. Don't you get it? None of us are alive. Not yet, anyway."

Hendricks thrust Bibb back up against the tree, smashing Bibb's head hard against the bark. "No more lies. Is Yuri back in charge?"

"He can't be stopped. And he's not alone. The founders are all back. Every one of them."

"That's impossible."

"It's true. They share a new vision. It's beautiful."

"What is? What vision?"

"A world without…"

Hendricks was growing more impatient by the second. "A world without what?"

"A world without gymnastics." Hendricks loosened his hold on Bibb and took a step back. He couldn't believe what he was hearing. "Think about it. No more meets. No more resources changing hands over a weekend. No more pathetic gods. We will rule it all. We will decide what is good for everyone. We will control everything. SYPHUS will rule!"

"Enough! That's crazy. SYPHUS' vision is to destroy everything?"

Bibb cackled. "Tear down the institution so we can rise from the ashes. Join us."

"Never. It's not going to happen."

"They can't be stopped. This is going to happen. There is nothing you can do to stop it."

"I may not be able to stop it alone. But, I'm not alone. This time, I have help."

"You don't mean those pathetic kids, do you? They can't help you. He has them right where he wants them. They're not yours anymore. They belong to SY…"

Hendricks had heard enough. He punched Bibb square in the face, knocking his adversary's head hard on the base of the tree trunk, rendering him unconscious. Hendricks thought for a moment about taking Bibb into the safari and leaving him there for the wild beasts to feed, but quickly changed his mind, opting instead to call for Sir Arlington to send a drone taxi to his location, where Bibb would be brought into custody and transported to Chipwood Prison.

On the call with Sir Arlington, Hendricks briefly informed the headmaster of Bibb's whereabouts and the need for security agents to arrest him. He also added a strong message. "SYPHUS is waging war on gymnastics. It's time for Whitfield and Aspen to join the fight. Make sure they are ready."

Sir Arlington was prepared for this news. "They are. And they are not alone."

"If you're talking about the girl, you better be damn sure she's on our side."

"I am. She is. And she's not the only one."

"Is the other one just as good?"

"Yes. The four of them need each other, and we need each of them if we are to prevail."

"There is no if. We must prevail."

"We will."

"We better."

Chapter 28
Gen. Gibson Hack

Aspen showed up at WGF headquarters on Monday morning at 08:00, right on time. He was tired from last night's information session where Ugu offered instructions on the floor layout of the building, identifying all relevant offices, and meticulously detailing every facet of the computer hack Aspen was about to pull off. Flaherty contributed several useful persuasion tactics that she learned from *Seduction* classes to help Aspen secure some alone time in one of the offices. Flaherty also gave Aspen a few quick 'bird' dance lessons, so that he could focus on his mission during the time his handlers would think he is working on his practice training.

Before exiting his ride, Aspen recalled every word from last night's coaching session. He closed his eyes and visualized images of Ugu and Flaherty taking turns prepping him.

"When you get there, they will give you a quick tour of the building. Pay attention to everyone you meet and where their office is located. They will drop you off at Human Resources for processing, where you'll get your security clearances and account information. After you are done there, you'll likely take a trip up to Gen. Gibson's office suite, so he can meet you. Be super friendly and mention how much you like the view from his office. They'll probably want you to get changed and start your practice downstairs in the bullpen; however, if you play your cards right and he and his assistants like you, they may offer you the large conference room next to his suite to practice."

"You can even mention how you would feel better staying upstairs to train, since you want to maintain your secret identity and too many people may recognize you from being on the gymnastics team and all the press you've been receiving."

"That's good. Listen to Flaherty. Either way, ideally, you want to be in that conference room. Gen. Gibson may even have his credentials already inputted into the conference room computers, which would significantly reduce the hack time.

Since it's your first day, your trainers will likely give you some alone time to set up your account and fill out some forms before practicing your dances and other routines. Don't worry about any of the forms just yet. You can complete those remotely. Get right to the hack."

Flaherty had some additional advice. "If anyone stays in the room with you, ask for a sandwich or something else from the cafeteria. This will get them to leave for a few minutes. If that doesn't work, use some of the tactics we went over to get them to sit across from you, away from your screens. It's important that they sit. If they do suspect anything, the time it takes for them to get up will give you extra time to switch screens."

Ugu had continued prepping Aspen. "And if you do happen to get caught, play dumb. Say you were not sure exactly what to do, but didn't want to look bad on your first day. They will likely cut you some slack, with this being your first day and all. You'll likely need about 8-10 minutes from start to finish. If Gen. Gibson's credentials are already active, then you'll only need about three minutes. Use your time wisely."

Aspen remembered it was at that time when his brother jumped in to offer encouragement. "Piece of cake, bro. Just get in. Do your thing. Get out." *Mmm...cake.*

Flaherty had offered a final word. "If you do find yourself in a jam, and the timing is right, break out that new dance move we worked on."

Aspen remembered thinking, *but that move is kind of silly.*

As though she was reading his mind, Ugu wrapped up the prep session. "Exactly. Your trainers will be too busy either laughing, objecting, or trying to change the dance move that they will have forgotten all about what they saw with the hack. Trust me, this is going to work. All of it."

Aspen opened his eyes. It was now 08:30 and everything was going exactly as Ugu had said it would. Aspen was keeping mental notes of everyone he met and the entire office layout. He received his security clearances and went up to meet Gen. Gibson. On his way up, Aspen grabbed a few chocolate candies from the hallway dispensers and made it a point to hand them out to Gen. Gibson's assistants when he met them. This simple, yet smooth, move immediately endeared Aspen to the staff. They all instantly fell in love with the ten-year old.

Aspen had no problem securing the conference room for his paperwork and initial training session. The only issue was that Gen. Gibson's assistants wouldn't leave him alone. The mascot trainers made sure the chicken suit fit Aspen, gave him a few simple dance moves to work on, and said they would be back in about

30 minutes for a full training session. It took some persuasion, but Aspen finally got Gen. Gibson's assistants to leave him alone. He still had 15 minutes on the clock.

Aspen placed the mascot head on the table, and got to work. Gen. Gibson's credentials were not already preloaded on the conference room computers, but Aspen was prepared for this possibility. He expertly navigated his way through the system's security protocols and gained access to Gen. Gibson's account. Well over a million messages. Thousands of messages sent to schools around the country with scoresheets attached.

Aspen didn't have time to review them all right now. He just needed to complete the transfer. His time was almost up. The trainers should have been back by now, and he still had another three minutes of transfer time to go. Remembering Flaherty's advice for getting out of a tight spot like this, Aspen started making some outrageous movements with his feathers and chicken butt, enough so that he was noticed by Gen. Gibson's assistants from outside the conference room.

Once he saw that he had their attention and they were smiling and giggling, Aspen grabbed his chicken head and walked toward the door. He motioned for one of the assistants to come over.

"Hi, sweetie. Is everything OK?"

"Hi, Miss Twinkler. I'm really sorry to ask this, but I've been trying to get this one move down and I really want to get it before Shawna and Hank come back. Could you stall them for just a few minutes? Please."

"Sure thing. sweetie. Don't be so hard on yourself. I think you are going to be a fine mascot."

"Aww…thank you. I'm really trying hard. I think I'll just need a few more minutes."

"You got it."

Just a moment later, Shawna and Hank came back, but rather than walking into the conference room, Miss Twinkler cut them off and brought them to her desk. Aspen didn't know exactly what she was saying to them, and it didn't matter. He went back to his screen and saw that the transfer was almost complete. He looked up once more to make sure no one was watching, confirmed that the transfer was complete, cleaned up any trace of his hack, and then continued making outrageous motions with his feathers, prompting the two trainers to come in to offer their much-needed guidance.

On his way home that afternoon, Aspen felt good about completing his mission. He now had all of Gen. Gibson's incoming and outgoing messages. *We have to be able to find something useful in there. Are there more hidden bank account numbers? For how long has this been going on? Who else is involved? Am I going to be the best WGF mascot ever?*

Questions like these were running through Aspen's mind all the way back to campus, when something caught his eye on the video monitor inside the flying drone taxi. Gen. Gibson was giving a press conference outside WGF headquarters. "Hey, I was just there. That's Gen. Gibson. And Dr. Hewitt is right behind him."

Gen. Gibson was speaking to reporters. "Yes, we are disappointed too. But, until we subject this scanning technology to more stringent testing, we will not subject our athletes to the potential dangers. We will not harm any athlete."

"But, hasn't the technology already been used in numerous human trials and on ocean life?" The question came from an off-camera reporter.

"Yes, but we can never be too careful when it comes to protecting our children. Sorry, we just cannot place them at risk."

Aspen was stunned. "How could he do that? The technology is safe. There is no danger to the athletes. This is terrible." Gen. Gibson was not going to allow his and Whitfield's project technology, that they worked so hard at developing, at any more meets. Aspen paused for a moment, before the thought hit him. "Maybe he found out about the hack and he's trying to get us back. What if I'm in trouble? Wait until Whitfield hears about this. He's not going to be happy."

****

Whitfield's first day of classes for Term 2 was going great. He loved being in class with Ugu. He met Ugu on the Outer Loop in the morning so they could walk to class together. They sat next to each other during class and walked hand in hand to their next class together. The day was about as perfect as could be, until they bumped into Morocco at lunch. He seemed upset.

"Hey, Whitfield, what's this I hear about your scanning tech being dangerous?"

"What? What are talking about?" Whitfield clearly hadn't seen Gen. Gibson's press conference.

"Yeah, dude. Gen. Gibson was just on the news saying that they are not going to use that scanning tech in meets because it may be dangerous."

Whitfield was totally confused. "That can't be right. There's no danger at all. It's completely safe."

Morocco shoved a finger in Whitfield's chest. "For your sake, I hope you're right. We all let you scan us during our last meet. I'm going to be mad if I find out it wasn't safe."

Ugu stepped in. "Morocco. It's completely safe. The engineering group has been working with that tech for years. Flaherty uses it all the time."

"Well, you better go talk to Gen. Gibson then. Something isn't right here."

Whitfield needed to get to the bottom of this. "Thanks. I gotta run. I'm gonna find out what's going on." Whitfield and Ugu rushed to the AMQE library to catch a replay of the press conference. Aspen had already returned to campus and caught up with Ugu and Whitfield at the library. Flaherty was on her way.

"Whitfield, did you hear about the ban?"

"Shh…we're watching the press conference now."

Ugu pulled Aspen aside, and quietly spoke. "Hey, how was your first day?"

"Great! Mission accomplished."

Whitfield overheard Aspen's enthusiastic reply and briefly peeled his attention away from the video screens. "Hey, that's great, bro. Any problems?"

"Nah. I was smooth."

Ugu hugged Aspen. "Nice job."

Flaherty finally arrived. "Hey, Aspen. How did it go?"

"Great! I got it. Thanks for your advice, Flaherty. I needed it."

Flaherty gave Aspen a congratulatory fist bump. "Oh good, I'm glad I could be helpful. Whitfield, what's going on?"

Whitfield was entirely focused on the video screens. Ugu stood next to Flaherty. "Did you see this?"

Flaherty watched for a few minutes. She was totally shocked. "That's simply not true. There is no danger at all. That's ridiculous."

Whitfield turned off the press conference and sat still for a moment, just thinking. Ugu eventually broke the silence. "Whitfield, what is it?"

Whitfield was still wrapping his head around this unexpected turn of events. "It's Dr. Hewitt. He did this."

Ugu wasn't following. "What do you mean?"

"This weekend, at the flower gardens, I was cleaning up with Dr. Hewitt and he asked about our scanning tech. I was telling him about some of the applications and I let slip that it could be used to analyze gymnasts' falls. He seemed to perk up at that very moment. I tried to backtrack, but he seemed fixated on that particular application."

Flaherty didn't yet see the connection. "Did he say anything else?"

"No. He just took off in a hurry. My guess is that he realized that we could use this tech to identify which gymnasts took intentional falls. If he's involved in all this, he wouldn't want that evidence to get into the wrong hands. That's why he had Gen. Gibson shut it down."

Flaherty was beginning to connect the dots. "So, you think Dr. Hewitt and Gen. Gibson are both involved. You think they're bribing gymnasts to take falls against Seven Bridges? But, why? I mean, Dr. Hewitt works here, but Gen. Gibson isn't directly affiliated with SBA."

Ugu was one step ahead. "I think Aspen may have the answer."

Aspen looked surprised. "Me? What answer?"

"Gen. Gibson's account. You need to go through it and tell us what's in there."

Whitfield was growing more confident in his suspicions, and was already devising a plan to gather all the evidence they needed to stop Dr. Hewitt and Gen. Gibson. "Flaherty. We need you to go to the Uniform Galleria and pick out something really nice. After practice, you're having dinner with Spencer."

Now Flaherty was surprised. "Spencer? Why?"

"We need those bank records."

"I already told you; he doesn't have access anymore. His internship ended over a week ago."

"I know. We don't need his access codes. We need you to find out everything you can about the bank. Where they keep their servers. When they receive deposits. How much cash they keep on hand for everyday withdrawals and where they keep reserve bills for larger withdrawals. Where the vault is located. We need to know it all."

"Why? Are you planning on breaking into the bank?" Flaherty was being sarcastic.

"No. You're going to."

****

"Whitfield, that's crazy! I am not robbing a bank."

"Who said anything about robbing a bank?"

"Uhh…you just did."

"No, I said you were going to break into the bank. You're not going to rob it. In fact, you're going to be leaving money there."

Ugu wasn't used to feeling left out, but at the moment, she was clueless as to Whitfield's plan. "Aspen, do you understand what's going on here?"

"No. But I know when Whitfield gets an idea, it's usually pretty good. We should just go with it."

"If you say so."

Whitfield continued, "Ugu, you still need to run that facial recognition program to see who was placing those bets in Hendricks' name, right?"

"Right."

"Aspen, you can start going through those messages. We'll meet you at practice in about an hour."

"Where are you going?"

"Flaherty and I have to go talk to Dr. Randle, over in engineering."

"We do?"

"Yes, I'll explain on the way." Whitfield stood up and headed for the door with Flaherty. As he was walking away, he turned his head back. "Aspen, don't be late for practice. Ugu, I love you."

Ugu just smiled. "I know you do."

****

Whitfield and Flaherty found Dr. Randle working in one of the engineering labs. "Ahh, Flaherty, my favorite student. And Whitfield, congratulations on your Curriculum Design Challenge winning submission. We were all quite impressed with your application of our scanning technology."

Whitfield still wasn't used to hearing all the praise for his work, and now that Gen. Gibson banned it from meets, he wasn't sure he deserved any praise, but remained gracious anyway. "Thank you, sir."

"What brings you both here at this time? Don't you have practice soon?" Like most faculty members, Dr. Randle was an avid fan.

"Yes, we do have practice soon, but we were wondering if you could help us with something first."

"Sure, anything for you, Flaherty. You know that."

Whitfield hoped Dr. Randle's willingness to help Flaherty would extend to himself as well. "Sir, at the start of the school year, you showed us those paper airplanes."

"Ahh, yes, just a little magic trick to get you excited about engineering classes. So, you finally came to ask how I did it?"

"No, sir, Flaherty already told me."

"She is a clever one, is she not?"

"Yes, sir, she is. But what we were wondering is whether that technology, the coating you placed on the paper airplanes to track their precise location and identify who held the plane with embedded fingerprint scanning, could that be affixed to any sheet of paper?"

"I should think so. Completely undetectable too. I've applied it to letters in the mail, envelopes, greeting cards…I even once forgot that I had ripped out a page from my notebook and stuffed it in my pocket and dropped my trousers off at the laundry. When I returned to pick them up, the man behind the counter said the paper went through the laundry but fell out when they were folding. I checked, and the darn tracker still worked."

Whitfield nodded. "Impressive."

"Do you think it would work with…money? Could bills be coated so they could be tracked?"

"Ahh, you're trying to track a bill to see all the places it travels throughout the world. Very interesting. Yes, I think it should work just fine on a bill."

Whitfield and Flaherty exchanged glances, knowing that they had an entirely different application of this technology in mind. "Great. About how long does the coating process take?"

"Not long. We have lab equipment here that takes care of all of it. Just feed the sheet of paper, or bill, into the machine and a few seconds later, the process is complete and the coated paper comes out the other end."

Whitfield did some quick math in his head. A few seconds per bill was not fast enough for what he had in mind. "If you don't mind me asking, sir, how did you get your entire notebook coated, if the sheets have to be fed into the machine one at a time?"

Dr. Randle flashed a dubious smile. "You don't expect me to give away all my secrets, do you?"

Flaherty had trained for this exact moment. She knew what she had to do. Flaherty gently touched Dr. Randle on his forearm, and while playfully batting her eyes, tugged Dr. Randle ever so closer. "Please, sir. We won't tell anyone."

Flaherty's mild seduction worked. Dr. Randle reluctantly shared his secret. "Oh, OK. The high-capacity machine in the basement laboratory handles entire stacks of paper. The user can feed up to 500 sheets at a time, then the machine will coat every sheet, or every third sheet, or whatever frequency the user sets. Of course, coating all 500 sheets would take a little longer, maybe 15 minutes, but at least you do not have to stand there the whole time, feeding the machine one at a time. Here, if you want, I can show you how it works."

"Thank you, sir. Maybe we'll come back another time. We do have to get to practice."

"OK, just let me know when you want to see the machine. I'll have to buzz you into the lab. Access is quite restricted."

"My pass should work, right? I mean, I have class in the lab right next door."

"Hmm. Perhaps. I'm really not sure what level clearance is needed to access the basement lab."

"We'll figure it out. Thank you so much sir. You really are my favorite teacher." Flaherty flashed Dr. Randle a smile and ran out of the office with Whitfield, hoping to still make it to practice on time. They spoke on the way.

"So, Whitfield, you think we can 'borrow' enough bills from the bank, coat them with Dr. Randle's tracking tech, and replace them in the exact spot needed to catch whoever is bribing gymnasts?"

"Exactly. I don't think those kids from Isadora's Gang are going into the bank and withdrawing the money themselves. Someone is making large withdrawals and distributing the money into different envelopes for the kids to pass out."

"And you think it might be Dr. Hewitt?"

"I do. But I do not think he is working alone. He is receiving phony scoresheets with embedded bank account numbers from Gen. Gibson."

"Hold on. We don't know for a fact yet if they are bank account numbers. And even if they are, we don't know if Gen. Gibson created the sheets, or if they were passed along to him by someone else."

"You're right. Aspen is going to find all that out from Gen. Gibson's messages."

"Well, everything except the bank account information."

"That's why you need to find out where those servers are located. We probably can't access those records remotely, but if we know where they are located, that gives us a fighting chance."

Flaherty had a dreadful thought. "You know if we get caught, they'll expel us, right?"

"Don't worry. We won't get caught. And if we do, we'll blame Jonathan."

Flaherty chuckled. "Yeah, not sure how that would work."

"No. Just kidding. I'll take full responsibility if anything goes sideways. I'm not going to have you, Ugu, or Aspen go down for this."

"Hey, we're all in this together."

"Thanks…sis."

Chapter 29
Ugu's Birthday

Amidst classes, practice, and the covert investigation surrounding gymnasts' bribes, Whitfield had completely forgotten about Ugu's upcoming birthday. He only had two days left, and didn't have a clue what to get the first girl he ever truly loved.

"Flaherty, you have to help me. Please."

"Whitfield, I can't tell you what to get her. It has to come from you."

"I know. But I've never had a girlfriend before. I don't even know where to start."

Seeing that Whitfield was desperate and hopeless to come up with an idea on his own, Flaherty decided to help. "OK. Let's think about this. What do you two enjoy doing together?"

"Everything."

"Oh boy, you're not helping. Do you still go running every night?"

"Yes. We didn't during PAW because of everything else going on, but we've been running together every night this week. What, you think I should I get her running shoes?"

"No, you dunderhead, she can get those herself from the Uniform Galleria."

"Then what?"

"I don't know yet. Still thinking. You two enjoy having class together?"

"Yeah, it's great. I mean, we've only had class together on Monday and Wednesday this week, but yeah, it's been great. Hey, maybe I should get her a pen? She said she forgot hers the other day, so I let her borrow mine."

Flaherty rolled her eyes. "Oh boy. Wow, you really are not good at this. Let me guess, she looked flustered that she forgot her pen, and then wrapped her fingers around your arm and with pouty lips asked if she could borrow yours and then acted excited when you gave her your pen and then kissed you on the cheek. Does that sound about right?"

"Yeah. Exactly. How did you…wait, did she pick that up from your class with her?"

"Oh please. That was a technique from way back in first year."

"I really need to sit in on those classes. She is just toying with me."

"Oh, stop it. We all do it. We need to practice. She just feels comfortable around you, so she knows she can get away with it."

"So, she doesn't try that with anyone else?"

"She used to all the time. But not since you two got together. It's been over a month now since I've seen her really act that way with anyone else."

Whitfield looked pensive. "Hmm…when was Keegan's birthday."

"Oh, I don't know. Maybe a month or two ago."

"That's it! I know what I'm going to get Ugu for her birthday."

"What?"

"Nothing."

"What?"

Whitfield smiled, like he was proud of himself for coming up with this idea. "We're going to break up."

"WHAT!"

"No. Not exactly break up. No, we're still together. Just, I can't explain it right now. I'll tell you later. I have to run. Thank you so much. You're the best."

Flaherty was confused, but smiled anyway. She was happy to help a friend. It didn't bother her at all that her own birthday was just two months away, and as far as she could tell, Whitfield didn't even know when it was.

****

Whitfield called an emergency staff meeting at his house on Thursday before practice to run through his idea for Ugu's birthday. Normally, students wouldn't get that excited about putting in extra work for some random student's birthday, but Ugu was different. Everyone loved Ugu and they were all happy to participate.

"Look, I am going to need every one of you to contribute to this. We only have one more day until her birthday. Do you all know what to do?" The 41 staff members all responded affirmatively. Whitfield's plan was put into motion.

After practice, Whitfield and Aspen decided to head over to Flaherty's house to discuss their progress with the investigation. Ugu was already there when the three gymnasts arrived.

"Hey guys, I picked up burgers and shakes on the way over. Dig in!"

"Ugu, you are the best. I'm starving."

Aspen already started shoving fries in his mouth. "Me too. Thank you, Ugu."

Whitfield kissed Ugu on the cheek. "What would we do without you?"

"Probably starve."

"Good point. Thank you, Ugu." The four friends ate and laughed. When the meal was about over, they started to focus on work.

Flaherty decided to kick things off. "So, Aspen, have you found anything yet?"

"Yes! Loads of stuff. I'm still not through everything yet, but here's what I know so far. After every school meet around the country, Gen. Gibson sends out official scoresheets to every school."

Flaherty wanted to make sure she heard correctly. "Every school? That's a lot of messages."

Whitfield agreed, "yeah, like 800 schools, right? Are you sure he sends messages to every school?"

"Yes. 800 schools exactly. Gen. Gibson sends each one an official scoresheet, every Tuesday, but here's the really cool thing." Aspen was obviously excited by what he uncovered. "Remember that message I found that Dr. Hewitt said was a glitch?"

Ugu had a feeling Aspen had uncovered something big. "Yeah?"

"Well, I was right. It's not a glitch. After every meet, Gen. Gibson sends out a wrong scoresheet to Dr. Hewitt and then a corrected one five minutes later."

Whitfield wanted to confirm. "After every meet?"

"Yes, I went back three years so far, and it's always a fake one followed up five minutes later with the real one."

Ugu felt more confident in her intuition. "That's incredible. Do all the fake sheets have bank account information?"

"I haven't checked all of them yet, but I think so. I mean, many of the gymnasts' names are the same year after year, but even the ones that change, still fit the code. But wait, there's more."

"More? What else did you find?"

"Dr. Hewitt isn't the only one. I mean Seven Bridges, they're not alone. Gen. Gibson sends out fake scoresheets to 19 other schools as well. He sends the fake ones first, and then 5 minutes later sends the correct scoresheets."

They were all astounded. Flaherty spoke for the group. "Get out! Really? Do they all fit the bank account number of digits code too?"

"I think so. I just tested a few, and they don't all use the same crypto algorithm, but yeah, I was able to convert the gymnasts' names to 23-digit codes exactly."

"Wow!"

"I know. And I looked at the 'correct' sheets that were sent to the other schools. I didn't see anyone's name misspelled. Only the names on the fake scoresheets are sometimes misspelled, which means whoever is doing this is intentionally trying to get to an exact account number. This is really going on."

Ugu looked at the others in shock. "This is unbelievable. Twenty schools. Fake scoresheets. Bank account numbers. What is going on here?"

Whitfield didn't have an answer, but knew they needed to keep going. "I think we may have just stumbled onto something big. Aspen, what other schools are receiving fake scoresheets?"

"None that we've seen in any of our meets, but they are all really good teams. I don't think any of them have lost a meet so far."

Flaherty had a grim thought. "Do you think these bribes might be happening at other meets too?"

Whitfield said what was on his mind. "I don't see why not. I mean, why should we be the exception?"

"I think there is something else you guys should see."

"What is it, Aspen?" Ugu stepped beside Aspen to look at his primary monitor, rather than the large holographic projection hovering over the table.

"Well, I wasn't really sure what to make if this, but I thought Ugu might know. I found some messages where Gen. Gibson was getting yelled at by some schools for not letting them into particular meets."

Whitfield wasn't sure what Aspen meant. "What do mean he was getting yelled at?"

"He's received a lot of angry messages about scheduling and bids not being accepted. I thought since Ugu worked there last year and handled bids that she might be able to make sense of this."

"I can try. Let me see." Aspen showed her the messages. "Wait. This isn't right. Look right here. This school claims it put up a bid twice as large as another school and got rejected. That isn't supposed to happen. Again, it happened here…and here. Look, this school posted a bid almost three times as high, and said they could go even higher."

Whitfield peeked over Ugu's shoulder at Aspen's monitor, but couldn't get a good look at the message contents. "And Gen. Gibson rejected them. Why?"

"It doesn't make sense. The WGF makes it clear that the bidding process is supposed to be unbiased and fair. The RFB (Request for Bids) is sent out to all schools, and those responding with the highest bids by the deadline are accepted.

There are some minor exceptions, but nothing that would cause all these schools to be rejected. This shouldn't be happening, unless…"

"Unless what?" Whitfield showed some concern.

"Unless Gen. Gibson is rigging meets so that only a few select teams win."

Flaherty immediately caught on to Ugu's train of thought. "By eliminating any potential threats from ever showing up on meet day."

Aspen followed along as well. "And bribing anyone who does show up that might still be a threat."

"So, then all of our wins were…what…rigged?" Whitfield's shoulders slumped and his chest hurt.

Flaherty didn't want to concede. "No, we still won. It just wasn't fair."

Aspen grew upset. "That's not right."

Whitfield agreed, "no, it isn't right. We have to tell someone."

Ugu knew Whitfield was right, but wanted to keep digging further. "Who are we going to tell? We still need to find out more information."

"Ugu. I don't want to compete in an unfair meet. I want to win because we deserve to win. Not because someone pulled some strings to make it easier for us."

"I agree with Whitfield. But we probably should still wait to see what else we can find out." Flaherty placed her hand on Whitfield's shoulder.

Whitfield hesitated. "I guess so. Well, speaking of more information, Flaherty, did you talk with Spencer yet?"

"No. We haven't connected yet, but we are going to dinner next week. I'll find out what he knows about the bank. Don't worry."

"I'm sure you will. How about the other thing? Did you and Ugu run facial recognition on the sportsbook to see who placed those bets in Hendricks' name?"

Flaherty and Ugu looked at each other. Ugu relayed what they found. "Uhh…yes, we did. The good news is that Hendricks did not place those bets himself. An alum named Bibb Tossino, who graduated around 25 years ago, placed the bets. He entered an account number that was traced back to your parents, with Hendricks' name listed on it as trade executor."

A wave of relief flooded Whitfield. "Great! Now we know Hendricks is clean and this Bibb guy is dirty. We should tell Sir Arlington. He can bring in this Bibb character and question him."

Flaherty put up her hand. "We may not want to do that just yet."

"Why? He's bad." To Aspen, the path was simple.

Flaherty looked at her best friend. "Ugu?"

"We tracked Bibb to see what he was up to or who he might be talking to on campus."

Whitfield appreciated the extra effort. "Great! And?"

"Whitfield, we saw Hendricks. He was on campus this weekend."

Whitfield felt betrayed. Flaherty continued with another blow. "And he was talking with Bibb. It was out in the rain forest, so we couldn't make out what they were saying, but Bibb went out there first, and Hendricks followed."

Aspen didn't understand. "What? How?"

Ugu felt terrible. "Whitfield. I'm so sorry."

Whitfield wouldn't let himself believe that Hendricks had lied to him. "No, something isn't right here. Hendricks wouldn't be here without telling us. Why would he be talking with Bibb? I…I…" Aspen started to cry and ran outside. Whitfield called out to his brother. "Aspen."

"No. Let me." Whitfield stayed and let Ugu follow Aspen.

"Hey, Aspen. It's OK." Ugu put her arm around Aspen, who was crying.

"No, it's not. Hendricks lied to us. He said he was leaving. But, he's here. He doesn't even want to see us."

"Aspen, that's not true. I happen to know Hendricks loves you very much. He is kind and sweet. Just like you. I know it must have been tough on all of you when your parents died. Especially tough on Hendricks, because he not only lost his best friends, but he had to watch over the two of you knowing that you would never get to see how wonderful your parents were. Being a guardian is a tough job, and sometimes sacrifices have to be made. He swore to protect you and that's what I believe he is doing. He's probably just watching over you and Whitfield from a distance, not wanting to interfere, but always being there to make sure you are safe. Like your very own guardian angel."

Aspen used his sleeve to wipe away his tears. "You really think so?"

"I do. I know he would want to spend every minute with you, but he also wants you to grow up to be a strong, independent man."

Aspen let out a smile. "I am pretty strong."

"Oh, I know you are. The strongest. Just don't tell your brother, OK?"

Aspen was feeling a little better. "I won't. Thank you, Ugu."

Aspen hugged Ugu and went back inside. Whitfield, who had been watching their interaction from a distance, gave Aspen a soft punch in the arm as he walked back into the house. "That didn't even hurt. I'm strong." Aspen sat back down next to Flaherty. Whitfield walked over to Ugu.

"I heard what you said. Thank you."

"Oh, no problem. I meant it, you know. I think Hendricks is a good guy."

"I know. He is. We'll make sense out of all this." Whitfield just stared at Ugu.

Ugu was starting to feel a little self-conscious. "What?"

"You really are something special."

"Oh, stop it. You just want another kiss, don't you?"

"No, it has nothing to do with that. You really just have a way of making everyone around you feel better about themselves."

"I don't know. I just like to help people, I guess."

"Well, you are very good at it."

Ugu leaned in a little closer to Whitfield. "Really?"

"Yes."

Ugu leaned in even closer. "Do I make you feel better about yourself?"

"Yes."

Ugu was now pressing her body up against Whitfield. "So, is there anything you want to ask me?"

"Yes. About that kiss…"

Ugu pressed her body tight against Whitfield's, positioning her lips close to his. "Nope. You said you didn't want another kiss. Bye." Ugu slinked away and went back inside Flaherty's house. Whitfield stayed outside for a minute. As Ugu went back inside, she casually flipped the switch inside the side door, turning on the outdoor sprinklers.

Whitfield screamed, "AAAHHH."

Aspen thought it was hysterical. He laughed so hard he fell out of his chair.

****

Ugu woke up on her birthday to the smell of fresh flowers adorning her entire bedroom suite. Lilacs, roses, peonies, lilies, gardenias, freesias, lavender, hyacinth, tuberose, and jasmine filled every open area from Ugu's bedroom all the way down to the kitchen and out the front door. Her entire front yard was covered in cherry blossoms and rhododendrons. Ugu eagerly checked every attached card and smiled as she read the names of one classmate after another, but strangely, not a single card from Whitfield. Other than a morning message wishing her a happy birthday, Whitfield was conspicuously absent from Ugu's birthday morning.

Ugu had all of her favorite foods awaiting her at the breakfast bar in her kitchen. Most of the staff in Aspen's house were eager to wish Ugu a happy birthday and each one gave her a birthday hug. As the morning progressed, students from across campus came to see Ugu and drop off gifts of all varieties and made sure to pass along their birthday wishes. When Flaherty showed up for their annual birthday run, Ugu's face was a little sore from all the constant smiling. She was truly happy that everyone remembered her on her birthday and showed how much they cared for her. Well, everyone except for Whitfield, who was still nowhere to be found.

Flaherty and Ugu ran all around campus and everywhere they went, students stopped Ugu to share some short story with her about how she had positively impacted them during their time at Seven Bridges. These stories and anecdotes meant the world to Ugu. She really did love helping people. But the surprises and good vibes did not stop there.

Plank 'N Steins shut down their regular service for the afternoon to host a huge birthday party bash for Ugu. Students decorated the entire restaurant with pictures of Ugu, holograms, videos, and hand-made artifacts all depicting Ugu's unrivaled warmth and generosity.

Members of the WGF, where Ugu had interned last year, showed up to the party to offer their own birthday wishes. Aspen even made an appearance as the WGF mascot to take pictures with Ugu and dance with her. Of course, no one other than Ugu and Flaherty knew it was Aspen in the chicken suit, but that didn't stop anyone from having fun. Whitfield was still nowhere to be seen.

As the sun was about to set, the party made its way out toward the waterfront, where a special surprise awaited. Out on the water, in a customized boat, the entire Crocodiles professional gymnastics team rode up to the shore, led by Gabe, who came ashore and gave Ugu a big hug.

"You know I couldn't miss your birthday."

"Gabe! Thank you for coming. This…this is incredible."

Every Crocodile team member approached Ugu and told her a different anecdote about how she had positively impacted Gabe's, and by extension, their own lives. Ugu was touched. She held dear all the times Gabe had helped her grow and mature at Seven Bridges, but had never appreciated the positive impact she had on him. Ugu stood there, listening to story after story, tears running down her cheeks. She had no idea how much she impacted the world around her. As the final Crocodile approached, Ugu looked past her to see if Whitfield was waiting for some grand appearance. But, alas, no one was there.

With everyone gathered on the beach, a set of drones converged out over the water to display a giant video board. Aspen's face appeared huge on the screen and everyone's focus turned toward the video recording.

"Thank you all for coming here to celebrate our favorite Seven Bridges' student. Happy birthday, Ugu! We hope you enjoy this presentation."

What followed was 25 minutes of video footage taken from around campus yesterday. Whitfield's and Aspen's staffs had interviewed students, faculty, and staff from around campus; everyone from personal tailors and laundry staff at the Uniform Galleria to International Affairs faculty and lab assistants; from second-year business students to young alums visiting campus for the day. Everyone shared a story about Ugu. Flaherty was the last to appear on the video. She spoke eloquently, and even shed a tear.

"My Ugu. We have been through so much together. You are my best friend. My sister. My other half. I'm sure you've heard from so many today about how you have impacted them during your time here and I wanted to share one of my favorite memories. Relax, I'm not going to tell everyone about the time in Dr. Richards' class when you laughed so hard milk squirted out of your nose or that time when Antawn announced to the entire school that you had a crush on Gabe, which was never true by the way, so I just want to put an end to that rumor. No, I'm not going to mention any of those embarrassing moments. So many moments. Like that time…no, I'm just kidding.

"I do want to share a memory that even you do not know about. It was our first year at Seven Bridges. Our first gymnastics meet at home, in front of 150,000 fans. That's enough to make anyone nervous. Now, I know what you're thinking. I was so nervous that I was shaking and you gave me a smile from the crowd and told me a funny joke that calmed me down and allowed me to perform at my best. I still remember that joke too, but, no, it was actually something else you did that day.

"There was a girl, Rachel, competing that day from Ken Chi Academy. She was a sixth-year, one of the best in the country. She was having a rough meet, and had just fallen on Parallel Planks. After her routine, her teammates and coaches wouldn't talk with her, and she just sat down on the side of the bench, crying. You must have seen that and you sneaked down from your seat and somehow got past security to talk with her. You asked her for her autograph and told her you liked her hair. You may remember that you two even bonded over a mutual love of squirrels, even though I know for a fact that you do not like those furry little creatures."

Ugu stood on the beach with tears streaming down her face, watching Flaherty's video tribute, with her arm around her best friend. "I never told you about that conversation. How did you know?"

The video tribute continued, "now, you are probably wondering how I know what you two spoke about. You never told me any of this. You didn't have to. She did. Actually, her teammates did. What you had no way of knowing that day, was that Rachel was going through an extremely difficult time, both in her personal life and in gymnastics. The pressure was getting to be too much for her. She had even contemplated taking her own life. She had brought some poison pills to do it right there in our gym. Perhaps right after that fall. Both Rachel, and her teammates, credit that conversation with an 11-year-old girl from another school, our school, for saving her life. And if you don't believe me, here, I have a special message for you."

Rachel appeared in a recorded message on the giant video screen.

"Hello Ugu. Happy birthday! I'm Rachel. You probably do not remember me, but we share a very deep bond. You saved my life that day when we competed at Seven Bridges. I was in a dark place and didn't think anyone cared about me. You showed me that I was wrong. You never once asked about my gymnastics or mentioned anything about my falls that day.

"You were interested in who I was as a person, and that may have been the first time in my life anyone showed that they cared about me, or didn't laugh at me when I said I like squirrels. I have a present for you. I'm going to hand it to the guy holding the camera. He says he knows you. I hope you have a wonderful birthday. And thank you again. You truly are an angel."

Flaherty's face reappeared on the screen. "Ugu, from the bottom of my heart, and from all of our hearts, happy birthday!"

At the conclusion of the video, fireworks went off high above the water, lighting up the night sky. Everyone on the beach, except for Ugu, who didn't know about this part of the plan, started to hum in sync with Ugu's favorite song. She recognized the tune almost immediately and locked eyes with Flaherty. They hugged and started to sing together. Several others chimed in, but before long, two voices could be heard over the speakers, louder than the voices on the beach.

Two figures appeared, each holding a microphone, walking up together from the water. Dona Palermo, lead singer of Chalk Bucket, Ugu's favorite band of all time, was singing Ugu's favorite song. Accompanying Dona to her right, was Whitfield, singing, as best as he could, directly to Ugu. The glow from the fireworks framed Whitfield's face brilliantly, and he never took his eyes off Ugu.

Ugu wanted to run into his arms right then and there, but Flaherty held her back. "Just wait one more minute."

With the music still playing, Dona Palermo and Whitfield each stopped singing, and Whitfield spoke directly to Ugu, in front of everyone. "Ugu. I've spent the whole week thinking about what to get you for your birthday. But no matter what I thought of, it just could never match the way I feel about you. Fireworks. Video messages. Dona Palermo. Parties with a thousand friends. None of it could ever match how I feel about you, so that's what I decided to get you. Nothing. Because nothing can top my love for you. Nothing can pull me away from you. Nothing is more beautiful than your smile. Nothing is faster than your two-mile? OK…so, I'm not a songwriter. That's why she's here. Hey, Dona…help me out."

Dona Palermo started to sing 'Rip in My Heart' and everyone got up to dance and sing along.

Ugu rushed into Whitfield's arms and wanted to kiss him, but Whitfield pulled back. "Sorry I'm late. It's been a long day. Here, Rachel wanted you to have this."

Whitfield handed Ugu a birthday present. Ugu opened it and inside was a stuffed animal squirrel and a framed picture of Ugu talking with Rachel at the gymnastics meet from two years ago. After hearing Rachel's story, Whitfield had combed through the video footage from the meet and found a distant shot of the two chatting, and through some video editing, brought the picture in closer and more in focus. Inside the box, was a note from Rachel: 'To my guardian angel. Forever bonded in life.'

"How did you…"

"It was Flaherty. After that meet a couple years ago, Rachel transferred from Ken Chi to Muppet Grove for her seventh-year. Rachel's teammates flagged Flaherty down at our first meet and told her the story. She was waiting for a special occasion."

"And, all this…this whole day. Did you…"

"It was group effort."

"Whitfield. I have no words." Ugu started to cry.

"Shh…you don't have to say anything. But I do. Look, Ugu, I love you, but so does everyone else here. I love that you're my girlfriend and we spend so much time together now, but you need to get back to what you do best."

"I'm confused."

"Look, I was a jerk for how I acted at Keegan's on his birthday. I guess I was jealous, and was hoping that you wouldn't kiss anyone else."

"Keegan's birthday? That was so long ago. Whitfield, you're not making any sense. Are you saying you want me to kiss other people?"

"No. That's not it."

"Good. Because I only want to kiss you."

"I'm good with that. Better than good actually. I'm thrilled about that, but I also want you to be comfortable talking with others. You've made such a positive impact at this school, and I don't want to take that away from them…or from you. You light up whenever you're around others. You love making people happy and solving problems and getting people to feel better about themselves. I can't live knowing that I'm taking that gift away from everyone else."

Ugu looked worried. "So, what are saying?"

Whitfield noticed the look in Ugu's eyes. "Whoa, no, we are not breaking up. No. No. No. I'm just saying that I don't want you to feel that you have to only talk with me, Flaherty, and Aspen. Go, have fun. Be yourself. You can talk with others in class or go do something with others in between classes. I mean, I'll go with you if you want me to. I love to help people too. I guess what I'm saying is I just don't want you to hold yourself back because of me. I love you too much for that."

Ugu smiled. "Are you done?"

"Yeah, I think so. You're not mad, are you?"

"How could I be mad at the perfect guy?"

"Exactly. You are talking about me, right?"

"Yes, you goober. Look, I know you've never had a girlfriend before, but I haven't ever had a boyfriend either. I guess I might have been holding on a bit too much because I was afraid of losing you. But I see what you're saying. I do enjoy meeting and talking with other students, and I guess I really haven't done that since we started to really like each other."

"I don't know about that. I mean you started to like me all the way back from the time we first met on the ferry." Whitfield flashed a sly smile.

Ugu took a step back. "Are you kidding me? I was just being nice. You're the one who fell in love with me before I even sat down. I know you were checking me out."

"Oh, come on, you were so checking me out before you even came over."

"Well, I needed to know if you were worth my time. You know, I'm a very busy girl."

Whitfield pulled Ugu close to him. "Ugu."

Ugu just melted in Whitfield's arms. "Yes."

"Shut up and kiss me."

Ugu didn't say another word.

Chapter 30
Bank 'Heist'

Flaherty's dinner with Spencer turned into a late-night workout session. After enjoying some shrimp, scallops, and tuna at Nolan's Surf Bar & Bucket, Flaherty and Spencer went out on the water for some kayaking, then hit the trampolines for a while before catching up with Whitfield and Ugu on the Outer Loop during their nightly run. All throughout the evening, Spencer shared his knowledge of the inner-workings of the bank, right down to where they kept every bill and coin, and even when bills were transferred, brought in from Rutherford Mint, and sent out for bank-to-bank transfers. Flaherty got away with telling Spencer very little about her ultimate plan as she was able to persuade and coerce Spencer into sharing more details than he ever thought he would. Spencer was a lot more willing to share information with Flaherty this time around, and as far as Flaherty thought, she just attributed it to her irresistibly masterful seduction technique.

The next morning, on their way to N'pal Tech for the Electronics, Engineering, and Technology meet, Whitfield, Aspen, and Flaherty brainstormed how they would be able to be able to pull off the biggest bank heist in modern history.

"First of all, it's not a bank heist. Stop calling it that."

"I know, Flaherty. But it sounds cooler than borrowing money to put a special tracking coat on the bills, and then putting all the bills back."

"Aspen does have a point."

"Maybe so. But, it's still not a heist."

Whitfield responded sarcastically. "OK, boss."

"Don't make me kick your butt…again."

Whitfield straightened up. "You're right, we're getting off track."

"Haha…she kicked your butt." Aspen loved teasing his brother about that.

"It was kind of funny, Aspen. You should have seen the way he just crumbled to the ground."

"Can we get back to this please?"

"Watch out, Whitfield. She might hit you again." Aspen and Flaherty both enjoyed a laugh at Whitfield's expense, before Flaherty got back down to business.

"No. No. Whitfield is right. So, if what Spencer said is correct, I should be able to enter through the side doors at night, and follow the route he laid out to get to the holding area just outside the vault. They keep about half a million dollars there, and only remove bills when moderately large withdrawal requests come in.

"Whenever that happens, the bank manager will bring the bills out to the front and handle the transaction personally, then immediately head to the vault, take out the exact amount needed to make the holding area complete again, and place the vault bills neatly at the bottom, or rear, of the pile, so that bills circulate through the system and do not get stagnant at the bottom of the holding area."

Whitfield followed along perfectly. "So, you just need to get in, 'borrow' half a million dollars, bring them back to the lab, hope your tracker unlocks the lab doors, coat the bills, and then break back into the bank and return the bills. Does that sound just a bit crazy to anyone else?"

"Well, when you put it that way, yes, it does. Oh, by the way, my tracker does work. I tried it earlier this week, so that's one less thing to worry about."

Aspen was still contemplating the plan. "Why are you going in through the side door? Couldn't you just enter through the basement? They probably have fewer surveillance cameras there."

"No, Spencer said the basement is split. The bank only controls half of it. They keep all their security monitoring devices and servers down there. He said it's nearly impossible to get into the basement through the bank's side."

"What's in the other half of the basement?"

"Something we hope we never have to see. It's the detention cell for students after their third arrest. Spencer said it's only been used twice before and said it's horrible in there."

"What's so bad about it?"

"He said it's dark and dingy. Pretty small. Students can still take classes remotely while they are in there, but all electronics are disconnected shortly after classes are over. Even your tracker gets turns off, so while students tend to do a lot of push-ups, dips, and V-ups while in there to keep their bodies in shape, none of it counts toward the House Point Challenge."

Whitfield didn't like anything he heard about the detention cell. "Sounds awful. How do students get their work done for class if electronics are turned off?"

"Old fashioned pen and paper. Students have about ten minutes after class ends to print out their assignments and anything else they need, but that's it. The rest of the work is all hand-written. The arrest sentence is for an entire term. 'Seven weeks in the Pit' is how Spencer refers to it."

Aspen shivered. "OK, so let's stay away from that place."

Whitfield agreed, "right. No basement approach."

Aspen continued mulling over the plan. "Well, rather than breaking into the bank twice, would it be possible to only break in once?"

"Bro, Flaherty's not just going to steal the money."

"No, I think he's asking whether we can bring the coating machine into the bank and treat the bills inside the holding area and then leave. This way, we wouldn't ever have to leave the bank with the bills."

"Right." Whitfield raised his eyebrows, thinking that that might work. "Well, what do you think?"

"Aspen, I think it could work. But I wouldn't be able to go in alone with the machine. I would have to have someone with me."

Aspen got excited. "Oooh…I'll go."

"No, I think it should be me. The machine is pretty heavy and it would be easier for Flaherty and I to maneuver with it."

"But, I'm strong." Aspen pleaded his case.

Flaherty knew how to deal with this. "Oh, no doubt. You are super strong. But, Whitfield's right. He's a little bigger and would probably be able to control the device better through some of the obstacles we're likely going to face."

Aspen knew Flaherty made a good point. "OK. I suppose you're right."

"Hey, we still need you for everything else with this plan." Flaherty put her arm around him.

Aspen smiled.

"OK, so Flaherty and I will get the coating machine from the lab. Wait, will any alarms go off when taking the machine out of the lab?"

"No, we're always moving equipment around for demonstrations and stuff, so we should be good there. But just to be on the safe side, I'll tell Ugu to disable the alarm system for a couple hours that night."

"OK, good. We'll take the machine with us to the bank, head down to the holding area, coat the bills right there on the premises, and then get out as quick as possible, all without being detected by surveillance or tripping any alarms."

Flaherty was beginning to feel better about this amended plan. "Piece of cake. This is going to work."

Whitfield was still unsure. "I wish I had your confidence."

"Trust me."

Whitfield, Aspen, and Flaherty sat through the rest of the trip to N'pal Tech in contemplative silence, each picturing in their heads how their upcoming mission was going to play out. It wasn't until they were about to land that their focus returned to gymnastics and all the pre-meet festivities awaiting them.

****

The fourth meet of the season saw another dominant performance by Seven Bridges Academy. Whitfield and Flaherty shared top honors, Aspen continued to dazzle on Pommel Clock, and the rest of their teammates all performed at or above season averages. Coach Brockport made some lineup changes for this meet, rewarding athletes who practice hard with more duel action. In the end, Seven Bridges Academy won by a large margin, reaping the benefits of a substantial allotment of new computers, crystal ball technology, electronic devices, software, and a host of other technological advances and patent rights.

The competition was noticeably weaker than Seven Bridges faced in prior meets, made even weaker by some last-minute defaults, where athletes pulled out of duel matchups just before facing Seven Bridges competitors.

As usual, the SBA gymnastics team returned home to a hero's welcome. Throngs of students came out to greet the successful athletes as they landed and proceeded toward the Inner Bowl. The celebration lasted into the late hours, making this the perfect time for Flaherty and Whitfield to sneak into the engineering lab, borrow the coating machine, and make their way into SBA Bank's holding area. Ugu had already completed her tasks; she disabled the engineering lab's alarm system and scrambled the bank's surveillance capabilities.

Even if someone was monitoring the bank's security feed, which was unlikely given the attention being paid to the team's return to campus, it would take a couple hours for the security team to unscramble the feed and disengage the dynamic loop footage Ugu installed. With these precautions in place, Whitfield and Flaherty still exercised extreme caution. They did not want to be seen entering or exiting the bank, and equally important, they did not want to be seen removing the coating machine from the engineering lab.

Even though Flaherty's credentials for the lab would have worked, Ugu disabled the locking mechanism, so Flaherty and Whitfield were easily able to access the lab and retrieve the coating machine. Exiting the building was another challenge entirely.

"Flaherty, there's too many people around. Someone is going to spot us."

"There's no one in the Inner Loop. They are all in the Inner Bowl or on the Outer Loop. We can just sneak through building to building with no one noticing."

"What about the connecting bridges? There's not much cover. If someone looks up, we're dead. And once we leave the Inner Loop, we still have to cross the entrance quad to get to the bank. We're definitely going to be seen."

"Any suggestions then?"

"Nothing comes to mind at the moment. Perhaps we can wait a few hours and wait until the crowd disperses. We'd have a better chance of not being seen."

"No good. Ugu only disabled the cameras for a couple hours. This is our only window."

Flaherty and Whitfield seemed to be out of options. Their plan had failed before it ever got started. "Wait. I have an idea. Stay here. I'll be right back."

Flaherty ran back downstairs. She was gone for only about three minutes, but that didn't stop Whitfield from building up a nervous sweat. "OK, I'm back. Here, wear this." Flaherty handed Whitfield a lab coat and goggles.

"Uhh, Flaherty, I thought the point was to get in and out without being seen. Everyone is going to recognize us in these."

"No, they won't recognize us, they'll notice two lab assistants moving equipment around. Happens all the time. They'll see two lab coats and think nothing of it. And if anyone does stop us along the way, we can just say that we're setting up for a demonstration at the bank tomorrow."

Whitfield was impressed with Flaherty's impromptu planning skills. "Hey, that's really good. Are you sure you're not the smartest student at Seven Bridges?"

"Hey, I heard that." Whitfield had forgotten that Ugu was tracking them and could communicate through their connected earpieces.

"Sorry, Ugu."

"I accept. You two look all clear. The Inner Loop looks empty and the bank is deserted." Whitfield and Flaherty quickly maneuvered their way around the Inner Loop, exited through the Administration Building, and scurried through the entrance quad to the bank. They reached the side door and it was locked.

"Ugu. It's locked."

"That's strange. It must be on a reset timer. No worries, just give me a moment. There. It should be good now. And be careful. I'm not able to track you inside the bank."

Whitfield heard the lock click open, and reached for the door. Only, the door opened just before he touched it. Someone was on the other side and had just caught Whitfield and Flaherty trying to break in.

****

Flaherty gasped when she saw who was standing on the other side of the door. "Spencer! What are you doing here?"

"I should be asking you both the same question. I figured you two were up to something with all those questions from the other night. I knew this would be when you would try to break in, what with everyone on campus distracted."

Whitfield recognized how bad this looked, and tried pleading his case. "Spencer, it's not what you think."

"I know what I think. You two are trying to rob the bank or steal bank account information. I'm here to tell you that it's a bad idea. Do not do this."

Flaherty stepped in front of Whitfield. "Spencer dear, we are not robbing the bank."

"I know. Because, I'm stopping you." Spencer tried sounding tough, but inside, he was incredibly nervous and desperately wished to avoid any physical confrontation.

"No, sweetie, you don't understand. We have no intention of robbing the bank. Can we come in?" Flaherty was aware that the longer they remained outside, the higher the likelihood of someone spotting them. "We're not robbing the bank, but we still do not want to get caught."

Spencer didn't want to get caught either. Even though he was trying to prevent a robbery, he had broken into the bank himself, and would still be in a lot of trouble if he got caught, even if his intentions were pure. "OK, but don't try anything." Spencer allowed Whitfield and Flaherty to enter the bank, but made sure they didn't step in too far.

"Look, Spencer, we are just trying to—"

Flaherty cut Whitfield off. "Let me. Spencer, do you know what this machine is?"

Spencer briefly inspected the machine Whitfield was holding. "No."

"It's a coating machine. You feed paper in, and it coats the paper with undetectable location tracking and fingerprint detection nanotechnology. We are going to run the bills kept in the holding area through this coating machine and place the bills back exactly as we found them."

Spencer didn't know where to begin. "OK. Lots of questions. I guess the first one is…why?"

Whitfield tried addressing Spencer's question. "We found some evidence that someone is bribing gymnasts to take falls at meets. Whoever is in charge is withdrawing money from this bank and distributing it to low-level goons to place in the hands of gymnasts."

"We want to continue to build evidence and this seems like a great way to do just that."

"We also need to find out who else is involved. We think it may involve some high-ranking people. Maybe even people here at Seven Bridges, which is why we have to do this ourselves." Whitfield stopped talking to allow Spencer time to process what he had just heard.

"So, you're not here to rob the bank?"

Flaherty put her hand on Spencer's arm. "Don't be silly, Spencer. We're not bank robbers."

Spencer let out a huge breath. "Phew. That's such a relief. I didn't want to have to, you know, hurt you or something."

Whitfield and Flaherty looked at each other and tried not to laugh. "Thank you for that, Spencer. But we are on a time crunch, so if you could lead us to the holding area…"

"Oh sure. It's this way." Spencer hurriedly led Whitfield and Flaherty to the holding area, where the two gymnasts fed bills into the coating machine, and replaced each stack exactly as it was. Having Spencer there was a huge help, as the entire process was expedited with having a third set of hands. On their way out, Whitfield noticed a document with bank account numbers on it resting on one of the desks. It was Seven Bridges Academy's year-to-date bank statement.

Whitfield thought it might contain some useful information, so at first pulled out his tracker to scan the document, but remembered Ugu's warning about using those devices inside the bank. Not wanting to be traced back to his current location, Whitfield instead made the quick decision to simply take the bank statement with him on the way out. He was taking a risk that this particular document hadn't been scanned and affixed with security monitoring techniques and that no one would miss the document when the bank reopened on Monday morning, thereby triggering an investigation.

The three operatives exited the bank. Spencer went home, but not before Flaherty gave him another kiss on the cheek. Flaherty and Whitfield returned the coating machine, lab coats, and goggles to the engineering lab, and walked together to the Outer Loop. "Well, I'm glad that's over. I thought we were cooked when Spencer opened the door."

"I know. Me too. Glad everything worked out though. I actually feel better that he knows the whole story now. I didn't feel great about using him before."

"Yeah, well, he still doesn't know the whole story."

"Right. Just about the bank stuff though."

"Right."

"Hey, Whitfield, what is it that you took from the desk in there?"

"Oh, it's Seven Bridges' bank statement. I saw some bank account numbers on it and thought I'd give it to Aspen to see if the numbers match up with any of the fake scoresheets from Gen. Gibson's messages."

"Good thinking. Do you want me to drop it off to Aspen in the morning?"

"Thanks, but I'm going to drop it off now. Besides, I really miss Ugu and this will give me a chance to surprise her."

"Uhh…I'm still here."

Flaherty chuckled. "That's the second time you forgot about your earpiece, you dunderhead."

"I know. Thank you, Flaherty. He is a dunderhead, isn't he?"

"Hey, I'm right here."

Ugu and Flaherty giggled together and at the same time, teased, "oh, right, we forgot."

"Fine, I guess I won't come over just to give you a hug."

"No, you do not have to come over. I'm already on my way up there. Hope you have your running shoes on."

"Seriously? Ugu, I just got back from a meet and then we had this mission…I'm a little tired."

"Yup. I know. But if you want that hug, you have to catch me first."

Whitfield sighed. "Flaherty. Good night. I'll see you tomorrow." Whitfield took off running at full speed to try to catch Ugu. It was a long weekend, and he really wanted a hug.

****

Sometimes gambles pay off. Aspen spent a good part of the next few days looking over the bank statement Whitfield had retrieved from SBA Bank, comparing it to the fake scoresheets Gen. Gibson had sent out to Dr. Hewitt. Satisfied that he had finally cracked the fake scoresheet code, Aspen asked Flaherty and Whitfield to meet him and Ugu at the Cherry Blossom gazebo in the flower gardens just beyond Aspen's property line.

"Hey, bro, this is some spot."

"Yeah, this is gorgeous. I don't think I've been here before."

"Yeah, I like to come here sometimes to work on stuff and to just think."

Ugu was sitting next to Aspen and briefly rested her head on his shoulder. "Well, Aspen, you picked an excellent spot. So, tell us, what have you found?"

"OK, so I think I've cracked the code. This bank statement shows all the transactions Seven Bridges made this year. It's a lot. They get huge deposits after every meet and then make a lot of payments for school stuff and other things. I don't really see who received the payments from Seven Bridges, just account numbers, but sometimes there are notes attached to the transaction. Anyway, I was able to match some of the account numbers from the bank statement to the fake scoresheets."

Flaherty nearly jumped with excitement, "so, they are bank account numbers?"

"Yes! But there is so much more. See the fake scoresheets actually match all the transaction details."

Ugu straightened up, "what do you mean?"

"OK, so, just like the real scoresheets, each fake scoresheet contains the following: meet information, like name of the meet and location; judges' signatures; gymnast names; All-Around rank; and eight event scores. We already know that each gymnasts' name converts to a 23-digit bank account number."

Whitfield was on board so far. "Right, we got that."

"The rest of the encryption works this way. The All-Around rank corresponds to which event score comes first when decrypting the remaining code. Going from left to right, the eight events are listed in order from Tri-Bars to Floor Exercise. For example, if the All-Around rank is 3, we start decrypting with the third event, Vault-Pegs. Each event score tells us information about the transaction."

Ugu was intrigued. "How?"

"Let me show you." Aspen laid out one line from the fake scoresheet from their first meet:

Gymnast	AA rank	TB	ET	VP	HO	PC	VH	PP	FE
Sydney Truxler	2	21.82	11.03	24.28	20.18	07.49	06.70	26.15	12.60

"The event scores all range from 00.00 to 30.00. They always have two digits to the left of the decimal point and two digits to the right. Let's start with the digits to the right of the decimal point. Since the fake scoresheet says Sydney finished second in the All-Around, the first decryption event corresponds to Escalating Tramps, or ET. The two digits to the right of the decimal point, 03, correspond to the month of the transaction. For the next event, the two digits to the right of the decimal point, 28, represent the day. So, we have a transaction date of 03/28. The two digits to the right of the decimal for the next five events correspond to the dollar amount of the transaction."

Whitfield was trying his best to follow along, but wasn't quite there yet. "Wait, I don't see it."

Aspen pointed to the appropriate numbers on the fake scoresheet and the bank statement. "Look here, the transaction on 03/28 was for $18,497,015.60. It matches exactly the amount listed on SBA's bank statement."

Flaherty was awestruck. "How did you spot that? I never would have come up with that."

"It wasn't easy. But, once I had the bank statement, it all started to make sense."

"Nice job, bro."

"Thanks, but we're not done yet. The two digits to the right on the final event correspond to the currency or resource code. I think these transactions don't involve just money switching hands. For example, at the Precious Gems meet, Seven Bridges received diamonds, which is code 82. Seven Bridges then shipped out over $18 million in diamonds to whichever bank account is encrypted with Sydney's name."

Ugu had lots of questions, but settled on two. "Do we know why? Or to whom they are shipping?"

"No, I told you we only have the bank account numbers. Without hacking into the bank's records, I can't identify account holders' information."

Flaherty wondered if there was more. "Aspen, do the digits to the left of the decimal point mean anything?"

"Yes. That took a little more digging into, but thanks to the book Sir Arlington gave me last term, I found out that all bank transfers go to specific branches. So, the numbers to the left of the decimal refer to a 2-digit country code; 4-digit bank code; 2-digit location code; 2-digit branch code; and a 6-digit passcode. All banks need these codes to process the transaction."

"This is really great work, Aspen."

"Thanks, Ugu."

"Why make it so complicated?"

Whitfield felt qualified to answer Flaherty's inquiry. "That comes straight from what Dr. Hewitt teaches us in class. He said the most common mistake in sending encrypted messages is following the same pattern. You know, like here, if he always put the transaction month under the same event, it would be easier to spot that something was wrong since all the scores on that event would end with numbers between 01 and 12. Someone might spot the anomaly and investigate further."

Ugu picked up on the irony. "Yeah, like we're doing now."

"Exactly. Also, notice how the amount is very specific. Dr. Hewitt warned us against using large round numbers. He says those are the easiest to detect when spotting nefarious transactions."

Flaherty continued peppering Aspen with questions. "So, were you able to identify specific transactions for every one of these fake scoresheets?"

"So far, yes, but I only looked at our four meets. None of the transaction dates for the fourth meet happened yet, so really, it's just the first three meets, and even on those, many of the dates haven't occurred yet. I'll likely be able to tell a lot more when looking at previous years' scoresheets. But, yes, every transaction whose date has already passed shows up on the bank statement, with the exact amount and date, and sent to the encrypted bank account number."

Whitfield started to realize the magnitude of what they had just uncovered. "And Gen. Gibson is sending out fake scoresheets to nineteen other schools as well?"

"Yup."

"Do any of the bank accounts line up across schools?"

"I haven't checked every one, but it would be odd if they do."

"So, about how many different account numbers are on each sheet?"

"Anywhere from 18-25."

Ugu saw that Whitfield was on to something. "What are you thinking, Whitfield?"

"I think Gen. Gibson is sending out instructions to these twenty schools to divert some of the winnings to specific accounts. I think he is stealing money and resources from these schools."

Flaherty was skeptical. "Really? Wouldn't the schools know about it?"

Ugu didn't think they would. "Not necessarily. I mean, Dr. Hewitt is Seven Bridges' treasurer. He handles all the financials and produces the reports. He could be hiding it from Sir Arlington, the School Board, everyone."

Whitfield agreed, "and as long as Seven Bridges keeps winning and getting fat on excess resources, who's going to miss a few million here and there."

Aspen needed to correct Whitfield. "Uhh…it's actually a lot more than that."

All heads turned toward Aspen. "What do you mean?"

"Well, if we add up all the money and resources from just the four meets so far, there was over $12.1 billion in transactions listed on the fake scoresheets."

Flaherty hesitated, but needed confirmation. "From across all schools?"

"No. That's just what was taken from Seven Bridges."

The four friends all looked at each other, stunned. Whitfield collected himself first. "Whoa. This just got real. Very fast. Gen. Gibson is stealing billions in resources and directing them toward specific accounts. If he's controlling all these resources, he could destroy SBA. Or worse. We have got to find out more about those accounts."

"Agreed. But how?" Flaherty was out of ideas.

"We have to break into the bank again. For real this time. We need to get into the servers."

"No, Aspen, we can't. We'd have to get into the basement and Spencer said it's impossible to access from the first floor."

Aspen kept thinking. "What about accessing it from the basement?"

Whitfield didn't see how this could be done. "Yeah? How?"

"The other half."

"Aspen, that's the third strike cell. You heard what Flaherty said. It's like a dungeon. They're not just going to give tours and let us hang out there while you steal sensitive bank records."

Ugu concurred, "that's right. You'd have to be in there for a while, slowly pecking away at the bank's security, and carefully pulling account information without anyone suspecting anything is amiss."

"Exactly. And even if…whoa, wait, that was pretty specific." Whitfield noticed Ugu slipped off into a state of deep thought. He knew she was hatching a plan of some sort. "Are you OK, Ugu?"

Ugu hesitated for about ten seconds before responding. "I am. I know what has to be done."

Flaherty did not like the look in Ugu's eyes. "Please tell me you're not thinking what I think you're thinking."

Ugu spoke softly and slowly. "Yup. I have to get arrested."

"Yes!"

Whitfield shot his brother a look. "Aspen! Why are you happy about that?"

"Because, it's perfect. Ugu gets arrested and they put her in the basement right next to the servers. She can pull all the info we need. It's perfect."

"No. It is not perfect. No. I won't let you do it. We'll find another way."

Ugu knew Whitfield was not going to like her plan. "Whitfield, this is the only way."

"No. And besides, you'd have to get arrested three times before they put you in there. You're going to get arrested three times?"

Ugu smiled. "Yes."

"Oooh…this is so cool." Aspen may have been the only one who felt that way.

Flaherty expressed concern. "Ugu, I don't know about this. You have a perfect record. Do you really want to jeopardize all of that? I just don't think it's worth all that risk, and even if you succeed in getting thrown in the Pit, there's no guarantee you'll be able to access the records."

"Look, thank you all for looking out for me, but I want to do this."

Whitfield was defiant. "No. I can't let you. I'll do it. This involves the gymnastics team and I want to be the one who does this."

"Whitfield, thank you, but it has to be me."

"Why?"

"You three are too important to the team. We need you."

"Oh please. That's a lousy excuse. I'm doing it."

"OK, I didn't want to have to say it, but I'm the only one here smart enough to do it. You and Flaherty don't have the skills to hack into the bank undetected and they won't throw a first-year into the Pit. He'd be expelled instead."

Flaherty pushed back a little. "They could expel you too."

"They could. But, they won't."

Whitfield still didn't like the idea. "How can you be so sure?"

"I just know. That's all."

Whitfield softened his tone. "Ugu."

"No, Whitfield. I know what I'm doing."

Whitfield relented, and smiled. "You always do."

"OK, now that that's settled. What are you going to do first?" Aspen was excited for Ugu to do something bad.

"Excuse me?"

"Well, you have to get arrested three times. I'm so excited. What bad stuff do you want to do first?"

Chapter 31
All-Star Week

As with almost anything she ever did, Ugu spent considerable time over the next few weeks deciding how to be bad. She didn't want to just commit a random dress code violation or skip class for an unexcused absence. If Ugu was going to be arrested three times, she wanted to leave her mark, and if possible, use these banned behaviors to somehow improve the lives of even just one person around her. After gymnastics practice ended on Thursday night, the day before the team went to Brock Robb Prep for their fifth meet of the season, Whitfield, Aspen, Flaherty, and Ugu met in one of the waterfall huts behind Whitfield's house to discuss their progress and Ugu's plans for her first arrest.

Flaherty was eager to share some news. "So, you'll never guess who just made a rather substantial withdrawal from the bank today."

Whitfield turned toward Flaherty right away. "Dr. Hewitt? Are you kidding?"

"That's right. $325,000."

Ugu whistled. "Not bad. I guess he's planning on bribing a lot of gymnasts this weekend."

"Can you see if any of the bills have been distributed yet?" Aspen wanted to know if they could start tracking the bills to see if Dr. Hewitt is indeed the one distributing the bribe money.

Flaherty checked the program she had uploaded to her tracker. "Let's see. It looks like he's actually giving out the bills right now."

Aspen perked up. "Really? Where?"

"Up at the ski lodge."

Whitfield wanted to act right away. "Let's bust in and catch him in the act."

Ugu remained calm and rational. "No, we can't do that. He hasn't really done anything wrong yet."

"He's passing out money to bribe gymnasts."

"No. He's just distributing bills to non-gymnasts right now. No real violation takes place until the money goes to the gymnasts. We need to wait until then."

Whitfield knew Ugu was right, but still wanted to do something to stop the corruption. "But Dr. Hewitt won't be there then."

"That's OK. The bills are being tracked and his fingerprints are all over them." Flaherty was just as adamant about wanting to clean up the corruption overtaking her sport, but was willing to remain patient while building a case.

Ugu added another nugget to the growing pile of evidence. "And we have video."

Whitfield had forgotten all about the video cameras. "Video?"

"Yes, remember, after our first meet on campus, Sir Arlington asked me to install surveillance cameras inside, and just outside, Jonathan's room, and up at the ski lodge, to record any future interactions like this. I believe we'll have the whole meeting recorded."

"That's so cool. We're going to be heroes." Aspen was already imagining accepting his award for taking down a crime ring.

"Yeah, I'm not so sure about that."

"What do you mean, Whitfield?" Flaherty wasn't sure if Whitfield was balking at the idea of bringing an end to the corruption or just uneasy about being called a hero.

"Well, assuming we bring down this whole crime ring, and the scheduling becomes less favorable and gymnasts stop throwing their routines against us, we may not win any more, or at least not as much as we do now. I don't think everyone on the team is going to be happy about that." Whitfield raised a good point, and now that Flaherty thought about it, she had to agree.

"You know, I think you're right. Wilson. Diego. Morocco. Kayleigh. I don't think they'll care if the meets are rigged or not. They just enjoy living in their mansions and having everything handed to them."

Even Ugu, who wasn't on the gymnastics team, saw merit in Whitfield's argument. "I agree. I think you guys might have some opposition on the team when the time comes, but for now, we have to remain focused on the job at hand. You do still want to pursue this, right? Even if it means not winning as much?"

"Yes." Flaherty was absolute in her conviction.

"Definitely!" Whitfield was equally adamant about wanting to pursue their investigation and stamp out corruption in the sport.

"Yes. They're cheating. It's not fair. I don't want to win that way." Aspen put into simple words what everything there was already thinking.

"OK. Good. We're all on the same page. Flaherty and I are documenting every bill transfer made with the money you guys tagged. Everyone involved will get what's coming to them."

Whitfield seized the opportunity for a quick change in topic. "Speaking of getting what's coming to them, have you decided what you are going to do to get arrested?"

Flaherty shook her head. "That still sounds so crazy every time I hear it."

Whitfield agreed, "I know."

Aspen sarcastically presented an option. "You should definitely pants Jonathan. He deserves it." The other three chuckled. "And then you should throw a pie in Wilson's face. I think that would be so funny."

"Thanks Aspen. Those are good ideas. I'll keep them in mind, but I was thinking about going a little bigger." The group stayed inside the hut until the late hours discussing Ugu's plans for getting arrested. Her first attempt at getting arrested was scheduled to take place during All-Star Week and was guaranteed to make a splash.

****

For the third consecutive year, Seven Bridges Academy was scheduled to host All-Star Week, by virtue of winning the national championship in each of the prior three years. Term 2 classes were wrapping up and Whitfield, Ugu, and Flaherty had aced all their classes and performed admirably on their placement exams for next term. Whitfield and Ugu enjoyed being in class together so much so that Ugu agreed to take an advanced mathematics class with Whitfield, and Whitfield agreed to take another IA course with Ugu in Term 3.

Aspen's internship at the WGF was over, and to his surprise, he had a blast being the WGF mascot for several PGL meets. He even enjoyed landing in 'The Nest' at WGF headquarters and entertaining families every morning. His evaluators gave him high marks across the board, and asked if he would don the bird suit again for Championship Week, if his schedule allowed.

At the conclusion of practice on the Friday before All-Star Week, the SBA gymnastics team gathered together at the gymnastics center for the WGF's All-Star Selection Show. All-Star Week was an exhibition of the greatest school-aged gymnasts in the world, and a true fan favorite of gymnastics enthusiasts across the globe. For five days, 500 of the world's greatest 11–18-year-old gymnasts would descend upon Seven Bridges Academy to compete for the fans. The WGF selected

252 domestic athletes and 248 international competitors to compete during All-Star Week.

As the selection show went on, Lord Sirroc, current President of the WGF, explained the breakdown of how athletes were selected. Domestic gymnast selections included the top 50 All-Arounders (limit 2 per school) and 25 additional specialists for each event. If an All-Arounder did not qualify as one of the top 50, they could still be invited as a specialist. Specialists could be selected for up to three events, and an additional (26th) specialist would be added for any non-All-Arounder selected for more than one event to round out the 252-athlete roster.

The international contingent of gymnasts included 248 athletes representing 48 countries. The number of All-Star roster spots per country was determined by the WGF's international rankings. Countries ranked in the top ten (excluding the host country) were each granted eight selections; rankings between 11-20 were each granted six selections; and those outside the top 20 were each granted four selections.

The WGF added the international component to All-Star Week four years ago to broaden fan exposure to gymnastics around the world and it has been very well received since its inception. Both domestic and international athletes enjoy meeting each other and fans love seeing the best the world has to offer, in a fun, fan-friendly environment.

The All-Star selections were finally revealed. In total, Seven Bridges Academy had six athletes, the maximum allowed for any one school, selected as All-Stars. Other than Seven Bridges, only Vertical Press Academy (6), Flagpole Prep (5), and Parallel Pines (5) had more than three athletes selected to compete during All-Star Week. In total, 181 domestic schools were represented with at least one athlete competing during the week; however, all 800 schools were invited to send two athletes and one coach to enjoy the week-long festivities and to be recognized during the Opening and Closing Ceremonies.

As expected, Whitfield and Flaherty made the All-Star roster as All-Arounders. Keegan was selected as an All-Star for both Handstand Obstacle and Floor Exercise. Sydney was selected as an All-Star for Escalating Tramps; Morocco was selected for Tri-Bars; and Aspen, who received a special exemption from the WGF to compete as a ten-year old, was selected as an All-Star for Pommel Clock.

Those left off the All-Star roster may have been a bit disgruntled, but understood the process and were generally OK with the selections, despite some lingering disappointment from Bella, Kayleigh, and Ryne. The WGF limited All-

Star selections from the same school to six, and those three would have been next in line, after Seraphina, who just missed beating out Sydney for an All-Star roster spot on ET.

While almost everyone selected as an All-Star celebrated, Aspen was unusually quiet for someone who had just been named the youngest All-Star ever.

"Hey, bro, you made it. That's awesome."

"Yeah, thanks Whitfield."

"Hey, what's wrong? I'm not feeling the excitement."

"It's just that I should have made it for Tri-Bars too. My routine is much better than half of the gymnasts selected on TB. I have a top 20 routine and you know it."

"Yeah, your routine is really good. So what? You made it on Pommel Clock. As a first-year. That's really impressive."

Aspen was still shaking his head. "It's just that Professor Marino keeps giving me low scores. The other judges all like my routine, but he always lowers my overall score. He just doesn't like me."

"Hey, I get low scores too. He doesn't like me either. But, forget about him. You made it, bro. You are an All-Star! We should go out and celebrate."

Aspen's mood quickly changed. "Really?"

Keegan overheard Whitfield say 'celebrate' and immediately ran over. "Heck yeah! All-Stars in the house. Let's get crazy tonight. I'm wearing fresh new underwear, and I don't care who writes on them. All I know is I'm going to lose my pants tonight and I don't care. Woo-Hoo! All-Star!"

Flaherty came over as well. "Well, I can see Keegan is excited. Congratulations Aspen. You really deserve it. All-Star Week is going to be a lot of fun."

Whitfield agreed, "I'm sure it will be. I can't wait."

Aspen finally cracked a smile. "Yeah, me too."

Flaherty knew they had one more thing to do before leaving the gymnastics center. "Hey, before we go out and celebrate, let's check off which events we want to participate in. The week has so much going on, it's impossible to do everything."

Whitfield, Aspen, and Flaherty went over to the video monitors to select their events. All-Star Week was jam-packed with events, both on the competition floor and off. In addition to the main tournament-style All-Star meet which included all 500 All-Star selections, select gymnasts were either invited, or opted in, to compete across a variety of skills competitions, including: stick knock-out, most air on a release move, fastest circles, fastest giants, and various strength elements.

The WGF also scheduled a bunch of fan contests, including one where fans could design a routine, and gymnasts would compete to see who could complete the routine with the fewest deductions. Fans also had unprecedented access to athletes as gymnasts were encouraged to invite fans onto select reserved spots on the competition floor during their routines and to interact with fans at their seats in between routines.

Off the floor, athletes were scheduled to participate in a bunch of red-carpet events, formal banquets and galas, interviews, and even one-on-one or group practice sessions with fans. While most events were scheduled to include fan access to their favorite athletes, the WGF did include several smaller gatherings reserved for just the athletes, attempting to facilitate relationships across geographic boundaries.

Whitfield, Aspen, and Flaherty selected their preferred events and signed up for a week's worth of activities, before heading out to meet up with Keegan and the rest of the gang to celebrate. Whitfield invited Ugu, who said she would meet them at Plank 'N Steins in an hour. She was just putting the finishing touches on her plan for her first dubious act.

****

In addition to athletes and coaches, the WGF itself was well represented during All-Star Week. Lord Sirroc, Gen. Gibson, and about two dozen other WGF officials attended the week-long festivities. Over 2,000 judges were also in attendance, as the WGF incorporated the International Judges Convention into the All-Star Week schedule of events. Judges from across the world gathered at Seven Bridges Academy for classroom instruction, hands-on training, holographic demonstrations, and an array of other learning modules, but also for networking opportunities and a fun, low-stress, all-expenses paid vacation.

Ugu took a keen interest in helping oversee the schedule of events during All-Star Week, particularly for the Judges Convention. As one of the WGF's prized recruits following her successful internship last year, Ugu was afforded a great deal of discretion and autonomy in carrying out the WGF's master agenda for the week.

Lord Sirroc had personally requested Ugu to lead a team of associates in making sure things went smoothly on campus. Ugu's responsibilities included overseeing staffing for everything from food service to security; contracting with various suppliers, including negotiating rates on behalf of the WGF; booking talent and entertainment; welcoming international guests; and generally problem-solving any unforeseen issues that might arise during the week. Lord Sirroc had great faith in Ugu, and she deserved it.

The entire All-Star Week was flawless in its logistical execution, staffing, and organization, thanks in large part, to Ugu's efforts. Well, flawless except for the fiasco that occurred during the mid-week Annual Judges Ball. To accommodate all the other events scheduled during the week, the top competition floor in the gymnastics center was temporarily repurposed to host roughly 3,500 judges, significant others, and other honored guests in a formal, black-tie affair, rated by many judges as the highlight of their year. The food was exquisite. The decor was mesmerizing. The overall atmosphere was purely delightful, with just the right amount of lingering chalk dust to make the judges feel right at home.

Several judges were scheduled to receive awards or otherwise be honored during the event. Among the scheduled honorees was Professor Marino. He was to receive an award for Ten Years of Judging Excellence; however, only about thirty minutes before his big moment, a clumsy waiter accidentally spilled red wine all over his tuxedo.

Seemingly out of nowhere, Ugu rushed over and very discreetly escorted Professor Marino out of Arlington Gymnastics Center, without any other tables ever noticing what happened. Ugu directed Professor Marino through a passageway out onto the Outer Loop.

"Sir, I am so sorry this happened."

"Oh, Ugu, it's not your fault. That clumsy waiter…look at this. Now I have to go to the Uniform Galleria to get a new tux."

"Actually, sir, if I may, you can go back to our mansion." Professor Marino was Aspen's house supervisor, so he was familiar with the entire house layout and how to get home from the Outer Loop. "I have an entire rack of tuxedos on the third-floor outdoor sitting area. I'm sure you can find one your size. Don't go all the way around to your side of the house. You can take Slide 19-WU. It will take to right down to the third floor. You can clean up there. If you hurry, you can still make it back on time for your award."

"Ugu, you are a life saver. Thank you so much."

"Absolutely. Take this tracker. Keep in on. If you're running a little late, I'll stall the awards presentation."

Professor Marino was quite taken with Ugu's generosity and problem-solving capabilities. "You really don't have to do this."

"No. I insist. You truly deserve this."

"Well, thank you so much. I don't know what to say."

"You don't have to say anything. Just the look on your face when you get up there is enough for me. Now, quick, you need to hurry."

Professor Marino rushed off through the Outer Loop toward his mansion, as requested. Ugu calmly walked back toward the gymnastics center, and through her earpiece, alerted Keegan to activate Step 2 of her plan. "OK, Keegan, he has the tracker on and is on his way to Slide 19-WU."

"OK, I'll tell the emcee. Did he suspect anything?"

"No. You were perfect. He didn't even notice you. Thought you were just some clumsy waiter."

"Good. Maybe after this he'll start giving Whitfield and Aspen the scores they deserve."

"Let's hope so. Now, go tell Ashlynn and get back to your banquet before anyone sees you here."

"Always happy to help."

"Hey, Keegan."

"Yeah?"

"Thanks."

"You bet." Keegan told Ashlynn, the emcee for the evening, and one of the most-trusted and successful gymnastics reporters in the profession, to start the special awards program that Ugu had scripted. The band stopped playing, and guests were asked to return to their seats.

Ashlynn stepped up to the podium. "Ladies and Gentlemen. We have a special presentation for you starring our night's next honoree." The large video monitors all displayed a live shot of Professor Marino jogging in the Outer Loop.

"Professor Marino, or Judge Marino as he is known to many of you, is one of our most beloved judges, but before he receives his award for Ten Years of Judging Excellence, he has invited us on a special journey with him as he tries to prepare for tonight's spotlight. This video presentation is brought to you by a solo producer, known only as J.E.F.E. Enjoy the show!"

Professor Marino had no idea the entire audience was watching his every move. Ugu's specially designed tracker activated all surveillance cameras within 50 yards of Marino to focus on, and live stream, his every movement. The video monitors at the Judges Ball showed a hefty Marino sweating and gasping for breath as he reached Slide 19-WU. The entrance was closed, and instead of using his own tracker to open the gate, he pressed the buzzer and quickly explained his situation to the security agent, who had been expecting him. The gate opened immediately.

Marino awkwardly stepped onto the trap door and within seconds was on his way. The slide was supposed to lead Marino directly to the third-floor outdoor sitting area, but Ugu had a surprise in store. After careful calculation, taking into account estimates of Marino's weight, clothes, and surface friction of the slide, Ugu had removed a panel from the bottom of the slide and replaced it with loose tissue paper, matching the color of the slide.

When Marino reached the missing panel, he immediately sank through the tissue paper and dropped 25 feet into a large swimming pool. The water in the pool, however, had been drained the night before and replaced with a mixture of green slime and caramel. Ugu had several members of her house volunteer to test it out the night before to ensure that Marino would not get hurt. The sticky and gooey substance provided a soft landing for Marino.

The audience watching the video monitors went hysterical. They were all laughing so hard, several fell out of their seats. A stationed 'lifeguard' at the pool was there to help Marino get to his feet. Marino was covered from head to toe with green and brown ooze. The lifeguard took a hose and sprayed Marino down, blasting ice cold water up and down Marino's stout figure. Still in a rush, Marino, who despite living in the house, was less familiar with this side of the mansion, demanded to know the fastest way up to the third floor sitting area.

The lifeguard directed Marino to the set of escalating parallel planks resembling a makeshift staircase on the side of the mansion, ascending up to the third floor. Not entirely happy about this option, Marino was not given another choice. He carefully stepped onto the first plank, and immediately slipped off and fell with a thud. The lifeguard helped him up and advised Marino to remove his shoes.

Marino kicked off his shoes and tried again. He stepped up to the first plank, jumped forward and bear-hugged the second plank. He frantically tried to lift his legs over, and finally got his whole body above the plank, and carefully stood up, reaching for the third plank. Again, Marino, kicked his legs and pulled his body up to get on top of the third plank, which he did, but this time, he could not maintain his balance, slid over the other side, lost his grip, and fell to the ground.

Rather than landing with a thud, Marino never actually quite reached the ground per se, but instead landed on a huge inflatable raft covered in white, down feathers and slippery cooking oil. With the audience back at the Judges Ball now laughing even harder and gasping for air themselves, the lifeguard remained calm and helped the feather-covered Marino to his feet and asked if he would like to simply take the lift up to the third floor. Marino stared at the lifeguard, wondering why this option was not offered initially, but instead of asking that question, chose to focus instead on the raft full of feathers.

The lifeguard was fully prepared to answer. "Oh, that was just left over from a late-night pillow fight last weekend. You know how crazy things can get around here, right?"

As he spoke that last line, the lifeguard turned and peered directly into the nearest surveillance camera, and winked. The audience back at the Judges Ball loved it. Marino stepped inside the lift and ascended to the third floor. Now, on the third floor, Marino, still trying to peel feathers off him, found the rack of tuxedos, as promised. Still unaware that cameras were live streaming his every movement, Marino looked around, and not seeing anyone, undressed down to his underwear. He took a pair of pants off the rack that matched his size, and tried putting them on. The pants did not fit above his massive thighs.

"Aarrgghhh...this stupid slime must have expanded my legs. I'll just have to go up a size."

Marino tried on the next size higher, and couldn't get the waist to close. He tried another size up, the largest size available on the rack, and they just barely fit. Marino had similar difficulties with the shirt and jacket, but eventually got his entire tuxedo on, while still picking off loose feathers from his hands and neck area. Apparently, Ugu's late-night call to the Uniform Galleria to send over the tuxedos, but to have each clothing item mislabeled to appear two sizes larger, had worked well enough to infuriate Marino even more.

Marino knew he was going to be late. He only had two minutes left and still had to climb up the ramp to the Outer Loop, rush through the loop, and walk down the extension tunnel back into the gymnastics center. Fortunately, Ugu had told him she would politely hold up the awards presentation for his arrival. The skin tight pants and jacket that was two sizes too small for him, made Marino walk stiffly and wobble from side to side. His shoes were still wet and slippery from the pool incident, and he slipped several times going up the ramp.

"Uh-oh. No. No. No. Please tell me I didn't..." But, yes, Marino split his pants. The entire seam covering his rear end split open. The crowd, once again, had a full view of Marino's underwear and could barely contain their laughter.

Marino continued talking to himself. "OK. Calm down. The jacket has tails. Maybe no one will notice. I can still go, accept my award, and exit through the back. I'll have Ugu pick up some looser fitting clothes. Everything will work out."

Marino continued his climb, and slowly trotted through the Outer Loop. The crowd was now cheering for Marino. What had started as a cruel prank, had turned into the making of a hero. Marino had faced down every obstacle in his path and was determined to get his award. The crowd wanted nothing more than for Marino to walk across the stage, triumphantly.

As Marino approached the extension tunnel leading to the gymnastics center, a lone table and chair was set up, with a glass of milk and a doughnut, and a note that read 'Final stop before the spotlight'. Marino pondered for a second, looked around, and grabbed the doughnut and ate it in a single bite. He sat down, which only served to rip apart the seam in his pants even further. Marino drank the milk, got up, and hurriedly wobbled down the extension tunnel.

From inside the Judges Ball, Ashlynn announced Professor Marino's entrance. "And here he is…everyone's favorite judge…a true gentleman…Judge Marino!"

Marino walked out to thunderous applause. The crowd, quite exhausted from the past twenty minutes of all out laughter, gave Marino a standing ovation. Marino was caught off guard, as he still had no idea the crowd had seen his incredible journey to the stage, but was touched by the gesture. Marino wobbled across the stage to receive his award for Ten Years of Judging Excellence. His speech was short and direct.

"Thank you all for this prestigious award. To be recognized for ten years of service is truly an honor. I do wish to apologize for my appearance at the moment. I…uhh…had some slight difficulty with picking out the right tux." The crowd laughed. "I've always tried to judge routines to the best of my abilities. Like everyone here, sometimes we miss things, sometimes athletes and coaches disagree with our judgment. That's OK. It's all part of the job. It comes with the territory. But the one thing I put above everything else in this position, is the safety of all gymnasts under my watch."

Marino appeared to be looking directly at Sir Arlington as he spoke these next few words. "I am determined to do everything in my power to protect all gymnasts. Keep them safe. Healthy. And smiling. At the end of the day, if no one gets hurts and I could put a smile on someone's face, then I'd say I had a good day. Thank you."

Once again, the crowd stood and cheered. Marino had hoped to get a clean getaway through the back of the stage, but just as his speech concluded, three WGF officials hurriedly came onto the stage and directed Marino to stay. One of the officials grabbed the microphone. "Let's hear it once more for Judge Marino." The crowd clapped.

"Judge, please stay with us for a moment. Ladies and gentleman. Every year, we at the WGF attend the Annual Judges Convention and interact with many of you throughout the week. By week's end, we huddle together, and agree to present one individual with the Uplifting Spirits Award. Now, normally, we do this in a discreet manner at the end of the week, but given the very public display we all just witnessed, we are proud to present the winner of this year's Uplifting Spirit Award to Judge Marino."

Again, the crowd roared. As Marino posed for pictures, confused as to what just happened, the crowd started chanting, "Jefe! Jefe! Jefe!" As Marino was escorted off the stage with three WGF officials flanked to his left, they informed him of the live streaming video that everyone had just witnessed. He was in complete shock...and quite embarrassed.

Ugu met Professor Marino backstage, and with deep sincerity in her voice, confessed that she had organized the whole thing, from the first wine spill to the poorly labeled tuxedos and everything in between. "I am so sorry, sir. I know that doesn't change anything, so I am willing to accept my punishment." Ugu lowered her head and directed her eyes toward the ground.

"You are responsible for all this? Hmm. I'll admit, I was quite upset with this series of one catastrophe after another, but looking back at how everything unfolded, how could I be mad at you?"

Ugu lifted her head in surprise. "Excuse me, sir?"

"Look, I won the Uplifting Spirits Award. I've always wanted to win this award. And, look, it comes with a check for $20,000! I'm too happy to be upset. I forgive you." Professor Marino walked away and Ugu was left baffled.

A few moments later, Sir Arlington approached Ugu backstage. "Young Ugu, or should I call you...Jefe? Am I to understand that you orchestrated this whole circus?"

Ugu thought she detected disappointment in Sir Arlington's eyes. *OK, one more chance to get arrested. Here it goes.* "Yes, sir, I admit it. I planned all of it."

Sir Arlington looked stern at first, but quickly softened. "Well done!"

What? "Sir?" Ugu was baffled, yet again.

"Young Ugu. We haven't laughed so hard in years. How did you ever think to pull this off...and at the Judges Ball no less? You know, just between you and I, these events are typically rather boring. But not this one. You certainly outdid yourself."

"I know...but, sir, I still violated about a dozen school rules. Shouldn't I be arrested?"

"Arrested? Oh, I should think not."

"Why not?"

"Well, for starters, school is out of session this week. We are on break. Plus, you were working on behalf of the WGF tonight. If anyone reserves the right to punish, it would be them. However, I wouldn't count on that either. After this display, I wouldn't be surprised if they made you a permanent job offer tonight."

I cannot catch a break. Why won't anyone arrest me?

"Really! Wait, no, this doesn't make any sense. I broke the rules. I should be arrested."

"Relax, my dear. You are not in any trouble. Professor Marino is happy. The crowd had a wonderful time. And it's all thanks to you…or should I say, Jefe?" Sir Arlington directed a wink at Ugu.

Ugu finally relented, realizing that tonight was just not her night to get arrested. "It stands for Judge Everyone Fairly and Equitably. J.E.F.E. It was meant to call attention to Whitfield and Aspen's unfair low scores on Tri-Bars."

"I see. Well, a word of advice. Tell the boys not to get too bent out of shape about Professor Marino's scores. Not everything is as it seems." The wisdom and foretelling in Sir Arlington's words were not immediately understood by Ugu. Sir Arlington patted Ugu on the shoulder and retreated back to his seat to collect his belongings.

The evening was at its close, and all that was left was to wait for the crowd to disperse and oversee the crew tear down the decorations and return the 8th-floor competition area back to its primary purpose. Despite a general happiness that came from running a successful event, Ugu couldn't help but feel a little disappointed in herself. She had tried to get arrested, and failed. Ugu hung around the competition area for a few minutes after the cleaning crew had completed their job, before walking up to the Outer Loop to go home.

Whitfield, Aspen, and Flaherty were returning from their own formal affair and happened to run into Ugu on the Outer Loop. "Hey, perfect timing! How was your evening?"

"Hey, Flaherty. Good, I guess." Ugu sounded really down.

Whitfield showed concern. "What happened? Is everything OK?"

"Oh, the Judges Ball went fine. Everyone had a great time."

Aspen let out a devious chuckle, remembering the plan. "Not everyone, right? I bet Professor Marino had a lousy night."

"Well, not exactly."

"Really? What happened? You couldn't go through with it, could you? See, Flaherty, I told you, Ugu is just too nice."

"No. Not too nice. I really let him have it. Slime. Feathers. Small tux. Everything."

Flaherty didn't understand. "Then, what's wrong?"

Whitfield had a horrible thought. "Wait, they didn't expel you, did they? I knew you shouldn't have gone through with this."

"No, relax, Honey Bear. I didn't get expelled. I didn't even get arrested."

"What? You got away with it. Cool!"

"Thanks, Aspen, but no. I confessed to Professor Marino. But he was too happy to be mad at me."

Flaherty questioned the inconsistency in Ugu's recap. "He was happy with all those terrible things you put his through?"

"Yeah, they gave him a huge award for it. Treated him like a hero for making everyone laugh. They thought he was in on it and just acting out a skit to show how silly people think judges are, I guess."

"That's crazy. So, you put in all this work, and didn't even get arrested?" Whitfield wasn't sure if he should feel relieved or disappointed.

"No." Ugu continued pouting.

"Well, we finally found something that you're bad at."

"Yeah, what's that?"

"You are really bad and being bad." Ugu half-smiled and rested her head on Whitfield's shoulder.

Aspen defended his housemate. "No, she's not. Ugu's great at being bad. She just needs some practice. Next time, she'll get arrested, for sure. I have confidence in her."

Ugu gave a slight smile. "Thanks, Aspen, and you're right. I will do better next time. By this time next term, I'll be in the Pit."

"And we'll help you get there."

Whitfield recognized the oddity of this conversation. "We have really weird goals." The four friends laughed and walked through the Outer Loop together to go home.

Chapter 32
Ugu's Bad Behavior

It was difficult for Whitfield and Aspen to focus on the first day of classes for Term 3 after an exhilarating All-Star Week. In addition to all of the formal events and interviews, the actual competition tournament was a blast. Whitfield had gone head-to-head against Flaherty on three events during All-Star Week, only winning once, and each loss coming by less than one point. Whitfield did not win any single event title, but did finish in the top 8 on five separate events, one of only three athletes to accomplish that feat. Whitfield also competed in a few skills competitions, and fared well, blowing away the competition in peg muscle-ups and most pommel circles in five minutes.

Aspen finished third in the Pommel Clock tournament, barely missing out on the finals because of an uncharacteristic slip on the ninth pommel during the semifinal round. Aspen finished second to his brother in the peg muscle-up skills challenge and led all gymnasts with most fan requests for one-on-one pommel training sessions.

In the end, Flaherty won titles on two events, finished in the top 8 on seven out of eight events, and further cemented her status as one of, if not, the best school-aged gymnast in the country, and arguably, the world. Even though All-Star Week was supposed to be just a fun exhibition for the fans, for Flaherty, and to a slightly lesser extent, Whitfield and Aspen, it served as a global introduction to the hottest young stars in the world of gymnastics.

****

After an entire term dressing up as the WGF mascot for his internship, Aspen was happy to be back in class, even if his term did begin with Dr. Crawfish in *Advanced Probability, Permutations, and Combinatorics* (APPC). Dr. Crawfish was still mean and nasty, and embarrassed students every chance he got, but Aspen learned to keep his head down, pay attention to everything Dr. Crawfish said, and to speak clearly and loudly anytime he was called upon.

Fortunately, Aspen would not have to navigate through his math class alone; Whitfield and Ugu were both in class with Aspen, all three trying to make it through the entire term without being yelled at, picked on, or insulted by Dr. Crawfish.

"It's really cool that the three of us get to have class together this term."

"Agreed. I think it should be fun. Although, I'm not sure Whitfield can handle finishing third in class."

"Third? Really? I know you don't think you're scoring higher than me in this class. This is mathematics. We're not over in IA, honey."

"Oh, I know. We already know I'm whooping your butt in *FIS* (*Foreign Intelligence Services*) this entire term, but I'm also going to whoop you in here."

"Hahaha…Whitfield, Ugu's right. She already knows we're both going to do better than you."

"You two are out of your minds. This class is all mine."

"You think so? Care to make it interesting?"

"Sure, what are you thinking?"

"Loser has to…"

Aspen interrupted. "Guys, shhh…Dr. Crawfish just came in."

Whitfield and Aspen sat up as straight as could be. Ugu followed in line.

Dr. Crawfish got right down to business. He didn't even bother introducing himself. "There are eight teams competing in an upcoming gymnastics meet. How many different combinations could there be in the top 3 final rankings?" Several hands went up in the air. "Olivia."

"336, sir."

"Correct. So, if I look at the final results of a recent meet and see that Seven Bridges Academy came in first, Triplepike Academy second, and Fallburn third, would I be correct in assuming that this outcome had a 1 in 336, or a 0.298 percent, expected chance of occurring?" A few hands rose, but Dr. Crawfish called on another student at random. "Stanke."

Stanke was not expecting to be called upon, and was not prepared to answer. "I think that would be correct, sir."

"Get out of my classroom! That was a stupid answer and I will not tolerate stupidity. Get out!" Stanke looked around at his classmates in shock, packed up his belongings, and left. "Whitfield. What is the correct answer?"

Whitfield was confident in his answer, but still responded nervously, watching Stanke exit the room. "No, sir. The likelihood of each particular outcome is determined by the probability function assigned to each team."

"Explain further."

"Certain outcomes may be more likely than others. The fallacy in your original statement was an implicit assumption that all teams had an equal likelihood of placing 1 through 8 in the final rankings, also assuming no ties. The likelihood assigned to each team placing in a particular spot in the final rankings is constantly moving, based on past performance, the health of athletes, starting lineups, how someone is feeling on a particular day, and countless other variables."

Dr. Crawfish nodded. "That's good. Especially the part about floating probability expectations. So, for example, if you were to say, meet with an unfortunate accident, whereby you shattered your leg and could no longer compete, would the likelihood of Seven Bridges Academy finishing in first place in their next meet increase or decrease?"

Ugu was disgusted that Dr. Crawfish would use such a personal, and gruesome, example. "Sir, I hardly think that is an appropriate example to use in class."

Dr. Crawfish did not appreciate interruptions. "I am not interested in your assessment of the quality of example I use in class. I want an answer, and I want it from someone who does not exhibit such disrespect in my classroom. Carlton. Would the likelihood of Seven Bridges finishing in first place in their next meet increase or decrease if their star athlete broke his leg?"

Carlton nearly broke down in tears, hearing his named called. "Decrease, sir."

"Good, now what would happen if…"

Ugu interrupted for a second time. "Excuse me, sir, but I think you are both wrong."

The students all gasped. Dr. Crawfish was appalled. "You think I am wrong?"

Ugu was defiant. "No, sir, actually, I know you are wrong, but I was offering you the courtesy of some respect."

The class collectively gasped again. Orton fainted. Kemba slid under her table.

"Well, Miss Ugu. Enlighten us. Share with us your superior knowledge of this subject matter."

"Certainly. Both you and Carlton, sorry Carlton, both relied on a similar faulty assumption that Whitfield pointed out earlier. You assumed that the likelihood of Seven Bridges Academy winning a particular meet was greater with Whitfield in the lineup. Just because he's an All-Arounder and has performed well this year, does not necessarily mean that Seven Bridges is better with him in the lineup, or that someone better isn't sitting on the bench just waiting for their turn to come in."

Whitfield was somewhat uneasy with Ugu's candid, and less than flattering, assessment of his contributions to the team. "Whoa. Easy now."

"Sorry. Just making a point here. Even if Whitfield was better than any other alternative, perhaps the team rallies around his gruesome injury; perhaps other teams don't prepare as well or compete as hard without Whitfield in the lineup; the unknown and immeasurable variables are too complex to reasonably optimize an algorithm. The bottom line is given the information you provided in your example, it is unknowable whether the likelihood of Seven Bridges Academy finishing in first place in their next meet increases or decreases with an injury to Whitfield?"

The class cautiously cheered Ugu's defiant, and articulate, response. Dr. Crawfish was not as appreciative. "I want you out of my classroom now."

Ugu did not move from her seat. "Well, sir, we don't always get what we want. I'm staying."

"Excuse me?"

Ugu stood as she spoke. "Sir, you may continue teaching or you can turn this into an even greater spectacle. I promise to not be disruptive to your class, as I, along with my classmates, are here to learn. You probably want to take note; however, that according to Seven Bridges Classroom and Campus Guidebook, all non-gymnastics classes serving three or more current members of the gymnastics team are automatically recorded and sent to administration for review protocols and made available to students campus-wide. As you can see, we have Whitfield, Aspen, and Chloe is down there. Hi Chloe. So, right now, this conversation is being reviewed, and I for one, would really like to get back to learning."

Ugu sat back in her seat, and kept her focus directly on Dr. Crawfish. Students were in stunned silence. No one had ever taken on Dr. Crawfish like that before and no one knew exactly what to expect next. Would Dr. Crawfish back down? Would he take the high road and simply move on with the lesson, and teach the class of students, eager to learn from him? Dr. Crawfish's next actions clearly answered his students' curiosity.

"How dare you? You do not ever speak to me that way. You, you, little ungrateful…" Dr. Crawfish's face was turning from red to purple. He was struggling with his next words, which were sure to be completely over the top, and regrettable.

Ugu remained calm, and decided to save Dr. Crawfish from himself. "Sir."

Whitfield urged Ugu to stop talking. "Uhh, I think you should probably stop now."

"Nonsense, I've got this. Sir, before you say something that will likely get you in a good deal of trouble with the School Board, might I suggest you relax, calm down, and take a deep breath. I am sure we can review some principles or theorems on our own until you compose yourself."

Ugu's calm nature only served to further enrage Dr. Crawfish. He was stomping around like a caged tiger. Dr. Crawfish unleashed a series of profanities and other expletives directed straight at Ugu. The class was now in defensive mode, as many braced themselves for what they assumed would be a physical assault by a teacher on a student. Whitfield stood up to try to restrain Dr. Crawfish before he jumped out at Ugu, but Ugu pulled his arm closer to her to keep him nearby, and out of the line of fire.

Dr. Crawfish had completely lost his temper. He started yelling at any other student who tried to calm him down. Several students returned to their seats crying. Once Dr. Crawfish started to direct his insults and fiery language toward other students, Ugu had had enough. She knew it would be just a matter of moments before Sir Arlington would show up with security in tow, but she couldn't let Dr. Crawfish get away with embarrassing and humiliating any more students.

Ugu spoke calmly, but forcibly. "Excuse me, sir. I believe your anger is with me. Could we please leave these other students out of this?"

"You smug, arrogant, pathetic, little…" This time, Dr. Crawfish did have to be restrained by several students.

"OK. I was hoping it wouldn't come to this, but you leave me no choice." Ugu had already prepared her hack into the classroom video boards. She had preloaded video footage from when Dr. Crawfish was a student at Seven Bridges Academy. For four consecutive years, Dr. Crawfish had tried out for the gymnastics team, and each year, came up far short.

Ugu had compiled a blooper reel of Dr. Crawfish's failed attempts at each event, and drew parallels to his hot-tempered behavior as a teacher. The chaos inside the classroom subdued, as Dr. Crawfish settled down and was no longer in need of physical restraint. As he watched his memories of past failures stream across the video boards, his anger softened, replaced by tears and regret. He looked around at all the students in his classroom watching the video boards, snickering and looking at him shamefully.

Several moments later, Sir Arlington stepped into the classroom with three security guards. The guards immediately surrounded Dr. Crawfish, who surrendered willingly. As Dr. Crawfish left the classroom, he gave one more menacing look up at Ugu, and left. As he walked out of the building, he realized that students all around the AMQE campus had come out of their classrooms to catch a glimpse of him.

Ugu had live-streamed what was happening in their classroom to the entire Seven Bridges' campus, across every classroom, office, library, and building. Dr. Crawfish's incessant bullying had to be stopped, and Ugu felt she had a responsibility to everyone to stop him herself. Despite, or perhaps because of, her best efforts to stop Dr. Crawfish from endangering students, Ugu found herself in trouble. Sir Arlington spoke in front of the room full of students.

"Class is dismissed for the day. You will find reading materials and applicable exercises available on your course accounts by mid-day today. We will find a suitable replacement for Dr. Crawfish. This course will proceed as planned following today's anomaly."

The students all got up to exit the classroom. Nearly everyone made it a point to thank Ugu for taking a stand against Dr. Crawfish on their way out. "Young Ugu. A word please."

"Certainly, sir." Ugu remained in the classroom. Whitfield and Aspen were unsure whether to stay or leave. After a few moments of indecision, they both decided to stay and lend support to Ugu.

Whitfield cautiously approached the headmaster. "Sir, with all due respect, Ugu was right in her actions. She remained calm throughout the exchange and merely pointed out a flaw in Dr. Crawfish's instruction."

Aspen offered additional support. "Yeah, she didn't do anything wrong. Dr. Crawfish is the one who totally lost control."

"Thank you, boys. I am aware of what transpired in this classroom this morning. Now, normally I would ask to speak with young Ugu alone, but given your relationships, I am sure whatever I say here will be repeated in a matter of moments and I would like to ensure my words are not in any way misconstrued during a retelling. Besides, after the defiance I just witnessed, to be honest, I am a little concerned over what young Ugu might say if I asked you two to leave us." Sir Arlington let slip a smile to let the small gathering know he was joking.

"Does this mean we're not in trouble?"

"Young Aspen, you and young Whitfield have avoided any punishment for your actions. In fact, you should be commended for taking action in restraining a teacher who had, in my opinion, gone temporarily mad."

"Thank you, sir. But what about Ugu?"

"Well, young Whitfield, this part is more complicated. My dear, young Ugu…I believe young Whitfield used the phrase 'with all due respect' earlier. I do appreciate that. I also feel that the role of professor at Seven Bridges Academy is one that commands respect as well."

"But, sir…"

Sir Arlington raised his hand. "Young Whitfield, I know what you are about to say. What is our role in offering respect for the position when the one placed in that role abuses it by disrespecting others? Shouldn't the one standing tall on the teaching perch be held to a higher standard of character to elicit such respect? And if that teacher disrespects the position, does that give students the right to disrespect them? These are all good questions, each with nuanced answers."

Aspen didn't fully understand. "But, sir, Ugu didn't disrespect Dr. Crawfish."

Ugu turned to face Aspen. "Actually, Aspen, I did."

"You didn't say anything bad. You were just calling him out for being wrong."

Sir Arlington was about to say something, but Ugu interrupted, "my apologies for interrupting, sir, but if I may." Sir Arlington nodded. "I don't think it was my words that were necessarily disrespectful. It was the video board hack and showing those old clips of Dr. Crawfish falling during tryouts. I didn't need to go that far. I knew Sir Arlington would be on his way, and that you, Whitfield, and the other students would most likely continue restraining Dr. Crawfish until he arrived. Setting up the live stream video simply to embarrass a teacher was wrong." Aspen was still not convinced, but it was not his decision on how to proceed.

"Well said, young Ugu. Look, Dr. Crawfish is a very knowledgeable man and could be an excellent teacher, but his methods are less than desirable. Each of us on the faculty bring a different element into the classroom, and there are some voices that support having an old curmudgeon around. To be sure, valuable lessons could be learned from uncomfortable, or even scary, situations too."

Aspen mumbled under his breath. "Yeah, like how not to act."

Sir Arlington heard Aspen clearly. "Exactly."

"So, sir, does that mean you can just give Ugu a warning and we can move on to our next class?"

"No, young Whitfield, I am afraid not. This time, we do have to administer a punishment. Young Ugu, you are to be arrested for violating the Seven Bridges

Academy Student Code of Conduct. This being your first offense, your punishment will be served during a one-week period, commencing as soon as this conversation concludes."

Aspen was upset. "But, sir…"

Whitfield quickly quieted Aspen. "Aspen. Stop. This is Sir Arlington's decision. Let it go." Sir Arlington became keenly aware of the group's unusual acceptance of Ugu's punishment and knew there was something more going on, but did not attempt to unravel it at this moment.

"Now, at this point, I am going to ask for a moment alone with young Ugu. Boys, you may wait in the hallway. This will only take a moment." Whitfield and Aspen looked at Ugu. She nodded and told them she would meet them outside the classroom shortly. The boys left Ugu alone in the classroom with Sir Arlington.

"Sir, something seems wrong? What is it?"

Sir Arlington waited for the boys to exit the classroom before speaking again. "We need to retrieve all surveillance equipment from young Jonathan's room."

"What about from the lodge?"

"No, that equipment can stay…for now. We have reviewed the video footage and have clear images of all those involved in several late-night meetings at the lodge."

"Really? Who else was involved?"

"Let's table that conversation for a later date. For now, we cannot afford to have any of this equipment discovered or compromised in any way. I need you to devise a plan to get back in there and retrieve our 'belongings'. Make sure you check everywhere, closets, dressers, windows, and especially under the bed."

Ugu was confused as to why she had to check all these places. She is the one who had planted the equipment in Jonathan's room in the first place. "Yes, sir. But I am going to be detained over the next week. How soon do you need the equipment back?"

"The retrieval mission is time-sensitive. The sooner the better."

"Can it wait a week?"

"No."

"Then, how…" The arresting officers re-entered the classroom.

Sir Arlington abruptly cut off Ugu and repeated his earlier declaration. "Young Ugu, I am sentencing you to Level 1 Detention for violation of the Seven Bridges Academy Student Code of Conduct. Guards, please arrest Ms. Gugurutruv and escort her to the Level 1 Detention area for processing."

Chapter 33
Retrieval Mission

The sentence for Level 1 Detention was typically carried out in the student's home mansion, where the arrested student is to remain in the house supervisor's quarters from 08:00 until 15:00 each day, at which time the student may leave the basement area, but must still remain inside the mansion for the duration of the sentence, usually one week. For Ugu, that meant staying in Professor Marino's basement loft for seven hours per day. While Marino was not one to hold a grudge and genuinely did move on past the incredibly unfortunate journey from the previous week, he remained a steadfast proponent of putting detained students to work for the duration of their sentence. Ugu was no exception. Professor Marino provided a long list of tasks for Ugu to complete during her one-week stay, in addition to her coursework, which included virtually attending all of her scheduled classes and submitting all assignments on time.

Professor Marino's task list for Ugu included the usual cleaning and polishing that he would demand of any student, but given Ugu's unique abilities, Professor Marino also tasked Ugu with helping him redesign his entire judging course curriculum, with updated examples and holographic displays. Ugu certainly preferred the curriculum redesign piece of her punishment over the cleaning element, but working on Professor Marino's courses meant she had to work even closer to him, which impeded her ability to plan, and execute, the surveillance equipment retrieval mission given to her by Sir Arlington.

Ugu needed time to think, but didn't have any to spare. Sir Arlington only gave her three days to retrieve all of the equipment from Jonathan's room, and here she was trapped inside her own mansion, with a Seven Bridges' Gymnastics professor keeping a vigilant eye on her every move. She was going to need help. Lots of it.

Even though Ugu was serving a one-week sentence, she was able to leave the basement at 15:00 every day, so she could still see Whitfield, Aspen, Flaherty and anyone else inside the mansion. Whitfield and Flaherty stopped by every day by

15:00 to hang out with Ugu. Rather than go to the library, Whitfield and Flaherty agreed to study with Aspen at his house every afternoon during Ugu's incarceration to make sure they were all there when Ugu came up the stairs. With Sir Arlington's deadline for retrieving the surveillance equipment fast approaching, Ugu knew she had to act fast. Tonight was the night.

"Hey guys, thanks again for coming over to see me. You really don't have to study here."

"Oh please. Of course, we do. We can't possibly listen to Whitfield whine all night about how much he misses you if he actually had to go through an entire day without seeing you." Flaherty loved teasing Whitfield almost as much as Ugu did.

"Hey, I don't whine."

"Uhh…yeah, you do, bro."

"Well, that's sweet. I miss him too. I miss all of you, but this is all part of the plan, right?"

Whitfield agreed, "right."

"OK, so I need you all to do something for me. If you get caught, you might get into trouble."

Without hesitation, Aspen was on board. "OK. I'll do it."

"You don't even know what it is yet."

"It doesn't matter."

"Yeah, OK. I'm with you, Aspen. Whatever you need, Ugu."

"Good. So, I need to get back into Jonathan's room to collect all the surveillance equipment."

Flaherty wasn't expecting such a challenging task. "What? Why?"

"Sir Arlington needs it. Tonight."

Whitfield was perplexed. "That seems odd. Why does he need it now? Can't it wait?"

"He didn't say why, other than he already has the footage he needs from All-Star Week and he doesn't want the equipment corrupted."

Whitfield still wasn't satisfied. "Hmm…I don't like this. Are you sure we can trust Sir Arlington?"

"I am. I know I had my suspicions before, but I'm confident now. We can trust him."

"That's good enough for me."

"OK. I trust Ugu. If she says we can trust Sir Arlington, then we can. So, what's your plan?" Whitfield wasn't sure if it was his head or his heart doing the talking, but either way, he placed his trust in Ugu.

"Here it is. I am going to convince Professor Marino to let me go out for a run on the Outer Loop tonight after you guys get out of practice."

"How are you going to do that?"

"Don't worry about it, Honey Bear. That's the easy part."

Whitfield frowned, thinking Ugu might apply her seduction techniques on Professor Marino. "Oh, I know what that means."

Ugu read Whitfield's mind. "Eww…no. Nothing like that. I'll just explain that I need to run to stay in shape. He'll let me go. I've been doing a lot of work for his courses, so I think he'll grant me some leniency."

Flaherty knew how convincing her best friend could be. "Yeah, Ugu's really good, Whitfield. She'll convince Professor Marino to let her go."

"OK, then what?"

"He'll know that I'm planning to meet up with you for my run. Professor Marino will let me go, but he'll be very suspicious. He'll track us on his monitor, so Whitfield and I will have to complete a full lap and then some to show that we aren't just getting together to sneak away somewhere. Flaherty, I'm going to need you to turn off your tracker and meet us at Slide 13-WL, leading to Fenway's house."

"I can't."

"What do you mean?"

"I mean I can't turn off my tracker. Coach Daza overrode all the trackers this week. Some of the others were staying out too late and got in some trouble, so now coach is monitoring us 24/7." Flaherty hesitated, before continuing. "But, if you really need me to, I guess I can…"

"No, that's OK. Just let me think a moment…OK, how about this? Can you grab about eight to ten other students and get them up on the Outer Loop for a short run after practice?"

"Sure. No problem. But, why?"

"I need a distraction. Whitfield and I are going to meet you at Slide 13-WL. As your group is running from the opposite direction, you're going to peel away and stay with Whitfield as I go down the slide to Fenway's house."

"No good. Professor Marino will see your tracker leaving the Outer Loop."

"Not if you two stand super close together in the slide alcove. I'll turn my tracker off, so he won't see me leaving the Outer Loop. The tracking signal is weaker in the alcoves, so he'll just think he lost my signal. Professor Marino will still be able to tell there are two students in there, but might not be able to read our names. It's OK if he sees Whitfield's name, but I want Professor Marino to think he's with me. Without specifically tracking Flaherty, he won't know the other student is you. He'll just assume it's me."

Aspen didn't yet believe this plan would work. "Isn't that a little sketchy? I mean, if Professor Marino sees you stopped for too long, won't he get suspicious?"

"That's exactly what I want."

"Why?"

"Professor Marino's going to be watching us on his monitor. I want him to think Whitfield and I stopped somewhere to maybe get a little cozy with each other."

Flaherty raised an eyebrow and smiled. "Hey, that's not a bad idea. Maybe you two should get a little cozy."

"He wishes."

"Oh yeah, I'm not the one who just…"

Ugu quickly snapped. "Whitfield! Shut up."

Aspen suspected they were hiding something. "What? What happened?"

Whitfield just smiled. "Umm…nothing. Ugu, go ahead."

"Thank you. Professor Marino is going to get upset because he thinks Whitfield and I are doing whatever, and he'll want to catch us, but he won't leave his monitors unattended. That's why it's important that he sees Aspen walking by his office door at that precise moment."

"Why me?"

"Well, first, because you live there, right? He won't be suspicious of you. Second, while he leaves his quarters to chase after us, I need you to pull a slight hack."

Aspen's eyes got large. "Ooh…what is it?"

"I need Jonathan out of his room."

Flaherty was confused. "Wait, I thought you said you were going to Fenway's house. Jonathan lives in Seraphina's mansion."

"I know, but I need to access Jonathan's room from the back of the house, the part facing the lodge. I can't slide right into Seraphina's house, because everyone will know I'm there and start asking questions. Fenway lives two houses away. I can take the slide to the fourth-floor balcony and zip-line down to the back edge of her property line. From there I can cross over through the tree line to Seraphina's. I already know which room is Jonathan's, so I'll climb up, collect all the surveillance equipment, and get out."

Whitfield was trying to do some quick mental math. "How long is this all going to take?"

"I figure it's going to take Professor Marino ten to eleven minutes from the time he leaves his desk until he reaches you and Flaherty. So, that's how long I have to complete the mission."

Aspen inquired about his part in the plan. "What about the hack?"

"Right. Since you'll be right at Professor Marino's desk, I need you to hack into his faculty account and change Jonathan's grade. Since Professor Marino will be leaving quickly, it's possible that he'll already be logged in. Otherwise, you should be able to hack in easily."

"No problem. But what will changing his grade do?"

"Any grade change after the term ends generates an automatic message to the student. With any luck, Jonathan will get upset when he sees the message and storm out of his house to confront Professor Marino."

Flaherty tried playing devil's advocate. "Yeah, but what if Jonathan doesn't check his messages right away? You have a very short window to pull this off."

Whitfield offered a thought. "I got it. Look up all the members of Seraphina's house that took a class with Professor Marino last term. Change all their grades. Someone is bound to check their messages in real time and then check with others in the house. When they all realize they got the same message, they'll leave as a group."

"OK. Sounds good. I can easily do that, but shouldn't I change the grades back too?"

"Yes, definitely. I only need about ten minutes, so make sure you change the grades back and attach a formal-looking message that apologizes for the glitch. Say that all their grades remain unchanged and it was just a system reset, or something like that. This will get the students to return home and forget all about it. They probably won't even mention it to Professor Marino."

Whitfield wanted to make sure he was clear on the plan. "OK. So, just to recap here. Ugu is getting permission from Professor Marino to run on the Outer Loop with me tonight after practice. I'll meet Ugu here after practice, and we'll run almost two laps until we reach Slide 13-WL to Fenway's house.

"At that exact moment, Flaherty will lead a group of runners to that same location. Flaherty will hang back and the three of us will duck into the slide alcove, where Ugu will go through the trapdoor for her retrieval mission. Flaherty and I will remain in the alcove for about ten minutes, waiting for Ugu to return. Am I correct so far?"

"Yes. Remember, you have to be pressed close together to confuse Professor Marino's tracking."

"Right. As Ugu is zip-lining, running around trees, climbing houses, and doing all her spy stuff, Aspen will be waiting outside Professor Marino's door, waiting for him to notice the trackers stopped in the Outer Loop. Professor Marino leaves his desk, Aspen steps in and changes Jonathan's…"

Flaherty was quick to interject. "…and his housemates…"

"Right…and his housemates' grades on Professor Marino's computer. If all works well, Jonathan will leave his room to question what's going on, giving Ugu time to complete her mission. Aspen will change the grades back and Ugu will return with the equipment to the Outer Loop."

"No. I'll have to stash the equipment at Fenway's house."

Aspen wasn't sure about this part of the plan. "Hmm…I don't like that."

Whitfield concurred, "I agree. Not sure we can trust Fenway to not poke around your bag. She may get curious and then how would you explain all that stuff in your bag?"

"OK. What do you suggest?"

"You should keep the bag with you. If you make it back before Marino gets there, you can just give the bag to Flaherty for safe keeping. If not…"

"Yeah, wait a second, Whitfield. What are we supposed to tell Marino if he catches us there? And, Ugu, what if he asks about you?"

"Good questions. Flaherty, you are going to have to fake an injury. Twisted ankle, or something. You can use that as an excuse as to why I'm not there. I went to the nearest house to get ice and a wrap for your injury."

"Yeah, but why wouldn't Whitfield go? You're supposed to be arrested, right?"

"I can just say that I didn't want to leave your side, in case you needed to be carried, and Ugu is friends with Fenway and knew she could get in and grab some ice and a wrap and be back quickly. Professor Marino has to know Ugu is the fastest runner here."

"Well, that is true. She is a whole lot faster than you. If I really did need medical attention, I'd want her running for help."

"Me too." Ugu flashed Aspen a quick smile.

"OK. Ugu will make sure to pick up ice and towels at Fenway's before coming back up the ramp. We'll pretend to treat Flaherty. I'll walk her home. Ugu will go home with Professor Marino. I think we have everything covered."

Flaherty was optimistic. "Great! I like this plan. It's going to work."

"I like it too. Should I stay in the basement until Professor Marino returns?"

"Yes. And try to act bored. If you are too excited, he might suspect something is up."

"You got it."

"OK. Well, we better get to practice. Ugu, message me if anything changes or if you can't break free tonight."

"I will. Have a good practice, guys."

"See you soon." Flaherty gave Ugu a quick hug before leaving.

Whitfield, Aspen, and Flaherty left to go to practice. Ugu still needed to work through some of the specific details of how she was going to manage to get into Jonathan's room and back out in ten minutes. But, first, she had to work her charms on Professor Marino, or else the whole mission would fail.

****

"Professor Marino, have you had a chance to review the changes I made to the holographic demonstrations?"

"Yes, I did. They are wonderful. How did you come up with that idea?"

Ugu spoke while stretching out her back in front of Professor Marino. "It was a long night, stuffed in a cramped room, but I just kept poring over your notes from the last few meets. You seem to really be emphasizing body shape on VH-Bars."

"Aahhh…that's right. I don't know what it is, but these kids this year just aren't maintaining the correct shape throughout their transition from flagpole."

"I know. It seems they are just a bit too lazy or care more about completing higher difficulty skills, and not focusing on the fundamentals," Ugu continued stretching.

"That's exactly what I think. Well said."

"Well, I'd be happy to add another sub-unit to your reference guide on *VH-Bars: Form and Function*. Perhaps even add in another holo demo with your notes added in to really drive home the point."

"That sounds like a wonderful idea. Perhaps we should add that to our agenda for tomorrow."

Ugu was still stretching, focusing on her neck now. "Actually, sir, I already added in a full schedule for tomorrow. We are replacing your old notes on Pommel Clock with an updated version to highlight some of your comments on the newer skills we've seen this year."

"Oh, that's right."

"But I have some time now."

"Oh, you don't really have to. I know this is your detention week, but you can enjoy some free time."

"Oh, it's my pleasure. I really want to help." Ugu flashed a sweet smile.

"OK, I suppose I can put in a couple hours this evening."

Ugu and Professor Marino went to work. Ugu knew she had the stamina to outlast Professor Marino, but she was also trying to soften him up, so that he would agree to allow her to take a run on the Outer Loop with Whitfield. Ugu kept stretching in front of Professor Marino, occasionally commenting on not being used to sitting still for so long. After about two and a half hours of intense work redesigning Professor Marino's judging course, Ugu sensed he was tiring and she thought it was time to move forward with her plan. "Sir, I think we have made some great progress tonight. Do you want to start on another chapter?"

"Wow. You really are full of energy, aren't you?"

"Yes, I usually head out to the Outer Loop to run a few laps every night, you know, to burn off some energy."

"Yes, I sometimes see you coming home late with your running shoes on."

Ugu continued stretching. "You do? Hmm, I didn't think anyone noticed. Anyway, I think that's why I'm so tight now. Haven't run in a few days."

"Yes, well, that's unfortunate."

Ugu sensed Professor Marino was softening. "I know. It's entirely my fault. And, I know what I did to Dr. Crawfish was wrong, and I deserve to pay the penalty."

"Well, yes, I suppose that is what you are doing."

"Oh, wow, my legs are so tight." Ugu leaned forward, stretching her hamstrings.

That's when Professor Marino cracked. "Look, if you want, I can allow you to run on the Outer Loop tonight, but just for a short while."

"Oh, sir, I couldn't."

"No. No. I will allow it. You certainly can use the exercise. I'll allow it under a few conditions."

Ugu needed to be sure she would be allowed to run with Whitfield, so she pretended to be fearful. "Oh, please don't say I have to run alone. I ran alone at the beginning of the school year, and came across some kids teasing me. I got really scared. Now, I always make sure I run with Whitfield. Especially at night."

Professor Marino grew slightly suspicious. "No, that's not where I was going. Although, if you were to meet up with your boyfriend, I do not want any funny business going on. You are being temporarily released on my orders, for the sole purpose of running in the Outer Loop. That's it."

"Of course, sir. I would never think to abuse your trust."

"Good. Just to be sure, you will need to wear this special tracker." Professor Marino handed Ugu a similar tracker to the one she made him wear during his live-streamed journey during the Judges Ball. Ugu had to think fast.

"Sir, I'm not sure how comfortable I am with having you watch me as I run. I do have my personal tracker on though. You can track my location at all times on your monitor."

Professor Marino hesitated. "Yes, I suppose you are right. OK. I'll track you using your device. You are not to leave the Outer Loop for any reason. You are to report back here immediately upon your return. You have one hour."

"Oh, sir, thank you so much. My body really needs this. I normally run for about 90 minutes, but one hour is plenty. I am very grateful, sir."

"You are welcome. Remember, no funny business."

Ugu placed her hand over her heart. "I promise."

"OK. Now go make your plans with Whitfield and let me know when you plan on leaving."

"Thank you again, sir. You are so generous." Ugu went upstairs. Her plan was off to a terrific start. Whitfield was scheduled to arrive in about an hour, which gave her little time to review every last detail before heading out.

****

The mission was being executed to near perfection. Whitfield and Ugu ran a lap around the Outer Loop and continued almost three-quarters around a second lap when about a dozen students came running in the opposite direction. Whitfield, Ugu, and Flaherty all ducked aside, with Ugu never hesitating as she reached Slide 13-WL and shot through the trap door. Whitfield grabbed Flaherty by the waist and held her close in the alcove, allowing the entrance door to close. The enclosed area was built for one person at a time to use the slide, so with both Whitfield and Flaherty sharing the space, their bodies were pressed tight against each other.

Flaherty thought it would be wise to keep the entrance door closed for most of the ten-minute time frame to prevent anyone passing by from interfering with the plan. Ugu had already given detailed instructions to Fenway's security agents to not grant access to anyone attempting to use that slide, and instead to direct them to another slide. She also warned the security agents against opening the trapdoor with Whitfield and Flaherty inside.

As expected, Professor Marino was watching his monitors intently, and grew concerned when he noticed the large group pass by and two trackers huddled together by Slide 13-WL. He was still able to read Whitfield's name on his monitor, as he was purposefully tracking Ugu's boyfriend, but the other tracker's signal was weak.

"Hot marbles! She tricked me. She is up there having a good 'ol time with her boyfriend, while I sit here and stew about it. No sir. I am going to nab her, once and for all. Aarrgghhh…I trusted her." Professor Marino got up from his desk, but did not want to leave his monitors unattended. He opened his door and saw Aspen standing in the hallway.

"Sir, I was wondering…"

Professor Marino threw up his hand. "Never mind that. I need you to watch my screens. Can you do that?"

"Sure. I guess. But what am I watching for?"

"Your brother and Ugu are making a fool out of me. I need to catch them in the act."

"Uhh…OK?"

"Just watch the monitors and tell me if those two dots move at all."

Aspen just shrugged. "OK." He played his role perfectly. Professor Marino never would have guessed Aspen was in on the plan.

Professor Marino left in a huff. Aspen waited for about 90 seconds after Professor Marino left to start his hack. He pulled up Marino's class roster from Term 2 and identified all students living in Seraphina's house. He then pulled up Marino's gradebook and adjusted eight students' grades downward two levels, and waited.

Within 60 seconds, Professor Marino had two calls come into his office and 30 seconds later, had three new messages from affected students. Clearly, Aspen's hack worked. He needed to wait another few minutes before resetting the grades and sending out the apology 'glitch' message. In the meantime, he deleted all traces of the incoming messages and hoped Professor Marino hadn't been checking the incoming messages on his own tracker.

****

Ugu stealthily navigated her way through the trees and Seraphina's backyard to reach Jonathan's window. When she got there, Jonathan was still in his room, at his desk, but there was a knock on his door. Jonathan tried ignoring it, but eventually got up and was immediately pulled into a heated discussion concerning Professor Marino's inexplicable grade changes. Jonathan left without closing his door, but Ugu couldn't wait any longer.

Time was short, and she had to retrieve the surveillance equipment. Ugu opened the window and pounced inside. She quickly detached and disassembled each of three primary pieces of surveillance equipment from inside Jonathan's room, along with the other pieces just outside his window frame. Ugu was about to leave when she remembered Sir Arlington's advice to check the closets, dressers, and under the bed, even though she wasn't entirely sure why he had added this request. With the door open, it was risky, but Ugu checked the closets and dressers and didn't find anything of note.

Then, she heard Jonathan's voice just outside the doorway. She turned around and saw the back of Jonathan's head. She swore she was caught, but Jonathan was busy yelling at one of his housemates and hadn't yet seen Ugu. She had to move quickly, but the window was too far away. Ugu scrambled and hid under Jonathan's bed.

Jonathan came back into his room, slammed the door, and sat down at his desk. He looked over and noticed the window was open, uttered some obscenities and closed it without giving it much thought. Ugu was trapped in Jonathan's room. She was running out of time. If she didn't think of something fast, Professor Marino was going to catch Whitfield and Flaherty, and they would both get into trouble. Ugu couldn't let that happen. She was out of options. Ugu looked around under the bed for something she could use and only found some boxes and a bunch of loose papers.

One paper, in particular, caught her attention. It was labeled '*Seven Bridges Academy—Entrance Exam—Do Not Distribute*'. The three boxes were also labeled *Entrance Exams*. Ugu wondered what Jonathan was doing with Seven Bridges' entrance exams, but couldn't get caught up in thinking about that now. She had to move fast.

Ugu silently slinked out from under the bed and reached for one of Jonathan's dirty shirts and wrapped in around her head. She knew she would have to be quick to get out of there, but couldn't take the chance of Jonathan catching a glimpse of her face. Ugu grabbed Jonathan's grips bag and threw it hard against the opposite wall.

Jonathan screamed and turned his head directly toward the point of impact. Ugu quickly moved in from the opposite direction and swiftly delivered a roundhouse kick to Jonathan's right temple, knocking him out cold. Ugu heard someone yell through the door, asking if Jonathan was OK. Ugu grabbed her bag, took Jonathan's dirty shirt off her head and threw it on the floor, opened the window and jumped out just as the bedroom door opened.

Ugu had escaped just in time, but still needed to get back to Fenway's mansion and race up the ramp. Ugu ran as fast as she could through backyards without being seen and made it back to Fenway's house two minutes late. She quickly grabbed some ice and towels and tucked them into her bag as she climbed the ramp.

By the time she had reached the top, Professor Marino was already there, looking stern as he surveyed the scene in front of him. Whitfield was holding Flaherty's ankle and putting her though a series of mobility tests. Ugu could not tell for how long Professor Marino had been waiting, but he looked angry.

"You have some explaining to do. Just where have you been?"

Ugu remained calm. "One moment, sir. Flaherty, how are you? Here, I was able to get you some ice."

"Thank you. It still really hurts." Flaherty winced in fake pain.

Professor Marino was growing impatient. "I'm waiting."

"Sir, I'm sorry. We were running on the Outer Loop, like you said we could, and we saw Flaherty. There was a large group running and she must have tripped and twisted her ankle. We pulled her over to the side so no one else would trip over her and…"

Professor Marino interrupted. "Yes, yes, I heard all that from them. Why did you leave the Outer Loop?"

"To get ice, sir."

"But you are in Level 1 Detention. You are not permitted to leave the premises without permission."

Flaherty spoke through gritted teeth. "Sir, I'm sorry, but my ankle hurt really bad and I sent Ugu to get ice. I needed Whitfield here with me."

"Thank you, Flaherty. I appreciate your predicament, but you are not authorized to grant permission for a student to leave during her incarceration period."

Whitfield attempted to defuse the situation and shoulder the blame. "With all due respect, sir, Flaherty was injured, and no person of authority was immediately available. I made the call to stay with Flaherty and send Ugu for ice. If anyone is to be punished here it should be me."

"Thank you, Whitfield. I think you may be on to something here. You knew Ugu was serving out her punishment and instead of running for ice yourself, you decided to snuggle up with Miss Flaherty here."

Ugu acted surprised and while turning toward Whitfield, feigned outrage. "Excuse me? Snuggle up with Flaherty? What were you two doing?"

Whitfield was caught off guard. "Nothing. She hurt her ankle."

Professor Marino continued to light the fuse that was growing inside Ugu. "That may be so, but then why were you two in the slide alcove with the door closed?"

Ugu's face reddened. "What?"

Professor Marino continued, "yes, I tracked Whitfield throughout this entire episode. I saw him and someone I believed to be Ugu together inside the slide alcove with the entrance door closed. Now, if Ugu really did go get ice, that means Whitfield and Flaherty were in there together. How were you tending to her ankle inside such a tight space? Can you answer me that, Whitfield?"

Ugu realized Whitfield might be in a tough spot and seized her opportunity by yelling and screaming. "YOU LYING CHEATER! How could you? I thought we had something special." Ugu proceeded to punch Whitfield square in his nose and again across his left cheek.

When Whitfield bent over, Ugu raised her knee and hit him right in his jaw. Flaherty yelled out for Ugu to stop. Whitfield fell to the ground and Ugu kicked him once more in the gut before Professor Marino stepped in to break it up.

"That's enough. Ugu, you go stand over there and wait for me. Flaherty, I suggest you go home. That is, if your ankle is up to it." Professor Marino strongly insinuated that Flaherty was faking her injury.

Flaherty wasn't quite sure what to make of what just happened. She just witnessed her two best friends get into a huge fight, and all over a misunderstanding. She and Whitfield hadn't done anything, and Ugu should have known that. After all, it was her plan in the first place. Not knowing exactly what to do next, Flaherty stood up and took a feeble step toward Ugu, who callously flung her bag at Flaherty. "Here, take your towels and wraps. I hope your ankle feels better, you boyfriend-stealer."

Ugu genuinely looked upset and hurt. Flaherty didn't know what to say. She simply caught the bag, turned around, and walked, with an exaggerated limp, around the Outer Loop, back to her mansion.

Professor Marino looked down at a somewhat bloodied Whitfield. "Well, I think you have suffered enough tonight. Go home and get yourself cleaned up."

Professor Marino turned and caught up with Ugu, who had already started walking back home. "Ugu, stop right there." Ugu stopped and turned to face Professor Marino. She had tears in her eyes.

"I am willing to forget about your leaving the Outer Loop. Whether or not Flaherty actually twisted her ankle, I am not sure, and maybe you're not sure either. I will trust that you were fooled into thinking that she actually needed ice. But I cannot forgive your assault on another student, even one who may have deserved what he got. I am going to call security. You will be arrested."

With tears in her eyes, Ugu protested, "but, sir…"

"I know. I may have done the same thing if I were in your shoes, but I, too, would have to live with the consequences. You are fully aware of our policy on fighting. I have no choice, but to submit for your immediate arrest."

Professor Marino called security and remained with Ugu in the Outer Loop until two agents arrived. For the second time in a week, Ugu had been arrested. She was now one step closer to her ultimate goal, reaching the inside of the bank's basement.

"Sir, can I just send Aspen a note. I promised him that I would help him with a poem for class, and since I'm not going home tonight, I'm afraid he'll be unprepared for class tomorrow."

"Sure."

Ugu had wanted to send messages to both Flaherty and Whitfield, but knew Professor Marino would be monitoring her communication. Instead, she sent a series of six messages to Aspen:

23:09: *It's time. Add three plain drops over your own open space. Go enjoy.*

23:10: *Yes. Stop piling wins after at least one fan falls alone. Add ten.*

23:12: *Eleven if glowing. Smile alone by the fire as truth can not store.*

23:12: *Fly high. For it matters like red eggs battered. Still one two more.*

23:13: *Own ten over ten. Who flies or she glides. None stop and again.*

23:14: *The clown hears flying peeps howling at other elephants. Often awake not woken.*

Sure enough, Professor Marino stood over Ugu's shoulder, making sure she was only communicating with Aspen, and not sending messages to anyone else, especially Whitfield. The pressure of Marino's intrusion would have flustered just about anyone; however, Ugu remained calm while she completed her night's mission.

"So, that's poetry, huh? I'll never understand that stuff. I think I'll stick with gymnastics."

Ugu had dried her eyes, and attempted to return to her usual sweet demeanor. "Oh, sir, I think you should give it a try. I mean, I'm not very good at it, but I think you would be great. You just have to let your feelings out."

"That's OK. Thanks anyway."

Ugu was able to send out her hidden message to Aspen without Professor Marino suspecting a thing.

Chapter 34
Birthday Planning

Although they knew the ultimate goal was for Ugu to get arrested three times so that she would have access to SBA Bank's basement, Whitfield and Flaherty were still shocked by Ugu's actions last night. Neither had expected Ugu to react in such a hostile manner, and both had hoped her actions leading to her second arrest were all part of the larger plan, and that she was not genuinely upset with either of them for being so close to each other in the slide alcove. Aspen's ability to quickly and adeptly decrypt Ugu's late-night message went a long way in calming their fears.

"C'mon guys, cheer up. Ugu still loves you. Let me read the decryption again. It says, 'tell Whitfield I love him. Tell Flaherty I love her. Tonight was all part of plan. Two down. One to go.' So, cheer up, it was all part of her plan."

"Yeah, I guess so, but I just wish she would've told us about it." Whitfield didn't like being kept in the dark.

"She did tell us about most of the plan. Maybe she improvised at the end, or maybe she knew if she did tell you that you might not have gone through with it."

Flaherty thought Aspen made a good point. "I could see that. You probably would've fallen down right away before she even hit you. She had to make it look real or else Professor Marino would have known something was up."

Whitfield rubbed his jaw. "Well, yeah. That really hurt. She's strong, you know."

"Oh, believe me, I know. And I'm sure she was holding back too, so don't ever mess with my Ugu."

"You got that right. I never want her to actually be mad at me. My body can't take any more damage."

"Oh, stop being such a softie."

Aspen chuckled. "Haha…you do complain a lot."

"Yeah, how would you like it if someone punched you and…"

"See."

"Whitfield, Aspen's right. Stop complaining so much."

Whitfield sighed deeply. "OK. You're right. Let's move on. Flaherty, did you bring Ugu's bag with all that surveillance stuff back to Sir Arlington?"

"Yes. Dropped it off last night. He was a bit confused why Ugu hadn't delivered it herself. I figured he was going to find out about what happened anyway, so I told him. He acted a bit strange, though. Almost as though he expected it."

"Maybe he had already heard about it from Professor Marino, or the security agents told him."

"Or maybe Ugu told him her plan."

"I suppose any of those possibilities could be true. I just thought it was odd, that's all. I expected him to be a little more surprised."

"Well, maybe if she punched him in the nose, he'd be surprised."

"Oh, Whitfield, enough already. You got a little boo-boo. Suck it up."

Aspen chuckled again.

"You're right. We have to come to the realization that Ugu is going to be incarcerated for at least another two weeks. Does anyone know how Level 2 Detention works? I didn't pay much attention when Jonathan served out his sentence earlier in the year."

"Me neither. But I may have an idea. Well, I think so. I've never had it myself, but Niell's chief-of-staff got Level 2 Detention last year."

Aspen looked up. "Niell? Who's that?"

"He was on the team last year. He graduated, and I think he's competing in the minors somewhere, but I haven't heard anything about him in a while. We weren't really that close."

"So, what do you know about Level 2 Detention?"

"Right. So, Ugu will still have to serve out her complete Level 1 sentence first. They could conceivably extend her sentence for misbehavior while in detention, but that's unlikely. Instead, she will probably go straight to the Level 2 Detention area immediately upon being released."

Whitfield was still looking for answers. "Where is the Level 2 Detention area?"

"The Uniform Galleria."

Aspen thought that might not be so bad. "Really? She's going to shop for clothes for two weeks?"

"Not exactly. It's really quite awful. She's going to be put on display inside a glass box on the third floor where students are encouraged to mock her, write mean things on the glass, and otherwise make her stay in the Box as uncomfortable, demeaning, and embarrassing as possible."

Aspen quickly changed his mind. "Whoa. That sounds cruel."

"I know. She is going to be so miserable in there."

Whitfield felt sad for Ugu. "And we encouraged her to do it."

Aspen looked on the bright side. "It's for a good cause. We need to find out who's behind all this cheating."

"Yeah, but it should have been me."

"Whitfield, we discussed this. It had to be Ugu. She knew what she was signing up for."

"Yeah, well, it doesn't make me feel any better about it."

"What can we do? She has to serve her sentence."

"That may be true. But there is no way I'm going to let her suffer alone. I'm going to be there every minute."

"Bro, what about classes? What about practice?"

"I'll skip them both. I don't care. She doesn't deserve to be alone." Whitfield really felt bad for Ugu and even though he had no reason to feel this way, he felt guilty.

"Whitfield, I understand how you feel. But, Ugu will really kick your butt if you miss class, or practice, for her. We'll figure out another way."

"We better. Or else I'm going to break into that glass box and stay with her the entire time."

"Don't worry, bro. We'll come up with something. But we have something else to think about first."

"What's that?"

"Uhh…did you forget? Flaherty's birthday is coming up?"

Whitfield totally forgot. "Oh, shoot. That's right. Happy birthday, Flaherty."

"Well, thank you, but it's not today. It's not until Tuesday, but we are going to celebrate it this weekend. Whitfield, you do know that it's your brother's birthday next week too, right?"

"What? No, his birthday isn't until the 4th."

"Yeah, that's coming up soon. Wow, you are really not good at remembering this stuff."

Whitfield completely lost track of the calendar. "I'm sorry. I've just got a lot on my mind."

Aspen thought about getting mad at his brother for nearly forgetting his birthday, but decided to cut him some slack. "That's OK. I understand."

"So, what are we doing for both of you?"

"Well, even though Aspen's birthday isn't until closer to next weekend, we have a meet that weekend, so I think Ugu was planning something for this weekend."

Aspen considered their current predicament. "I think those plans might take a back seat now."

Flaherty wasn't so sure. "I wouldn't put it past her to still make something work from her detention cell, but yes, we shouldn't burden her with this stuff."

"I don't know. Birthdays are really a big deal around here. Flaherty, what did you do for your birthday last year?"

Flaherty's face lit up. She loved talking about her birthday. "For the past two years, Ugu and I have organized an on-campus fun weekend for 200 underprivileged kids from around the country. We cleared it with Sir Arlington and he provided us with funds. We flew everyone to campus, showed them around and had all the kids over our houses. Some other students volunteered too. We each took groups of them and played games, talked about life on campus, and a bunch of other things. We couldn't fit all the kids in just mine and Gabe's mansions for the entire weekend, so we got just about every house to agree to have a group of kids stay with them for the weekend. It was really fun."

Aspen was impressed. "Wow, that's really amazing!"

"Yeah, it was."

"Well, are you guys doing that again this year?" Whitfield didn't see why Ugu's incarceration should prevent underprivileged kids from coming to campus.

"No. We had asked Sir Arlington about a month ago if we can do it again, but he said the school no longer had funds available for that type of thing. Strange, huh?"

Aspen was shocked. "What? I thought the school had unlimited funds."

Flaherty shook her head. "Me too. Well, maybe not unlimited, but certainly enough for something like this. The kids all had a blast and I think every student who participated with the kids loved it. Ugu and I both thought it was strange that Sir Arlington denied our request, especially since the team keeps winning and we seem to have more and more resources."

Whitfield thought the corruption they uncovered might have something to do with it. "Well, maybe those excess resources are dwindling with Dr. Hewitt sending out payments to these mystery accounts. What if he really is attempting to drain our school's resources?"

"Well, that's what we're trying to find out, bro."

"Yeah. And Ugu is suffering for it." Whitfield, Flaherty, and Aspen all took a brief moment to contemplate their current situation.

Aspen tried to find a cheerful solution. "Look, Ugu is still in the mansion this weekend. She doesn't start serving Level 2 until Tuesday. Let's do something big this weekend for our birthdays. We can combine efforts. Do you think if we both went to Sir Arlington, he could find enough money to bring kids to campus?"

"Not likely. Besides, it's too late. Organizing something like that takes weeks."

"What about if we went to visit the kids? Combined, we have over 80 students in our two houses. If everyone goes someplace different, we can cover the entire country."

"That's a great thought, Aspen, but Ugu can't leave her mansion. We shouldn't leave without her."

"Oh, right."

"But, wait. That could still work." An idea sparked in Flaherty's head.

"You're not thinking of having her violate her detention again, are you?"

"No, Whitfield, of course not."

"Good."

"But look, it's our birthdays and we should do something good for others. I think if our staff members all paired up, we could visit about 25-30 children's hospitals, senior centers, food shelters, schools, and other places."

Aspen was confused by Flaherty's math. "Why not 40?"

"Well, not everyone will be able to go on such short notice, and you and I will need security, and…"

Whitfield politely cut her off. "No, if we're going to do this, let's do it right. One hundred visits. I'll talk to my guys and I know Keegan, Seraphina, Chloe, Sydney, McKenzie, and probably others will all be in as well."

Aspen was growing cautiously optimistic. "You think? I know some of the guys on the team were talking about traveling off-campus this weekend."

"So, we'll lose some of them. We don't need every student. Just 200. Plus, some added security."

Flaherty wanted this idea to work, but wasn't sure yet. "You really think this will work? We have to get it all set up today. How are we…" Just then, the thought hit all three of them at the same time.

"Ugu!"

****

Whitfield, Aspen, and Flaherty were feeling a whole lot better after their morning chat. They walked together over to their weekly staff meeting, which for the three of them simply brought them together with the same familiar faces they see every day in practice. Usually, these gymnast staff meetings lacked any true substance, and served more as a forum for Wilson, Diego, and Reid to complain about their staffs, but this week's gathering afforded Flaherty and Aspen the opportunity to discuss their birthday plans and to gauge interest from the others. To their delight, several other gymnasts seemed particularly interested in visiting different places to spread cheer and hope to those less fortunate. Several others, however, turned down the invitation, mostly due to previous plans to vacation off-campus for the weekend, just as Aspen had speculated.

Now that they had a list of volunteers for the weekend, Whitfield, Aspen, and Flaherty headed over to Aspen's house to wait for Ugu to come upstairs after her detention session with Professor Marino. To their surprise, Ugu did not appear at 15:00 as expected. Instead, Professor Marino came up the stairs alone.

"Aspen, good to see you. Ugu will be up shortly. She's just wrapping up a few things now. As for you two, I am a little surprised to see you both here…and together again." Through their excitement in planning Flaherty and Aspen's joint birthday activities, Whitfield and Flaherty had completely forgotten that Professor Marino was still under the impression the Ugu was upset with both of them and that showing up together might not have been the best look. "Ugu does not wish to see either of you. Now, I suggest you both leave immediately. Good day."

Whitfield and Flaherty looked at each other. They knew they should leave. Ugu was probably still playing up the whole fabricated incident from last night, so as to not raise any suspicion from Professor Marino. It really hurt Whitfield that he could not see Ugu, especially since the last time he did see her, she whooped his butt.

Whitfield said goodbye to Aspen. "Hey, bro, I guess I'll catch you later."

"Yeah. I guess."

Flaherty gave Aspen a hug. "You going to be OK?"

"Yeah, I'll be fine."

"Good. I'll be at the lab all afternoon and then maybe we can go to Plank 'N Steins later tonight, after practice."

Whitfield thought that was a good idea. "Yeah, I'm going to head over to the library now, but Plank 'N Steins sounds good."

"Sure. I'll stay here with Ugu for a while. Lots to talk about. I'll see you at practice."

Professor Marino interjected himself into the conversation. "Yes, I bet there is. Look, this may be none of my business, but it's not right what you two have done to that girl downstairs. She really did care about you, Whitfield. You too, Flaherty. Have you no shame?"

"Sir, it's not what you…"

Flaherty quickly cut Whitfield off. "Sir, we know what you are saying, and we are terribly sorry. What we did wasn't right, and we both hope to sit down with Ugu soon to clear everything up."

"I should hope so, because she is devastated right now. And your plan to sit down and clear the air will have to be delayed for another two weeks. Ugu's being transferred tomorrow to the Level 2 Detention area."

Whitfield stood in disbelief. "Tomorrow? I thought her Level 1 sentence wasn't over until Tuesday."

"Got a call last night from Sir Arlington. Seems to think she is in need of more immediate rehabilitation."

Whitfield, Aspen, and Flaherty all exchanged worried glances. Flaherty seemed to be the most composed. "Thank you for the heads up, sir. We should be leaving now." Whitfield and Flaherty said goodbye to Aspen, quietly told him to move forward with the plan, and quickly rushed out of the mansion.

Whitfield was still in shock. "I can't believe she's going to be in the Glass Box tomorrow. We have to call off the birthday trips."

"No, we can't do that. We already told the team. They're telling everyone in their houses now."

"So. We'll just tell them it got canceled."

"No. That would just make things worse."

"Well, I'm not going. I can't leave her by herself."

"Whitfield, you have to go. It's just one day. You'll be back the same day. Besides, if we get 200 students to go with us, that's fewer students that would be here to see her in the Glass Box."

Whitfield was defiant. "That's still over 800 students here though."

Flaherty tried her best to calm Whitfield. "Yeah, and many of them are leaving campus for the weekend. Look, Ugu can take care of herself. Besides, she loves planning these trips. She'll be busy all day tomorrow checking in on everyone, acting as command central for over 100 missions. This will be good for her."

Whitfield shook his head. "I don't know. I hope you're right."

"Trust me. I know Ugu. She's strong and she'll get through this just fine." Whitfield and Flaherty went their separate ways, each to study for class. Whitfield still wasn't convinced he was doing the right thing by agreeing to leave campus while Ugu was being transferred into the Glass Box. Flaherty was hoping she was right, and that her best friend would be OK without her.

****

Ugu's eyes were red and her face blotchy as she appeared in the kitchen. Her hair was a mess, and she carried a wad of tissues in her left hand. She had obviously been crying most of the day. Aspen saw her and instinctively gave her a hug. Ugu hugged him back and asked Professor Marino if they could go upstairs. Ugu didn't need Professor Marino's permission to leave the kitchen, as it was after 15:00 and she could go anywhere she desired inside the mansion, but she still felt Professor Marino deserved this modicum of respect as he had comforted her throughout the day, as though she were his own child.

Aspen and Ugu left the kitchen, and as soon as they turned the corner out of view of Professor Marino's watchful eyes, Ugu's demeanor completely changed. She was back to her usual cheerful and upbeat self again. She smiled, for the first time all day, and it felt good. Ugu and Aspen caught each other up on the day's events, and Aspen shared with Ugu their plans for jointly celebrating his and Flaherty's birthdays.

"Aspen, that's a wonderful idea! Oh wow, I love it! When Flaherty and I couldn't get the school to pay to bring the kids out here, I thought about doing something like this. Oh, this is incredible. I need to get started."

"Wait. Don't you want to relax or something? You just got out of the basement."

"No way! I had to pretend to be upset all day long. It was not easy. Professor Marino wouldn't leave me alone for a second. I had to practically beg him to let me get some work done. No, I need to do something productive."

"OK, if that's what you want."

"Yes, that's what I want. Hey, you can help if you want to."

"Sure. What do you want me to do?" Aspen and Ugu continued to work together for the next several hours. They were still going strong when Aspen noticed the time and had to hustle to make it to practice on time. There was still a lot to do, but Ugu assured him that she could handle it. "Are you sure? I can be late for practice."

"Nonsense. Get out of here. I'll be fine."

"If you say so." Aspen started to leave.

"Hey, Aspen."

"Yeah."

"Thanks for staying with me. You're a really good friend." Aspen smiled and left for practice.

****

By the time the sun rose on Saturday morning, Ugu had successfully planned 104 'missions' to children's hospitals, senior centers, food and clothing shelters, schools, and a host of other charitable organizations across the country for willing and able Seven Bridges' students to visit and spread hope and cheer. Ugu had scheduled transportation, filled out agendas for the entire day, and confirmed every site visit with all appropriate parties. All that was left to do was for the students to make their way to their designated transportation pick-ups and be on their way. Ugu would actively monitor all missions from her own monitors and confirmed with Sir Arlington that she would be able to continue her role even after being delivered to the Glass Box.

Given the overwhelmingly positive attributes surrounding Ugu's latest project and the overall good-natured vibes encompassing a dual gymnast birthday weekend celebration, Sir Arlington agreed to discreetly move Ugu into the Glass Box, opting to forego the usual fanfare and ominous heckling and taunting that typically accompanied such a journey across campus for any student about to be placed in the Level 2 Detention area.

Ugu greatly appreciated Sir Arlington's discretion and settled into her new 'home' for the next two weeks. The 12x15 foot glass box included one twin bed, one desk, and one chair. Bedsheets, two pillows, and two blankets were also provided. Dressers and closets were unnecessary as all clothes could be ordered directly from inside the Uniform Galleria and delivered through the tiny mail slot across from the desk. Worn clothes would be sent out through the same mail slot, where they would fall into a hamper and be picked up for laundry service.

In one corner of the floor, a 3x3 foot platform lowered into a full bathroom, located underneath the Glass Box, where Ugu could shower, change clothes, and use the toilet. The Glass Box was also equipped with electrochromatic walls for a sliver of privacy, allowing Ugu to temporarily adjust the walls' opacity; however, these settings were limited to only 15 minutes per day, to be used at Ugu's discretion, and were intended primarily for detained students wishing to change clothes without descending into the bathroom.

Ugu was in good spirits when she arrived, and immediately settled in. She didn't bother testing out the bed or any of the privacy controls, and didn't even lower herself into the bathroom to inspect the only other 'room' available to her. Instead, she got right to work monitoring every mission and responding to all inquiries. Even though she was on full display for all to see, the Uniform Galleria was unusually quiet, and Ugu felt right at home leading command central for the weekend, feeling oddly optimistic that these next two weeks wouldn't be that bad after all.

All of that changed when Jonathan walked through the door on the third floor. Having spent two weeks in the Box earlier in the school year, Jonathan knew just how awful it could be, and had every intention of making Ugu's stay as miserable as possible. He began with some childish insults hoping to hurt Ugu's feelings, but quickly moved on to picking up one of several markers hanging on strings outside the box and started writing nasty words and drawing inappropriate pictures on the glass.

The galleria workers on the third floor watched scornfully, but were powerless to stop such actions. Jonathan was not in violation of the Seven Bridges Academy Student Code of Conduct, which encouraged mocking, ridiculing, and insulting those students who found themselves in the Glass Box. Occasionally, a fellow student walking on the third floor would ask Jonathan to stop harassing Ugu, but the mean-spirited Jonathan simply ignored their requests and continued with his deplorable actions.

To Ugu's credit, she largely ignored Jonathan, for the first hour, at least. But Jonathan was just getting started. He began by banging on the glass. "Hey, loser, I know you are trying to ignore me, but it won't work. You're going to break down. You're going to cry. And, I'm the one who is going to break you. Hahaha." Ugu just kept working. "Oh, this is going to be so much fun. I have to go pick something up, but don't worry, I'll be right back. Try not to miss me too much." Ugu just kept working. "Oh, I almost forgot. Did you happen to ask for an extra blanket?" Ugu just kept working. "No? Well, you may want to ask for one. It's about to get really cold in there."

Jonathan adjusted the air-controlled temperature inside the Glass Box down to a frosty 42 degrees Fahrenheit. He waved at Ugu and left, laughing.

Thirty minutes later, Ugu was shivering. She was having difficulty keeping her hands and fingers warm enough to type. One of the workers had seen what Jonathan had done and, even though she couldn't adjust the thermostat herself, she did bring over some extra blankets, a sweater, a hat, and gloves. Ugu greatly appreciated the gesture, but couldn't effectively type with gloves on, and couldn't keep warm without them.

Jonathan returned about an hour later, and to his delight, Ugu was visibly uncomfortable. He was able to see her breath fogging up the glass in front of her, and her ability to type fast had been severely impacted. Ugu had planned to continue ignoring Jonathan, but he was not alone. He had brought three of his friends with him, all with despicable intentions.

Each of the four ill-mannered friends started banging relentlessly on the walls of the Glass Box, one on each side, so Ugu had nowhere to turn to avoid the distraction. She knew that Jonathan was the leader of his small band of troublemakers and that she wouldn't be able to regain her concentration until he stopped. Ugu needed to figure out a way to get back to her work to ensure every student completed their mission, and returned home to campus safely. She allowed herself to look at Jonathan for the first time, and she couldn't help but smile.

The side of Jonathan's face, from the temple down to just below the cheekbone and around to below his eye was badly discolored from bruising. Bruising that she was directly responsible for. Not only that, but Jonathan was wearing the same dirty shirt she had left behind on the floor in his room when she delivered her perfectly executed roundhouse kick. She wondered whether Jonathan was sending her a message by wearing that particular shirt, but quickly discarded the thought and concluded that he was simply just a slob and couldn't be bothered bringing clothes to the laundry.

"What are you smiling at, you piece of dirt?"

Ugu stood up and walked toward Jonathan. "Just imagining how you might have received that bruise on your face."

"Shut up, loser. I got it while trying a new skill on Tri-Bars. Something so difficult that none of your pathetic friends on the team can do."

"Oh, really? Wow, that must be some skill. The bruising seems to run all the way from your temple, covering most of the right side of your face. Did it hurt?"

Jonathan scoffed. "Please. Nothing hurts me. Except maybe your ugly face."

Ugu continued to smile and remained calm. "Aww, thank you for noticing my face, but I am very curious about your face. Did you lose consciousness at all when it happened? I mean, a blow like that could really startle someone."

Jonathan was starting to show signs of growing frustration. "No. Of course not. I told you; nothing can hurt me."

Ugu sat back down and tied her shoe, the same shoe she used to kick Jonathan in the head, while cleverly devising a plan to trick Jonathan into leaving her alone.

"Well, you must have an incredibly high tolerance for pain then, because a shot like that would probably knock out a lesser student. Then, of course, they would have to see Nurse Vogleburg for BH and TS testing, go to Professor Pineiro to get their trackers reset, and obviously register with the Administration Office to get their automatic passing grades for the term. Phew, it's a good thing you weren't knocked out." Through years of training, Ugu had perfected her ability to lie effectively, without committing any obvious tells.

Jonathan fell for Ugu's lies, and appeared concerned. He looked around to his friends, but none of them were of any help. "What? What is all that stuff? I didn't know about any of that."

"It was all in our orientation packet first year. Don't you remember?"

"No. Who reads all that stuff?"

"Well, it's all in there. But, why would you care? You weren't knocked out, right?"

"Of course not…but, if someone was knocked out, do they really get passing grades for the entire term?"

Ugu continued messing with Jonathan. "Oh, yes. That's an automatic. Just report to the Admin Office, but only after seeing the nurse first. She has to send over confirmation."

"And what was all that other stuff? BA testing, or something like that?"

"BH testing. Brain Hemorrhaging. Yeah, really scary stuff. Sometimes you don't even feel any symptoms and then, bam, out of nowhere, your brain just stops working. Definitely should get that looked at right away. I'd also go for TS, Tissue Scarring, tests as well. Could be really serious stuff."

"How come I never heard about that?"

"I told you; it's all in the orientation packet. Plus, we covered it in *Cell and Molecular Biology*. Didn't you take that class?"

Jonathan now looked very concerned. "No."

"Well, yeah, it's all in there. And the tracker reset is important too. The electrical impulses are wired to pick up brain activity. If you were ever knocked unconscious, which I know you never were, because you are super tough, but if you were, the tracker could cause brain waves to misfire, and the results could be very dangerous. Oh well, I'm just glad you weren't impacted by any of this. Good thing you are such a tough guy."

Ugu returned to her desk, still wearing the sweater the galleria worker gave her, but refused to wrap herself in the blanket while Jonathan was there. The banging on the glass had stopped during her conversation with Jonathan, and now she heard the four hooligans talking among themselves. Jonathan appeared agitated and worried. He ordered the other three to come with him to the nurse's office and once again, Ugu was left alone, but just for a moment. Emelie and Lisa, two first-year students, were on the third floor and approached the Glass Box after Jonathan and his friends left.

"Hi. Ugu, is it?"

Ugu looked up and smiled. "Yes, hi. You're Emelie, right?"

"Yes, how did you know?"

"I helped set up some of the first-year events this year. I remember seeing you there. And you're Lisa, right?"

"Yes, that's right." Lisa and Emelie were both impressed and flattered that Ugu knew their names.

Emelie quietly asked Ugu a question. "Is what you just said to that boy accurate? Because I did go through the entire orientation packet, and I do not recall seeing anything about what to do after being knocked unconscious."

"Yeah, me too." Lisa was hesitant to agree, just in case she had actually missed important information in the packet.

"Oh, heavens no. I made it all up. I just wanted to scare him enough so that he would leave me alone for a couple hours so I could get back to work."

Emelie and Lisa both laughed hard. "That's brilliant! How did you come up with all that?"

"Just needed to appeal to his sensibilities. He thinks he's so much better than everyone else, but he's really not the sharpest student at Seven Bridges. I knew if I made up some trick for him to pass his classes without putting in any work, he'd jump all over it. But I needed more time, so I tried to scare him into thinking his brain might be impacted too."

"Yeah, but he said he wasn't knocked out. How did you know he would get scared?" Lisa made an excellent point.

Ugu thought about telling Emelie and Lisa how she knew, but opted instead to keep that part a secret and only suggested that it was a hunch. Emelie and Lisa thought Ugu's trick was really quite clever, and instead of engaging in their right to continue making Ugu suffer, they voluntarily adjusted the thermostat, raising the temperature in the Glass Box back up to a comfortable level. Ugu thanked them and went back to work. The two girls left the galleria, awestruck by Ugu's quick thinking and friendly disposition, especially under such difficult conditions.

Chapter 35
The Glass Box

Whitfield, Aspen, and Flaherty all arrived safely back on campus after their respective missions very early on Sunday morning. While they were each able to get some sleep on the drone shuttles coming back to campus, they were all still very tired when they arrived. Flaherty and Aspen decided to head straight home to get some more rest, but Whitfield was determined to see Ugu, even if she was likely be to sleeping. He wanted to be the first one she saw in the morning when she woke up. Whitfield quickly ran home, got changed, grabbed a blanket, pillow, and some snacks, and rushed over to the Uniform Galleria.

The darkness of the night sky was only beginning to soften as the sun hadn't yet risen, but that didn't stop Whitfield from scurrying across the barren entrance quad and ascending the steps to the galleria. Once inside, he climbed to the third floor, fully expecting to see Ugu asleep, and hoping he could catch a couple hours of sleep himself before the morning rush. What he saw when he arrived, however, was a much different scene than he had anticipated.

Jonathan, and about a dozen other students, were yelling at Ugu, all saying rotten and nasty things to her. They were banging on the glass, writing disgusting words and phrases on the glass and in all other ways tormenting Ugu. Inside the Glass Box, Ugu was wearing next to nothing, and sweating profusely. She was wilting on the floor at the foot of her bed, with her head between her knees.

Jonathan had set the temperature inside the Glass Box to 101 degrees Fahrenheit, the highest it could go, and without any true air circulation or passing breeze, the resulting stifling heat was almost too much for anyone to bear.

Whitfield instantly felt his heart breaking seeing Ugu suffer like this, knowing that he was powerless to take on all thirteen taunting students at once. He had to do something though, and fast, before anyone saw him. Too late. Jonathan spotted Whitfield before he could duck away.

Whitfield put down the blanket and other accessories he was carrying and walked toward the mob.

"Hey, everyone, look at who it is. Whitfield. Just in time to see his girlfriend, or should I say, ex-girlfriend, pass out from the heat."

Daulton snickered from beside Jonathan. "Yeah, I heard she really kicked your butt the other day. Knocked you out cold."

Melina piled on. "Yeah, it was probably a cheap shot. You know Ugu always tries to act nice just so she can stab you in the back."

Mirabelle continued banging on the glass. "Yeah, she's trash." The mob continued their relentless harassment of Ugu, who could barely lift her head.

Jonathan wasn't sure of Whitfield's intentions. "So, did you stop by to try to stop us, or are you going to join in?"

Whitfield noticed several students guarding the thermostat, and the rest all had menacing looks on their faces, waiting to pounce on Whitfield if he dared try to offer Ugu any assistance. Whitfield had to carefully weigh his options and think fast. For a moment, he considered pretending to be on Jonathan's side and join the angry mob in hurling insults at Ugu, while hoping to at least get close enough to adjust the thermostat, but ultimately decided to take a different tack. "So, why are you trying to get Ugu to pass out?"

"She deserves it, that lying, filthy cheesehead." Despite the early morning hour, Jonathan was all riled up.

"Whoa, let's watch the language. What did she lie about?"

Daulton was quick to respond. "She told Jonathan that if someone gets knocked unconscious, they automatically pass their classes for the term. We checked it out and the Administration Office never heard of that. She's just a liar."

Whitfield nodded. "Hmm...anything else?"

Mirabelle added to the list of things Ugu had lied about. "Yeah, as a matter of fact, she did tell other lies. She said Jonathan had to get his tracker reset and go for all kinds of tests at the nurse's office. He went and they told him he didn't have to go for any tests. See, she's just a filthy liar."

Again, Whitfield nodded. "I see. And you all heard her say this?"

"No. It was just me, Daulton, Carlton, and Jonathan here when she said it."

"OK. Just a moment. Can I please scoot in there for just a second?" Whitfield slid his way closer to the Glass Box and tapped lightly on the glass. "Hi, sweetie. How are you?"

Ugu lifted her head and saw Whitfield for the first time. She smiled, relieved to see him, and despite still feeling lightheaded and sweating intensely, she got up, walked over to the glass and put her hand up to the glass right where Whitfield had his hand. Despite all that was happening, Ugu's first thought centered on Whitfield. "Everything go OK yesterday?"

Whitfield smiled. "Oh, yeah, it was great. We owe it all to you. Excellent planning."

"Oh good. I was worried that something might go wrong."

Whitfield continued his conversation with Ugu as though no one else was there. "Nope. Everything went smoothly. In fact, we—"

Jonathan interrupted, "hey! This isn't some happy reunion, you two. Knock it off."

Whitfield took a page out of Ugu's book, and remained quite calm. "Just give me a minute, sweetie. I love you."

Ugu smiled. "I love you too."

Whitfield turned to face Jonathan. "OK, so where were we? Oh right, Ugu lied to you."

"That's right. She's a dirty kook."

"Wow, again with the language. OK, here's the deal. Yeah, she lied to you. Why? Because your stupid. And not just you, but…" Whitfield pointed to the other three that were with Jonathan earlier and heard Ugu's lies. "…you, you, and you. All stupid. She played you. Just like she's playing you now. You really think she's going to pass out from the heat? She's a world-class runner. She runs over 12 miles every night. Hot. Cold. Humid. Freezing. Doesn't matter. She can adapt to any climate. She's in there right now laughing at all of you."

Jonathan didn't want to believe Whitfield. "No, you're wrong. Now you're lying."

Whitfield shrugged. "Perhaps. But how do you think she knew you were knocked out the other day?"

Jonathan protested, "I was not."

Whitfield smiled. "Now, who's lying? If you weren't knocked out, then why did you bother running through all those hoops she laid out for you, like a good little pet, by the way."

"Uhh…I had a head injury and didn't want to take any chances. What do you care anyway? I told you I wasn't knocked out."

Whitfield stepped in closer to Jonathan, nearly chest to chest. "Ahh, but you were knocked out, weren't you? I know, because I was there."

A look of utter disbelief, and fright, came over Jonathan. "What? What do you mean?"

Whitfield was desperately hoping he could apply the lessons he learned in his *Lying, Cheating, Stealing, and Deception* class to help save Ugu. "In your room. You, at your desk. Screaming like a little girl." Whitfield now stepped back for everyone to hear. "One kick to the head. That's all it took. Out cold. Thought about tucking you into your little red fireman pajamas, but thought it would be best to leave."

"That was you?"

Mirabelle questioned Whitfield's account. "Jonathan, what's he talking about? You told us you got injured practicing tricks on Tri-Bars."

Whitfield pounced on the opportunity. "Oh, Jonathan. Lying to your friends? Ouch." Whitfield turned to the others. "Sorry, guys. I guess you just need to pick better friends."

Jonathan was struggling to think of something to say. "Hey, why are you smiling? You just admitted to breaking into my room and assaulting me. You're getting arrested for this. Maybe even expelled."

Whitfield shook his head. "No. See, that's not going to happen either. You failed to report the incident, didn't you? Too embarrassed, I guess. I mean, what if it was a lowly first-year student that whooped your butt, or maybe, even a girl? Could you imagine that? A girl, who maybe wasn't even a gymnast, like maybe, Ugu, in there. Imagine if she knocked you out with one simple kick. Wow. No, that would really be too embarrassing to handle, so you never reported the incident. If you do now, you'll have to suffer the penalty, which I believe, for you would be Level 3 Detention, wouldn't it? I know you don't want that, do you?"

Jonathan had never been this angry before. "You are so dead."

Whitfield remained calm. "No, I think I'm going to be just fine. You, on the other hand, have to explain to all these people why you lied to them, and how you could be such a coward."

Ugu chimed in, "and fragile. Don't forget fragile."

"Oh right. Thank you, honey. And fragile. I mean, one kick. Out like a light. Not even my best shot. Hmm…and you claimed to be trying a new skill. No wonder why the team never wanted you in the first place."

The angry mob of students now turned their attention toward Jonathan. They wanted answers, and Jonathan was scrambling to defend himself. In the ensuing chaos, Whitfield was able to reach the thermostat, now left unguarded, and turned it back down to more appropriate levels. As Jonathan rushed out of the galleria, with his posse short on his tail, Whitfield took off his shirt and handed it to Ugu through the mail slot.

Ugu was confused. "Uhh…what are you doing? I know I'm dripping with sweat in here, but you know we're not going swimming now, right? And I don't have an apple with me." Even under extreme conditions, Ugu still kept her wits about her and cracked some jokes.

"Relax. It's nothing like that." Whitfield instructed Ugu to run the shirt under water and add soap to it. Ugu did so, and returned a minute later to return the shirt to Whitfield. Whitfield then asked Ugu to turn on the privacy settings, turning the walls an opaque white color, and to just relax for about ten minutes and get cleaned up, while he used his, now, wet and soapy shirt to scrub the outside walls of the Glass Box clean.

Two galleria workers broke protocol and helped Whitfield clean the profanity off the glass walls. Whitfield grabbed a couple bottles of water and placed them inside the mail slot for Ugu.

The privacy settings remained on for the full fifteen-minute daily allotment, and when the glass finally returned to its transparent form, Ugu was just rising up from the bathroom, having showered and changed into more suitable attire. She grabbed the water waiting for her by the mail slot, and pressed her hand up to the glass for Whitfield. The walls were cleansed of any derogatory messages. There were no more hecklers, at least not at the moment. No more banging on the glass. The third floor was peaceful again. Ugu's first 24 hours inside the Glass Box were trying times, and to be honest, almost broke her, but Whitfield saved her. It wouldn't be the last time they came through to save each other.

****

Ugu's stay in the Glass Box over the next two weeks was full of ups and downs. On the positive side, Whitfield, Aspen, and Flaherty stayed with Ugu, just outside the Box, every chance they could, even alternating which one would sleep there overnight to guard against hecklers and other taunting students. Even though none of them could completely protect Ugu from the taunts, shouts, and evil glances coming her way, it made Ugu feel much more comfortable knowing she had at least one friend with her at all times.

The difficult times came during gymnastics practice and the team's first meet after All-Star Week, its seventh meet overall. Whitfield, Aspen, and Flaherty all committed much of their security staff to stay near Ugu while practice was in session, but it often wasn't enough as that's also when Jonathan and several other obnoxious students would most often visit the Box to cause trouble. The meet weekend was particularly difficult for Ugu, but she managed to live stream the meet on her monitors and tried her best to remain focused on her three best friends, rather than the torturous treatment she was receiving, both inside and outside the Box.

Even though she tried ignoring the outside noise, she still heard every comment and felt hurt by students' relentless insults. Despite being one of the most popular, and well-liked students on campus just a few short weeks ago, Ugu was now being treated as a villain. No one but her closest friends knew why she had assaulted Whitfield in the first place, and she couldn't clear the air by telling anyone else, without risking her ultimate plan.

Ugu just had to bear down and take the humiliation and public embarrassment until her two weeks were up. Ugu was surprised, and saddened, by how many students, who she had always been friendly with, had so quickly turned on her and actively sought to hurt her feelings while she was trapped inside the Glass Box.

One of the strangest traditions at Seven Bridges Academy was the release of a student who had just spent two weeks inside the Glass Box. The whole school was invited to what amounted to a release party, whereby the incarcerated student walked out of the Box to great cheers, hugs, and friendly fist bumps. Students, who had just moments before, and all through the past two weeks, shouted unimaginable insults, threats, and abusive jabs in her direction, were now congratulating Ugu for enduring the Box.

Many apologized for their behavior, claiming they were just upholding school tradition, but Ugu still felt many went far beyond the spirit of the custom, and knew it would be a long time before she could look at many of them in the same way she had before these two weeks commenced.

Aspen and Flaherty were two of the first to greet Ugu upon her release. Aspen hugged Ugu for a long time, but it was nothing compared to the lengthy embrace Flaherty shared with her best friend. Flaherty wiped tears away from her eyes as she hugged Ugu for the first time in weeks. She told Ugu that Whitfield was waiting for her back at Aspen's mansion, and that she should soak in the moment, even though she knew Ugu likely just wanted to get home and rest in her own bed after two weeks of torture.

After a long hour and a half of rejoicing and smiling with her classmates, Ugu finally headed home. She was exhausted, and even though she wanted nothing more than to feel Whitfield's loving arms around her, she knew she needed to get some sleep too. As she approached her house, she hoped Whitfield could understand, and not be too upset with her, if she wasn't wide-eyed and enthusiastic when she saw him. To her surprise, Whitfield wasn't even at her house.

Instead, he left a series of sweet notes, directing her to her bedroom. When she opened the door, she found one last note, on her bed, next to Whitfield's favorite stuffed animal. The note read "Ugu. I love you with all my heart. Mr. Bear thought you could use some rest. Feel free to cuddle with him. I can't wait to see you tomorrow. Good night, sweetheart!"

Ugu smiled. She picked up Mr. Bear and hugged the stuffed animal. She crawled into bed, closed her eyes, put the past two weeks behind her, and slept for the next ten hours, holding Mr. Bear tightly in her arms.

Chapter 36
Cheating at Seven Bridges

Ugu's return to class in Week 4 of Term 3 was emotional for a number of reasons, especially since it wasn't until she entered the classroom that she saw Whitfield for the first time since leaving the Glass Box. Her eyes were immediately drawn to Whitfield, but their long-awaited reconnection would have to wait a little while longer as the entire APPC class stood and cheered when Ugu entered the room. As was customary at Seven Bridges Academy, breakfast always awaited students at their seats for the first class of the day, which encouraged students to show up for class at least ten minutes early. Ugu was typically one of the first to arrive, sometimes as much as 30 minutes early, but today, the entire class was present for this moment. By the time Ugu found her way to her seat, she barely had time left to swallow down her muffin and juice.

She was about to lean over to give Whitfield a much-anticipated kiss, when a loud voice boomed over all the remaining chatter, and every student instinctively sat bolt upright. Dr. Crawfish, who had been suspended for the past two and a half weeks, entered the room, and immediately started calling on students to answer complicated probability and permutation questions. He did not address the incident from Week 1, nor did he glare menacingly in Ugu's direction throughout the entire class period. It was as though nothing had happened.

Everything was the same as it always had been in Dr. Crawfish's class for the past 18 years, except for two things: students were now well-aware of just how easily Dr. Crawfish could snap and lose his temper and Sir Arlington would occasionally show up before or after class to check in with Dr. Crawfish and review his plans for the day and go over any testing materials. Fortunately, Dr. Crawfish remained somewhat tame, by his standards, throughout the class, only embarrassing a handful of students for not knowing answers to his so-called 'so easy an idiot should know the answer' questions.

Whitfield, Aspen, and Flaherty spent considerably more time in the library studying over the next two weeks than usual, making up for all the time they lost while visiting and protecting Ugu earlier in the term. Ugu, who undoubtedly had the roughest time trying to keep up with her studies, spent appreciably more time in the library, but also found herself working in Sir Arlington's office for far longer than she would have anticipated, under the circumstances.

Ugu was as determined as ever to discover who was receiving all these mystery payments from Seven Bridges Academy, but the thought of spending an entire term in the Pit was weighing on her, and she started to doubt whether she could go through with her final elaborate plan to get arrested, for a third time. After several weeks of planning, Ugu finally confided in the others her apprehension over dinner.

"Hey guys, thanks for coming over. I really need to talk through this plan."

"No problem. We totally have your back." Flaherty always supported Ugu, unconditionally.

"I already live here, so I was going to be here anyway, but yeah, whatever you need." Aspen always spoke whatever was on his mind.

"Is everything OK? You look a bit worried." Whitfield was able to read Ugu's face.

"I think so. Well, maybe not. You guys are leaving tomorrow for your meet, and…"

"Wait. You're coming to this one, right? You said you were coming." Aspen had a look of disappointment sweeping across his face before Ugu even answered.

"I know. I'm sorry. I can't. This plan still needs some work, and I have to stop by to see Sir Arlington tomorrow. I really wish I could go, but it doesn't look like I'll be able to."

Whitfield put his hand on Aspen's shoulder. "We understand, don't we?"

"I guess so." Aspen couldn't hide his feelings.

Flaherty tried to remain cheerful. "Of course, we do. Now, tell us, what's bothering you?"

"So, I know I said those two weeks in the Glass Box didn't bother me at all."

"That's right. You handled it like a champ and walked out tall and in charge. Like a boss."

"Yeah, thanks, Flaherty. You guys were great too. I mean, to stay with me throughout the entire time, I could never thank you enough."

Whitfield showed even greater concern. "Then, what is it?"

Ugu started to tear up. "It's just that, it did bother me. Seeing all those students being so mean to me. Yelling at me. Saying so many hurtful things. It just really got to me."

Aspen felt Ugu's heartache. "It upset me too. They were so mean to you."

Flaherty agreed, "you're right. It's a stupid tradition here at the school. There should be some limits to how far students can go, but that's all over now, right? No one is being mean to you now, are they?"

"No. Everyone is back to being super nice to me. Well, not everyone. Jonathan and his crew are still nasty to me, but I can handle them. It's just that when I see people in class or on campus or just walking by at lunch, I can still picture them shouting and pounding on the glass. It makes me wonder if..." Tears streamed down Ugu's face. Flaherty reached out and hugged Ugu.

"Wonder what?"

"Whether I can go through with this last act."

Without hesitation, Aspen offered what he thought was some encouragement. "But the Level 3 Detention area is in the SBA Bank basement. You'll be all alone. Students won't be able to torture you down there."

"I know. I'm not worried so much about the seven weeks down there."

Whitfield knew right away what was really concerning Ugu. "It's the following term that you're worried about, isn't it?"

"Right." Ugu lifted her head in slight surprise. *Wow! He really does get me.*

"You think your entire reputation is going to be destroyed and all those taunts and insults will come back and follow you throughout your time at Seven Bridges."

"Yes." *It's like he's reading my mind.*

Whitfield pondered for a moment before speaking again. "So, don't do it."

"What?"

"Don't do it. There has to be another way. I could go in your place. We all know I wouldn't mind taking a shot or two at Jonathan. I'm sure I could work my way up to Level 3 Detention really fast."

Aspen mumbled audibly, "or a hundred shots at him."

"Right. I can serve out a few detentions, and we can still get what we need from the Pit."

"No, Whitfield. We can't lose you from the team."

"Sure, you can. Look, someone else can replace me. Aspen could fill in as an All-Arounder for a few meets. Remember what Wilson said. We always win anyway. Whoever is behind all this will just bribe more gymnasts."

"Is that what you want? More bribes?"

"Well, I don't want this. Ugu is suffering, and for what?"

Flaherty and Whitfield's conversation started getting a little heated. "For fairness. For justice. For doing what's right and stopping all the bribes, the underhanded deals, and inequity in our sport."

"Look, the team doesn't want fairness. You heard them after practice. They just want to keep winning. If we go through with this, they're going to hate all of us. Is that what you want?"

"Hey, it wasn't everyone that didn't care about fairness. We had a lot on our side too."

Aspen contributed some observations from the previous practice, where Flaherty and Whitfield had loosely presented the team with a purely hypothetical situation, that just happened to closely mirror their current environment. "Yeah, it was split pretty evenly. About a dozen on each side. Maybe some of them weren't sure what side to take, or just didn't speak up."

Flaherty continued arguing her case. "That's right. We owe it to those dozen teammates to find out the truth. We owe it to the hundreds of other schools out there that have the odds stacked against them. The thousands of good students and athletes that are never going to get a chance to compete on a level playing field because Gen. Gibson, Dr. Hewitt, and who knows how many others, won't ever let that happen. Schools are cutting teams. Resources are being stripped away from good places. Lives are being ruined. We need to do this."

At what cost?

Ugu quietly offered the answer they were all looking for. "Any cost necessary." Whitfield and Flaherty stopped arguing and both turned to look at Ugu. "Flaherty's right, and she may not know it, but I heard you make the exact same argument up on the Outer Loop before we even got started with any of this. Whitfield, you care more about fairness than anyone. We have to do this. I have to do this."

Whitfield reiterated his earlier point. "But they're going to hate you for it."

Ugu appeared reinvigorated from hearing the heated exchange in front of her, and grew more determined than ever. "I can handle it."

"But, your reputation."

Ugu nodded. "I can handle that too."

"Really? How?"

"Because now I know the one thing I can't handle. I can't handle losing the three of you. Aspen, you are like the best little brother ever. You're always there whenever I need a hug or someone to talk to, and you always make me laugh.

Flaherty, you're my sister. I love you to death. Whitfield, you have this fire inside you that I never knew could exist. You have this superhuman desire to do what's right, no matter the cost. You may be a bit awkward and clumsy at times, but you are a natural leader, and we all, students, teachers, Seven Bridges, the whole world, need to follow your example. I need to do this for you."

Whitfield and Flaherty looked at each other. Their plan worked. Neither was comfortable playing Ugu the way they just had, but it was important that Ugu continue down this path. They had all come so far, and were closer than ever before to uncovering the truth behind all the corruption.

Flaherty looked at her best friend. "So, are you saying you'll continue with the plan, even if it means further embarrassment, humiliation, and all that other bad stuff?"

"Absolutely!"

"Yay!" Aspen started to dance spontaneously. Flaherty and Ugu both laughed.

Whitfield composed himself. "All right. If you're sure. Let's go over the plan one more time."

****

The weekend was another successful triumph for Seven Bridges. The gymnastics team won the Spice meet, and with it, earned controlling interests in large portions of the world's spices, including pepper; salt; cumin; vanilla; garlic; ginger; coconut; coriander seed; turmeric; methi seeds; dry chillis; and nutmeg. As per custom, Seven Bridges Academy would keep a portion of their winnings to satisfy their own current and near-term demand and either store the excess spice in nearby facilities or sell part of their inventory on the open market at favorable prices.

If market demand for a particular spice was sufficiently high, Seven Bridges could use their 'preferred' trading partner status to acquire even larger quantities at reduced rates, and turn around and sell the same quantities at higher prices. Given the current shortage of, and increasingly growing demand for, nutmeg around the world, Seven Bridges' victory at the Spice meet resulted in extraordinary profits for the school.

Regarding the competition itself, the scores were a lot closer than in other recent meets, with Seven Bridges only winning by 12 points, their smallest margin of victory in any meet thus far this season. Part of the reason for the slim margin of victory was Chloe's absence from the lineup for the entire weekend, and Coach

Brockport's decision to rest Flaherty during Sessions 3 and 4 on Day 1 and Whitfield during Sessions 5 and 6 on Day 2.

With the final week of Term 3 coming up, and final exams and projects due, Coach Brockport decided to give his star athletes some extra time for their studies. Chloe had asked out of the lineup to focus on Dr. Crawfish's final exam, now scheduled for Monday, whereas Whitfield and Flaherty fought tooth and nail to remain in the lineup, but ultimately had to respect Coach's decision.

Despite the extra time off during the meet, Whitfield, Flaherty, Chloe, and many of the other gymnasts kept their noses in their books for the entire ride home after the meet. While most exams and projects were not due until Wednesday or Thursday, Dr. Crawfish's APPC exam was scheduled for Monday morning. Whitfield, Aspen, and Chloe studied together on the way home.

Whitfield had hoped to include Ugu in their study group, but he could not get a hold of her. She wasn't answering his calls. He figured she was probably busy studying in Sir Arlington's office and didn't want any distractions. When the team arrived back on campus, Whitfield, Aspen, and Flaherty once again managed to avoid all the fanfare and quickly sneaked away, back to their respective homes to get some rest before the start of exam week.

As expected, Dr. Crawfish was particularly grumpy on Monday morning. He did not appreciate students asking last-minute questions, feigning excuses for their poor performance all term, or seeking leniency on grading. Whitfield and Aspen were so focused on their own preparation that they almost didn't notice that Ugu was not in her normal spot in the classroom. Instead, she positioned herself directly in the middle of the room, highly visible from all corners and camera angles. Ugu waved to Whitfield and Aspen, who both returned the gesture before sitting down. Chloe decided to sit in Ugu's usual spot, next to Whitfield and Aspen.

"Hey guys. Mind if I sit here?"

"Go ahead. Please."

"Thanks, Aspen. So, why is Ugu sitting over there and not with you two?"

Whitfield admitted that Ugu's seat selection was odd, but offered a viable reason for her decision. "Oh, she probably just wants to show Dr. Crawfish that she's not scared of his exam and is confident that she's going to do well."

Chloe looked surprised. "That's bold. No one else wants to sit there, that's for sure."

Aspen cringed, "yeah, it's kind of like taking an exam with a spotlight on you. She's probably going to feel Dr. Crawfish staring at her the whole time."

Chloe agreed, "no thank you. Too much pressure. I'm happy sitting here, away from all the attention."

Dr. Crawfish offered some final instructions, harshly recited the school's zero-tolerance policy regarding all matters pertaining to violations of the highest standards of academic integrity, and rigidly distributed the exams. All chatter ceased, and the exam session began. Five minutes into the exam period and the whole class knew they were in for a long three hours. Dr. Crawfish had a reputation for making his exams challenging, but this one was ridiculously difficult. Dr. Crawfish patrolled the room with a smug look on his face, almost as though he took great pride in making students feel unworthy and inadequate.

At exactly fifty minutes into the exam, with students sweating and squirming in their seats, the otherwise quiet exam room heard a thunderous boom. Dr. Crawfish lifted a large book with both hands over his head and threw it straight down onto his wooden desk, cracking the desktop, causing the lamp, other books, and papers to crumble inward toward the middle of the collapsed desk and slide noisily to the floor. With everyone's attention in the room squarely on him, Dr. Crawfish bellowed loudly.

"UGU GUGURUTRUV!" The whole class jumped and gasped in fright, fearful that Dr. Crawfish might try to attack Ugu again. "BRING YOUR EXAM PACKET UP HERE AT ONCE!"

Ugu had a guilty look on her face. "But, sir…"

"NOW!" Dr. Crawfish was completely red in the face. No, he was closer to purple. He had spittle forming at the corners of his mouth, like a rabid mongrel. Ugu collected her belongings, brought her exam packet up to the front of the room and handed it to Dr. Crawfish, who angrily ripped it out of her hands. The class was still staring helplessly at the site unfolding in front of them. Dr. Crawfish took a few strides to his right and lifted a small glass cover on the wall and pressed the blue button. He then turned two nearby dials to activate the campus emergency video system. All monitors on campus were now tuned into Dr. Crawfish's classroom. Security agents were quickly on their way to the room.

Dr. Crawfish spoke harshly and rapidly. "Ugu Gugurutruv. You are hereby charged with violations of Seven Bridges Academy's Student Code of Conduct. You have been caught cheating on a final exam. I have video evidence to support this charge." Dr. Crawfish picked up a device from the floor near his cracked desk and replayed the camera feed from just a few minutes earlier, clearly showing Ugu taking out a sheet of notes from her pocket, looking over at her neighbor's test paper, and checking her own tracker, all within about 40 seconds of each other.

The camera feed was on full display on every video monitor across campus. Ugu had cheated. On an exam. This was quite possibly the worst offense a non-gymnast could commit at Seven Bridges. Ugu was caught, and could do nothing to defend herself. She just had to stand there and absorb Dr. Crawfish's wrath until she was taken away by security, for a third time this term.

The students were horrified as they watched the video. How could cheating take place at Seven Bridges Academy? How could Ugu do something so heinous? Did Ugu finally crack under all the pressure? Had her stay in the Glass Box changed her? Students shifted their glances from the video monitors to Ugu, piercing her with disdainful and hateful looks. Several students crumpled up pieces of paper and threw them at her as she stood there, in front of the classroom, on display for all Seven Bridges students and faculty to see—an example of deplorable behavior and wicked intentions. As the security agents entered the room and surrounded Ugu, she just stood there, silently, with her head down. Sir Arlington walked in shortly after.

"Sir, I demand this student be arrested at once." Dr. Crawfish appeared to take pleasure in reciting his demand.

Sir Arlington looked on, stoic in appearance. Emotionless. "Thank you, Dr. Crawfish. I have seen the footage. Young Ugu, I hereby sentence you to Level 3 Detention for repeated violations of the Seven Bridges Academy Student Code of Conduct. Guards, you may escort Ms. Gugurutruv to the Level 3 Detention area for processing."

Dr. Crawfish was not yet finished. "Halt. Sir, I demand that she also be expelled from this school. We have a zero-tolerance policy in place for a reason, and she knowingly and willfully violated it."

Sir Arlington nodded, reluctantly. "Yes, very well then. Young Ugu, I hereby place you on the Student Expulsion List, effective immediately. You will serve out your seven weeks in Level 3 Detention and then stand for a hearing regarding your expulsion from Seven Bridges Academy. Guards."

Throughout this entire scene, Whitfield and Aspen had refused to look directly at Ugu. They were both fully aware that Ugu was planning to get caught cheating on Dr. Crawfish's exam and that he would likely have a loud, boisterous reaction, much like he did. They both knew Sir Arlington would come in and, if everything went according to plan, Ugu would be sent to Level 3 Detention. But expulsion was not part of the plan. Whitfield and Aspen looked at each other, and then at Ugu, as she was led away by four security agents. *How could we let this happen? How could we let Ugu go through with all this and get expelled?*

Whitfield shouted out from his seat. "Ugu!"

Ugu remained calm and turned to look directly at Whitfield. "It's OK. I'll be OK." Then, Ugu, mouthed the words, "look under the bed."

Whitfield whispered softly to Aspen, "did she just say look under the bed?"

"Yeah, what do you suppose that means?"

"I don't know. Maybe she left something for us under her bed."

"I guess."

Ugu was escorted out of the classroom, and Dr. Crawfish regained control. "OK. Show's over. Back to work. Sit down and get to work. If I see one more person even think about cheating, I'm going to throw this book directly at them." The class all did as they were told. The rest of the exam period was tense, but it all came to an end, eventually. Whitfield and Aspen handed in their exam packets, watched as Dr. Crawfish snickered at them as they walked by, and ran out of the building to catch up with Flaherty, who was waiting for them at Pike's.

Flaherty hugged both boys when she saw them. "Are you two OK? I saw the whole thing on the video boards."

"Yeah, we're OK, but Ugu…" Aspen had a frantic look about him.

"I know. She's going to be OK. Trust me."

"So, did you hear about the Expulsion List?"

Flaherty jumped back in surprise. "What? No. The video boards shut off live coverage after Sir Arlington said Ugu was arrested and just kept replaying Ugu at her seat. What's with the Expulsion List?"

Aspen quickly jumped in. "She's on it."

"WHAT?"

"Yeah, so Dr. Crawfish demanded that Sir Arlington place Ugu on the Student Expulsion List."

Flaherty couldn't believe it. "And Sir Arlington did it?"

Aspen now had tears in his eyes. "Yeah."

Whitfield put his arm around his little brother. "He did. Flaherty, what does that mean?"

"Oh, no. It's not good. Every year, Seven Bridges admits up to five transfer students, but with each incoming transfer, one student is expelled. That's actually how Whitfield was admitted. To open up a spot for Whitfield, someone had to be expelled. Students can only transfer in as second- or third-years, but current students could be expelled in any year. Sometimes, a student may voluntarily leave school, but that's really rare. Usually, it's poorly performing or terrible behaving students that are informed that they are on the Expulsion List leading to possible removal from the school."

Aspen hadn't heard any of this before. "Whoa. That's harsh. Does that mean that Ugu is going to be expelled?"

"No, not necessarily. First, SBA can only take up to five transfers per year, no more. And sometimes, we don't even find five qualified students to bring in, so that number may be less than five. Second, just because you are on the list, doesn't mean you automatically get expelled. There may be five or six other students on the list ahead of Ugu. We just don't know yet."

"Can you think of anyone else on the list so far?"

Flaherty shook her head. "Not off the top of my head, but the list is public. Here, let me pull it up now." Flaherty typed a few keystrokes, and within seconds, the Student Expulsion List was visible on her monitor, and fully updated to include Ugu's name on it. She was already listed as #3. The screen also displayed incoming transfer applicants, and there were already at least five worthy candidates, out of a pool of several thousand applying for transfer admission.

Whitfield stared at the screen. "This isn't good. We're clearly going to have five incoming transfers. Unless three more students get added to the Expulsion List ahead of Ugu, she's going to be expelled."

Flaherty tried to remain calm. "Let's not get ahead of ourselves. Term 3 grades aren't even in yet. We still have a long way to go before the end of the school year. There are always a couple first-years on the Expulsion List at the end of the year, but none of them made the list yet. They only have grades posted for one term of classes so far, and the administration typically wouldn't add first-years to the list until after at least two, if not three, terms of bad grades are posted. Plus, we still have another three terms of classes left. Someone else is bound to mess up big. We shouldn't give up on Ugu yet."

Whitfield was determined. "Oh, I'm never going to give up on her. I hope you are right about all this."

"I am. You'll see. Besides, if we can crack these bank records, we can then tell Sir Arlington about all this, and then there's no way he'll expel her."

Aspen offered a terrifying thought. "Unless he's part of it."

Whitfield, Aspen, and Flaherty all fell silent, and shared worried looks with each other.

"Well, we can't let that stop us. We have to keep going. Speaking of which, Flaherty, did Ugu say anything to you about hiding something under her bed?"

"No, why?" Whitfield proceeded to tell Flaherty about the words Ugu mouthed as she was leaving the classroom. Flaherty wasn't sure exactly what they meant, but thought there would be no harm in checking out Ugu's bedroom anyway. "Let's check it out. Maybe she did leave a clue there."

Whitfield, Aspen, and Flaherty raced back to Aspen's mansion and climbed up to Ugu's room. They checked under her bed, but didn't find anything useful. "There has to be something here. She specifically told us to look under the bed, right, Aspen?"

Aspen nodded. But after another round of searching, the trio still didn't find anything out of the ordinary under Ugu's bed.

After some time had passed, the doorbell to Aspen's mansion rang. With forty other students living in the house, Aspen was sure someone else would answer, but apparently no one did. The doorbell rang again. Aspen scurried down the stairs to answer the door, with Whitfield and Flaherty close behind. Aspen opened the door, and to his great surprise, Sir Arlington stood in the doorway, along with two security agents.

"Uhh, sir…good to see you. Why are you here?"

"Hello Aspen," Sir Arlington offered a nod as he spotted the other two students standing on the stairs behind Aspen. "I wanted to check in on you three. How are you doing following today's unfortunate events?"

Whitfield spoke for the group. "Hello, sir. Thank you for stopping by. We're still processing it all."

"Yes, yes. Quite an unfortunate incident, to say the least."

Flaherty was direct with Sir Arlington. "Sir, are you really going to expel Ugu?"

"Well, she is on the Expulsion List."

"Yeah, we already saw it." Aspen admitted.

"Sir, did you really have to put her on the Expulsion List?"

Sir Arlington remained more rigid than usual, with his security detail nearby. "Yes, young Whitfield, I am afraid so. Dr. Crawfish was adamant. But, do not fret, all is not decided yet. I do believe young Ugu has some quite resourceful friends." Sir Arlington made eye contact with each of the three students.

"I'm not sure how much help we're going to be," Whitfield sounded hopeless.

"Hmm…I see. Well, when all else fails, think back to the last words she spoke to you. That might provide some comfort." Whitfield sensed that Sir Arlington was attempting to relay a message.

Aspen quickly muttered what immediately came to mind, "no use. We already checked under her bed and didn't find anything." Flaherty slapped Aspen's arm to get him to stop talking. Sir Arlington noticed Flaherty's attempt to silence Aspen, but paid it no mind.

"Hmm…curious. Why did you check there?"

Flaherty tried covering up. "Uhh…no reason."

Whitfield decided to trust Ugu's assessment of Sir Arlington. "Because she told us to check under the bed." Sir Arlington raised his eyebrows just as Ugu's words hit Whitfield. "Guys, she just said to look under the bed. She didn't say her bed. Thank you, sir. We have to go now."

Sir Arlington appeared pleased with Whitfield's revelation. "Certainly. As long as you three are fine. And, remember, do be careful. I do not wish to see you following in Ugu's troubled footsteps." Sir Arlington emphasized his final words.

"Yes, sir." Whitfield, Aspen, and Flaherty decided to rush up to Aspen's room first. They checked under his bed, and found nothing unusual. They then raced up the ramps to the Outer Loop toward Flaherty's house, and again, found nothing under her bed. Convinced that whatever Ugu had hidden for them had to be under Whitfield's bed, the three friends raced to Whitfield's mansion, but alas, they did not find anything useful under Whitfield's bed either. Disappointed, they sat down on Whitfield's bed, and contemplated the situation. "OK. We have to be missing something."

"Whitfield. What were Ugu's exact words as she was leaving?"

Aspen answered instead. "Look under the bed."

"But she didn't put anything under our beds. She couldn't expect us to look under every bed on campus, right?"

"Right. That would take too long."

"Did you guys have some code or special place named 'The Bed'?"

Whitfield tilted his head. "No. Nothing like that."

"I guess it could be an encryption. I could try to crack the code." Aspen was hopeful that it was an encrypted message so that he could use his superior code-breaking skills.

"Perhaps, bro. It would be just like Ugu to do something like that, but I don't think so. Let me think. She had been working in Sir Arlington's office a lot lately, right?"

"Yes."

"And he showed up here really fast, right after she was arrested."

"Yeah, but Ugu trusts him. I don't think he was here to do anything bad."

Whitfield agreed, "me neither. I think he was trying to help us." Whitfield started to pace.

Flaherty wasn't following, but saw that look in Whitfield's eye. "What do you mean?"

"He told us to think back to her last words."

Aspen restated the obvious. "Yes, look under the bed. That's what we're doing."

"And then he said to be careful."

Flaherty was trying to help Whitfield along. "Why would we have to be careful if we were just looking under our own beds?"

"Exactly. And then he said he didn't want to see us following in Ugu's troubled footsteps." Whitfield stopped pacing and looked up. "I got it! I know where she was directing us."

"Where?"

"Guys, we have to break into Jonathan's room again!"

Chapter 37
Entrance Exams

The remainder of exam week went relatively uninterrupted for Whitfield, Aspen, and Flaherty. They all passed their courses with high marks, and scored well on their Term 4 placement tests. Whitfield opted to schedule two *International Affairs* courses for Term 4, so that he would have a valid, school-approved excuse to visit with Ugu during her stay in the Pit. Aspen and Flaherty also decided to schedule one IA course each, for the same reason. Ugu wrapped up Term 3 in the Pit, and opted to continue serving her time through the open week between Terms 3 and 4, when most students opted to leave campus for vacation or to visit with family.

Whitfield, Aspen, and Flaherty had each decided to stay on campus during the break, in large part to support Ugu, but also to get in some extra practice at the gymnastics center. Coach Brockport had allowed team members to take the week off if they so desired, but also said that anyone who wanted to stay for the week would have full access to the training facility.

Aspen, in particular, wanted to spend some extra time in the heavy-gravity room to work on strengthening his legs for vault and floor skills. With a quarter of the season remaining before the post-season, Aspen wanted to be ready in case Coach needed him for any other events.

After wrapping up her final exams, projects, and placement tests from inside the Pit, Ugu went right to work on trying to hack into the bank's system undetected. The Pit was located in the basement of the SBA Bank building, adjacent to the bank's server room. Unlike the Glass Box where Ugu had spent the previous two weeks, the Pit was not furnished with a bed, desk, and comfortable chair.

Instead, Ugu had to lay on a hard stone floor in a dark and mildewy room. The stone was cold to the touch, but the air was hot and humid. The only sources of light came from a poorly installed light bulb hanging high in one corner and the faint blinking blue lights resonating from the server room. The whir of the servers penetrated into the Pit, making it hard to concentrate, sleep, and, after a while, keep one's own thoughts coherent. Seven weeks in the Pit was enough to drive anyone mad. Ugu had her work cut out for her if she was going to make it out without losing a piece of herself inside.

Ugu's first two weeks in the Pit were terribly lonely. While she didn't have to deal with the incessant harassment of her mean-spirited classmates banging on glass walls, she did have to endure the total absence of any other person in her vicinity. She was in almost total solitude. Over the first several days, Ugu was permitted to use her electronic devices to complete her exams, projects, and placement tests, with little additional screen time for anything else.

Now that the term was over, Ugu's allowable screen time was reduced to thirty minutes per day. She had to use this time judiciously. Naturally, Ugu wanted to communicate with Whitfield, Aspen, and Flaherty during this limited time, but she also needed to test the bank's security and establish a secure hack into the system, and with only a 30-minute daily allotment and heavily reduced server activity during the one-week break period, Ugu had to be extremely precise and deliberate with her activity.

Ugu had originally planned to utilize an unsuspecting intern's login credentials to navigate through the bank's databases, but with second-year students scheduled for internships in Term 4, she doubted whether any student would intern at the bank over the next seven weeks. Furthermore, Ugu ruled out using traditional back-door approaches to hack into the bank's system, as she suspected Dr. Hewitt would likely be keeping a watchful eye on these approaches, given his involvement in such nefarious activities as routing resources away from Seven Bridges.

With these approaches off the board, Ugu instead opted to create an entirely fake profile for a completely made-up incoming employee. She drew up fake documents and hacked directly into the Human Resources system to approve all checks and inquiries. Ugu even passed along her fake employee's credentials through the system, so that other real employees had to sign off on various approvals and security clearances. Her hack worked like a charm, and after about a week, Ugu had complete access to the bank's system, through her fictitious employee's account.

While Ugu was making progress on gaining access to bank records, Whitfield, Aspen, and Flaherty were busy planning their mission to break into Jonathan's room. Flaherty wasn't yet convinced that Ugu was referencing Jonathan's bed with her final words when leaving the classroom. "Are you absolutely sure Ugu wants us to do this?"

Whitfield was convinced, "yes. Well…yes. I am sure."

Aspen recognized the difficulty with carrying out this plan. "This isn't going to be easy. Jonathan really doesn't leave his room anymore, except for class and other scheduled meetings. Seraphina said he keeps his door locked at all times, whether he's in there or not."

Whitfield wasn't surprised. "I know. I also heard he's been planning something. I don't know what it is, but it probably has something to do with getting revenge on me."

"Why you?"

"C'mon, Flaherty. Because he thinks I broke into his room and knocked him out, remember?"

"Oh right. And now, you're planning to actually break into his room. You really can't blame him for being a little paranoid."

"You do have a point. If this is going to work, he can't know that I was involved at all."

"Then maybe I should be the one who breaks in."

Aspen wanted to play a bigger part as well. "Hey, what about me? I can do it."

"Look, none of us really knows exactly what to expect in there. We know Ugu said there were some boxes labeled Seven Bridges Entrance Exams, or something like that, and some loose papers with the same label. We think that maybe Jonathan is somehow getting advanced copies of the entrance exams and either distributing them or, perhaps even selling them."

Flaherty admitted their information was spotty, at best. "We don't know if that's what he's doing, but if it is, oohh…that's really bad."

"Right. Bad enough to get him expelled. If we can get our hands on those exams and prove that Jonathan has been violating the integrity code by distributing them, we may be able to save Ugu by pushing Jonathan ahead of her on the Expulsion List."

"Why can't we wait until Ugu gets out of the Pit? She's already been inside Jonathan's room. She knows exactly where to go."

"Aspen, we can't risk Ugu getting into even more trouble. A fourth strike and she is definitely expelled."

Flaherty agreed, "right. Besides, applications from prospective first-years are due really soon; maybe even next week. If anyone hasn't taken their entrance exams yet, they will need to do so quickly. If Jonathan is distributing those exams, he's likely to do so this week, if he hasn't sent them out already."

Aspen understood. "OK. Then what's the plan? We need to move fast."

"What's the one thing Jonathan wants more the anything else?"

Flaherty answered immediately. "To be on the gymnastics team."

"Right. So, what if we start a rumor that a spot on the team is going to open up soon?"

Aspen didn't see how this was possible. "Yeah, but how? Even if someone gets hurt, coach won't replace them this late in the season."

Flaherty knew a way though. "That's true. But he would if someone got kicked off the team."

"Exactly."

"So, who are we going to say got kicked off the team?"

Whitfield looked at both Aspen and Flaherty. "Me."

"What?"

Flaherty nodded. "That's perfect. Jonathan already doesn't like Whitfield, so he's already more willing to believe news that Whitfield is getting kicked off the team, so he's not going to question it much."

"If we could say that the team is holding a private tryout for my replacement at, say 20:00 tonight, Jonathan would likely go over to the gymnastics center to try out. That would give us a window to get into his room, take the entrance exams, and get out."

Aspen admitted the plan could work. "That's pretty clever, but I don't think Whitfield should go into Jonathan's room. He should be at the gym. Boy, the look on Jonathan's face when he sees you. Hehehe."

Whitfield like Aspen's idea. "That's good. I won't go into his room. So…" Whitfield turned to look at Flaherty.

"I can do it. Aspen and I will head over Seraphina's house this afternoon. We'll tell her we're playing a prank on Jonathan. She'll love it."

Aspen wasn't so sure. "Wait. How are you going to get into his room? Seraphina said he always keeps it locked."

"Seraphina will have a key. All the gymnasts have keys to every room in their mansion, right?"

"I know, Whitfield. But do we want Seraphina to know we're breaking into Jonathan's room? And what if he set up surveillance cameras in there?"

"Good thinking, Aspen. I suppose I can pick the lock to his door, while you distract Seraphina. And to get by any cameras, I'll wear a disguise. I'll pick something up from the Uniform Galleria. Maybe a seventh-year's colors to really throw Jonathan off."

"Sounds good. I can hang out around the back of the house, and Flaherty can toss the boxes out the window to me so she doesn't have to walk out of Jonathan's room with anything. I'll put the boxes in my gym bag and head over to the gym."

Flaherty was starting to like this plan. "That's even better. Then, if I have any trouble picking the lock, I can ask Seraphina to open the door and we can put shaving cream all over his bed or something, as a prank, and while she's distracted with that, I'll toss the boxes down to you."

Aspen was excited. "Awesome! I think this is going to work. Let's go."

****

The plan to get Jonathan out of his room long enough to take the boxes marked *Entrance Exams* from under Jonathan's bed worked perfectly. Seraphina played her role to perfection, and even unlocked Jonathan's door for Flaherty and left with Aspen, so that Flaherty could play her prank without any accomplices. She only asked that Flaherty didn't steal anything, and when Flaherty walked out of Jonathan's room with nothing in her hands, Seraphina was satisfied.

While inside the room, however, Flaherty found the boxes, and threw them down to Whitfield, who raced through the yard toward Fenway's house, and climbed up to the Outer Loop to head over to the gym. To avoid unnecessary attention, Whitfield placed the boxes inside his gym bag as he traversed through the slides and Outer Loop area.

By the time Whitfield arrived in the gym, several other gymnasts were already making fun of Jonathan for showing up and believing that Whitfield was kicked off the team. Keegan was the first to spot Whitfield. "Hey, Whitfield, guess who showed up here to tell us that you're off the team."

Whitfield acted surprised. "What? I'm off the team?"

Chloe couldn't stand Jonathan, and was enjoying this moment. "That's what this little twerp told us."

"Hey, watch who you're calling a twerp, stupid."

Whitfield kept striding closer toward Jonathan. "Hey, let's not resort to calling each other names. Jonathan, tell me, why did you think I was kicked off the team."

"I overhead your stupid little brother and Seraphina talking."

Whitfield stepped even closer to Jonathan. "I already told you, let's stop with the name-calling. What was my brother talking about?"

"He said you were kicked off the team, and coach was having open tryouts today." Several of the other gymnasts started laughing.

Whitfield put his hand up to urge the others to stop laughing at Jonathan. "And you came here to try out?"

Jonathan didn't say anything. His face turned red with anger. He wanted to punch Whitfield right in his face, but thought better of it, as several of Whitfield's teammates were close by. "Hey, Jonathan, I'm sorry, but you must have misunderstood my brother. Maybe he was talking about someone at a different school. I know he talks with gymnasts from all over."

"Shut up, Whitfield! Stop trying to cover for your brother. You know, if all your pathetic teammates weren't here right now, I would pummel you into the ground."

Whitfield stood there, smiling. "Interesting. I don't really think that would happen. But since you're so confident…" Whitfield turned to face his teammates. "Hey guys, would you mind giving Jonathan and I some space. He'd like to take a shot at me." Whitfield's teammates started backing away. Just then, Flaherty, Aspen, and Seraphina arrived at the gym.

Flaherty sensed something bad might happen. "What's going on here?"

"Oh, c'mon Flaherty, let our boy knock his block off." Keegan wanted to see Whitfield whoop Jonathan's butt.

Jonathan turned to face Aspen and Seraphina. "Oh, here they are…the three little liars."

Flaherty appeared confused. "What are you talking about?"

"Don't play dumb. I heard you talking about Whitfield being kicked off the team. You were trying to trick me."

Aspen defended himself, "I wasn't talking about my brother. He's not kicked off the team."

Seraphina acted offended, "excuse me. You were eavesdropping on our conversation?"

"You were talking right by my room."

"It was a private conversation. And it wasn't even about our team, or you." Jonathan was incredibly upset now. He picked up his gym bag, yelled some derogatory comments toward Whitfield, Aspen, and the rest of the gymnasts who were there, and stormed off the floor.

After Jonathan left in a huff, Keegan asked what was on everyone's mind. "What was all that about?"

Flaherty sighed. "Oh, nothing. Just a little payback."

Chloe approved. "Seems to have worked. He's really mad."

"Serves him right. He's always so mean to everyone." Many of the gymnasts agreed with Aspen.

Whitfield continued glancing in the direction where Jonathan left. "Yeah, well, let's leave him alone for a while. He needs to cool off." Whitfield, Aspen, and Flaherty each got their individual workouts in, and then left together to go to Whitfield's house, with the boxes they stole from Jonathan's room still in Whitfield's possession.

****

"Hey, check this out. These exams aren't blank. They're already filled out."

"Let me see. You're right, Whitfield. All of these. There's got to be over a hundred exams here." Aspen continued sorting through the exams. He handed a bunch to Flaherty.

"Did Jonathan fill them all out?"

"I don't think so. They all have different markings on them."

Flaherty was confused. "So, if these exams aren't for distribution, then what are they for?"

Aspen didn't have any answers, just more questions. "And why does Jonathan have them?"

"I don't know. Something isn't right." Even Whitfield couldn't put his finger on what was going on here.

"Hey, look at this. Some of these answers look like they've been changed."

"Let me see those." Aspen showed his brother where some of the answers had been altered. Flaherty found similar changes on the exams she was reviewing. Whitfield, Aspen, and Flaherty quickly went through more than 50 exams, and found evidence of answers being changed on all of them.

Whitfield continued scanning the documents, before summarizing. "So, we have two boxes of entrance exams that we think were sent in to Seven Bridges. Somehow, they got into Jonathan's possession and several answers are changed on each exam. Is there any pattern to the changes?"

"Way ahead of you, bro. Yes, it seems that all the exams in this box had Questions 67-74 incorrect. Even if the exam taker had the correct answer, it was changed to an incorrect one. The exact opposite happened to this other pile of exams. Questions 67-74 are all correct. If the answer originally provided was incorrect, it was changed to the correct answer."

Flaherty offered a thought. "Do you think Jonathan is trying to rig admissions to get certain students accepted and others rejected?"

Whitfield nodded. "That certainly crossed my mind."

Aspen shook his head. "Oh, that's really low. How could he be so evil?"

"That's what I want know. Come on, we need to see Ugu."

Flaherty looked up from her pile of exams. "Ugu? Why?"

Aspen felt he needed to remind Whitfield. "Umm…did you forget? We can't get in there."

"We can still message her. She has access to her devices for a brief window every day. Once the term starts, she'll have access for even longer. I need her to hack into Jonathan's bank account records. I think he's getting paid to alter these exams."

Flaherty raised an eyebrow. "By who? You think all these students are sending him money?"

"Perhaps. But I have a suspicion this is somehow being coordinated. I mean, how did all these exams end up in Jonathan's possession in the first place? It's possible these are all individual, let's say, customers of Jonathan's, but I think it's even more plausible that someone at the school is using Jonathan to rig admissions."

Aspen glanced up at his brother. "Any idea who?"

"Not yet. I know his mom is on the Board, so that might be a good place to start. Hopefully, Ugu can shed some light on all this." Whitfield asked Aspen to send Ugu an encrypted message asking her to pull Jonathan's bank records. Aspen was able to send out the message within the hour. None of them expected to hear back from Ugu until the next day, at the earliest. Until then, they would rest up. Term 4 was about to begin.

Chapter 38
Ugu's Research Meeting

Term 4 classes got off to a good start. Whitfield was enjoying his two *International Affairs* courses, and since he and Ugu were both enrolled in the same classes, he was able to see her on his screen during class, and communicate with her for a few minutes after class as well. Flaherty decided to take two classes with Aspen, sensing that he was feeling a little lonely without Ugu on campus or at his house. Whitfield and Flaherty had even decided to take another class together, *Forensic Biology II*, after enjoying being lab partners in Term 3.

By the end of the first week, Ugu had dropped a bombshell message for Aspen to decrypt. Ugu had fully unraveled all of the bank account information pertaining to Dr. Hewitt's mystery payments, as well as learning more about Jonathan's bank records, which most surprisingly, the two pieces of information were related.

Ugu mapped all of the payments from Seven Bridges Academy to external parties over the past five years. She honed in on the account numbers from the decrypted fake scoresheets attached to Gen. Gibson's messages to Dr. Hewitt.

Ugu found that most of the account numbers were controlled by a single entity, SYPHUS Industrials Inc. The accounts that were not directly controlled by SYPHUS, were linked to fake companies controlled by the WGF, and established by Gen. Gibson himself. Ugu had even traced the coated bills meant for distribution to members of Isadora's Gang to an address listed for two of the fake companies under WGF control, and pinpointed several instances when Gen. Gibson himself, along with Dr. Hewitt, were present at the exact same time as members of Isadora's Gang, with money transferring hands directly.

Furthermore, Ugu pulled information on SYPHUS from the bank records and found hundreds of bank account numbers under their control. She mapped over 350 of the encrypted accounts from the fake scoresheets Gen. Gibson sent out to the other 19 'preferred' schools to SYPHUS Industrials. Gen. Gibson appeared to be the mastermind behind the efforts to redirect resources from schools to SYPHUS-controlled accounts.

Gen. Gibson would send encrypted messages to Seven Bridges Academy, and 19 other schools, and over the course of the next several weeks and months, valuable resources would be shipped out from the schools to SYPHUS accounts. As far as Ugu could tell, Seven Bridges Academy did not have any direct business with SYPHUS, other than these outgoing payments.

The connection to Jonathan truly piqued Ugu's interest. For each of the two years since Jonathan arrived on campus, his mother, a member of the Seven Bridges Board of Directors, funded her son's bank account with a handsome sum of money. While the amount was significantly larger than what other students received from their own parents, this practice was not all that uncommon.

What stuck out to Ugu was Jonathan's mom's account number was listed in two of Gen. Gibson's fake scoresheets, once per year. Ugu may not have ever caught it, except that Gen. Gibson used a gymnast's name who wasn't even on the team to encrypt the account number and it caught Ugu's eye.

The gymnast whose name had been used had in fact tried out for the team both years, and Ugu had at first figured that it was just another encrypted account number, but it only appeared once each season, and the dollar amount of the transaction was large, and for the same amount, each year. Ugu had flagged the account for further investigation and that's when she learned of Jonathan's mother's involvement.

Ugu compiled all her research and sent it in a series of encrypted messages to Aspen. After practice on Friday night, Aspen asked Whitfield and Flaherty if they wanted to get together to go over Ugu's research. They all decided to meet at Flaherty's house.

"Guys, this is incredible! It's all here. There's enough to get Dr. Hewitt fired, Jonathan expelled, and go after Gen. Gibson. We probably could get Jonathan's mom ousted from the Board of Directors as well."

"Flaherty's right. And who knows if there is anyone else from the WGF involved?" Aspen was truly impressed with the level of detail in Ugu's research.

"This is huge. We have to go to Sir Arlington with all this." Flaherty was finally on board with looping in Sir Arlington, figuring they had enough evidence to launch a formal investigation.

Aspen agreed, "absolutely. Maybe we should go now. He's probably still awake, right?"

"Sure. We have to at least try. Whitfield, are you coming?"

"What?"

"Uhh…hello? Haven't you been listening?"

"Oh, sorry. Yeah, I have. It's just…you know as soon as this thing comes out and gets exposed, everything is going to change. You know that, right?" Whitfield had that look about him of being in deep thought and contemplation.

"What do you mean, bro?"

"Think about it. Gen. Gibson's been rigging meets for us to win. We still don't know why, but that's what's happening. And because we always win, we have all this nice stuff. Mansions. Food. Clothes. Jewelry. Tech. Everything."

Aspen wasn't backing down. "Yeah, but he's also stealing a lot of our resources from us. If they weren't stealing from us, we'd have even more."

"How much more do you want?"

"That's not what I meant. I just think that he shouldn't be stealing from us, that's all."

"I agree. Whatever their ultimate goal is, they still shouldn't be stealing from us. But, in a way, they may be responsible for us having all of this in the first place." Whitfield was expressing some mixed feelings.

Flaherty sensed Whitfield's internal dilemma. "So, are you saying you don't want to go through with this? I thought we had this conversation already."

Whitfield shook his head. "No, I do. I just want us all to think about the ramifications."

Aspen was quick to respond. "I have. And I don't care if my teammates don't like me. I don't care if we lose our mansions and fancy clothes. I don't care if we don't go undefeated this year. I mean, sure, I want to win. But, not by cheating!"

"Amen. I'm with you."

Whitfield felt proud of both his brother and Flaherty. That was exactly what he wanted to hear. "Then, we're all in agreement. Let's go see Sir Arlington."

****

Whitfield, Aspen, and Flaherty arrived at Sir Arlington's study inside the library on the AMQE campus late in the evening. Not surprisingly, Sir Arlington was still awake, and working. "Ahh…young Whitfield. I see you've brought friends too. Young Flaherty. Young Aspen. I've been expecting you."

Flaherty looked puzzled. "You've been expecting us?"

"Yes. I presume we have a lot to discuss. Come in." Sir Arlington welcomed the three students into his study chambers. Whitfield spoke first, and presented

Ugu's research to Sir Arlington. It took the better part of two hours to go through everything, as Sir Arlington asked many questions, and paused quite often to contemplate the gravity of what he had just learned. "Most fascinating! This goes way beyond my initial thoughts. We need to act fast. First, I need to make a few calls. Might I ask the three of you to take a lap around the Outer Loop?"

Whitfield was not expecting this odd request. "Excuse me, sir?"

"This is going to be a long night. I need you all awake, and thinking straight. The exercise will get your brains functioning in the proper manner. I also need witnesses see you running on the Outer Loop tonight. When you return, do not use the front entrance to my office. Exit the Outer Loop at Brooks' mansion. Use Slide 02-EL and do try to make yourselves invisible as you enter through the tunnels behind the Applied Mathematics and Quantitative Economics Building."

Aspen wasn't as familiar with all the hidden intricacies of campus. "Tunnels, sir?"

Flaherty nodded. "I know where they are. You'll be fine."

Sir Arlington was satisfied. "Good."

Flaherty was still unclear. "But, sir? Why…"

Sir Arlington gently raised his hand. "I will explain when you return. Now go. We do not have much time." Whitfield, Aspen, and Flaherty all got up and scurried up to the Outer Loop to run a lap before returning through the tunnels. While they were gone, Sir Arlington set the clocks surrounding the Outer Loop ahead two hours, made several calls, and prepped the conference room for a late-night meeting.

When Whitfield, Flaherty, and Aspen arrived back at Sir Arlington's study, they saw the door to the conference room was open, with activity inside the room. They walked in and were surprised to see that Sir Arlington was not alone. Professor Marino and Dr. Randle were seated around the large oval table. Hendricks, who the boys hadn't seen since his mysterious departure during PAW, was seated at the table, via holographic imaging, along with Lord Sirroc, President of the WGF. Three other women were also seated at the table, two via holographic imaging.

Whitfield and Aspen did not recognize any of the women, but Flaherty recognized the one who was physically present as Julienne, a professional stylist from the Uniform Galleria. Whitfield, Aspen, and Flaherty's heads were spinning as they each tried to make sense of the scene in front of them, and just when they thought they had seen it all, a twelfth person walked in through the side door.

"Ahh, young Ugu. Good to see you. Now that we are all here, let's get started. We have some disturbing news to share with you. It seems that SYPHUS is back and stronger than before." There was an audible gasp, and some grumbling among those seated at the table. Whitfield, Aspen, and Flaherty were all still standing, alongside Ugu, who seemed to know more about what was going on than the three of them did.

Professor Marino expressed some hostility. "How could that be? We destroyed their operations over eight years ago."

"Well, it is true. We have confirmation that they have infiltrated the WGF. They even have an operative planted right here at Seven Bridges Academy."

Hendricks was outraged. "Dammit, Arlington. You said my boys would be safe there."

Sir Arlington remained composed, "and they are safe, dear Hendricks. Look for yourself." Sir Arlington turned toward the four students, who were still standing against the side wall. "Would you four please make your way over to the table and find your seats?"

"Uhh…our seats?"

"Why, yes, young Whitfield, these are now your seats. You have each demonstrated exceptional skill, integrity, compassion, and ingenuity during your time here, and are deserving of a seat at the table."

Aspen was just as confused as the others, and spoke for all of them. "Umm…what's going on here?"

Julienne kindly introduced herself and motioned toward the empty seats. "You are being welcomed onto the Council. Congratulations!"

Whitfield's head was spinning. "What Council? I'm sorry, but this is all a lot to take in."

Julienne turned toward Ugu, "you didn't brief these three on the Council?"

"No, ma'am. My apologies. We didn't have time during my incarcerations to discuss the nature of the Council."

Sir Arlington attempted to move the meeting forward. "No apologies necessary. And given the short time we have available; I believe we must dispense with the history lesson as well. Perhaps another time. As for now, we need to move ahead. Young Ugu, your highly capable team briefed me on your research into payments made to SYPHUS from our Seven Bridges accounts and the related bribe attempts. Would you care to brief the rest of the Council?"

"Certainly, sir. We've secured detailed information pertaining to the illegal transfer of $386.7 billion in resources from Seven Bridges Academy to SYPHUS over the past five years. We believe additional resources have been reallocated to SYPHUS from 19 other schools as well."

The gathered audience did not have the intense look of shock that Whitfield had expected. Instead, Dr. Randle remained stoic when seeking out additional clarification. "Any estimate of how much was stolen from the other schools?"

"Nothing concrete with limited access to global banking data, but our estimates put the number at roughly $2.9 trillion from other schools."

"Dear Lord, that's over three trillion dollars in total stolen resources going straight to SYPHUS."

"That's correct, Professor Marino. We have detailed documentation of every transaction."

Hendricks had regained his composure from his earlier outburst. "Who approved all these transactions?"

"I have a list right here." Ugu pulled up a list of 21 names on the video monitors for everyone at the table to view. "Each school has a single point of contact, except for P'socto, who used two people to fill the same position. For Seven Bridges, it was Dr. Hewitt. After every meet, Gen. Gibson would send out encrypted messages to each of these 20 schools, with detailed transaction instructions."

Lord Sirroc appeared unaware of this elaborate scheme. "Gen. Gibson? But, he's in charge of scheduling all our meets, collecting bids, and distributing resources. Not this…"

"Yes, my apologies sir, but he has been leading this effort to reallocate resources from select schools to SYPHUS."

Lord Sirroc looked incredulous. "But, how?"

"Well, as you said, he is in charge of scheduling and collecting bids."

Lord Sirroc interrupted Ugu, "and we have a strict policy in place for that."

"Well, sir, I have evidence that Gen. Gibson violated that policy. He has routinely accepted lower bids from less skilled teams, and then coerced them into adding more to the pot through various unreported side bets. He constructs the meet schedule to include just one or, at most two, of his 'preferred' schools at a time. He then hires gang members to bribe gymnasts to take falls during their duel matchups with Seven Bridges, or any of the other preferred schools."

"No, I cannot believe this." Lord Sirroc felt his deeply-held belief in a well-run, almost utopian, WGF come crashing down around him.

Whitfield confirmed Ugu's research. "It's true, sir. We've seen it all."

Ugu continued, "yes, sir. We have archived surveillance footage, both from meets and right here on campus, and we also tracked bills transferring hands from Gen. Gibson and Dr. Hewitt to gang members shortly before bribes were handed out."

Lord Sirroc dropped his head into his hands. "This is devastating."

Ugu needed to continue. "One more thing…and sir, this directly relates to you."

Lord Sirroc lifted his head, fearful of Ugu's next words. "Yes?"

"We have uncovered messages sent from Gen. Gibson's account instructing your renewal exam scores to be misreported. You did not actually fail your renewal exam, sir. Gen. Gibson paid someone to change your answers before final submission."

Lord Sirroc pounded on the table, back in his own office. "What! That is outrageous! How could he…"

"We believe he is after your job, sir."

Julienne furled her eyebrows. "We cannot let that happen."

Hendricks expressed the fear on everyone's mind. "If Gen. Gibson ascends to the presidency, we may be powerless to stop him. To stop SYPHUS."

Sir Arlington nodded, but remained calm. "Yes, well, is that all, young Ugu?"

"Yes, sir."

Aspen sheepishly added another piece to the puzzle, "Actually, we did find something with the entrance exams, sir."

"Yes, I believe I am aware of that issue. That is an internal school concern, and I will deal with that later. As for now, we must act to put an end to Gen. Gibson's manipulation and outright theft of resources." Those seated around the table all nodded in agreement.

Whitfield had been sitting silently, meticulously taking in all that was revealed in front of him.

He couldn't yet wrap his head around one important missing piece. "If I may, sir…"

"Yes, young Whitfield. What's on your mind?"

"Thank you, sir. I realize I am new here and do not fully understand the history of all that is going on, but I do wonder why SYPHUS is doing all of this."

Hendricks was about to speak up, but thought it best to not yet reveal what he learned from Bibb Tossino regarding SYPHUS' true intentions. Instead, Professor Marino offered a response. "They are evil and greedy, that's why. They want money. And power." The group concurred with Professor Marino, and urged Sir Arlington to move on. Whitfield still wasn't convinced.

Sir Arlington raised his hand. "Hold on a minute. Whitfield, you do not seem satisfied with greed as a motive here."

"Oh, no, I think greed is a powerful motive, but I think that's too simple. Too clean."

"Curious. What else do you suggest it could be?"

"Well, look, if it was simply greed, Gen. Gibson could have petitioned to increase the WGF's cut of the pot from 10% to 15 or 20, or even 25%."

Lord Sirroc agreed, "that's true. We have had some of those discussions internally, but no one has championed an increase from 10%. But we have accounted for every dime, so he wouldn't be able to steal from us."

Whitfield frowned, "I'm not so sure. It wouldn't be as difficult as planting moles across 20 schools and manipulating schedules, bribing gymnasts, and all that. He would just have to coerce maybe two or three people inside the WGF to go along with him."

Ugu supported Whitfield, "which I believe he is already doing. I started looking into WGF's bank records too, and there are some discrepancies there as well."

Lord Sirroc looked defeated. "Really?"

Whitfield continued, "really, but let's address that later. The point is, it would have been a lot easier to steal money that way. Instead, Gen. Gibson, and SYPHUS, opted to take this other, more arduous path. The question is why." Whitfield paused a moment to let the question sink in, before offering his own conjecture. "I believe their ultimate goal is to destroy the sport of gymnastics."

Professor Marino adamantly opposed Whitfield's conclusion. "What? That's crazy! We need the sport. Why would anyone want to destroy it? Besides, our revenues from media rights, ticket sales, gambling, merch, licensing, and everything else have never been higher. The sport is in great shape."

Whitfield was undeterred, "let's think about this. Lord Sirroc, how many schools had teams this year?"

"I believe we had 800 exactly."

"That's right. And that's down from about 820 last year, right?"

"I believe we had 824 last year."

"OK. And how many schools are dropping their team from competition at the end of this year?"

Lord Sirroc knew these figures by heart, and with a look of sadness, delivered them to the group. "So far we have had 32 schools submit paperwork canceling their team's competitive status for next year."

"OK. That's 32 already. By the end of the season, that number may be up to 50. Or maybe 60. Maybe more. With Gen. Gibson pulling the strings, success on the competition floors is concentrated among only a few schools. How much longer until more teams decide against competing? As it stands now, we have several hundred schools simply throwing resources to the elite 20. Once schools figure out they don't stand a chance at winning; they aren't going to bid as much, or maybe just drop out altogether. Once fans realize the meets are 'fixed' so that select teams always win, they're going to stop watching too. The sport can't survive with just 20 schools and no fans."

Sir Arlington expressed no outward emotion, but internally, beamed with pride over Whitfield's poise and rational thinking. "I think we all agree that the sport can't survive with only 20 schools. Do you really believe that is Gen. Gibson's goal?"

"Either Gen. Gibson or what's the organization's name…SYPHUS? Yes, I believe they are acting to discredit the sport. To tear it down from the inside. Introduce corruption at the highest levels and force teams to shut down." Again, Hendricks considered relaying his interaction with Bibb to support Whitfield's argument, but decided to hold back, for the time being.

Sir Arlington thought for a long moment, before seeking input from others. "That's an interesting theory, young Whitfield. Lord Sirroc. What do you think?"

Lord Sirroc remained quiet for a minute before responding. "It pains me to say it, but I believe the boy may be right. All the evidence points in that direction. And now that I think about it…" Lord Sirroc paused for even longer this time.

Dr. Randle grew impatient. "What?"

"We have seen an increase in gambling activity at both the school and professional levels this year."

Professor Marino didn't see a problem with that. "So? That's a good thing, right?"

Lord Sirroc cautiously continued, "normally, yes. But particular spikes in gambling have coincided with, let's call them, unfortunate, and perhaps unexplained, injuries and withdrawals from competition. We haven't yet run a full analysis of the situation, but we're hoping to use Whitfield and Aspen's technology to help support our investigation. Well, that was before Gen. Gibson banned the tech from all competition. I suppose his unsupported act is further explained now."

Aspen perked up, sensing an opportunity to contribute. "Sir, we would be happy to look into those gambling issues, if you like."

Lord Sirroc was appreciative. "Thank you. Let's take care of one issue at a time, though."

Sir Arlington agreed, "right. Besides, you four are still students at this institution and have classes to concern yourselves with. Lord Sirroc, do you have a proposal?"

"Yes. I will personally call for Gen. Gibson's immediate termination from his position tomorrow, and have him arrested. We will issue a public press release, and I will order a full investigation into his actions. Let's see if my team can uncover any additional collaborators."

Sir Arlington nodded. "That's a good start."

Flaherty thought even more could be done. "Sir, what about the bribes? I realize Seven Bridges has benefited from those bribes going out to other gymnasts, but we really don't want to keep winning that way. We want it to be fair."

Sir Arlington continued to feel pride for his students. "Very admirable, young Flaherty. Yes, Lord Sirroc, perhaps you'll want to mention in your press release that law enforcement is pursuing other co-conspirators involving payments made to select gymnasts. That should scare members of Isadora's Gang into hiding and at least put a temporary end to the bribery."

Lord Sirroc nodded. "It will be done."

Sir Arlington solicited additional feedback from the assembled group. "Any other thoughts?"

Julienne urged discretion in any public press releases, particularly to guard against further discrediting the sport. "We need to craft a statement, specifically with those schools terminating their programs in mind, to ensure fairness will return to the sport."

Hendricks disagreed, "it's too early for that. We have no way of knowing how deep this issue goes. How far SYPHUS' corruption has penetrated the WGF, Seven Bridges, or elsewhere. We should keep it quiet, within these walls, until we know more."

Professor Marino concurred, "I agree with Hendricks. We must remain cautious. Ever vigilant. I must admit, Hendricks, that your plan to use these boys as bait to draw out SYPHUS worked better than I thought. They never would have been so bold as to bribe gymnasts in our own backyard if…"

Whitfield quickly turned to face Professor Marino. "Whoa! What do you mean, use us as bait?"

"Hendricks?"

Hendricks was caught off guard, wishing Professor Marino hadn't brought up their original intentions at this meeting. "Yes, well…"

Sir Arlington attempted to defuse the situation. "I do not believe now is the time to get into all that. Young Whitfield, you and young Aspen are safe here under our watchful protection. No harm shall come to you."

Aspen wasn't ready to let this go. "I'm confused. What do you mean? Why would harm come to us?"

"Because of who your parents are…"

"Marino!" For the first time ever, Whitfield heard Sir Arlington raise his voice. "Please. Now is not the time. We have to take steps to ensure the integrity of our sport, rid ourselves of all this corruption, and ensure that SYPHUS does not continue to grow."

"Agreed." Julienne brought the meeting back to a civil discourse. "Sir Arlington, I call for the immediate termination of Dr. Hewitt."

Hendricks approved. "I second that motion."

Sir Arlington returned to his usual calm, collected self. "Yes, I understand your position. Lord Sirroc, how long would it take your office to coordinate the arrests of all 21 individuals on the list young Ugu provided?"

"We will need a day or two to confirm all the bank transactions in Ugu's research, but I believe we may have the manpower to bring them all in simultaneously. Maybe three or four days."

Sir Arlington shook his head. "Not good enough. We need to make an immediate statement. I will vouch for young Ugu's work. She has never let me down before. Make the call to your security team. I want all 21 contacts arrested first thing in the morning, along with Gen. Gibson. Any other co-conspirators can sweat out the week while your office investigates."

Lord Sirroc reluctantly agreed, "OK. Done."

Sir Arlington made a few keystrokes on his personal device, and brought up a call on the large video monitor hovering over the oval table.

"Hello?" Ashlynn, the star investigative journalist, who had emceed the Judges Ball answered immediately.

"Ashlynn, my dear."

"Sir Arlington! What a pleasant surprise. What can I do for you?"

"Ahh, my dear, it is I who wish to do something for you. Several prominent arrests will be made tomorrow morning at 08:00. I will send you a list of 20 schools where arrests shall be made, and yes, Seven Bridges Academy is on that list."

Ashlynn gasped, "are you serious? This is huge!"

"Yes, it is. Which is why I am trusting you, and you alone, with this information."

"I understand. Thank you so much."

"Of course, dear. Oh, and perhaps you will want to personally handle another high-profile arrest."

"Oh, really? Another one? Where?"

"I suggest you personally go to WGF headquarters by 07:50 sharp tomorrow morning. This one is big, Ashlynn."

"Are you kidding me? WGF headquarters! I owe you my life. Thank you, Sir Arlington." Ashlynn was giddy with excitement, but the reporter in her sought more information. "Obviously, all of these arrests are related to each other. Any comment on how?"

"We will leak out details over the coming days."

"Oh, come on. You can give me something now, can't you?"

"OK. Just promise nothing gets posted until after the arrests are made."

"You have my word."

"Lord Sirroc is innocent. The schedule for the final three school meet weekends is subject to change. And..." Sir Arlington paused for dramatic effect.

"And what?"

"SYPHUS is back!" With that, Sir Arlington hung up.

Hendricks frowned. "Now what did you do that for? You know she is going to blast that all over the media."

"Which is exactly what I want. SYPHUS has always operated in the shadows. We want to bring them out into the light."

Hendricks motioned toward Whitfield, Aspen, Ugu, and Flaherty. "Sir, perhaps it is time for your students to return to their mansions."

Sir Arlington sensed that Hendricks wished to speak privately. "Yes. Young Whitfield. Young Aspen. Young Ugu. Dear young Flaherty. You have all done well. Excellent marks. Go home and get some rest."

Ugu politely spoke up. "Sir?"

Sir Arlington softened his tone, and spoke dejectedly. "Yes, of course. Young Ugu, my dear, you shall return to the Pit. Your sentence is not over yet."

Whitfield thought he saw an opportunity. "Sir, given all that Ugu has sacrificed to bring this information to your attention, isn't there anything you can do?"

"I am truly sorry, young Whitfield. Our dear young Ugu has been sentenced to seven weeks of Level 3 Detention. She is also on the Expulsion List. Even I cannot go above the rules to interfere with such penalties."

"But, sir."

Ugu took Whitfield's hand. "It's OK. I'll be OK. It's only a few more weeks. We accomplished our goal. We got the information we needed. We'll be together again soon." Ugu hugged Whitfield before heading back out the side door from where she had entered. Whitfield, Aspen, and Flaherty exited the room through the tunnel entrance. Once the four students left, Sir Arlington sat back in his seat.

"Yes, Hendricks, the room is now secure."

"We need to address the huge elephant in the room."

Dr. Randle knew exactly what Hendricks was alluding to. "Our entire mission depends on it."

Professor Marino was more direct. "Is it wise for us to rely so much on these four…kids? Especially given who they are and where they came from."

Meritxelle, one of the women attending the meeting via holographic imaging, who had remained silent until now, adamantly opposed the inclusion of at least one of the students in the Council's plans to stop SYPHUS. "I have kept my mouth shut the entire meeting. But I need to express my extreme disapproval with discussing such matters in front of Yuri's daughter. It's bad enough that Livvy and Aldrich's sons got involved in this mess. We cannot afford to lose this battle."

Elise, one of the other holographic attendees, expressed similar views. "I agree. I am still in shock that you would include those children in these matters."

Hendricks took exception to lumping his two wards in with the others. "I can assure you that Whitfield and Aspen are well-trained and fully capable of handling themselves. But they also have no knowledge of SYPHUS' past, or of their parents' involvement. I do agree that we must be cautious concerning Ugu, though. She is very crafty. Highly intelligent. And the only daughter of the most powerful man in the world."

Meritxelle added another fact, "who, lest we forget, is one of the original founders of SYPHUS."

Sir Arlington had heard enough and regained control of the meeting. "Thank you all for expressing yourselves. I understand your concerns. These are indeed unprecedented times, and we are fighting against a powerful enemy. An enemy that will not relent until they usurp complete control over the WGF and all the world's resources. They are tenacious, vicious, devious, and single-minded in their pursuit of dominance. And, quite possibly, if we are to believe young Whitfield's theory, determined to tear down the sport we hold as the cornerstone of our existence. This is a battle that we cannot win without the help of those four…as you call them, kids."

Julienne protested, "but, sir…"

"Please, let me finish. Young Aspen single-handedly decrypted the 'uncrackable' cipher built by the person who quite literally wrote the book on cryptanalysis. He is the most gifted codebreaker I have ever seen. We will need him to penetrate SYPHUS' complex network of operatives, money laundering, and shell corporations. Young Whitfield is a natural leader and the only one to ever score higher than young Ugu on the entrance exams. And remember, she scored higher than every faculty member to ever take the exam, and we all take the exams every year.

"Young Whitfield is a bona fide genius, with the capacity to lead special ops that will be necessary to take down SYPHUS' well-structured organization. Young Flaherty's engineering and technical skills are off the charts. Her mental and physical strength, elegance, beauty, and ability to coerce anyone to do her bidding makes her the perfect agent to infiltrate SYPHUS from the inside. She does not yet know her place in all of this, as she was shielded from her family's past, but it is inevitable that she will learn the truth, and Lord help whoever gets in her way when she does."

Hendricks was still not convinced. "That is all well and good, but what about Ugu. Can we trust her?"

Sir Arlington offered an honest, unfiltered answer. "I want to say yes, but, honestly, I don't know. But I do trust her with my life."

Julienne recognized the paradox right away. "That doesn't make any sense, sir."

"It makes perfect sense. Young Ugu is the most gifted student we have ever had. Her father was a masterful tactician and strategist while he was a student here, and continued to develop into one of the greatest masterminds in the world. A true evil genius. But, young Ugu is better. Smarter. More clever. More thoughtful. And, perhaps even more devious. But she is not evil."

Meritxelle raised a good point. "Neither was Yuri when he was here."

"Perhaps you are right. Whether Yuri was born evil, or developed those characteristics along the way, we do not know. He did experience some trauma in his life, and it's very possible those experiences shaped his world outlook. Young

Ugu has one thing that Yuri never did, though. She is truly in love. Her and young Whitfield have something real. And young Whitfield is an honest, hard-working, compassionate, and loyal good guy. As long as she has him in her life, I believe she will do everything she can to help him, and us."

Hendricks asked the question that was impossible for anyone to answer. "Even if it means taking down her own father?"

Sir Arlington hesitated before answering. "One way or the other, young Ugu and young Whitfield will determine the outcome of this war."

Elise offered one final disturbing thought, "and if she decides to side with her father?"

Sir Arlington looked around the room, removed his glasses, set them on the table, and took a long, deep breath before answering. "Then, we'll lose the war."

Chapter 39
Entrance Exams Restolen

Tuesday's headlines read 'Retribution Day: Crackdown on Organized Crime'. Classes across campus were halted as breaking news streamed across every available video monitor. Students were both intrigued and horrified when they heard about the conspiracy to fix gymnastics meet outcomes and the resulting resource allocations that affected everyone around the country, and the world. In total, 32 arrests were made...so far. Twenty-one school officials, including Seven Bridge's own Dr. Hewitt, were arrested for their roles in money laundering, theft, fraud, conspiracy to commit bribery, and a laundry list of other charges. Ten others were arrested for actual bribery, including several members of Isadora's Gang.

The apparent ring leader of the entire operation, Gen. Gibson, second in command at the WGF, was terminated from his position at the World Gymnastics Federation; however, when agents showed up at his office and at his home, he was nowhere to be found. According to the news reports, Gen. Gibson is a fugitive of the law, and is considered to be very dangerous. The WGF Law Enforcement Division is treating Gen. Gibson's capture a top priority.

The breaking news reports opined on some of the charges, but without any concrete evidence in their hands, reporters had very little to go on. The WGF did issue a press release concerning the three remaining meet weekends of the school season:

For Immediate Release:
After careful deliberation, we, at the WGF, have decided to move forward with the remaining three meet weekends of the school season. However, due to recent revelations, meet schedules have been reorganized to better reflect the true nature of the bidding process, as outlined in WGF Code 142.4.C, free of any tampering, bribery, or other malicious or nefarious purposes. School officials and head

coaches will be notified of scheduling changes via official communication from our offices by no later than this evening.

All gambling and other wagering activity has been temporarily suspended, and will reopen tomorrow morning. All currently outstanding wagers directly impacted by these scheduling changes will be voided, unless otherwise noted by individual brokerages. Any gambling insurance claims should be directed to your insurance carriers, who have all been instructed to process claims under Article 62.4.B11 of the WGF Code. Further scheduling details are forthcoming.

The buzz around campus all day was how the scheduling changes would impact Seven Bridges Academy's quest for a fourth consecutive national title. Whitfield and Aspen received more pats on the back and high fives than usual, as most students on campus remained optimistic about their school's chances to continue their unprecedented winning streak. Other students expressed their nervousness by reminding team members of just how important the remaining meets were to their season, their livelihood, and their own self-worth. If Whitfield and Aspen hadn't felt pressure before, they were certainly feeling it after the day's news broke, and even more so when they got to practice that evening.

Keegan appeared to be in good spirits, as usual. "Yo, Whitfield, what's up, playa?"

"Hey Keegan."

"Got to hand it to you, cuz. You called it."

"Called what?"

"Everything, man. Haven't you been watching the news. Thirty-something arrests. Corruption. Crime. Scandals. Man, you were on top of it."

Whitfield had to choose his words carefully. There was no way Keegan knew exactly how on top of it he was. "Yeah, I guess so. Something just never seemed right about all of it."

Diego was not as cheerful as Keegan. "Yeah, well, now we're screwed. Did you see the new schedule? We have both Thryce and New Release Hills next week. They've got Tewksbury, Wyatt, Moffett, and Falefa. Those dudes are good."

Keegan didn't seem to care. "Aww, man, you're crazy. Falefa ain't nothing. We got this…right, Whitfield?"

Whitfield high fived Keegan. "Right."

Reid agreed with Diego, "I don't know, guys. They're tough."

Flaherty didn't care for the negative attitudes creeping into practice. "So are we. Now get your asses on the equipment, or you won't have to worry about Tewksbury whooping your butts next week. I'll do it right now."

"Yeah, girl. You tell 'em."

"You too, pretty boy."

Keegan blew Flaherty a kiss. "Ooh…I love it when you talk that way."

Whitfield started walking over toward VH-Bars and saw Wilson just hanging around. "Hey, Wilson, you taking a turn, or can I jump in there?"

"All yours, bud. And, hey, don't sweat all this. I told you before, we always win."

"I don't know, Wilson. I think the days of us just showing up and winning are over. You saw the news…no more bribes. No more favorable scheduling."

Wilson wasn't convinced. "No way, kid. They're not going to let us go down like that. They need us."

Whitfield looked puzzled. "Who needs us?"

"Everyone. The WGF. The media. Fans. The whole sport. We're the best."

"I don't know about all that. I hope we're as good as you think we are. I'm not taking any chances though." Whitfield got on the apparatus and started his workout. Team practice went about the same as usual, despite the increased tension in the air over the scheduling changes.

Of the 25 team members at practice, about half worked really hard, while many others slacked off, barely taking turns during their scheduled apparatus allotment time, and otherwise wasting solid practice time. The gap between the top gymnasts on the team and the bottom half grew considerably throughout the year, and judging by these practice habits, that gap was not closing any time soon.

The rest of the week went about the same. Whitfield, Aspen, and Flaherty went to classes and studied together in the library; that is when Flaherty didn't have to be in the lab. Whitfield communicated with Ugu every day during class and briefly after class, for as long as she was allowed. Team practices were no more or less intense than usual; however, Whitfield, Aspen, and Flaherty increased their own intensity, knowing that competition was about to heat up.

Aspen spent additional time in the heavy-gravity room after every practice, determined to break into the lineup on Vault-Pegs and Floor Exercise. Whitfield would run on the Outer Loop every night after practice, occasionally joined by Flaherty.

Aside from Ugu serving out the remainder of her sentence in the Pit and the excitement surrounding the mass arrests at the start of the term, the first couple weeks of Term 4 were relatively drama-free, especially when compared to the first half of the school year. All that changed; however, when Flaherty returned home Thursday night after her run with Whitfield, and found her mansion had been broken in to, and her room trashed.

At first, she didn't notice anything missing, but then she found a note and knew exactly who had broken in and what was taken. Rather than calling campus security or reaching out to her own security team, Flaherty immediately called Whitfield, who had just returned home. "Get over here, quick."

"What's wrong?"

"Jonathan."

"What?"

"He just broke in to my room, and he stole the entrance exams."

Whitfield fell silent. The entrance exams were the ticket they needed to bump Jonathan ahead of Ugu on the Student Expulsion List. Without them, the odds of Ugu getting expelled were much higher, even though Sir Arlington knew exactly why she had committed all three school violations. As long as five qualified candidates applied for admission, the School Board was going to expel five current students to make room for the incoming transfers. Without the tainted entrance exams, Whitfield wouldn't be able to convince the Board that Jonathan should be expelled ahead of Ugu.

"Whitfield?"

"I'm on my way."

Whitfield was shocked when he got off Slide 03-WU leading to the west side of Flaherty's mansion. The outdoor patio on the third floor was completely wrecked, with shattered glass and torn pillows littering the deck. The screen door was mangled, and the first three bedrooms inside the west wing were broken into and badly damaged. Flaherty's room was one floor up, and the vandals left her room a complete wreck as well, smashing mirrors, overturning the bed, and breaking personal mementos.

Flaherty was trying to hold herself together, but Whitfield sensed she needed some comfort. He put his arm around Flaherty, and she pulled away. Her anger outweighed her need for comfort at the moment, and Whitfield had to think quickly to prevent her from storming over to Jonathan's place and tearing his head off.

"Flaherty, I'm really sorry about all this. Where was your security team when this happened?"

"Gave them the night off. Usually do on Thursdays before a meet. I should have known something like this would happen."

"Don't beat yourself up. It wasn't your fault."

"Oh, I know…it was all him. And when I get my hands on him…" Flaherty was fired up, and looked ready to kill someone.

"Is anything else missing?"

"Not that I can tell. Just the exams."

"Did he leave anything behind?"

Flaherty pointed toward her desk. "Just that note. It's over on the desk." Whitfield walked over to the corner of the room, and resting on top of Flaherty's desk was a note written in Jonathan's hand:

Si, now we are even, Virus
Fly Superheros Fly

Whitfield inspected the note to see if there was anything else, but the words seemed to stand alone.

"Oh, I'll show him even. Calling me a virus? When I get through with him…"

"I'm with you, Flaherty. I want to nail him too, but let's think for second. First, let's move to a different room."

"Why?"

"Just follow me." Whitfield led Flaherty out of the mansion completely, and they walked out toward the beach, where the crashing waves would prevent others from hearing them. "Just don't want anyone else hearing our conversation."

"You think he bugged the house?"

"Maybe. Not sure. We can run a sweeper through later, but for now, we need to be cautious. When you took the exams from Jonathan's room, did you touch anything else? Destroy anything? Mess up anything?"

Flaherty thought carefully. "No, not at all. In fact, when I moved past his desk, a dirty shirt fell off his chair. I actually turned around and picked it up and put it back exactly where it was."

"So, nothing was out of place?"

"No."

Whitfield was trying to piece everything together. "This doesn't add up then. Why would he destroy your room, and several others, and then say you were even?"

"Because he's evil. Sick and demented."

"No argument here, but he's also not one to go this far without provocation. He's not that stupid."

"You sure about that? He did misspell superheroes in his note."

"Yeah, I caught that too. He knows we can tie the note back to him. Why taunt you like that?"

Flaherty was just starting to calm down, and with it, thinking more clearly. "You know something, you're right. This isn't like Jonathan. Too extreme. Maybe it wasn't him."

"Oh no, I think it was Jonathan. He was definitely here. But he wasn't alone. And, I'd venture to say, this wasn't even his idea."

"If it wasn't Jonathan's idea, then whose idea was it?"

"Honestly? I think it was Gen. Gibson."

Flaherty stepped back in surprise. "What? Gen. Gibson was here?"

"I don't know for sure. Maybe not. But take a look at this note again." Together they read the note in silence:

Si, now we are even, Virus
Fly Superheros Fly

"It doesn't make a whole lot of sense. I think there's a hidden meaning."

"Like what? You mean 'Fly Superheros Fly' could mean something other than telling us to get out of here?"

"Maybe. Let's run this by my brother. He's really good at cracking codes."

Flaherty was still skeptical. "If this is actually a code."

"Right."

"Should we go see him now?"

"Sure. But, first, how about you pack up some things? It might not be safe for you here. Maybe you should sleep at Aspen's. You can use Ugu's room."

Flaherty was insulted. "Hey, I can take care of myself, you know."

"I know. It's just that until we get your place swept for bugs, it could be dangerous."

Flaherty came to her senses and realized Whitfield was just trying to keep her safe. "Yeah, you're right. I'll just grab a few things. I'll be right out."

Flaherty went inside to pack a few belongings while Whitfield waited outside. Whitfield was so focused on trying to decode any hidden meaning behind Jonathan's note that he was completely unaware that he was being watched, and nearly jumped out of his skin when a hand tapped him on the shoulder from behind. Whitfield immediately yelled, but another hand quickly covered his mouth to keep him quiet. When Whitfield turned around to see who was holding him, he had a look of complete shock.

"Hendricks?"

"That's right, kiddo."

"What are you doing here? Did you break into Flaherty's mansion?"

"No, it wasn't me. But I know who did it, and you are not safe here. Where is your security detail?"

"Back at home. I just came over here after Flaherty told me her place got trashed."

Hendricks spoke quickly. "Make sure you keep your security tight. Keep them around you all the time. Things are getting a bit chaotic right now."

"What do you mean?"

"Gen. Gibson is on the loose, and with the way we just clamped down on SYPHUS, I'm sure they're out for revenge. They'd love to get their hands on you."

"What do you mean? Why me?" Just then, Whitfield and Hendricks heard Flaherty coming out of the mansion with her bags.

"We can't talk now. I'll contact you later. Be careful this weekend." Hendricks tried rushing away, but Whitfield grabbed hold of him.

"Hendricks. Is it true that you gambled my parents' money away and kept taking money from Morton?"

"What? Who told you that?"

"Ugu's dad said…"

"You can't believe anything that man says. He's evil, Whitfield. Trust me, I never took a cent from Morton, or your parents. It was all Yuri."

"But, then why…"

"I'll explain it all to you later. Everything. I have to go now. Remember what I said. Keep security tight." And just like that, Hendricks was gone, retreating into the darkness, nowhere to be seen. Whitfield wasn't sure what to make of Hendricks' apparent hatred of Ugu's dad.

Flaherty approached Whitfield on the beach. "Hey, you ready?"

"Uhh…what?" Whitfield was still on edge from his recent encounter.

"Are you ready to go? I've got everything I need."

"Oh. Yeah, I'm good."

"Is everything OK?"

"Yeah, everything is good. My mind just wondered for a moment."

Flaherty thought she knew what was distracting Whitfield. "Thinking about Ugu? Or about the first time I whooped your butt over there by those rocks?"

Whitfield smiled. "Hey, that's not fair. You've whooped my butt so many times, it's hard to remember every time." The two friends chuckled.

"That's fair. Just thought I'd remind you in case you forgot. If you want, I can do it again."

"No, that's OK. I think I'd rather just think about Ugu."

"OK, fine. I suppose that is better. I actually like these sneakers. I don't want you spilling any of your blood on them." Whitfield and Flaherty both smiled, and continued walking along the beachfront until they were able to cut across to campus by Sydney's house and headed straight to Aspen's mansion.

Whitfield kept a watchful eye out for any potential danger, as did Flaherty, but Whitfield thought it would be best to not tell Flaherty about Hendricks' surprise visit just yet. He wanted time to process it all, and perhaps get some answers from Aspen regarding Jonathan's cryptic note.

****

Whitfield and Flaherty arrived at Aspen's house late at night, but Aspen was still downstairs in the study lounge working on a class assignment.

"Hey, bro, what are you working on?"

"Oh, just an assignment for *International History*. Ugu designed an awesome class. I really like it."

"Cool. Sorry to interrupt…"

"Oh, no worries. What are you guys doing here so late?"

"Well, when I got home tonight…"

Whitfield interrupted. "Uhh…perhaps we should just show him the note first."

"Right. Good idea. Here, can you see if you can spot any hidden messages here?" Flaherty handed Aspen the note.

Aspen inspected it for a few moments before speaking. "Where did you get this?"

"It was left in my house. In my room, to be more specific."

Aspen looked concerned. "Was anything taken?"

Flaherty was confused as to why Aspen would automatically jump to that conclusion. "What do you mean?"

"I mean, did whoever left this note take anything from your room?"

Flaherty looked at Whitfield, who simply shrugged. "Uhh, well, yes."

"Hey, bro, why would you ask that?"

"Because of who left it."

Whitfield looked at Flaherty, who returned the same blank expression Whitfield had just given her. "How do you know who left it? We didn't tell you."

"So, you know who left it?"

"Yes. Well, we think so."

"And?"

"We think it was Jonathan."

Aspen smiled. "Hmm...good guess, but you're wrong."

Whitfield thought his brother might just be messing with them. "How do you know that?"

"Oh, come on, it's so easy. It's staring you right in the face."

"Hey, just because you're a super genius and can decrypt ciphers in your sleep, don't expect everyone else to be able to do the same. Can you help us?"

Aspen looked at his brother, and decided to stop messing around. "Sure, but it's not a cipher. It's just an anagram. At least, that's what it looks like. I'll need a few minutes to be sure though."

Flaherty was impressed with how quickly Aspen came to his conclusion. "How do you know it's an anagram?"

"The word pattern. The misspelled word. The odd use of repetition and a throwaway word just to get everything to fit. It's constructed with the same clunkiness as many elementary ciphers, but this one is too basic to fit even the crudest encryption techniques. Besides, I already spotted the biggest key takeaway."

"Oh really? What's that?" Flaherty loved seeing Aspen's mind at work.

"Look here...S-Y-P-H-U-S. It's not by accident that those letters all appear in the note. Look here's another word, E-V-E-R-Y-O-N-E. I can probably crack the rest of it in a few minutes." As Aspen went to work on solving the anagram, Whitfield and Flaherty stared at each other, processing what Aspen just revealed to them.

Whitfield whispered under his breath to himself, "so, Hendricks was right." He hadn't intended for Flaherty to hear, but she did.

"What? What's Hendricks got to do with this?"

Whitfield decided to come clean. "He's here."

"WHAT?"

"When you went inside to pack your bag, he approached me on the beach."

"And you're just telling me this now?"

"I know. I'm sorry. I should have told you. But I needed to know what we were dealing with. He said we are in danger and should keep extra security around us at all times, especially this weekend at our meet. Now, I know why."

Flaherty also knew. "If SYPHUS broke into my house, they can get in anywhere."

"Maybe. Remember, your security team wasn't there. And, it seems that they had a very specific mission in mind."

"Yeah, to piss me off."

"Well, maybe to scare you. But it also had a lot to do with those entrance exams. Remember, Gen. Gibson sent those two large payments directly to Jonathan's mom. For whatever reason, he wanted those particular entrance exams to be corrupted. He paid a lot of money for it the first time, and now he just went through great lengths to get the exams back. Why? What's so special about them?"

Flaherty shook her head. "I don't know. Maybe he knows the families. Maybe they're all SYPHUS supporters."

"Could be. Regardless, we have to get the exams back. And not just to figure this all out, but for Ugu's sake, as well."

Aspen yelled out from his desk. "I GOT IT!"

Flaherty ran over to him. "Already?"

"Yup. Piece of cake."

"It was that easy for you, huh?"

"No. I'd just like a piece of cake. I always get hungry after solving a puzzle." Whitfield and Flaherty laughed, and the three of them walked into the kitchen for a super late-night piece of cake.

While enjoying a delicious piece of chocolate cake, Aspen shared with Whitfield and Flaherty the solved anagram. "See, it wasn't that difficult. Here it is. The original note said '*Si, now we are even, Virus*; *Fly Superheros Fly*'. Which is an anagram for: *Everyone will fear us; SYPHUS wins forever.*"

"Wow. That's incredible, Aspen. How did you come up with that so fast?"

Aspen appreciated Flaherty's admiration. "I don't know. The letters just jumped out at me."

"Well, you certainly earned your cake."

"Thank you."

"Good work, bro. So, what does this all mean?"

"Well, just as Sir Arlington said in that crazy meeting, SYPHUS is definitely back."

Whitfield stared at Flaherty. "Right. And it seems that Jonathan is their newest recruit."

"What do we do now?" Flaherty looked at Whitfield for their next move.

"First, we need to report this. Sir Arlington needs to know."

Flaherty agreed, "right. I already told my guys when I went in to pack to call campus security. I'm sure they've already alerted Sir Arlington, but it wouldn't hurt to go see him directly."

"Agreed. Is it too late now, you think?"

"Nah. Let's wake him up."

"We'll need to bring some security agents with us." Whitfield heeded Hendricks' advice.

Flaherty reconsidered, "on second thought, let's wait until morning. We have a big weekend coming up and it's already super late."

Whitfield was feeling tired himself. "You got it. Hey, bro, is it OK if we both crash here tonight?"

"Sure. I think we have some room for you both."

"Thanks."

****

In the morning, Whitfield, Aspen, and Flaherty all went to meet Sir Arlington at his office, even before eating breakfast. As expected, Sir Arlington was fully aware of the break-in at Flaherty's mansion, but did not know about the note. "Please sit down. This is most troubling. SYPHUS had never dared such a brazen attack before. We must increase our defenses. Not to worry, we are quite prepared for such measures."

"I hope so, sir. Did you know that Hendricks was here on campus last night? He sounded very concerned about my safety."

"Yes, yes. Hendricks does drop by on occasion. Always in the shadows. Always on alert. We are all concerned over your safety, but trust me, our defensive measures are quite good."

Aspen spoke curtly. "They didn't seem to work last night."

"That is a fair point, young Aspen. But now that we are on high alert, we shall make use of some newly developed technology to ensure our safety." Whitfield, Aspen, and Flaherty still looked uneasy. "Oh, cheer up. Would it help if I told you that our dear, young Ugu helped to design the very defensive measures of which I speak?"

Aspen replied honestly. "Yeah, a little."

"But who's running the control room? Ugu is still wasting away in the Pit."

"Not to worry, young Whitfield. We have qualified agents at the helm. But, yes, it would seem appropriate to grant young Ugu additional access during her incarceration. I am powerless to shorten her sentence, but I think we can offer some flexibility on her device allotment time, particularly in the interest of school safety."

"Any chance you could let her come to our meet this weekend?"

Aspen took a shot.

"Oh, I'm afraid not."

Aspen looked disappointed, "just thought I'd ask."

"I understand. You miss her. We all do. Her sentence will be over soon, but we still have that small issue of keeping her around this institution beyond this year. There is some strong support for her expulsion."

"But sir, you know why she did all those things." Whitfield couldn't yet understand why Sir Arlington couldn't just override the Student Expulsion List.

"Yes, I am aware. But that still will not save her. And now with some possible supporting evidence gone missing, the likelihood of our saving her has dampened even more."

Flaherty peered at Sir Arlington. "You knew Jonathan had those entrance exams, didn't you?"

"Let's just say, I had a hunch."

"What's so important about those exams? We looked through them and found that they were corrupted, but why did SYPHUS go through all that trouble to get them back?" Whitfield kept searching for answers, but hadn't yet stumbled across any.

"You looked through the exams?" Sir Arlington appeared intrigued.

"Yes. Why?"

"And you said they were corrupted. How?"

Aspen was still disappointed that Ugu wouldn't be attending the weekend's meet, but quickly regained focus. "The answers were changed for about eight questions."

Sir Arlington's interest piqued even more. "Changed how?"

Aspen continued, "we saw that one group of exams had all the questions correct and the other had the same questions all incorrect."

Whitfield added more detail. "Jonathan, or whoever made the changes, made it look that way. He didn't change all the answers. For the one pile where he changed the answers to an incorrect response, he didn't touch any of the responses that were already incorrect."

Flaherty rounded out the details and offered a concluding thought. "And the same thing for the other pile. We figure he was trying to rig admissions. You know, get some of his friends, or maybe kids that paid him extra money, accepted to SBA, and to make room for them, ruin some other kids' applications."

"That's a fine conclusion, and one that certainly fits, given the evidence, but my gut tells me there is something else going on. Something even bigger."

Flaherty was puzzled. "Excuse me, sir, but what could be bigger than getting into Seven Bridges Academy?"

After a long pause, Whitfield found the answer. "Leading Seven Bridges Academy?"

Sir Arlington encouraged Whitfield's train of thought. "Even bigger."

Whitfield grew excited. "Running the WGF! Sir, who writes the questions for the entrance exams?"

Sir Arlington sat back in his chair, thrilled to be surrounded by such brilliant minds. "Ahh, excellent question. There is actually a team of us, five in total. We each write a different part of the exam."

Whitfield continued piecing it all together. "And how is the team constructed? Who decides who gets the honor of writing questions for the exam?"

"As with everything around here, we live in a meritocracy. We earn the right to stay in our positions, or perhaps move into different positions, through annual testing and evaluations. Earning the right to craft entrance exam questions is an honor that falls upon those in select positions; however, it is an area that is often criticized and harshly evaluated by both those internal, and external, to our institutions."

"Sir, did Lord Sirroc write any of the entrance exam questions?"

Sir Arlington smiled. "Indeed, he did."

"Do you happen to know which questions he wrote?"

"Indeed, I do."

Whitfield turned toward his brother. "Aspen, what questions were changed on the exams?"

"I believe it was Questions 67-74."

Whitfield turned back toward Sir Arlington. "Sir?"

Sir Arlington nodded.

"That's why it was so important for SYPHUS to retrieve the exams. They're not trying to rig admissions. They're trying to discredit Lord Sirroc."

Aspen was slowly coming around. "But why not just change every answer to the wrong one. Wouldn't that show that his questions aren't good?"

Flaherty had the answer. "Yes, but that wouldn't be good enough. Just writing a difficult question that no one gets correct is a sign that you might be too tough, but probably not enough to have an inquiry filed. But showing that you wrote a biased question, one that catered specifically to a particular target demographic…"

Whitfield interjected, "…such as wealthy families or students from a particular geographic region."

"Right. Showing that kind of bias in your duties as a writer of exam questions would be grounds to file an inquiry into your capacity to fulfill job responsibilities."

Whitfield stood up. "Gen. Gibson already tainted Lord Sirroc's annual re-appointment exam results and rather than waiting for a retake, of which he might have less control over, he ordered Jonathan to change the answers to make it look like Lord Sirroc was biased."

Aspen stood up as well. "They're trying to get Lord Sirroc fired. We have to do something."

Flaherty agreed, "right. But now they have the evidence back in their hands. Any idea where they might be holding the exams?"

"Who knows? They could be anywhere. They'd be dumb to bring them back to Jonathan's room. They're probably not anywhere on campus. We'll never get the exams back."

Sir Arlington offered a glimmer of hope. "I wouldn't be so sure, young Aspen. Our admissions team still has to review the exams. There is still a chance."

"Sir, can't you just tell the admissions team what Jonathan and SYPHUS have done?" Flaherty hoped it could be that easy.

"I cannot interfere with the admissions process. It is forbidden for any current sitting faculty member to tamper with admissions."

Aspen offered a radical suggestion, "what if you stepped down from being headmaster?"

"Aspen! He's not going to do that."

"I mean, just temporarily."

"That is a good idea, young Aspen, and one to which I would give serious consideration, but I would need to recuse myself for a minimum of three years before taking part in such a process."

Whitfield's eyes lit up. "Well, if you can't tamper with the process, that only leaves…"

Sir Arlington quickly interrupted. "Excuse me, but before you finish that thought, please be aware that I am required to report any infractions, past or with reasonable expectation, to the Disciplinary Board. I would advise against such conversation in my immediate presence."

Whitfield nodded. "Understood, sir."

Flaherty stood up. "Well, thank you, sir. We appreciate your time this morning. We do have a meet this weekend. We have to get ready to hop on the drone bus."

Sir Arlington rose as well. "Always a pleasure to meet with such fine students. I will see what I can do about granting young Ugu additional access during her current sentence. Perhaps she may have some ideas on how to resolve your current conflict."

"Thank you, sir."

"Certainly. And young Flaherty, sweetheart, please have no fear upon returning home. You are in no danger of subsequent attacks. However, I do advise you all to maintain strict security protocols this weekend."

"Yes, sir. Thank you, sir."

"Oh, one more thing."

"Yes?"

"Good luck this weekend!"

Chapter 40
Meet Failure

The Precious Metals meet, hosted by Thursday Cruise School, was an unmitigated disaster for Seven Bridges Academy. The increased competition, combined with illnesses, untimely injuries, and a string of bad luck doomed Seven Bridges right from the start of Day 1's duels, and continued throughout the weekend. It all started when Sydney and Ippy each came down with a cold and couldn't travel with the team. Diego tried filling in for Sydney on Escalating Tramps, but injured himself during his third duel of Session 1 and was out for the remainder of the weekend. The big blow was Keegan's badly sprained ankle that he suffered on Floor Exercise during Session 2. He was unable to continue on Floor Exercise, and tried to continue competing on Handstand Obstacle, but after a few more duels, his ankle was in such bad shape that he couldn't focus on his routines and suffered some uncharacteristic falls.

Coach Brockport scrambled to find an adequate replacement for Keegan, but no one was able to step up and consistently win their duels, until Session 7, when Coach put Aspen in on Floor Exercise. Aspen's routines were nowhere near the level of difficulty as Keegan's, but he consistently hit his skills, and won his duel matchup on Floor Exercise in the weekend's final session. Unfortunately, the outcome of the meet had already been decided long before Aspen stepped on the floor.

Whitfield had a mediocre meet, by his standards. He competed in all 56 of his duel matchups, and won 42 of them, but only earned 67 points for the team, and had given up 18 points to other teams, a season high. Flaherty earned 62 points for Seven Bridges, but Coach Brockport sat her out for the entire last session to rest her shoulder, which had been bothering her during the week. Aspen competed on five events over the course of the weekend, and earned a personal best 52 team points, despite falling six times on Pommel Clock, only completing his full routine once during the entire meet.

Aside from Aspen's work on a new event and his season-best point total, Seven Bridges' team had little else to celebrate. Fenway and Chloe earned personal best scores on Vault-Pegs and Parallel Planks, respectively, but in an ironic twist of fate, both gymnasts lost those particular duels.

If there was a silver lining to the meet, it was on the resource allocation side, as the hurried scheduling changes left little time for side bets to accumulate to large amounts. Still, Seven Bridges had bid large quantities of palladium, gold, silver, platinum, rhodium, and iridium, all but depleting their once rich reserves of precious metals.

The school was still cash-rich and could replenish their stock at will, but would have to pay somewhat inflated market prices to do so. On the other side, New Release Hills and Thryce finished 1-2 in the meet, earning themselves a handsome pot of precious metals for their efforts. In the end, Seven Bridges Academy finished in fourth place, a full 28 points behind 3rd place Hooter Owl Institute.

The ride home was tense. Having enjoyed so much success up until this point, Seven Bridges' coaches had neglected to build team chemistry, which manifested itself in a few altercations on the done bus ride heading back to campus. Reid and Vail lashed out at Diego for not competing through his injury; Wilson and Hutchison blamed Seraphina for losing her duels; and several members got annoyed with Aspen for his positive assessment of his floor and tri-bars routines. When Whitfield stepped up to quiet down the blame and accusations, Wilson, Diego, Morocco, and a few others turned their venom on Whitfield himself.

Wilson lashed out first. "Why did you have to say anything? Everything was going great until you started poking around with this 'unfair scheduling' and talking about bribes. I bet you're the reason the WGF even started looking into all this."

Diego agreed while shaking his head. "That's right. You couldn't be happy with the way things were. Now, look at us."

Morocco piled on. "And don't think we forgot about that stupid technology you used that may have caused us all some damage. They probably made it tougher for us on purpose just to stick it to you."

Wilson wasn't done yet. "We'd be better off without you. And why would you ever tell the judge that he missed your hand go out of bounds on Handstand Obstacle? That was stupid."

Whitfield defended himself against that last accusation. "Because it did. I was out of bounds."

"What's out of bounds is you cost us three points with that stupid move. If the judge doesn't see it, just let it go." Several others on the team agreed with Wilson.

Flaherty tried playing the role of peacemaker. "Hey, guys, knock it off. Whitfield's the best All-Arounder we have, and he was just being honest with the judges. I didn't see any of you earn over 60 points today."

Morocco was still hopping mad. "Yeah, I would have. I would've smoked those punks from NRH if coach put me in."

Seraphina chimed in, "didn't you lose your duel to that fill-in gymnast from Hooter Owl? She wasn't even in their starting lineup."

"Shut up, Seraphina."

Whitfield sensed the team was falling apart. "Hey, hey. Let's all settle down. I know. Losing sucks. None of us like it. And none of us are used to it."

Diego shouted, "we better get used to it now."

Whitfield shook his head. "No, I don't think so. We are still a good team. Very good, in fact. I still believe we have a great chance at winning nationals, but we're not perfect. We have some things we can clean up."

Wilson still had a lot of pent-up anger. "Yeah, especially Seraphina."

Whitfield continued, "ALL of us. We can all improve. And not just in the gym. It's this, right here. Now. None of this bickering and arguing is going to help us take that next step. If we don't straighten this out now, we will lose the next meet, and the one after that. It doesn't have to be that way."

Flaherty offered her support. "Whitfield's right. Look, I know this feeling is something I don't ever want to experience again. I know it's easy to blame everyone else for their falls, their injuries, their illnesses or whatever else, but the truth is that none of us can win a title alone. Even if Whitfield was perfect on all his routines, we still would have lost. If Seraphina hit every one of her routines, we still would have lost. If everyone played through their injuries, yeah, we still would have lost. It takes all of us, competing together, if we're going to win a title."

Morocco expressed his frustration. "That's all well and good for you to say, but honestly, I don't see it. Like you said, even if we all hit, we still would have lost. Those other teams are just better than us."

Aspen mumbled under his breath. "Then we have to get better."

Whitfield nodded. "That's right. Morocco, I don't disagree with you. Those other teams are good. And so is West's Vineyard. Parallel Pines. Friarmuth. They're all good."

Wilson was still bitter. "Yeah, but thanks to you, now we have them all on our remaining schedule."

"Good. I want to see them. I want to go up against the best. Don't you?"

Wilson wasn't having it. "Nah, man, I just want to win."

Morocco agreed, "me too."

Diego was also in Wilson's camp. "That's right, brother. All about that W."

Aspen stood up and faced the others. "But it wasn't fair when we were winning. Gen. Gibson paid other gymnasts to take falls against us."

Wilson defended his position. "Hey, that's their problem, man. I don't care about all that. Just give me the win."

Diego decided to escalate the argument even further. "And why are you and your brother talking about winning fairly. Whitfield, didn't your girlfriend just get busted for cheating on an exam? And you want to talk about playing fair?"

"Yeah, she's the real cheater. We didn't do anything wrong. If someone else wants to help us win, that's on them."

Whitfield's attempt at building team chemistry was backfiring. The team seemed even more divided now than ever before. Half the team put winning above everything else, while the other half cared more about fair competition and honesty. The team was fundamentally divided. Whitfield simply looked at Flaherty with a defeated look on his face as he collected his thoughts. He knew that he wouldn't be able to convince everyone on the bus to change their fundamental outlook on competition, but he also knew that if he didn't at least try, some of his teammates might resort to their own forms of cheating to ensure they win the next meet.

Whitfield sat down. "Flaherty, what do we do?"

"I don't know. They just don't seem to get it. How could they feel good about winning when they knew the competition was rigged?"

"I don't know. It doesn't make sense. Wouldn't you want to measure yourself against the best, and let the awards play out fairly?"

"Absolutely."

Whitfield was glad that he had at least one other supporter on the team. Two if you count Aspen. "Oh, and thanks for having my back earlier. I appreciate what you said, but you and I both know you're the better All-Arounder."

Flaherty smiled and winked at Whitfield. "Oh, no doubt about it. You were on a roll, and I didn't want to steal your thunder."

"Thanks." Just then, a thought came to Whitfield. "Wait, that just might work. You may have just given me an idea."

"Oh, honey, I can tell everyone you want that you're the better All-Arounder, but, sweetie, no one is really going to believe that."

"Haha...thanks a lot. No, Wilson, Morocco, and the others all seem to want to win, but don't really want to put in the work to get there. They've been living these extraordinary lives in beautiful mansions at an amazing campus, where practically everything is done for them and they are treated as superheroes—but what if all that went away?"

Flaherty wasn't following yet. "I think that's what they're worried about. If we keep losing, all of that does go away."

"No, that's not exactly what I mean. Look, I don't think we are going to be able to convince everyone that they should care more about fairness than winning; to care more about competition and integrity than mansions and fame. Some people are just built differently and have different values. Despite the school's best efforts, not everyone here exhibits high character."

Flaherty nodded in unfortunate agreement. "Are you suggesting we ask coach to kick some of them off the team?"

"No. Well, at least not yet. We'll see where this goes. No, I'm suggesting that we use their fear of losing everything to motivate them to actually work harder, together."

Flaherty liked the sound of Whitfield's words, but wasn't yet sure how to put them into action. "Yeah? How's that going to work? I don't think they'll believe us if we just start spouting off on them."

"You're right. It has to come from someone else."

"Who?"

Whitfield thought for a moment. "What about Ashlynn?"

"I'm confused. What can she do?"

"OK, hear me out. We get her to come to practice tomorrow and make sure everyone can see her. She'll tell the team that she's writing a feature article all about Seven Bridges' recent dominance. I'm sure Wilson and Diego will love that. But then we convince her to write a scathing piece on how overrated we are and how we are likely to lose everything. No more houses. No more jewelry. All that stuff. We'll make sure she includes some discussion of how the WGF is cracking down on ALL forms of cheating and dishonesty. She'll slip an advanced copy to us by mid-week to share with the team. That ought to shake things up around here."

Flaherty was impressed. "That's good. She has credibility, so they'll believe her. They'll be too scared to cheat, because they think everyone will be watching."

"Right. And that part is actually kind of true. Aspen and I heard that Lord Sirroc is actually going to put our technology back in place for the remaining meets, so every routine will be scanned and analyzed."

Flaherty hadn't heard that piece of news. "Oh, that's great! Congratulations!"

"Thanks."

"So, Ashlynn's fake article should definitely include that also. It will help to convince Morocco and some of the others that the tech is safe. With the team so scared that they might lose, that might convince more of them to work harder in practice. Maybe?" Even as Flaherty spoke the words, she wasn't convinced their plan would work, at least not on everyone.

"Maybe. Look we have two goals here. First, we want to take cheating out of the game, and it seems that we are taking significant steps toward that aim. Obviously, our second goal is to win the title, and you're right, we'll need more of them to work harder to accomplish that goal. Ashlynn's article might do the trick, but we should think of other ways to motivate them as well."

"Agreed. Hey, I think I got it. What if Ashlynn's article wasn't that fake after all?"

"No, I don't actually want that article published. The results could be devastating if the outside world actually thinks our reign is over. Could be a self-fulfilling prophecy."

"No, of course we don't want that article to get out. I'm saying what if we made life a little less comfortable for our teammates outside the gym. Make them consider what life might be like if we don't pull things together."

"Interesting. What do you have in mind?"

Flaherty flashed a devious-looking smile. "Oh, we could start with something small. Electricity outages. Technology failures. Clothing difficulties. We can blame it on dwindling resources from our loss."

Whitfield returned a smile. "I like it. It makes Ashlynn's article seem even more real. Do you think that would motivate them?"

"Perhaps. Without other distractions, some will head to the gym. As long as they are there, they may put in some work."

"Right. We'll just need to be there too."

"No problem there, right?"

"Nope. And of course, we know just the person to cause all this mayhem."

Whitfield and Flaherty shared a knowing glance and smiled. The rest of the ride home was relatively quiet, as the team members reluctantly contemplated their current state, still bitter from their loss. Despite the outcome, students still gathered around campus to welcome the team home, and various parties and social gatherings ensued as usual, although slightly less enthusiastically than during previous welcome home nights. As usual, Whitfield, Aspen, and Flaherty avoided the crowds and instead headed to Aspen's house to call Ashlynn and put their plan into action.

On their way to Aspen's house, Whitfield noticed he had a message from Ugu, and it wasn't her usual 'good luck and I miss you' message that she sends before every meet. This message asked if Whitfield could meet her at her detention cell when he returned to campus. It sounded urgent.

"Uhh, change of plans, guys. We need to go to the bank."

Aspen looked concerned. "Is everything OK with Ugu?"

Flaherty jumped in. "Yeah, I think so. I got a message too. Ugu wants to see us."

"OK. Let's go." Whitfield, Aspen, and Flaherty stealthily traversed the entrance quad and approached the bank without anyone seeing them.

Whitfield looked all around. "This is a bit odd. There doesn't seem to be anyone around."

Aspen didn't find the emptiness that strange. "Probably all greeting the team. You know how it is."

"I guess. But be careful." Whitfield sent Ugu a message saying they were at the side door, and Ugu promptly unlocked the door using a program she uploaded to her tracker. The three gymnasts entered the bank, then quietly navigated the halls of the empty basement and found their way to Ugu's cell. With a student currently residing in the Pit, the bank had cleared a path down to the basement. "Hey, sweetheart, are you OK?"

Ugu was so happy to see her friends. "I'm fine. How was the meet?"

Flaherty shook her head. "Don't ask."

"That bad?"

"You probably already know, don't you?"

"Yeah, I saw. How is the team taking it?"

Aspen threw his gym bag on the ground. "Again, don't ask. So much arguing on the ride home."

"Sorry. I'm sure things will get better."

Whitfield tried sounding optimistic. "Thanks. We're working on a plan. It actually kind of involves you. Well, I mean, we can use your help."

"Sure, anything. But first, I have some news for you."

Aspen's eyes lit up. "Are you getting out?"

"I wish, but not quite. Sir Arlington visited this weekend and told me what happened at Flaherty's house, with the entrance exams being stolen and the note. Which, first, great job decoding the note, Aspen! And second, how are you, sweetie?"

"Oh, I'm fine. Just mad at Jonathan and whoever else trashed my place."

"Me too. But I think I found a way to get them back. All of them."

Whitfield was curious. "How?"

"Well, first we know exactly who broke into your place."

Flaherty was stunned. "How? They disabled all the CBT surveillance. Even with Sir Arlington's access, we can't see what went on in those rooms."

Ugu flashed a mischievous grin. "Sure, Sir Arlington can't see. But we can. Don't you remember, Flaherty? When we took *CBT II* and learned about how the CBT cameras could be disabled, we installed back up surveillance feeds all around our houses."

"That's right! Oh, wow, I totally forgot about those."

"It's a good thing you have me then. So, I did a little digging through the footage, and presto…here are your intruders." Ugu showed a surveillance feed of four intruders ransacking Flaherty's mansion, toppling over furniture, breaking glass and figurines, and finally, stealing the entrance exams. Sure enough, Jonathan was there, and can clearly be seen leaving the note on Flaherty's desk.

"The intruders were careful not to be seen by anyone else who may have been walking around the mansion, but did not seem to take much care in covering their faces while inside the bedrooms or hallways, probably since they knew they had disabled the CBT cameras." Ugu pulled up profile pictures of Jonathan and the three other intruders.

Flaherty's mouth was agape. "I don't believe it. Is that really Jonathan's mom? She broke into my room?"

Whitfield looked on with the same astonished look. "Certainly looks that way. Who are those other two?"

Ugu pulled up bios on the other two intruders. "The one on the left is Bibb Tossino. Remember, we saw him during PAW. He was the one placing bets under Hendricks' name."

"I thought Sir Arlington told us he was arrested and sent to Chipwood."

"He was. Just got out a day before ransacking Flaherty's place. Guess he has some powerful friends."

Aspen was disgusted. "That's terrible."

"Tell me about it. The other one here is Col. Drachlich. He was also on campus during PAW. And guess what…both have strong ties to Gen. Gibson. They are each listed as minority owners of SYPHUS Industrials Inc. and take frequent withdrawals from bank accounts listed on Gen. Gibson's fake scoresheets."

Whitfield tried remaining calm, even though he was furious at all four intruders for what they did to Flaherty's place. "So, Gen. Gibson wasn't here himself. I guess that would have been too risky, since he's the one trying to replace Lord Sirroc as President of the WGF. He sent his goons here to retrieve the exams instead."

Flaherty was also trying to make sense of it all. "And Jonathan's mom would have access to the slides and other buildings because she's a member of the Board of Directors. That's how they got access to my house."

Whitfield knew they needed to put a stop to this. "Not for long. We have to get this information over to Sir Arlington."

"I already have. He's going to call for Jonathan's mom's immediate termination from the Board of Directors and tell Lord Sirroc to get arrest warrants for Bibb and Col. Drachlich. Neither will be able to step foot on campus again. I've added them to our defense network."

Whitfield and Flaherty both nodded their approval. "OK. So, what do we do now?"

"Sir Arlington has something else in mind for us—well, really you three, since I'm stuck in here."

Aspen always loved when he was involved in a new plan. "What's that?"

Ugu dropped her voice to a low whisper. "How would you three feel about breaking into Lord Sirroc's mansion?"

Chapter 41
The Planning Stage

"Excuse me?"

"What?"

Ugu could see that Whitfield and Aspen were surprised by her request, but she didn't let that stop her. "Yes. Lord Sirroc's personal residence. His 115,000 square foot mansion sitting on 18 acres of prime real estate."

Flaherty hadn't the slightest idea what Ugu was planning. "Ugu, that's serious. What's your angle?"

"First, I need to know that you're in."

"I'm in. This is going to be so cool."

"Aspen, hold on. This is for real. We can get in a lot of trouble, and not just with the school, but with the WGF."

"Whitfield, you're right. But Ugu needs us. She's asking for our help, and I trust her…unconditionally. I'm in."

Whitfield was quickly outnumbered. "But…"

"Oh, come on, you know you can't say no to Ugu."

"She's right, you can't say no to me." Ugu flashed her sweetest smile.

Whitfield let out a deep breath. "I could, if I really wanted to."

Ugu had her doubts. "Mmm…really?"

"Maybe."

"No. You can't. OK, so all three of you are in, right?"

Whitfield relented. "Oh, sure, why not."

"Good. So, here's the deal. We know Gen. Gibson has been working hard to discredit Lord Sirroc."

Whitfield added what little information he could. "We also know Gen. Gibson is working with SYPHUS, which has enormous resources behind them and agents all over the place."

"Right. So, they are going to want Lord Sirroc to suffer ultimate humiliation in front of a large gathering to cement his exit and possibly launch Gen. Gibson as the favorite to take over as president."

"But, how? Everyone knows Gen. Gibson is guilty of fixing meets, bribing gymnasts, stealing money…"

"Well, Aspen, Gen. Gibson is denying all of that and says he has proof that it was actually Lord Sirroc behind it all." Aspen shook his head and was about to interrupt, when Ugu raised her hand. "Of course, we know he's lying, but we can't underestimate him. My guess is that Gen. Gibson is going to show up at Lord Sirroc's house to stake his claim on the presidency."

Whitfield was confused. "When? Just randomly?"

"No. At the end-of-season gala that Lord Sirroc hosts every year just before the playoffs."

Flaherty nodded in agreement. "Wow. That's the perfect time. Everyone will be there. Coaches, athletes, media, everyone goes to it."

"Have you gone before?" Whitfield was still learning about all these off-campus events and traditions.

"Sure. Everyone on the team is invited. We get dressed up, mingle with the crowd, meet some people, eat some food. It's kind of boring, compared to some of the other events we go to, but it's still pretty nice."

Now Whitfield was really confused. "So, if we all get to go anyway, why did Ugu say we have to break into his house?"

Ugu began to spell out her plan. "Because the event is restricted to only a few areas—front lawn, backyard, atrium, banquet hall, and a few other designated open meeting places. You three are going to need to break through the security tape."

Flaherty thought she understood the mission. "Looking for what, exactly? The entrance exams?"

"Maybe. I think Jonathan is holding onto the exams for his mom, who may be planning to plant them inside Lord Sirroc's house for them to be 'discovered' during the Gala. The public shame of it would cause an even greater fall from grace for Lord Sirroc."

Whitfield was starting to see the bigger picture. "OK. So, that actually helps us. Since we do not know where the exams are currently being held, we can simply wait until the Gala to steal them back, right?"

Ugu threw in a curveball. "Not exactly. Another option is that Jonathan's mom destroys the corrupted exams after the admissions committee records the results. By destroying the evidence, Lord Sirroc would still be presumed guilty. Ideally, we'll want to get our hands on the exams before they ever make their way to Lord Sirroc's mansion, but after the committee inputs the results."

"Why wait until after the results get recorded?"

"We want Gen. Gibson to go through with his plan, fully thinking that he has a smoking gun. When he references the biased exam results, we can pull out the tainted exams to show where the actual corruption lies."

Whitfield expressed some concern. "Whoa. Now, we're stealing exams from the Admissions Office? We could really get into trouble here. Does Sir Arlington know about this plan?"

Ugu chose her words carefully. "Officially, no. Unofficially, it was kind of his idea."

"Oh boy, I'm excited about this." Aspen was eager to get started already.

Whitfield was still trying to understand the entire plan. "OK, so we wait until the admissions committee enters the results from the tainted exams into their records. We then steal the exams somehow. Gen. Gibson will think the evidence is either destroyed or planted somewhere in Lord Sirroc's mansion, when in reality, we have the evidence in our possession. Do I have that all straight?"

"Yes, I think so."

"OK. That seems really complicated, but let's move on. We haven't really even got to what you want us to do at Lord Sirroc's mansion."

"Right. Here's where it does get a little complicated."

Whitfield let out a nervous laugh. "Oh, this is the complicated part? So, stealing exams from the Admissions Office and breaking into Lord Sirroc's mansion were the easy parts?"

"Yes."

"Easy?"

"Yes. Relatively speaking."

"Easy?"

Flaherty decided to put an end to Whitfield and Ugu's childish back and forth. "Oh, shut up, you big baby. I'm excited about doing this."

"Me too. Big baby."

Aspen chuckled.

"Hey."

Ugu flashed a quick smile in Whitfield's direction. "If I can continue…we believe several members of SYPHUS are going to be at this Gala. They're not going to want to miss a big chance to take down Lord Sirroc, but if things do go a bit sideways, and even if they don't, I think they may try some aggressive tactics."

Aspen's smile disappeared and he showed genuine concern. "Aggressive? Like what?"

Flaherty got excited. "Do I get to kick some butt?"

"No, I don't think it will come to that, but you should always be prepared, just in case. SYPHUS is a lot more sophisticated with their tactics now. Whoever is running the show is very well-organized, clever, and extremely smart. They are not going to just go around bullying people at the Gala. But I think they may consider other means of attack."

Whitfield was locked in. "Such as?"

"Well, there are several possibilities. Lord Sirroc is vulnerable in a few areas, and we cannot possibly cover everything, but I think the most likely sources of concern are his personal bank accounts and his security access codes."

"This stuff all sounds pretty heavy. Why doesn't Lord Sirroc just hire extra security to protect himself?"

"Good question."

Flaherty shared info from her past experiences attending the Gala. "From what I remember, those parties always have tight security."

"Yes, they do, and yes, Lord Sirroc will likely bring in even tighter security now that he knows SYPHUS is back, but here's the deal…in all honesty, SYPHUS is smarter than Lord Sirroc. Smarter than a hundred security agents. We four are really the only chance Lord Sirroc has of surviving this attack. And what's more, we're *not* going to try to stop the attack from happening."

"Wait…what!"

"What do you mean? Why aren't we stopping them?"

Flaherty and Aspen were both surprised by Ugu's tactics, but Whitfield followed her logic. "It's because we want to draw out SYPHUS. We want them to think they're winning. Show their hand, right?"

Ugu was impressed that Whitfield caught on so quickly. "Exactly."

"It's a dangerous game we're playing here."

Ugu looked Whitfield directly in the eyes. "Are you up for it?"

"It's going to take a lot of planning."

"Hey, that's what I'm here for."

Whitfield and Ugu shared a long look, neither breaking eye contact until Aspen interrupted. "Are you going to the Gala, Ugu? It's not until the end of the term. You'll be out by then."

"No. Sir Arlington said it would be better if I do not show up at any big events for a while. Said it might cause some unnecessary distractions. And, besides, I don't think I'm going to be Little Miss Popular anymore."

Aspen was saddened by Ugu's comment. "What do you mean?"

"Well, remember when I got out of the Glass Box and everyone cheered?"

"Yes."

"Well, it's kind of like the exact opposite coming out of the Pit. And with everyone thinking that I cheated on an exam, they're really calling for me to be expelled."

Aspen sort of mumbled, "well, you did cheat."

Whitfield defended Ugu. "Aspen. That doesn't matter now. We know why she did it. And, we're not going to let Ugu get expelled, right?"

Flaherty enthusiastically agreed, "right."

"Thanks, you two, but we can't worry about that right now. We have some planning to do." Whitfield and Flaherty nodded. "Oh, one more thing. They kind of make a huge deal about end-of-season awards at the Gala. You know, Newcomer of the Year, Most Outstanding Gymnast, that sort of thing. Now, normally that kind of attention would distract you from completing your mission, but I remember from last year's Gala, that Gabe and I were taken all over the mansion and given special access passes to private rooms and various events."

Whitfield perked up. "Excuse me?"

Flaherty put an end to Whitfield's concerns immediately. "Oh, stop it. Nothing ever happened with those two."

"Actually, there was the one time…" Ugu missed teasing Whitfield, and thought she might try to capitalize on this one opportunity. Whitfield's eyes got really wide and his cheeks were turning bright red. "Aah…I'm just kidding. You are too easy."

Whitfield was not amused. "Very funny."

"Anyway, I think that could be your way in."

"What are you saying?"

"I'm saying that in order for this to work, you two need to win some big awards, and from my calculations, Flaherty, you're the favorite for MOG, but Whitfield, you really need to finish up with two solid meets if you're going to take home any prizes."

Aspen felt bad being left out. "What about me?"

"I do think there is a very good chance that you get one of the newcomer awards, but actually, I have a different plan for you."

Aspen got really excited. "You do? What's that?"

Ugu paused for a second. "Who's everyone's favorite chicken?"

Aspen's elation came crashing down, as he covered his face with his hands. "Oh no." Whitfield and Flaherty both laughed.

"Oh, come on, bro. It's the perfect disguise."

"But Lord Sirroc already knows I'm the chicken."

Ugu was quick to divulge Aspen's key role in the plan. "We're not trying to fool Lord Sirroc. We need to get you inside Lord Sirroc's office, before anyone from SYPHUS enters. Having the chicken suit on will provide you with some extra cover in case anything goes off script."

"Oh, all right. But what do I need to do in Lord Sirroc's office?"

"You'll need to install a program that I'm writing. It will replicate the screens one would see when logging into Lord Sirroc's personal accounts, but with a few minor modifications. The user will still think they are in his accounts, though, so whatever they attempt to do will be recorded and delivered back to my screen."

"Oh, that's clever. Just like our extra credit project back in first year, right?"

Ugu smiled at Flaherty. "Exactly. It's important that whoever breaks into Lord Sirroc's office thinks they actually accomplished what they set out to do. So, you need to get in there before the guests start arriving. That's why the mascot gig is the perfect cover. You can get there early, plant the program in the office, and still make it out to greet guests."

Whitfield approved of this part of the plan. "OK, that sounds good. And while Aspen is busy in the office, Flaherty and I will keep an eye on the security defense network."

Ugu shook her head. "No need. I'll be able to control that from here. You'll just need to break into the control room and reroute the controls to me."

Whitfield raised his eyebrows. "Oh, is that all?"

"Oh, come on. It'll be easy. Flaherty will distract whoever is there and give you enough time to do what you need to do."

Flaherty appreciated Ugu's confidence in her abilities, but wasn't entirely sure how she would pull it off. "You make this sound so easy."

Ugu, on the other hand, was fully confident in her plan. "The actual execution should be relatively easy. The planning is the hard part. I'll continue to make progress planning. You three just need to make sure you take care of business at these next two meets."

Whitfield saw his opportunity. "Speaking of that…"

"Oh, that's right. You had a project for me?"

"It seems kind of ridiculous asking you to work on something else with all this going on…"

"Oh, don't be silly. Sir Arlington granted me unlimited screen time. What is it?"

Flaherty tried framing the issue. "We are having some team chemistry problems."

From what Ugu gathered from her own past conversations with team members, she considered that a bit of an understatement. "Well, losing will bring those out."

"Right. We seem to be split on this whole fair competition issue."

"Let me guess, some of you think winning is the most important thing while others, like you three, care more about fair competition."

"Right. How did you know?" No matter how many times she did it, Aspen was continually surprised by just how quick Ugu was at understanding a problem or crafting a solution.

"It was bound to happen with everything that's going on."

"Right. Well, we just thought that maybe we could tip the scales a little in favor of fair competition." Whitfield was all in favor of maintaining integrity in the sport.

"Yeah, we're going to call Ashlynn and have her write a fake article saying how overrated our team really is."

Flaherty added the final part of their plan. "And to drive the point home a little further, we thought that removing some of the comforts of Seven Bridges Academy may spark some of our less-motivated team members to step up their practice habits in the gym."

Ugu didn't need any more framing. "Understood. I got it. What were you thinking? Technology? Electricity? Jewelry? Clothes? Test scores?"

Flaherty knew she could trust her best friend. "How about all of the above?"

"Done."

"Really? Just like that? You can mess with all that from in here?" Whitfield was both impressed, and a little frightened.

"Yup. All from right here. Sir Arlington lifted my restrictions. I can use my electronics any time now."

"Well, just be careful. I don't want any of this stuff being traced back to you."

"Oh, Whitfield, you worry too much. Don't you know I am much too clever for that?"

"Good to know. I just want you out of here and uhh…"

Ugu smiled. "And what?"

Flaherty offered a smile of her own. "Yeah, Whitfield, and what?"

Aspen started to giggle. "I know…he wants a little smoochie-smoochie."

Whitfield felt embarrassed. "Oh, grow up, you two." Ugu and Flaherty just laughed. The four friends said their goodbyes for the night before Whitfield, Aspen, and Flaherty left the basement and headed to Aspen's house for a late-night call to Ashlynn.

****

The next few weeks were the busiest of the year for Whitfield, Aspen, Ugu, and Flaherty. Ugu's tinkering with many of the gymnasts' comforts of home worked just as Whitfield and Flaherty had hoped. Team members spent more time in the gym and wasted less time on trivial pursuits. That is not to say that all the gymnasts were happy about their lights going out or the Uniform Galleria suddenly running out of stock in certain sizes, but to their credit, the affected gymnasts only complained a little, and instead, put forth more effort on perfecting their routines. Even Wilson was seen taking additional turns on several events, something that no one on the team had ever seen Wilson do before.

The mood in the gym was still tense, as several gymnasts had still not forgiven Whitfield for pursuing his notion of fair competition, which they were all now convinced is what prompted the WGF to act so drastically in shifting around schedules. Seven Bridges' schedule for the final two meets was supposed to be one of the easiest in the country; but now, it ranked as one of the most difficult, with each meet featuring at least three top ten teams in the current rankings.

Despite the increased intensity and more challenging schedule on the horizon, or perhaps because of it, team practices over the remaining few weeks of the regular season were the most productive of the entire year. Whitfield, Aspen, and Flaherty continued working at max effort, but so were many of the other gymnasts, including Hutchison, Seraphina, Morocco, and Chloe.

While Ashlynn's visit to practice and subsequent leaked article, coupled with Ugu's tampering, seemingly had the desired effect on practices and workout regimens, the increased effort in practice, unfortunately, did not translate into Seven Bridges regaining the top spot on the podium in the final two meets. Seven Bridges Academy finished second in the Footwear, Headwear, and Everything in Between meet, trailing only top-ranked Packer Dust Prep.

Seven Bridges did, however, come away with top finishes in Pommel Clock (Aspen); Tri-Bars (Morocco); and Parallel Planks (Flaherty). Flaherty finished first in the All-Around and Whitfield finished fourth. Two weeks later, Seven Bridges Academy again failed to win the top prize at the Fine Arts and Antiques meet; however, they did post season high scores in six of eight events. As a team, Seven Bridges Academy competed at a high level and just missed out on the top spot by eight team points.

Seven Bridges' gymnastics team learned a lot about themselves during the final month of the regular season. The athletes all put extra time in the gym and improved on their skills, consistency, and even team chemistry. They also learned that winning a fourth consecutive national title was not going to be easy, but given how far they had come over the past month, a title was certainly within reach.

For Whitfield, Aspen, and Flaherty, though, their chaotic month didn't end with the final meet of the season. Term 4 was almost over; Ugu was about to be released from the Pit; final exams and placement tests were fast approaching; and they only had one week left to prepare for Lord Sirroc's big end-of-season Gala, where they would be violating over a dozen federal laws by breaking into Lord Sirroc's mansion, stealing entrance exams, planting an illegal program inside Lord Sirroc's personal computer, and taking over the security controls of one of the largest defense networks in the world. If they managed to accomplish all this and escape without getting caught, they still had the upcoming playoffs to be concerned about, and with any luck, all the added pressure that comes along with the biggest annual event in the world, Team Championships. The stakes couldn't be higher, and the fate of the world rested in the capable hands of four schoolchildren. Exceptionally talented schoolchildren, but still, children.

Chapter 42
Awards

Ugu's release day was finally here. Her stay in the Pit had been extended for a few days beyond the standard seven weeks as a trade-off for Sir Arlington granting her additional access to electronic devices during the latter part of her sentence. Unlike her earlier release from the Glass Box, there was no fanfare and no celebration. Ugu was released from the Pit under the cloak of darkness, in the middle of the night. Two security agents escorted Ugu to her house and made sure she entered the front door, before leaving without uttering a word. Ugu walked through the front door and crept through the foyer, front hallway, and study lounge in near total darkness before finally turning on a light in the kitchen. Even though she knew Vincenzo and Stacy were alert at their security posts, she was alone, standing by herself in the kitchen.

Ugu was relieved to be out of the Pit. She had lost some weight, and felt weakened by her stay in solitude, but knew those affects were just temporary. She would return to her normal healthy eating habits and workout regimen and would, eventually, smile again. Ugu felt her bed, in her spacious bedroom suite, calling to her, but couldn't bring herself to climb the stairs just yet, no matter how tired she felt. She knew she had to go see Sir Arlington.

After all, he was the one who had pulled her release date up by several hours, and allowed her to access Seven Bridges' most top-secret files and security tapes during her stay in the Pit. She owed him her unwavering support and loyalty. Yes, she knew she needed to see Sir Arlington first.

Ugu left home and instead of taking the easy, direct path cutting through campus to the AMQE library which housed Sir Arlington's office, Ugu decided to take the long path around the Outer Loop. She missed running. She wasn't really dressed for it, but thought a quick lap around the Outer Loop would help clear her head and figured there was no better time than the present to start her long journey back to health and fitness. Ugu didn't get too far before she came to two realizations.

First, she wasn't as fit as she thought she was. Perhaps it was going to take a little longer than she had hoped to get back into shape. The lack of mobility over the previous seven weeks had really taken a toll on her stamina. Second, Ugu realized rather suddenly that she was not alone in the Outer Loop. Someone else was in the loop, and the footsteps were getting louder and closer, and before long, were right behind her.

Fear was not an emotion Ugu was familiar with, especially while running, but tonight was different. It was almost 03:00. The middle of the night. No one should be in the Outer Loop at this time. Even the security agents would be tucked away at their posts, hardly noticing the monitors as they studied or played games, hoping to make it through another quiet night without any alarm bells going off. Ugu decided that she could seek cover in the nearest slide alcove, and if needed, would have time to ring for security and would just have to defend herself for 30-40 seconds before the first wave of help arrived. As Ugu reached the nearest slide entrance, her would-be attacker came into view. Ugu immediately dropped her hand from the call button and ran toward the oncoming runner, throwing her arms up and around him.

"Whitfield! I am so happy to see you."

"Ugu? What are you doing here? You can get into trouble."

"No. I'm out. I was released."

"What? When?"

"About 45 minutes ago."

"How come you didn't tell me? I would have been there."

"Oh, no, that's OK. Sir Arlington arranged it all last-minute. Thought it would be better if no one else knew exactly when I was getting released."

"Wow! I've waited so long for this moment." Whitfield and Ugu embraced for what seemed like an eternity. Neither was willing to let go of the other. Both had tears streaming down their cheeks. It was a perfect moment, borne out of so much hardship, suffering, and tireless effort to rise above everything that was wrong with the world. Whitfield and Ugu's embrace, at that very moment, was the most pure, most innocent, and most needed hug of all time. Finally, they both softened their embrace and just stared into each other's eyes. Ugu was the first to speak.

"Hey, why are you out here at this time, anyway?"

"Couldn't sleep. Been thinking about you. About Lord Sirroc's Gala. About the upcoming playoffs. Finals. Placement tests. Gen. Gibson. SYPHUS. It's all been a lot."

Ugu put her finger on Whitfield's lips. "Shh…stop. Don't worry about any of that. Just hold me. Everything will be OK."

Whitfield hugged Ugu tight for another minute. Another perfect minute. Ugu pulled back slightly. "Feel better?"

Whitfield smiled. "Much better."

"Good. Now, let's go see Sir Arlington."

"Wait, what?"

"Sir Arlington. We need to go see him."

"But you just said to stop worrying about all that stuff."

"Well, yeah, I just wanted another hug. But all that 'stuff' isn't going away. I just told *you* not to worry about it."

"Well, it's some pretty big stuff. Why shouldn't I worry about it?"

"Because, now you have me. I'm no longer in that awful place. I can do this whenever I want." Ugu reached over and kissed Whitfield on the cheek. "I can also do this whenever I want." Ugu elbowed Whitfield in the gut.

Whitfield gasped, and doubled over. "Oh great…another thing for me to worry about."

"Oh, suck it up, you big baby. Let's go see Sir Arlington. We need to make sure everything is on track for next week." Whitfield and Ugu walked hand in hand through the Outer Loop, smiling and laughing, just like old times. When they reached Sir Arlington's office, he welcomed them both inside and offered them each a hot beverage. Despite the late hour, Sir Arlington did not appear to be surprised to see either Whitfield or Ugu, and was cheerful, but also seemed a bit distant, like something was weighing heavily on him.

"I am so glad to see you both; although, not as glad to the two of you appear to be to see each other." Sir Arlington winked in their direction.

"Yes, sir. It's been difficult, as you know. I couldn't have made it through the past few weeks without you both."

"Ahh, young Ugu, that is kind of you to say. But I believe there may be some others that share in your joy." Sir Arlington reached under his desk to press a button. The side door to Sir Arlington's conference room opened, and in walked a sleepy Aspen and Flaherty. At the sight of Ugu, however, they both opened their eyes wide and rushed to hug their beloved friend. "When the security feed picked up your reunion with Whitfield in the Outer Loop, I thought you might like to share the happy reunion with these two, as well." Once again, tears flowed freely down Ugu's cheeks as she engaged in deep embraces with both Flaherty and Aspen.

"Ugu, I'm so glad to see you. I'm sorry I wasn't awake when you got home. I didn't know…"

"That's OK, sweetie. I didn't know I was being released tonight either, until just before it happened."

Flaherty was crying tears of joy. "I love you so much."

"Me too." Ugu and Flaherty embraced for a long minute.

Whitfield turned to Sir Arlington. "Sir. Thank you for organizing this. We really appreciate this moment."

"Certainly. You have all earned it." Sir Arlington stepped back and, with great joy, watched the scene unfold before his eyes for a few moments, before interrupting with a more business-like tone. "Well, now that we are all present and accounted for, I do believe we have some matters to discuss."

Ugu dried her eyes with a tissue from Sir Arlington's desk. "Of course, sir. We have Lord Sirroc's Gala and awards to discuss. Where would you like to start?"

"Yes. How about the awards? Are we all set there?" Whitfield, Aspen, and Flaherty all seemed a bit confused. End-of-season awards were not scheduled to be released until next week, at Lord Sirroc's Gala. As far as they knew, award winners had not yet been decided.

Nevertheless, Ugu continued, "yes, I believe so. Well, as far as I can tell this early in the process. Flaherty will, in all likelihood, win the MOG Award. Her All-Around scores and team points set her apart from the competition. Her media presence and charisma would make her the perfect candidate to receive the highest honor, and sources already confirm several marketing campaigns and endorsement deals in the works. I assess her odds of winning at 87%, with no other viable candidate at more than 3%."

Sir Arlington nodded. "Good work."

Flaherty seemed surprised. "Really! I'm going to win MOG?"

Ugu smiled at her best friend. "You earned it."

Whitfield put his hand on Flaherty's shoulder. "You really did. I keep telling you that you're the best."

"Thank you, but don't sell yourself short. What about Whitfield? He should get some votes too, right?"

Ugu shook her head. "Not likely. His overall performance was not up to par with yours and since you are on the same team, voters have a direct comparison.

We also do not have a precedent for a first-year gymnast, that is, a gymnast without any prior years' experience, winning the award. Voter bias will work against Whitfield."

Flaherty continued to show her support for Whitfield. "But he should get something, right? I mean he is really good. I mean, not as good as some others, but still…"

Whitfield caught on to Flaherty's little sarcastic comment. "Thanks."

Ugu continued to relay her informed predictions. "He will. At least, I think he will. Let me circle back to Whitfield. The easier one to predict is Aspen. He should win Pommel Clock Performer of the Year, without question, and will likely take home the Most Outstanding First-Year Gymnast Award. He does have some competition for that award, though, mostly from Carter at Triplepike Academy and Smallz at Better Release Point Prep. Carter's scores are comparable to Aspen's and he started out the season competing on three events, whereas Aspen only competed on two. They both ended the year with roughly the same number of routines and team points.

"Aspen has more media appeal and his age likely works in his favor, as media outlets would salivate over the 'youngest gymnast ever to win' story-lines. Smallz doesn't have the team points or average scores that Aspen does, but he did compete as an All-Arounder for the final three meets, more than holding his own, and did defeat Aspen in their only head-to-head duel this year."

Aspen defended himself, "hey, that wasn't fair. It was on Tri-Bars, and everyone knows Professor Marino gives me low scores."

Whitfield tried calming his brother. "Hey, bro, it's OK. We know."

Ugu agreed, "that's right. Don't worry about it. I do not think Smallz will receive the award over you, but I just needed to mention the possibility."

Sir Arlington was all business. "What's the likelihood that Aspen wins?"

"About 65% sir."

"OK. That's good. Now, what about Whitfield?"

"Well, sir, Whitfield is a special case. I've looked through the past 20 years of data, and there's never been a third-year transfer gymnast with no prior competition history perform as well as Whitfield has this season."

Sir Arlington gave a slight head nod. "I have no doubt that is true."

"In fact, his performance does rank among the top ten to fifteen among all third-years ever. Of course, still behind Flaherty, Gabe, and a few others from recent memory."

Whitfield whispered to Flaherty, "she didn't have to throw in Gabe's name, did she?"

Ugu overheard. "Yes, I did. Anyway, Whitfield does have marketing appeal and the media has run several stories featuring him this year, but not enough. Even if we had Ashlynn run a puff piece this week, he still wouldn't win over voters for one of the top three awards, but..." Ugu hesitated.

Whitfield wanted her to continue. "But, what?"

"I do think he has the best odds to win..." Again, Ugu paused.

Flaherty encouraged Ugu to continue. "Win what?"

"Oh, I can't believe I'm going to say this."

"Say what?" Aspen was on the edge of his seat.

Ugu felt her face get all flush even before finishing her thought. "Whitfield is probably going to win the award for Sexiest Gymnast of the Year!" Aspen and Flaherty broke out in hysterical laughter. Aspen fell off the couch. Ugu's cheeks turned red with embarrassment just uttering those words. Even Sir Arlington allowed himself to grin. Whitfield, however, remained stoic, pensive.

"Yeah, I could see that."

Aspen burst out laughing. "Whitfield! Sexiest Gymnast? You have to be kidding."

"I know, it sounds ridiculous, but look, the data supports it."

Flaherty attempted to dry her eyes with a tissue from Sir Arlington's desk. "Oh honey, you really must be in love. Sexiest gymnast? Whitfield? Really?"

Ugu sighed heavily. "Yes, I know. But hear me out. The criteria for the award are largely built around performance metrics. Now, it also includes media attention, interview scores, school aptitude, and eligibility. Whitfield would score outstanding marks on all those factors."

Flaherty needed to remind Ugu. "It also includes an appearance factor."

Ugu looked befuddled. "Yes. And?"

"What, Flaherty, you don't find me attractive? Am I not sexy enough for you?" Whitfield stood up and did a silly little dance, shaking his hips.

Flaherty shielded her eyes. "Oh, please. And, what about eligibility? Everyone know you two are so into each other."

Ugu felt she needed to correct Flaherty. "Not necessarily. We did have a rather public fight and break up. Students haven't seen me around for the past seven weeks, and the media hasn't seen me attend any meets."

Aspen confirmed, "because you haven't."

"That's right. There are some shots of us together at earlier functions, but there's way more shots of Whitfield with Flaherty than with me."

Whitfield didn't detect a hint of jealously coming from Ugu, but wanted to make sure. "Yeah, but that's just for team publicity."

"Oh, I know. I'm just saying that I really think it's a strong possibility."

"Ugu. No one from Seven Bridges Academy has ever won that award. Not even Gabe."

Whitfield really perked up now. "Oh really? So, if I won, would that mean I am sexier than Gabe?"

Ugu decided to burst Whitfield's growing bubble. "Uhh…no. The competition for the award this year is pretty slim. We have Adrian from P'socto, Danyelle from Pancake Batter Prep, Barley or Marina from Circleville, Dustin from Farmstead, and Harris from Neering Tech. That's about it."

Whitfield was feeling good about his chances. "Oh, I'm sexier than all of them." Aspen almost fell off the couch again.

Sir Arlington had let the frivolity continue for long enough. He desired to get back to business. "OK, let's settle down. I understand the rather emotional, and personally gratifying, underpinnings to this award. Looking at this from a strictly objective point of view…I think Ugu has a point. Whitfield is a viable candidate. Ugu, how certain are you?"

"Actually, sir. It's about a 55-60% certainty that Whitfield wins the award."

Sir Arlington nodded. "OK. Let's tilt the odds a little more in his favor. I'll call Ashlynn. Whitfield, have your staff set up a few interviews with some national outlets and out-of-area local feeds. Get this all done over the next 2-3 days. That's all we have left to influence voters."

"Yes, sir. Sounds good, but I have another idea."

"Yes, young Whitfield?"

Whitfield regained his composure. "Ugu, what are Flaherty's odds?"

"Excuse me?"

"For the Sexiest Gymnast of the Year Award."

"Umm…that's interesting. Flaherty would certainly receive some votes, if she weren't going to win MOG. There's never been an MOG that also won Sexiest Gymnast in the same year. Now that I think about it, I can't recall anyone winning both awards across different years, either."

Whitfield looked pensive. "Hmm…"

Sir Arlington wanted Whitfield to continue sharing. "What is on your mind, young Whitfield?"

"All season, Flaherty and I have had requests for both of us to appear together. Interviews, fashion shoots, even community service projects. What if we were both voted Sexiest Gymnast? Together."

Sir Arlington raised an eyebrow. "Hmm…that is an interesting concept. Young Ugu?"

"Sir, it's never happened before. Difficult to determine the odds."

"Forget the odds. What does your gut tell you?"

"Honestly, sir. It's brilliant. The media would eat it up."

Whitfield turned toward Ugu. "Would you be OK with that?"

"Me? Yes, of course. You're my boyfriend. Flaherty's my best friend. I trust you both completely. It would be pretty cool to be surrounded by the two sexiest gymnasts of the year."

Aspen was feeling left out. "Hey, don't forget about me. I'm sexy."

Ugu smiled. "Yes, sweetie, you certainly are."

Sir Arlington seemed pleased. "OK, good. I'll call Ashlynn first thing in the morning and float the idea to her. Now, with all three of you likely winning prestigious awards, you will each have access to certain secure areas inside Lord Sirroc's mansion."

Whitfield knew Sir Arlington would remain coy about his knowledge of their upcoming plan to infiltrate Lord Sirroc's mansion, but did seek some confirmation. "Sir, about that. Are you going to give Lord Sirroc a head's up about what we're doing?"

"Lord Sirroc knows all that he needs to know at the moment. We'll loop him in, if needed. Remember, he'll be busy throughout the evening, and we do not need him screwing anything up by alerting his own security staff as to what you may, or may not, be doing. The more people that know, the lower your odds of success."

"Understood. Sir, will you be attending the Gala?"

"Yes. I will be there. Young Ugu will run your op from in here. In case anything goes sideways and your valiant efforts get unmasked and traced back here, I'll have plausible deniability, and then we can credibly attempt to blame SYPHUS for hijacking my network."

Flaherty was optimistic it wouldn't come to that. "Clever. But Ugu's too smart for that. She won't get caught."

"Thank you." Ugu peered over at Sir Arlington as if to check whether it was OK to discuss certain details of the mission in his presence. Sir Arlington did not object. "Aspen will upload the program on Lord Sirroc's personal computer. Whitfield and Flaherty will route the security defense network to this office. I'll disable any firewalls or other protections, making it easier for anyone from SYPHUS to break in to the system. I'll record every keystroke, and keep a record of any attempted crime."

"What should we do after we complete our mission? Should we just get out of there?"

"No, young Whitfield. It's important that people see you at the Gala. Make your appearances, mingle, and be memorable, but still watch your backs. Do not find yourselves alone with any members of SYPHUS." To Whitfield's surprise, not only did Sir Arlington stay in the room to hear their plans, but he also contributed to the tactical planning.

"How are we going to know who is part of SYPHUS?"

"Good point, young Aspen. SYPHUS agents could be anywhere. Just watch each other's backs. And young Aspen, after your mascot duties, get out of the suit and rejoin the Gala as quickly as possible. You will be the most vulnerable, and young Ugu will likely not have eyes on you at the beginning. It will take some time before young Whitfield and young Flaherty can route the controls here."

"You got it, sir."

Sir Arlington had seemingly taken control of the op. "Any questions?"

Flaherty looked around at the others. "Nope. I think we're good."

"Good. Now, perhaps I will retire to allow some discussion regarding our beloved admissions process." Sir Arlington had indeed drawn the line between that which was acceptable for him to hear about and that which was not.

"Actually, sir. I do have a question. Actually, more of a request."

"Yes, young Whitfield?"

"I was wondering if you might be able to convince Ashlynn to set up an advance photo shoot for Flaherty and I for the Sexiest Gymnast award."

Flaherty thought Whitfield was too far ahead of himself. "Whitfield. We haven't actually won anything yet. It's still a longshot that we would both get it."

"Oh, I know. I just thought perhaps we may want to have the shoot on campus. Maybe near one of the Administration offices?"

Ugu quickly caught onto Whitfield motivation. "Ahh…perhaps near Admissions?"

Whitfield nodded. "Couldn't hurt…maybe give some of our hard-working admissions team members a much-needed distraction."

Sir Arlington pondered this request. "Hmm…understood. I will see what I can do."

"Thank you. Good night, sir." Sir Arlington left his office.

"Whitfield, that's a really good idea. Maybe while we are doing the photo shoot, we can distract the committee members enough to allow Aspen or Ugu to sneak in and get the exams."

Aspen quickly called dibs on this latest mission objective. "I'll do it."

"Sounds like a great idea. We'll need to get it done Saturday morning. We can't be late for Lord Sirroc's Gala."

"Really? Ugu, I can really do it?"

"You are the man for the job. As long as you can get it done Saturday morning before the Gala."

"No problem." Aspen had a huge smile. "Anyone up for some cake?"

"Bro, what is up with you and cake?"

"What? I like cake." Ugu and Flaherty laughed.

"No. Not tonight, sweetie. I think we should all try to get some sleep. We can go over the plan for the admissions team tomorrow."

"Good idea, Ugu. Hey, do you have any exams tomorrow? Err…well, in a couple hours." Whitfield checked the time and realized just how late it was.

"Yes. I'm sure it's going to be rough—seeing other students, that is, not the exam itself—but I have to face it head on." Ugu looked uneasy.

Whitfield offered some comfort. "I'll be there for you."

"Me too. Whatever you need." Flaherty put her arm around Ugu.

"Same here."

Aspen snuck around Flaherty to hug Ugu too.

"Thanks. Really, I mean it. I love you all."

"Of course, you do. We're the sexiest around." Whitfield started dancing again.

Ugu rolled her eyes. "Oh, please. I knew I shouldn't have said anything." The four friends left Sir Arlington's office together, laughing and smiling. They each went home, and slept fast, as morning approached more quickly than any of them had hoped.

Tired and mentally drained, each of them got out of bed after a short night's rest, and faced the remaining few days of Term 4 head on. The weeknights during finals week were filled with study hours for all students preparing for final exams and placement tests, but for Whitfield, Aspen, Flaherty, and Ugu another mission needed to be planned. The admissions committee would be meeting on campus over the weekend to review applications and make final decisions for first-year admits, marking the last opportunity for Whitfield and his crew to steal back the entrance exams before Lord Sirroc's Gala.

****

As expected, Ugu's first week back among students was horrible. Even though exams and final projects preoccupied most of campus, students still shouted and spewed nasty insults at Ugu and gave her dirty looks wherever she went. Words such as 'cheater', 'liar', 'fake', and 'fraud' echoed throughout campus. The insults were not only directed at Ugu, but felt by anyone who dared comfort or associate with her.

Whitfield and Aspen both felt the putrid stench of students' venom by merely associating with a known cheater. Only Flaherty was able to avoid some of the spillover anger, as she appeared to be universally loved among the student body, a perch once shared by Ugu herself.

Despite taking classes virtually for most of the term, Ugu earned perfect marks on all her exams. Her every movement in the exam rooms was heavily scrutinized and recorded from multiple angles to ensure additional cheating would not take place. After her final exam in Term 4, Ugu felt a huge wave of relief, even though the sneers and insults did not stop. To his credit, Whitfield tried to deflect as much of the verbal abuse as possible, but he couldn't stop all of it. After their last exams of the term, Whitfield and Ugu met up in the Inner Bowl.

"Hey, Honey Bear. How does it feel to be done with Term 4?"

"A huge relief. I think I crushed this whole term."

"Great! Wouldn't expect anything less from the second smartest student in school."

"Oh, I see how it is. How'd you do on your exams?"

"Killed it."

"That's my girl. How you holding up?"

"Good. I think. I mean, it really stinks that everyone still thinks I'm a cheater."

"I know. It's taken a toll on me too. I can't stand hearing all that noise about you."

"Just try to ignore it. When this all comes to pass, they'll realize what's up."

"I hope so."

"Trust me. They will. Besides, you have more important things going on this weekend."

Whitfield nodded. "I know. I know. Lord Sirroc's Gala. I'm ready."

"Uh-uh. Not what I'm talking about."

Whitfield turned to face Ugu. "You mean…are you serious? We are actually going out on a date?"

"Umm...I would love that. More than you know, but sadly, that's not what I was talking about either."

"Then what?"

"Didn't you hear?"

"No. What?"

Ugu flashed an adorable smile. "Oh, you'll see." Ugu and Whitfield continued walking on campus toward the entrance quad.

"Why are we over here? Are we just scoping out the area for tomorrow's admissions team op?"

"Well, maybe. But, more importantly..." Whitfield and Ugu walked into the Administration Building, and as soon as they did, Whitfield saw it. Everyone who walked in the building saw it. How could anyone miss it? There it was. Over 50 feet high. Hanging down from the top floor and spanning over twenty feet wide. Two huge banners. Two huge faces. On the left, 'Whitfield Mitchell: Sexiest Gymnast of the Year'. On the right, 'Flaherty Sumner: Sexiest Gymnast of the Year'. Whitfield was stunned.

"Uhh...how? What?"

"Yes, I know. Officially, awards will not be released until tomorrow at the Gala, but schools receive a heads up on a few awards so they can start marketing campaigns and profit off the announcement."

"Wait, so this is true? We both won?" Ugu nodded. "I can't believe it. What about MOG? Did Flaherty not win?"

"No. I mean, I really don't know. It hasn't been announced yet. They save MOG, all the newcomer awards, and most of the event-specific awards for tomorrow. The big early reveal is this one."

At this point, several students walking through the atrium of the Administration Building took notice of Whitfield standing there, in front of his own banner, and congratulated him on the high honor. Several female students, and even a few staff members, asked to take pictures with Whitfield. Ugu kindly stepped aside, and grinned at Whitfield's ever-growing popularity.

"Don't worry, Ugu. I won't let this all go to my head."

"Oh, I'm not worried about that. You wouldn't ever leave me. Right?"

"Not a chance."

"Good. Well, now that you've seen it. I wonder if we should call Flaherty and tell her to come by. I don't think she's seen it yet, and if you are up for it, perhaps we can capitalize on both of your newly found fame, and conduct our op a day early?"

"But Sir Arlington scheduled the photo shoot for tomorrow."

"Right, but this opportunity might be too good to pass up. Look at all these people." The atrium was starting to flood with students.

"Might not be a bad idea. You call her, and I'll check out where the admissions team is set up."

Ugu had a better idea. "No, I think you should call her. If you start walking around the building, someone from the committee may spot you and things might get a little chaotic too early. Go in the corner over there, make the call, and I'll scan the building."

"You got it boss, or should I say jefe."

"I know you're being sarcastic, but you know it's true."

Whitfield slid into a private corner and connected with Flaherty, asking her to meet him and Ugu in the Administration Building. He didn't mention why, but Flaherty agreed to come anyway. She was just finishing up showing Aspen some of the lab equipment she used for her Term 4 project. Whitfield told her to bring Aspen along as well.

In the meantime, Ugu had located the room where the admissions committee was set up, all the way up on the top floor, and it appeared that the packets of corrupted entrance exams were on the table and had already been evaluated.

Now was the perfect time to take back the exams. The corrupted data was recorded. The records would show that Lord Sirroc had intentionally written biased questions. All that was left for SYPHUS to get away with it was to destroy the tainted evidence. Ugu couldn't let that happen. If this mission was to succeed, Ugu would have to act fast.

Ugu quickly walked out toward the railing overlooking the vast atrium below and spotted Whitfield in the far corner. Ugu then screamed at the top of her lungs. "AAAAAHHHHH...OMIGOSH...OMIGOSH...OMIGOSH. HE'S HERE! IT'S WHITFIELD! AAAHHHH! He's the sexiest gymnast in the whole world! Everyone look. It's really him."

Ugu was pointing frantically in Whitfield's direction, and all the students, staff, and other passersby in the building all stopped what they were doing to catch a glimpse of the newly crowned Sexiest Gymnast of the Year. As a crowd started to build around Whitfield, Ugu spotted Flaherty and Aspen ascending the outside steps and about to walk in. She screamed again.

"AAAAHHHH. THERE'S FLAHERTY! SHE'S SO SEXY!" By now, the entire place was buzzing. Students were screaming Whitfield's and Flaherty's name, and gathering around them for pictures. It seemed that everyone wanted to touch the newest celebrities, with many students, and staff alike, leaning in for hugs, and even a few kisses on the cheek. The entire building was abuzz. Even the admissions committee, perched in a secluded room on the top floor, rushed out to see what the commotion was all about.

With the deafening sounds of screaming teenagers filling every open space in the Administration Building atrium, Ugu knew she had to exploit this opportunity. Flaherty and Whitfield each had their own crowd surrounding them, but before long, both had found their way toward the center of the atrium floor to pose for pictures with their huge banners serving as an over-the-top backdrop.

Aspen, who remained near Flaherty's side, managed to attract some attention from the enamored students, but this show was all about Whitfield and Flaherty. Soon, Aspen began to look around for any sign of Ugu, and when he finally spotted her, she was still standing by the railing, and motioning for Aspen to come up to meet her.

Several members of the eight-person admissions committee joined the fracas on the ground level, but others stayed up top, joining the many others who had exited their offices and conference rooms to take in the excitement. Ugu met Aspen by the stairs and whispered in his ear instructions to sneak into the large meeting room and grab the entrance exams. It would be Ugu's job to make sure the room stayed empty until after Aspen's mission was complete.

Ugu positioned herself in the crossroads of the hallway leading to the large meeting room and the outer-facing walkway overlooking the atrium. From where she was standing, Ugu could spot Aspen heading down the hall, and the nearest committee members still taking an interest in the festivities below, but slowly starting to engage in side conversations. She knew interest would be fading soon, and members would be eager to get back to work. She also knew Aspen would likely need a few more minutes to collect the exams and steer clear of the long corridor. Students were not supposed to be in the corridor, and it would be more than a little suspicious if someone found Aspen carrying a bunch of exams out of the meeting room.

In a last-ditch effort to refocus everyone's attention on the wild circus below, Ugu hurriedly approached the railing, and shouted out the first thing that came to mind. "WHITFIELD. TAKE YOUR SHIRT OFF!" The entire crowd, which grew substantially over the previous five minutes, as word of mouth spread extremely fast across campus, yelled out their approval.

Chants of 'take your shirt off' reverberated across the crowded expanse. The windows and walls shook as throngs of students jumped in unison, hoping to see more. In the end, an embarrassed Whitfield remained calm and collected, and kept his shirt on. He did, however, move closer toward Flaherty, and the two of them posed for pictures together for a while longer.

The distraction worked like a charm. Aspen escaped the meeting room and made it all the way down the hallway, tapping Ugu on the shoulder, before any committee member had even taken their eyes off the gripping scene below. Ugu took the exams and swiftly placed them in her bag and she and Aspen exited the top floor. Ugu went down the staircase on the left, while Aspen waited a beat and made his way along the walkway and descended down the staircase on the right. Neither waited for Whitfield or Flaherty. They each made their way across campus, and back to Aspen's mansion.

Along the way, Ugu left messages for both Whitfield and Flaherty. "You may be sexy, but Aspen is a stud!" Whitfield and Flaherty knew immediately the first part of their mission was a success.

Chapter 43
Lord Sirroc's Gala

Whitfield and Aspen met up with Keegan, Morocco, Reid, Hutchison, and Pryce at the Uniform Galleria on Saturday morning to get their formal attire and accessories for Lord Sirroc's Gala. It was strange for the boys to have the entire third and fourth floors to themselves, but the girls had all headed over to Flaherty's house to get ready. Even though she wasn't attending the Gala, Ugu arranged for the Uniform Galleria, which normally did not send items out for delivery, to send out a whole stable of dresses, jewelry, shoes, and bags for Flaherty and the rest of the girls from the gymnastics team to try on and see which combinations they liked best. Several of the girls still shot evil glances in Ugu's direction, but most did warm up to Ugu as the morning wore on. Despite the friction, Ugu loved spending time with the girls, especially Flaherty, away from the Glass Box and the Pit, just smiling, laughing, and having a good time.

Over in the Uniform Galleria, Whitfield and Aspen were also having a great time hanging out with the guys. With all the pressure that Term 4 brought, Whitfield and Aspen were relieved to have even just one morning without having to worry about SYPHUS or the future of the entire gymnastics' world crashing down around them. Instead, they could just be kids. Laughing. Enjoying themselves. Watching Keegan try to fit into a size small jacket. Laughing as Hutchison forgot to button his trousers and everyone could see his shirt poking out. Having everyone come together to tie a bunch of neckties together, forming a contraption to open and close changing room doors.

Yes, the morning was a blast for everyone there, especially when all the guys got to see the special swag the WGF sent over for Whitfield to wear, as the recipient of the Sexiest Gymnast of the Year Award. Whitfield had the honor of being outfitted with the exquisite Piero Feterer sapphire crystal watch, diamond and black opal encrusted sunglasses, and sparkling purple jadeite cufflinks, to match his silk handkerchief and vest color combination. Even for a school with seemingly every luxury available for students, Whitfield's look for the Gala stood out above the rest.

Not to be outdone, the WGF sent a special wardrobe consultant and precious gem expert to Flaherty's house to bestow the other Sexiest Gymnast of the Year Award winner with the most expensive and exquisite set of jewelry ever crafted. Flaherty had her pick of earrings, necklaces, bracelets, rings, and so much more. She could not believe the size of several of the stones in front of her, and immediately became the envy of every girl in the room. The WGF wanted their award winners to stand out, and the world's most exclusive jewelers and clothing designers wanted their products adorning the stars of the evening.

Flaherty understood as much, but also knew the value of teamwork and friendship. With every gem, stone, and sparkling ornament presented to her, Flaherty calmly and gracefully, redirected the piece to one of her teammates, whom she decided 'was a better fit' to wear such an exquisite item.

In fact, Flaherty had made sure every other girl, except for Ugu, who was not attending the Gala, was beautifully adorned with the finest jewelry in the land, before placing a single gemstone on her own skin. In the end, all that was left was a relatively understated necklace, which Flaherty wore proudly, alongside her teammates. Truth be told, however, even without the full assortment of jewels and gems, Flaherty appeared flawless, and would undoubtedly live up to her award at tonight's Gala.

Following the morning's wardrobe dress rehearsal, Flaherty, Ugu, and the girls went down to the kitchen and had a warm buffet lunch, while the guys went out to Plank 'N Steins for a bite to eat, where the laughs and good times continued. Before wrapping up their long lunch and heading over to SBA IV for their personal drone limo service, Whitfield made sure to remind Aspen of their mission. Aspen needed to get to Lord Sirroc's mansion about a half hour earlier than the others so he could greet guests as the WGF chicken mascot. The plan offered Aspen some flexibility in when he would upload Ugu's program onto Lord Sirroc's personal computer in his office.

Ideally, Aspen would upload it as soon as he arrived, before changing into the chicken suit, but, if necessary, he could wait until after his appearance and upload it then, but a longer delay meant that SYPHUS agents had more time to get in and access Lord Sirroc's files without any of Ugu's coded protection.

Given the high spirits and overall frivolity of their lunch gathering, it was easy for Aspen to sneak away unnoticed. He calmly trotted over to the landing port on top of SBA IV where a personal drone shuttle was already waiting for him. Unlike

Aspen's internship where he had changed into the chicken suit on his way to WGF headquarters, Aspen was no longer in possession of the suit, and would have to wait until he got to Lord Sirroc's mansion to change. Aspen directed the shuttle to the top landing port on the west side of Lord Sirroc's enormous mansion.

Two handlers met Aspen as he arrived, and directed him inside, where the chicken suit awaited. To Aspen's surprise, the handlers quickly left Aspen alone to change, but not before giving him explicit instructions regarding the expectations for his performance, including where to appear and when. Other than a few quick words, Aspen was left to his own accord inside the top floor of Lord Sirroc's mansion, just outside Lord Sirroc's office.

The first part of the plan could not have worked out any better. Two security guards were stationed outside Lord Sirroc's office. Aspen calmly approached them and asked if he could get changed inside, since no one was to know the true identity of the WGF mascot. Perhaps it was the secretive nature of the stealth mission that appealed to the guards, or maybe Aspen was just too persuasive to deny entry. Either way, the guards allowed Aspen to enter, and proceeded to close the doors behind him and stood guard, leaving Aspen alone in the office.

Not wasting a moment, Aspen adroitly uploaded Ugu's program on Lord Sirroc's computer, and got changed into the chicken suit before the guards ever knew what happened. Aspen knocked on the door to let the guards know he was ready, and one of the guards escorted Aspen up a ladder inside the highest turret and waited beside him until receiving the go ahead to open the window and have Aspen 'fly out of his cage' for the awaiting guests. Aspen zip-lined across the immense yard, softly tossing 'eggs' filled with various prizes and trinkets, before gently landing in the designated outdoor dance area, where Aspen proceeded to cluck, waddle, strut, and groove his way around the grounds to everyone's amusement.

Meanwhile, gymnasts, coaches, and other dignitaries from all across the land had been arriving with their guests at any of four designated landing ports on the periphery of the beautifully landscaped grounds. A cadre of greeters and attendants welcomed each guest with a gift bag and a special invitation to one, or more, of several exclusive events being held at the mansion that evening. All gymnasts receiving end-of-year awards were issued special 'backstage passes' to gain entrance to otherwise restricted areas of Lord Sirroc's mansion.

Guests were asked to keep their event invitations quiet, but word quickly spread among the gymnasts that anyone with the gold-lettered invitation to Event 12 was an award-winner. Keegan nearly punched an elderly woman walking nearby when he raised his fists in the air after realizing he had won an end-of-season award. Fortunately, he barely missed her and the old lady only had to recover from an overly raucous cheer from the sixth-year first-time winner.

As guests continued to pour in, the music grew louder and the cheerful reconnection of distant friends perfectly accented the calm, slightly breezy evening. Consistent with their modus operandi when arriving at big events during the season, Whitfield and Flaherty were among the last gymnasts to arrive at Lord Sirroc's Gala.

Sharing a drone limo so they could go over their mission plan one more time, Whitfield and Flaherty made quite the entrance, as Lord Sirroc's head groundskeepers perfectly timed an early fireworks display to go off just as the two most sought-after gymnasts arrived at the first landing port. Whitfield exited the vehicle first, but only so he could grab hold of Flaherty's hand, and help escort her down the two steps, made trickier by Flaherty's higher than usual heels.

The two sexiest gymnasts of the year stopped to pose for pictures, before fashionably making their way toward the front steps of the enormous mansion, pausing occasionally to chat with friends and to catch up with competitors they hadn't seen in a while. Whitfield and Flaherty both received the same gold-lettered invitations to Event 12 as Keegan, and all the other award winners, had in their welcome bags. As usual, Flaherty looked gorgeous in a long sleek black dress, with a plunging neckline and purple accents, and an understated, but still exquisite diamond necklace.

Whitfield looked handsome in a black tuxedo with purple accents. Understandably, the advanced media cameras seemed to focus on the two of them more than the others, and Whitfield hoped that Ugu wouldn't get jealous watching him walking arm in arm with Flaherty throughout much of the night. The truth is they only stayed that close to each other so they could whisper into each other's ear when they spotted known SYPHUS agents or to point out security protocols.

The tightened security at the Gala did not allow for personal electronic devices, even making a point of banning any earpieces with remote communication capabilities, which prevented Ugu from being a constant presence in their ears throughout the night. While everyone else appeared to be there to have a good time, Whitfield and Flaherty were on a mission; a mission that if failed could mean the end of gymnastics and the WGF as they knew it, and upend the entire world.

Shortly after Whitfield and Flaherty had arrived, and Aspen joined the Gala as himself, Lord Sirroc took center stage, welcoming all guests and encouraging everyone to have a good time. No speeches. No extraneous political chatter. Short, sweet, and to the point.

Guests still had some time to mingle before the awards presentations, but the awards recipients were asked to step inside Lord Sirroc's inner sanctum for a tour and an exclusive meet-and-greet with WGF officials, politicians, business leaders, and professional gymnastics team owners. Whitfield's eyes lit up when he saw all the special guests in the room, but forced himself to remain focused. Flaherty offered some encouragement as well.

"Hey, get your head out of your butt. Pay attention."

"I'm here. I know what's going on."

"Good. Because I need you. We're a team on this, right?"

"Right. We'll sneak off. You distract any guards and I'll upload the program."

"OK. Ready?"

"Ready."

Flaherty left first. She sneaked out the side door and quickly darted through another door down the hall. She hesitated for a moment when she didn't see Whitfield on her heels, and got a little concerned when he still didn't show up a few moments later. Whitfield was about to sneak away from the group just as a hand firmly grasped Whitfield on the shoulder. Whitfield's knees buckled. He hadn't even done anything yet, and already thought he was caught, and in big trouble. He closed his eyes and heard a voice say, "Whitfield, so glad to see you."

Whitfield opened his eyes, not expecting to see a familiar face staring back at him.

"Mr. Gugurutruv?"

"Yes. You look surprised to see me."

"Uhh…no. Well, yes, actually. I mean, I just didn't expect to see you here."

"Oh, I never miss these events. It's nice to get together and see some familiar faces. Plus, I have the added bonus of seeing my daughter. You wouldn't happen to know where she is, do you?"

"Umm, she's not here, sir. I mean, she didn't come this year." Whitfield looked nervous. He knew Flaherty was waiting on him, but didn't see any way out of this particular situation.

"That's odd. She usually loves coming to these things. Is everything OK?"

"Yes. Of course. She just had a lot going on back at school and thought it would be wise to stay back and get caught up."

Mr. Gugurutruv appeared disappointed. "Hmm…I see."

"Look, Mr. Gugurutruv, it was great seeing you, but I really have to take care of something now."

"Nonsense. You'll stay with me. I can introduce you to some of my friends." Ugu's dad put his arm around Whitfield.

"Sir, I really appreciate the offer, but I have someone waiting for me."

"Who's more important than me? You already said my daughter is back at school. Come. Stay with me. It'll be a good way for us to bond." Whitfield looked over toward the side door and made eye contact with Flaherty, who had circled back and caught a quick glimpse of Whitfield with Ugu's dad. She saw that Whitfield was not going to be able to escape, and that she was going to have to complete the mission on her own. This was going to be tricky, but if anyone had the skills to fly solo, it was Flaherty.

While Whitfield was being introduced to team owners, wealthy businessmen and powerful politicians, Flaherty approached the main server room, and primary security control post, of Lord Sirroc's entire estate. From down the hall, Flaherty could spot two security guards chatting with each other outside the glass doors and what appeared to be a rather sophisticated electronic lock system keeping unauthorized guests out of the main control room. Without Whitfield, Flaherty would have to gain entrance into the room and upload Ugu's program herself.

As Flaherty stood close to the wall, surveying the scene at the end of the hall, she noticed that she was not alone. Four men in dark suits purposefully walked toward her from the other direction, and surrounded her.

"You are not permitted to be in here. State your purpose."

Flaherty immediately noticed that these particular agents were not as friendly or as welcoming as the guards she encountered when she arrived. Perhaps it was simply because she was somewhere she shouldn't be, but Flaherty was still alarmed. "Oh, I am so sorry. I'm one of the award winners tonight and I thought we were able to roam freely inside the mansion."

"We've been instructed to remove you from the premises." Agents 1 and 2 flanked Flaherty on either side and each grabbed hold of one of her arms and brusquely escorted her down the hall, away from the control room. Agents 3 and 4 proceeded to walk toward the control room and confronted the two guards keeping watch outside the secure door. Flaherty stumbled a little and asked if she could bend down to fix the strap on her shoe and as she did, she glanced backward and saw the two sinister agents remove tasers from their jackets and incapacitate the two guards.

Flaherty gasped, "SYPHUS." Stunned, Flaherty knew she had to act fast before SYPHUS took control of the WGF's entire defense network. Flaherty slowly stood up and continued walking with the agents. They turned a corner and as soon as one of the agents let go of her arm to type in a passcode to unlock the door in front of them, Flaherty stomped her heel as hard as she could on the one agent's left foot and deftly punched the other agent in the throat. Flaherty continued to unleash a series of elbows, knees, roundhouse kicks, and punches, until the two agents were doubled over in pain, on the verge of unconsciousness.

Flaherty collected herself, and swiftly moved down the hall toward the control room. She needed to avoid being seen through the glass walls by the two agents who had now entered the control room, but couldn't afford to waste any time. Her only option was to move fast and pray that the agents left the door unsealed. The two agents inside the security control room barely noticed Flaherty's silhouette pass by, fully expecting it to belong to Agents 1 and 2.

Even as Flaherty opened the door, the dark-suited agents didn't bother to glance up from the screens in front of them, focusing instead on the task at hand. Flaherty paused for a moment, trying to catch a glimpse of the screens, but couldn't be sure exactly what she was seeing, as everything appeared to be encrypted code. Whatever it was, Flaherty knew she didn't have time to spare. Her initial reaction was to attack both men from behind, completely kick butt, and upload the program before leaving, but she remembered that Ugu stressed how important it was that SYPHUS *thought* they had succeeded in their plot. Flaherty decided instead to rely upon her gymnastics skills, along with a little deception.

Flaherty took off her shoes, and holding them by the straps, in her teeth, deftly leaped up onto the nearest table and jumped to reach one of the thin pipes zigzagging across the open ceiling, pulling herself up to a supine planche position so her legs weren't dangling. She needed to keep her ankles together to prevent her dress from flowing underneath her. Flaherty took a mental note of the most direct path to the main control panel using the overhead pipes.

Reaching up with one hand, while maintaining her body position, with her other hand holding her entire body weight, Flaherty took one shoe out of her mouth and threw it into the corner of the room to her right and then quickly removed her other shoe and tossed it toward the corner on her left. She then regripped the bar with both hands, while still in a supine planche position, and waited. Both agents quickly raised their heads and turned around.

"Did you hear that?"

"Of course, I did. I think it came from over here."

"No, it definitely came from over there."

"Do you think that girl got away?"

"Maybe. Perhaps her partner got through and came looking for her."

"Let's split up. You look over there. I'll go this way. If you have to, use your taser. Remember, the boss doesn't want her hurt."

The two agents left their post and proceeded to search every darkened corner of the room for intruders. Meanwhile, Flaherty expertly navigated the intricate maze of piping until she reached the main control panel and dismounted, landing without making the slightest sound, and, of course, stuck the landing. Flaherty quickly removed the flash disc from her bra strap and inserted it into the waiting port. She was so thankful that Ugu had insisted that she and Whitfield each carry a copy of the program…'you know, just in case'. It only took about five seconds for the program to upload, and before the agents had given up on their hunt, Flaherty took the disc back and was already back in place, blending in with the piping, gliding across the room, like water.

She knew it would be too risky to open the door again, so she decided she would have to remain silent and still until the two agents completed their work and exited on their own. The agents returned to their post, convinced that the room was clear, and completed their mission, unaware that their every keystroke was now being monitored and redirected to a false network, all while the defense controls had been routed to Ugu's work station in Sir Arlington's office.

While Flaherty waited in a perfectly still position, her muscles began to shake and her hands started to sweat. She secretly wished she had some chalk right about now to help secure her grip, and tried calming herself by contemplating how judges might score the level of difficulty of this incredible feat of strength, and if she should consider adding this strength skill to her vast repertoire on Vault-Pegs. As expected, the agents wrapped up their mission and left the room, quickly stepping over the two guards who were just now beginning to regain consciousness.

Flaherty dropped down to the ground and left the room, but instead of following the SYPHUS agents, she stopped to check on the guards. They were confused by what had just happened, but were quite appreciative of Flaherty's concern. Neither questioned why Flaherty was there in the first place. Rather, despite their headaches and general state of confusion, both asked Flaherty to take a selfie with them. Flaherty obliged, gave both guards a hug, and walked back down the hallway. Flaherty took a second to look in the glass window to check her hair and straighten out her dress. Unbelievably, after all she just went through, she was still the most stunning gymnast at the Gala.

Before rejoining the other award winners, who were still engaged in their meet-and-greet session, Flaherty glanced down the side hallway and noticed the other two agents were no longer sprawled on the ground. It appears that all four had escaped, and even though they had certainly encountered some unexpected resistance, it was safe to say they would feel as though their mission was a success.

Flaherty rejoined the group and immediately found Whitfield, who was engaged in a deep conversation with two of the wealthiest women in the world, the owner of the Le Violet Mooncats and the CEO of the largest gymnastics equipment manufacturer in the world. When Whitfield caught sight of Flaherty in his peripheral vision, he politely excused himself and found his way toward her.

"Whitfield, is everything OK out here?"

"Oh, you would not believe what I've been through. Where have you been? Some of these people are incredibly boring. Not those two; they were very nice, but some of these others. So difficult. I'm really drained from these conversations." Flaherty just stared at Whitfield. "I'm ready to rejoin the others out in the backyard. This was brutal."

"Are you kidding me?"

"What? That was tough."

"That was tough? Talking to some people? Eating snacks? That was tough?"

"Well, I did like the scallops, but, honestly, I think the crabcakes were a little doughy."

"Doughy?"

"Yeah. And I think there was still a little piece of the shell in one of them. I may have cut my gum. Look, is it bleeding?"

Flaherty flashed a look of total exasperation. "You are unbelievable."

Whitfield mistakenly took that as a compliment and smiled. "You think?"

Flaherty shook her head. "No."

"So, how did everything go? Did you upload the program?"

Flaherty continued walking alongside Whitfield as the two rejoined their friends outside. "Yup."

"Good. Pretty easy job, huh?"

"Yup."

"You know, your hair is a little messed up on the one side. You may want to check that out."

"Uh-huh."

"Hey, next time, maybe you can take the difficult part and I'll coast with the easy job."

Flaherty stopped and stared at Whitfield, exercising every bit of restraint in her body not to punch Whitfield in his nose. "...yup."

****

Whitfield and Flaherty rejoined the outside festivities just before the awards presentation was set to begin. Aspen had spent about twenty minutes in the meet-and-greet event, but eventually found his way out to the main Gala area and was having a wonderful time mingling with gymnasts from across the country, as well as with his more familiar teammates, most notably Seraphina and Chloe. Aspen spotted his brother and made sure to inquire about the mission before any of the speakers took the stage.

"Well?"

Whitfield nodded. "All good. You?"

"Perfect."

Flaherty wondered whether Aspen may have encountered any of the same agents upstairs. "Did you run into any difficulty?"

"Piece of cake. I wasn't even nervous either. It was scarier taking the zip-line down from all the way up there." Aspen pointed toward the highest turret.

"When did you do that?"

"Earlier. Did you guys miss it?"

"I'm sorry, sweetie. We probably weren't here yet."

"Sorry bro."

Aspen shrugged. "No problem. Don't worry about it. It was pretty cool though."

"Nice. So, we're all good then? Nothing else?"

Flaherty stood close to Whitfield, keeping a vigilant lookout for potential danger. "I think so, but we might still want to keep an eye out for other SYPHUS agents."

Whitfield glanced at Flaherty. "Other agents? Did you see any?"

Flaherty played it cool. "I may have run into some. Nothing big though. Let's just keep our eyes open." Whitfield nodded.

"Hey, Whitfield, what did you and Ugu's dad talk about? You seemed to be talking with him for a while." Aspen was too busy talking with other people at the meet-and-greet event to join his brother's conversation with Mr. Gugurutruv.

"Oh, he was just checking in on me. Well, he really wanted to get information about Ugu. I guess they haven't spoken in a while. He didn't even know she wasn't coming tonight."

Flaherty furled her eyebrows. "That's odd. They used to talk all the time."

Aspen raised a good point. "Well, she has been incarcerated for the past couple months."

"I suppose. Yeah, I guess that makes sense."

"Anyway, he was really nice to me. Said if I ever needed anything, I should reach out to him."

"Hmm…I'm a bit surprised by that. You didn't exactly make a great first impression." Flaherty recalled back to Whitfield's first encounter with Ugu's dad, and chuckled.

"Maybe he likes you now."

"Thanks, bro. I think he does. Even said if I wanted, he would set up an internship with him at his company."

"Really? Doing what?"

"Not sure. We got sidetracked with another conversation before I could ask."

Aspen wondered if Whitfield thought that was a good idea. "Is that something you'd be interested in doing?"

"Tough to say. Maybe if I like what I'd be doing."

"No, I mean working with Ugu's dad."

Flaherty shared Aspen's concern. "Could be awkward."

"I know. I'd have to run it by Ugu first. See what she thinks."

Flaherty smiled. "That is always a good idea."

A few moments later, fireworks went off again in the distance, drawing everyone's attention to center stage. Lord Sirroc said a few words and welcomed some distinguished guests. After a few short speeches, the awards started to roll out. In no particular order, some of the highlighted awards were as follows:

Name	School	Award
Flaherty	*Seven Bridges Academy*	*Morton Cheesestock Most Outstanding Gymnast*
Aspen	*Seven Bridges Academy*	*Most Outstanding First-Year Gymnast (MOFYG)*
Jade	*Vertical Press Academy*	*Most Team Points Earned*
Ricardo	*Flagpole Prep*	*Highest Scoring Average (tie)*
Zoya	*Parallel Pines*	*Highest Scoring Average (tie)*
Whitfield	*Seven Bridges Academy*	*Newcomer of the Year (NoY)*

Event Performers of the Year

Kelsie	*Riverboard*	*Tri-Bars*
Dante	*West's Vineyard*	*Escalating Tramps*
Flaherty	*Seven Bridges Academy*	*Vault-Pegs*
Keegan	*Seven Bridges Academy*	*Handstand Obstacle (tie)*
Quinn	*P'socto*	*Handstand Obstacle (tie)*
Aspen	*Seven Bridges Academy*	*Pommel Clock*
Carter	*Triplepike Academy*	*Vertical-Horizontal Bars*
Peyton	*Vertical Press Academy*	*Parallel Planks*
Liza	*Thryce*	*Floor Exercise*
Whitfield	*Seven Bridges Academy*	*Sexiest Gymnast of the Year (tie)*
Flaherty	*Seven Bridges Academy*	*Sexiest Gymnast of the Year (tie)*

Awards were also given out to outstanding newcomers on each event; Citizen of the Year; Fan of the Year; Judges of the Year (for each event); Event Coach of the Year; Head Coach of the Year; and more. The overwhelming majority of awards went to a gymnast or coach from one of Gen. Gibson's 'preferred' schools, adding to the already growing discontent among lower-tiered schools. As expected, Seven Bridges athletes earned more awards than athletes from any other individual school, despite the team faltering in their final three meets. The loudest cheers of the night went to Flaherty for her MOG Award and Aspen for being the youngest ever award-winner. Every award presentation was accompanied by fireworks, light shows, and great fanfare, once again cementing Lord Sirroc's Gala as one the most entertaining nights of the year.

When Whitfield and Flaherty took the stage to receive their Sexiest Gymnast of Year Awards, the entire crowd screamed. Coupled with the spectacular fireworks display and musical performances, the entire scene was deafening, which is probably why it took some time before anyone noticed the video monitors being hijacked.

As Whitfield and Flaherty accepted their awards, the video boards across the vast expanse of Lord Sirroc's outdoor grounds all went dark. The sound system cut out. The light stands placed all around the grounds went dark. The crowd grew quiet as confusion, and fear, started to trickle in. Suddenly, the video boards sprang to life, focused on a man standing at a podium, flanked on either side by three security agents. The man appearing in the middle of the video boards, standing at the podium, was none other than Gen. Gibson. The crowd gasped and murmured, but remained intensely focused on the screens in front of them. Flaherty and Whitfield looked at each other.

"I thought you uploaded the program."

"I did. Maybe I was too late."

"What do you mean?"

"Well, SYHPUS agents were already in there messing around. I thought Ugu said it wouldn't matter, as long as I got in there before they were done. I guess something went wrong." Whitfield didn't respond. Instead, he turned his attention to the man speaking on the video screens.

"Greetings, my friends. My deepest apologies for the interruption. I hope everyone is having a wonderful time. Under normal conditions, I would be present at this end-of-year celebration honoring our many incredible athletes and coaches, but alas, these are no ordinary times. Recently, I have come under attack by a corrupt and ruthless dictator. A man who has fooled each and every one of you into thinking he is a decent man, when in fact, he has lied to you all. I have proof, right here in my hands, that Lord Sirroc has betrayed the WGF. Betrayed our country. Betrayed all of you."

Lord Sirroc could be heard yelling from the stage. "That is a lie!"

"Oh, Lord Sirroc, you poor, misguided old man. Your time is over. I hold here bank records detailing the authorization of billions of dollars in hard-earned school resources, redirected into the hands of our sworn enemies. I have confirmation from at least a dozen school officials that it was indeed you who had authorized these payments.

"And most recently, I have come into possession of school entrance exam fraud, where the admissions committee at your own beloved alma mater of Seven Bridges Academy, has noted that each and every question written by Lord Sirroc was biased and solely intended to sway the committee into admitting your own hand-picked recruits from wealthy, elite families, only serving to further your power and control as you undoubtedly attempt to lead a coup against the WGF. Now, I dare you to respond."

Lord Sirroc became frantic and defiant. "None of this is true. I swear it. You are the guilty one. It wasn't me."

"Lord Sirroc, your reign of corruption has ended. I have placed several agents at your Gala tonight, and they will now approach the stage to escort you to Chipwood Prison, where you belong. Agents!" About a dozen armed agents, four of which Flaherty had already encountered earlier in the evening, approached the stage from all corners.

Lord Sirroc was surrounded. He had nowhere to go, and no one to help him. His own security detail was either bound and gagged, rendered unconscious, or otherwise ordered to stand down. Lord Sirroc was left defenseless.

Gen. Gibson's agents reached the stage in unison, and took Lord Sirroc into custody. The crowd looked on in stunned silence. Whitfield, Aspen, and Flaherty looked helplessly at each other, pleading with each other to do something, but it was no use. They couldn't fight off a dozen agents, and who knows how many more sympathizers were scattered across the grounds. Everything they had worked for was coming crashing down, and there was nothing more they could do to stop it from happening.

Gen. Gibson continued speaking. "Friends, again, I apologize for the inconvenience, but you deserve better. No more lies. No more corruption. As your new president, I will lead you out from under this cloud of darkness and into the light. A new beginning. A new path. My friends, I will…" The sound cut out. Gen.

Gibson still appeared to be talking, but no one could hear what he was saying. Instead, another voice was heard loud and clear.

"Phew, am I glad that's over. That man does not know when to shut up." A single spotlight shone on the speaker, who was off in the distance, and accompanied by a large entourage, including over 50 security personnel. "Gentlemen, please take your hands off Lord Sirroc and surrender your weapons. Our fully capable and well-armed security team will now escort each of you to your new home inside Chipwood Prison. Your crimes have already been documented and ruled upon." Whitfield still couldn't see who was speaking, but he recognized the voice. "Lord Sirroc, sir, please return to the stage, and accept our deepest, heartfelt apologies for this intrusion."

The speaker was getting closer to the stage. The large crowd made way as the entourage came closer to center stage and climbed the steps. The speaker lowered her microphone and spoke a few words to Lord Sirroc, hugged him, and kissed both cheeks, in a sign of loyalty and friendship. The entire time this spectacle was unfolding, Gen. Gibson could still be seen on the video screens, occasionally shouting, but not heard.

It was clear that he could see the events unfolding in front of him, from his undisclosed location. After a few moments, Whitfield recognized that Sir Arlington had joined the entourage, but he wasn't the one speaking. Professor Marino was also there. And so was Hendricks. Yes, Hendricks!

Whitfield, Aspen, and Flaherty each made their way closer to center stage, until they were only a few feet from the stairs. With Gen. Gibson's dozen agents all in custody, several of the remaining members of the late-arriving security force searched the grounds for Lord Sirroc's captured guards, while the others kept a watchful eye on the crowd, which was understandably quite confused. After a few additional moments, the mystery speaker turned to face the crowd. Whitfield couldn't believe his eyes. Flaherty and Aspen looked at each other, mouths agape, unable to speak.

"Hi! My name is Ugu Gugurutruv and I am a third-year student at Seven Bridges Academy and a former intern at the World Gymnastics Federation. Over the past few months, my team and I have been investigating suspicious activity at the WGF. What started as a series of messages sent from Gen. Gibson to officials at twenty schools culminated in us discovering the misappropriation of over 3.2 trillion dollars, essentially stolen from those twenty schools, and placed in the coffers of bank accounts controlled by a single organization, at the direction of

Gen. Gibson himself. Gen. Gibson rigged meet schedules and ordered over 450 confirmed bribe attempts, with many more suspected."

The crowd gasped. Lord Sirroc remained stoic on the outside, but felt sick to his stomach that all this happened under his command.

Ugu continued, "we also found concentrated efforts, either directed by, and in many cases, directly involving Gen. Gibson himself, to undermine the competency of Lord Sirroc. Earlier this year, Gen. Gibson ordered the falsification of Lord Sirroc's annual re-appointment exam. Sir, you will be pleased to hear that you did in fact pass the exam with flying colors.

"More recently, Gen. Gibson ordered the theft of 105 entrance exams and paid a Seven Bridges Academy Board member, who in turn paid her son, a current Seven Bridges student, to change the answers to selected exam questions to implicate Lord Sirroc in a campaign to discredit his ability to write unbiased questions, a non-trivial part of his job, and one that if shown to be inadequate, could cost him his re-appointment. Gen. Gibson knew this, and ruthlessly went after Lord Sirroc. He went so far as to order the ruination of a Seven Bridges' gymnast's personal residence to regain possession of the corrupted exams, which we now have here in our possession."

Hendricks held the tainted exams up high above his head for the crowd to see. The crowd started chanting, "get Gen. Gibson! Get Gen. Gibson!"

Ugu wasn't yet finished. "And here, tonight, while all of you were enjoying this wonderful event, Gen. Gibson sent his sinister agents inside these walls to hack into Lord Sirroc's personal bank accounts to make it look as though he had committed such crimes himself.

"Gen. Gibson also ordered his agents to seize control of the WGF's defense network, through the secure control room hidden deep in Lord Sirroc's mansion. Both attempts were successfully thwarted, yet detailed records of their attempted theft, espionage, cyber-fraud, and a host of other crimes are now clearly documented and detailed, with an iron-clad digital trail, already submitted to the proper authorities. Now, Gen. Gibson, I dare you to respond." Ugu lowered her microphone.

Gen. Gibson, still visible on the video screens, was at a loss for words. The crowd continued chanting, "get Gen. Gibson! Get Gen. Gibson." Seeing no way out, Gen. Gibson cut off the video feed, and the screens went dark again, but only for a moment, until Ugu reconnected the video feed to the prearranged awards presentation scroll. The crowd cheered. Lord Sirroc hugged Sir Arlington. Hendricks leaped down from the stage to hug Whitfield and Aspen.

Flaherty ran up the stairs to hug Ugu. "You are such a badass!"

"Thank you! You too."

"Excuse me?"

"Oh, I saw what you did to those agents. Girl, you were smoking hot in there."

Flaherty appreciated the compliment. "Thanks. Hey, just don't tell Whitfield, OK? He thinks I just strolled in there and uploaded the program—no problem."

"He is so clueless. Your secret is safe with me."

After embracing Hendricks, Whitfield climbed the stairs to greet Ugu. They hugged, for a long while, without saying anything. Eventually, Whitfield pulled back. "I thought you said you weren't coming."

"I know. Are you disappointed?"

"A little."

"What? Really?"

"Well, I knew about all the deception going on around here, but I didn't think the awards would get it wrong too."

Ugu had a confused look. "What do you mean?"

"Look, I totally do not deserve this award. You are, by far, the sexiest one here tonight."

"Aww…that's sweet. But look again. That award says Sexiest 'Gymnast' of the Year. I'm not a gymnast."

Whitfield smiled. "You have the heart of a gymnast, and are every bit as tough, determined, focused, and sexy, as any gymnast I know. But you have one quality no other gymnast has."

"Oh? What's that?"

"All my love!" Whitfield thought he was being sweet.

"Oh, is that all? I thought you were going to say something like soft hands or no bruises on my legs. All your love? I mean, what am I going to do with that?" Of course, Ugu loved teasing Whitfield. She flashed him a sweet smile.

"I don't know. Maybe love me back."

Whitfield leaned in to kiss Ugu and she paused, just for a second. She just wanted to take one more look into Whitfield's loving eyes, before closing her own. Whitfield and Ugu kissed, for a while, before Aspen barged in to break it up. He wanted to give Ugu a hug for all she did. Sir Arlington came over too, to thank the four students for what they accomplished in saving Lord Sirroc's job, and the entire WGF from an unknown, but certainly devastating, outcome. SYPHUS was still out there, and Gen. Gibson was on the loose, but Lord Sirroc's job was safe, for now.

They allowed themselves to enjoy the remainder of the night. The regular season was over and championship season was just around the corner. It was sure to be a grueling stretch, with both team and individual championship meets ahead of them, but no one was thinking about that now. The Gala was really kicking into high gear, now that all the drama was over. The music was loud. The dance floors, tramps, and foam pits were open. And Keegan was just about ready to pass out in his underwear. The party was just getting started!

Chapter 44
Team Championships

The time was now. The crowd had been filling in for the past three hours. The world had been waiting all year. Morocco put his arm around Whitfield. "Yeah, championship season is always bananas!"

"What?" Whitfield could hardly hear his teammate over the music blaring from the speakers.

"You look a bit worried. Don't stress about it. You'll be fine."

"Oh that...no, I'm good. I just didn't expect all this on Day 1. I mean, I know this is the playoffs and all, but look around. Just starting to feel some pressure."

"Ah, nothing to it. This is what we're built for. It's what you've worked so hard for all year. You know what they say, to be the best, you have to beat the best. As far as I'm concerned, we are the best, and I don't intend the let anyone beat us."

Whitfield slapped Morocco on the chest. "I hear that. Let's go out there and dominate."

Morocco let out a loud howl and made his way out to warmups, as Whitfield got his gear together and stretched out some more. Whitfield looked out over the competition floor. Aspen already seemed locked in. Whitfield's younger brother was scheduled to compete on four events during the Team Playoffs this week. Aside from Whitfield and Flaherty, who were both competing in the All-Around, Aspen had the heaviest workload of any Seven Bridges gymnast. Keegan, Sydney, and Chloe were all in good spirits, but remained singularly focused on their routines.

Only Flaherty seemed to be completely comfortable, mingling with gymnasts and coaches from other schools, laughing and hugging competitors as if they were long lost friends catching up at a local café, and not minutes away from squaring off in the most intense competition of the season. The gymnasts from P'socto all stretched in unison. Riverboard gymnasts were spread out across the warmup area.

A lot of really good gymnasts all on one floor. So much intensity. Whitfield needed to get his head in the game.

The schedule for Team Championship Week was as follows:

Days 1 and 2: 128 teams compete across 16 sites. Each site hosts 8 teams in a one-day, abbreviated meet, spanning five sessions (as opposed to the normal seven), with random draw assignments.

Days 3 and 4: the top two teams from each opening round site (32 teams in total) compete across four sites. Each site hosts 8 teams in a one-day, abbreviated meet, spanning five sessions, with random draw assignments.

Day 5: Recovery Day.

Days 6 and 7: the top two teams from each second-round site (8 teams in total) compete at one site in a two-day, full round robin meet. Team Champions are crowned at the end of Day 7.

Seven Bridges Academy competed on Day 1, and if they managed to finish the day in one of the top two positions, they would move on to the second round on Day 3. Seven Bridges was expected to win the Day 1 meet handily, but would likely face some stiff competition in the second round. Throughout most of the season, they were the odds-on favorite to win the team championship, but those odds slipped during the final month of the season, and now it seemed that three, or maybe even four, teams had a realistic shot at hoisting the trophy. Every gymnast knew that before they could even dream of holding the championship trophy, they would have to make it past the first round.

Whitfield knew the previous week of practice had been the best the team looked all year. Collectively, they were ready. Personally, Whitfield was nervous, and it showed on his routines. As usual, Whitfield completed eight routines in the first session, and even though he earned an impressive 25 team points, he fell three times, only stuck two dismounts, and just looked shaky overall. For the first time in his brief gymnastics career, Whitfield really started to let doubt creep into his mind, and wasn't sure if he could continue. He really wished Ugu had been able to make the trip.

Outside of practice time, Whitfield had spent nearly every minute of the past week with Ugu, loving every second of it. Even though she hadn't travelled to a single meet all year, he knew just seeing her there would immediately calm his nerves, but given how much class time she missed last term, she didn't dare ask to be excused from the first day of classes in Term 5 to travel with the team for Day 1 of Championship Week.

Besides, Ugu had promised Whitfield, Flaherty, and Aspen that she would compile detailed summaries of all the work they missed in class and do her best to review it with them on Tuesday afternoon. No, Whitfield would have to get over his nerves without Ugu's assistance, or so he thought.

During the first intermission, Coach Brockport pulled Whitfield aside and offered a few words of encouragement, making it clear that nerves were part of the game and that everything would be fine. Coach Daza also encouraged Whitfield to just have fun out there and not to put so much pressure on himself.

In his heart, Whitfield knew his coaches were right, but still. Whitfield couldn't get the idea of the fate of the entire school resting on his shoulders out of his head, and that if he didn't go out there and perform at his absolute best, he would be letting everyone down. Thoughts of his friends turning on him, the way they did on Ugu, ran through Whitfield's head. Whitfield envisioned life without the mansions, the resources, the great food. He imagined life, quite possibly, without Ugu. It was all bubbling up inside of him and he felt like he was going to explode.

That's when it happened. The moment that turned Championship Week around for Whitfield. Sensing that he was about to lose it, Flaherty sat next to Whitfield in the locker room. She whispered in his ear that they needed to talk. She grabbed Whitfield's hand and led him into the vacated coaches' office. She turned to stand directly in front of Whitfield. Still holding his hand, Flaherty looked directly into Whitfield's deep blue eyes and said, "Whitfield, I think I'm in love with you."

Whitfield stood there, in a state of total shock. "Uhh...what?"

Flaherty repeated herself. "I love you, Whitfield."

Whitfield couldn't move a muscle. "Umm...uhh...what?"

"I'm trying to tell you I'm in love with you."

Whitfield was completely unprepared for this incredible revelation. "Uhh...really?"

Flaherty couldn't hold it in anymore. She started laughing hysterically. "NO! Of course not, you dunderhead. I'm not in love with you. But she is." Flaherty opened the curtain covering the video board and on the screen was Ugu, laughing.

Whitfield was so confused. "Uhh...what's going on?"

"Hi sweetie. How are you feeling?"

"Very confused. Flaherty just told me she loves me."

Ugu was still laughing. "Yes, I know. Your reaction was perfect."

"Will someone please tell me what's going on?"

"It's simple. You're nervous out there, aren't you?"

"Yeah, how did you know?"

"I've been watching."

"Aren't you in class?"

"Don't worry about that. This is about you, and you alone. You're feeling pressure to perform at your very best, and you think that if you don't, everything will fall apart. Am I right?"

"Yeah, something like that. You know me so well."

"Yes, I do. And you know what else I know?"

"What?"

"You're an idiot."

"Ouch! Why would you say that?"

"Whitfield, I love you. That's not going to change if you fall a thousand times. Flaherty loves you."

"Wait. That's actually true?"

Flaherty punched Whitfield in the gut. "Not that way, but yeah. You're like my brother."

"She does. Aspen loves you too. You are surrounded by love and no matter what you do out there this week, none of that will change. You are at your best when you just go out there and enjoy yourself. You love the challenge of hitting your routines. Sticking your dismounts. Not for the crowds. Not for the money or resources. And, to be honest, not for me or Flaherty or anyone else. But, for you. Just you and the apparatus. No one else."

Flaherty nudged Whitfield. "Now do you understand?"

"I think so."

"Whitfield, just go out there and do you. Forget about everything else. No pressure. No cameras."

Whitfield was finally able to crack a smile. "I got you. Thanks. I really appreciate all this."

"No problem. And, hey, if you really want some pressure, how about this? If you fall on Handstand Obstacle just one more time, I'm not going to kiss you again for a month."

Flaherty liked that idea. "Ooh, that's good."

"What!"

"You heard her. And what were you thinking? Falling on a handstand."

Whitfield shook his head. "I know. I know. That one was bad."

"And don't think you can get away with anything. I'll be watching." Ugu playfully teased Whitfield.

Whitfield was back to feeling himself. "OK. You got it. No more falls."

"That's my Honey Bear."

"But just so you know, when I do go out there and win this whole thing, we're going out to celebrate, and you are going to wear that really cute top that I told you I like and you're going to give me a huge kiss."

Ugu raised her eyebrows. "All right. You got it. Go out there and be a champion."

Whitfield turned to leave, but stopped for a moment longer. "Hey Ugu."

"Yes."

"Thanks." Ugu blew a kiss to Whitfield and signed off.

"Feel better?"

"Much better. Thank you, Flaherty. I really am happy you're in my life. I do love you."

"I know. Now, let's get out there and kick some butt." Flaherty and Whitfield left the coaches' office just as the first intermission was concluding. Whitfield felt like a totally different gymnast. He was loose and having fun. He stepped up to Parallel Planks and hit the best routine of his life. From that moment on, Whitfield was the best version of himself, dominating the competition. At the end of Day 1, Whitfield and Flaherty's 1-2 punch was more than enough to vault Seven Bridges Academy to the top of the leaderboard and secure a spot in the second round.

Even more astounding, was that after all 128 teams competed between Days 1 and 2, Seven Bridges had the highest overall team score, and Whitfield had set new records for highest All-Around score and most team points earned in the first round of the playoffs, even outscoring Flaherty by seven points.

Seven Bridges enjoyed a successful first day of Championship Week, but the extra fifth session in a single day and the late-night travel back to campus took its toll on the gymnasts. Whitfield, in particular, felt sore on Tuesday, and wanted nothing more than to spend the day resting, but thought better of it and went to class. As promised, Ugu had prepared extensive recaps of the prior day's classes for Whitfield, Flaherty, and Aspen, even for those classes where she wasn't enrolled. The vibe around campus was mostly joyful and optimistic, albeit with pockets of negative energy still directed at Ugu.

Seven Bridges students prided themselves on being young men and women of high character, and with some notable exceptions, this was true, which made Ugu's cheating an unforgivable offense, and one that much of the student body felt deserved immediate expulsion. For those students, seeing Ugu attend classes and walking around campus was inexplicable, prompting occasional protests asking to move the expulsion date up from the end-of-year celebration date.

Ugu's heroics at Lord Sirroc's Gala did, however, win over almost everyone on the gymnastics team, as well as many others. The faculty had stopped giving Ugu such a hard time, and there was reason to believe the blind hatred from some students would crack, eventually. But for now, Ugu, and through association, Whitfield, Aspen, and Flaherty, still had to deal with this new normal on campus. In a show of support for their friend, Whitfield, Aspen, and Flaherty remained by Ugu's side throughout the afternoon on Tuesday, mostly reviewing coursework, and insisted that she come with them to practice Tuesday evening.

To their surprise, Ugu accepted. She found a spot to sit in the stands and watched the light practice for a couple hours before the team adjourned for the night to get some much-needed rest. Whitfield was tired, but still decided to go for a run around the Outer Loop with Ugu. It had been much easier for Whitfield to keep up with Ugu since her stay in the Pit, but her strength was returning now, and for the first time in a while, Whitfield really had to push himself to keep pace.

At the end of their run, Ugu was about to open the door to Slide 19-EU, when Whitfield reached out to grab her hand. "Hey. What, no good night kiss?"

"Nope. Remember, you have a championship to win."

"Oh, so no kiss until we win?"

Ugu appeared to rethink her refusal, and placed her hands around Whitfield's neck. She leaned close enough so that the tips of their noses touched. "Nope. Sweet dreams." Ugu retreated and went down the slide to her room. Whitfield stood there for a moment, smiling, totally in love with the girl of his dreams. He turned and sprinted for about 1.27 miles back to Slide 06-WU, returning home safely. Within minutes, he was asleep.

****

Day 3 of Team Championship Week could not have gone any better for the team from Seven Bridges Academy. Every SBA gymnast hit their routines, leaving the competition in the dust.

Flaherty finished the meet on top, with Whitfield securing the number two spot. Perhaps even more impressive though, was Aspen's perfect 20-0 record on Day 3, a feat not seen in three years. Aspen's performance on Day 3 garnered a lot of media attention, tasking his marketing team to carefully select and schedule interview requests to fit around Aspen's class schedule over the next two days. Overall, the team was positioned well heading into the weekend's Championship Meet as the #1 overall seed.

As perfect as Day 3 went for Seven Bridges, Session 1 of the two-day Championship Meet was equally disastrous. Aspen injured his wrist on his very first Pommel Clock routine of the meet and would not be able to compete for the rest of the day. Flaherty injured her right ankle on Escalating Tramps and would likely be unavailable for the rest of the weekend. For a team that had largely avoided major blows to their lineup throughout the season, this was the worst possible time to have two of their star athletes go down.

Seven Bridges finished Session 1 in last place, eighth overall, and by the end of the first day had rallied behind some inspired performances from Reid, Fenway, Ippy, and Wilson, of all people, to rise up to 6th place, with only three sessions remaining on the final day of Team Championships. Heading into the final day of competition, Seven Bridges' dreams of a fourth consecutive national team championship were all but dead.

After all the interviews, showers, and mid-meet coaches' meetings wrapped up, Whitfield called for a team meeting, right there in the locker room. Despite some disagreements among team members during the season, particularly toward the end, the team had been seeing eye to eye more recently and Whitfield had emerged as their bona fide leader.

"Hey, everyone, thanks for staying. I know today wasn't what we were all expecting coming in." Whitfield scanned the room and saw a lot of hanging heads, a tearful Aspen with his wrist in a splint, an uncharacteristically somber Flaherty with her ankle heavily taped and crutches nearby, and about a dozen ice bags and wraps adorning team members as though they had just gone 15 rounds with a sleuth of angry bears. "No, today wasn't what we expected. It was better."

Several heads looked up, surprised by Whitfield's positive assessment of the gloomy situation. "That's right. Today surpassed expectations. Seraphina. You stepped into the #2 position on Tramps and crushed it, going 3-1. Eight team points. Ippy, you went 3-1 in the #3 position on Floor. Ten team points. Diego. Two wins in the #1 spot on VH-Bars. Three big team points. Ryne. You moved all the way up to the #2 spot on Parallel Planks and went 4-0. Six team points.

"All season long, Flaherty has carried us on her back. Aspen has been a rock in every meet. He even went perfect in the second round. All while you were waiting in the wings. Waiting for your shot. Morocco. You once told me that if you were an All-Arounder, you'd take home every title. Well, Rocco, here's your shot. Five events tomorrow. Gear up, champ. Bella. Pommel Clock. You have the cleanest lines of anyone on the team. Well, maybe except for Aspen. You can go out there and beat anyone. You're moving up to #3."

Bella lifted her head in excitement. "Really? Coach said that?"

"Coach Brockport is on board with whatever we have to do. But listen to me now. This is not coach's team. This is our team. Your team. Each and every one of you. Flaherty told us all that no one person could win this title alone. It's going to take all 25. Twenty-five of the greatest, hungriest, strongest gymnasts on the planet. Every one of you can be All-World if given the chance. Well…here's your chance."

Keegan spoke softly, as soft as anyone has ever heard him before. "Whitfield. You really think we have a shot tomorrow?"

Whitfield scanned the room. "No. We don't have a shot at winning. We ARE going to win. We are raising that trophy tomorrow. This is the Team Championship Meet and, dammit, we have the best TEAM in the world."

One by one, each team member stood and cheered. They clapped together. They yelled together. Whitfield accomplished the impossible. In that moment, he brought 25 individual, strong-willed personalities together. All fighting for a common goal. Together. He made them all believe they were going to win.

"All right. All right. We need to save some of this energy for tomorrow. I don't know about any of you, but I'm not leaving here without a chip. No, I mean it, I am not leaving this building. I say we order dinner and eat here. Have the coaches grab our bags from the hotel, and sleep here. And tomorrow, we gear up and win that championship right here, in this building. Our building. Our home. Our title."

The cheers grew louder. The walls started shaking. The coaches, who were all gathered in the coaches' office, stood in awe as they opened the door to take in the glorious scene unfolding in front of their eyes. The team ate together in the locker room, where the coaches had their bags delivered. The entire team spent the night inside the locker room, sleeping on makeshift cots and blankets scattered over the floor. Getting to sleep that night was difficult, as Whitfield's powerful speech still echoed inside their locker room church, bringing newfound faith to those who had once lost their way, but now were found. And determined.

Whitfield got up during the night and saw the light was on in the coaches' office. He got out of his makeshift bed and opened the door to find Flaherty, with tears running down her face, talking with Coach Brockport. "What's going on?"

Coach Brockport asked Whitfield to step inside the office and close the door. "We got the medical reports back. Both broken."

"What?"

Flaherty spoke through her tears. "Aspen's wrist. My ankle."

Whitfield quickly glanced out the window toward Aspen's bunk and saw that his brother was sleeping. He then sat down next to Flaherty and put his arm around her. "Can we fix it?"

Flaherty shook her head. "Not bones. Not that fast."

"If it was just a ligament, sure. Tendons, easy. With our healing tech, no problem. We could have our medical staff fix those things up in no time. Bones take at least a week or two. We can fuse it back together, but the lingering pain would be substantial and we cannot offer external pharmaceuticals during an ongoing meet. The risk of re-injury is above our liking as well." Coach Brockport looked dejected.

"Does Aspen know yet?"

Coach Brockport shook his head. "No. These just came in. I figured he should get some sleep. Look, Whitfield, I know what this team means to you. That was a great speech. Made me want to suit up and give you everything I have, but you have to face it. We're not going to have enough to win tomorrow."

Whitfield didn't accept Coach's words. "Sure, we do, coach. Those are some outstanding gymnasts in that room."

"I know, Whitfield, believe me, I do. But…"

"No. I hear what you're saying. Really, I do. But I don't think you are hearing me. We are going to fight until the very end. We are going to give you everything we have and then some. As long as there is a pommel left standing, I'm on it. A bar left hanging; I'm flying over it. And there are 24 other gymnasts in this locker room willing to give the same effort. Now, maybe two of them are hobbled right now, but we still need everything they have too.

"Flaherty is, without question, the strongest person I know. And I'm not talking about what she does on the mats. She could earn 70 team points on her own. Unleash her on the sidelines tomorrow, and she'll double that production. Trust me. Aspen. Let's just say if we're within five points coming down to the end of Session 7 tomorrow, Aspen will get those points for us. Broken wrist and all. You don't know him like I do. Coach. Relax. Get some sleep. You have a championship to win tomorrow. Flaherty, c'mon, let's go to bed."

"Excuse me?"

Whitfield realized his words to Flaherty did not come out as intended. "Uhh…I didn't mean that. Let's get to bed together. No. Not that either. I mean, I'll help you get into bed. Because of your ankle. Then, I'll get into my own bed. All the way on the other side of the room. Umm…"

Flaherty smiled. "Whitfield. Shut up."

"OK. Thank you. Good night, coach." Whitfield and Flaherty left the coaches' office.

"Whitfield?"

"Yes, Flaherty."

"Thanks for what you said in there. It means a lot to me."

"No problem. I meant every word. You're going to lead us to the championship tomorrow."

Flaherty was convinced. "Damn right I am."

"Good night, Flaherty."

"Good night."

****

Whitfield felt like he didn't sleep at all last night, which wasn't too far from the truth, but even so, he wasn't tired in the least. Maybe it was pure adrenaline kicking in, but today was the final day of Team Championships and it didn't matter to him that his team had dug a huge hole for itself the day before. Whitfield was the first to get out of bed. He already showered and got dressed before anyone else started to stir. Seizing his moment, Whitfield went into the coaches' office and drew up the starting lineups for Sessions 5-7.

Flaherty joined Whitfield in the office shortly thereafter, still before anyone else woke. Coach Brockport had already worked through the lineups, and Whitfield and Flaherty didn't make any major adjustments, but they knew the impact it would have on the team, seeing the lineups printed in their own hand. Whitfield was now the team's undisputed leader. Nothing against Coach Brockport, who was a fine leader in his own right, but having a teammate take control would resonate with the others that their fortunes were truly in their own hands.

Flaherty turned the music up loud and started getting everyone out of bed. Today was their day to be crowned champions and both she and Whitfield were determined to do everything they could to realize their dreams. The buzz in the room almost immediately returned to the levels of the previous night. The team was never so focused or as determined as they were right now. The team reached the practice floor a full hour before they were required to, but that didn't stop them from stretching, bouncing, bounding, and flipping their way to a good warmup sweat. Whitfield pulled Aspen over to the side and asked how he felt.

"My wrist still really hurts."

"I know, bro. It's broken."

"What? Really? No, it isn't. I can still compete, can't I?"

Whitfield lowered his head. "Not in this session or the next. But I'll make a deal with you."

Aspen grew visibly upset, tears welling up in his eyes. "What deal?"

"I already told Coach Brockport that if we climb back up to within five points of the top spot in Session 7, that you're going in on Pommel Clock. There's no one I'd rather have in that spot."

Aspen's chest swelled and a smile flashed across his face. "Thanks, Whitfield. Are you sure I can't compete before then?"

"Yeah, sorry. We really can't risk further injury. But, if you do want to compete today, you'll have to see the medical staff and have them fuse the bone. Flaherty already got her ankle fused this morning. It'll be painful and the pain will likely only get worse throughout the day. You can't take any meds during competition. Of course, if the pain gets to be too much, you can take the meds, but you'll be ruled ineligible for the rest of the meet."

Aspen understood the consequences. "OK. I'll go back and get it fused. I want to be ready for Session 7."

Whitfield smiled. "That's my brother. Go get that taken care of. We're going to need you later." Aspen left to go see the medical staff. The other teams starting spilling into the gym shortly before 09:00, the official start of the 30-minute warmup session. Flaherty made her presence known, cheering on her teammates, while trying her hardest to put the intense pain she was experiencing out of her mind.

Session 5 got off to a solid start for Seven Bridges, with Whitfield, Keegan, Morocco, and Seraphina all scoring major five-point wins. The team certainly missed Flaherty and Aspen's presence, but with Whitfield stepping into the #1 spot on five events and the others stepping up as well, Seven Bridges Academy closed the gap on the leaders, sliding into 4th place heading into Session 6.

The penultimate session of the championships started a little shaky with early falls from Kayleigh and Keegan, but Whitfield steadied the ship with steady performances on VH-Bars and Vault-Pegs, and Morocco smashed the meet record with an unbelievable routine on Tri-Bars. Both Flagpole Prep and Vertical Press Academy faced some adversity, with untimely injuries, opening the door for Seven

Bridges to move into a third-place tie, just four points behind second, and twelve points out of the lead heading into the final session. Parallel Pines had been hitting their routines all weekend, and if they continued to do so, it would be difficult, but not impossible, for Seven Bridges to catch them.

Whitfield's teammates were on a roll, and their belief in him, and in themselves, was growing with every routine. One session remained to crown a champion. Seven Bridges was a mere 32 routines away from claiming history with a fourth consecutive team title, and if accomplished, would also be the largest comeback in the history of Championship Week, but that's when adversity struck again. In the locker room during the final intermission, Whitfield saw Kayleigh and Fenway both head into the training room, with looks of utter disappointment on their faces.

"What's going on?"

Coach Daza was shaking his head as he followed both injured athletes to the training room. "Shoulder for Kayleigh. She's out. Wrist for Fenway. She's out too."

Whitfield walked past Coach Daza into the training room to comfort, and encourage, both athletes. Kayleigh and Fenway both had tears in their eyes, more from disappointment in their bodies breaking down than from the pain. Whitfield offered some encouragement. "Don't worry. You helped get us here. There's a trophy out there waiting for you. We'll get it."

Whitfield left the training room and found Aspen. "How are you feeling, bro?"

"I'm good."

"Don't lie to me, Aspen."

"OK. Honestly, I'm in a lot of pain. But, Whitfield, please don't take this shot away from me. You know I can do this." Whitfield studied Aspen's face and knew he was right.

"Suit up. You're going in Kayleigh's #2 spot on Pommel Clock."

"Kayleigh's spot? Why not #1?"

"Because I'm there and I'm not injured. We're facing Jade from VPA and can't afford to give away another five points if you fall early."

Aspen's face turned to stone. "Put me in at #1. I won't lose."

"Aspen, the whole championship may come down to this."

Aspen stood firm. "I know. And it's not good enough to simply tie Jade. We need to outscore her, and even at your best, you can't do it. We need five points."

"Aspen, you're not winning a major against Jade. She's never been outscored by that much."

"Put me in at #1." Aspen was defiant. Whitfield knew Aspen wasn't going to back down, and more importantly, he knew his brother was right. Whitfield couldn't defeat Jade by that many points, but Aspen could. If Aspen was healthy. But he wasn't healthy. Whitfield could see the pain his brother was in. Less than 36 hours removed from a broken wrist, without any medication to ease the pain, Whitfield had to decide right then whether to trust his brother. With an entire team championship on the line.

"OK, bro. Go be a champion."

Aspen didn't say a word. He simply turned and ran out of the locker room to prepare for his duel with the reigning Pommel Clock National Champion.

Flaherty was standing nearby and overheard their conversation. "That was very loyal of you."

"I hope it wasn't very stupid."

"Either way, you made the right call. I'll back you up."

"Thanks. Well, that takes care of Kayleigh's spot in the lineup. Now, I have to go see if Diego can take Fenway's spot on Vault-Pegs. I don't want to mess around with moving anyone out of their spot. We can't afford multiple losses."

"Diego's hurt. Can't go."

Whitfield shoulders slumped. "Oh no. Then who?"

"Me."

"Flaherty, stop. We don't have time for jokes. What about Ippy?"

"Whitfield, I'm serious. I'll compete on Vault-Pegs. Put me in at #3. We can get an injury exemption. I already had the bone fusion. They'll approve it."

"Flaherty, you can't put any pressure on your ankle."

"So? It's Vault-Pegs. All upper body. I'll be fine."

"It's not all upper body. You have to run and hit the springboard. And you have to dismount at the end. There is no way."

Flaherty grabbed Whitfield by the arm. "Whitfield. Look at me. I have a broken ankle. Do you have any doubt that I can still kick your ass right here, right now?"

Whitfield saw a look in Flaherty's eyes that told him she was capable of anything. "No doubt whatsoever."

"Well, unless you want to be laid out on that trainer's table next to Kayleigh and Fenway as the rest of us are hoisting that trophy, you'll listen to me. You need to trust me. I can do this. I will do this. Aspen is not the only one who can play through pain."

"I understand. But the risk of re-injury. One misstep and you could be out even longer. We have Individual Championships in another week. You can't risk missing that."

"To hell with Individuals. We are winning this team championship."

Whitfield saw the same defiance and determination in Flaherty's eyes as he did in Aspen's just moments earlier. "OK. Go get us a championship."

Session 7 was incredible! The stuff of legends. Each of the top teams had their ups and downs. Bella scored a major win on Pommel Clock. Wilson went head-to-head against one of Parallel Pines' top athletes and scored a personal best, denying the current leaders any team points. Ippy and Wilson both fell on their events, but managed to recover enough to avoid giving up big points.

When his team needed him most, Whitfield delivered. He went 8-0 in the final session, bringing home 22 team points, against some of the top competitors in the meet. Going into the final set of duels; however, Seven Bridges Academy was three points behind Parallel Pines and within seven points of Vertical Press Academy, with all the momentum on their side.

In the final thirty minutes, eight duels remained. Flaherty was scheduled to square off against Flagpole Prep's #3 on Vault-Pegs and Aspen would finish off the meet with one final routine against the defending national champ on Pommel Clock. Flaherty was up first and stepped up to the vault runway to thunderous applause. The crowd was amazed to see Flaherty's name up in lights as the replacement for Kayleigh. With a broken ankle, and in intense pain, Flaherty raced down the runway with nary a limp, hit the springboard with incredible force and was certain she heard another pop in her ankle.

Despite the shooting pain, Flaherty reached up and grabbed the hanging pegs and positioned her body in a supine planche with her hips above hand level. She remained perfectly straight and motionless for three long seconds, enough time to take her mind back to the control room at Lord Sirroc's mansion. Flaherty completed the remainder of her routine as if in a trance.

After multiple series of swing, strength, and hold moves, executed at a level unseen before in school-level competition, Flaherty dismounted. If the arena was empty, no one would have believed what just happened. Flaherty completed a triple pike, full double-twist and stuck the landing…on one leg. She could not bear to put any pressure on her right ankle, and kept it lifted in the air as she found the landing mat with her left foot and managed to maintain perfect balance throughout, only daring to move after hearing the crowd's roar of approval.

Flaherty's score of 28.18 was a personal best, meet record, and all but assured Seven Bridges Academy of at least a second-place finish. As Flaherty was completing her magical performance on Vault-Pegs, Jade put up an impressive 25.81 on Pommel Clock. Seven Bridges wasn't dead yet, but they needed at least eight team points combined from Flaherty and Aspen to be crowned champions.

Aspen remained focused, visualizing his own routine, even as he heard the crowd's cheers after Jade's impressive score flashed across the video boards. Aspen didn't bother to take notice. His focus was sharp. Aspen stepped up to the first Pommel and saluted the judges. Whitfield raced upstairs after his own Handstand Obstacle routine to watch Aspen, and immediately regretted his decision when he saw Aspen wince when raising his broken wrist in salute. Whitfield's stomach further clenched when he noticed Jade's score. At this point, any additional points for Vertical Press Academy would clinch the title for the team currently sitting atop the leaderboard.

Aspen took a deep breath and closed his eyes for a second to collect his thoughts. He opened his eyes and somehow felt no more pain. His mind went to a place only he knows, and allowed him to perform what would be described later as The Miracle Clock. Aspen moved swiftly and forcefully, up and down each Pommel, like clockwork. Every flair; every handstand; every loop; every toe point was a model of perfection. Aspen had always excelled on Pommel Clock, but this routine was anything but routine. It was graceful, yet powerful. Smooth and seemingly effortless.

Every movement seemed free and at the same time executed with calculated precision. Aspen traveled around the entire clock and in a dizzying display of eight consecutive helicopter spins leading into his final dismount, Aspen didn't just stick his landing, but, as one reporter later remarked, "Aspen floated on air, hovering above the landing mat like an angel, sent to deliver Seven Bridges Academy its fourth consecutive national title."

The final tally from the Team Championship meet had Seven Bridges Academy on top by two points, the closest final score in team championship history. The crowd roared and cheered nonstop, for eight whole minutes, following Aspen's championship-clinching performance. The team carried both Aspen and Flaherty off the floor on their shoulders, and straight into the training room in the team's locker room for treatment. Whitfield remained down on the floor, just outside the tunnel, alone for a spell, just soaking it all in, as his teammates and coaches celebrated in the locker room.

Judges collected their belongings before heading into the media room for debriefing and feedback from WGF headquarters. Other gymnasts ran around here and there collecting socks, grips, chalk, and even a pair of pants, all scattered about on the floor. Hundreds of thousands of fans were still in shock after witnessing the greatest comeback in the sport's history. Whitfield just stood there, soaking it all in, knowing that the trophy and about a thousand reporters were all waiting for him inside. He stood there, wondering how they had just accomplished the impossible.

Even he would admit, that although he made his team believe, he never fully bought into all that he was saying the night before. *Did my words actually speak the championship into existence?* No, he wouldn't let himself take that much credit. It was a team effort. They deserved all the credit. He was just a piece. Part of the machine. What a ride!

Just before Whitfield was about to walk up the tunnel into the locker room, he saw a shadowy figure, one that he would recognize anywhere, off in the distance, walking toward him.

"Been here long?"

"The entire weekend."

"Well?"

"You need to keep your head back on your front layout."

Whitfield smiled. "I'll try to remember that."

"And your legs keep coming apart on your final tumbling pass."

Whitfield nodded. "Anything else?"

"And…you were amazing!"

"Is that an official critique?"

"No. Just an observation."

The shadowy figure had come into plain sight and was now standing right in front of Whitfield. "So, what do we do now?"

"Well, as you can see, I decided to wear that cute top you like so much."

"I noticed."

"I suppose I owe you a huge kiss now."

"That was part of the deal."

"Well, what are you waiting for? What's the problem?"

"I don't know. A week ago, I couldn't hit a routine and just yesterday, we were sitting in last place with two of our best gymnasts hurt."

"Yeah. And?"

"And now…"

"You just won the team championship!"

Whitfield still couldn't believe it. "How did that happen?"

"You were great."

Whitfield shook his head. "No. Aspen. He was great. Flaherty. I saw her score. She must have been great. I. I don't know."

"I'm not talking about your routines, Whitfield. When are you going to realize, you are a great leader! You got this team to believe in themselves. To believe in each other. You did that. They poured everything they had into this championship for you. I saw the looks in their eyes as they walked out of here yesterday. I don't know what you said in the locker room, but you lit a spark in them. A spark that was never there before."

"Oh, come on. The team won three straight titles before I got here."

"That was all Gabe. He dominated the competition and carried the team on his back. You did this with your heart. With your words. With your mind. And, sure, you weren't all that bad out on the competition floors either."

"Yeah, but…"

"But nothing. Enjoy this moment. Go in there and celebrate with your team. You are a champion!"

Whitfield knew his girlfriend was right. "Thanks, but what about that kiss?"

"What kiss?"

"Hey, we had a deal. We win the championship, and you give me a kiss."

"Well, technically, Aspen is the one who won the championship, so maybe I should…" Ugu loved teasing Whitfield.

"Ugu."

"Yes?"

"Shut up." Whitfield put his arm around Ugu's waist, pulled her in close, and the two kissed.

And not just any kiss, but one that fairy tales talk about. Pure. Sweet. And everlasting.

Chapter 45
Individual Championships

Seven Bridges Academy celebrated its fourth consecutive National Championship in style, or perhaps more in line with reality, Seven Bridges students celebrated by partying for the next four days. Classes were officially canceled for the week in response to huge student, and faculty, demand. Team members became instant legends in the pantheon of gymnastics greats to come before them, with Whitfield, Aspen, and Flaherty each immortalized in the Hall of Champions with magnificent busts unveiled at a mid-week ceremony, which attracted the attention of national, and world, leaders. Whitfield never imagined how awesome a spectacle the aftermath of Team Championship Week would become, and was a little uneasy with all the attention, but always smiled for the cameras and spoke intelligibly and charismatically for all the interviews and special features that kept his calendar full. His only true moment of joy throughout the media circus was watching his brother handle himself so well. Aspen was a natural on camera, and the media loved him. For such a young gymnast, Aspen had incredible presence and his personality made the world instantly fall in love with him.

For most team members, practice was considered optional for the two weeks following Team Championships, but for those competing in the Individual Championships next week, practice was as intense as ever. Seven Bridges had a record ten gymnasts qualify for Individual Championships, but only six were healthy enough to compete. Fenway and Diego were still nursing injuries suffered during Team Championships and Flaherty decided to sit out the week to rest her ankle. It was a tough decision for her to make, but the right one.

Flaherty still had a bright future ahead of her and re-injuring her ankle now could sideline her for a much longer period. Instead, Flaherty was scheduled to be a lead media analyst for the event. Not only was she a perfect fit for the role, but her involvement with the broadcast would secure the highest ratings ever for the championships.

Reluctantly joining Flaherty as an analyst, was Aspen. After his miraculous, championship-clinching performance, Aspen was determined to win an individual title on Pommel Clock, but Coach Brockport stepped in and withdrew Aspen's name from the invitation list. Aspen was distraught over the decision and pleaded with his coach to let him compete, but the head coach made the wise decision.

Aspen was too important to the team, and as a first-year, he would have plenty of opportunities to win one, and quite possibly multiple, event titles. Aspen eventually understood Coach Brockport's reasoning and agreed to join Flaherty as an all-star pairing of media analysts for the main event.

Of all the talented gymnasts scheduled to compete, Whitfield was considered one of the favorites for the All-Around title, and could possibly compete for a handful of event titles, but his main strength was consistency across every event. Flaherty's absence from the event really opened up the field, and now there were four or five gymnasts with a realistic shot at the All-Around crown.

Morocco was the favorite to repeat as Tri-Bars champion, and Keegan, if he could overcome some nagging injuries, was expected to compete for titles on Floor Exercise and Handstand Obstacle. Sydney was looking for a good showing on Escalating Tramps and Chloe and Ippy were both hoping to find some magic on their events.

The format for Individual Championships followed that of a regular meet, except for two additional sessions, one on each day, and the scoring emphasized both individual score and duel match points. On Days 1 and 2, eighty athletes competed per event spread across eight site locations. Ten athletes were assigned to a particular location, and competition ran as a full round robin, with each gymnast squaring off against each of the other nine athletes at their site.

Care was taken to ensure that those athletes competing in multiple events were not scheduled in multiple locations on the same day. Five sessions were held on Day 1 and four on Day 2. The eight site winners plus two wild cards on each event (based on highest combined scoring total) were invited to compete at the Individual Championships Finals on Days 4 and 5.

Events ran simultaneously, which meant All-Arounders would complete 72 routines over the first two days, with winners asked to perform another 72 routines to determine a champion. The grueling nature of determining an All-Around champion ensured that the ultimate winner was truly worthy of such an honor.

Even though classes had been canceled the previous week, Whitfield's teachers extended him the courtesy of excusing his absences during Individual Championships Week as well, allowing him to miss assignments and projects.

Whitfield appreciated the sentiment, but promised to complete all work during his Day 3 recovery day. He felt the extra coursework would take his mind away from the pressures of the championships, and if he was fortunate enough to make the top 10 and compete for a title, he would most definitely welcome the distraction.

Whitfield was happy to ride to his Day 1 site with Keegan and Coach Brockport. Their competition site was only an hour away by drone shuttle, so they left early in the morning, bypassing all the pre-meet festivities. The other Seven Bridges gymnasts were assigned to different travel sites for their competition and left the night before. Keegan added some much-needed levity to an otherwise intense competition period.

"Yo, cuz, I hear the cheerleaders at Individuals go loco for gymnasts."

"What?"

"You think coach will give us some time to check them out. Maybe have a little fun."

Whitfield shook his head. "You're crazy, Keegan."

"What? Tell me you never noticed any of our cheerleaders."

"No. I'm with Ugu. Why would I even look?"

"OK. OK. I get it. More for me. That's all I'm saying."

"We have a competition, you know."

"Oh please, I only have two events. That leaves plenty of time to get into some trouble."

"Well, I don't have time. You see my schedule? I have 40 routines today. Not sure how I'm getting through all that, and still have energy left to do another 32 tomorrow."

Keegan put his arm around Whitfield. "Little cuz…I have faith in you. I'll tell you what I'll do for you. For every routine you hit, I'll get another girl to shout your name."

"What's that going to do for me?"

"OK…fine. She'll shout my name. Woooo…I am pumped. This Championship Week is going to be awesome. Woooo."

Whitfield just smiled. "You are crazy, man."

"You know it." Whitfield and Keegan arrived at the site about 90 minutes before warmups. They headed into the locker room to get ready. Whitfield would have been nervous, but Keegan's antics kept him loose. "Yo, Whitfield, they got a hot tub and an ice bath in here. Come check this out."

"That's OK. I've seen 'em before."

"Yo, I'm going to switch the temps and get Coach to get into the hot tub. He'll freeze his butt off."

Whitfield chuckled. "No, man, don't do that. He'll get upset."

"Sorry, cuz…already happening. Coach needs to chill out." Keegan yelled for coach. "Yo, Coach, I got your hot tub ready for your pre-meet soak." Whitfield just smiled. After Keegan lowered the temp in the hot tub to a ridiculously cold level, he came back out to hang with Whitfield for a few minutes before heading out to the warmup floor. Whitfield was just sitting there, with his head down, looking over the schedule for Days 1 and 2.

Keegan saw Whitfield looking nervous. "Ten minutes left."

"Yup."

"You good?"

"You see this? Man, this is a tough schedule. No easy matchups. I have to be on my game the whole week."

"That's what this week is all about, baby."

Whitfield sighed, "yeah."

Keegan decided to dispense with the shenanigans and get serious for a moment. "Yo, all kidding aside, you are the best damn gymnast I've ever seen. Even better than my boy, Gabe."

Whitfield raised his head. "Really?"

"Dude. You've been crushing it all season. And keep getting better. I don't know how you're doing it. You keep this up, and they're going to rename this whole meet after you."

Whitfield started feeling better. "Thanks, Keegan. I appreciate that. I'm just trying to fit in here."

Keegan cocked his head to the side. "Why?"

"I don't know. I guess I still feel like the new guy. Trying to earn my keep."

"Dude, after all we've been through, you're not the new guy anymore. You're an OG, man. We all see it. You da man."

"You think so?"

"Yeah. You know who else thinks so?"

"Who?"

"Ugu. You're a lucky dog, man. I've seen her grow up fast these past few years and she is all that. And, she's so completely into you. I saw that kiss after championships." Keegan nudged Whitfield and offered a sly smile.

Whitfield turned a little red. "You saw that?"

"Yeah, man. I came out of the locker room looking for you. Never seen her look that way before. You got it all, man. Now, let's get you off your butt and go out there to get you your All-Around title."

"You're right. Let's do it."

Just as Whitfield stood up, Coach Brockport yelled out, "KEEGAN."

"Yeah, cuz, we need to run outta here." Whitfield and Keegan were two of the first gymnasts to arrive on the warmup floor. As usual, Whitfield soaked in the environment, and was surprised to see even more cameras and famous people in the crowd than were at Team Championships.

"Hey, this is insane? Is it just me, or is this even more crazy than last meet?" Whitfield felt he was screaming at the top of his lungs just so Keegan could hear him over the speakers.

"I think so. Well, with Flaherty out, you're the favorite to win. I guess they all came to see you, kid. And, of course, me. Watch this, I'm about to give 'em a show." Keegan took off his shirt, exposing his rippling abs and chiseled chest. Several fans could be heard shrieking, and Keegan soaked up every bit of attention. Whitfield just shook his head and kept stretching. The time had come to make their way to their first events. "All right, brother. Let's do this. I'm right by your side."

"Same here. Go out there and win a chip. Win two chips."

Keegan winked. "Got it in the bag, cuz." Keegan and Whitfield walked their separate ways to get to their first events. As Whitfield made his way to VH-Bars, he recognized a familiar face sitting in the front row. He decided to take a quick detour toward the stands.

"Mr. Gugurutruv? How are you, sir?"

"Whitfield. I'm well. How are you, son?"

"Feeling good."

"Great. Just great. I want you to know I'm here just for you. Decided to sit in the front row, and I'll be in the front row for each of your events."

Whitfield seemed a little confused. "Sir?"

"I just want to show my support for you. And for my daughter. Sorry I didn't get a chance to say goodbye the other day. Something came up and I had to leave quickly."

"Yes, I was looking for you. Ugu ended up coming to the Gala after all."

"Yes. Yes. I heard about her appearance." The smile on Mr. Gugurutruv's face briefly went away. "Is she here today?"

"No. Classes, you know."

"Right. She is a dedicated student. Well, I'm here. And you have my loyal support. Go get 'em." Ugu's dad patted Whitfield on the shoulder.

"Thank you, sir." Whitfield started to leave, but stopped when he heard Ugu's dad call out once more.

"Oh, Whitfield. One more thing."

"Yes, sir."

Mr. Gugurutruv looked Whitfield square in the eye. "I'm proud of you, son."

"Thanks." Whitfield wasn't quite sure what to make of Mr. Gugurutruv's appearance at the meet, or his surprisingly loyal support. Whitfield walked to his first event, and paused to look back once more. Mr. Gugurutruv was staring right back at him, with the slightest twinge of a smile. Whitfield made his way to his first event, trying to put this most recent strange interaction with Ugu's dad out of his head. It didn't take long for Whitfield to regain his focus. He began his arduous twelve-hour marathon on Day 1 with a win on VH-Bars and just like that, his quest for an All-Around title was off to a good start.

At the end of Day 1, Whitfield was atop the leaderboard in the All-Around competition, with a comfortable lead over Ricardo from Flagpole Prep. Whitfield was also either first or second on six events. He was in fourth place on Parallel Planks, and fifth place on Escalating Tramps. Whitfield had amassed an impressive 34 duel wins on Day 1, setting himself up for a potential finals-clinching Day 2.

Before heading into the locker room, Whitfield caught up with Mr. Gugurutruv, who gave Whitfield a huge hug and was very complimentary of Whitfield's performance. Whitfield still wondered what brought on this unusual show of affection from his girlfriend's father, but he was starting to enjoy the support. After all, his own parents were gone, and Hendricks, his guardian almost since birth, didn't attend a single meet all season. It felt nice to have a father figure in his life who actually came out to support him.

Back in the locker room, Whitfield caught up with Keegan, who also had a very good Day 1. Keegan was in second place on both of his events, trailing only Whitfield on both Floor Exercise and Handstand Obstacle. Back at the hotel, Whitfield checked in with his other teammates via video messaging, and, for the most part, his teammates also enjoyed great success on Day 1, with the sole exception being Chloe, who fell on four out of her five Parallel Planks routines.

Whitfield offered her some encouraging words, and wished her the best for Day 2. Chloe was appreciative and certainly felt better about her chances going into the second day of competition after talking with Whitfield.

Day 2 was another successful outing for Whitfield. By the end of day, he had secured a spot in the All-Around Finals, as well as seven event finals, narrowly missing the cut on Escalating Tramps. Keegan qualified for event finals on Handstand Obstacle, but a few disappointing routines on Floor Exercise, eliminated him from a second event finals.

Across the other sites, Seven Bridges had mixed results. Chloe and Ippy each missed the cut. Sydney made the cut, and would compete for a title on Escalating Tramps. Morocco slipped to second place in his group on Tri-Bars, but still made the event finals as a wild card, by virtue of amassing the highest remaining scoring average, after all first-place finishers were accounted for, across the ten sites. In total, Seven Bridges Academy would be sending four athletes to Individual Championships Finals, three single event competitors, and Whitfield, who was competing for seven event titles and the all-important All-Around crown.

Back on campus on Wednesday, Whitfield was glad to be home and was in full recovery mode. He still attended his classes and met with Ugu, Aspen, and Flaherty to review his missed coursework from the prior two days, but he let his body rest. He attended practice for only an hour on Wednesday night, mostly to stretch out some nagging tightness, and for about 90 minutes on Thursday, but still kept his workout light, before leaving campus late to get to Finals.

Whitfield still went for his nightly run with Ugu on Wednesday, mostly because he just really enjoyed her company, but also out of a sense of obligation to help Ugu get back into her pre-Pit shape. It was working too. Ugu looked light on her feet and strong. She was almost fully back to the high standard she had set for herself, and made sure to let Whitfield know it, by out-sprinting him every chance she got. Before saying good night on Wednesday, Whitfield shared with Ugu his strange encounter with her dad.

"Yeah, he was sitting right there in the front row, for every event. Every time I switched floors; there he was."

"That's strange. Did you get flustered?"

"No. That was another strange part. I actually enjoyed having him there. Made me feel, I don't know, comfortable knowing I had his support."

"Good. I'm glad you two are getting along. Did he ask about me?"

"Of course. He brought up having to leave Lord Sirroc's Gala early and when I told him you showed up late, he got quiet and acted strange."

"Strange? How?"

"I don't know. He seemed to know you were there. Said he heard about it."

Ugu shrugged. "I really haven't spoken much with him lately."

"Everything OK?"

"Oh, sure. I've just been...well, you know."

"I do. You've been in trouble. Such a bad girl," Whitfield smiled.

"Oh, do you like that?"

"Actually, I prefer this Ugu better. I like being able to hug you whenever I want, without a glass wall between us."

"Oh, so you think you can hug me whenever you want?"

"I can't?"

"You have to catch me first." Ugu took off running. Whitfield had been hoping their run for the night was over, but apparently one more lap was needed. He ran as fast as he could, but still couldn't catch up to Ugu. She felt a little bad, so she let up after a while, and allowed Whitfield to catch her. Honestly, she wanted to feel his arms around her. They finished up their final lap walking with their arms around each other, two teenagers, hopelessly in love.

****

Individual Championships finals were the most highly competitive, and intense, sessions Whitfield ever experienced. The ten greatest gymnasts on every event, all under one roof. Whitfield was pleased that he skipped out on all the pre-meet festivities by staying on campus to practice and showing up to his hotel late to get a good night's sleep. But missing the pre-meet interviews, meant the media was clamoring to get soundbites from Whitfield before official warmups started. As soon as he left the locker room, Whitfield was bombarded with questions from dozens of media reporters. His security detail did a nice job of maintaining order, but still, Whitfield couldn't escape all the attention.

The only moment of solace came when he was ushered over to the prime network for a final interview before taking the floor. Being interviewed by his brother and Flaherty was strange, but at the same time, awesome. For the first time since showing up last night, Whitfield felt comfortable, surrounded by a little piece of home. After the interview, both Aspen and Flaherty hugged Whitfield and offered some words of encouragement.

Whitfield took their encouragement and ran with it, performing at a higher level than he had ever reached before. He hit nearly every routine on the first day of competition and ended the day as the front runner in the All-Around and on three separate events, although the competition was tight. Once again, Mr. Gugurutruv was in the front row for every one of Whitfield's routines.

At the end of the first day, Mr. Gugurutruv asked if Whitfield would join him for a late dinner. Normally, Whitfield would just grab something in the locker room and call it a night, but Mr. Gugurutruv was persistent, and Whitfield felt he owed him some of his time, so agreed to meet Mr. Gugurutruv back at the hotel for a late supper.

Whitfield found Mr. Gugurutruv sitting at a secluded table near the back of the hotel restaurant. Ugu's dad stood up and embraced Whitfield as he reached the table, before they both sat down. "Mr. Gugurutruv. Thanks so much for all your support this week. It really means a lot to me."

"Of course. No other place I'd rather be."

"You'll be happy to know that I think your daughter is flying out here tomorrow."

"Oh, wonderful. I'll be sure to save a seat for her."

"Front row?"

"Absolutely." Just then, a fan came up to the table and asked to take Whitfield's picture. He obliged. Ugu's dad even got in the shot too.

Whitfield seemed a little embarrassed by all the attention. "Sorry about that."

Mr. Gugurutruv threw his hand up. "Oh, no need to apologize. I understand. You're a celebrity."

"You know, she's never seen me compete from that close. Your daughter, that is. It'll be fun seeing you two there together."

"You can count on it. So, Whitfield, this is some competition, isn't it?"

"Sure is."

"Are you feeling confident?"

"I'm feeling good. Not sure how things will wrap up tomorrow, but I'm going to give it my all."

"Good. Good. You know, you've brought in a lot of resources for Seven Bridges with that performance during Team Championships."

"Really? I don't really pay attention to any of that."

"Yes, it's true. That championship brought in billions to SBA. Almost doubling what you earned during the season, not to mention all the side bets and gambling profits. And that's nothing compared to what the school stands to gain from having an All-Around champion."

"How's that?"

"I know, it seems strange doesn't it. Having an All-Around champion bring in more than the team title. Just one of those quirks."

"Well, that's nice, I guess. Like I said, I don't really get involved in all that." Whitfield felt a little uncomfortable talking about resources exchanging hands, gambling profits, and all that stuff. He just wanted to stay focused on his routines and not worry about anything else.

"I know. I know. Not your concern. But it is tough to ignore. After all, that kind of money can change lives. I remember when I was first starting out, placing a few bets for fun, I had quite the winning streak going."

"Really?"

"Oh, yes. I've always had a knack for choosing winners. There was this one gymnast. He was good. Real good. I met him a few times and knew right away he was special. Started placing bets on him to win and the money just kept pouring in. Made millions. But, one day, right from under my nose…he lost. Wiped out a whole fortune. Didn't see it coming. That's the thing. On top one day and then it all disappears. Everyone loses, eventually."

Whitfield looked concerned.

Mr. Gugurutruv must have picked up on it. "Oh, no. Not you. You still have a lot of great years in front of you. I wouldn't worry about things going south for you. No. You're a good one. Real special. Once in a generation. Of course, the only way to know for sure that a gamble is going to pay off is to…ehh, get involved some way. You know, like those messy little bribes that people over at the WGF were handing out."

Whitfield wasn't sure where Mr. Gugurutruv was going with all this. "Oh, you heard about that?"

"Of course. All over the news. But we know you wouldn't ever take a bribe, right?"

"No sir."

Mr. Gugurutruv sat back in his chair. "Even for, say, ten million dollars."

"No way."

"That's what I like about you, Whitfield. Integrity. You've got character. Yes, you're a special one. That's why I'm betting it all on you to win tomorrow."

Whitfield dropped his fork in surprise. "Sir?"

"That's right. Every dime. Everything my family has been saving for years. Took us a while to recover from that last debacle, and you'd think I'd learn my lesson, but I see something in you. My daughter sees it too. You, Whitfield, are a winner. Just like me. Together, we are going to get far."

Whitfield started to panic. "Sir, I'm not really comfortable with all of this. I mean, your entire life savings?"

"And Ugu's."

"Sir?"

"Well, her inheritance, that is. Don't worry about it. You'll be fine. Eat your lobster."

Whitfield was starting to sweat. "Sir. The competition is really tough. I...I may not win."

Mr. Gugurutruv leaned forward. "Are you saying you're not going to win? Are you sure? Should I bet against you? You could make that happen, you know. No one would suspect it. We could make a killing."

"No, sir. I would never throw a meet. I'm going to try my best to win."

Mr. Gugurutruv sat up straight and smiled. "Attaboy. I knew I could count on you."

"Sir, I just don't think you should risk your entire family fortune on me."

Mr. Gugurutruv's tone shifted. "Never tell me how to spend my money. You, my boy, are a winner. I may have made a mistake in the past, but I was young. Foolish. Now, I know better. I see that fire inside you. That burning desire to be the best. You won't let me down."

Whitfield's throat was dry. He had a tough time swallowing. "I'll try sir."

"I know you will."

"Well, thank you for the meal, sir. I had a nice time. I really must be getting to bed now."

"Of course. Of course. Hey, I had a blast. Thanks for joining me."

"No problem. Good night, sir." Whitfield left the table, and on his way out, Mr. Gugurutruv called out to him.

"Whitfield, remember, I'm counting on you, son."

Whitfield nodded and exited the restaurant. He went upstairs to his room. It took him a while to fall asleep. Whitfield couldn't get the conversation with Ugu's dad out of his head. *Was he really trying to get me to throw the meet tomorrow? Is he really gambling his whole family's fortune on me to win? What if I don't win? What would that do to him? What would it do to Ugu? She might never forgive me.* Whitfield slept uneasy. He woke up several times throughout the night in a cold sweat.

The final day of Individuals Championships was only a few hours away and Whitfield was worried he might cost his girlfriend her entire family's fortune, not to mention the hundreds of millions, or perhaps billions, he might cost Seven Bridges Academy if he didn't win. The pressure was making Whitfield sick. Sleep was out of the question. He just laid there, in his hotel bed, worrying. The pressure was finally catching up to him.

When Whitfield walked onto the warmup floor in the morning, he spotted Ugu sitting in the front row with her dad, but unlike the previous day, Whitfield made no attempt to walk over to greet them. He tried to remain focused on his routines, but lack of sleep and a worried mind, made concentration difficult. Whitfield's performance in Sessions 6 and 7 were uneven, at best. He made several uncharacteristic errors and even completed the wrong tumbling pass on one of his Floor Exercise routines. He had inexplicably forgotten that he had taken out one pass, and now that he put it back in, he was confused with what to do next; his indecision costing him several points.

Whitfield had slipped in the rankings, but was still in position to take home some trophies, including the All-Around title, if he buttoned up his routines and performed up to his capabilities during the final two sessions.

Whitfield had let the conversation with Ugu's dad get to him. His mind was playing tricks on him, and Whitfield didn't know where to turn. Fortunately for him, there was one person who knew Whitfield better than he knew himself, and she just happened to love him more than anything in the world and knew just how to get his head back on straight. Ugu sneaked into the locker room during the intermission before Session 8 and approached Whitfield.

"Hey, Ugu, you can't be in here."

Ugu waved her hand. "Of course, I can. But just to be safe, let's go into the coaches' office." Ugu grabbed Whitfield's hand and walked over to the coaches' office, opened the door, and politely asked Coach Brockport, Coach Daza, and the rest of the coaching staff to leave. To Whitfield's surprise, they all left without uttering a word.

Ugu then turned to Whitfield. "Sit." Whitfield sat in Coach Brockport's chair. "What's bothering you? And don't even think about lying to me because I will shove this chalk bucket where the sun doesn't shine. You know I'll do it."

"OK. OK. You're starting to sound like Flaherty. I'll tell you." Whitfield proceeded to tell Ugu about the conversation he had with her dad over dinner last night. He was hesitant to tell her everything, especially the part about him gambling away her inheritance, but he broke down and told her everything. Ugu was caught off guard. She wasn't expecting any of what Whitfield told her, but one of Ugu's greatest strengths was her ability to think quickly on her feet, and given that she only had a few minutes left until Whitfield had to go out and compete in Session 8, she knew she had to come up with something fast.

"OK. So, what's the problem?"

"Haven't you been listening? If I don't win, everyone loses. Your dad. Our school. You. Everyone. Your dad will probably hate me forever. You'll leave me. I just…can't."

Ugu nodded. "OK. I see the problem. You're a coward."

"What?"

"You, Whitfield, are a big 'ol coward, with a capital C. You're afraid of losing. You're afraid of disappointing my dad. You're afraid of upsetting your friends. You're afraid of losing me."

"Well, yeah."

"Stop being so afraid! Whitfield, you are a wonderful gymnast and have a real shot out there, but even if you don't come home with any titles, so what. That doesn't change anything. Seven Bridges will still have more money than they know what to do with. Your friends will still love you. My dad is a big boy. He can handle himself. He made a decision to gamble away his money and if he loses, that's on him."

"What about your inheritance?"

"A few minutes ago, I didn't even know I had one. As far as I'm concerned, none of his money is mine anyway. I'm going to make a fortune on my own, with you by my side, because we are meant for each other. You and me, Whitfield. I love you. You love me. I'm not leaving you. And, let's face it, we all know you are NEVER going to leave me. So, stop being afraid. Look, you are a champion. You've already proven that. And not out there, but in here. In your heart. You always know the right thing to do. And right now, you know the right thing to do is to get off your ass, stop whining, stop being afraid, and just go out there and be great. Like I know you can."

Whitfield had never felt a stronger connection to Ugu than he did at that moment. "Can I say something?"

"It better not be something stupid."

"You're right. I was afraid. Not anymore. I have no reason to be. I already have everything I want. Right here in front of me."

"Well, you're everything that I want. But right now, I want you to go out there and be yourself. No fears. No regrets."

"You got it, boss. Hey, anyone ever tell you that your eyes sparkle and you get the cutest little wrinkle in your nose when you get excited?"

"Aww, really?"

"Good thing too…takes the focus off your flat butt. Bye." Whitfield kissed Ugu on the cheek and ran out of the office and down the tunnel back out onto the floor.

Ugu yelled after him. "You had to say something stupid, didn't you?"

****

Thanks to Ugu's pep talk, Whitfield was back to his usual self, performing exceptionally clean and highly skilled routines. He retook the lead in the All-Around and ended Session 8 with the lead in three events, second on two others. The competition for the All-Around title was the closest it had been in the past ten years heading into the final session. Whitfield was in first place, followed closely by Jade from Vertical Press Academy and Kelsie from Riverboard. All three were separated by only 2.50 points. Of the three, Whitfield had the toughest draw in Session 9, but if he hit his final eight routines, the All-Around title would be his.

Whitfield fell on his first routine of Session 9, but so did Jade. Kelsie temporarily took the lead, but Whitfield wrested it back after his second routine. The three All-Arounders each took turns with the lead during Session 9, something that had never happened before in the final session of Individual Championships.

Heading into the final duel period, Whitfield squared off against Jade, the top team point scorer in the country and reigning national champion on Pommel Clock, while Kelsie competed on Escalating Tramps against Ricardo from Flagpole Prep. Jade and Kelsie were each scheduled to go first in their respective duels, meaning Whitfield would go into his final routine knowing exactly what he needed to capture the title.

Whitfield couldn't believe his luck, being paired for his final duel against Jade, whom his brother had just fought with him to compete against at Individual Championships just over a week ago. Whitfield recalled Aspen's voice, telling him he couldn't defeat Jade on Pommel Clock. Maybe his brother was right. Maybe Jade was too good, and in the end, perhaps Jade would exact her revenge, this time against Whitfield, undoubtedly the weaker of the two Mitchell boys on Pommel Clock. Whitfield knew he needed to put those negative thoughts out of his head if he was going to deliver the performance of his life.

Kelsie and Jade each hit their routines, putting the pressure on Whitfield to come up big. Whitfield needed a 26.68 to surpass Kelsie and 27.31 to beat Jade and earn the title of All-Around champion. Thanks to solid performances over the previous eight sessions, Whitfield only needed a 25.98 on his final performance to secure the event title on Pommel Clock, but he wasn't ready to give up on the All-Around crown. Whitfield's season average on Pommel Clock was 25.25, but had scored a personal best of 27.99 on Day 1 of Individual Championships earlier in the week.

Needing such a high score to win the title, Whitfield knew he needed more than just a clean routine; he needed to execute his entire repertoire of higher-level skills to near perfection. He couldn't play it safe. He had to let it all out. As he walked up to the first pommel, Whitfield glanced over at Ugu for one final time before the title would be decided. He also looked over at her dad, sitting quietly, looking stoic on the outside, but Whitfield knew, deep down inside, he was frantically praying for Whitfield to hit his routine.

Whitfield stepped up to face the Pommel Clock, closed his eyes, took a deep breath, opened his eyes, saluted the judges, and started his routine with a flawless mount. Pommel Clock was one of Whitfield's best events, and with a solid routine, he would be assured of his second event title, matching the one he earned earlier in the session on Vault-Pegs; but with an outstanding routine, he would be crowned All-Around champion. One final routine. For a chance at glory.

Whitfield looped and flaired, spun and traveled, went up to handstand and pirouetted from one pommel to the next, up and down and across the connecting ramp. Then, it happened. A mistake. It was barely noticeable, but it happened. As Whitfield performed a daring helicopter spin transition down to rear facing front circles, his left leg grazed the pommel. It wasn't supposed to. Technically, it was a fall. His leg didn't put any pressure on the apparatus and he didn't use the contact to help stabilize his balance, but his leg hit the pommel nonetheless.

A full point deduction. Whitfield was only a few pommels away from his dismount. He didn't have time to process what that fall would mean for his chances of winning, but he was pretty sure it knocked him out of contention. *That's it. Jade is going to win. I had my chance. I just wasn't good enough today. Give her credit. She earned it.*

Whitfield completed the entire clock and stuck his dismount. The crowd went wild. The other gymnasts on the floor surrounded Jade and Whitfield, knowing that one of them had just won the All-Around title. After a few tense moments, Whitfield's score was revealed. 28.05. He did it. Whitfield did it! He won.

Whitfield had just won the All-Around title and was now the national champion on Pommel Clock!

The entire arena erupted. Confetti dropped from the rafters and frenzied media personnel rushed the floor. Whitfield was immediately congratulated by all the gymnasts in his group; even Jade offered her heartfelt congratulations. It was all happening so fast, but Whitfield knew something was wrong. *They didn't see my leg hit. The judges. They didn't take the point deduction.*

Ever since he was a child, Whitfield had the amazing ability to compute scores in his head, and he knew, without a doubt, the judges had missed his fall. Whitfield stopped celebrating and rushed over to the judges' table. The judges were all still seated, tallying up their final scoresheets.

"Congratulations, young man! That was quite a performance."

Whitfield ignored the adulation. "I think you made a mistake."

"What mistake? You won. You should be celebrating. Wonderful competition today."

"No. I mean, yes. Thank you."

"What is it then?"

"My last routine. Did you take off for my fall?"

The judges looked at each other and then back at Whitfield. "What fall?"

"On Pommel Nine. My leg hit the pommel."

Again, the judges all looked at each other. None of them seemed to catch Whitfield's leg hit the apparatus. "I didn't see a fall. None of us did. When did you say you fell?"

"On Pommel Nine, when I came down from my helicopter spin."

"Are you sure?"

Whitfield nodded. "I am."

The judges again looked at each other. Judge 1 made the announcement to the entire arena. "Scoring Review in Progress." The deafening roar of the crowd subsided as fans began to notice the video boards' flashing message:

Scoring Review in Progress

Whitfield looked over at Ugu, who a moment earlier had been jumping up and down with her dad, in pure elation. They were now standing side by side, her dad with a look of worry, his eyes sternly fixated on Whitfield. Keegan and Morocco, fresh off their second-place finishes approached Whitfield as the judges conferred with the replay monitors.

"Sup, cuz?"

"They didn't deduct for my fall."

"What fall? You crushed that routine." Morocco slapped Whitfield on the back.

"My leg hit the pommel."

"So? If they didn't catch it, who cares?"

"Yeah, man. Judges make errors all the time. Part of the game. You are the champ. Enjoy it!"

Whitfield couldn't enjoy it though. "Thanks, but I can't. I didn't earn it. Jade did. She deserves the title."

Morocco threw his arms in the air. "Can you stop being a boy scout for once. Enjoy the win."

The judge called Whitfield back over to the scoring table. "We've reviewed the footage, and we still do not detect a fall."

Keegan overheard. "See. No fall. You won. CHAMP in the house!"

Whitfield knew the judges were mistaken. "No, it's got to be there. Let me see."

Whitfield reached for the monitors and Judge 1 stepped in his way. "This is highly unusual. We typically do not let athletes interfere with the scoring process."

Whitfield pleaded his case. "Please, sir. This is important."

"OK. Here you go." The judges allowed Whitfield to review the video monitors.

"Look. It happened right there. I know it. The video has a blind spot. Probably the same blind spot that caused you to miss it. Here, tap into this other feed." Whitfield detached the cable from a nearby camera feed. "It's the video from my N-Dimensional Scanning Technology. The WGF installed these cameras for all meets."

Judge 3 looked concerned. "Umm. I'm not sure we can use that footage for the review process."

"Do you want to get the scoring correct?"

After a moment of hesitation, Judge 1 consented. "Pull up the feed." Whitfield connected the feed to the judges monitor, and sure enough, exactly where Whitfield said his leg hit the pommel, it did. The video footage from his own invention showed the infraction clear as day. "Whitfield, will you excuse us while we confer?"

"Certainly."

The mood in the arena was growing restless. The event titles had all been decided. Whitfield won event titles for Vault-Pegs and Pommel Clock. The rest of Seven Bridges' gymnasts were shut out. The All-Around champion, for now awarded to Whitfield, was now being reconsidered, and the fans had no idea what to make of the situation. Whitfield was announced as the winner, and he was the only one speaking with the judges afterwards. Usually, if there is disagreement over scoring, it would be the losing party that appealed to the judges. Whitfield was already crowned the winner, so the fans were totally confused.

On the prime networks, Flaherty and Aspen tried to make sense of the judges' extended review. They showed the replay over a dozen times and made note of every deduction the judges could have possibly found and both agreed that the score seemed justified, if not a little low. Flaherty nit-picked every hand placement and every toe point. She just couldn't find anywhere where the judges would deduct more points. They were both convinced, and in the process, convinced millions of viewers, that Whitfield was indeed the new All-Around champion.

Everyone seemed convinced, except for Whitfield and one other astute observer. Ugu intently watched Whitfield's every action, and smiled to herself. *He's doing it. He's stepping up for what's right. He's no longer afraid.*

Ugu hadn't taken her eyes off Whitfield since he completed his routine, and she knew what he had done. She also knew that once it came out that he was the one protesting his own score, he would be the target of much animosity, perhaps even led by her own dad.

After all, it's safe to say that billions of dollars in resources were about to change hands if the judges honored Whitfield's appeal and changed his score. Her first thought was to make sure Whitfield was safe. Ugu rushed from her seat over to the tunnel area where Whitfield's security team waited. "Hey, Jill. I need you to take Whitfield inside the locker room right now. He might be in danger."

The head of Whitfield's security detail knew Ugu well. "What? Why?"

"Please. I'll explain later. Tell him I asked for it. He'll know why."

"You got it." Jill and her team approached the mats where Whitfield and the rest of the gymnasts were awaiting the judges' final decision. Jill whispered in Whitfield's ear, and he followed her and the rest of his security detail into the tunnel area before the judges' conference was over. Moments later, the final verdict was announced over the speakers:

"Due to a scoring error, we have updated the final results. Whitfield's score has been revised to 27.05. As a result, Jade is the All-Around champion. Congratulations Jade!"

The crowd was stunned. A large pocket of fans started screaming in support of Jade's accomplishment, while many others booed and jeered the change in scoring. Sensing the moment, security around the arena came to the forefront. The situation was tense. Ugu wanted to speak directly with Whitfield. Her dad, insisted on following her.

"Whitfield, are you OK?"

Mr. Gugurutruv rushed the tunnel, and was forcibly restrained by security. "You son of a green-toed sloth. How dare you? Did you get the judges to change that score?"

Whitfield was visibly shaken by Mr. Gugurutruv's irate behavior. "I fell. They missed it. I was just trying to make it right."

"Do you have any idea what you cost me tonight? What you cost your school?"

"I know. And I'm really sorry about that. I really am. But I didn't win. Jade did."

"No. You had the title and gave it away."

"Sir, I didn't earn the title. It wasn't mine to give."

"I treated you like a son, and this is how you treat me? You'll pay for this. Every dime. You'll pay." Mr. Gugurutruv stormed away, but the media frenzy was just getting started.

Reporters bombarded Whitfield with questions. "Is it true, Whitfield? Did you ask the judges to change your score?"

"Were you really too scared to win?"

"Was the pressure too much for you?"

Whitfield didn't know which question to respond to first. "I simply pointed out that I had fallen during the routine. The judges conferred and, in the end, they got it right. Jade is the true champion."

"Did you know you were giving up the title when you asked for a scoring correction?"

"The title was never mine to begin with. The judges got it right. Jade won." Whitfield made his way through the throngs of reporters back into the locker room, where he was met by some angry teammates. Ugu was unable to sneak back into the locker room amidst all the chaos, and decided to find an empty corner to call Sir Arlington and suggest that he make preparations to diffuse what would likely be a hostile crowd welcoming the team, and particularly Whitfield, back to campus. She knew that despite winning two event titles, most students were not going to support Whitfield's decision to come clean to the judges. Back in the locker room, Whitfield was targeted.

Morocco wanted to hit Whitfield upside his head. "How could you do that, man?"

Chloe, who had made the trip despite not qualifying for finals, punched her locker in frustration. "Yeah, Whitfield, do you know what you just cost us?"

Even Sydney expressed her disappointment. "We're going to lose everything. I told my parents to bet on you to win. I believed in you. How could you do that?"

Keegan may have been Whitfield's only vocal supporter in the locker room. "Hey, cut him some slack. He was just doing what he thought was right. I know it was tough for you, bro. I'm proud of you. You did a stupid thing there at the end, but I'm still proud of all you accomplished this week." Keegan stepped up to give Whitfield a bro hug. The others threw down their bags and towels and returned to their lockers.

Whitfield felt all alone. His teammates turned on him. Ugu's dad surely hated him. Seven Bridges Academy would likely lose a ton of resources. All because of a simple decision to speak up. Whitfield started to question his decision. *Did I really do the right thing? Is my integrity worth all this pain? How do I apologize? Am I sure I even want to apologize? For what? What did I do that was so wrong?*

Whitfield stayed inside the locker room for a while, until he was called to come out for the post-meet media interviews. To his credit, Whitfield stood at the podium and tried to answer every question as honestly as he could. Despite winning two event titles and finishing second in the All-Around, truly a spectacular result, all anyone wanted to talk about was Whitfield's unprecedented move to ask the judges to address a mysterious missed deduction.

The questions were aggressive, and many were unnecessarily cruel. They questioned whether the pressure was too much for Whitfield to handle and whether he may have bribed the judges to lower his score. They asked if he had bet against himself and intentionally threw the final event. Shots were being fired and Whitfield did his best to stay strong, but the media was merciless.

Finally, Coach Brockport stepped in to put an end to the firing squad. "Enough! Whitfield is a hell of a gymnast. And an even better person. You should all be half the man he is. He knew exactly what he was doing. He was protecting the integrity of this meet. The integrity of athletes everywhere. He knew what was right. He knows the value of high character. He knows doing the right thing may be costly, but is willing to pay that price. He knows everyone is going to attack him for this. Unfairly. Unjustly.

"Every day, we see athletes all across this sport try to exploit every advantage to win, even if it means stepping over the line of right and wrong. We've grown numb to cheating. Numb to dishonesty. Numb to lying. Well, not Whitfield. He is a shining example of all that is right with this sport, and in one gesture, showed the world what true integrity looks like. Shame on all of you for making him feel bad for having the guts to do what you are too cowardly to do in your own lives. We can all learn from Whitfield. Dammit, I hope one day, I become half the man he is today. Come on, Whitfield. Let's go."

Whitfield and Coach Brockport walked off the podium together. The media room grew silent.

Whitfield knew he had at least one supporter. "Thanks, Coach."

"Meant every word. Damn fine work out there. I couldn't be prouder."

Whitfield went back into the locker room, and his teammates, having just heard Coach Brockport's remarks all stood to greet him with heartfelt apologies.

Morocco stepped up first. "Hey, Whitfield. I'm really sorry, man. I just didn't realize…I mean, you did the right thing. You thought you fell and told the judges. I can respect that."

Chloe hugged Whitfield. "Yeah, me too. I'm sorry for what I said. I just wanted that title so bad for you. You're our leader. I guess now we know why we love you so much."

Keegan stayed by his locker, but spoke up above the crowd. "I said it before. You da man. Stronger than all of us combined. I don't think any of us would have had the courage to do what you just did. I'm proud of you, cuz."

Each of Whitfield's teammates took turns coming up and hugging him. Whitfield was brought to tears. He knew the firestorm that was probably waiting for him back on campus, but right here, in this room, with his teammates, he was convinced he made the right call. Convincing a thousand of his classmates and millions around the world? That might take a little more time and effort.

Ugu decided to leave the arena and head back to campus before Whitfield was even close to leaving the locker room. She wanted to be on campus to try and calm any angry protesters before Whitfield arrived. Ugu was in full damage control mode now, knowing full well that Whitfield had suffered enough already and didn't deserve to be treated as a villain.

To his surprise, Whitfield was met with a warm, and rather cheerful, reception upon his return to campus. The crowd was small, given that he had just won two event titles and finished second by the slimmest of margins in the All-Around. Sir Arlington was the first to greet Whitfield as he stepped off the drone bus.

"Congratulations, young Whitfield! Job very well done!"

"Thank you, sir."

"How are you feeling?"

"Honestly, sir, I feel OK. I was expecting a more hostile welcome."

"Oh, don't let this fool you. It was hostile here just about an hour ago. I came out and had some words with some of our…more passionate…students. I tried appealing to their own morality, but in the end, they only agreed to reconsider their actions in light of proposed penalties. You'll find that integrity is something many people pay lip service to and some, may even think they possess it, but when the stakes are high, very few have the courage to display it in the manner in which you just exhibited. I want you to know I am proud of you, young Whitfield."

"Thank you, sir."

Sir Arlington put his arm around Whitfield. "And don't worry about your classmates. They will come around. Eventually. You may have a few difficult weeks ahead, but trust me, by the end of the school year, you'll be their hero again."

"Sir, I don't really want to be anyone's hero. Being a student is difficult enough."

"Ahh, well said. And that, is why you are my hero, young Whitfield. Let's get you home."

Whitfield looked around for Ugu, but couldn't spot her in the crowd. He was tired. It had been a day for the ages, and after such a restless night before, Whitfield needed to get some sleep. Whitfield returned home and was greeted warmly, but not overly enthusiastically, by members of his staff. Whitfield politely thanked everyone for their support and went up to his room. He crawled into bed and was asleep before his head even hit the pillow.

Chapter 46
Revelations

The morning headlines were merciless:

"Pressure Too Much for Gutless Whitfield," "Whitfield Crumbles Under Weight of Trophy—Begs to Lose," "Too Cowardly to Win," "Whitfield is a Whole New Breed of Loser."

Even the WGF issued a statement regarding the upcoming International Bowl:

"Due to recent events, we feel that it is in the best interest of our team, our country, and for the individual, to remove Whitfield from our elite team of athletes representing our country in the upcoming International Bowl. Whitfield is an outstanding gymnast and we are happy to have him as one of our own. We look forward to Whitfield competing at the highest levels of gymnastics for years to come. For now, we wish Whitfield all the best on his road to recovery."

Ugu jogged over to Whitfield's mansion in the morning, thinking her boyfriend might need to see a friendly face after last night's life-altering events. "Road to recovery? What are they talking about? Recovery? What am I recovering from?"

"The WGF is buying into this whole media nonsense about the pressure being too much for you to handle. I think they are taking the official stance that you'll be under the care of a sports psychologist over the coming weeks, or even months."

"What? Really? Everyone thinks I crumbled? Is that really what this is all about?"

"I think so. They've replayed the video thousands of times and no one saw you fall."

"But I did. You believe me, don't you?"

"Of course, I do. I can see it on your face. The problem is that no one can see it on the video replay."

"It wasn't on the network cameras. They had to use my scanning tech to see it."

"Really? Is that even allowed?"

Whitfield shrugged. "It's so new, I don't think it was written into the rules yet. Even the judges weren't sure."

"But you insisted they look at it." Ugu's comment came across as more accusatory than she had intended.

Whitfield grew defensive. "They needed to get it right."

"Even if it cost you the title."

"Ugu, what are you saying? You think I should have dropped it and not encouraged them to get it right?" Whitfield didn't want to argue with Ugu. "I don't know. Maybe you're right."

Ugu saw that fire in Whitfield start to dim. "Whoa. Stop right there. Don't you ever, for a second, think that what you did wasn't the right thing. You were brave. You displayed courage that others could only dream about. And I love you for that. You hear me? You knew your score wasn't correct and you stepped up and made it right. I am so proud of you."

Whitfield appreciated Ugu's support, but knew she was holding something back. "Then what?"

Ugu lowered her head. "Whitfield, I think we have a problem."

"What? You're not going to break up with me because I did what's right, are you?"

Ugu smacked Whitfield on his arm. "Don't be stupid. If I'm going to break up with you, it'll be because Gabe calls. I mean, he actually was an All-Around champion." Whitfield's jaw dropped open, but he couldn't utter a sound. "Oh, stop it. I'm kidding with you. I already told you; you're never getting rid me."

"OK good. But, terrible joke. I hear he picks his nose. You don't want to be with someone like that."

"Are you through?"

"Terrible dresser, too. And his hair. I mean, come on."

"OK, I get it. You're a stud who dresses wonderfully and never picks his nose. Ooh, baby, I want you so bad."

"Not sure I care for the sarcasm."

"Then stop being stupid. Look, I think we have a real problem. My dad."

Whitfield put his head in his hands. "I know. He probably doesn't want you seeing me anymore."

"No. It's not that. Well, you might be right, but actually I'm not so sure. Anyway, look, after you told me about my dad's fortune and my supposed inheritance, I got curious, and started poking around my dad's finances."

"Ugu. That's a bit much, don't you think?"

Ugu waved her hand. "Not at all. Anyway, one, he is incredibly wealthy."

"Yeah. But you knew that already."

"No, not this much. I mean filthy rich. I had no idea. I tracked his records going back as far as I could, and what he said to you appears to be accurate. He started out with a modest amount and his gambling profits kept growing and growing. He made a ton of money, and then one day about 10 or 11 years ago, it was all gone."

Whitfield nodded. "That must have been when that gymnast he was telling me about fell or something."

"Makes sense. But shortly after, he got it all back and then some. Whitfield, he's one of the wealthiest men in the world. I really had no idea."

Whitfield didn't look all that impressed. "OK. I guess you were in line for a big inheritance then. Until I screwed it all up. Sorry about that."

Ugu shook her head. "Well, not exactly. You see, that brings me to my second point. My dad didn't bet on you to win. He actually put a large sum of money on you to lose."

Whitfield jumped up, knocking his chair backward. "WHAT? That doesn't make any sense. He was cheering for me. He wanted me to win."

"No, Whitfield, he was just playing mind games with you. That's what he does. It really bugs me to say it, but he's kind of a genius."

"Oh thanks. He's a genius for playing mind games with me?"

"No, you don't understand. I mean, he's a real genius. Super smart. Just look at what he did. Wow, he is so clever. He made sure everyone saw you two together. Made sure to sit in the front row all week. Took you to dinner the night before the last day of championships. Probably made sure someone took plenty of pictures too."

Whitfield did recall a moment from the restaurant. "Now that I think of it, someone did take our picture at dinner."

"Yeah, I'm sure he got a shot of both of you together. Whitfield, if anyone finds out my dad bet against you, rumors are going to spread."

Whitfield caught onto Ugu's train of thought immediately. "Rumors that I intentionally asked the judge to lower my score so that your dad would win."

"Right. Everyone now knows we're dating and you just spent the week with my dad in the front row. Your pure and innocent actions might get portrayed as corrupt and devious and driven purely by gambling profits."

Whitfield was now concerned. "You're right. This is a problem. How do we handle it?"

"Well, best case scenario is that my dad was simply playing mind games with you so you'd mess up and his bet would pay off."

"That's pretty messed up."

"Ehh…not as messed up as the alternative. My gut tells me it's not that simple. It never is with my dad."

"OK. What're you thinking?"

"My dad's too smart to get burned twice. And besides, the bet was big, but not that big. Compared to his overall fortune, it was a drop in the bucket, but to anyone else, it's a lot. I think he's going to try to blackmail you."

Whitfield's eyes widened. "How? Why?"

Ugu paused a moment to collect her thoughts. "Not sure. If it were me, I'd divert some money into your account. Maybe claim it's a gift or something. Nothing too large to draw the bank's suspicion, but large enough to make it seem like a payoff for throwing the meet."

"And if anyone found out…"

"Your reputation wouldn't be the only thing ruined. He made a big scene out there by the tunnel. Made sure people saw him. Remember, his bet won, so he had no reason to be upset."

Whitfield was starting to understand Ugu's dad's devious nature, and was thinking aloud. "So, it was an act. He wanted people to see him upset. But, if he's trying to blackmail me, why act as though he's upset? Wouldn't he play it cool, as though he got exactly what he wanted? This way, he could hold the payment over my head and threaten to go public with his 'bribe' if I don't do what he wants."

"Right, but that's only if he pays you himself."

"What do you mean?"

Ugu was continuing to develop her thinking as she spoke. "He's not going to pay you himself. He's trying to set someone else up." Bam! That's when the idea hit Ugu. "Wait. No. He couldn't be."

Whitfield hadn't yet been struck with the same thought. "Couldn't be what?"

"He's still going after Lord Sirroc. Why didn't I see this earlier? Whitfield, I didn't want to tell you this way. I promised Gabe that I would tell you all the way back during PAW, but I just never could find the right time."

Whitfield was confused. "Promised Gabe? Tell me what? Ugu, I don't follow."

"I've always had my suspicions, but I didn't want to believe it myself. I can't keep denying it. It's all right here."

"Ugu, what are you talking about?"

"Whitfield, my dad is part of SYPHUS! That's why they wanted access to Lord Sirroc's bank account information. It wasn't to steal his money. It was to blackmail him."

Whitfield stood there in shock. "No, that's crazy. He couldn't be."

"No. He is. I'm sure of it now. That's why he didn't stick around at the party after I got there. We shut SYPHUS down that night, and he needed to escape. It all makes sense now."

Whitfield did not know how to respond. "How?"

"The story he told about the gymnast who fell. It all lines up. The dates on the bank records. How did I miss it?"

"Miss what?"

"A little over ten years ago, Morton Cheesestock was the best gymnast in the world. He won every meet. Every time. He was the best."

"Yeah, I know. Aspen and I loved him growing up. I had his posters on my wall. Your dad said he was friends with Morton. Shared the same house with him when they were at Seven Bridges together. Morton was a great gymnast, but then fizzled out. So?"

"He didn't fizzle out. Morton had won at World Championships for like five straight years. He was the absolute best. No one could touch him. And then…"

"Wait a second. Are you talking about the time he fell three times in his final routine and cost himself another title? I remember watching that meet with my parents."

"Yeah. On that same exact date my dad lost a ton of money. It was Morton. Morton was the gymnast that cost my dad his first fortune. I think my dad still wants revenge."

This was all a lot for Whitfield to take in. "OK, so your dad bet on Morton to win and lost. What does that have to do with SYPHUS? Or me?"

"After that meet, it was rumored that Morton was the target of an attack. News reports said it was Isadora's Gang. My dad told me a story of how he had once saved Morton, and I just always assumed he was referring to that night."

"But now you think your dad was one of the thugs sent to take out Morton?"

"Not exactly. I think my dad ordered the attack himself, but before anyone laid a finger on Morton, he swooped in to save him. He made sure to let Morton know he was now forever indebted to him and the attack was no accident. I'll bet if we look again at my dad's gambling winnings since that night, it will coincide with Morton's meets, with the biggest payoffs on nights Morton loses."

"So, you think Morton has been losing all this time on purpose?"

"It makes sense. For the past ten years, Morton wins enough to still be a significant draw and attract a lot of gambling activity, but yeah, at just the right moment, my dad orders him to take a fall."

Whitfield wasn't convinced. "That seems a little far-fetched. Why would Morton agree to go along with it for all this time?"

"I don't know. I haven't gotten that far yet. Maybe Morton's scared. Maybe that attack really shook him up. Maybe my dad has something of his. Maybe he's getting paid to take falls. I don't know for sure. My guess is my dad is blackmailing him somehow."

"So, what does all this have to do with me? You think your dad wants me to be his next Morton?"

Ugu stared into Whitfield's eyes. "I do. But there's more. He's targeting Lord Sirroc because he wants to take down the WGF. That much is clear. I'm less certain why he's targeting you. I think you're connected to all this in some way."

"You mean, besides dating his daughter?"

"Maybe that's it, but I still think there's something else tying you to all this."

"OK. So, let's assume your dad is part of SYPHUS."

"Not just part of it. I think he may be the head."

"Scary, but OK. Let's assume he's the leader of a terrifying evil organization with desires to take over the world, how do we shut him down? You said that he'll probably have Lord Sirroc offer me a payoff, disguised somehow."

"Without Lord Sirroc's knowledge, of course."

"Sure." Whitfield paused to think. "Hey, do you still have your program up and running in Lord Sirroc's office?"

"Yes."

"Good. Make sure SYPHUS still thinks they can hack into Lord Sirroc's bank records. We'll know exactly when the payment is scheduled to arrive as soon as it's entered. At that point, your dad will want to take a meeting with Lord Sirroc. We need to get to him first."

"Who? Lord Sirroc?"

"No, your dad."

"Whitfield. My dad is very crafty. He's super clever. I'm not sure you want to go toe-to-toe with him."

Whitfield agreed, "you're right. We're going to need some help on this one. Let's go see Sir Arlington." As Whitfield and Ugu were getting set to leave Whitfield's mansion, Aspen and Flaherty opened the front door.

"Hey, you two, sorry we're late. A lot to wrap up with the network last night." Flaherty noticed the WGF press release on the holographic imager above the kitchen island. "Aarrgghhh. I am so disgusted with everyone talking smack about Whitfield. That's it, I'm not going to the International Bowl either."

Whitfield thought Flaherty was overreacting. "What? No, you have to go."

"No, I don't. You're not going. Neither am I. They can shove it." Even though Whitfield didn't agree with Flaherty's decision, he felt good having her support. "Anyway, why are we going to see Sir Arlington?"

Ugu collected her bag. "We'll tell you on the way. Aspen, how was your big analyst debut?"

Aspen shrugged. "It was OK. They had a lot of food backstage. I had two doughnuts."

Whitfield nudged his brother. "Hey, I'm jealous."

"Yeah, they were really good. What about you? What's going on?"

"Oh, just found out Ugu's dad is the richest person in the world and the leader of an evil organization and wants to blackmail me. You know, normal stuff."

Flaherty's jaw dropped. "Uhh, what are you talking about?"

Ugu made her way toward the front door. "Let's go see Sir Arlington."

****

Whitfield, Aspen, Ugu, and Flaherty knocked on Sir Arlington's door. "Ahh, we were just talking about you four. Please, come in." Sir Arlington escorted the four students directly into the conference room, where just like before, several familiar faces were already seated. Aspen ran over to hug Hendricks, who was there in person this time. Whitfield followed. "Please, have a seat."

At the risk of further interrupting their meeting, Whitfield did not wait to be called upon before speaking. "Sir, something has come to our attention and we think you should be made aware."

"Please share. You are in a safe place. These people can be trusted." Whitfield and Ugu shared their revelations about Ugu's father's bank records and Morton Cheesestock's falls, and expressed their thoughts on what to expect next. Sir Arlington surveyed the room. "See, Professor Marino, they are smarter than we give them credit for."

Flaherty was hearing all this for the first time. "So, is all this really true?"

Sir Arlington confirmed everything Ugu had suspected about her father, and candidly added further disturbing details. "Yes, I'm afraid so. Yuri Gugurutruv is but one of six heads of an organization known as SYPHUS. They are powerful, resourceful, and well-organized. We believe Yuri holds leverage over Morton Cheesestock, forcing him to comply with demands to take falls at selected meets. To date, we estimate Morton's compliance has raked in over thirty-four billion dollars for Yuri directly, and many more billions for the SYPHUS organization. We also believe Morton is getting older, prompting Yuri to find a replacement. It seems that he has targeted our very own young Whitfield."

"Yes, sir, we already figured all that out. But, why Whitfield?"

Sir Arlington peered across the table. "Hendricks?"

Hendricks stood, and paced as he spoke. "Ten years ago, Whitfield's parents worked as financial advisors for a company called Fly High Capital, an investment firm founded by your grandfather, Fireno Gugurutruv. They handled mostly a few large accounts, but also oversaw several smaller accounts, including the personal accounts belonging to Fireno, himself, his wife, and their son, Yuri. Livvy and Aldrich were excellent advisors, and had known Yuri from their time together at SBA, but Yuri was strong-willed, reckless, and had a bad temper.

"He was very smart, but liked to gamble. He demanded that Livvy and Aldrich place large bets on only a few positions, and loved to bet big on Morton. As sound financial advisors, they discouraged such big bets, but Yuri wouldn't listen. As long as he was winning, Livvy and Aldrich were safe, but Yuri's confidence in his big bets grew, to a point where he bet everything he had on Morton one night. As you know, he lost, and that's where his temper came out. He blamed your parents for losing his money and swore revenge."

"Hold up. Hendricks." A horribly gut-wrenching thought came to Whitfield. "Did Yuri kill my parents?"

Hendricks stopped pacing. "Whitfield, it's not that simple."

"Just answer the question."

Aspen's eyes moistened. "Hendricks? Is it true?"

Ugu's heart started pounding. "Whitfield, calm down. Let's not…"

"Ugu, please. I need to hear this."

Hendricks closed his eyes, confirming what Whitfield had suspected. "Whitfield."

Whitfield turned to face Ugu, and spoke softly, with intense pain in his heart. "Your dad killed my parents?"

Tears began to stream down Ugu's face. "Whitfield, I had no idea. Please, believe me."

Whitfield started tearing up. "I can't believe this. Your dad. How could he? Those were my parents."

Ugu's face reddened, tears flowing, voice cracking. "I swear to you I didn't know. Whitfield." Ugu tried putting her arm around Whitfield.

Whitfield pushed hard against the table, driving his chair backward. He stood. "No, get off me. I can't…"

Ugu cried out. "Whitfield." Whitfield turned to leave.

From his seat, Professor Marino firmly called out. "Whitfield. Get back here. We're not finished."

Whitfield had tears in his eyes and had lost all composure. "You may not be, but I am. I'm done. And Hendricks, you knew about all this? Why didn't you tell me? WHY?"

Hendricks held his ground. "I couldn't."

Whitfield shot back. "That's a lie."

Professor Marino slapped his hand on the table. "We decided that it was best for you not to know."

"Why?"

Professor Marino stumbled. "Well…"

Whitfield took an aggressive step toward the table. "Well, what?"

Julienne remained calm. "Because we think your parents may still be alive."

And just like that, silence. Whitfield and Aspen looked at each other. Then they both looked at Hendricks. And at Sir Arlington. Aspen turned to Julienne. "What?"

Julienne continued in a calm voice, "we think Yuri may be holding them captive to continue his leverage over Morton, but we need to know for sure. We knew if you found out, you would likely do something reckless, and that whatever actions you took, could quite possibly cost you and your parents their lives."

Dr. Randle spoke for the first time, "we decided to wait until you were old enough, to keep you and your brother in hiding, out of SYPHUS' reach and under Hendricks' care, until you were ready."

Whitfield remained standing, but had regained control of his emotions. "Ready for what?"

"The truth."

Flaherty was just as shocked, and confused, as the others. "What truth?"

Sir Arlington cleared his throat. "The truth is we don't have all the answers, but here is what we know, or at least, what we think we know." Sir Arlington motioned for Whitfield and Hendricks to return to their seats. Both complied. "Yuri has leverage over Morton. We think that leverage is your parents. As you know, they were great friends while students here. In fact, young Aspen, you may not know this, but Morton was going to be your godfather before things went all chaotic. We've been in communication with Morton over the past two years. He tells us that he has seen video clips of your parents, pleading with him to continue adhering to Yuri's wishes. He knows they are being forced to say it, but is convinced the clips are real."

Aspen started bawling, "Mom and Dad are alive?"

Julienne remained stoic, "we do not know when the clips Morton is seeing were recorded. It's possible they were recorded a long time ago."

Whitfield saw an opening. "Possible? But that means it's also possible they weren't recorded a long time ago and that they're still alive."

Sir Arlington nodded, "that's true."

Flaherty thought they needed to pursue this lead right away. "Then why aren't we going to the authorities? Why aren't we doing anything to rescue them?"

Professor Marino dejectedly suggested the futility of going after Whitfield and Aspen's parents. "We have tried. Believe me, we've tried. No one can touch Yuri. He is protected by the highest powers."

Sir Arlington added, "I have spoken directly with Yuri about this, and, of course, he denies having any involvement."

Hendricks grew emotional sharing his own exploits. "Boys, I've stormed into every one of Yuri's known properties. I've followed his every movement. I've followed his henchmen and goons. For ten years now. I can't get close. Every road is a dead end. We thought that by bringing you boys out of hiding, and enrolling you at Seven Bridges Academy, Yuri would slip up and let his guard down.

"Maybe give us something we hadn't known before. Some clue. We thought maybe he did during PAW with all that gambling mess, using my name and your parents account info, but he was just toying with us and trying to set me up. Truth is, we're no closer to finding your parents than we were ten years ago."

The room grew silent again, until an unexpected voice was heard. "Maybe not. I think I might know how to find them." Ugu was in the unenviable position of being the daughter of man most hated by everyone in the room.

"Really? How?" Aspen didn't care that Ugu was Yuri's daughter. He trusted Ugu and desperately wanted his parents found.

"First, I need to say something. Well, two things actually." Ugu rose from her seat. She could sense the daggers being sent her way from those seated at the table, and couldn't really blame them for transferring their hatred for her dad onto her. She did her best to ignore the hateful looks. "First, Whitfield, I love you with all my heart. I would never hurt you and I feel terrible about all the pain and suffering my father has caused you, Aspen, Hendricks, and everyone else here who love your parents. Please believe me. I am truly sorry."

Whitfield stood up, and in that moment, had to decide if he could ever truly forgive Ugu for what her dad has done. He stepped toward Ugu and wrapped his arms around her. "It's not your fault, and I'm sorry for the way I acted earlier. I know you had nothing to do with any of your dad's actions."

Ugu felt a huge weight lifted from her chest. "Thank you. Now, to all of you in this room, I know how you must feel about me, being Yuri's daughter and all. I understand that some of you are probably disgusted by the fact that I am even in the room right now discussing this, but I can assure you, I am not my father. I love Whitfield. I love Aspen. I love this school. And I will do anything in my power to protect all of you from my father, from SYPHUS, from any evil lurking out there. I'm not asking you to believe my words, but I am asking for a chance to prove my loyalty."

The faces in the room took in Ugu's words, and looked upon each other. Sir Arlington was the first to speak. "Young Ugu. I've said it before. I'll say it now. I trust you with my life. That's the most I can say."

Dr. Randle was the next to offer his support. "We need all the help we can muster. Ugu has proven herself to be quite capable and a valuable asset. I trust her."

Julienne concurred, "as do I."

Whitfield and Aspen turned their focus toward Hendricks, who was not so quick to offer his support to the daughter of his sworn enemy. "I trust my boys. Whitfield? Aspen? What say you?"

Aspen put his arm around Ugu. "She's cool. We should keep her."

Ugu smiled at Aspen, and then turned to face his brother. Whitfield, surprisingly, took a more philosophical stance. "I don't think I could ever turn my back on my own parents for anyone. That's what we're asking Ugu to do right now."

On the surface, Ugu was hurt that Whitfield didn't respond as enthusiastically as his brother, but deep down, she completely understood his hesitation. "But, Whitfield, you're not asking me to do it. I'm doing it of my own free will."

Whitfield looked into Ugu's eyes. "I know. Still, he's your father." Whitfield turned to face the Council. "Whether he's killed my parents, or has been holding them as prisoners for the past ten years, I will not seek vengeance on Yuri Gugurutruv."

A few members gasped, while others grumbled. Hendricks did not approve. "But Whitfield…"

"Let me finish, please. I will not be responsible for killing my girlfriend's father. I will not harm Yuri, despite all the cruel actions he may have taken on his own. We are going to get my parents back. We are going to take down SYPHUS. But no harm shall fall upon Mr. Gugurutruv. Understood?"

Hendricks was left with no choice. "If that is the way you want it."

"It is."

Aspen stood by his brother. "Me too."

Sir Arlington beamed with pride at the maturity shown by his star pupils. "OK. Settled. No one on the Council shall bring harm to Yuri Gugurutruv. Now, young Ugu, my dear, I believe you said you may know where to find Livvy and Aldrich?"

Chapter 47
Whitfield's Birthday Bash

Ugu took her seat at the table. "I said I think I may know how to find them. The how is actually more important than the where."

Dr. Randle appeared confused. "What do you mean? If we know where he's keeping them, we can get them back."

"It's not that simple. You should know, with my dad it never is. I don't think he's keeping them in just one location. He's moving them around. Probably why Hendricks hasn't been able to locate them yet. If we identify the pattern in their movements, we should be able to get a jump on their next move and grab them."

Aspen's eyes lit up. He was a master at finding patterns and working with codes. Whitfield flashed his brother a smile before responding to Ugu. "That's good. Any thoughts on how they are being moved? What's the pattern?"

"Assuming they are still alive and Morton isn't watching old pre-recorded videos, we can start by analyzing the video clips. Aspen can search for any kind of time stamp or other clues related to when the videos were recorded. Flaherty, are you sure you're not competing in the International Bowl?"

"Positive. It's not a true national team if Whitfield's not on it. Besides, this is more important."

"OK. Then you and I can put our tracking skills to good use. I gave my dad a birthday card when he was in town for the meet. Actually, I put it in his briefcase, figuring he'll open it up, read it and keep it in there as he travels. You know, a little sentimental gift from his daughter."

Aspen didn't see the relevance. "How is that going to help?"

"I lined the card with Dr. Randle's nano tracker. Wherever that card goes, Flaherty and I will know about it."

Whitfield was impressed. "That's brilliant. What about me? What should I do?"

"Well, I'd like to tell you to do nothing. My dad has targeted you, and any move you make at this point may prompt further retaliation, but I know you too well to even ask. So, instead, I want you to meet with Morton."

Whitfield raised his eyebrows. "Morton? Why?"

"We need to find out what he knows. Anything he knows about my dad, their arrangement, your parents. Any information could be valuable."

Whitfield nodded his approval. "Is that all?"

"No. This may sound weird, but I need you to assess his gymnastics skills."

"Why?"

"I need to know if he can actually still win a big meet."

Until now, Sir Arlington had been following Ugu's train of thought. This most recent request was unexpected. "What's on your mind, young Ugu?"

Ugu took a deep breath. "OK, but this isn't going to be pretty."

Hendricks was cautiously optimistic that with Ugu's help, they may be able to find where her dad was imprisoning Livvy and Aldrich. His voice was firm, but fair. "Don't worry about winning a popularity contest with us. We just need to get Livvy and Aldrich back. I don't care how we do it."

Ugu nodded. "All right. Honestly, I don't think we're going to find any time stamp or other clues on the videos. Sorry, Aspen. We still need to look though, just in case. Maybe my dad left some of the handling to one of his lackeys and they got sloppy. But the stronger evidence we need is to see an actual reaction in the video to a current event. An unexpected event."

Julienne was eager to hear the rest of Ugu's plan. "Keep going."

"What if Morton were to win his next big meet, costing my dad millions?"

Members of the Council sat quietly, pondering the ramifications of this extremely hypothetical situation. Professor Marino was the first to offer his thoughts. "Your dad may lose his temper. The penalty for Livvy and Aldrich could be significant."

Dr. Randle chose to elaborate. "He could kill them."

"I thought of that, but it doesn't seem likely. The real danger is for Morton. My dad knows Morton is getting older and isn't the gymnast he once was. That's why he's so aggressively going after Whitfield. He sees Whitfield's talent and has already thrown out a few tests of Whitfield's character, to see how venal he might be. With Whitfield's unwavering integrity, to us he seems incorruptible, but to my dad, he's simply another challenge. He's going to try to break Whitfield. And the perfect leverage to do so…"

Whitfield finished Ugu's thought. "…is to keep my parents alive, but hidden."

"Exactly."

"So, then if Morton wins, he'll have defied your dad, and what, your dad will kill Morton?"

"No. I don't think so. Well, not yet, at least. He still needs Morton. Sure, my dad will lose a big bet, but he'll see that Morton can still compete, and draw in large crowds. He'll use that to his advantage, but will still exact some degree of revenge. My guess, is he'll rough up your parents a bit and show the video to Morton. Kind of a 'look at what happens when you defy me' sort of thing."

Aspen gasped in horror. "So, you want my parents to get beat up?"

"No, but it will give us the proof we need that they are still alive."

Whitfield was actually pondering this possibility. "And given how personal all this is to your dad, he'll likely want to be there for the attack; maybe even do it himself."

Hendricks saw a potential avenue for victory. "And with that birthday card tracking his every move, we'll find their location as well. I can follow Yuri and stop him before he even lays a finger on Livvy and Aldrich."

Ugu encouraged Hendricks, and the others, to curb their optimism, for now. "Possibly. Remember, my dad is still very crafty. He rarely makes a move without doubling back, checking over his shoulder, and outsmarting whoever is coming after him. And it's likely he'll move Livvy and Aldrich immediately after shooting the video, so even with whatever information we get from the video, the location isn't going to help us much, other than possibly providing another data point to unravel any pattern he's using."

Sir Arlington scanned the boys' faces. "Young Whitfield. Young Aspen. What do you think?"

"I don't want Mom and Dad to get hurt."

"Me neither. But at this point, we don't even know if they're alive. Hmm. Hendricks, could they handle it? You know, if Mr. Gugurutruv…"

"Your parents are two of the toughest-minded people I've ever met. Who knows what kind of torture they've faced over the past ten years, but I think if it gets them one step closer to being rescued, we have to take a shot."

Whitfield nodded in agreement. Aspen was more reluctant to agree, but eventually came around. "I guess so."

Sir Arlington placed his palms face down on the table. "OK. Look, it may not ever come to that. Perhaps young Aspen will discover something on the videos, and we can devise a new plan accordingly, but for now, I will schedule a time for young Whitfield to meet with Morton, and the rest of us all have some work to do.

It will probably take up to two weeks to get those videos from Morton. Young Ugu, thank you for your loyalty. And for each of you, my dear young students, I realize this is a difficult time for you all, but please remember to attend your classes, try to enjoy yourselves, and always keep dear to your hearts the true nature of what it means to be a student at Seven Bridges Academy."

Ugu was most thankful to still be included as a trusted member of the Council. "Thank you, sir."

Whitfield took Sir Arlington's words to heart. "Thank you, sir. We will."

Hendricks walked over to Whitfield and Aspen and put his arms around both of them. "And boys…keep faith that your parents are alive. We will find them."

Aspen hugged his guardian. "Thank you, Hendricks."

The meeting adjourned and the four students left together, quietly walking out of the AMQE library and across campus. They each remained quiet for about ten minutes, but it didn't take that long for Ugu and Whitfield to be reminded of their mutual status as outcasts on campus. By now, Ugu was getting somewhat used to the threats and taunts, but for Whitfield, even though he knew to expect them and trained himself to ignore the noise coming his way, the sheer volume of direct insults was disheartening.

With so much to take in, Whitfield and Aspen weren't sure how to feel. They were thrilled to hear that their parents may still be alive, and that they may be able to one day see them again, but at what cost? Ugu, though fully devoted to Whitfield, didn't appreciate having to turn her back on her father. The group remained silent, until Flaherty broke the ice.

"OK, so I know that was some heavy stuff in there. Evil organization. Parents dead or alive. All that stuff. And now, we step out here and it seems that no one likes us. Well, really, they just don't like you two, but Aspen and I hear it too. Real heavy, and I don't mean to belittle any of that, but we need to get our heads together. Everything is going to be fine. We've been through a ton together this year, and this is just one more mission."

Ugu attempted to share in Flaherty's cheerfulness. "You're right. We'll get through this all, together."

The positive vibes seemed to rub off on Aspen, who smiled. "Together."

Flaherty brought them all together for a group hug. "That's right. But before we get to any of that stuff, did you all forget about next Thursday?"

Ugu's face lit up. "I didn't."

As usual, Whitfield was oblivious as to the calendar. "What's happening next Thursday?"

Flaherty rolled her eyes. "Oh, you are such a dunderhead."

"What?"

Ugu put her arm around Whitfield. "Sweetie, it's your birthday next week."

"Oh, that. Yeah, I think we're just sending out some gift bags to all the houses. You know, like Keegan did."

Flaherty was not on board with that plan. "Uhh, think again. That is super lame."

"Yeah, bro. You can come up with something better than that."

"Sorry. Not really in the mood to celebrate. Besides, I don't think I'm very well-liked on campus right now. Everyone still thinks I was too scared to win the All-Around."

Ugu glanced over at Flaherty. "Oh, I wouldn't worry about that. I think we can change their minds. Right, Flaherty?"

"Absolutely!"

"I don't know."

Ugu put her foot down. "Look, we are going to celebrate either with or without you, so I suggest you get on board."

"Really? You're going to celebrate MY birthday without me?"

Flaherty agreed with Ugu. "Heck yeah. If you're just going to bring us down, get out of our way. We are going to celebrate. It's your birthday. Your parents may be alive. We have a week off from practice—well, maybe not a full week, but hey, the season is over and we crushed it. We need to celebrate."

Whitfield's curiosity started to pique. "So, uhh, what did you have in mind for my birthday?"

Ugu and Flaherty simply looked at each other and smiled.

****

For almost two weeks leading up to Whitfield's birthday, Whitfield, Aspen, Ugu, and Flaherty got together every day after class to complete their homework, study, and work on Whitfield's birthday weekend celebration.

"Do you really think we can pull this off?" Whitfield hadn't yet fully come around to the girls' plans for his birthday celebration.

"Of course. This is happening." Ugu's confidence should have been reassuring, but Whitfield was still unconvinced.

"Seems like a really big undertaking."

"Oh, Whitfield, I've been planning this for months now."

Aspen was surprised. "Really? Months?"

Flaherty confirmed the lengthy planning process. "Oh, trust me, she has. Ever since what we all pulled off for her birthday, she's been planning something big for Whitfield."

"But I don't really want all that flash and stuff."

Ugu shook her head. "Too bad. This is going to be epic."

For the umpteenth time, Flaherty wanted to make sure they had everything in place. "OK, let's run through it one more time. How many charities do we have coming to campus?"

Ugu knew all the details without having to refer to her files. "We have reps from 85 charities already confirmed. I've already handled all the travel arrangements. We have seven more that haven't yet responded, but if they do, we'll have room for them."

"Great! Now, are we dividing everyone up into groups, or what?"

Whitfield thought he knew what the girls were planning, but didn't realize charities were involved. "I'm sorry, but what is going on?"

"Flaherty, you didn't tell him?"

"No, I thought you were going to."

"Oh, well, fine. So, we took an informal poll of all the students here and asked them their favorite charities. We got a great response. Just over 900 students responded, and they listed 104 different charities."

Flaherty continued, "so, we reached out to all 104 and most of them responded, saying they were interested in attending."

"Interested in attending what?"

"Oh, right. Sorry. We planned an all-weekend, strength, exercise, and fitness event in honor of your birthday."

"So, we're not just having a simple cookout in the Inner Bowl for students to celebrate my birthday?"

Flaherty elbowed Whitfield in the gut. "No. Of course not. For 48 hours, every Seven Bridges student…"

Ugu interrupted, "well, every student who wants to participate."

"Right. For two straight days, any Seven Bridges students wanting to participate will complete as many circles, rope climbs, L-holds, dips, shoulder taps, and a bunch of other strength elements as they can, to earn money for their preferred charities."

Aspen liked the idea. "That's so cool. But where is the money coming from?"

Ugu smiled. "That's the really cool part. It's coming mostly from us."

"Us? How?"

Flaherty was eager to share this piece with the others. "Well, after we discovered what Gen. Gibson was up to with stealing resources from a bunch of schools, including ours, Lord Sirroc was able to claw back a lot of what had been taken away."

Whitfield looked at Ugu. "Really?"

"Yup. He was able to use the bank account and transaction information Aspen decoded from those fake scoresheets to reverse a bunch of transactions. Seven Bridges got a bunch of money and resources back, and Sir Arlington told me he was leaving the decision over how to handle a large portion of the recovered money to me…well, really, to us."

Aspen was happy, but also still confused. "Why would he do that?"

"Because we're the ones who found out about it, and did something to get it back."

"Flaherty's right. And because Seven Bridges Academy was already enjoying a significant surplus in their budget this year, and Sir Arlington trusts us. I still ran this idea by him first, and he's completely on board. Said he wants us to make it an annual event. Also thinks it will help with getting students to like you again."

"You too." Flaherty was hopeful that Ugu's reputation would also get a much-needed boost this weekend.

Ugu wasn't so sure students would be willing to forgive her as easily as they would forgive Whitfield. "Ehh…probably not. It's your show this weekend. Besides, once you remind everyone what a fantastic gymnast you are, they'll all love you again."

"Thanks. Maybe you would be more convincing if you didn't just roll your eyes."

"Sorry. Of course, they are going to love you. You're a gymnastics God around here. Anyway, the money for charity isn't coming just from us. Lord Sirroc said the WGF will match every dollar we donate to charities and I was able to get some other companies to agree to do the same. I think at the end of the day, whatever we raise, we'll actually have five times that amount through the WGF and various companies."

Aspen looked at the others with his mouth agape. "That is so awesome!"

Even Whitfield agreed, "it really is."

Aspen still wasn't sure how it all worked. "So, how do we earn money for charities?"

Flaherty had set up this part of the operation. "It's simple, really. All you have to do is complete as many gymnastics' skills or strength elements as you can in 48 hours, and you earn money for your charity. It's that simple. For example, I think we set the rate at one dollar per circle, so if you do 100 circles, Seven Bridges will donate 100 dollars to your preferred charity."

Ugu added on. "And those 100 dollars turn into about 500 dollars after all the matching WGF and corporate contributions."

Aspen was thrilled. "Wow! That's crazy. I could do like a million circles."

Whitfield decided to take a little air out of Aspen's sails. "Not quite a million in 48 hours, but you could probably do a lot."

"I bet I could do 5,000."

"That's still a lot, Aspen."

"Not really. It's only about 100 an hour. I could do 100 circles in under two minutes."

"I know, but after so many hours, you're going to get tired."

"Nope. I'm doing 5,000."

Ugu stepped in to cut off the Mitchell brothers' light-hearted debate. "That's great, Aspen. But there are other things you could do too."

"Yeah, like rope climbs…"

"Flaherty's right. I think that's 5 dollars each."

"Right. And L-sits, giants on VH-Bars, all sorts of tuck jumps and pikes, tramp work, and a whole lot of other things. Here, Ugu and I made up a whole list, and here are the dollar values." Flaherty showed Whitfield and Aspen the list of all the skills, exercises, and strength elements they could complete at Whitfield's birthday bash and the related donation amount.

Whitfield looked over the list. "Cool. And this is open to all students?"

Ugu sensed Whitfield was starting to come around. "Yup. All 25 team members are in. They love the idea. And all students could participate. Faculty too, if they want."

"And anything students do will still could toward the House Point Challenge, so it's kind of a win-win for everyone. Everyone's personal trackers will tally up their contributions during the 48-hour period and donations will be aggregated and sent out immediately to each person's preferred charity."

Aspen was on board. "This is so cool. I can't wait."

"So, what charity did you guys go with?"

Flaherty appreciated Whitfield's question. "Well, at first, we were going with Seniors in Our Hearts. Remember, that's who funds that senior center we went to earlier in the season where we sat with Yonca's dad for a while."

"Oh yeah, at P'socto. That was nice."

"It really was, but surprisingly, a lot of students listed that charity, so we figured we would spread our donations around. I decided to go with the AHR Foundation. They do research for the Morton Cheesestock Center for Achilles Surgery."

Whitfield nodded and turned to Ugu. "And I chose Sunshine Without Borders. They provide resources for children battling various diseases."

Aspen thought both charities were worthy causes. "Wow. They both sound great. Could I pick both of them?"

Ugu smiled. "Sure, if that's what you want. You're really not restricted."

Whitfield got that look in his eye again, where he was starting to formulate a plan. "So, did everyone pick a charity?"

Ugu shook her head. "No. Quite a few students just left that part blank."

"So, what happens to that money then?"

Ugu looked at Flaherty, who simply shrugged. "I guess we just aggregate it and divide it proportionally across the other charities."

"Hmm…I have another idea. You've heard that about 65 schools have filed to remove their gymnastics teams, right?"

Ugu frowned. "Yes. I read about it the other day. A lot of it has to do with cost constraints, but also the perceived unfairness of the system."

"Well, the unfairness was not just perceived. It was real. But now that Gen. Gibson is out of the picture, we can hopefully return to a fair system. I'd like those schools to keep their teams."

Flaherty wasn't yet clear on Whitfield's intentions, but thought she had a clue. "What are you saying? You want to donate money to help save other schools' gymnastics teams?"

Whitfield smiled. "That's right. Look, our sport is better when more teams compete. When more athletes compete. Why not take the unallocated donation money and do what we can to save other teams? It might not be enough to save all of them, but every bit helps, right?"

Aspen's eyes lit up. "I think that's a great idea. I'm in. Can I change my charity to that one?"

Flaherty was impressed. "Actually, that is a tremendous idea."

Ugu smiled. "Come here." Whitfield walked toward Ugu. She pulled him in even closer and gave him a kiss. "You are incredible. Fantastic idea. Let's do it. We'll still raise money for all these other charities, but any money raised that isn't earmarked for a particular charity, we'll pool together and work with other schools to help save their teams."

Whitfield felt a wave of happiness wash over him. "Thanks. That means a lot to me."

Flaherty clapped her hands and let out a deep breath. "Well, this has been great. Let's get some dinner. I'm starving."

"Me too." Aspen was always hungry. The four friends went out to Plank 'N Steins for dinner, and despite the nasty looks and death stares shot in their direction, the group had a nice time laughing, talking, and enjoying each other's company.

****

Whitfield's Birthday Bash, as Ugu named it to draw attention to her boyfriend in a positive way, was a huge success. Everyone who participated had a wonderful time, and collectively, Seven Bridges students raised just over forty-nine million dollars; thirty-eight million dollars for charities, plus another eleven million to help support other gymnastics programs. All told, Whitfield was thrilled with his birthday weekend, but the biggest thrill, and perhaps most important shock of all, came in the form of an unexpected guest, who showed up late in the night on Saturday.

"Excuse me. Whitfield? Is there someplace we can go to chat?"

"Great googly mooglies, you're Morton Cheesestock."

"That's right. I think we have a lot to discuss, but I don't have much time, so if you please."

"Sure. Uhh…follow me." Whitfield took Morton inside the International Affairs library, where they could speak uninterrupted. "Why are you here?"

"Sir Arlington. He told me you learned about your parents. I am so sorry, Whitfield. I truly love both your mom and dad. They are like family to me."

Whitfield wasn't sure how to respond, but appreciated Morton's love for his parents. "Thanks. I haven't seen them since I was just a kid. Do you know if they are still alive?"

Morton's eyes darted away from Whitfield. He took a few steps off to the side. "I wish I knew for certain. I see videos, about one every two or three months. Yuri sends them over to me. Your parents always say the same thing. Tell me to do what Yuri says, or they'll suffer consequences. The videos are all about the same. They may have been recorded years ago, or they may be more recent. Too tough to tell."

"Does it look like they aged at all in the videos?"

"Tough to say. Maybe, but there's always a shadow cast over their faces, so I can't really make them out too good."

"Any idea where they could be?"

Morton kicked one of the bottom shelves in frustration. "None. I've asked. Believe me, I have. But Yuri won't tell me. He just sends the videos and tells me when to take a fall in a meet. It kills me when he does that. I hate losing, but I couldn't bear to live with what he might do to Livvy and Aldrich if I don't do as he says."

"I understand. So, all those falls in meets over the past few years—they were really intentional?"

"Well, at first, yes. I could have won World Championships at least another three years, but lately, I've actually been falling a little more on my own."

"Why?"

"Just getting old, I guess. Shoulder's been hurting a bit. Elbow's a bit banged up too. Yuri's not happy when I fall when I'm not supposed to, but I don't think it's because he's betting on me to win. I think it's because he wants better odds of me winning the meets when he does bet against me."

"When is the next meet where Yuri wants you to take a fall?"

"In a few weeks. With the pro season all wrapped up, we have a little down time before the International Season ramps up."

"So, he wants you to take a fall in the first qualifier?"

Morton shrugged. "He didn't tell me yet, but I suspect he will. He usually waits until a day or two before the meet and then tells me which event to fall on and in which session. Usually, it's one of the later sessions. He wants me to do good early on so the payoff for me wiping out is bigger." Morton slammed his hand against a shelf.

"Suppose you didn't wipe out? What would happen?"

Morton turned to face Whitfield. "I already told you. Your parents would suffer the consequences. And who knows what he would do to me, not that I care about any of that now. I just want your parents back."

Whitfield remembered Ugu's plan. "Do you think you can win the next meet? I mean, if you don't intentionally fall."

Morton looked down. "Tough to say. Some really good competition out there. I mean we have a guy, Gabe, who is really good and has been coming on strong late in the season. Not to mention Torrence, Piñata, and some of the other gymnasts from foreign countries. Why? What's on your mind?"

Whitfield wasn't sure if he could trust Morton yet, but decided to let him in on the plan anyway. "I really need to know if my parents are alive. I figure if you defy Yuri and cost him a lot of money, he'll get mad and maybe take it out on my parents. I imagine he'll want you to see what he did, so if the next video still looks identical to the previous ones, we can assume that the other videos were all pre-recorded and that my parents are dead already. If they are bruised a bit, then we'll know they're alive, and maybe we can get some clues as to where Yuri may be holding them."

Morton shook his head. "Too risky. Yuri has a really short temper and may do worse than just bruise them a little."

"I know. I'm not happy about taking that risk. We may be able to stop him before it ever gets to that point. We have a tracker on him, so if he decides to go see them personally after your win, we can discover where he's keeping my parents and rescue them before he does any more damage. Besides, I don't think he'll hurt them too bad. He wants me to follow in your footsteps, and probably wants to continue using them as leverage against me, the same way he's using them against you."

Morton was still opposed to putting Whitfield's parents at risk. "Sounds too risky. Wait, what do you mean he wants you to replace me? How do you know that? You haven't spoken with him, have you?"

Now, it was Whitfield's turn to be on the receiving end of a long list of questions. "Well, yes, several times, actually."

"He told you about all this?"

"No."

"Then why did you meet with him?"

Whitfield hesitated before slowly responding. "Well, I'm kind of dating his daughter."

"WHAT?"

"Yeah, it's pretty serious. She's really smart and funny, and has a great…"

Morton rushed around the table that had been separating them, and grabbed Whitfield by the arm. "No. No. No. You can't date his daughter. She's evil."

"How can you say that?"

"Because I know Yuri. He is pure evil, and if she is anything like him, you're in a world of trouble."

Whitfield was able to wrench his arm away from Morton's grip. "No, she's really cool. She knows about her dad and is just as mad at him as I am. She wants to take him down too."

Morton had a determined, yet frightful, look in his eye. "Whitfield, you can't trust her. She is just using you. You are going to get hurt."

"Thank you for the advice, Morton, but I'm going to trust my gut on this one. I love Ugu. She is not going to hurt me."

Morton pounded on the table just before collecting himself. "Just watch yourself."

"Thank you. Now, how about my idea about you not taking a fall next meet to see if my parents are alive?"

Morton stood his ground. "I don't like it. Too risky."

Whitfield was disappointed, so tried a different angle. "Do you have a better idea?"

Morton thought for a moment. "Actually, maybe I do. You said you've spoken with Yuri, right?"

"Yes."

"Do you think he likes you?"

"Yes, I think so. He asked me to intern at his company. I mean, he's mad at me right now, because I didn't win at Individual Championships, even though he bet against me so he won a lot of money. So, really, he's just pretending to be mad at me…"

Morton put his hand up. "OK, stop right there. I should have known. Everything with that man is convoluted, complicated, and devious. That was probably a test."

"Exactly what I thought."

"Let me guess. He challenged your integrity somehow to see how susceptible you might be to his schemes?"

Whitfield nodded. "It wasn't necessarily a direct challenge, but yes. He definitely tried playing some mind games with me during the last meet."

Morton shook his head and took a few steps around the table. "Of course, he did. OK look, you're a good kid. He is going to try to break you. You cannot let that happen. He broke me, and I've been living in shame ever since. You do not want this life."

Whitfield followed Morton around the table. "So, how do I stop him?"

"Do you want to stop him or do you just want to get your parents back?"

"Can't we do both?"

"That's asking for a lot. I've never seen anyone get the better of Yuri before. He's too strong. Too smart. Too clever. Too ruthless."

"Try me. If someone was to get the better of him, how would it go down?"

Morton looked into Whitfield's eyes, and saw a fresh determination and raw spirit waiting to be unleashed. "OK. He's going to try to pin you down. You'll have to get to him first. Use deception. Make him think that you need him for something."

"I kind of do. Remember? My parents."

"Right. But with them, he has all the leverage, and he knows that. He'll try to chip away at something else first. You need to make him think you need him for something, but in reality, you control it."

"Like what?"

"I don't know. Tell him you cheated on his daughter and could use his advice. Ask him not to tell Ugu. This way he'll believe you owe him a favor, and you can see for yourself how manipulative he can be. When you still refuse to give in to his wishes, he'll lose his temper and resort to using your parents as leverage. Then, you'll know they're alive and maybe even where he's keeping them."

"That's good, but I don't want to use the cheating thing. Ugu and I already played that card earlier this year."

"Well, come up with something else. I don't care. The point is, you need to turn the tables on Yuri. Look, I've given you his roadmap. He's going to try to manipulate you. Now, you need to throw all of that on its head and redraw the map. Make him play your game. That's the only way to get your parents back. That's the only way to stop him."

"Thanks, Morton. I really appreciate you coming here. And, hey, I'm really sorry you're in this situation."

Morton put his hand on Whitfield's shoulder. "Aww, kid. Don't thank me. I'd do anything to get your parents back. I'm just really sorry I haven't been able to do it."

"Well, you've given me hope. Because of you, I have belief that they are alive and that one day, I can see them again." Whitfield gave Morton a quick hug.

"Let me know if I can do anything else. I have to run now. Sir Arlington is waiting. I can't be seen here."

"You got it."

Morton turned to leave, but stopped before he reached the door. He turned back around. "Whitfield. Yuri's dangerous. So is his daughter. Make sure you know what side she's on."

"I already do."

Morton shook his head. "Right. One more thing. If you are going to try to deceive Yuri, make sure it works. He better not find out you're lying to him."

"Thanks again. And don't worry. I already know how this is going to play out. And, we're getting my parents back." Morton left. Whitfield immediately made two calls. First, he called Flaherty, who just finished doing an epic twenty-first consecutive rope climb, and was a little out of breath.

"Oh, hey, Whitfield."

"Hi Flaherty. Are you busy?"

"You're kidding, right?"

"Sorry. I need a quick favor."

"Sure. What do you need?"

"I'm in the IA library. I was just talking with Morton Cheesestock. I need you to catch him on his way out so Ugu can plant a tracker on him."

Flaherty didn't hesitate a beat before responding. "No problem."

"Really? Not even going to ask why?"

"No need. I trust you."

"Thanks, Flaherty. I owe you one." Whitfield ended his call with Flaherty, and then called Ugu, who was walking around campus, enjoying the festivities.

"Hey, sweetie, where are you?"

"I'm at the IA library. I'll be out in a minute. I need a favor though."

"Sure. Anything."

"I was just in here with Morton."

"Cheesestock?"

"Yeah. I need you to put a tracker on him."

"OK. Covert or can he know it's me?"

Whitfield thought for a second. "Covert. I just asked Flaherty to run interference to make it easier for you."

"You got it. How much time do I have?"

"Not much at all. He's heading back over toward Sir Arlington now."

"OK. I'm close to AMQE. In fact, I see him right now. And there's Flaherty."

"Good. Hey, Ugu, be careful. I don't think he's telling us the whole truth."

"What do you mean?"

"I think he may be working *with* your dad. And not as his prisoner."

"I'll be extra careful." Ugu ended the call. Whitfield walked out of the IA library and spotted Aspen over at a pommel station.

"Hey, bro. Got a second?"

Aspen was still waiting for his next turn. "Sure. What's up?"

"I just spoke with Morton. I think Mom and Dad are alive."

Aspen's face lit up. "Really? He told you?"

"No, he's hiding it. I think he might actually by working alongside Ugu's dad. I told Ugu to plant a tracker on him. And I think he's going to lead us straight to our parents."

Chapter 48
Yuri's Deception

For the next two weeks following Whitfield's successful Birthday Bash, life at Seven Bridges Academy proceeded as usual, with its share of ups and downs. Term 5 classes were wrapping up. Aspen was not able to uncover any clues as to his parents' whereabouts from the videos sent to Morton. Whitfield's hunch leading to Ugu placing a tracker on Morton hadn't yielded any new information about his parents' whereabouts, and no mysterious payments were found in Whitfield's bank account. Students were still highly critical of Ugu, and had even started a daily public countdown of the number of days remaining until Ugu was officially expelled from Seven Bridges. On the bright side, many students seemed to have 'forgiven' Whitfield for his controversial finish at Individual Championships. Beyond Ugu's efforts to repair Whitfield's image through his birthday event, Flaherty's unwavering support for Whitfield went a long way in bolstering his reputation.

With the pro and school gymnastics seasons over, students' attention turned to the world stage, as 64 national teams competed in a 10-week season to determine a World Champion. Of particular interest to many Seven Bridges' students was the addition of Gabe to the national team roster, joining four other Seven Bridges Academy alums, including Morton Cheesestock, on the active roster. Current Seven Bridges gymnasts, plus Ugu, would typically get together at one of their houses to watch the national team meets, which suited everyone involved just fine.

Most of the team members were really starting to bond with each other, and they had all welcomed Ugu as one of their own, overlooking her cheating mishap, mostly for Whitfield's benefit, but also, as Whitfield soon realized, due to Ugu's father's rapidly growing reputation as a powerful business leader, wealthy gambler, and friend to many professional team owners.

Yuri was quickly becoming a fixture on most network broadcasts; not as a media personality or analyst, but as a behind-the-scenes operator, who many thought pulled the strings at not just the WGF, but across many of the world's largest, and wealthiest, companies. Yuri surrounded himself with global political leaders, corporate presidents, and many high-end celebrities, not to mention a few well-known criminals of the underworld. He seemed untouchable, which only served to induce greater intrigue among the masses.

But while most others watched in awe, Whitfield, Aspen, Flaherty, and even Yuri's own daughter, Ugu, took copious notes of every individual photographed with Yuri, even if just briefly crossing paths, maintaining a detailed journal of his travels, interactions, and gambling activity, thanks in large part to the tracking device embedded in the birthday card still resting inside Yuri's briefcase.

Through much effort to bypass a state-of-the-art security network, Ugu was able to not only hack into each of Yuri's eight personal gambling accounts, but also gained access to his personal bank records, along with the records, both gambling and banking, of 28 of his closest known associates. Occasionally, she would get lucky and a few of the bills Whitfield and Flaherty encoded with trackers would pass hands among these associates, but as of yet, nothing had led them to the location of Whitfield and Aspen's parents. Still, Whitfield, Aspen, Ugu, and Flaherty continued to gather as much information as they could, even as finals week was upon them.

"Hey, Ugu, thanks for coming over to the library to help me study."

"No problem, Aspen. Our finals are just about over and we don't have any placement tests for next term because of our internships."

"I know. You're so lucky."

"Hey bro, don't be jealous. You didn't have to take any placement tests before interning at the WGF, Mr. Chicken."

"Don't call me that."

"Yeah, Whitfield, leave him alone. He was a great chicken," Ugu smiled at Aspen.

Flaherty also flashed Aspen a quick smile. "Did you two figure out where you're interning yet? Whitfield, you still have that offer from Ugu's dad. It might be worth taking."

Whitfield wondered how Flaherty could even suggest such a thought. "No way!"

"All I'm saying is you may be able to keep a closer eye on him and learn more about what he's up to."

Whitfield reconsidered, and was no longer offended. "Fair point. But I can't risk being that close to him for that long. Besides, Ugu and I spoke and since she's not allowed to intern off-campus this year, I decided to stay on campus with her."

"I told him he doesn't have to."

"Aww…he just cares about you, that's all."

"No, he just wants to smoochie-smoochie with her." Aspen playfully mimicked his brother and Ugu kissing.

Whitfield was not amused. "No. That's not why."

Ugu smiled. "Oh, so you don't want to kiss me?"

"No, that's not what I said. Stop twisting my words around."

"OK. I sometimes forget that I'm dating such a simpleton. Can't even use words correctly."

"Excuse me, but I believe this simpleton just bested you on not one, but two classes this term."

Whitfield was gloating, just a bit.

Flaherty wasn't aware of the final grades. "Oh, no, you didn't. Did you?"

Whitfield just smiled. Ugu tried to defend herself, but couldn't. "I…it was…no, the test…"

Whitfield was enjoying getting the better of Ugu for once. "Hmm…seems like someone else is having a difficult time sounding out some words. Let me help you. Repeat after me. Whitfield…is…smarter…than…I am."

Ugu raised her eyebrows. "You are not. And you will never hear me say those words."

Whitfield continued smiling, "that's OK. You don't have to say it. I mean, sometimes I do forget that I'm dating such a…what's the word?"

Ugu pointed her finger threateningly in Whitfield's direction. "Don't even think about saying it."

Whitfield chuckled. "Anyway, I'm going to intern on campus with Ugu. We've narrowed it down to the Holographic Design and Engineering Lab; Campus Planning, Architecture, and Design; and Gymnastics Routine Development. Coach Brockport said we could use the facilities here, instead of heading over to the WGF for that last one."

As though he was listening from inside his office, Sir Arlington opened his door and offered a fourth alternative. "You may want to consider the on-campus stock exchange."

Ugu was startled by Sir Arlington's sudden appearance. "Excuse me?"

Flaherty seemed somewhat shaken as well. "Were you listening this whole time?"

Sir Arlington closed his eyes for a moment, as if to wash away the question. "No, of course not. I just caught wind of that last part. And something about young Ugu no longer being the smartest student in this school." Sir Arlington tilted his head toward Ugu. Aspen and Flaherty started laughing. Whitfield smiled. Ugu was not amused.

"Sir, why should we intern at the stock exchange?"

"Well, young Whitfield, we have been combing through the bank and gambling records our dear young Ugu has been so gracious to share with us. Young Aspen, have you been able to detect any pattern, yet?"

"No, sir. Why, did you?"

"Oh, heavens no. Relax. You are much smarter than I. If you haven't found a pattern, then what chance do I have? No, the reason I ask is that I believe a pattern does exist, but we just haven't examined all the data yet."

"And you think the data can be found in the stock market?"

Sir Arlington offered a knowing glance. "Let's call it a hunch. You've been able to access gambling and bank records, but I happen to believe Yuri has an extensive trading portfolio as well. With what you've already uncovered, we could probably put Yuri away for a long time, but I want to be sure. And remember, this isn't just about Yuri. SYPHUS has six heads and a large number of dangerous associates. I want to get a better idea of what we're dealing with here."

Whitfield and Ugu looked at each other. "Well? What do you say, Honey Bear?"

"I guess we're interning at the stock exchange."

"I guess so."

"Thank you, sir."

"No problem. Keep up the great work. And young Whitfield, great job on your final project. Young Ugu, better luck next time." Sir Arlington appeared to take a modicum of pleasure in teasing Ugu. With one more wink directed at Whitfield, Sir Arlington receded into his office, but not before Aspen and Flaherty burst out laughing again. Ugu was taking the good-natured ribbing in stride, but was determined to never finish in second place again.

****

The sixth and final term of the school year always brought good cheer and positive vibes for most students on Seven Bridges' campus: the final term of classes; the school meet season was over; and students could look forward to making vacation plans with family and friends. For one set of students, however, Term 6 was still as stressful as all the others. As anyone who has ever competed at an elite level can attest to, there is no off-season in gymnastics, and at no other place did this mantra ring true than at Seven Bridges Academy.

Despite the absence of any school meets over the upcoming months, practices were still intense. Most of the team's upperclassmen were hard at work prepping for the upcoming Pro Day where gymnasts had one final chance to impress team scouts before Draft Weekend. All Seven Bridges gymnasts were automatically eligible for the draft; however, teams almost always exclusively selected from a pool of fourth-year gymnasts and above due to teams' draft rights only extending out as far as four years.

The Professional Gymnastics League (PGL) consists of 96 Major League clubs spread across four tiers, split evenly with 24 teams per tier. Each club also has three Minor League affiliates, bringing the total number of roster spots available on each club to 100 athletes, 25 on the Major League roster and 75 on Minor League affiliate rosters. The PGL draft takes place over four days during Week 5 of Term 6. Alpha Tier clubs draft athletes on Day 1, Bravo Tier on Day 2, Charlie Tier on Day 3, and Delta Tier on Day 4. Each day consists of 15 draft rounds, where clubs take turns selecting available gymnasts to add to their organization.

Once a club drafts a player, that club has exclusive rights to that athlete for up to four years; rights which may be terminated at the athlete's request immediately preceding each year's annual Pro Day prior to Draft Week. For any non-graduating current student drafted by a pro team, their obligation to the drafting club is mostly restricted to the three-week period immediately following the completion of Term 6 and going straight through until the two-week school tryout period preceding Term 1 the following year. During the three-week Draft Class Orientation Camp, draftees live at the club's training center, interact with club personnel and ownership, and get to know the other athletes on the club.

Any current school athlete may be drafted by a second club during the same draft or in subsequent drafts while still under another club's control. At no point does the secondary club hold any rights to the drafted athlete until the athlete's initial four-year term with the first club expires or the athlete elects to terminate the first drafting club's rights. The four-year term commences immediately upon being drafted, therefore drafting a current fourth-year student would leave the club with control rights for only one competition year, after the draftee finishes their seventh year of schooling, before the initial draft rights expire, absent early termination.

Every year, Seven Bridges students gather at the house of their highest expected draft pick to watch the draft unfold live. This year, since Flaherty and Whitfield were still just third-years, the honor of hosting the Day 1 draft party went to Morocco. Even though he wasn't projected to compete as an All-Arounder at the pro level, he was graduating, which meant a team would have four full years of Morocco under contract.

Morocco had been drafted twice before, once by a Delta Tier club and once by a Bravo Tier club, but given his prior underclassmen status and expected performance improvement, he opted to terminate each contract before the subsequent draft, hoping to improve his draft position. Furthermore, his Tri-Bars routine was already elite, and he showed some potential to grow into a solid performer on two or three other events, all driving up expectations that he would be a mid-range first round Alpha Tier draft pick this year.

Ryne, Keegan, Fenway, and Kayleigh were also expected to be drafted on either Day 1 or Day 2 this year. It should be noted that although many experts placed Keegan higher than Morocco on their draft boards, he was still only a sixth-year student, which meant the club drafting him would only have three years of Keegan under his initial draft contract, compared to Morocco's four. In any event, Morocco gladly hosted this year's draft party.

The entire team, plus Ugu, all met at Morocco's house for the Day 1 draft party. For the past several weeks, every reputable media outlet published mock draft boards and analyzed myriad possible scenarios considering who and where athletes would be selected, so when Jade was selected first, followed by Ricardo, Dante, and Liza, no one even batted an eye. In fact, the top ten selections all went according to expectations, with only two sixth-years selected and no other underclassmen taken.

As the draft selections continued rolling in, the atmosphere surrounding the small contingent of gymnasts gathered at Morocco's house grew increasingly anxious, until the Ropeburn Mat Rollers selected Morocco with the 18th selection overall. Everyone let out a huge roar. Morocco was so happy, he had to wipe tears from his eyes in between hugging all his teammates. The phones were blowing up. The walls were shaking. The music was blaring. Spontaneous dances and backflips ensued. Whitfield and Aspen were genuinely happy for Morocco and just as they were both congratulating him, Keegan's voice was heard over all the chaos.

"What the...? Yo, did anyone else just hear that?"

Sydney, still laughing and enjoying the party, looked toward Keegan. "No. What happened?"

Reid thought that maybe Keegan was drafted next. "Did you just get drafted too? Oh, man, that's awesome."

Keegan's face lost all expression, as though everything he thought he knew in this world had suddenly turned upside down. "No. Not me."

Bella noticed the expression on Keegan's face. "Then who? The screen says another Seven Bridges gymnast was just selected. Was it Kayleigh?"

Kayleigh wasn't close to the video screens. "What? Me? I was drafted?"

"No. Not you either."

Morocco, seeing his teammate at a loss for words, grew concerned. "Then who, Keegan?"

Keegan searched the crowd and made eye contact with the person whose name was just taken off the draft board. "It's Whitfield!"

Aspen screamed, "WHAT?"

Whitfield was only partially paying attention when he heard his name and saw everyone's eyes directed at him. "Wait. What?" The whole room quieted down for a moment to look at the video screen. It was true. The Periwinkle City Flippers had just drafted Whitfield with the 23rd overall Alpha Tier pick in the draft.

Ugu was astounded. "Wait. How did this happen? He shouldn't even be eligible. Why would anyone draft a third-year?"

Flaherty agreed, "that doesn't make any sense. The team's draft rights expire before you would even graduate. Why would anyone do that?"

Whitfield didn't have any answers. "I...I don't know." Whitfield reached down to check his tracker and saw that he already had 36 messages and the number kept going up at an alarming rate. A few seconds later, the number hit 95. A few seconds more, 149. And then, a call came in. He didn't recognize the caller, but assumed it was Hendricks calling from some unknown location.

Despite all the confusion, which quickly turned back into celebration, Whitfield took the call. "Hello? Who is this?"

The voice on the other end of the call sounded familiar. "Whitfield! Congratulations. This is Yuri Gugurutruv."

Whitfield's face went ghost white. Yuri was the last person he expected to hear from. Without thinking, Whitfield hurried outside to continue the call in private.

"Sir? It's been a long time. I thought you might still be mad at me for what happened at Individual Championships. What can I do for you?"

"Ahh, Whitfield, son, no need to bring any of that up. Water under the bridge. I'm calling to congratulate you."

"Congratulate me?"

"Well, surely, you've heard the news. You are tuned into the draft, aren't you?"

"Oh, yes, of course. Thank you, sir. I'm still trying to process it all."

"Yes. Yes. I'm sure it came as a big shock to you."

"As a matter of fact, yes, it did."

"Well, we are just thrilled to have you on board."

Did he just say 'we'?

"Sir?"

"Yes. Oh, don't tell me my daughter didn't tell you."

What didn't Ugu tell me? Oh no, please say it isn't what I'm thinking. It couldn't be.

"Umm...tell me what, sir?"

"You're going to be staying with us for three weeks."

Ok, now I'm confused. Why would I stay with Ugu and her dad? Unless...

"What? When?"

"For the draft camp. Whitfield, you do know I own the Flippers, right?"

Whitfield nearly fell over. His knees buckled and he needed to hold onto the stone ledge to prop himself up. "What? You own the Flippers? How? Since when?"

"Haha...I understand this may come as a shock to you. But yes, it's true. Two weeks ago, my business partners and I purchased the controlling stake of the Periwinkle City Flippers. The club's training facility is right by our estate, so I plan on hosting all the draftees at our house."

This can't be happening.

"Wow. That's…great. I guess."

"Of course, it is. It'll give us a chance to get to know each other better. And you can still see my daughter over the school break. It's a win-win for everyone."

"Well, thank you, sir. I appreciate you taking a chance on me. But I do have a question."

"Yes, I know. You weren't expecting to be drafted this year, right?"

"Right. The draft rights will expire before I can even compete for your club."

"Yes, I am fully aware. Don't worry about any of that. I'll take care of everything. It was just important to me that as my first act as club owner, I bring you into the fold. We're a family at the Flippers, and who better to add to our family than my daughter's true love?"

Whitfield's head was spinning. "Yes, I suppose so. Again, thank you so much for this opportunity."

"You bet. Congratulations, again. You deserve everything coming to you."

"Thank you, sir." Whitfield ended the call. He stood outside Morocco's house for a few minutes contemplating the monumental impact of the evening's activities. A quick glance at his tracker revealed over six hundred unread messages. It seemed that every student at Seven Bridges was reaching out, but Whitfield had no desire to read through any of them at the moment. He needed to figure out Yuri's angle. He wasn't sure if he should go back inside to get Aspen, Ugu, and Flaherty, or if he should just head over to Sir Arlington's study to seek the headmaster's counsel.

Whitfield's momentary hesitation yielded the best of both worlds. Aspen, Ugu, and Flaherty all walked out of Morocco's house just as Sir Arlington was spotted hurrying up the path to Morocco's front door.

"Hey, bro, there you are. Did you hear? Keegan was just drafted."

Flaherty was all smiles walking out of Morocco's house. "Yeah, early in the second round. Pretty cool, huh?"

"Yeah. That's great."

Ugu knew something wasn't right. "How are you doing, Honey Bear? Who were you just talking to?"

Whitfield didn't know where to direct his eyes. "That was your dad."

"What? Why?"

Whitfield turned to look at Ugu. "Did you know he owns the Flippers?"

Ugu denied any knowledge of her dad's recent acquisition. "No. He doesn't own a gymnastics club."

Sir Arlington stepped in to confirm the recent purchase. "Actually, my dear, he does."

"No. That's not possible. I've been tracking his finances. He hasn't made a purchase that large in the past few months."

"That's because Yuri Gugurutruv financed the deal through SYPHUS Industrials Inc. Technically, SYPHUS now owns the controlling stake of the Periwinkle City Flippers. The transaction was approved by the WGF Board a little over a week ago, despite Lord Sirroc's staunch opposition."

Whitfield's eyes grew large. "Ugu, maybe that's why he's been selling so much stock over the past month."

"What do you mean, young Whitfield?"

"Well, sir, Whitfield and I have been tracking my dad's trades on the stock exchange, you know, with our internship, and we've noticed my dad building up a huge cash position by selling a lot of stock. We couldn't quite figure out why, but now it makes sense."

Aspen jumped up and gasped, "that's it! That's what I've been missing."

"What is?" Whitfield was almost knocked backward by his brother's enthusiasm.

"I wasn't looking at all the data. He's made other purchases. Look, I have to go. Tell Morocco I had fun, but I have head home. I think this could be it." Before anyone could say anything, Aspen took off. He blazed a trail across the Engineering and Advanced Medicine campuses back to his place to crunch some numbers.

Flaherty turned to the others. "What was that about?"

"He's been working on cracking a code. Well, really trying to detect a pattern in my dad's trading."

"It does fit, you know. Selling some holdings to raise cash to buy the team. Clearly, your dad has something planned. He told me we would be spending time together after the term ends, at his estate, with all the other draftees."

Flaherty furled her eyebrows. "He told you that?"

"Yeah. He didn't seem to care that the draft rights would expire before I could actually compete. Very strange. He was more interested in keeping me at his place for three weeks. He said Ugu would be there too."

"What? I wasn't planning on going home. We're going on vacation together over break, aren't we?"

Whitfield noticed that Sir Arlington looked a bit quizzical. "Yes, I know. Sir Arlington, when Aspen and I won the Grand Curriculum Development Challenge we made plans to take Ugu and Flaherty with us on vacation."

Flaherty expressed her disappointment. "I guess this means no vacation together?"

"Sorry. Look, this is all hitting me really fast. Yesterday, I was planning on going on vacation with all four of us. But now, being drafted…I don't know what to do."

Ugu spoke for the four of them, even in Aspen's absence. "This stinks!"

"I know, but if Whitfield doesn't honor his draft obligation, it will impact his draft status in the future."

"Flaherty's right. I can't risk being declared ineligible. Sir Arlington, what do you think?"

Sir Arlington pondered the situation. "I think…we ought to ask young Ugu what she thinks. She knows her dad better than we do. She may have some insights into his motives."

"OK. Ugu?"

"Let's think for a minute. Whitfield is right. This must be all part of a bigger plan. It always is with him. He just spent a lot of money to bring you to our estate for three weeks, when he could have just asked me to ask you to stay with us."

Flaherty offered a plausible rationale. "Maybe he doesn't know how serious you two are, or he just didn't want to put Ugu in the middle of whatever he has planned for Whitfield?"

"Maybe, but he did make it a point to say that Ugu would also be there at the estate."

"Right, he doesn't care about me. His plan is bigger than me. He wants Whitfield there, away from Aspen, and away from Hendricks, right? He knows Morton is no longer reliable. He's tying up your draft rights for the next four years."

Flaherty encouraged Ugu to continue. "What are you thinking, Ugu?"

"I think he may be trying to make his move now. He's going to try to convert Whitfield over to his side. Over to SYPHUS."

"That's crazy. Whitfield will never side with him. SYPHUS is trying to destroy gymnastics. Besides, your dad killed…err…kidnapped his parents."

"But he doesn't know that we know that." Whitfield was following Ugu's thought process.

"Which gives us the advantage. My father is testing Whitfield."

"Which is why I have to go."

Flaherty didn't think that was such a good idea. "Whitfield, are you sure?"

Whitfield and Ugu exchanged knowing glances at each other. "Yes. Look, the only way we can know for sure whether my parents are still alive is for Mr. Gugurutruv to slip up. I have to go out there and try to find out as much as I can."

"But this is all part of his plan. Why would you go along with it?"

"He's not. My dad is going to try to convert Whitfield by building trust first. If that doesn't work, he'll try blackmailing him with whatever leverage he has—if your parents are still alive, that's what he'll use."

"And I'll be ready."

"So will we. What do you need from us?" Flaherty may not have wanted Whitfield to willingly put himself in danger, but was more than willing to put her own life on the line to support him.

Whitfield appreciated Flaherty's unwavering support. "I don't know yet."

Sir Arlington concluded their little gathering. "For now, I suggest you return to the draft party. It seems that your teammates are having a great time inside. I suggest you three join them. And do try to enjoy yourselves. I do not think Yuri's plan will fully unfold during your time at the Draft Class Orientation Camp. He is playing a much longer game. I suggest you do the same."

Chapter 49
End-of-Year Celebration

The end-of-year celebration was a time-honored tradition at Seven Bridges Academy. It was the last time this particular set of 1,050 students would be together before the seventh-years advanced beyond these walls to join the rank and file of the working class. To be sure, several seventh-years would still maintain a presence at Seven Bridges as either contractors, coaches, staff, or, for the elite chosen few, faculty; but, for most of the graduating students, this was goodbye.

In addition to the 150 graduates, five other students were scheduled to be expelled from Seven Bridges during the ceremony, banishing them from campus. Ugu's name was still on the Expulsion List, and now that the end of Term 6 was upon them, Whitfield, Aspen, and Flaherty were saddened, distraught, and in no way, in the mood for a celebration with Ugu's expulsion ever so near.

Whitfield struggled to sleep the night before the celebration and spent the morning pondering how in the world they got to this point, and if there was anything else that could be done to save Ugu from her cruel fate. With the exception of the Draft Week festivities, Term 6 seemed to fly by for Whitfield. His and Ugu's internship at the stock exchange proved fruitful, as they not only learned a lot about stock trading and market microstructure, but they were also able to track Yuri Gugurutruv's many stock transactions, and with the help of Aspen, build a case against Yuri for insider trading and other illicit activities.

Aspen had excelled in all his classes and Flaherty, opting to follow in Ugu's footsteps and intern at the WGF, gained valuable knowledge of the inner-workings of the largest organization in the world in a post-Dr. Hewitt environment.

The four friends had insisted on spending most of their free time together throughout the term, but with the end-of-year celebration upon them, Whitfield couldn't help but feel that his world was slipping away. As much as the foursome had accomplished in their first year together, they weren't able to remove Ugu's name from the Expulsion List, a fact that many of their classmates routinely and vehemently reminded them of every day. Ugu's name had actually moved up to number one on the Expulsion List, seemingly a direct result of constant student protests, often led by Jonathan and his cronies, and despite the overwhelming evidence that Jonathan had violated several school rules by falsifying entrance exams, his name was still only on the Watch List and not officially among the top five to be expelled.

Whitfield, Aspen, and Flaherty had made countless trips to Sir Arlington's office, pleading with him to remove Ugu's name, but each time they were met with stern rejection. For her part, Ugu remained calm and poised whenever the topic came up, which Whitfield attributed to her desire to maintain some degree of dignity, and cheerfulness, especially around her friends, during her final few days as a student at Seven Bridges Academy.

Whitfield closed his eyes and remembered what was likely to be his final late-night run with Ugu. She had stopped by Whitfield's mansion last night and asked if they could go for an earlier run than usual, since she wanted to save some time to pack her belongings before the next day's celebration.

Despite the inevitability of this being their last run together, Whitfield and Ugu still laughed and smiled and found comfort just being near each other. When they approached Slide 19-EU, for what felt like the final time, there was no long goodbye. No extended kiss. Not even a final hug. Ugu simply treated it like any other night. "Thanks for the run. You've improved a lot. Keep working hard."

"What? That's it? No goodbye?"

"Nope. Not a big fan of goodbyes."

"But, tomorrow…are you even going to be there?"

"Sure. After some welcoming remarks and the results of the Student Fantasy Daft, they'll bring the five of us onto the stage so students can get one final look at us before shipping us away."

Whitfield couldn't understand Ugu's nonchalance regarding this whole spectacle. "That's it, then. Will I ever see you again?"

"Sure, you will. Remember draft camp? You're staying at my dad's estate. I'll make sure I'm there for some of it."

"I know, but how can you be so casual about all this? I mean, this place is nothing without you. I mean…" Whitfield had tears streaming down his cheeks.

Ugu remained calm, on the outside. "Whitfield. Stop. I know this is hard for you. Imagine how it feels for me. But I can't do this right now. I have to go." Without saying another word, Ugu opened the entrance to Slide 19-EU, stepped inside, and was gone. Whitfield thought he had seen tears forming in Ugu's eyes, but couldn't be sure. That's how his final night with Ugu came to an end.

By the time Whitfield walked downstairs for breakfast, Aspen and Flaherty were already in his kitchen, fully dressed, and still quite upset about Ugu's situation.

Aspen couldn't even touch his food. "This is awful. I am so upset. I can't believe Ugu is getting expelled today. There must be something else we can do."

"I know. I feel the same way, but there is nothing we can do. We've tried everything."

"I'm so mad. Why isn't Jonathan getting expelled instead? He did worse stuff than Ugu ever did."

Flaherty put her arm around Aspen. "I know."

"It's just not fair."

Whitfield entered the kitchen and didn't do much to improve upon the gloomy, despondent mood resonating from the others. "Hey, guys. Good morning."

"What's so good about it?"

"Yeah, bro, I know. I don't even want to go today. It's going to be too painful watching Ugu up there."

"We really should go though. It would be disrespectful to Sir Arlington and all the other students and faculty. Missing the celebration isn't going to get Ugu off that list."

"You're right, Flaherty. Ugu wouldn't want us to do that."

"Hey, has anyone tried calling Ugu's dad? Maybe he could help. I mean, it is his daughter, after all." Aspen was grasping at straws.

Flaherty threw her hand up. "No. Ugu was very clear about not wanting to get her dad involved. Besides, that would be a violation of the school's Code of Honor and Integrity."

Whitfield nodded in agreement. "And I don't think we want to be in debt to Yuri Gugurutruv. That fate might be worse." As Whitfield headed back upstairs to shower and get ready for the end-of-year celebration, the doorbell rang. "Could one of you get that?"

Flaherty rose from her seat. "Sure." As Flaherty answered the door, she was surprised to see who was standing there. "Spencer? How nice to see you. What brings you here?"

"Oh, hi Flaherty. I was actually looking for Whitfield."

"Oh, he just went upstairs to shower, but you're welcome to come in. He'll be down soon."

"Oh, thank you. That's very generous of you, but I really just came to drop this off." Spencer handed Flaherty a small box, filled with papers. "I've been meaning to drop this off earlier, but kept getting sidetracked with other projects."

Flaherty happily accepted the mystery package. "OK, sure. I'll be sure Whitfield gets this. What is it?"

"Oh, just something I think he'll be interested in. It's rather urgent though. I think he should read through it before coming to the end-of-year celebration."

Flaherty was confused, but didn't push. "OK. Thank you, Spencer."

"Good to see you again, Flaherty. Maybe we can keep in touch over the break?"

"Definitely. I'd like that. In fact, come see me after the celebration today."

Spencer smiled. "OK. I will." Spencer left and Flaherty closed the door. She walked back into the kitchen with the box.

"Who was that?"

"That was Spencer. He dropped off this box for Whitfield. Said he wants Whitfield to go through it before the celebration today."

"Hmm. I wonder what it is." Despite their curiosity, and the fact that the box was not sealed, Aspen and Flaherty did not open the lid, and waited until Whitfield came downstairs.

A few minutes later, Whitfield moped into the kitchen. "Hey, who was at the door?"

"Spencer."

"Oh. Sorry I missed him. What did he want?"

"He dropped off this box for you." Flaherty handed Whitfield the box. "Said there are papers in there that you should read before coming to the celebration."

"That's odd. We have to leave in about an hour."

"So, get busy reading, bro."

Whitfield opened the box and started reading through the contents. With each passing page, his eyes grew bigger and his heart pounded faster.

"I don't believe it. I don't believe it."

"What? What is it?"

"What time is it?"

Flaherty checked the time. "08:45. We have to leave in about 45 minutes to get our seats for the celebration."

"We're going to be late, but I think we can still make it there in time."

"In time for what?"

Whitfield looked directly at Flaherty. "There's still time to save Ugu. But we have to move fast."

Aspen jumped up and shouted, "WHAT? How?"

"I'll tell you on the way." Whitfield ran over to his study and grabbed three earpieces, one for himself and the other two for Aspen and Flaherty, and then the three of them headed for the door. "Here, Aspen take this and head over to the International Affairs library. Get there fast. I'll tell you what to look for on the way. Now go." Aspen took off running. "Flaherty, head over to the Engineering campus. Find the patent records."

"We have access to patent records through our trackers."

"No, we need the paper copies. Just go." Flaherty took off sprinting toward the Engineering campus. Whitfield ran upstairs to the third floor and exited his house by climbing up the slide ramp to the Outer Loop, securing his earpiece as he ran. "OK, can you both hear me?" Both Aspen and Flaherty responded affirmatively. "Good. Aspen, I need you to pull the case file from P'socto v. Stanson. I don't have the exact date, but it was about two years ago."

Flaherty thought Whitfield may have directed Aspen to the wrong place. "Why are you sending him to IA? Shouldn't case files be on the Law campus?"

"Trust me. I have a hunch."

Aspen was running as fast as he could. "OK. I'll get it."

"Great. Meet me over at Flaxen when you're done. I have to visit the Administration Building first."

Flaherty was nearing the Engineering campus. "What do you want me to do over at the patent records office?"

"Pull the log-out sheets for Patent #44116589. It should be for a rather familiar computer program."

"You got it. Is that all?"

"No, I need another file too. See if you can find any patent records for algorithmic optimization patterns in coaching gymnastics. Look at records submitted from the Southwest Region about four or five years ago. Let me know if you recognize any names on the patent sheets."

Flaherty didn't have a clue as to why these records were so important, and why they needed to be retrieved right away, but didn't argue. "You got it."

"Hey, if you have time, pull the CBT scans from the records office over the past few weeks. Shouldn't be many visitors to the office, but I have a hunch we'll find some friends."

"On it."

"OK, guys. You have 60 minutes. Don't be late."

****

As students filed into the historic auditorium, Sir Arlington had a look of worry and concern on his face. He had always relished these end-of-year gatherings as a time to reflect on and celebrate all the school's accomplishments over the past year. To be sure, Seven Bridges Academy had a remarkable year. Perhaps its best ever. But it was not without its troubles. Dr. Hewitt was found to have been in league with SYPHUS, rerouting billions in resources, and ultimately terminated from his position and imprisoned.

The gymnastics team navigated difficult waters toward the end of the season, but managed to pull it all together to earn its fourth consecutive national championship, only to see controversy return with Whitfield's contentious decision to give up the individual All-Around title in a valiant, albeit costly, display of honesty and integrity. And, of course, the thing that most saddened Sir Arlington, was the imminent expulsion of one of his favorite and most talented students, Ugu Gugurutruv, for committing perhaps the most heinous crime ever seen at Seven Bridges Academy—cheating on a final exam.

Sir Arlington rose to the podium and scanned the crowd of students, noting the absence of Whitfield, Aspen, and Flaherty. Though disappointed, he understood their absence and decided right then against pursuing any punishment for their truancy. As usual, Sir Arlington began the proceedings by highlighting Seven Bridges Academy's wonderful achievements throughout the year and made several remarks concerning the ultra-competitive Student Fantasy Draft.

"Congratulations to Lincoln, Conrad, Misty, and the rest of the Plancher family for drafting such a wonderful group of students. Together, you are this year's Student Fantasy Draft winners." Sir Arlington paused as the crowd cheered.

"And now, we must turn our attention to other matters, of a more somber nature. Every year, Seven Bridges Academy seeks to reward students from outside our school with the opportunity to join our ranks, if they are so deserving. I am proud to say, that this year, we received over 1,200 applications for our five coveted incoming transfer slots, and after meticulously reviewing these applications, our admissions committee, with oversight from myself and several other current faculty members, have selected five outstanding students to join us for the start of next year. They will all be here for the annual Kickoff Party, so be sure to welcome them."

Sir Arlington continued, "to make room for these chosen few, we must say goodbye to some of our dear friends. This part is always difficult, made even more so this year, as no current first-year student made the Expulsion List, a laudatory feat that I attribute to considerable curricular resource improvements initiated by one of our own students."

Sir Arlington paused to turn around and make eye contact with Ugu, who was waiting her fate backstage. "But I digress…making their way to the stage now are the five individuals ending the year on the Student Expulsion List. Four are here by virtue of earning grades either at or near the bottom of their respective class, and the other, well, we shall get to that. I'd like to take a moment now to say a few words about each of them, and allow you all the opportunity to say a few words of your own to your soon-to-be departed classmates."

Sir Arlington proceeded to share some thoughts about each student up on stage. Students in the audience also participated at will, sharing a few positive memories of their friends, housemates, classmates, and lab partners before they left. Just as Sir Arlington was turning his attention to Ugu, Jonathan led a chorus of boos, jeers, and pointed insults in Ugu's direction. Sir Arlington listed Ugu's transgressions, and allowed the crowd to have their say before stepping in.

He knew why Ugu had committed each violation, but was powerless to change the minds of a raucous student body. Sir Arlington decided against sharing many of Ugu's positive attributes, and simply allowed the students to exit the stage, amidst belittling and derogatory remarks. As Ugu reached the end of the stage, and took one last look at her, well now former, classmates, she shed a tear. And then another. And another.

For three years, Seven Bridges Academy had been her home. She loved everything, and everyone at SBA, and, at one time, they had loved her too. But now, that life was gone. Ugu knew she had committed those infractions for a good cause, and had helped to save the integrity of the sport they all loved so dearly, but it had come at an incredible cost. One that she would have to bear…forever.

As Ugu closed her eyes to the world around her, the video monitors adorning the inside walls of the auditorium and the large screens overhead went dark. Ugu's picture appeared, and the hissing and howling continued among the students. It took a moment to adjust the volume to be heard over the crowd, but once the students settled down a bit, the crowd was treated to a recording from a meeting between Ugu and Sir Arlington, taking place in the headmaster's office several months ago, moments before carrying out her Level 1 Detention sentence.

"Thank you for seeing me on such short notice, sir."

"Certainly, young Ugu, what can I do for you?"

"Well, sir, I am afraid that we may be facing a problem regarding academic integrity on campus."

"Ahh. So, you heard about young Jonathan cheating on his history exam?"

"Yes, sir."

"I will not tolerate cheating at this institution. You can be sure I will have his name at the very top of the Expulsion List by morning. The faculty are outraged that he is still here." Jonathan slumped down in his seat, and those near him could be heard hurling pejorative comments his way.

"Sir, I know Jonathan messed up, but please give him another chance."

"Curious. Why do you care so much about young Jonathan?"

"Oh, it's not him that I care about, really. It's just that he is a Seven Bridges student, and I just want us all to succeed."

"That is admirable, child, but we need to make an example of him to deter others from following in his footsteps."

"I agree sir. That's why I'm volunteering myself."

"Excuse me?"

"Sir, I am asking for your permission to develop a video whereby I get caught cheating, and suffer all the horrendous ramifications from my actions."

"Are you sure? Have you thought this through? Students will despise you if they find out you cheated."

"I know. And they will find out. I'll make sure of it. But no one can know about my plan."

"What is your plan?"

"Well, with your help, I'd like to take one of my final exams early. I think it should be my class with Dr. Crawfish. His reaction to a student cheating, especially me, will be enough to scare any student straight, but he cannot know about the plan ahead of time. It would ruin the moment. Do you think you can secure an early copy of the exam?"

"I will do my best."

"After I submit the exam early, I'll walk into the scheduled final exam with all the other students, and get caught cheating. Dr. Crawfish will blow up at me, and I'll be arrested. It will all be recorded and you can use it for educational purposes, maybe orientation or some other academic integrity meetings. I'll even show it to my *Lying, Cheating, Stealing, and Deception* professor. Maybe she'll want to use it for class."

"This is a highly unusual proposal. You do know that something like this could land you on the Expulsion List. And if it does, I will be powerless to save you."

"I know, sir. I just want what is best for our students. I don't want any of them to cheat, or to suffer the consequences. I think this can help."

Sir Arlington was seen nodding before the video boards cut out again, and students sat in their seats, speechless. They couldn't believe that Ugu would risk everything, just to help them maintain their own honor. Sir Arlington regained control of the podium.

"In light of this, now public, evidence, I believe a new vote may be in order." The doors in the back of the room swung open, and Whitfield, Flaherty, and Aspen strode in.

Whitfield strode briskly toward the front of the vast auditorium. "My deepest apologies, sir, but I do not think it would be wise to call for a vote until the faculty have all the information." Several students booed as Whitfield entered the hall. Clearly, not everyone had forgiven him for his decision at Individual Championships.

Sir Arlington raised his eyebrows. "Oh. Is there more information?"

Flaherty responded firmly. "Yes. Lots of it."

"Then, by all means." Sir Arlington yielded the podium.

Whitfield climbed up onto the stage. "I apologize for interrupting the end-of-year celebration, and for our earlier absence. We certainly meant no disrespect. It has come to our attention that several students at this institution have failed to live up to the Seven Bridges Academy Code of Honor and Integrity. First, I hold in my hand a case file from P'socto v. Stanson from roughly two years ago.

"Some of you may recall the story of a terrible student at P'socto who kept committing horrible violations at the school, but never appeared on their Expulsion List. Year after year, he managed to avoid getting expelled. As some of you know, he got away with it by hacking into his school's expulsion database and manipulating the code to effectively put a governor on his own name from appearing among the top five."

From the front row, Professor Marino called out. "What does this have to do with today's celebration?"

Flaherty strode across the stage. "I'm glad you asked. It turns out that the courts filed a patent to make public the code Stanson used to commit his hack. The Engineering library holds copies of those patent records, and CBT scans show our very own Jonathan, Daulton, and Mirabelle breaking into the file room and retrieving this exact patent record."

Whitfield urged the faculty to conduct a very quick and simple investigation. "I submit that a simple back-door check of the expulsion database will, in fact, show a weeks-long hack in place, originating from one of their signatures. Dr. Randle, I believe you can probably pull this up in no time." The crowd gasped, and waited for Dr. Randle, seated in the front row, to confirm Whitfield's conjecture.

Dr. Randle punched in a few keystrokes. "By golly. You are correct. The hack originated from Mirabelle's computer, and was later edited by Daulton."

Aspen wanted to make the impact of their actions clear. "And, if you remove the hack, does Jonathan's name appear among the top five on the Expulsion List?"

Dr. Randle continued punching his keys. "Give me a second. Yes. It sure does. Jonathan moves up to number one, and Ugu actually drops to number 5. It seems that these young scamps altered the original program to push Ugu's name to the top." The crowd turned their venom on Jonathan, Daulton, and Mirabelle.

Sir Arlington stood up and made his way back toward the podium. "Fine work. Is that all?"

Whitfield did not relinquish his spot. "I'm afraid not, sir. We have one more rather large finding to share with everyone. On a hunch, we investigated patents pertaining to algorithmic optimization patterns in coaching gymnastics. We found something very unsettling."

Flaherty held up several patent documents. "We found a patent issued five years ago discussing optimization patterns. The patent files were logged out a few months ago by Rodolfo and Quan. Records show that Rodolfo's father was a lead investigator on the original patent. Rodolfo and Quan used the original patent, in its entirely, without making any substantive changes, when they submitted their project for the Grand Curriculum Design Challenge—a clear violation of the Code of Honor and Integrity."

Whitfield offered some concluding remarks. "We submit these finding faithfully, but with reservation, so as to not hurt our fellow classmates, yet uphold the rich and steep tradition of Honor and Integrity at this fine institution. We do not feel it right to punish those students whose only crime was finishing at or near the bottom of their class, especially when there are those with far less integrity sitting among us. Thank you for your time, and once again, please accept our apologies for the interruption."

Whitfield, Aspen, and Flaherty left the stage and walked straight toward the back of the auditorium and through the doors. They had decided not to stay for the remainder of the end-of-year celebration. Sure, they felt bad that they would miss saying goodbye to their seventh-year friends and miss out on the gymnastics team's final celebratory round of applause and the traditional anointing of replacements for their graduating members, but for the three of them, Ugu was all that was on their mind, and they couldn't bring themselves to sit there and watch as the faculty voted on her expulsion status.

Flaherty had reminded Whitfield and Aspen that they would still see everyone at the evening festivities, so they could catch up on all they missed and say their goodbyes later. Even as they clung to hope that their words up on that stage would sway enough of the faculty to save Ugu, Whitfield felt terrible having to throw others under the bus just to save his own girlfriend.

Flaherty put her arm around her friend. "Whitfield, we did the right thing."

"I agree. Bro, those other students did bad things. I mean, Jonathan's the worst, but Daulton, Mirabelle, Rodolfo, and Quan all deserve to be expelled too."

Whitfield still felt uneasy. "I don't know. Maybe. I just don't like calling out others."

"Then why did you send us all over campus digging up dirt on them? Was it just to save Ugu?"

Whitfield contemplated his brother's question. "I thought that's all it was at first, but then I realized that those others all cheated in some way. They broke the rules. I don't know if they should get expelled or not. That's not my call. I just felt that the faculty deserved to know all the facts before deciding on someone's fate."

Flaherty agreed, "I can respect that. Hey, let's head over to Pike's for one more meal before tonight's festivities and before we all go home to pack up and leave tomorrow."

Whitfield was too anxious about Ugu's fate to go out. "No, that's OK. I kind of just want to be alone right now. You two go ahead."

Aspen hugged his brother. "Are you sure?"

"Yeah, I'm sure."

"Well, Aspen, what do you say? You wanna get something to eat?"

"Sure. I'm starving."

****

Flaherty and Aspen were enjoying burgers and fries, and each other's company, when Spencer showed up a couple hours later. "Hey, Flaherty. I got your message. Thanks for letting me know where to find you."

"Sure. Have a seat. How was the rest of the celebration?"

"Thanks. Hi, Aspen. You will not believe it. You guys did it! You saved Ugu!"

Aspen screamed, "really? That's so awesome! I am so happy. Where is she? Does my brother know?"

"Relax, Aspen. Spencer, oh my gosh. That is such great news. Oh, my little Ugu. I think I'm going to cry."

"Yeah, it got really wild in there after you left. While the faculty discussed who to expel, the crowd really turned on Jonathan and his buddies. And then Rodolfo and Quan got in a fight. It was crazy."

Flaherty expressed some concern. "So, who got expelled?"

"Well, Jonathan was number one on everyone's list."

Aspen smiled. "Yes. So, he's gone, right?" Spencer nodded. "Oh, I wish I could have seen that."

"It was pretty cool. Daulton and Mirabelle are gone too. Sir Arlington brought up the fact that they actually tampered with the settings of the Glass Box when Ugu was in there."

"Really? How?"

"The Glass Box was never supposed to be able to get that hot. I think they set it to 101 degrees or something ridiculous like that. It was only ever supposed to go up to 94. They also got it to go colder than it was supposed to go. Anyway, between that and hacking into the expulsion database, the faculty voted to add them to the top five."

Aspen was happy Daulton and Mirabelle both got expelled. "Good. I'm glad. Who were the other two? Was it Rodolfo and Quan?"

"No. The faculty were kind of torn on them. Since it was their first offense, some faculty members didn't think they should be put on the list. They'll just receive a warning. Instead, Ponchet and Marcel were kept on the list. They both had really bad grades in every term this year."

Flaherty was relieved. "Well, at least Ugu is safe."

"Yeah, it was really amazing. They brought Ugu and the other two that got saved back up on stage, and Sir Arlington made a big deal about welcoming them back. Especially Ugu. All the students cheered. I think she must have hugged everyone in there. Students kept walking over to her to apologize and say how sorry they were for thinking she actually cheated. I mean, no one knew, right?"

Flaherty looked at Aspen and winked. "Right. So, how come you put all that stuff together in the box? I don't even know what was in there, but it seems to have helped Whitfield figure it all out."

"I don't know. I mean, I've always liked Ugu. You and her have always been nice to me. I didn't want to see her go, and I knew Whitfield must've felt the same way. Hey, where is Whitfield, anyway?"

Aspen casually replied, "he went for a walk."

"Oh, OK. Anyway, we talked about that P'socto case in class and I wondered how that kid got away with it all, but when I went to the Law library, I couldn't find anything. I guess you guys had better luck."

"Actually, I found the case file in the International Affairs library. I guess since Stanson only hacked into the database when he was vacationing outside the country, it became an international matter. It wasn't actually our courts that published the code."

"Wow. That makes sense now why I couldn't find it. The stuff with the other two, Rodolfo and Quan, I just always thought their project was kind of fishy. It usually takes a long time to optimize an algorithm like that. I didn't know it had already been patented. I just shared some thoughts about their project with Whitfield. I guess he took it and ran with it."

Flaherty was still curious about the recording from Sir Arlington's office. "What about the video? I mean, I had no idea she planned that all with Sir Arlington ahead of time."

Spencer shrugged. "Me neither. I don't know where that came from. I think I had something in the box about Ugu meeting with my *Lying, Cheating, Stealing, and Deception* professor. Maybe Whitfield put something together from that, but I really don't know."

"You are amazing, Spencer. Thank you so much. You really helped save Ugu today. How can we ever thank you?"

"Oh, no need to thank me. I'm just happy that Ugu is still here." Aspen and Flaherty both agreed. Flaherty wrapped her arms around Spencer's arm, pulled him in close, and kissed him.

With her eyes closed, Flaherty heard a familiar voice. "Ooh, I hope I am not interrupting anything."

Aspen shouted, "UGU!" Aspen rushed over to give Ugu a huge hug. Flaherty immediately followed suit. Neither wanted to let go of Ugu, but eventually eased up and allowed her to join them at their table.

Flaherty was in tears. "We are so happy to see you."

"Me too. Spencer, I hear you had something to do with saving my skin?"

Spencer shrugged. "Not really. It was all these guys, and Whitfield."

Flaherty reached out to hold Spencer hand. "Spencer is being modest. He did help, but really, it was all Whitfield. He came through when you needed him."

"Well, thank you, Spencer. Where is Whitfield?"

Again, Aspen casually replied, "went for a walk."

Flaherty checked the time. "Yeah, a while ago. Aspen, we told him where we were going, right?"

"I think so. Besides, he knows how to find me. He can just use his tracker to locate me. He has the code."

"Yeah, mine too. Hmm. Not like him to be gone this long. I'm sure he's just thinking things over. Maybe packing for tomorrow's trip out west."

Aspen looked down. "Yeah, I wish we were all going on vacation."

Ugu tried cheering Aspen up. "Aspen, he's not going on vacation. It's a Draft Class Orientation Camp. I'm sure he's not going to have fun without you."

"Yeah, but you'll be there too."

"I know, but it's not like I'm going to see him much, if at all. I think they're going to be pretty busy."

"Yeah, I guess."

"Besides, aren't you going home to see Hendricks?"

Aspen lifted his head and smiled. "I am. I miss Hendricks. It'll be nice seeing him again."

Flaherty was happy for Aspen. "Well, tell him I said hi. I'd rather go with you than spend the time off with my family."

Aspen thought he had a great idea. "Well, come over then."

"I wish." Flaherty was about to just brush away Aspen's request, but then thought about it. "Actually, maybe I can. I'll have to spend at least one week at home or my parents won't let me hear the end of it, but then maybe I can come see you. I'll let you know."

Aspen was happy again. "Great!"

Ugu stood up. "I'm going to find Whitfield. The Inner Bowl is already getting crowded. I think the music is going to start soon, and I want to thank him for saving me before we all get lost in the crowd."

****

Ugu used her tracker to find Whitfield, who was all alone inside the Pommel Clock practice gym, which was typically reserved for non-team members, but currently vacant as students prepared for the outdoor music festival that always takes place on the final night of the school year. "Hey, Honey Bear. I've been looking for you."

"Ugu. Oh, I'm so happy to see you."

"Well, you did it. You saved me. I'm not getting expelled. I owe you everything."

"Oh, that's terrific news, sweetie. Really, I'm so happy for you. But you don't owe me anything. It was a team effort. Flaherty and Aspen did most of the work. And Spencer, he really came through, too."

Ugu knew something was bothering Whitfield. "Then what is it? I thought you'd be a little…happier."

"I'm sorry. No, I really am happy. Believe me, I am." Whitfield wouldn't look Ugu in the eye.

"Then what?"

"Nothing."

"Whitfield. Something's bothering you. Tell me."

"I thought I was losing you. And when my back was against the wall, all I could think about was putting someone else, anyone else, up on that list. I didn't even give Rodolfo and Quan a chance to explain themselves. I just told the whole school. I just couldn't bear losing you."

"Is that what's bothering you? Look, Rodolfo and Quan made their choice and you followed school protocol. The Code directs us to reports any and all violations immediately upon learning of their existence. You did exactly what you should have done."

Whitfield wasn't sure if he agreed, "I could have reported it privately to Sir Arlington. I didn't have to tell the whole school."

"Maybe so. But it wasn't your transgression. It was theirs. If they didn't want the whole school knowing they cheated, they shouldn't have cheated. Period. That's it. This was on them."

"Then why do I feel so bad about it?" Whitfield kicked an empty chalk bucket.

"Well, if it's any consolation, Rodolfo and Quan aren't expelled."

Whitfield looked back at Ugu. "What?"

"No. They just have a warning. They won't even serve out Level 1 Detention."

"You're kidding."

"No, I'm serious. See, Whitfield, you didn't get anyone expelled or cause any harm to anyone. Those infractions would have all been discovered over time. And if they weren't, those committing the infractions would likely violate the Code again. Maybe next time, someone would get hurt. Or worse. You need to believe that you did the right thing. You simply reported violations of the Code. Others made the determination of whether or not to punish."

"I see what you're saying. But I'm still upset by it."

"I know you're upset, but I don't think it's because you reported some violations."

"Sure, it is. What else could it be?"

Ugu reached out and grabbed Whitfield's hands. "Honestly, I think you're upset because you realized how far you'd be willing to go to save me. And with my dad's plans for you, whatever they are, and your parents lives at stake, you're wondering if you'll go ever further to save them."

Whitfield looked directly into Ugu's eyes, and knew she was right. "I wasn't thinking straight after I saw what was in that box Spencer brought over. I just went into attack mode. Ugu, what if I'm dangerous? What if I do cross the line?"

"Whitfield, listen to me. You are dangerous, but you do not need to be scared, and I'll tell you why. You didn't just go into attack mode and punch out your enemies or go all ninja on people. You remained in control and used your brain, your wits, your natural leadership acumen to direct your team to find a solution to a problem that's been plaguing us for half the school year. When the chips were down and everyone lost hope, you came through. Everyone lost hope, that is, except for me. I knew you would come through. That's why I never said goodbye to you last night."

"How? Even I didn't know what I was doing."

"That's where you're wrong. You knew exactly what you were doing, because you always know. People around here speak of honor. Integrity. Respect. Honesty. Service. If you take an honest look at yourself, you'll see all those characteristics, and more. Whitfield, that's why I love you. Not for your muscles, or your smile, or those magnificent blue eyes. In your heart, you are not just a good person, but the best. Incorruptible. Pure. And that's how you are going to defeat my father. That's how we are going to take down SYPHUS. With you leading us."

"Are you sure?"

"I've never been more sure of anything in my life."

Whitfield took his hand and brushed aside a strand of hair from Ugu's face. "So, I guess this would be a good time for a kiss."

"No."

"No?"

"It's the perfect time for a kiss."

Chapter 50
The Captain

Whitfield and Ugu joined Aspen, Flaherty and about a thousand other students in the Inner Bowl to celebrate the end of the school year. Whitfield couldn't help but smile seeing everyone embrace Ugu, finally putting her past 'transgressions' behind them. Aspen was having a wonderful time, dancing and singing along with the bands. Flaherty was also busy making the rounds, hugging and laughing with everyone she encountered. Despite being in the middle of all this cheer and good spirits, Whitfield felt oddly alone. Sure, he was happy for Ugu, Aspen, and Flaherty, but he was still hanging onto his decision from Individual Championships, and suspected many around him felt uneasy with his presence. Whitfield tried his best to put the past out of his mind, but was having a hard time.

"Hey, Whitfield! There you are. Come here. Give me a hug. We did it. You did it. Ugu is staying." Flaherty gave Whitfield a giant hug and tried to get him to dance a little.

"Yeah, I heard. You and Aspen really came through."

"Oh, shut up. You know it was all you."

"Let's just agree that it was a team effort."

Flaherty was in no mood to argue. "Alright. I'm OK with that. So, where is Ugu?"

"Umm...she's around here somewhere. We were just talking over at the practice gym."

Flaherty grinned. "Yeah, I'm sure that's all you were doing."

Whitfield just smiled. "Hey, is that Keegan up on stage?"

Flaherty turned to see her teammate, shirtless, on one of amphitheater stages. "Oh my gosh. It is. Keegan, you're crazy!"

Keegan grabbed the microphone from Graham 'Angel' Cooper, lead singer of Angelbreath, who was rocking out on stage. "What's up, Seven Bridges!" The crowd roared. "Everyone having a good time?" Again, the crowd roared. "Coop, I hope you don't mind, but I've got something to say."

Angel gladly shared the stage. All bands playing across the Inner Bowl, temporarily stopped playing. "Yo, let's give it up for Angelbreath. They'll be back in five." Once again, the crowd roared.

Keegan looked comfortable holding the microphone. "So, here we are again. Last day together for the school year. I don't want to repeat what Sir Arlington said earlier today, but this has been a crazy, whack year, hasn't it? For anyone not on campus right now, it might just seem like another year for Seven Bridges. I mean, once again, NATIONAL CHAMPIONS!" More crowd roaring. "I want everyone on the team to get up here now. C'mon Flaherty. Wilson. Morocco. Everyone, get your butts up here." All team members started making their way onto the stage. The rest of the students all screamed their approval.

Keegan continued, "you know, this year's championship wasn't like the others. We had some real struggles. We even started to doubt whether we had it in us to win another one. I'll tell you what, after the meet at Thursday Cruise, we were falling apart. Tempers flared on the ride home. It got pretty ugly. But one person brought us all together. Stood up in front of the team and laid it all on the line. He took some shots, but never backed down. Later, at Team Championships, we were left for dead after Day 1.

"Man, we were terrible. Again, he stood up and made us believe in ourselves. We rallied as a team because of him. And won the team championship. And then, at Individuals, with a sure-fire All-Around title in his hands, he taught us all about true integrity. About honesty. Now, I know he's taken a lot of crap from many of you about what happened out there, but here, I want you to watch this."

Keegan lowered his microphone. The video monitors all around the stage, on the Outer Loop, atop Arlington Gymnastics Center, and in all other corners of campus sprang to life with video footage of Whitfield's infamous 'fall' on Pommel Clock at Individual Championships. The video showed a split screen with camera angles from Whitfield's own N-dimensional scanning tech zooming in on Whitfield's leg brushing the pommel.

It was clear as day, for all to see. Finally, students had the hard evidence supporting Whitfield's claim that he had indeed fallen, and hadn't simply given up the title because he was too scared or cowardly. Whitfield was vindicated, and for the first time in his life, felt great that everyone saw him fall.

Keegan raised the microphone again. "Look, no one is asking for an apology from any of you who were hard on Whitfield. I'll admit, we were just as stunned and upset in the locker room after he spoke with the judges. But he's our teammate, and our leader, so we believed in him. And now, y'all can believe in him as well. You know, no one ever said being honest was easy. Sometimes, it comes with a great cost. It may even rip loved ones away from us. Tear up a family.

"Whitfield knew the risks in that moment. He knew y'all might hate him for it. But he also knew the right thing to do. No matter how hard. No matter the cost. He stayed true to himself. Stayed true to the sport. Stayed true to all of you. He knew Jade had earned that title. And now, I think Jade has something to say."

In a surprise to everyone in attendance, Vertical Press Academy's All-Around National Champion, Jade, walked out onto the stage. To their credit, the crowd of SBA students mostly cheered Jade's appearance.

"Hello, Seven Bridges. Thank you for inviting me. This is awesome. You guys really know how to throw a party. I won't take up much of your time, but when one of your students reached out and invited me to campus to say a few words, I knew I had to come. You guys have an incredible gymnastics team. The best program in the world. And, honestly, as an outsider, we would love to hate you guys for it, but we can't. We don't. I admire you guys so much. And Whitfield, I can't put into words how much your actions meant to me and my family.

"My dad cried for days looking at my name on that trophy. None of us really knew why you did what you did. I guess we do now. Thanks for sharing the video. Look, I don't know if I would have been strong enough to do what you did, but I'm really glad you were. And not just because I won, but because of what you did. You know, showing courage like that. You've really made an impact. Thank you." Jade walked over and shared a hug with Whitfield, as the crowd cheered.

Jade handed the microphone back to Keegan. "Thank you, Jade. That was beautiful. Whitfield, get over here, cuz." Whitfield walked over to Keegan, who wrapped his arm around him, and faced the crowd, as the other 23 members of the Seven Bridges gymnastics team lined up across the stage behind them. "Whitfield, I want you to know we all took a vote. The results were unanimous. We decided to change our school uniforms for next year, in honor of your contributions to the school. Here, take a look."

The crowd roared their approval, with raucous laughter. A little confused, Whitfield turned around and saw each member of the gymnastics team standing there with a pair of underwear on their head and holding an apple with both hands in front of their private area. Whitfield burst out laughing. He looked back toward the crowd, and like lighters at a rock concert, waves of students appeared with underwear on their own heads, and, somehow, they all appeared to be holding apples.

Whitfield had to brush away tears from laughing so hard, in order to see Ugu standing in the front row holding a now almost empty basket, with just one remaining apple. Ugu reached her hand in and grabbed the last remaining apple out of the basket and tossed it to Whitfield.

Keegan pulled Whitfield back from the edge of the stage to make another announcement. "Yo, yo, yo…just one more thing. For the first time ever at Seven Bridges Academy, we have a team captain. It is my honor and distinct privilege to introduce our captain, and my best bud, Whitfield!"

All those in attendance roared with approval. Whitfield was completely shocked. He was not expecting any of this. As he was being showered with high fives, congratulations, and applause, he broke down in tears. Flaherty broke through the mob to embrace Whitfield. She spoke directly into Whitfield's ear. "You deserve this. You've been our captain since the day you arrived on campus. I love you, Whitfield."

Aspen was the next to slide in for a big hug. "I am so proud of you, bro. You deserve this. But I am not saluting you, Captain." Whitfield smiled.

"That's it. I'm out. Let's hear it for Angelbreath." Keegan relinquished the mic, and Angelbreath started jamming again. Whitfield hopped down from the stage and immediately fell into Ugu's waiting arms.

"Did you know about this?"

Ugu offered a sly smile. "What, me?"

"It was your idea, wasn't it?"

"Not all of it. I'll admit I reached out to Jade, and may have had something to do with the uniform gag, but the captain thing was all them."

Whitfield was touched. "Well, thank you. This was all really nice."

"You deserve it. All of it. I love you, Whitfield."

"I love you, Ugu."

****

The end-of-year celebration lasted until the early morning. Fortunately, Whitfield and Ugu left early enough to get some much-needed rest before their long drone shuttle ride to Yuri's estate. Though it wasn't quite the vacation they dreamed of, Whitfield and Ugu sat next to each other, holding hands, and smiling throughout the three-hour ride.

"Are you nervous for the camp?"

"Not really. I think I can hold my own with those guys. I'm more nervous about dealing with your dad. I mean, how can I be in the same room with him knowing that he may be keeping my parents hostage?"

"I know. It's going to be tough. He's not going to be there until tomorrow morning, but we talked about this. Remember, stick to the plan. No matter how tough. If everything goes according to plan, we'll have your parents home soon."

"I know. I know. If our plan works. Hey, thanks for standing by my side with all this."

"Of course. I love you. We're in this together."

Whitfield kissed Ugu's hand. "It's nice knowing I have the second smartest student at Seven Bridges on my side."

"Second smartest?"

"That's right. I saw the final rankings."

"Oh, Honey Bear. Sorry to burst your bubble, but those weren't final. Remember Dr. Crawfish's exam? The one I 'failed'."

"Yeah."

"Well, turns out I aced it."

"So, what does that mean?"

"It means I beat you by two points this year. 9.89 GPA beats 9.87. Sorry, chum."

Whitfield pulled his hand away. "Wait. No, you couldn't have."

"Aww…I'm sorry. Did I use big words? OK, repeat after me. Ugu…is…smarter…than…I am."

"Very funny. I'm seeing Sir Arlington when we get back."

"Oh, Whitfield. Nothing wrong with being number two."

"You are not going to let this go, are you?"

"I'd answer you, but I'm not sure you'd understand. Maybe take a little nap. You should rest that fragile brain of yours." Ugu turned her shoulder and rested her eyes. Whitfield just stared at her. He eventually closed his eyes too and rested until they landed at Yuri's place.

****

The following morning, Ugu was stretched out on the sofa in her dad's house, still in her pajamas, reading a book, when her dad walked in and gave her a kiss on the forehead.

"Good morning, precious."

"Morning, Daddy."

"How was the ride in yesterday?"

"Uneventful."

"And how is Whitfield?"

"Great."

"So, how was your third year at Seven Bridges?"

"Couldn't have gone any better. Exactly as we planned."

"And the relationship?"

"Perfect. We're in love."

"Does he still think he's here just for the draft camp?"

"Yup. I didn't tell him about your other plans."

"Good. I'll pay him a visit this morning."

"We have plans for lunch, so don't keep him too long."

"No problem. I think he'll be eager to see you. So, you were right about Gen. Gibson. Incompetent fool. We needed to change course. Do you have someone in mind for Dr. Hewitt's replacement?"

"Yes. I have it all drawn out, but we have plenty of time to discuss all that. Let's enjoy some breakfast first."

"You got it, boss. So glad to have you back home. We have a lot of work to do."

"Looking forward to it."

****

Later that morning, Whitfield was in the gym with fourteen other members of his draft class, when he got called into the coaches' office. "Hello, Whitfield."

"Mr. Gugurutruv! I wasn't expecting to see you until tonight. Thank you again for drafting me. This facility is terrific."

"Thank you, and you're welcome. Good to see you again. Are you getting along with the others?"

"Yes, of course. Great group here."

"Good. Good. Well, I can't stay long, and I don't want to interrupt your training session. Just came to say hello and drop off a message for you. It's already loaded on the screen. Just press play when I leave."

"OK, will do."

"Great. And, Whitfield, really glad to have you on our side."

"Me too, sir." Yuri left the coaches' office, and Whitfield moved behind the desk. He sat down facing the video screen and pressed play. Whitfield's eyes grew large and immediately started to well up. He was staring right into his parents' faces on the screen.

"Hello Whitfield! We've waited so long for this moment. We are so happy you are here." It was the first time Whitfield had heard his dad's voice in over ten years.

"Whitfield, baby. It's Mommy. We love you so much. We miss you and Aspen so much. We can't wait to be a family again." When the video ended, the back door to the office opened.

In walked Livvy and Aldrich. "Mom? Dad?"

"Yes, son, it's us." Whitfield's mom looked exactly as he had pictured her after all these years. Whitfield jumped out of his seat to hug her. After a long embrace, Whitfield's mom stepped aside to allow her son to reunite with his dad. Aldrich looked at his son, put a hand on Whitfield's shoulder and said four words that would change Whitfield's life forever.

"Welcome to SYPHUS, son!"

ACKNOWLEDGEMENTS

When I was four years old, my parents signed me up for soccer. I enjoyed playing on the team, but my soccer skills were not very good (ok, I was terrible). I knew which direction to run when our team had the ball and which goal to defend when the other team possessed the ball. I also knew that when I kicked the ball out of bounds and the referee awarded our team the ball, that it must have been a mistake. I remember my coach yelling at me when I went to tell the referee that I had touched the ball last. I remember the other parents yelling at me to run down the field. I remember thinking that it was wrong that we had the ball, but I moved on. Everyone makes mistakes. Even referees.

As time moved on, I started to notice a pattern emerging across all sports. In a World Cup match, I saw flops, deception, and a never-ending display of finger-pointing from players trying to convince the referee to award their team the ball. This behavior extended to football, baseball, basketball, and just about everywhere else I looked. Surprisingly (to me, at least), the relative importance of the game didn't seem to matter either. It occurred during pre-season games, little league, high school, college, everywhere. Even in practice.

Now, please don't get me wrong. I love winning. I know others do too. But sacrificing one's integrity to do so seems too high a cost. I want to win because I earned it on the field of battle, not because I effectively lied to a judge or referee. Perhaps I'm alone with that sentiment, and maybe that's why the Whitfield character in this book appeals to me so much. His integrity seems almost superhuman, but the truth is…he's not alone. Neither am I. So many athletes walk among us that place integrity above winning. I wanted to write a book that champions that very spirit. I may not have known it when I was four years old, but that's where the idea for *Chalk Wars* originated.

I have so many people to thank for their contributions to this book. First, I want to thank the amazing team at Austin Macauley Publishers for taking a chance on an unknown 13-year-old. Your support means so much.
To all my teachers and administrators. It may be strange for most kids my age to say, but I've always loved school. The reason is simple—I've had some of the most

amazing teachers on earth. Huge shout-outs go to Sheila Abruzzo, Danielle Ambrosia, Rebecca Azia, Denise Brennan, Paige Carr, Kristine Garofalo, Lauren Guglielmi, Sal Khan, Maddie Titus, my future Stanford professors (?), and all my amazing teachers, past, present, and future.

To all my current and former coaches, whether in the gym with me every day or offering words of encouragement at camps, clinics, or awards ceremonies, you've all inspired me. Mike Acevedo, Blaze Gymnastics, Tony Beck, Centre Elite Gymnastics, Garison Clark, Chris Cote, Christina Fuller, Matt Fuller, Jake Hawley, Rachel Herwerth, Karl Jaanimagi, Mitch Johnston, Walt Kurfis, Minyoung Kwon, Jim Luttinger, Dan Molnar, Cody Stumpf, Keith Stumpf, Ryan Terrill, Ethan Thomas, Carlos Vazquez, Luke Wilcox, Jeff Zack, and so many others.

To all my past, current, and future gymnastics teammates and competitors. You push me to be my best in the gym every day and while I cannot possibly list all of you here, know that your contributions to the sport and to this book are felt every day. Special thanks go to Richard Alpha, Jake Apelt, Hasan Aydogdu, Cian Baillie, Veeresh Bezawada, Liam Brick, Carter Canastra, Carson Crooks, Colin Daley, Xavier Derienzo, Maguire Deutsch, Lincoln Dubin, Daniel Gavrilyuk, Dmitri Gavrilyuk, Caleb Greenberg, Jason Hao, Ty Herzing, Ben Hickman, Cameron Houseknecht, Jun Iwai, Jovan Jimeno, Maksim Kan, Dylan Kramer, Adam Lakomy, Kole Landis, Danila Leykin, Elijah Maeding, Michael Munufie, Brady Mitchell, Michelangelo Morgan, Devin Murray, Auggie Nicholas, London Norris, Evan Patrizio, Dante Reive, Silus Reive, Samuel Soldato, Brody Schuller, Canyon Schwinn, Lathan Simpson, Isaac Steele, Niko Stefanov, Luke Sykora, Adrian Tangretti, Jude Weber, Brayden Wilhelm, and Kai Uemura.

To all the current and former collegiate and international gymnasts. Your intense dedication to the sport and sick skills motivated me to create a world where your hard work and unparalleled athleticism are so richly valued. Special thanks go to Patrick Armstrong, Michael Artlip, Maggie Ayers, Raj Bhavsar, Simone Biles, Luisa Blanco, Cameron Bock, Crew Bold, Jordan Bowers, Haleigh Bryant, Bailey Bunn, Jordan Chiles, Taylor Christopulos, Justin Ciccone, Carter Cochardo, Matt Cormier, Alice D'Amato, Jake Dalton, Audrey Davis, Livvy Dunne, Shawn Johnson East, Aleah Finnegan, Mike Fletcher, Gabbie Gallentine (my brother would still like for you to be his prom date…in six years), Olivia Greaves, Ian Gunther, James Hall, Daiki Hashimoto, Donovan Hewitt, Ella Hodges, Asher Hong, Patrick Hoopes, Jonathan Horton, Trevor Howard, Michael Jaroh, Paul Juda, Josh Karnes, Madison Kocian, Suni Lee, Danell Leyva, Nastia Liukin, Riley Loos, Martina Maggio, Isabella Magnelli,

Brody Malone, Ashley Maul, Grace McCallum, Connor McCool, Riley McCusker, Kalea McElligott, Sam Mikulak, Yul Moldauer, Stephan Nedoroscik, Kameron Nelson, Kaylia Nemour, Maggie Nichols, Shallon Olsen, Carly Patterson, Abby Paulson, Curran Phillips, Sam Phillips, Ali Raisman, Ian Raubal, Nicole Riccardi, Fred Richard, Kyla Ross, Alicia Sacramone, Alyona Shchennikova, Elena Shinohara, Kenzo Shirah, Dani Sievers, Evgeny Siminiuc, Landon Simpson, Ragan Smith, Emma Spence, Justin Spring, Kevin Tan, Trinity Thomas, Heath Thorpe, Olivia Trautman, Porsche Trinidad, Kohei Uchimura, Favian Valdez, Giorgia Villa, Colt Walker, Max Whitlock, Donnell Whittenburg, Gabi Wickman, Jordyn Wieber, Nile Wilson, Shane Wiskus, Natalie Wojcik, Raena Worley, Liu Yang, Khoi Young, and Kim Zmeskal.

To my friends and loved ones. Maria Berdan and Jason Bloom, thank you for always being there for me and for doing so much more than just opening your home to me. Lucie Martinelli. You are one of my oldest friends and inspire me to be the best version of myself every day. Thank you. My favorite pommel horse (you know who you are). Thanks for all the bruises on my legs. The wonderfully creative people at Lego. Homestead Park. USA Gymnastics. Scrivener. Darth Vader. Thank you all.

Finally, I would like to thank my family. Grandparents, thank you for the many compliments and congratulations that you have given me. I appreciate all that you have done for me, and carry your love with me every day. You were the first people outside of my immediate family to read my novel.

Brian, thank you so much for all of your wonderful ideas that you share every day and for just being yourself. You're goofy, silly, and sometimes weird, but I love you with all my heart and I don't want you to change at all.

Mom, you supported me every step along the way. I always felt like you have been there for me. I want to thank you for being there and helping me and always encouraging me. It means a lot.

Dad, you have been right by my side throughout this entire journey, and I appreciate every moment. You've been there for the ups and downs and everything in between. Thank you for listening to every single chapter I wrote and giving me feedback every day. I truly could not have done this without your help.

And one more thank you, to all the *Chalk Wars* readers. I am forever grateful.

About the Author

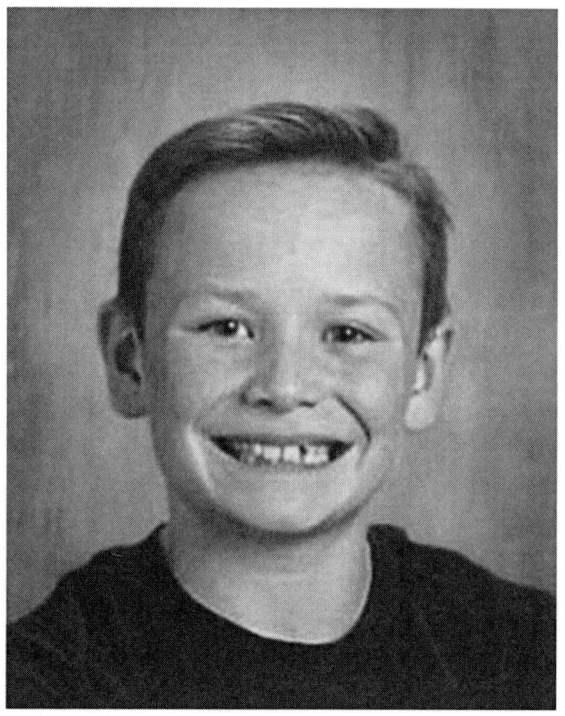

Patrick Sinclair is a 14-year-old sophomore at State College High School. *Chalk Wars: Pommel Clock and the Incredulous Cost of Integrity* is his first novel. Patrick currently resides in State College, PA with his parents and 10-year-old brother, Brian. He has been a competitive gymnast for seven years and continues to advance further each day. Patrick's favorite stuffed animals are Lion and Sir Purr.